DIGGING DEEP

The ups and downs of a 1960s
Yorkshire mining community

TREVOR MASSEY

First published 2012 by Mosaic (Teesdale) Ltd.

ISBN 978 0 956781 65 9

Typeset in Bembo by Mosaic Print & Design, Middleton-in-Teesdale.

Printed and bound in Great Britain by Biddles, King's Lynn.

Mosaic's policy is to use papers that are natural, renewable and recyclable
and made from wood grown in sustainable forests. The paper used in this
book is Vancouver 80gsm opaque – woodfree, high white offset paper,
FSC accredited (totally chlorine free) and PEFC accredited.

Mosaic (Teesdale) Ltd
Moor Edge
Snaisgill
Middleton-in-Teesdale
County Durham
DL12 0RP

www.mosaicprintdesign.co.uk

This book is dedicated to the memory of the four generations of my forefathers who worked in the coal industry in Staffordshire and Yorkshire. They helped to power the industrial revolution, but in their days the coal mines were a harsh and dangerous workplace.

For Beryl

Trevor Janey

Legal Disclaimer

Acknowledgements

I am indebted to Derek Hinchliffe, a life-long friend, for his comments on the draft of this book. His personal knowledge of coal mining, the Methodist church and Yorkshire folk allowed him to provide valuable and candid comment which contributed greatly to the final work.

I am also grateful to Judith Mashiter, of Mosaic, for her encouragement, patient editing and attention to detail in publishing this book.

Trevor Massey

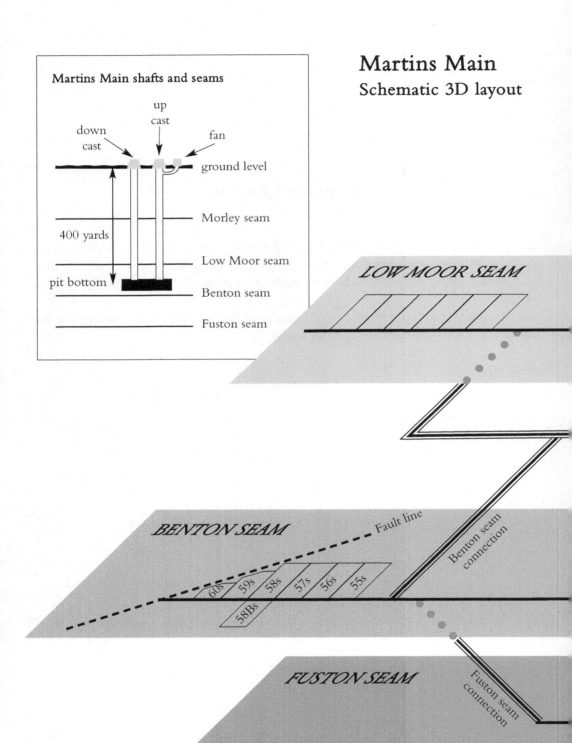

Martins Main
Schematic 3D layout

Martins Main shafts and seams

down cast
up cast
fan
ground level

Morley seam

400 yards

Low Moor seam

pit bottom

Benton seam

Fuston seam

LOW MOOR SEAM

BENTON SEAM

Fault line

60s 59s 58s 57s 56s 55s

58Bs

Benton seam connection

FUSTON SEAM

Fuston seam connection

MORLEY SEAM

Morley roadway

Morley trunk roadway (2 miles)

Cento roadway

pit bottom

Central Conveying Scheme

Benton roadway

Fuston One

Fuston Two

Characters

Norman Pickersgill   *Number Two Yorkshire Region General Manager*
Diane Parks   *Norman Pickersgill's secretary*
Mr Jones   *Number Two Yorkshire Region Production Manager*
Ralph Lacey   *Number Two Yorkshire Region Planning Manager*
Reg Jenkins   *Number Two Yorkshire Region Group Manager for six pits including Martins Main, married to Polly*

Roy Dobson   *Martins Main General Manager*
Helen   *his wife*
Robert and John   *their children*

Gordon   *Clerk to Roy Dobson*
George Turnbull   *Martins Main Undermanager*
Mike Darlow   *Martins Main Assistant Manager*
Jim Lord   *Martins Main Graduate Trainee*
Jeff Briggs   *Martins Main Finance Officer*

Joe 'Cobba' Green   *Martins Main Union President*
Sandra   *his daughter*
David   *his son*
Jimmy Bell   *Martins Main Union Secretary*

Gerry Moore   *Martins Main workman*
Peggy   *his wife*
Tony and Michael   *their children*

Bob Hall   *Martins Main fitter*
Janet   *his wife, a dress shop assistant in Doncaster*
Willie Carter   *Martins Main workman, trustee of Upthorpe Methodist Church*
Peter   *his son, organist at Upthorpe Methodist Church*
Dr Sloan   *organist in Leeds and Peter Carter's teacher*
Joe Horton   *farmer, trustee of Upthorpe Methodist Church*
John Warwick   *Headmaster of Upthorpe Junior school, trustee of Upthorpe Methodist Church*
Rev James Folds   *Minister for Upthorpe Methodist Church*
Gwen   *his wife*

Cliff Smith	*Enclosure member, former mine deputy at Martins Main*
Charlie Marshall	*Enclosure member, former miner*
Albert Dunn	*Enclosure member, former union official*
Cyril Mann	*Enclosure member, former winding engineman*
Bert Wall	*Enclosure member, former Surface Foremen at Martins Main*
Pat Mulligan	*Enclosure member, Irishman with no mining connections*
Richard Wallace	*Welsh Mining Contractor*
Denise	*his wife*
Mr Franks	*Mines Inspector*
Dennis Gates	*Gardener and driver for Roy Dobson*
Joan	*his wife*

Chapter 1

Thursday 16 April 1964

'Interview, love?' The girl slid the glass partition back and asked the question from her seat at the telephone board where she and three other girls criss-crossed the wires and plugs to keep the telephone exchange working.

'Yes,' the young man replied.

'Up the stairs, the door facing you at the top, number seventeen.'

'Thank you.'

The partition slid back and Roy Dobson turned to go and find room seventeen. He was in the hall of a stone-built country house used by the Yorkshire Region of the British Coal Executive as their headquarters, on the outskirts of Barnsley. On either side of the old hall, two rectangular three-storey office blocks had been built to house the many personnel and other departments associated with the running of twenty-five coal mines. As he climbed the stone steps he licked his lips, which usually went dry whenever he faced an interview panel, and he pulled out the flaps of his coat pockets. The door faced him at the top of the stairs. On it was a plaque which read 'Secretary Regional General Manager'. So they were holding the interview in the Big Chief's office. That was interesting. He knocked at the door and a female voice invited him in.

It was the usual sort of executive outer office: banks of filing cabinets, telephones, an intercom speaker, two typewriters and a desk and swivel chair for the lady in charge. She stood up and moved towards Roy as he entered the room. He thought she looked like a typical private secretary, too. She was in her early thirties, wore good foundation garments, well-cut clothes and looked super-efficient and not a little sexy. She gave him a questioning smile.

'Roy Dobson,' he said.

'Ah yes, Mr Dobson.' She crossed his name off a list on her desk. 'Well you are a little early, and of course the interviews are running behind schedule as usual. Will you take a seat over there please?'

Roy took one of the empty chairs at the end of the office. He smiled at the other fellow who was sitting there. The chap was older than Roy. He was nervously fingering his wristwatch, which he had taken off and he was obviously in no state to carry on a conversation. So Roy looked across at the secretary. He watched her eyes following the squiggles on her shorthand pad and her fingers tapping the squiggles into words on the typewriter and then, as his eyes drifted to her legs, his thoughts were arrested by a voice over the intercom.

'Yes, Mr Pickersgill,' the secretary replied. She stood up and showed the other fellow through the inter-connecting door into the Regional General Manager's office.

Another twenty minutes before my turn, thought Roy, and his mind drifted to his own position. He was thirty-two, and manager of his second pit in the Nottinghamshire coalfield. His job was nothing glamorous but he was still young and making progress quickly. Young mining engineers were being encouraged to move around the British coal industry. The British Coal Executive was still a large organisation with mines and coalfields widely spread around the country. It had over 600,000 men and the annual output was around two hundred million tons. There had been closures of some small coal mines which had limited reserves and very low productivity. For the first time since the start of the Second World War, the industry was facing competition from cheap oil, so coal no longer had a captive market. However, the construction of large, coal-fired power stations to generate electricity was giving the industry some security.

Roy was on new ground though, in Yorkshire. That might be a mistake and could be the reason for his lack of enthusiasm. He had always worked in the Midland coalfields. He was a product of D H Lawrence country and proud of it. His wife came from that part of the country, too. She would not be keen to move up to Yorkshire. But then, he reflected, she would not have to make that choice. This visit was only a day out and a bit of interview practice. He was too young for a General Manager's job. Martins Main was too big a pit for him, and anyway, there was sure to be someone local lined up for the job.

'Who is on the panel?' He decided to try and pick the brains of the secretary.

'The panel is the big three senior managers of the Region, along with Mr Watts, the Personnel Manager and Mr Reg Jenkins, the Sub-Region Manager. Martins Main is one of his pits.'

'Who do you mean by the big three of the Region? I am strange to this part of the country,' he continued.

'Oh yes, I forgot. Of course I'm really new here, too. Mr Pickersgill brought me along with him when he came to this job from London three months ago. You'll know Mr Pickersgill, though?'

'Yes, he's something of a phenomenon in the industry. I've never met him—I'm not sure I am looking forward to it either under these circumstances,' replied Roy.

'Well, the other two are Mr Jones, the Regional Production Manager and Mr Lacey, the Regional Planning Manager. They have both been in Yorkshire a good number of years but Reg Jenkins is new as well. He's only been here a matter of a few weeks.' Roy Dobson was making progress; he decided to push on—this might be a useful contact some day.

'How do you like Yorkshire then, after London?' he asked.

She threw up her arms in despair. 'It's dead, just dead after London. Prices are lower here though. I suppose it does cost a lot less to live here. But there is no life here at all, not the life we were used to in London. Anyway, I think that we'll be making our own entertainment now we are settling down. And I have heard that Reg Jenkins and his wife are great ones for entertaining. They might help to liven things up.'

She returned to her typing and Roy reflected on what he had heard of Norman Pickersgill. His nickname was 'the whispering administrator'. One of his physical anomalies was a very soft, high-pitched whispering voice. It was rumoured that he had sacked more men for disobeying instructions that they had never heard, than he had dismissed for genuine failures. He was small, fat and walked with a peculiar hobble. He wore thick spectacles for his bad eyesight and his hair and moustache were always untidy. All this against him physically, but at forty-two he was recognised as a brilliant administrator who was riding the crest of a successful career. He was a hard taskmaster to work for, ruthless to anyone who crossed him, and sparing in his praise, but he paid good money to anyone who got him the results he wanted. He had a beautiful wife and three teenaged children. His morals were impeccable up to midnight and the stories about him after midnight were persistent, but unbelievable.

The door opened and the previous candidate came out shaking his head and straightaway left the office without any comment.

'I think he had a hard time,' said Pickersgill's secretary with a knowing smile. After a couple of minutes the intercom sounded and the secretary stood up and led Roy Dobson in to the interview room.

The room was high-ceilinged and spacious. Two large windows let in the southern light and they overlooked a large lawn and flower garden. Roy took the chair obviously meant for him at one side of the large oval table and viewed the strange figures arrayed against him. Mr Pickersgill, who was sitting opposite Roy, introduced the rest of the panel and threw the questioning over to each of them in turn.

There followed the usual round of questions: production methods, wage controls, planned maintenance of equipment, communications to junior officials, and consultation with workmen. Each questioner pushed his own pet subject and then filled out the answer he received to show his own ability. Roy Dobson held his own, but he played it quietly and answered carefully. He didn't challenge any ideas; he was among strangers and he didn't know their bite. When each member of the panel had finished there was an expectant pause, until Norman Pickersgill looked up from his papers.

'It reads very good on paper; fully qualified, a good degree, some varied experience and your second Manager's job at thirty-two; but tell me this, Dobson. What is your ambition? Where are you going in your career? What are you aiming for?' He hunched his shoulders and glared across the table. Roy could feel the sweat from under his armpits trickling down his body. He had no stock reply for that sort of question. He pondered a moment.

'I don't have a clear ambition laid out, Sir. I never aim for rapid promotion, I always tackle each job as though I am going to be in it for twenty years.'

Norman Pickersgill threw out his arms with a cry of disgust.

'That's no way to carry on, lad. You will kill yourself that way. Stand on them underneath you; make them sweat and climb on their shoulders. That is the only way to get on in competitive management. And tell them that you are going to do it that way. They will be glad to help you on your way to get rid of you.'

Roy Dobson's reply was not heard by Mr Jones, the Regional Production Manager, or Mr Lacey, the Regional Planning Manager. Their feelings were numbed by their boss's short outburst that was intended for more ears than those of the lad being interviewed.

'Is there anything you would like to ask us, Dobson?' asked Pickersgill. Roy decided to try to make up for his last false move.

'Well, I am a stranger to this part of the country; I don't know Martins Main. Are there any exceptional problems at the pit? Has it any special features which I ought to know about?'

'It's a bloody pit, lad. They are all the same. They have all got problems. If they had no problems we should need no managers. That's about right isn't it, Reg?'

'Yes, indeed, Mr Pickersgill, you are right, Sir. Though I think it is fair to say to Mr Dobson that there are some problems at Martins Main which can be laid at the feet of former management over the pit.' He glared across the table at Mr Lacey and Mr Jones when he made that remark.

'Yes, yes, Reg, but that is why the British Coal Executive have brought you and me in here, and that is why we are going to appoint a new manager to put the place right. All right, young man, off you go. We will let you know the result of the interview in a few days' time.'

'Phew!' Safe in the outer office, Roy Dobson let out this expression of his feeling to Mr Pickersgill's secretary.

'Was it one of those experiences?' she said with a smile.

'Not half,' replied Roy as he picked up his coat. 'Anyway I know where I stand. I'll say goodbye to Yorkshire before I even arrive. I had better settle in my own nest further south, thank you very much.' He left her and went down the stairs to his car.

Tuesday 21 April 1964

Rob Dobson received a letter offering him the appointment as General Manager at Martins Main, with an increase in his salary of three hundred pounds per year.

Thursday 23 April 1964

BRITISH COAL EXECUTIVE
MARTINS MAIN COLLIERY
Nº2 YORKSHIRE REGION

The large notice board, with white and gold letters on a pale blue background, stood at the entrance to the surface buildings at the end of the only road leading to the mine. This road, Martins Lane, sloped slowly down from the mine until it reached the main road of the urban district of Upthorpe. Martins Lane was flanked on each side by a row of terraced houses. These houses, numbered one to one hundred and eleven on one side and two to one hundred and twelve on the other side, had been built when the pit was first sunk in the 1890s, and housed a significant proportion of the population of Upthorpe. The British Coal Executive now owned the houses and they were rented out to workmen at the pit. There had been a scheme in the 1950s to add a small inside bathroom and toilet, but the outside toilet buildings were retained in the back yards. On the main road opposite Martins Lane, the local council, during some road repairs, had constructed a low retaining wall and paved the area behind it. On the paved area had appeared an oak seat, with a suitable plaque, and on this seat, or on the wall, sat the retired old men of Upthorpe. It was known locally as 'The Members Enclosure', or just 'The Enclosure' because of its prominent position from which to observe the happenings in Upthorpe and at the mine. The old men could see the business of Yorkshire flowing past them on the main road as lorries and vans went towards Doncaster or Pontefract or Wakefield; they could learn a lot about Martins Main by the traffic or personnel going up Martins Lane to the colliery; and they could even guess the attendance, on Mondays and Fridays, by the number of empty seats on the busses taking miners up to the mine. Nothing happened in Martins Lane without their knowledge, and in the avenues and crescents of newer Upthorpe they had good contacts who brought them the news and gossip. Only in the new private residential estate being built on the outskirts of Upthorpe did their information sources dry up.

'Some bloody snooty folk moved in across there,' said Charlie Marshall, pointing in the direction of the new estate. Charlie was a restless character. He fidgeted about all the time and hardly ever sat down. His face twitched frequently, where it was scarred from a shot-firing accident.

'No good to Upthorpe folk,' agreed Cliff Smith. 'They're only interested in their houses and cars. Not bothered about anybody else.' Cliff was a retired colliery Deputy. A Deputy was responsible for the operations and the workmen in each working coalface at the mine. He dressed well and always wore a hat and carried a stick with a silver handle. His smart appearance disguised his seventy-two years and as the un-crowned chairman of the Enclosure he always sat in the middle of the seat.

'Not doing so well at Martins this morning.' Cyril Mann was a large, fat, former winding-engineman. He kept a careful watch on the pit headgear to see if the wheels were turning. With the state of his heart and the excess weight he carried, the doctor didn't give him much more time. Nobody commented.

'Look who's coming here,' said Charlie, looking down the main road. 'It's our Walter. Sun's got you out then, Walter.'

The little man who came up to them and sat on the wall did not reply. He only grinned and continued to gasp the air into his dust-soaked lungs. He only joined them on warm, fine days.

'Them bellows sound rusty today, Walter,' said Cliff.

'Aye, Cliff.' Walter White was proud to be accepted into the Enclosure.

A large car swung round from the main road and sped up Martins Lane. The horn sounded several times to send grubby children scurrying into the gutter. It was Reg Jenkins.

'Welsh bastard, that,' said Albert Dunn. He was an old union man and had strong views.

'It's queer that, bringing a Welshman up to show us how to run pits in Yorkshire,' said Charlie.

'It's bloody ridiculous, bringing him here,' put in Albert. 'I reckon old George Turnbull has had one go with him already.'

'Not surprised. George won't stand any nonsense,' replied Cliff. They all knew that George had worked under Cliff as a lad. George Turnbull's success, to get from a house in Martins Lane to be undermanager at Martins Mains, was one of Cliff's proudest achievements in life. He claimed more influence in this success than was due. 'George has been at Martins now for nearly forty years. If anyone knows the pit, he should. I can remember the day that he started, when he was fifteen. He was always a grafter. There will be some trouble at Martins if that Welsh fellow tries to push things around.'

'Who's going to get the manager's job? Anybody heard owt?' Charlie had been asking the same question every day for a week.

'He's got something on, whoever gets it,' said Albert.

'Still not heard anything,' said Cliff. 'I reckon it will be between young Darlow, the assistant manager underground here, and the fellow over at Lucy pit. A pity George Turnbull hasn't got a colliery manager's ticket. There would be no question then.'

'I've heard that a fellow from Nottingham has got it.' They all looked to the end of the wall to the big bald-headed Irishman, Pat Mulligan. He was not a native of Upthorpe, nor had he been a miner but, after living with his sister for several years, had been accepted in the Enclosure; firstly, because of his information on racehorses, and then because of his stop-press news. He was no conversationalist and never joined in the discussion unless he had something special to contribute, but he often had the punchline. The Enclosure took his news as gospel truth. Albert, summed up the members' thoughts on the subject. 'It's a bugger how Pat always gets to know first.'

Tuesday 12 May 1964

The sun shone all day and in the evening George Turnbull was inspecting the roses in the small front garden of his house, in a village a couple of miles from Upthorpe. He straightened his back and looked up at the early evening sky. He was fifty-three years old and his stout figure might well be taken for middle-age fat. In fact it was mainly muscle formed from an active life, and his practical policy in the pit that every man had to be shown how to do his job, not just told what to do. His hair was short and grey and his face lined, but his eyes were bright and keen and no-one ever suggested that George Turnbull was past it. He straightened up again as his wife called him to the telephone. He glanced at his watch; it must be the afternoon shift report.

When he returned from the house fifteen minutes later he had a worried look on his face. 56s coalface had failed to clear their coal again. He knew there were difficulties with bad roof conditions on the face, and water in the seam, but his thoughts were more influenced by the meeting he had had with Mr Jenkins that afternoon in the manager's office at the mine. Mike Darlow, who was acting as manager, had called him up to the office. As soon as he entered, Jenkins, who was sitting astride the manager's desk, had laid into him.

'Now then, Turnbull; tell me, when are you going to get some coal off 56s face?' He winced at the name Turnbull. He hated to be called Turnbull; everybody at the pit called him George, they always had done and always would.

'Well, Mr Jenkins, we have some problems on that coalface with the fault. It is only a small fault with a displacement of about twelve inches but there is water and bad roof conditions associated with it. I'm confident we shall master the conditions soon. And the men are doing their best in the circumstances.'

'Doing their best, Turnbull,' Jenkins repeated sarcastically. Then he had banged his fist on the desk and leaned over, pointing his finger at George. 'They don't know what fucking shovels are for in this part of the country. You will never get results at this pit with their effort.'

Young Mike Darlow kept quiet. He had not been brought up at Martins and he was thinking of his future. He had ambitions.

'I think they are giving us a fair effort, Mr Jenkins. Before you say too much you ought to have a visit down there and see things for yourself. That coalface has some rough conditions on it at the moment.'

'I don't need to look at the coalface to get to know the facts, Turnbull, I can sense them. I know that at this place no one gives a bugger about things. There is no organisation, no drive to get results. You are all letting things slide. I can feel it, man, when I enter the bloody pit gates.'

'Nay, don't say that. I have been there myself the whole day. Look at my clothes; you can see that they are wet through with trying to get the conveyor belt running through the water.'

'It should not need you on the fucking job to get things done, Turnbull. I'm telling you, other people are there to do that. Your responsibility is to organise them. Anyway, you are not up to date in this part of the world at all. You still talk about bloody men shovelling coal. It's 1964, man! Shovels are out of date, they want throwing away. What we need is machines to do the work, not men. And if I get my way we are going to have machines at this pit. But think on this, Turnbull. If we get machines, we shall want good management and good organisation–better than what there is at Martins now. And we shall bloody well get it you know, even if there has to be some new blood around here.'

'I'll go and get bathed.' George Turnbull didn't like that sort of talk. He didn't need threats to make him do his job.

He went back to viewing his garden. After all, he had not much left in his life but his job. His daughter was married to a schoolteacher and lived in Kent. His son was a draughtsman with Rolls Royce in Derby and he had his own life and family planned out there. No, there was just his wife and his job. But it was not an ordinary job, it was a way of life for him. His main tools were the men who worked for him in his part of the mine. He was dealing with the flesh and blood of the community. He had been born with them, brought up with them; he knew them, he understood them and they, in turn, trusted him. That was the main thing–they trusted him and respected him. George knew that no one gets trust and respect anywhere in five minutes. It takes years of hard work and good decisions to get where he had got now in the eyes of his men. He knew this, but did the new bosses know it? Did they understand? Did they care? He looked at his house and garden and at his wife standing in the window watching him; and then he looked beyond, over the fields, to the headgear of Martins Main sticking up on the skyline, and the first houses of Upthorpe. There were changes coming; changes that would affect Martins Main and Upthorpe, and possibly George himself. He liked new ideas, new plans and progress; he was not against change. However this change was tinged with panic. There was something ruthless about it, something dangerous, something cruel. He shivered. He did not know whether he shivered because of the cool evening air or from his thoughts, but he decided to get his coat and go back to the mine to have a word with the nightshift men before they went underground to their work.

Friday 15 May 1964

Sandra Green was parading in her underwear in front of her dressing table mirror, admiring herself. She was pleased with what she saw. Her body glowed with the potent vitality of a healthy eighteen-year-old girl. Her bust was full and firm, her waist tight and narrow and her legs, which she had inherited from her mother, were long and enticing. She ran her hands up her left leg to alter the seam of her stocking and then she adjusted her suspender. She smiled at herself in the mirror as she wondered what the local boys would give to see her dressed so scantily. Her face, which was plain and not distinctive without cosmetics, had every reason to smile and go on smiling, because events had turned very much in favour of Sandra Green.

Three years ago she had moved house from number eighty-one Martins Lane, in the middle of all the horror and squalor of street life, to number two Wilbur Crescent, the end house of a semi-detached council estate in Upthorpe. The change had been made as a result of the influence of her father, who was a local district councillor, and two years after he became President of the Miners' Union for Martins Main. To a girl who was going to High School in Doncaster, this move had opened up new friendships and given her a new status and more self-confidence. She even became ambitious at school and directed her abilities towards going into the sixth form, with the objective of possibly going to teacher training college. Her ambitions were short-lived because fate again moved for her benefit. Her mother died within the first year in the new house, after a recurring attack of bronchial pneumonia. Like her father and her brother, she did not mourn the loss because her mother had been a hard woman to live with. Continually affected by bad health, Mrs Green had demanded love and pity and service from her husband and the children alike. She had ruled all the activities within the household and then resisted every attempt by her family to go out and mix with other people. Her years of domination led to the escape of her husband through his complete involvement with the Miners' Union and as a local district councillor. Her children could not escape, though, and they had to conceal their pent-up frustration and desire for freedom. After her death there was talk in the wider Green family of some relative moving in to keep house, but Sandra's father, Cobba, let them all speculate and then gave his ruling which was simple and final.

'There is no other woman coming in to rule this house. The three of us that are left have wanted to be alone for a long time. We know what we want and we are going to have it. Our Sandra will be lady of this house from now on. She can run it. She knows how to.'

And so it was. The relatives were offended and kept to their own affairs, but Sandra was delighted and revelled in her freedom and importance. She mothered her younger brother, David, who was thirteen and still at school, and she coddled her father with his favourite food dishes. She even showed an interest in her father's many activities and responsibilities. This was so strange to him that he was embarrassed and pleased at the same time. In return, encouraged by her proud father, she filled her wardrobe with clothes, and went out whenever she liked with her friends. She was free—as free as a young bird when it flies the nest.

'I'm going to the meeting now, Sandra.'

It was her father calling from the bottom of the stairs. She opened the bedroom door to shout back to him.

'Alright, Dad. Have you got a key?'

'Yes, I'm taking the spare one for the back door. Where's David tonight?'

'He's playing cricket at school. He took a key with him because I won't be in when he comes home.'

'Where are you going?'

'I'm going into Doncaster with Pauline, to a dance. I might be late back so don't wait up for me. I'll take the front door key.'

'Alright. Look after yourself, lass.'

'Right, Dad.'

Cobba Green walked up to his front garden gate and down Wilbur Crescent. His mind was on the meeting he was going to and he was unaware of Sandra watching him from behind the bedroom curtains. She watched him go and smiled at his concentrated look. She was proud of her father; he was a real man in her eyes.

At forty-eight years of age, Cobba Green was a successful, working-class capitalist who had left-wing socialist principles. His appearance perfectly fitted that of a communist agitator. He was tall and thin; he had short, grey hair and his face was pale and well-lined for his years. His grey eyes often had the distant look of a thinker but, when the time was right, he never missed an opening that would help his cause and benefit Cobba Green. As President of the Martins Main branch of the Miners' Union, he saw to it that there was always sufficient business to keep him occupied full-time so that he had no job underground. On the District Council he served on several committees and sub-committees, some of which involved visits and inspections and the payment of expenses. He was chairman of the committee that supervised the non-profit making scheme for distributing free coal to the miners of Martins Main. The scheme had its own lorries and workmen. Accounts for this business were a closely guarded secret. Another of his lucrative activities was to chair the small committee that ran the Upthorpe Working Mens' Club. This magnificent institution, rebuilt by the brewery company from a wooden shack into a palace of chrome and glass, was the centre of Upthorpe nightlife. It provided cheap drink to quench any thirst, live entertainment at the weekend, bingo several nights each week, and the opportunity for speculation at any time of the day on the four one-arm bandits. Running a club like this was an important job for the community and it was accepted that the committee should pay themselves an appropriate level of expenses.

Sandra wondered how much money her father had tucked away in his building society account. He was certainly generous to her with the housekeeping money, although he had no plans about having a car or a house of his own. He always maintained that he was a working man and a fighter for the working man's cause. He lived the role, which probably accounted for his popularity in Upthorpe and at the pit.

Sandra glanced at her watch. It was time to go and meet her friend Pauline and then catch the bus to Doncaster. She poured some perfume down her bra and then slipped on her underskirt and dress.

It was in Doncaster that night that she first met Terry Lacey. He danced with her several times and near the end of the evening when the lights were low, he held her very close and tickled her ear with his tongue. He wanted to take her home in his car, but she insisted on going home on the bus with Pauline. She knew it would not be the last time she would meet Terry Lacey. Life was really opening up for Sandra Green.

Chapter 2

Wednesday 20 May 1964

'Send Dobson in now, Mrs Parks, will you please?'

Mr Pickersgill flicked the button of the intercom with his left hand, as he glanced through a pink-coloured form requiring his signature to authorise the money for another project. He looked at the signatures of all the other people who had signed their approval, until his eyes rested on that of R J Jones. It was on the line above the one for the signature of the Regional Director.

'Sign anything, some folk,' he mumbled as he tossed the form into his out-tray, unsigned.

'Come in, lad. Don't sit there, come a bit nearer,' he said, indicating a chair positioned alongside his desk.

'Thank you, Sir.' Roy Dobson was recalling his last encounter with Mr Pickersgill and he approached this meeting with caution.

'Now then, I understand that you have accepted the post at Martins Main.'

'Yes, Sir.'

'And that you will be starting there next week?' Roy nodded.

'Well, this meeting is something that I don't normally have with a new manager. But in your case, I decided that it is necessary for me to have a word with you before you take up the post. I had a lot to do with your appointment. That is one reason. The other reason is that Martins Main is losing a lot of money now for the British Coal Executive, so I have taken a particular interest in the pit and got to know something about it. I want to give you a few facts about the pit, rather than leave you to pick them up from other, less reliable, sources.'

'Thank you, Sir.' Roy was a little embarrassed by the fatherly approach.

'First of all, you have got a tough job to do. Life won't be easy at Martins Main, because the men don't take easily to change. But change they will have to have, because the pit has had a bad record of results for a long time. The original owner, a fellow called George Martin, made a fortune out of the pit at the end of the last century and in the years just before the First World War. The company he sold the mine to had lost the same fortune by the end of the Second World War. The British Coal Executive has not done much better and, along with the losses, goes a history of indecision and procrastination.'

Mr Pickersgill paused and pushed his hand through his hair. Roy took this as a cue for a question.

'Is the main trouble geological, Sir, or is it the organisation along with manpower problems?'

'There are some organisational deficiencies, but I think the main difficulty is the manpower. The men at Martins are very conservative. They remember the lean years and they cling to every old practice and concession they have ever had, and grab any more that may be going. The trouble is that, over the years, they have never had any good leaders among their own union men and, as a result, they don't like being led. Your first job is to get a contact within their ranks and there is one possibility. The chap to go for is Joe Green, the Union President. Everybody calls him Cobba; you'll meet him, he'll make sure of that. This must be your first job.'

He paused and gave Roy a searching look.

'You'll have to buy him. It might be expensive and it won't be easy.'

Roy Dobson nodded slowly, and the two men looked for a moment into each others' eyes. There was a link of conspiracy between them.

'As for the rest, you must get to know the set-up and the people at Martins as quickly as possible. Then we will strengthen the staff for you. You will see the obvious weak links soon enough.'

'Have you decided any set policy for the pit in the future, Sir?'

'I have my own ideas, but I don't intend to share them with you at this moment in time. I shall be interested in your ideas when you have had a look around.'

This rebuff sent Roy retreating into his shell again.

'One other thing, Dobson;' He paused again and gave Roy a searching look. 'I must tell you a bit about Reg Jenkins.'

There was another pause and a long look. 'He is a great fellow, is Reg. I have known him and his wife a long time; in fact, we were students at university together. Reg has a sharp tongue and it gets him into trouble from time to time. It got him into serious trouble in Wales. He caused some big disputes and the Coal Executive had more or less decided to throw him on the scrapheap. That would have been a shame really, so I agreed to take him up here and somebody else took the hammer for the trouble in Wales. Now he doesn't know this. He thinks this job is promotion for services rendered, so he will carry on in his old ways. You will have to watch this. Remember it's your pit and you are the one who will stand in the witness box if anything goes wrong. You'll find that Reg Jenkins will help you a lot in some things.'

He waved his arms to the side. 'Anyway you know what I mean, and you know now what to watch out for.'

'Yes, I will remember what you have said, Mr Pickersgill.'

'I don't think that there is anything else that I want to say, Dobson.'

'Right, Sir.' Roy stood up to leave.

'You will remember that this has been a confidential chat.'

'Of course, Sir.'

'I don't want anyone else to hear of anything from this conversation. I suggest not even your wife. They can forget and let things slip out at times.'

'Yes, I understand.'

'By the way, has your wife been up to see the house?'

'No. I am bringing her and the children on Saturday.'

'Well, I think she will approve of it. I have told the housing boys to get it ready for you as quickly as possible. It is a nice, large house not very far from the pit, but on the hill on the opposite side of Upthorpe. It has a large, walled garden and a very good gardener. I am told that the last Regional Director always got a supply of fresh tomatoes from there. I shall expect the tradition to continue, Dobson.'

'Oh indeed, Sir; I'll see to that.'

Roy took his leave more pleased with his second contact with Mr Pickersgill.

Monday 25 May 1964

They were crowding up to the barrier in the pit bottom and getting restless as the last few minutes dragged up to shift time at the end of the afternoon shift. Ben Holt dreaded this time of day; he was the onsetter, the man in charge of the pit bottom, and he operated the signals for the shaft to the pit top and to the winding-engineman. It was easy at the end of the dayshift as there were always some bosses around then; but, at the end of the afternoon shift, he stood alone against the mob of tired men. They were all anxious to get into the baths and off home or into the club for a drink. The cages in the shaft were at the top and bottom ready for winding the men because all the coal had been raised to the surface long before the shift time as it had been another poor day for output at Martins Main.

'Come on, Benny, get the cage moving. We shall be on overtime soon,' a voice yelled from the crowd.

'Aye, come on, Benny,' others echoed.

They were getting restless. Ben Holt took out his pocketwatch and looked at the minute hand. Five minutes to go.

'Throw that bloody thing away, Benny. It's a company watch. Look at a right watch.'

'Aye, come on, Benny. We're missing all the sunshine down here.'

Ben Holt moved towards the signals, and then he paused. It was the first day of the new manager. He must be careful. They said this chap was a stickler for the rules, and time was time.

'You've not filled enough coal today to deserve to go out,' he said to the black faces near the barrier.

'That's not thy worry, Benny,' said young Gerry Moore. 'Get us on't bloody cage. That's thy fucking job.' Gerry Moore was a noisy young fellow and very cocky since he had got a regular job on 56s coalface where his father was charge-man.

'What's the matter, Gerry,' said one of the older fellows. 'Tha's very restless. Has she promised thee a bit tonight?'

'Promised him a bit?' scoffed a young chap near Gerry. 'He daren't have any. Every time he has a sniff he drops her one in't pot. That's right, isn't it, Gerry?'

'Thee shut up, Bert,' said Gerry. 'Tha's no room to talk.' But Gerry Moore was embarrassed by the conversation. He was only twenty-two and his three years of marriage had produced two children and he was sure that his bed work was more successful than anything else he ever did.

The signals from the surface echoed around the pit bottom indicating that the shaft was ready for man-riding. The men crowded onto the cage and held tight to the hand rail as the cage raced the four hundred yards up to the surface in less than a minute. As they emerged into the pit yard, some of them with their cap lamps still lit, they were surprised to see the big bulk of George Turnbull stood in their path. They did not race as usual across to the lamp room and into the baths, but walked in an orderly way past him. Some mumbled 'How do?' but they could see by his face that George was in a tough mood.

'Where's thee dad, Gerry?' he pounced on Gerry Moore as he came up to him.

'He's behind George. He'll be up on the next cage.'

'I want to see him. And thee come over here, Willie, I'll have a word with thee as well.' Willie Carter was another older miner and an experienced face worker. He was a member of Upthorpe Methodist Church and although he had been a chargeman in the past, he couldn't reconcile the chargeman's responsibilities with his church beliefs.

Fred Moore, Gerry's father, was near the end of the next line of men who emerged from the shaft. He was a big fellow and he moved with long, deliberate strides. He saw George and Willie Carter, who were obviously waiting for him.

'Now then, George,' said Fred.

'Come over to the office, Fred; I want a word with you two. How much coal have you filled this afternoon?' George asked this question as they started to walk across the pit yard.

'Not much, George. We've had trouble with that conveyor belt all afternoon again.'

'I thought as much when they told me how many tubs had been filled at the loading point,' replied George. He unlocked the door of his office and they went inside.

It was a square office, with a square table in the middle of the floor, and along two of the walls were wooden forms. Plans of the underground workings were pinned to most of the walls and half the area of the table was covered with piles of reporting books and notebooks. In one corner was a rack which held several walking sticks and, in the same corner, two pit helmets were suspended from nails driven into the wall. Over everything was a layer of fine, black dust as the office was near the surface coal cleaning plant. George sat in the chair behind the desk and the two men sat on the form opposite him.

'What's the reason then for the belt not running?'

'It's the water, George. You can't expect a belt to run with all that water,' said Willie Carter.

'Willie Carter, I thought better of thee than to make excuses like that,' said George. 'There was the same water last Thursday and Friday but, because you did as you were told, and fed the coal on steady, the belt ran with no problems and you cleared all the coal on the coalface. That conveyor was running okay this morning because I saw it myself.'

The two men were silent. They both remembered that George had been up and down the coalface himself all through the shift on Thursday and Friday, supervising the work. Nobody had dared to do anything wrong with him there and he had also organised extra supports where the roof conditions had been bad.

'That coalface was much better today,' he continued. 'We've never had the roof conditions as good, and you know it.'

'Aye, it was better in my part of the coalface. I'll admit that,' said Willie.

'Aye, and because the roof was good you have all let go with them shovels like madmen at the beginning of the shift. I'll bet you bogged the conveyor down for a start and it never ran for the rest of the shift.' George was beginning to raise his voice.

'There is no doubt the lads went hard at it to start with, George,' said Fred Moore.

'And then I suppose they sat on their arses while the Deputy and the belt-man tussled with the conveyor. Well, you can tell them this, Fred. I'm only paying them for the coal filled. If they want to sit on their arses, they'll get paid arse-sitting money from now on. I told Mr Dobson that there should be no trouble from now on with 56s face. You filled the coal alright at the end of last week and there is no reason why you should not fill it this week. He'll think I am a grand one when he gets to know about this, and on his first day at the pit, too.'

'Now George, I don't think you should be too hasty. That coalface has been stood over the weekend. Conditions change you know. It wasn't like last Thursday and Friday today,' said Fred.

'Don't try it on, Fred.' George rose in his chair and raised his finger at Fred Moore. 'There's some bright lads in your team that will use any excuse to avoid working. I've seen them all before. I've made up my mind that I'm not having the same trouble on 56s as I have had with them on other coalfaces. You tell them that it is money for work done and nothing else from now on. Off you go.'

'If that's it, I'll tell them,' said Fred, as he stumbled out of the office.

George decided to wait until 56s Deputy came out of the pit. When he had spoken to him his suspicions were confirmed.

'Buggered it up, George, they did. Right at the beginning of the shift they piled the conveyor up until it couldn't run. I tried everything I knew, but the damage was done. There are some right bastards in that team.'

'Right,' said George. 'I'll show them where they get off. You book the amount of coal each man filled. We have a good case here.'

Tuesday 26 May 1964

Roy Dobson had arranged that he should meet the committee members of the Miners' Union for Martins Main in the pit conference room. He had spent his first twenty-four hours at the pit meeting a lot of people, asking a lot of questions and studying the facts and figures. The picture was evolving clearer and clearer. Martins Main workings covered a large geographical area and there were plenty of reserves of coal which were untouched. The trouble was that the reserves were split up with geological faults and these faults had a history of causing water difficulties from time to time in some seams. It was considered that there were twelve workable seams at the mine. The best two coal seams had been worked-out in the profitable period of the mine's history before the First World War. Six of the other seams had been worked at different times and, of these, three were being worked at the present. They were the Benton seam, the Morley seam and the Low Moor seam. They were all thin seams about three-feet thick and the coal was mined from nine coalfaces. The coal was of good quality and had plenty of demand from a range of customers.

The manpower, of sixteen hundred men, could not be used efficiently because the coalfaces were spread out into different parts of the reserves, and none of them were near the pit bottom and the shafts. Roy studied the plans for the future and they too continued the same dispersed system of working in various parts of the reserves. His last job the previous night had been to study the accounts for the mine. Back throughout the history of the British Coal Executive, the figures for Martins were in red, showing a significant loss for each year's operations.

'What do you think to the pit, then?' his wife had asked the previous night, when he had been talking to her on the telephone from his hotel.

'Oh, it's going to be interesting,' he had replied. 'There are a pile of problems as high as the headgear, but there are answers to a lot of them. It is all a question of whether the manpower is prepared to accept the answers and follow them up with some hard work.'

'You'll sort it out, love,' she'd said.

His wife had always believed in him and encouraged him, but as the union officials filed into the conference room he wondered if her confidence was justified. He shook hands with them all in turn as they introduced themselves. When he got to Cobba Green, the last one, he looked deep into the cold, grey eyes. There were no signs of warmth there. Roy took his chair at one end of the large, rectangular table.

'I've asked you to come in this morning to have a quiet chat with you and to give you a chance to meet me. I don't have a lot to tell you about Martins Main, because it is too early yet for me to have formed any impressions of the problems here, or of the solutions to them.'

The door opened and two canteen women entered with a tray of teas and a tray of coffees. Roy stopped his remarks.

The men were impressed by the treatment. They had never been accustomed to such consideration. As the conversation died down from the requests for sugar and milk, Jimmy

Bell spoke out. Little Jimmy, as he was known, was the Miners' Union secretary and he had a reputation for stating his views with no forethought for tact or personal feelings.

'I'll tell you one thing straight, Mister. There are a lot of fellows in Upthorpe not happy that this job has not gone to a local chap. We make nowt round here of fetching foreigners in to run our pits. That's right, isn't it, Cobba?'

'Aye, Jimmy, but I don't think it's Mr Dobson's fault that he got the job,' replied Cobba Green.

'That's true enough,' said Roy. 'I've no doubt that there are plenty of fellows in Yorkshire as capable as I am to do this job. Probably someone decided to get a few new ideas into the pit, and thought I might bring some with me from the Midlands.'

'New ideas are alright so long as you have brought some extra brass to pay for them. I reckon our lads will not object if your ideas put more brass in their pay packets. That's what we want.' Jimmy smiled round at the rest of the meeting, glad to have got the first blow in for the men. Roy treated his remarks as a joke and laughed them off, but he was not happy at the prospect of an enlightened understanding with Jimmy Bell.

The meeting continued with general talk about the pit and Roy briefly sketched out his early career and experience, dwelling particularly on his practical work.

'I want you to accept me,' he concluded, 'as a young fellow who has worked hard and studied hard to make mining his life. I'm like you all; I come from a mining background, it's bred in me. I think you will find that, while I am at Martins Main, I shall do my best to do a good job. If we all work together – and I mean work together – so that the management and men are all aiming for the same result, then I am sure that we can make Martins into a successful pit, and Upthorpe into a very prosperous place.' Roy finished to a silence that was impressive. He had rehearsed his last remarks a few times and he was confident that they had made the required impression.

There was a pause, and Roy was going to go on with other items he had prepared, when the door opened and Reg Jenkins strolled in.

'Good morning,' he said, addressing everyone together. 'I see you've got all the rogues of Martins together at one go, today, Mr Dobson. You know this lot will rob you and plunder you and never turn a hair. That's right, isn't it, Cobba?'

'You keep saying so, Mr Jenkins. Some day you'll find out,' replied Cobba guardedly.

Reg Jenkins sat beside Roy and assumed chairmanship of the meeting. He used the gathering to mount one of his attacks. He challenged the work performance of the men, the ability of the officials to supervise the work properly, and the lack of interest of anyone to make Martins a successful pit. The whole tone of the meeting changed to one of challenge and counter-challenge, defence and attack, placing blame and allotting responsibility. Like all such meetings, the only point of contact was an agreement that the past carried the blame for the present day problems. There was no concern for the future. As Roy sat back in his chair, aloof from the arguments, superseded by his superior who was in a militant, forceful mood, he was sad to see all his aims for the meeting shattered around him.

There was no talk of a new approach, no talk of a new future; no hope, no light on the black, industrial scene. Only the old prejudices showed themselves, the restrictions rose up alongside the old traditions, industrial sores and cancers openly bleeding and nobody was interested in applying first aid. Would there be any change? Could there be any change? Or was the whole set up entangled in an intertwining undergrowth from the past that choked everything?

When the union men left, Reg Jenkins stayed behind. He was proud of his performance. He wanted to underline the star points of it and leave the younger man impressed.

'That's the way you have to talk to these fellows, Roy, lad,' he said, striding around the conference table. 'It has got to be attack all the time. Get in there first. Show them who is tough. Show them who's the Boss. That's the way I have always dealt with men and that's the way they expect it. I don't go along with all this consultation and 'team spirit' business. It's soft; it shows weakness. A boss must be feared. That's the only thing workmen understand–fear. Fear for their pay packet, fear for their job. Don't you agree?'

'Well, I don't entirely go along with you, Mr Jenkins, in that approach.' The tone of Roy's reply made Reg Jenkins pause in his stride and lean over the table and talk down to his manager, but the young man sat fixed and huddled in his chair and their eyes never met.

'Now, now, lad,' said Reg. 'Think a bit before you try anything fancy at this pit. Take my tip. I've seen this place for a few months now. These boys are seeped in the old ideas. They are not the type for any new ideas or new notions. You get to know them a bit before you try anything. You're not in the Midlands now.'

Roy did not pursue the subject, but suggested that they return to the manager's office. There they talked about the operations of the pit and then, over a sandwich lunch, they discussed in detail the conditions and the results of the different seams being worked. The manager's clerk who came into the office interrupted them.

'Yes, Gordon, what is it?'

'It's 56s men, Mr Dobson. There is some trouble with them. They are all sat outside the canteen. They are not going down the pit this afternoon.'

'What is the trouble about, Gordon? Do you know?'

'I don't know yet, Mr Dobson, but I'll try to find out. I've been trying to get in contact with Mr Turnbull, but he's still down the pit. That is why I thought you should know.'

'Alright, Gordon; I'll try and get in touch with George. You had better send for Jimmy Bell and Cobba Green and we'll see if they know anything about it.' Roy picked up the underground telephone and asked the exchange man to try and find George Turnbull. Reg Jenkins, who was chewing his lunch with a hard look on his face, embarrassed him.

'They are trying something on, to test you, lad,' said Reg. 'I tell you, man, these fellows at this pit stink. They are the dregs of the barrel. They are always trying to cause trouble and go on strike.'

A few minutes later Jimmy Bell and Cobba Green came into the office. Dobson tackled Cobba from the start.

'Cobba, I understand that we have some trouble with 56s men. What's it all about? Do you know?'

'I have heard some rumours,' replied Cobba, guardedly.

'Is it true that they are not going down the pit this afternoon?' asked Roy.

'They have not changed into their pit clothes yet, as far as I can see,' replied Cobba.

'Well, this is no way to carry on, is it?' said Roy forcefully. 'You know what I was saying this morning. I am available to discuss any problems, at any time, but I will not be pressurised into discussions by threats and strikes. I have never been used to this, and I have no intention of starting. You go along and tell them to get changed and go to their work and then I will see the chargeman, along with you chaps, tomorrow, to discuss their grievances.'

'We've got some hope,' said Jimmy Bell. 'That team stick together and they don't put their problems off until tomorrow.'

'That's your problem, Jimmy. You are elected to handle their affairs, in your good time, not in theirs.'

Jimmy was going to reply to this, but Cobba moved to the door.

'Come on, Jimmy. Let's go and see these chaps.' The two of them left the office.

'This is the history of this place—threats and strikes all the time. Not enough firmness by the management,' said Reg. 'That's the job in front of you, lad. These fellows must be put in their place.'

The underground telephone rang and Roy heard George Turnbull's side of the story. He listened carefully, making no comments, but smiling at the graphic punctuations and images in Turnbull's account.

'And you will be on the surface in about fifteen minutes then, George? Right, you had better come straight up to my office.'

Roy put the telephone down and thought carefully. George had put forward a strong case; there was no doubt about that. This was Roy's first case with the men and he had got to win it. The men must understand that while he was Manager, they would only get paid for work done. He looked across at Mr Jenkins. Where did he stand in this matter? He had stated his views all morning, but if it came to the crunch would he back them up?

'This is a good case for my second day, Mr Jenkins. There is a principle involved here. We have got to win this one, you know.'

Cobba and Jimmy were shown back into the office.

'Now then, Cobba; what do you make of them?' It was Reg who spoke first.

'We have had a talk to them, Mr Jenkins, and the lads have a grievance. They want to know what they are getting paid for yesterday's shift.'

'That is a strange question,' said Roy quickly. 'How do I know what they are getting paid for yesterday? How does anybody know yet? The wages will not be prepared until the end of the week, and the men will get them a week next Friday. I think somebody is getting very particular if he wants to know now what he's getting paid for yesterday.'

'Come off it, Mister,' said Cobba. 'George Turnbull was back at the pit last night. He told the men what they were getting paid. He said they would only get paid for the coal they filled yesterday, and they are not satisfied. They want it clearing up before they go down the pit.'

'Aye, that's right,' said Jimmy. 'We have the chargeman and a mate outside if you want to hear their view.'

'I don't need to hear anybody else's views,' said Roy. 'I know all the facts in this case and the principle that George expressed last night is quite correct—payment for work done. There is nothing wrong with that. I have always paid that way and I intend to continue paying the same way at Martins.'

'That's alright if everything else is right. Our lads can't be expected to stand the cost if the management doesn't get the equipment working for them. That's where we stand, isn't it, Cobba?' Jimmy was warming to the argument.

'Are you going to see these two lads, then?' asked Cobba, who had been standing by the door all the time.

'I'll see these two if the rest of the team get changed into their pit clothes and go underground.'

'We'll ask them,' replied Cobba. 'But there isn't much chance of them going underground. These lads have always sorted things out together on the pit top. This team just don't trust management, I might as well tell you, Mister.'

Roy stood up sharply and raised his voice, pointing at Cobba and Jimmy.

'Well, somebody is going to have to start and have some trust around here. And they can start by having some trust in me. My word is my bond, Mister. I'll tell you that now before we start. And you can go and tell your men that. And you can tell them this as well; the first day they find that Roy Dobson can't be trusted they will not find me sitting in this chair, because I don't want to be a manager over anybody if I can't be trusted.'

There was a gripping silence through the office as Roy sat down, his face flushed and his eyes glistening.

'Come on, Jimmy, let's see what we can do,' said Cobba, and they left the office.

'This is typical of Turnbull, you will find,' said Reg Jenkins. 'He is crude. He goes at them like a mad bull. No tact. I can see who is behind this already.'

'He has a good case here, Mr Jenkins. He told me over the telephone. These lads filled all the coal on Thursday and Friday when George was there supervising them; but yesterday afternoon, when George was not there, they piled the conveyor up early on in the shift until it would not run and then they filled hardly anything for the rest of the shift. I'm going to stand behind George on this one. I know it's early days for me, but I think that these chaps want putting in their place. They can't be allowed to get away with performances like yesterday.'

'You try, lad, but you are on a poor wicket with this case.'

'Mr Jenkins, I might be on a poor wicket, in fact I've never been on a good one, but I am going to stick it out to the end, and I hope you are going to help me.'

'We'll see how it goes,' said Reg, very noncommittally. 'I'll hang on in case you need me.'

George Turnbull came into the office. He was black and dusty and still carried his lamps and his yardstick with him. He was surprised to see Jenkins in the office.

'Oh, how do you do, Mr Jenkins?'

'Good afternoon, Turnbull. Yes, I'm here again. Always at hand to sort out the problems you keep making for yourself. How did you get into this one, then?'

'It started with the performance on 56s face yesterday afternoon. They had filled bugger-all at the end of the shift, so I came back to the pit and saw the chargeman. I told him that his team might as well understand that they are going to get paid for work done from now on at 56s coalface. There is no reason why they can't do their job now on that face. Conditions are much improved. I know because I have spent a lot of time there this last week. In any case I am not having that team causing trouble on 56s like they did on their last coalface. You said yourself, Mr Jenkins, that we must put them in their place before they create more trouble.'

'Yes, I know what I said, but you have got to use tact, man. Do it cunning. Don't let them know what you are planning. You can't tell them straight out like you did last night; they're bound to flare up.'

'You have got to talk straight to these men, Mister. It's no use talking to them in riddles. They are as thick as this desk, all of them. They only understand straight talking. That's the only way to get through to them.'

'Alright, George, have the rest of the men gone to their work?' asked Roy.

'They were all going across to the shafts when I came up just now,' replied George.

'We'll wait for Cobba and his mate then, and see what they have made of these men.'

They fell into discussing details of another part of the mine while they waited. After about ten minutes Cobba and Jimmy were shown into the office, but this time they had with them the chargeman, Fred Moore, and his mate, Willie Carter.

'Now then, have your mates gone down the pit?' asked Roy.

The men looked at each other hesitantly before anyone replied.

'No, Mr Dobson,' said Cobba. 'They flatly refuse to go down until this job is sorted out. There is a principle involved here which needs settling and, as far as me and my colleagues are concerned, they have the union backing.'

Roy was going to speak, but Mr Jenkins got in first.

'Go on then, Cobba, put your case. You have the chargeman here now. We might as well sort it out.'

'Thank you, Mr Jenkins. Our case is that under the conditions prevailing on 56s face, our men can't be expected to earn their money under the existing seam contract. That's right, isn't it, Fred?'

'Yes,' said Fred. 'There's too much water and the roof condition isn't good enough.'

'But you did your work alright on Thursday and Friday, and the roof is a lot better than it was a week ago?' said George.

'Ah, yes, George,' said Cobba. 'But that coalface has been stood over the weekend and conditions don't improve in a pit by standing. We all know that.'

'But Mr Turnbull himself saw the face yesterday morning before these men went on the afternoon shift; he said it was no different from Friday. That's right, isn't it, Mr Turnbull?'

'Yes, Mr Dobson. These lads know what happened yesterday. They bogged the conveyor down early in the shift and never gave it a chance to run.'

'That's another thing, Mr Jenkins,' said Cobba Green. 'This team object to what George said last night. He said his piece without getting the full facts. He was only guessing and giving his views last night when he saw the men. He had not seen any other official at that time.'

'Yes, but all that the Deputy said confirmed my views,' said George, getting excited. 'I'll fetch him in here to tell you himself if you like.'

'There will be no need for that Mr Turnbull, I think that we can reach an understanding here without bringing the Deputy in,' said Roy. He looked across at the union officials. 'I accept what Mr Turnbull says that the men can now earn their wages on 56s face. What I am prepared to do though, as a compromise, is to pay for yesterday the average rate that the men earn for the rest of the week. This includes the wage earned today and I shall only pay it provided the men go straight to their work.'

'That's no good, Mister,' said Jimmy. 'The lads have made it quite clear to us that they are only going to work today if you guarantee them a full day's wage for yesterday, as the conditions on 56s face were not their fault.'

'I can't do that,' said Roy, amazed at the finality of the request. 'There is no doubt in my mind that the major part of the responsibility for yesterday's poor performance rests with the men.'

No one replied to this comment. The two workmen and the union officials looked at each other in silence. They had reached the waiting phase of the dispute. After a long pause, Cobba spoke.

'I think you should bend a bit here, Mr Dobson. We don't want to start our association with you in an antagonistic way.'

'And I don't want to start my association with you by appearing to be a soft Johnny, because I am not.'

Reg glanced at Roy at this remark but he did not say anything. After another pause the underground telephone rang. George answered it. He listened carefully and then put the telephone down. He looked at Roy and then he glanced at Reg Jenkins.

'All the rest of the afternoon shift men are still in the pit bottom and they say they are not going forward to their work until this dispute is settled,' he said quietly.

The workmen nodded to each other. Immediately Reg Jenkins stood up. He spoke quickly and waved the men out of the office.

'This is fucking stupid. I'll have to sort it out. Right, Cobba, I'll fix yesterday's wages for 56s men. Off you go and get these men down the pit. And let the men in the pit bottom know that it's sorted out and they can get off to their work.'

'Right you are. Thank you, Mr Jenkins, I'll see to it.' Cobba and the four men hurried out of the office.

'A poor case, that one,' said Reg. 'I told you it was all the time. We don't want the pit on strike for an argument like that. Well, I must be going back to Region Headquarters now. There you are Turnbull; I've sorted them out for you, again.'

With a flourish he left the office to silence. Roy leaned over the desk with his head in his hands. He had a fixed look on his face and his eyes were focused on the door through which Reg had departed. George understood his feelings.

'I'm sorry, Mr Dobson; I should never have started this so soon after your arrival. I ought to have let you get settled in first. You needed to win your first battle with that team.'

'Oh don't take that attitude, George. It's not your fault. I think you were right and I would have backed you all the way. The thing that worries me about this case is the way the heavy artillery have let us down.'

'He's very unpredictable is Mr Jenkins, from what I have seen. Sometimes he causes trouble the other way by blasting the men when it's not their fault at all. I don't understand him; it must be his Welsh blood. One thing is certain though: whichever way it goes, I always seem to be in the wrong.'

'Don't worry about that, we'll sort him out, somehow. At least I now know that I have problems above me, as well as the problems around me at Martins. I must say though, it has been a disappointing day. I had hoped to set a new pattern of communications and get a new understanding of some trust established. All that has happened today has been a continuation of the old regime. You know, George, as well as I do, that if you don't start by changing things in a job like this, you never get a chance. Never mind, it's not too late, yet. You go and get bathed, George, and then I will have a talk with you and Mike Darlow about the way I want us to operate together.'

After George left, Roy sat at his desk thinking about the events of the day. Eventually he went to the window behind his desk and looked out at the pit entrance road and beyond to Martins Lane and the houses of Upthorpe. He felt very lonely and isolated at the signs of so many homes and families. He realised that he was missing his wife and the children and he knew that the next fortnight, until they joined him in the new house, was going to be a trying time. He turned then and went to the window at the opposite end of his office. This looked down onto the pit yard, and there he saw 56s men walking across to the shaft. They were all laughing and joking together. Were they laughing at their victory? Was it a triumph for them and were they laughing at his humiliation? Or was it just that they didn't care, that nothing really mattered to them? That was the most important question that Roy needed to answer at Martins Main. Who cared among the men, who cared among the officials, and who cared among his superiors? It was very important that he knew the answers to these questions, because he cared; he cared about his responsibilities very much. That might be his problem, he told himself–he took things too seriously.

Thursday 28 May 1964

Willie Carter sat back in the pew and revelled in the scene. Around him, the trustees of Upthorpe Methodist Church sat, or stood, and listened to the organ demonstrating its range and rich sound. They were in strange surroundings, in a church, in Pontefract, that was to be demolished in the interests of industrial development and the finances of the Methodist church. They had all collected together and travelled from Upthorpe in a hired bus, to hear the organ before they considered whether it was worth the cost of having it dismantled and rebuilt in the Upthorpe church. It was Willie Carter's son, Peter, who was playing the organ. He was only sixteen years old, and he looked young to be sitting at such a large, two-manual organ.

'He certainly makes it sound a fine instrument, Willie,' said John Warwick, the Upthorpe headmaster.

'He does that, Mr Warwick,' replied Willie. 'He gets his talent from his grandfather, you know. A great man for his music, was my dad. He used to build his own violins and play them.'

'Where is your Peter having lessons now, Willie?'

'In Leeds, Mr Warwick; his teacher plays the organ at the Parish Church there,' replied Willie. 'I can tell the difference now; I think our Peter is making great progress.'

Peter was deputy organist at Upthorpe Methodist. Everybody knew that he was a much better player than Mrs Pearson, but she had played the organ, in her own way, for over twenty years and nobody dared suggest that she should be replaced. Willie stopped listening to the organ and concentrated on his arguments for the meeting later in the evening. Willie had been a regular at Upthorpe Methodist Church all his life and he had spent much of his spare time in all the various activities of the church. However he had never been one of the leading figures in the church, and his views had never counted for much. To some extent his job at the pit, with its shift work, was against him, and the fact that his wife played no part at all in the church, also didn't help. On this occasion, though, he was desperate to see the decision go his way, so he must make his views sound important. He passionately wanted to have that organ at Upthorpe. He could see it in the middle of the church, with his son Peter sitting at the keyboard leading the singing, and everyone marvelling at Peter's playing. Willie had never been an important person himself; this he accepted gladly, and now all his dreams lay in his son achieving distinction for the family. Peter was a good lad, he had great talent, and there was no reason why he should not achieve the honours his father prayed for.

Willie ran his hand through his thinning grey hair and he nervously twitched his nose and adjusted his spectacles. If only he had the ability to express his feelings clearly and so convince the rest of the trustees with his arguments. He knew what they would say: the church has only just paid off its debt from its initial building project; people are tired of being asked for donations and more donations; the structure of the church will need altering and the choir seats will need moving to get the organ in; the organ is too large for a church the size of Upthorpe. He knew all their views and the arguments they would raise, but somehow he had to get across his ideas and convince them to have this organ.

After they had listened to Peter for a while, they talked to a representative of the firm that had built the organ originally. He explained what would be involved in moving it, and the probable cost. Willie's heart sank when the figure mentioned was around £1,000; he was sure that the trustees would never enter into another debt of that order. The representative then played the organ to show its scope and variety, and the effects he achieved left them all, including Peter, amazed and impressed.

Peter sat with his father on the bus going home. He could not control his excitement and enthusiasm.

'She is a beauty, Dad. How long do you think it will take to get it transferred to Upthorpe? I can't wait to have an organ like that to practise on every day, and it will only be a few minutes' walk from our house.'

Willie was feeling sad, and the lad's excitement made him feel it more.

'Don't build up too much, lad,' he said. 'It's not been agreed to have the organ yet, and there's a lot of money involved. Nothing is settled at this stage, and I don't think it's a foregone conclusion.'

'But Dad, you have all heard it. You can't let that beautiful instrument go to scrap. It's got to come to Upthorpe.'

'We'll see, Peter, lad. I'll let you know how the meeting goes when I get home tonight.'

Willie sat back in his seat and closed his eyes. It is so easy to make a decision when you are young, he thought. There are no complications at that age—everything is either black or white.

When they reached Upthorpe, they left the bus at the church gate and Peter turned for home while his father followed the others inside the church. Unlike the usual trustees' meetings, that were held in the vestry, at John Warwick's suggestion they were holding the meeting in the main part of the church. As they filed in they all looked to the end of the church where the new organ would have to fit. Then they looked to the side of the church at the old harmonium, with its handle sticking out for the organ blower. To Willie, that harmonium was his enemy. He had a great desire to see it destroyed to make way for the other organ, and his son Peter. Five minutes with his hammer and pick out of the pit, he thought, and he could reduce that harmonium to firewood. These thoughts were boiling over in his mind during the prayer, with which tradition dictated they started the meeting. Then John Warwick, the chairman, addressed the meeting.

'Now then, brothers and sisters, as we arranged at our last meeting, we have been to hear the organ in Pontefract, and we are here now to decide whether we shall go ahead and have it or not. What are your feelings?'

Willie remained silent. John Warwick had given no clue to his feelings on the subject and he normally carried most weight among the trustees. So it was an open question, which way the meeting would go. Then the others began. Willie sank lower in his seat as the first three speakers all criticised the Pontefract organ as too large, too expensive to move, too loud for the choir and generally not suitable for Upthorpe. All the arguments flowed out and hardly any were in favour of the organ. Joe Horton then cleared his voice to speak. Joe was a farmer and he never did anything in a hurry, including speaking. He looked a bit more anxious than usual and Willie had an idea that he had been told what to say by his sister, Bertha Pearson, who was the regular organist. She had made her views well known to everybody that she was against the new organ, and some folks were sure that this was because she was not able to play anything more complicated than the old harmonium.

'I suppose I am a bit old-fashioned,' began Joe. 'But I have got used to this place as it is. It has served us well for thirty years and during all that time we have sung to that old harmonium there. I don't think that it has ever let us down and it seems a bit wrong, to me, to throw it on the scrapheap now that we have a chance of having something bigger and more complicated. We'll probably end up dragging the piano in out of the schoolroom every other week because the thing has gone wrong. They do go wrong, you know, these complicated machines. We've had some on the farm and I've had my bellyful of them lately. No, I'm not for changing that old harmonium, I think we should stay as we are.'

'You surprise me, Joe,' said John Warwick. 'You didn't have those views thirty years ago when we wanted to build this new church. You were all for change, then, and I remember it was you who made the first move, by giving us the land on which to build the church. And another thing that we all should remember is that this organ is not a new one; it's a hand-made, craftsman-built instrument that has mellowed and matured over its sixty years in use. It is not a modern machine, and I don't think that it'll cause a lot of trouble like your new harvester, Joe.' John Warwick was beginning to show his hand, and some of the trustees stirred in their seats. They had misjudged his views.

'There is one point, more important than all the others, that I think we should consider,' continued John Warwick. 'And that is the hard work that was done by the church members in Pontefract to buy that organ in the first place. They are our bothers and sisters in Methodism. There must have been some hard-earned pennies put towards the cost of that instrument around the turn of the century. I think we should forget our own selfish position and remember those past members of Methodism. I don't see how we can let such a lovely organ go to scrap. We have a responsibility to the people who bought it, to keep it in use in a Methodist church. How do you feel Willie? Do you want us to have that organ?'

Willie jumped up from his seat. The words came tumbling out as he addressed the meeting.

'Oh I do that, Mr Warwick, I want it more than anything I have ever wanted for this chapel. I'm praying that we shall have it. You know, brothers and sisters, I can see it up there now, and I can hear it playing, and it is a wonderful sound. I know it will be a great blessing to this place. I'll do all I can, Mr Warwick, to raise money so that we can have it. I've always done my best for this chapel, but this time I'll do even better. I'll not leave a stone unturned to raise money for that organ. I can't say more than that.'

'Thank you, Willie,' said John. 'I'm sure you mean all that you have said.'

There was not much more talking, but during the discussion Joe Horton forsook his sister and changed sides to support the organ. The meeting decided to go ahead and form a special organ fund, and an organ fund committee. Willie was made secretary of this committee, and Joe the treasurer. He was so excited, Willie could hardly wait to get home.

★

'What happened, Dad?' asked Peter, as soon as his father got through the door.

'We are going to have it,' replied Willie. 'It was a struggle at first, but John Warwick changed their minds for them. And do you know what? They have made me secretary of the organ fund committee. I'll need some money-raising ideas from you, young lad.'

Willie hardly slept that night, and when the alarm clock went off at four-thirty next morning, he opened weary eyes as he got up to go to Martins Main and 56s coalface.

★

Martins Lane was wilting under the hot, afternoon sun. Along the fronts of the houses the little children lounged in the gutters, apathetic, sticky and dusty. They ran the dust through their fingers and drew strange shapes in the same dust on the footpath. There was no fighting, no shouting, no crying and no games to disturb their parents. They were good, unobtrusive children, slowly tiring in the sultry heat and slowly getting dirtier with each passing car or lorry. At worst, an evening breeze might revive them, at best they would succumb gladly to the water and soap and be put to bed early. Martins Lane was no place for young children on a hot summer's afternoon. The maroon-blue bricks of the houses, weathered and cracked from their sixty-year life, absorbed the blistering heat of the sun like firebricks, and longed for a shower of rain to wash away the dust from their crevices and cool their burning faces. The chimneys stood erect and purposeless because all the fires were shut down or burning low, and some had never been lit. Behind the houses of Martins Lane, in the rectangular bricked-off back gardens, all was still. The little squares of grass in some of the gardens were brown and withering; the flowers in others were drooping and dying. In the shelter of the walls of the outside toilets, mongrel dogs lolled and panted away the afternoon. Doors were open to welcome any breeze, and curtains flapped over the upstairs windowsills, begging for air for the bedrooms. On such an afternoon, everybody who could, stopped completely what they were doing, and the rest went at half pace.

Peggy Moore, her husband at the pit, her little baby fed and changed, her bigger baby asleep upstairs, wiped her perspiring brow and decided to sit down for a rest. She was soon disturbed.

'Are you in, love?' said her friend, Janet Hall, walking straight in at the back door. Janet had been in the same class at school with Peggy, and she lived at number sixty Martins

Lane, ten houses further along from the Moore's house. Janet had been married just one year less than Peggy and the two women had remained friendly even though their circumstances were rapidly diverging. Janet had no children and, with her husband in a good job as a fitter at Martins Main, and with her job in a shop in Doncaster, they were well-off by the normal standards of Martins Lane residents.

'Can you find a seat, Janet? I'm all upset as usual,' said Peggy, indicating the room littered with baby clothes and toys, and the sink in the corner piled high with washing up. 'It's too hot to do owt today. I'm like a dried-up lettuce leaf. I can't stand weather like this.'

'You don't look too good, love,' said Janet. She looked at the straight hair, the pale face and the dull, darkened eyes of her friend. 'I must say I was glad to get home from the shop today and take off my stockings and roll-on. I'll tell you what; let me make a cup of tea while you have five minutes.'

Janet went to the corner and put the kettle on the gas ring. Then, under the tap, she began to wash out two cups and saucers from the heap of dirty pots in the sink.

'What's that you've brought me?' asked Peggy, indicating a small parcel on the table.

'It's the wool you asked me to get for you to knit that jersey for your Michael. It's the colour you wanted.'

'Oh, I must pay you for it while I remember.' She reached up for her purse on the mantelpiece. It was a large purse with many compartments. She searched in various pockets and then put the purse back.

'Do you know, Janet, I could cry. He's done it again. It's Thursday and he's run out of money so he's been in my purse and pinched a pound note. I don't know, I'll have to pay you when I get my money this weekend. But then he's only got four shifts in for last week, so I suppose there'll be an argument before I get enough out of him.'

'Don't worry about that, Peggy. Any time will do; I'm not fussy, you know that.' Janet poured the boiling water into the teapot. 'Bob was saying there was nearly a strike with them last Tuesday.'

'That doesn't surprise me. There's one thing certain; if anybody suggests not working, Gerry will support them. He's not partial to work. I don't know what I saw in him. His mother is always saying what a good lad he is, but I don't think she knows him as well as I do. Anyway, it's too late to worry now.'

'By, but you do sound depressed, love. Here, drink this, it will pep you up.'

They both drank their tea in silence—Peggy her head bowed in despair and nearly in tears; Janet sitting erect, healthy, well-groomed and well-dressed. They were so apparently different that it seemed incongruous that they should remain friendly.

'I don't know why you bother with me, Janet. I seem to have slipped since I got married,' said Peggy at last.

'Don't say that, love. We've been pals for a long time. I think you are just run down, Peggy. You haven't got over having your Michael yet. What you need is a holiday.'

'That's a good one. Some hope of a holiday at this house! The way Gerry gets through the money at the Club, we can hardly make ends meet as it is. And then there are the kids to stop us. How can we go on holiday with them? You don't know how lucky you are, not having a family. I envy you and Bob your freedom.'

Janet paused before replying.

'You might be surprised, Peggy, but we envy you. Do you know Bob would give anything for a baby? I think it may be with him being older than me, but he has wanted one ever since we got married. Nothing ever seems to happen though. Bob wanted me to see a doctor about it a few weeks ago.'

'Are you going to?'

'No. Not yet anyway. Bob was talking to one of his mates at the pit who went to see a doctor with his wife. And do you know what the doctor told them?'

'No.'

Janet laughed to treat it as a joke.

'He told them they were not trying hard enough. He said they had to get stuck in every night. I don't know what else he told them, but it worked–she's pregnant now.'

'What did Bob say to that?'

'Oh, he thought we should try the same idea, so we've been on the same hop. I've bought three sexy nighties from Marks and Spencer to encourage him, and we've had a go. I'm not bothered either way, but Bob is on his knees. I think he has had enough to last him a long time, these last few weeks.'

They both had a good laugh together.

'Has it had any effect then?'

'Well, I'm a week late this month, but that doesn't mean much with me. I never was predictable.'

'I wish I had the same trouble. With me, it's the opposite way. When Gerry has had a few drinks he's always on the go.' She turned very serious. 'I think it might be that what's getting me down, Janet.' She looked down at her cup, very embarrassed. 'You see, he won't wear anything, and we've had two kids easy enough. I can't stand the thought of a third. In any case, I don't think I am up to it. I have thought about that Family Planning place.' She looked at Janet. 'Do you know anything about it, Janet?'

'I don't know anything because I don't have to bother. But I'll find out while I'm at the shop, when I have a bit of spare time next week. If there's a clinic I'll go with you one night, when we can fit it in. Can you get your mother-in-law to have the kids for a couple of hours?'

'Oh, I don't know; she's not keen to have both of them together. It's a lot of trouble. I'm not used to that sort of thing and I never like doctors examining me.'

'Don't be daft. I'll be with you. It's a lot better than getting upset like you are now. You'll end up seeing a doctor anyway, if you go on like this.'

'You've got to pay at those places, anyway,' said Peggy, with a sigh of despair.

'Yes, but it won't be much. Anyway, I'll see to that side till you get a bit by you. Don't worry, Peggy. You leave it to me.'

Peggy Moore sniffled into her handkerchief. She had never dreamed that the friendship of Janet Hall would mean so much to her.

However their planning was all in vain. That night, Gerry Moore went straight from the pit to the Upthorpe Club and spent his wife's money. He came home late for his supper, his belly full of beer, and visions before his eyes of the writhing glittering body of the young female singer at the Club. He took his wife that night and, despite her cries and protests, he stayed, and the seed was sown and the egg was ripe.

Chapter 3

'It's a grand place you have here, Cobba. There must be some thirsty fellows in Upthorpe to keep a place like this going.' Roy Dobson knew that one of his extra jobs would be to act as a member of the Welfare Club Committee and he had persuaded Cobba to show him round so that he was familiar with the Club before the first committee meeting. He did have other objectives for the evening, if the opportunity arose.

'I can tell you this, Mr Dobson; the brewery has not regretted the money they spent here. We are good customers and I think we shall do even more business with them. This is the committee room.' Cobba Green showed the way into a plush room on the second floor over the Club entrance hall. The carpet was thick, the walls papered, and the long table down the middle of the room was covered with a fine green cloth and in front of each chair was a block with a writing pad and notepaper.

'This is really something. You must feel like directors of a nationalised industry when you have the meetings in here.' Roy sat down on one of the chairs. 'To think I'll be attending the meetings here… Is it as easy as running a pit, running this place, Cobba?'

Cobba sat down at the end of the table and looked at his visitor. He had been surprised when Roy Dobson had asked outright when Cobba was going to show him the Working Men's Club. He had never known a manager before who was so keen to establish some sort of personal contact with his union officials.

'How long have you been a union official at Martins, then, Cobba? It must have been a long time, because everybody talks about you as though you are a permanent feature of the pit.'

Roy was starting his third week at Martins Main. His attempts to get close to Cobba in their meetings at the pit had proved futile. The quiet of the committee room was an opportunity not to be missed.

'I've been on the union committee for fifteen years. I was Secretary for eight years and then I've been President for nearly five years,' replied Cobba, quietly. He was still puzzled at the interest.

'You'll know a lot about Martins' men, then?' Roy Dobson looked across at the grey hair and lined face staring impassively at him. 'Is it right that they are a bad set of men? There are a lot of folk at Region level very keen to tell me so. I'd like the benefit of your views on this, Cobba. I think it will help both of us if I get the right picture.'

So that was it, thought Cobba. He was after some information about the men. That was easy.

'You don't have to believe all they tell you at Region,' he replied, with a faint smile on his face. 'Some of the bosses there know nothing about pits, and they never come near to find out.'

'Yes, but you know, Cobba. You've been around and dealing with the men a long time. You know the sort of men they are. How do you rate them?'

'Well, they're not soft men. They know their rights and they'll stick out for their rights. And there are some good miners among them; some of them as good as you'll find anywhere. I don't know what you expect me to say about my own men?'

'Yes, I suppose I was a bit vague, and in any case it's not an easy subject,' conceded Roy.

'You'll not find them bad if you play fair with them.'

'It's not that side that worries me, Cobba. At a pit the size of Martins Main, I think the main problem is getting things over to the men and establishing communications with them. They tend to be suspicious of management at most pits. My feeling is that at Martins they are worse than most.'

'That may be true. They have reason to be suspicious, you know. We've had two strikes in my memory that the management dragged out through Christmas. There were some empty stockings and poor Christmas dinners those years, I can tell you. And folks remember things like that.'

'Well, how do you rate my chances of getting through to the men and persuading them to take on new ideas? Go on, say what you think. You've seen me long enough to have formed some views about me, Cobba.'

'It all depends what the new ideas are, and what they mean for the men. I think you'll be alright from what I have seen,' said Cobba, sitting back in his chair.

There was a pause while Roy Dobson doodled on the notepad in front of him.

'I think you are wrong, Cobba. I don't think I have an earthly chance here. I'm a foreigner in these parts, for one thing. I'm a young man, for another. And in any case, I think that this job has to be tackled a different way.'

'How do you mean?'

'I want somebody who knows the men to put my ideas over to them.' Roy saw a flicker of suspicion pass through Cobba's eyes. He was quick to plug the gap. 'There will be no trickery in this, you need not worry about that. You see, Cobba, I don't want Martins Main to fail because the men get hold of the wrong end of the stick. I want to know there is somebody among the men who understands what is happening at the pit, and can explain it to them. I'll do my share in communicating to the men, but I can't be there to squash all the rumours. It's hard to explain clearly what I'm after. Have you got the idea?'

'In a way; but we've never had any of this stuff in the past.'

'That's true. I am sure that you are right there, Cobba. That may be the cause of some of the problems at Martins. All I am suggesting is good consultation and communications all the time, simply that. Telling everybody where we are going, and what we're trying to do. I think miners like to be talked to about the plans, and they can often make good suggestions when they know the facts. Now do you get it? Do you see why I need someone who understands the local men and the pit?'

'Yes, I think you'll be able to find somebody who'll do that for you.'

Cobba Green was showing no interest. He was not impressed with this new approach to running a pit. He looked away and stirred in his seat as though he was ready to move.

'Cobba?' Roy Dobson paused until the other man looked back at him.

'Yes?'

'I don't want somebody, or anybody, to do this job for me, I want you to do it.' Cobba was obviously shocked at the suggestion.

'Me? I can't do it, Mr Dobson,' he said hurriedly. 'I'm a union man. I'm not for the management. My men come first, so my interests are not the same as yours.'

'They are, Cobba; that's where you're wrong. I want a Martins Main that is a successful pit, and a successful pit is a good pit for the workmen. You know that. It's the same in any industry. So really you want the same as me—a successful pit for the benefit of your men, and for the benefit of yourself.'

'What d'you mean by that last bit? You made it sound as though it has two meanings.'

'It has. I've been looking at the way you get paid at Martins.'

Roy Dobson made this remark sound casual. He paused to see if Cobba drew him on.

'And?'

'Well, to be honest, I'm not impressed, Cobba. I've been at a pit where the union man—the one in the confidence of the manager—gets paid a good wage, almost a salary for doing his job.'

'And how does this affect me?' asked Cobba, showing more interest.

'I want to do the same for you, if you'll go along with me. It's a tough job, when you have to persuade the men to go against their old habits on some issues, for the benefit of the pit. So the job wants to be well paid. And to have the responsibility for passing on the new ideas to the men is very important. A man doing that job needs paying well.' Roy Dobson stopped talking and looked at Cobba.

'You're trying to buy me off. That's it, isn't it? You want to buy me. Well, nobody has bribed Cobba Green so far, so I suggest you stop trying, Mister.'

Roy Dobson was disturbed that his remarks had been interpreted in this way.

'Buying you was the last thing in my mind, Cobba; I want you to believe that. I've looked around the pit to try to find somebody—somebody I can trust. You are the only one I can see around who I could have enough confidence in to do this job. Buying you was the last thing I had in mind. You will still function as a union man; there will be plenty for you to do in that capacity. Of course, the knowledge that you would have of pit plans would avoid you following wild goose chases on some issues. You would be saved embarrassment that way. Anyway, tell me this Cobba. If you were in my shoes, who would you pick among the union officials for a responsible job? Would you try Jimmy Bell for a job where tact and diplomacy are required?'

Cobba smiled.

'I'm not for these new ideas; I'm for the old setup of two sides, and running the pit that way.'

'It doesn't work, Cobba; you know it doesn't work from the problems we have at Martins now. Management and unions have got to talk to one another, and work together, to get good results in any industry.'

The door opened and a young fellow popped his head into the room.

'Oh, there you are. We wondered if you had gone off somewhere. If you want to see the turns, Cobba, they are just going on now.'

'Right lad, we were just going to come down into the bar.'

They moved out of the Committee Room onto the stairs.

'Good lad, that,' said Cobba, indicating the young fellow who had gone down the stairs before them. 'He's the Steward, you know. He's straight, as well, which is more than can be said for most stewards at local clubs.'

In the bar, the noise was slightly subdued and all faces were turned towards the stage. On the stage, an old man on the electric organ and a young fellow on the drums were gazing, like everybody else, at the young female vocalist who was reaching the end of her song. The pianist and drummer were waiting for the cue from her to strike the final chord on the organ and give a roll on the drums as her voice reached the last piercing, amplified note of an emotional ballad. The drums rolled and the chord sounded, and the whole resounding noise was further confused as the applause started long before the singer ran out of breath. Early applause, though, is a good sign to a club artist.

'She's going down well, Cobba, and there's a good crowd in tonight.' The concert secretary was using his position to have a word with Cobba and get an introduction to his guest. Roy Dobson shook hands with him and he could feel the buzz of interest around the bar at his presence. It was obvious that Cobba was finding things a little embarrassing, being host to the manager, but in his quiet way he was fending off the approaches by nods and noncommittal replies. They all relaxed a little when the next turn, a comedian, took the microphone. Roy clutched his half-pint of beer and leaned on the bar. He might as well enjoy himself; at least he had made a start with Cobba, and he had tried his best. Whether or not he had been successful, he was still uncertain.

The comedian was warming to his audience, which was reasonably impressed with his first few jokes, but then he made an unsuspecting error.

'The other day, the manager at the pit…,' he began.

'Watch it, cock,' a voice called from the bar. 'He's here listening to thee. Tha'll have thee cards in a few minutes if tha's not careful.' Eyes from all directions focused on Roy, and the whole audience had a good laugh at the expense of the comedian. He tried to recover his position by explaining that the pit concerned was not the local one.

An hour later, Roy Dobson decided it was time to take his leave.

'I guess I'll have to be going now, Cobba. I have a bit more work to do before bedtime, and then I have to ring my wife up at home and give my report.'

'Right you are, Mr Dobson. I think I'll go as well and have an early night.'

'I might as well give you a lift, then,' said Roy. 'It's on my way.'

The eyes around the bar watched as the two of them drained their glasses and nodded to the barman.

'Tha's more in favour with t'manager than I am, Cobba, if tha can get a ride in his car,' said Gerry Moore. 'He never saw me yesterday when I was walking down Martins Lane and I could have done with a lift.'

'I should think nobody would give thee a lift, Gerry. Thy tongue's that long, and it never stops wagging. No fellow dare risk having thee in his car and getting nattered at all the time. Good night, lads.' Cobba nodded to the others round the bar. The drinks had awakened a slight sense of humour in him that was not normally evident, and his eyes had a mischievous twinkle.

The car drove out of the Club car park and into the road. Cobba directed them past the bottom of Martins Lane and into the Council estate, winding in among the houses until they reached the end of Wilber Crescent.

'You might as well come in a minute, seeing as you're here,' said Cobba. 'I haven't got a wife, as you know, but our Sandra is in tonight. She can find us a bit of supper and it will be better than the stuff you get in a hotel.'

'It's good of you to ask me, Cobba. I'll have a few minutes but I mustn't get settled.'

Roy Dobson was wondering if this was the chance to finish off their earlier conversation. He could not miss such an opportunity. He followed Cobba along the garden path and through the back door into the kitchen.

'Is that you, Dad?' a female voice asked from the living room.

'Yes, Sandra. I've brought a gentleman to meet you, and have a bite of supper with us.'

'Stay there, then. Don't come in here,' the voice replied, with a note of panic. 'I've just had a bath and I'm not decent, especially for meeting strange men.'

The two men looked at each other and grinned as they stood in the kitchen. Roy caught a brief glimpse through the open door of a scantily-clad figure wrapped in a towel, as Sandra Green made a dash for the stairs and some more clothing.

'She is a right hothouse flower, is our Sandra,' said Cobba. 'She always likes to dry off in front of the fire after she's had a bath. I keep telling her she is too old to walk about the house like she does. Come on, let's go in now.'

Cobba found the incident highly amusing, not least because of Roy's embarrassment. They sat down in front of a large fire, and several minutes later the door opened and Sandra appeared. She was covered now by an expensive dressing gown, and her hair was concealed by a headsquare. Her face was glowing pink from the bath and the fire, and she kept her eyes down in mock embarrassment. When she had shaken hands with Roy, she turned to her father.

'You are a right one, Dad. Why didn't you tell me you were bringing someone home with you? Mr Dobson will think we have a right carry on at this house.'

Cobba laughed. 'I didn't know, love,' he said. 'It was all done on the spur of the moment as we were leaving the Club. Anyway, nothing's spoiled. Rustle up a drink of tea and a bite of supper, will you? Mr Dobson is staying in a hotel until his wife comes up into their house; he'll welcome a bit of homemade stuff.'

The conversation stayed on family subjects. After his drinking, Cobba talked much more freely, but to Roy's dismay he showed no signs of letting the subject return to work and the pit. When Sandra joined the two men with sandwiches and a pot of tea for supper, all hope of discussing Martins Main was gone. Roy decided to follow out another line of conversation.

'I'm surprised to find a young lady of your age staying at home on a night, Sandra?' he said.

'This is the exception, not the rule, Mr Dobson, but I wanted to wash my hair tonight,' she replied.

'That's true,' put in Cobba. 'She has a free hand with what she does with her time. She was on a chain long enough when her mother was alive.'

'Is there a young man at home on his own tonight then? Or haven't you got to that stage yet?' asked Roy, smiling at Sandra.

Sandra did not say anything, but she smiled back at Roy.

'She hasn't told her Dad about him yet,' said Cobba. 'Of course, I suppose I shall be the last to get to know.'

'You know perfectly well that I shall tell you if anything serious comes along, Dad.' She turned to Roy. 'No. I'm a spinster housekeeper, and I shall be on the shelf a long time with that fellow and this house to look after.' She laughed out loud and Cobba pulled a face at her.

'If this is a sample of your baking, I think you will be in demand before long,' said Roy, sampling a lemon cheese tart. 'I must say one thing though, Sandra; if you are not too busy, I am sure that my wife will be on the look out for a babysitter when she gets moved in up here. We shall have quite a few functions to attend through the year, and babysitting has often been a problem. I don't know if you are interested?'

'Yes, I don't mind,' she replied. 'I'll look after the children. If your wife will let me know a day or two before, so that I can make arrangements, I'll be glad to oblige. How many children do you have, Mr Dobson?'

The conversation again returned to family affairs, and stayed on that subject until Roy decided he must leave. The close, independent atmosphere that he had found in Cobba's house impressed him. There was evident harmony on show. This was definitely a home, not a house. Which then was the real Cobba, thought Roy? Was it the cold, hard, calculating man on show to the outside world, or the smiling, family man, proud of his home and proud of his family, especially his lovely daughter?

When Roy announced his departure, Sandra Green went across to take his cup and plate. As she bent over the coffee table, her dressing gown parted and he had a glimpse of her full, round breasts, and through their cleavage, her curving stomach. Roy Dobson's heart kicked and his stomach muscles tightened, and he knew in that moment how much he was missing his wife. When he glanced up into Sandra Green's face, her eyes flickered and her lips parted slightly. She knew what he had seen, and she knew the effect it had produced on him, and she felt a resurgence of the strange new power in her life.

I wonder if Cobba Green understands that he has not got a little girl on his hands any longer, thought Roy, as he walked with Cobba down the garden path to his car. It was dusk at the end of a fine day, and the sky was a mixture of shades of blue and purple. The street lamps were not lit and the cul-de-sac was very quiet.

'I've enjoyed myself tonight, Cobba,' said Roy softly. 'It's been a real change. You must thank Sandra again for the supper. And you'll not forget that other matter we were talking about earlier tonight? I'd like to finish that discussion and then we can arrange something.'

'Aye,' said Cobba. 'We'll do that sometime.'

The last word gave the reply an evasive sound. As Roy drove to the hotel, he wondered over and over if his night had achieved its purpose, or whether had he failed to pierce the hard shell of Cobba Green.

Saturday 13 June 1964

Cliff Smith walked slowly up to the seat at the Enclosure, and the others on the form shuffled away to release his place in the middle. Cliff had his raincoat over his arm, a small case in one hand, his stick in the other, and he wore a straw hat on his head. Everybody knew that Cliff was an umpire of some distinction in Yorkshire cricket, and he was dressed for an umpiring trip.

'Where are you today, then, Cliff?' asked Charlie Marshall, walking around behind the seat.

'Other side of Doncaster, today, Charlie. I'll have to go on the eleven o'clock bus to give me plenty of time to get there. Why don't you come with me, Charlie, you'd enjoy the change?'

'No, I'll not bother, Cliff. I've arranged to watch Upthorpe.'

It was a custom in the Enclosure for Cliff to suggest that Charlie went with him. Charlie liked to be invited but he never accepted, even if the distance to travel was short. It was rumoured that Charlie had not been on a bus for years, as the vibrations affected his nervous system.

'Anyway, I've got a mate today,' said Charlie. 'Our Walter is going to watch the locals this afternoon. That's right, isn't it, Walter?'

'Aye,' said Walter with a toothless grin. 'I think I have enough puff to make it today.'

In the middle of the conversation a large furniture van slowly pulled across the main road and parked at the bottom of Martins Lane. The driver's mate got out of the cab and crossed the road to the Enclosure. He was a tall lad with blonde hair and he looked self-conscious as he approached the locals wearing the long white apron of his trade.

'Now then, lad,' said Cliff, sitting forward on the edge of his seat and taking charge of the situation.

'Is that Martins Main pit?' asked the lad, pointing over his shoulder at the colliery headgear.

'It is that,' replied Cliff.

'Well, can you tell us how to find the manager's house? We've got his furniture here and we are not sure of the directions his missus has given us.'

'Oh, he's flitting in today, then, is he?' said Albert Dunn. 'He must fancy this place. He hasn't wasted much time. I wonder if he'll be as keen when he's lived here a bit? I reckon he's still a lot to learn about Yorkshire folk.'

While Albert gave his commentary to the Enclosure, the lad stood in front of them with a puzzled look on his face. Cliff came to his rescue.

'You want to go back into the main road and follow it through the village. Then take the first road on the right after you get past the last of the houses. You can't miss it. The house stands on its own about half a mile up that road.'

'The house is on the other side of the valley from the pit,' put in Albert. 'You'll see it. It's a bloody big square house, set in its own garden, with a wall round it. It was built out of the losses at Martins.'

The young lad thanked them and returned to his mate, who reversed the large van out of Martins Lane and they continued their journey along the main road.

'Have you seen the new manager yet, then, Albert?' asked Cliff.

'No, I'm not one for mixing with management; you know that Cliff.'

'I've met him,' said Charlie. 'He was in the Club the other night, with Cobba. He seemed a decent sort of fellow to me. I'll bet he's clever, from the look of him.'

'I've heard he's one of these modern young managers,' Albert said sceptically. 'All schooling and no practical experience. I'll bet he's never filled any coal with a shovel in his life.'

'You don't sound very happy?' said Cliff.

'I'm not, Cliff. I heard about him going to the Club with Cobba Green. I thought Cobba had more sense. You can't mix bosses and union men together, even in social life. If Cobba lets himself be tempted into management's pocket, he'll be a bloody fool. He wants to carry on fighting for the lads at Martins. I'm sure Cobba could get the better of this manager like he did the last one.'

'Now don't talk like that, Albert,' said Cliff, joking. 'It's common knowledge that all union men are in the pay of management. I know Albert Dunn got a turkey every Christmas out of the Company when he was a union man, which is more than I got.'

'Christmas is a bit different,' said Albert. He could never stand the taste of turkey now, after the number of times he had been ribbed about his Christmas turkeys when he was a union official.

'Cobba had him home for supper this week,' said Pat Mulligan.

They all looked to the end of the seat, shocked by the news.

'Was it the same night they went to the Club?' asked Charlie.

'Aye, I think it would be,' said Pat.

'Well, that does surprise me,' said Cliff.

'There you are, what did I tell you?' said Albert, spitting on the floor in his disgust. 'It's bloody ridiculous. You don't know where you are these days. They are all pissing in the same pot.'

★

A large fire burned brightly in the fireplace and the flames were reflected in the windows and on the new paintwork. The curtains were not drawn and an open window let in the cool evening air. About the room the furniture was spread haphazardly, with no look of permanence. Around the carpet, floorboards, newly scrubbed, stood out blankly. The only article that appeared to be in its final position was the television set tucked into a corner; the picture was flashing across the screen, but the sound was turned down to a whisper.

Roy Dobson entered the room and glanced briefly at the television and then went and stood by the open window. He could hear the sound of his wife moving around upstairs in their bedroom, but the sounds of the children had ceased. They must have gone to sleep at last, after their exciting day. It had also been an exhausting day, and Roy laid his arm on the windowframe to form a cradle for his head, and he drank in the tranquil evening scene.

The air was cool now, and refreshing. The garden on which he looked was at peace; the lawn closely cut and the flowers neatly arranged along the borders, where there were no signs of any weeds. Everything had been prepared by the gardener to impress the new tenants. An occasional bird flitted by, but their evening songs were ended, leaving a dead quiet and stillness. Just occasionally the slightest breath of wind stirred the poplars along the fence by the road, but evening was turning into night calmly, inevitably, but with a promise for tomorrow. Did the promise hold anything for Roy Dobson and his family as they began their new life in Upthorpe? Roy reflected on this and his thoughts went back to his early life in Nottingham.

He was the son of a dustman. His father had been the youngest of five boys, and the weakest. All the others had followed their father into the mines, but Roy's father had spent his life in menial jobs for the local council, when he was not in the doctor's surgery. The strange thing was that he had attracted and married a healthy and industrious wife, whose efforts had made up for his deficiencies. She had raised him a son and daughter to be proud of. Roy had felt no great remorse on his father's death when he was fifteen, but his admiration for his mother grew as she continued to work selflessly for her family.

Prompted by his grandfather, Roy had left grammar school when he was sixteen, and gone into the mines to answer the traditions in his blood. His mother had accepted this move, provided that he studied to gain some qualifications, and there he had made his mark. Learning came easily to him, and after four years working in the pit and studying part-time at the local Technical College, he gained a scholarship to take a mining engineering degree at university.

A smile crossed Roy's face as he recalled those four years spent at university: four years of freedom, friendship and challenge to him as an individual; four years to think, and plan, and develop mentally, and each summer a spell back at the pit with the miners to readjust and focus his new knowledge; four unforgettable years as a student with a million memories of student pranks and light-hearted revelry. Then, near the end of those four years, a chance meeting with a ward sister from the local hospital.

★

Roy listened to his wife still arranging things in the bedroom above his head. He had never understood their meeting or its consequences. He had been slightly drunk at the time and, as a result, his memories of that first meeting remained somewhat hazy. She was two years older than him and in a responsible post, so she should, by rights, have rebuffed his advances and sent him back to the bar. Instead, she had smiled back into his flushed face and accepted his invitation to dance. She had even allowed him to guide her back to the nurses' hostel at the hospital, and agreed to meet him the following day. From that start, a match was made—of two dissimilar people forming a working partnership.

He heard the bedroom door close and her footsteps approaching the stairs and, as she descended the stairs, his mind cascaded through their life together. Their marriage, the little flat, their ghost-like life as they both worked on peculiar shifts; their first baby, a boy named Robert, and the realisation, then, that it was his responsibility to earn all the income for the family. He recalled their first house, and the drunken neighbours; his job as an official, and then the second baby boy, John. Two lean years of hard work and frustration followed in his career, to a backcloth of nappies and disturbed nights. Through it all, an understanding wife, quietly confident, always prompting, always hopeful and never admitting defeat. While he raged and fumed with an untamed temper, she matured, and the difference in their ages seemed to grow greater. During the last three years, when success had crowned his efforts, Roy had grown to love his wife deeply, but with a love made up more of respect and admiration than of physical passion. He turned to her as she entered the room with several cushions in her arms that she distributed to the chairs.

'Stop sorting things out tonight, love; the rest will wait until morning. Come over here and look at this garden which we shall have to live with for the next few years. Do you think it will be for better or for worse?'

Helen Dobson went over to the window and looked out. Her husband put his arms around her waist and they both stood and quietly watched the light fade.

'I think it will be very nice here, Roy,' she said at last. 'I like the house. I am sure we shall be happy here, but then the house has nothing to do with that. We have been happy before. I suppose happiness depends on us, not on our surroundings.'

'That's a bit philosophical, isn't it?' said Roy, smiling.

'Yes, it is. I think I must be ready for bed. It's been a long day. Such thoughts are not normal for me. Come on, let's call it a day.' She broke away from him and walked across the room to turn off the television. Roy watched her, with proud possession in his eyes.

Helen Dobson had a large frame and a well-defined figure, but she carried no excess flesh, and her whole body radiated good health and the physical strength of an athlete. In her hospital career she had been noted for her strength and her ability to easily handle heavy patients. Her face was always a dark tan and, within this tan and beneath her jet-black hair, her eyes and her smile shone out brightly and displayed for everyone her open sincerity.

Roy closed the window and went into the kitchen. He dawdled over locking the door and making the fire safe. He followed his usual late night routine of time wasting until his wife had prepared herself for bed, and then spent her time in prayer, knelt by the bedside. He never disturbed her at this time; this was her own period of supreme privacy that she required every night. When she had realised that there would never be a contact between herself and her husband in sharing her beliefs, she had gone on alone in her faith. It was a peculiar arrangement, almost a partial estrangement, but each night the estrangement was ended by the smile that Helen gave her husband when he joined her in the bedroom. On this night, when Roy entered she was sitting up in bed reading a book, and rubbing lotion into her hands.

'I feel different, somehow, tonight in this house,' he said.

'Do you, Roy? How do you mean?' she asked, looking across to where he stood by the wardrobe with his back to her.

'I've never felt so positive about life, or so enthusiastic about my prospects. I feel that I'm in the right place at the right time, at last. I know I've bitten off a big job, but I feel I can do it.'

'I'm sure you can.'

'But it's something more than that, even. I feel happy at the prospect of dealing with awkward men and officials, and sorting out problems with my superiors. I don't know; I feel like a superman.'

'You are, love,' she said, teasing him.

'Yes, or else I'm sickening for a dose of flu!' He turned round and looked at her, feeling ashamed that he had not been able to transmit his enthusiasm to her. He eyed her appraisingly, picking out the curves of her body through her nylon nightdress.

'That nightdress looks very fetching; I don't think I've seen it before?'

'No, you won't have; it's a new one. I decided to celebrate the first night in our new house by wearing it. You don't mind, do you?'

'No, you look very provocative, and I'm a bit starved after the last fortnight in the hotel.'

'Well, you can abandon any of those thoughts for tonight; I'm too tired. In any case, you mustn't waste your strength. You'll need it all for this bright new future you are forecasting for yourself in Upthorpe.'

Helen Dobson giggled as she slipped down beneath the sheets; but she was happy to see her husband so full of hope, and she was looking forward herself to this new phase of her life.

Monday 22 June 1964

'Gerry, come on, open thee fucking eyes. There's a light coming down the roadway and it must be an official 'cos he's got an oil lamp.'

The two young men put their snap tins away and hung up their coats and prepared to go back onto the coalface. Gerry Moore stirred, but did not open his eyes. One of the lads pushed him again with his boot to try to wake him.

'Come on, look theesen sharp, Gerry. We've been having our snap too long as it is. Tha's like a sleepwalker, today. Get theesen up.'

Gerry Moore got to his feet slowly, and hung up his coat.

'What are you panicking about? It'll only be t'Deputy. We can shout him down, anytime.'

'I think the way that light's coming down here, Gerry, it's somebody more than t'Deputy. It's a bright light. It might even be George. We'll soon know.'

The three young fellows moved back towards the coalface.

56s coalface was like hundreds more in the English mining industry. It was two-hundred-and-twenty yards long, and the thickness of the seam being worked was two feet nine inches. The coalface was divided into two parts by a central roadway that was enlarged from the seam height to be twelve feet wide and nine feet high. At each end of the coalface was another roadway, nine feet wide and six feet high. A flow of air passed along the central roadway to the coalface and, after passing through the coalface, returned along the other roadways into the main mine airways. The air was essential to cool the workmen and dilute the methane gases. The method of working the coal was to cut a slot five feet deep under the coal seam, with a special coal-cutter machine. The coal was then drilled, and the shot holes were fired with explosives, to loosen the coal. The men then filled the coal onto conveyors on each side of the coalface. These conveyors tipped the coal onto a larger conveyor in the central roadway. That conveyor carried the coal away from 56s' to join the coal from the other coalfaces in the Benton seam. All the coal from the seam was conveyed to a loading point where it was filled into half-ton pit tubs. The tubs were then hauled to the pit bottom and raised to the surface up the number one shaft. Each man filled a length of the coalface equivalent to about fifteen tons of coal and set wooden supports to hold up the roof. The objective was to complete a cycle, so that the coalface advanced five feet each day. The roadways were supported with steel girders to give a permanent travelling way, but the rest of the strata, behind the coalface, was allowed to collapse.

It was George Turnbull who arrived at the coalface. He was perspiring freely and the sweat was trickling down his cheeks from under his pit helmet.

'Now then, what are you lot doing?'

'We've been having our snap, and we're just going back onto t'face, George,' said Gerry Moore.

'Having your snap at this time?' replied George. 'You want to get some work done and give your bellies a rest. You'll get like fat cows so that you can't fill any coal.' He pushed past them and went forward to the coalface. He knelt down and looked along the coalface to see how much coal had been filled. When he realised the position he let out a shout.

'Gerry Moore, just thee come here. There's only five yards of coal filled out here by two of you, and the supports are not set as they should be. I think the lot of you have been buggering about here this morning.'

'It's been hard coal this morning, George,' said Gerry.

'Hard coal me bloody Aunt Fanny. I could fill that coal with me bare hands. See thee here, Gerry, I'm getting bloody fed up of all thy excuses. I'll bet there are some fellows in other parts of this coalface nearly filled all their coal, and you lot have only just started.' He rounded on the other two young fellows. 'And if you two let this young idle bugger lead you into his ways, you can expect what is coming to you. Thee Dad's not going to cover up for thee much longer, Gerry. Tha's going to have to earn thee own corn here before much longer.'

'Leave my father out of this. I can look after myself without him in this job,' replied Gerry, at George's remarks.

'Aye, tha wants to talk like that about him. He's a better worker now than tha will ever be, despite his age, and it was only with him and Cobba putting in a good word for thee, that tha got this job. Only thing tha can beat thee Dad at, is supping pints at yond bar in Upthorpe Club. Tha'd do better to spend a few less hours there and a few more at home with thee wife and kids, if tha asks me.'

'Nobody asked thee, George. Leave my wife and kids out of this. I'll ask for thy advice when I need it.' Gerry was very sore at George's remarks. He violently threw some pit props over the conveyor into the coalface, and then he climbed over himself.

'I've been around a long time, Gerry, lad. I know what's going off. I'm not blind. Tha'll grow up, happens, some day.' He knelt by the conveyor and watched the men start working. 'Come on now, get those arms moving with a swing. Let's see some coal filled, and a bit of sweat on your brows. Mr Dobson is coming down here today, and I want him to see some action from you.'

This remark prompted some response from the young lads, and one of them took off his vest as he began to sweat. Soon they all had their foreheads and shoulders running wet with sweat—sweat that slowly picked up the fine dust particles in the air to form a slimy, oily paste on their bodies. George knelt and watched them without sympathy. He shone his light about, and shouted instructions to them from time to time. Gerry, who had less muscles than his mates, worked jerkily and with less rhythm, and his efforts showed less results. His arms began to ache and he kept changing his crouched position to relieve the aches in his legs and thighs. As the coal stuck up before him and sometimes refused to yield to his shovelling and prodding, he spat out at it and cursed under his breath. Then he remembered the pale look of his wife the night before. She was looking under the weather these days.

'It's a bastard dog's life, is this,' he spat at the coal as he struck at it with his pick. A large block of coal rolled down to the floor and he moved back quickly out of its path, but not before a small piece had hit the back of his hand. The sharp edge cut through the layer of dust and pierced the skin in a long line. At first, the wound was white, but then the blood pushed its way out and trickled down his hand and finger. He lifted it up to look at it more closely.

'There's bugger all wrong with that, Gerry. Spit on it, it'll be all right. Get thee shovel going, it'll not feel so bad then.'

'That's all tha's bothered about, George. It'll be another mark for life, and I don't get paid for them in this job.'

Gerry picked up his shovel and began violently thrashing away at the coal, pushing it and throwing it onto the conveyor belt, conscious all the time of being watched. He was determined not to appear weak before the older man. His teeth were gritted and tears were smarting in his eyes, and rolling down his cheeks with the sweat.

'It's a bastard dog's life, this,' he mumbled to himself again.

As the men filled out more coal, they moved along the coalface, away from the front of the roadway. When George was satisfied that the work was progressing satisfactory, he busied himself in the roadway making the store of wooden pit props as tidy as possible, checking the ventilation, and seeing that everything was in order for the arrival of Roy Dobson. It was the last coalface at the pit to be visited by the manager, and George had given strict instructions to his officials what to attend to before the visit. He had a respect for the mining standards of his new boss who, in his visits to other parts of the pit, had demanded high standards of tidiness and workmanship. Roy had surprised everyone at the mine by his habit of returning for a second inspection to each part of the mine, a few days after his first visit, to see if his requests and instructions had been carried out.

Roy had already been to all the other coalfaces at the mine twice. He had been manager at Martins Main for five weeks, before the day of his visit to 56s. When he arrived, accompanied by Mike Darlow and the Deputy for 56s coalface, he was relaxed and at ease. He was beginning to feel in touch with the pit, and hopeful that his ideas would improve the performance.

'It looks a reasonable seam of coal, anyway, George,' he said, as he looked at the coal seam in front of him.

'That's nothing to the seam beyond the major fault that we are going to look at. It's more than twice the thickness of this seam,' replied George.

'I think your mouth will really water when you see it, Mr Dobson,' said Mike. 'There's a seam of coal there six-feet three-inches thick, and a large area of reserves which have not been worked at all.'

'Let's look at this coalface first; we have more coalfaces that can be worked in this seam before we need to work the coal beyond the major fault. The first objective is to improve the results on this face.'

By general coal mining standards, Martins Main had good geology. The coal seams had no steep gradients, but dipped in a gentle gradient west to east. The fault density was low, but there were significant major faults about two miles apart, and they ran in a northeast/southwest direction. It was one of these major faults that was near 56s district. Roadways had been driven forward to prove the fault and its displacement. This had shown that the Fuston seam was easily accessible, and a roadway had been driven down into the seam. As well as visiting 56s coalface, Roy intended to see the new development into the Fuston seam. He knew that both George and Mike were keen to develop the Fuston seam into a major part of the mine's production, because of the thickness of the seam. Roy had decided to look at the seam, and see the natural conditions, before attending a planning meeting at Regional Level to discuss the future plans for Martins Main.

When Roy had checked the ventilation for methane, and the supports, he set off along the coalface, laying on the conveyor and riding around the blocks of coal to where each man was working. Roy spoke to each man, and made a few comments, as George told him the man's name.

'Have you been cutting yourself?' he asked Gerry Moore.

'Aye, just a nick from a sharp-edged piece,' replied Gerry, passing it off casually.

'You ought to wear gloves, lad. It would avoid cuts like that.'

They passed along the coalface, spending quite a bit of time with Fred Moore, who was working with a helper in the fault area. The roof conditions were quite good, and there was little water. Fred agreed that the fault should not affect production if it could be controlled to that standard. When they were near the centre roadway, they stopped at a man who wore steel-rimmed spectacles and had an oil lamp hung near him.

'This is Willie Carter, Mr Dobson. I think you have met before,' said George.

'Oh, yes, I've met Willie.' He looked along the coalface where Willie had been working, and he saw all the neatly set pit props and the cleanliness of the floor. 'I can see some good old mining standards when I look along your stint, Willie.'

Willie took off his spectacles, which were covered in dust, and wiped them on an old piece of rag. He looked at Roy, a little embarrassed at the compliment he had received.

'I've been at it a long time, Mr Dobson. I ought to know how to do my job,' he said, grinning. As the others moved off, Willie crawled after Roy. 'Can I have a word with you, Mr Dobson? It's nothing to do with the pit,' he added hurriedly.

'Yes, Willie; what is it?' The others had gone off along the conveyor.

'Well, you see I am on the committee for the new organ at Upthorpe Methodist Church, and I wondered if I could have a word with you sometime about it?' said Willie.

'Oh, you're better talking to my wife about that sort of thing. She's the religious one in our family. Pop up to the house and see her some night; I'll tell her to expect you.' Roy jumped on the conveyor and left.

'Thank you, Mr Dobson,' Willie called after him.

Willie returned to his work and picked up his shovel with a smile on his face. His arms moved rhythmically, but his mind was on other things. Mrs Dobson interested in the organ fund! Invited up to the house to see her! Wait until Joe Norton hears that! As the shift went by, Willie had more and more ideas for the organ fund and Mrs Dobson figured in many of them. He could hardly wait until the evening to tell his son, Peter.

Roy was very thorough in his inspection of 56s district, and he ended by giving the Deputy a lecture on the district, and the matters to be put right before his return visit. As the time passed, Mike became very restless and impatient. He was afraid that they would not have enough time to go from 56s coalface down the roadway that led to the Fuston seam. His impatience was obvious to George, who went over to him and whispered in his ear.

'Don't fidget, lad, he'll come in his own good time. This fellow doesn't rush things.'

'I know, George, but I don't want him to miss seeing that seam of coal. It's going to make a big difference to this pit, is that seam, and it's very important that he sees it for himself. Then he'll understand my ideas.'

Mike Darlow was a young fellow, who had only been qualified as a mining engineer for a few years, and he was well informed on the latest techniques of mechanisation and modern pit planning. His ideas for improving Martins Main involved concentrating the production onto fewer coalfaces and introducing the latest systems of mechanisation. He had studied the plans for a long time before reaching his conclusions, and George, who had initially been sceptical of the suggestions, was beginning to realise that they were far-reaching and held great potential. He respected Mike for his ideas, but he had less confidence in his ability to handle the workmen and officials.

Eventually, they left 56s district and Mike led the way along the roadway that descended into the Fuston seam. The roadway was a hundred and forty yards long and dipped at a gradient of one in five. Air was pushed to the far end of the roadway through ducting by an auxiliary fan, and it returned as a slow flow, back up the roadway. The result was a damp atmosphere, with moisture clinging to the strata. As well as sweating freely, the three men had difficulty keeping their feet on the slimy floor as they descended the gradient. Several times along their route, Mike tested for any accumulation of methane in the roof. Each time he was satisfied, and they moved forward. Near the bottom of the incline, a sump had been excavated at the side of the roadway to collect the water produced from the strata. At the bottom of the incline the roadway went forward ten yards at a level gradient, and at the end was the Fuston seam that stood out black against the pale yellow of the sandstone roof.

'There it is, Mr Dobson,' said Mike, as though he was showing off a prize pig. 'Six-feet three-inches of coal and only one small band of dirt in the section.' Roy took out his steel tape and checked the measurements. He was impressed.

'What's the quality? Has that been checked?' he asked.

'Yes, the scientific lab has had a sample,' replied Mike. 'The ash content is similar to our other seams, but the sulphur content is a little higher. There should be no problems with the quality of the coal.'

'And the seam keeps this section, as far as you know, from those two boreholes you mentioned to me?'

'Yes. There is an area of coal clean of faults, that is well over a mile wide at this point and stretches for nearly three miles in front of us. In fact, it goes right beyond our boundary and into the reserves of Lucy Pit.'

'If it's as good as this, why haven't you worked this area before now?' Roy directed his question at Mike, but he referred it to George.

'You fill in the history, George. It goes back before my time here.'

'Well, this roadway has been down here two years now. But we were told that we couldn't work this area of coal until we had worked out the coal above the fault. That was 54s, 55s, 56s and then there are more faces at least to 60s face. There was no chance of speeding up those coalfaces because of the haulage system which could not take any more coal. Mind you, we should have been a lot further forward, if Fred Moore and his merry men had played the game with us.'

'The haulage system has affected all the previous planning for the pit, as far as I can see, Boss' said Mike. 'But I think I can see a solution to the difficulties. What I propose is a connection from 56s roadways in the Benton seam up into the Low Moor seam. We could then drive a new trunk roadway to the pit bottom. If we then installed conveyors in that roadway, all the coal from the Benton, Low Moor and Fuston seams would be conveyed to the pit bottom. The Morley seam would be closed. It would save lots of manpower and give the pit a real chance to hit the headlines.' Mike paused for breath, so George took up the theme.

'Aye, and if we could bring the men out of the Morley seam into this area here, we might get some better results. There are some good lads in that seam. You said so yourself when you saw their work, Boss.'

'It all adds up fairly conclusively,' said Roy. 'I'll have a session with the Surveyor and get it all plotted out before I go to the planning meeting at Region. If they agree in principle, it will be a real fight to get the capital allocation to drive the roadway and buy the conveyors for the project. It appears to be a good scheme, but it will cost a lot of money, and Region may not be keen to allocate capital to Martins, unless we get some better results.'

A light appeared, hurrying towards them.

'Now then, Charlie, what is it?' asked George.

'It's for Mr Dobson,' replied the young lad, panting for breath. 'From the office at the pit top; they say to tell him that Mr Pickersgill is coming to see him at three o'clock, and he wants to see Cobba Green as well.' The lad took a deep breath. 'That's all,' he concluded, and wiped his forehead.

'Right, lad; thanks very much,' said Roy. 'We had better head for the pit top, then, and get ready for the big man. He would pick today for his first visit to see me, when I am down the pit! I suppose it might impress him if I am all black and in my pit clothes when he calls on me.'

They set off for the pit bottom. It was a steep climb up the roadway, so conversation was sparse. Mike did ask one question, though. 'I wonder why he wants to see Cobba?'

'I have an idea what it might be,' said Roy, but he did not enlighten the other two. He was not very pleased with his own performance in the Cobba Green affair, and he was a little concerned how Mr Pickersgill might react.

As they walked and slithered up towards 56s district, Roy recalled his contacts with Cobba since he had visited Upthorpe Working Men's Club and put the proposition to him.

The matter had not been raised for nearly two weeks, until Cobba remained behind in the office with Roy after they had been discussing a suitable job for a man who was disabled with a back injury.

'What about that subject I was discussing with you at your house the other week, Cobba? You don't seem keen to raise the subject again. What's the trouble?' Cobba had remained silent for a few moments before replying.

'I'm not happy about the idea. There are too many complications for my liking.'

'Well, tell me what the complications are – let's see if we can sort them out.'

'Am I the only one for this treatment, or have you other folk lined up as well?'

'There will be no others. This is a solo job. I can't afford the cost of more than one on this job.'

'That's another thing,' continued Cobba. 'You haven't showed your hand with the money, yet.'

'I don't want to talk money until I get some sort of understanding with you, Cobba,' replied Roy, moving carefully on the matter. 'We can easily reach an agreement on that side.'

'I'm a bit worried about my colleagues on the union. They might suspect something and I'm not very good at covering up underhand jobs.'

You lying sod, thought Roy, but he said, 'I'm sure you can carry that off, Cobba.'

'I'll think about it, and let you know in a week or so,' concluded Cobba, as he turned for the door.

'Don't take too long, Cobba. This is a job that needs doing now.'

After Cobba had left, Roy had sat in his chair pondering, and the conclusion he reached was that he, Roy Dobson, was the poor one at underhand deals. He felt lacking in experience at cloak-and-dagger negotiations.

The next move on the matter had been a phone call from Mr Pickersgill.

The efficient voice of Mr Pickersgill's secretary had come over the telephone.

'Mr Dobson?'

The telephone clicked and the voice of Pickersgill came through, amplified to a coarse whisper.

'Dobson. Now then, boy, how are you getting on? You haven't sent much more coal out of that hole yet. Mind you, the pit has not been on strike for the last few weeks, so I suppose you have made some impression. Have you sorted that fellow Green out yet, like I told you?'

'Well, Sir,' replied Roy, taken aback by the conversation on such a matter over the telephone. 'I have made a couple of approaches and discussed the idea with him, but he seems reluctant to go along with me.'

'He will be cautious, of course. Cobba Green will not be an easy bird to coax over. I never thought he would jump straightaway.'

'He's going to see me this week to tell me his final answer, Sir. I hope that I can settle it then.'

'Well, come on, boy. You need him to help you, and you must get it sorted out quickly. Don't let it drag on.'

'No, Sir, I'll get it finalised as soon as possible.'

'Let me know how you go on then.'

As the telephone went dead, Roy put the receiver down and rubbed his chin thoughtfully. What a position to be in, he thought, failing at the first objective that the Region General Manager had set for him. Roy decided that he should see Cobba as soon as possible.

Roy Dobson called Cobba into the office to organise a domestic matter that his wife had pressed onto him.

'Cobba,' he began straightaway. 'Me and my wife are invited back to a dinner and dance in Nottingham. My wife wonders if your Sandra can babysit for us? We shall be very late back, so I think it would be better for her to stay the night at our place. Can you ask her to give Helen a ring to make arrangements? There's no panic, because it's not for another six weeks, but it is on a Saturday night.'

'I'll tell her, Mr Dobson. I'm sure she will be able to oblige you.' He stood up to go.

'Wait a minute, Cobba. There's that other matter you were going to discuss with me. Remember?'

'Oh, there's no need for any more discussion on that subject,' said Cobba, not resuming his seat. 'It's not on, as far as I'm concerned. I know which side of the fence I'm on.'

'Just a minute, Cobba, I don't think you should be as definite as that.' Roy was stalling for time. 'We've discussed all the implications of the job before, and I can't see you throwing it out so easily.' He paused before using his last trump card. 'I might add that this idea has the blessing of someone above me at Region.'

'You needn't have told me that, Mister, I knew this wasn't just your idea. It smells of bigger things. You had better tell that fellow above you to come and do his own dirty work himself. If he wants me bad enough he'll pay a bigger price than you dare pay.' Cobba Green continued his walk to the door and marched out.

'You bloody scoundrel, Cobba,' muttered Roy under his breath after the door closed.

Roy decided to wait a few days before he reported his failure to Mr Pickersgill. In the meantime he needed to consider several alternative ideas. Already he thought that he probably would not involve anyone else and admit his defeat.

Two days later Roy had rung Mr Pickersgill.

'Dobson here, Mr Pickersgill,' he said, when he was put through to the big chief. 'I am afraid I have had no success with Cobba Green. He seems set now on not joining in with my ideas.'

'Really, Dobson?' The voice at the other end of the telephone was cold.

'Yes, I am afraid so, Sir.'

'Have you discussed money with him yet?'

'No, Sir. I wanted to get him to agree first.'

'Yes, well you did right there. I must say though, Dobson, I am surprised that you could not carry this off. It only needed tact and diplomacy.'

'I'm sorry, Sir.'

'I will have to come over and see him myself then. I'll let you know when I can come and sort it out. I'll do it as soon as possible.'

'Thank you, Sir.'

Roy put the telephone down feeling depressed, despite the previous day's output for the pit being the highest since his arrival.

★

When they reached the conveyor road for 56s coalface, Roy Dobson used the pit telephone system to ring his office.

'Get hold of Cobba, Gordon, and tell him to wait in the canteen this afternoon, until I send for him. I'm coming out of the pit as quickly as I can now.'

'Right you are, Mr Dobson. I've already made arrangements with Cobba,' replied his secretary.

At last I've got a secretary who uses his head, thought Roy, as he continued the walk with the others to the underground man-riding train station. Mike tried several times to raise a further discussion on the planning suggestions he had raised earlier, but Roy showed no inclination towards the subject, his mind was too full of the meeting in the afternoon and the form it might take.

On reaching the surface he had a quick shower and returned to his office. He had no appetite for his sandwich lunch, and he could not concentrate on the reports and papers on his desk, so he spent half an hour walking his office and looking down into the yard watching for Mr Pickersgill's car. When the car pulled up, Norman Pickersgill got out and entered the office building with no papers and obviously in a hurry. He soon climbed the stairs and entered the office.

'Good afternoon, Dobson. I've only got a few minutes to spare before I rush off to catch a train to London. Where is Cobba?'

'I'll send for him straightaway, Mr Pickersgill.'

'What have you told Cobba, then?' asked Pickersgill, taking a seat by the desk. Roy outlined his proposition in general terms until Cobba was shown into the office.

'Good afternoon, Cobba. Sit down.' They had certainly met before, thought Roy.

'Good afternoon, Mr Pickersgill,' said Cobba.

'I won't keep you a minute, Cobba, but I think I have something to say that I'm sure will interest you. Mr Dobson has suggested to me that someone from the union side could do a good job for him as a sort of intermediary between the management and the men. It has to be a person who can be trusted and who can put over the management's ideas. Now, I think it is a good idea for the pit and that we should try it straightaway. How do you feel about it, Cobba?'

'Well, it might help us, Mr Pickersgill, and I'm for anything that will help us.'

'Good. Now how do you feel about taking on this work, Cobba? I am sure you fit the bill for it. You know the pit, and you know the men.'

'I might be interested.'

'Oh, well that is a start. Now for the money side,' continued Mr Pickersgill, taking Cobba's consent as read. 'I suppose you have some key development workers at the pit.' He looked across at Roy.

'Yes, we have a team of men doing a job in the Morley seam who I think are about the best in the pit,' replied Roy.

'And have they been earning good money of late?'

'Yes, they've done pretty well,' replied Cobba, before Roy could reply.

'In that case, you can have the same weekly wage as they earn. That should settle the money, Cobba.'

'Right. Thank you, Mr Pickersgill,' replied Cobba.

'Don't thank me, thank Mr Dobson. It was his idea. He'll arrange the money on a time basis.'

'Right you are, Mr Pickersgill,' said Cobba, and he prepared to leave.

'Now think on, Cobba, we want to keep the wheels turning now, and we want to see some progress at this pit. I am sure that we can succeed with some co-operation all round. That will be your job.'

'Don't worry, you can rely on me, Mr Pickersgill.' Cobba left the office and Roy was amazed at the ease of the negotiation, and astounded at the price offered. Cobba Green would be one of the highest paid men at the pit. Pickersgill stood up, ready to leave.

'I must be going or I shall miss the train. Get to work, Dobson. I think you should make some progress if you use Cobba the right way. Lead him in quietly, and don't push for too much at the start. Good afternoon.'

'Good afternoon, and thank you, Sir.'

To think of the way I have puzzled over that matter, pondered Roy Dobson, when he returned to his desk. I could have settled it in five minutes, if only I had known that the job was valued at that price by Mr Pickersgill.

Chapter 4

'Dad, do you know a fellow called Lacey, who works for the Coal Executive at Region?' Sandra Green was on the point of going out of the house when she asked this question. She was wearing a pale yellow dress, with matching gloves and handbag, and she carried a cardigan over her arm and a headsquare framed her face. In the warm evening sunshine flooding through the window, she looked fresh and exciting.

'He's the planning fellow at Region, if that's the fellow you mean?' replied her father, without looking up from the newspaper he was reading.

'Is it a good job?'

Cobba looked up, suddenly taking an interest.

'Yes, he'll get a good salary. Anyway why the interest?'

'Nothing, really; it's just that I have met his son,' replied Sandra, smiling.

'And how long has this been going on?' asked Cobba, with a fatherly interest.

'I've seen him several times, these last few weeks. It's nothing serious; don't get excited. But I wondered who his father was, to be able to buy him a car. I must be going, he'll be waiting for me.'

'Enjoy yourself, lass,' said Cobba, as she put a kiss on his forehead before running out of the back door.

Sandra walked along Wilbur Avenue, nodding to the neighbours, and then, after winding through the estate, she emerged onto the main road. She turned up the hill towards the bottom of Martins Lane, her eyes scanning the road looking for the dark green Morris 1000 car. She had arranged no definite meeting place along the road, in an attempt to avoid any prying eyes. She had not walked far before she saw the car coming towards her on the road past the bottom of Martins Lane. As it stopped beside her, she jumped in quickly and closed the door.

'Hello,' she said, smiling and putting her handbag near her feet.

'Hello. Sorry I'm a bit late; Dad was late back from the office today, from some meeting or other, and Mum wouldn't let me start the meal until he arrived.'

'Never mind, I'd only just walked out.' The conversation was a little strained.

'Where shall we go, then?' asked Terry. 'You choose.'

'Really? You want me to choose?' She was excited at her thoughts.

'Of course,' he replied.

'Let's not go into Doncaster, then. Let's go to the hills, right away from the pits and the factories. Let's find the moors and enjoy the lovely evening sunshine. Let's go somewhere beyond Penistone, on the road to Manchester. I remember going in a bus on that road once, when we went on holiday. Have we enough petrol?'

'Yes, I filled it up this morning.'

Terry Lacey drove the car away at speed. He knew the route and turned west, towards
the evening sun. They passed through several villages, all similar to each other, with long
rows of brick houses nestling near the pit headgear; each with its fish and chip shop, and
pub, and chapel; with its allotments, and gardens, and cricket field. Then they left the pits
behind them and the villages were further apart and tucked low into the narrow valleys.
The houses were made of solid, square stone, and little cobbled streets shot up from the
road to the higher houses. The focal point of each of these villages was a mill straddling
the river. The mills were large, rectangular and stone built, with rows of windows along
the sides. But it was still Yorkshire, and the people still had a broad accent, and there was
still the fish and chip shop, the pub, and the chapel. But now the cricket fields and the
gardens, with their little greenhouses, were wedged in, to take advantage of any level
ground. As they climbed up from the valley, the fields changed from rich green in the
bottom to rougher grass and, eventually, when they were near the top, into true moorland
vegetation. The hills had a coarse brown appearance and, in places, deep channels had
been cut into the peat, forming dark brown gashes which contrasted with the sheep
dotted around the view.

Terry pulled the car off the road, onto a track, before they reached the Manchester road.
They left the car and walked along the track and then took a sheep path to climb up to
get the view from a nearby hill. The path was narrow and steep, and he had to take Sandra's
hand to help her, as she stumbled from time to time. They laughed together at her comic
appearance, trying to mountaineer in high-heeled shoes. When they reached the top they
had a rewarding view. They could see the reservoirs stepping down the valley, on each
one the water gleaming in the sunlight. On one side of the reservoirs was the railway,
which in the distance looked to be in miniature, and on the other side the road wound
in and out, clinging to the valley side. On the road, little matchbox cars and lorries jostled
each other for position and, from time to time, one of them would explode with light as
the sun hit its windscreen.

'This is just like being on top of the world; we can see everything, but no one can see
us,' said Sandra.

'It's really lovely,' replied Terry, who could not take his eyes off the traffic below him.

'Let's enjoy it while we have the chance. We shall never have an evening like this again.'
Sandra let go of Terry's hand, released her headsquare, and turned her head into the breeze.
Her hair flew out behind her as she ran away from him into the wind, stumbling over the
tufts of grass. About thirty yards from him, she fell down and rolled over onto her back.
At first, he thought she had hurt herself and he set off towards her. But when he got near
to her, she kicked off her shoes, threw her cardigan out of her hands and lay her arms out
behind her head. She gazed up at the cloudless sky, laughing, half hysterically, and shaking
her head from side to side.

'Did you hurt yourself? Are you all right?'

'Of course I'm all right, I'm just happy. I've never been happier. I never thought I could find such a beautiful place, and feel so wonderful.' She closed her eyes. 'Make it complete, Terry. Kiss me,' she whispered through parted lips.

Terry looked down at her relaxed body. His eyes took in the heaving chest, the forced breathing; he noted her long legs, inviting and apart, and he could see her stocking tops where the wind had blown up her dress. What a girl this is, he thought. What an invitation.' He dropped onto the ground beside her.

'Just kissing, Terry. That's all. No more, not yet,' she whispered, as his face bent over hers.

They lay together kissing for a long time, and the nearness of her body stirred up new passions within him that he had never known before. He made several attempts to explore her body with his hands, but each time she pushed him away.

'Just kisses, Terry. No more, not yet.'

When they had finished, he helped her to her feet, and he recovered her shoes and her cardigan, while she straightened her dress and hair.

'I'll never forget tonight, Terry, not as long as I live. I really relaxed. I'm glad you did as I asked you, and only kissed me; you didn't spoil it.'

'It's not easy to hold back when a girl really lets herself go like you did,' he said, looking away from her.

'Oh, I know it isn't easy, Terry. I know it's very difficult for you, and I like you more because you were strong enough to do as I asked. You won't always have to hold back, I promise you.'

They walked back towards the sheep path.

'You are a strange girl, Sandra. I've never known anyone like you. You are so open about your feelings. You don't suppress anything.'

'I know, Terry. You might as well hear the truth.' She stopped walking and sat down on a ridge beside the path. As he sat down beside her, she took his hand and held it tightly in hers. She fixed her gaze on the hillside opposite, before she began talking.

'You have got to understand that I was suppressed for years while my mother was alive. Everything I felt, everything I longed for, had to be pushed back and choked. Well, now I'm free, and I'm grown up at the same time. I've got a body that wants loving. I've got desires—lots of them—that I want to know about, and I've got a boyfriend.' She squeezed his hand tighter, and turned to look into his face. 'Terry, I am not going to hold anything back, not ever again. Really, that's the truth. But I don't want it all at once. I want it to grow slowly, step by step. I don't want to rush things. I want to enjoy every new experience as it comes. If you love me, Terry, you stay with me and it will all be yours. I don't want to fight with you over it. Be patient; it won't be too long, and then I'll give you what you want—this body, all of me, everything that I've got. I promise, you can have it all, given free, when we have grown closer and we are sure we're in love.'

'You frighten me when you talk like this, Sandra. How can a fellow resist loving a girl like you?' He kissed her, and then they resumed their walk back down to the car.

★

Cobba passed his evening calmly reading his newspaper and a book, quietly happy that his daughter was innocently watching a film and holding a young lad's hand.

Tuesday 30 June 1964

'Willie, I think you have a good idea, there,' said Joe Horton. He had always been sceptical of Willie Carter as a source of original ideas, but this new organ was certainly bringing out the best in him. 'Let me get this straight. What you're suggesting is a social evening, like the usual thing, and at it we auction off the organ, so much for a note, so much for a pipe, so much for a pedal. Hmm, it should work. And how much do you think it could raise?'

'Well, our Peter listed all the parts, and if we have any luck and get half a crown for each key, and ten bob for a pipe, we could end up with over a hundred pounds,' replied Willie.

'That would be a good sum to raise at one go,' said Joe, ruminating over the prospects. 'Bright lad, your Peter. I think he's helping us grand with this new organ. We shall have to ask John Warwick to be the auctioneer, as usual. He makes a good job each year at the Harvest Festival; I'm sure he would do it.'

'I did have another idea that I thought you might like to consider,' said Willie hesitantly. 'I mentioned the organ to our new manager, Mr Dobson, down the pit the other day. He said I was to see his wife, and that she was sure to be interested. In fact, he said I should go up to their house and see her. I've heard that she is a very nice woman. Some folk say she is religious, like, but I don't know which church she goes to.'

'There's one thing, Willie; all the women of this place would come to the event if she were involved. They are all that inquisitive they'd come to see what she's like, and I've no doubt they'd spend a bob or two to find out.' They both laughed. 'I think you should go up and see her, Willie, and get it fixed up. We can make something out of this job.'

'But it's not as simple as that, Joe. Our Peter has had a word with her, and arranged for me to see her tomorrow night. But I daren't go up to see the manager's wife on my own, Joe. I'd get all tongue-tied and mixed up. You'll have to come with me. Can you make it tomorrow night?'

'Aye, I'll go if you like. But I'm no speechmaker, Willie, and I'm certainly not used to dealing with women. I'm all right with cows but not two-legged ladies. Anyway, I'll pick you up at half past seven, when I've finished milking.'

Willie left Joe Horton's farm that night very satisfied at the progress of the organ fund, and heartily relieved that he would not have to make the visit to the manager's house alone. When he arrived home, he asked his wife to have his best Sunday suit and his white shirt ironed ready for the following evening, as he was going out on business for the organ fund with Joe Norton. His wife shrugged in disgust at his enthusiasm.

Wednesday 1 July 1964

'This is a very interesting proposal,' said Mr Lacey, the Regional Planning Manager, to Roy Dobson, as they looked at a plan of Martins Main laid out on his desk. 'It is really two schemes. There is the concentration scheme to convey all the coal to the pit bottom. That is some project in its own right. Then there is the development of the Fuston seam and increasing the output from there.' He was stroking his chin, and he had a worried look on his face. 'Assuming we can get agreement to these plans, and get the money allocated, it will place a major strain on all of you at Martins, to carry out the work on time, and keep the results of the pit at a reasonable level. Do you think you can do it?'

'Yes, I am sure we can do it, but we need to have authority so that we can get started as soon as possible. The conveyors will have to be installed during the holiday week next year. There will be quite a bit of preparatory work to do before the holidays, but I think we can fit that in and keep production going.'

Roy spoke with enthusiasm. He'd gone into the ideas in great detail, and followed them through with careful calculations. And he'd illustrated them with detailed drawings by the Surveyor. There was no doubt in his mind that the ideas were sound, and would greatly improve the efficiency of Martins Main. He'd brought all the drawings along to the planning meeting at Regional Headquarters, and put the plans forward near the end of the meeting, when it was obvious that no one else was going to propose any significant changes to the layout of the workings at Martins. He was quietly amused at the embarrassment of Ralph Lacey and his staff, who regarded the plans with some scepticism and suspicion.

'Have you discussed these plans with anyone else on the production side – Mr Jones, or Mr Pickersgill?' asked Ralph Lacey, tentatively.

'Oh, no. This is purely a draft layout. I thought it should be brought to this meeting, and put to your department, first.'

'Quite. Quite. Yes, well we shall need a little time to absorb the implications and if it is acceptable it will need a proper scheme drawing up for approval etc. I'm sure you realise, Mr Dobson, this all takes time. What do you say, Mr Jenkins?' asked Lacey, looking across at Reg, who was the only person who'd remained in his seat while the plans were being discussed.

'The layout is all right, and the conveying scheme should have been put in years ago,' replied Reg, without any enthusiasm. 'It's a pit idea. I was only shown the plans yesterday. I don't mind where we get the coal from at Martins so long as someone authorises us some money to mechanise production at the pit. That's what will get results at Martins—mechanisation; getting machines to do the work and throwing the shovels away. We might keep the men at work, then.'

'I think you will agree though, Mr Jenkins, that you get the best results from mechanisation where you have concentration of workings as well. That is what these plans offer,' said Roy.

'Yes, it helps,' replied Reg, lighting a cigarette and turning to his notepad to continue doodling.

'I do want to emphasise though, Mr Lacey, that we must get the paperwork through as quickly as possible,' continued Roy. 'We need to be starting on the mining work within a few weeks, to keep time on our side. And the conveyors will have to be new ones, so they will need ordering fairly soon. I think this layout is first class and wants authorising without delay.'

'We will push things from our end, Mr Dobson,' said Ralph Lacey. 'We try to keep things moving in our department,' he added, with a little half-confident smile.

Ralph Lacey was not happy in his job, and because of this he was losing his nerve. His apprehension and hesitancy with anything new showed to his staff, and he knew it. At fifty-six years of age he had given a lifetime to the industry, but always in production posts. His pits had always been successful and recognised as good pits. He had held the respect of his men and his officials, as a gentleman of sound experience whose word could be trusted. Some people said he was too much of a gentleman for the mining industry. That could have been his downfall because, even though he was the senior production official in the Region, he had been overlooked for the post of Regional General Manager. He could have accepted that without hard feelings, but he was bitterly disappointed when Mr Jones, who was younger than himself and had always been his junior in experience, was given the Regional Production Manager's post. He had been left as Regional Planning Manager. It was obvious that he was regarded as an old man who was past it, and this was also evident in the rough treatment he had been given on a few occasions by Mr Pickersgill, who openly favoured the ideas, and blunter approach, of his Production Manager.

He nodded at the plans and then looked at one of his staff. 'We must go into this in detail. I want you to do a full profitability exercise on these plans, and assemble all the details for me to see, so that I can brief Mr Jones and Mr Pickersgill. They will want the answers to a lot of questions before they give their approval to these ideas.'

'Right, Mr Lacey, I'll get to work on it straightaway.'

'I think that covers everything for this afternoon. You have no more matters to raise, Mr Jenkins?'

'No.'

'Or you, Mr Dobson?'

'No. You have the meat of my thoughts for Martins Main in those plans.'

'Good. Well that ends our meeting, gentlemen.' He indicated to his staff to leave and they dispersed through the office door and into the main planning building, leaving Roy and Reg alone.

'I think that has been a good meeting, Mr Dobson. I know it has been your first meeting, but you have got an idea of the way we work.'

'Yes. The system is similar in most Regions, as far as I know.'

'I must admit, Martins Main has been a bit of a problem in the past, from a planning point of view. No one can plan well for a pit like that. Nobody knew from one day to the next whether the men would be working or on strike. There have been thoughts a few times over the years that the best plan would be to shut the pit. How are things now? I haven't heard of any trouble over the past few weeks.'

'We are doing a little better,' conceded Roy. 'Relations are always delicate, and liable to flare up, but I am trying to establish some form of stability before we start making changes. That will be the real test, when we start altering things.'

'You're not doing too bad,' said Reg Jenkins. 'Of course, you're only a new starter. Come on, I want a word with you in my office.'

They walked to Reg Jenkins' office. As they settled in their seats, the secretary entered in response to the buzzer on Reg's desk.

'Get us a couple of teas, Rita, that's a girl,' he said.

'You and your tea, Mr Jenkins,' she replied, with a familiar grin on her face. 'Do you take sugar?' she asked Roy.

'Yes, please; just one teaspoon.'

'That's all you'll get, love,' she replied pertly, as she left the room.

'I'll tell you what I want to talk to you about,' said Reg, searching in his diary. 'I've arranged to have a meeting with Watts, the Personnel Manager, and Mr Pickersgill, next week some time. Here it is, Thursday afternoon at half past three. I want you to come along. I've asked to talk to them about the staffing issues at Martins. I think we need some new blood and some extra strength.'

'I agree we're a bit thin on the ground, particularly in the engineering departments,' said Roy, with interest.

'You see I know the old man—Pickersgill I mean—is going to push mechanisation at Martins. I feel it coming. In fact, I guess that is one of the reasons he asked for me as the Sub-Region Manager over Martins.' Roy Dobson smiled at his thoughts at that remark. 'And before he pushes lots of machinery at us I want to get the staff strengthened and sorted out.'

'That is a very sound policy,' replied Roy, very pleased that Mr Jenkins was thinking on these lines. 'I hope Mr Watts and Mr Pickersgill can help us.'

'Oh, they'll help. I'm confident of that. What you need is a few young electrical and mechanical engineers—lads who are up to date with the new ideas on coalface equipment.'

'Yes, I agree with you there.'

'They're the ones needed to supervise the installation of modern coalface equipment. That is a must, the way you are fixed with your engineering teams; they are still in the steam age.'

Roy laughed, but he knew that the remark was to the point after his discussions with some members of his engineering departments.

'And then, of course, we need a replacement for George Turnbull,' concluded Reg. Roy caught his breath with shock at that statement.

'George Turnbull?' he said, his voice disclosing his amazement. 'Why? What's the matter with George?'

'He's no good,' replied Reg, coldly. 'I can't stand the man. He's one of the old school of undermanagers; he knows everybody, and they know him, and because they know him they get away with all sorts of things. He's out, as far as I'm concerned. We need somebody younger who can think new and big.'

'Well, I don't agree, Mr Jenkins,' said Roy, regaining some of his control. 'I've worked with a few undermanagers in my short experience, but I have never met anyone as thorough, or as good, as George. I think he's a first class chap, and I can't imagine what would happen at Martins if a younger, inexperienced chap replaced him. It would be chaos. I think George is sometimes let down by the officials who work for him. If you suggest some new blood and quality there, then I will go along with you. But a change for George? No thank you.'

'You had better think about this, and make your mind up before the meeting next Thursday,' Reg gave Roy a cold, icy stare. 'I've made my mind up. I have had enough of George Turnbull and I want him out. And you can remember this, Dobson; if Turnbull is any use to you now, he'll be no use at all when we start mechanising. He'll be like a fish out of water then, and you know it.' Reg concluded his remarks forcibly as the door opened and his secretary entered with the two cups of tea. Roy was shaken by the remarks. As they drank their tea, he mentioned one or two other items, but didn't refer again to the proposed staff changes before he left to return to Martins Main.

★

As he entered the pit yard Roy was surprised to see that George's car was still parked outside the offices, meaning that he had been at the pit for over twelve hours that day. Roy left his car outside the offices and went upstairs.

'George is in your office waiting to see you, Mr Dobson,' said his secretary.

'Right you are, Gordon.' He passed through into his office.

'Now then, George, you are late going home. What's the trouble?'

'No trouble, Mr Dobson. In fact things are going well down the pit today. I just stayed on to see how you got on at the planning meeting. What did they think of the new plans?'

'I think that they are impressed with our ideas, George. Of course, it will take a few weeks to get everything drawn up and sorted out, I have no doubt. You won't be able to start on the mining work tomorrow, you know. I think in the end the plans will be approved. Anyway, you get off home, George. I'll have a word with you and Mike about the details tomorrow.'

'Right you are, Boss. I'm real glad that you have made so much progress with the Region team. Good afternoon.'

George left the office and, though he little knew it, his interest had gone a long way towards Roy making his mind up on the future of George Turnbull.

★

The children had gone to bed in the Dobson household, and Helen Dobson took up her embroidery in a chair by the window while her husband fidgeted restlessly in another chair as he watched television. She was aware of his restlessness but she made no comment, until he stood up and switched off the set and came to her at the window. She looked up from her work.

'You seem very tense tonight, Roy. What are you worrying about?'

'Something that happened today at work.'

'I could have guessed that much. Do you want to tell me a bit more about it, or is it a great secret?'

He turned towards her.

'Reg Jenkins has set his mind on moving George from his job at Martins. He told me this afternoon in his office at Region.' His voice had a weary, hopeless tone.

'But I thought you said George was a good undermanager? That was one of the first things you told me about the pit.'

'I know, and I still think the same. George is a first class chap and one of the few with guts enough to stand up to the men at Martins. I don't agree with Mr Jenkins' views on this matter at all.'

'Then tell him you don't agree.' Helen said calmly. 'After all, you should have the biggest say in who you want on your staff.'

'I did tell him, but he is going to have a meeting with Mr Pickersgill about staffing issues and ask for a replacement for George. I shall look a grand one if he puts this forward and I disagree with him in front of Pickersgill. He was quite fixed in his views, this afternoon.'

'You say what you feel, and be honest about it. Things should sort themselves out then.' She resumed her embroidery.

'I'm going to have a walk around the garden and have a think about it,' said Roy, and he started for the door.

'Remember that the fellow from the church is coming tonight, about the organ,' said Helen, as he went.

'Give me a shout when he comes.'

★

Outside, the sky was overcast, and clouds were building up for another shower of rain. The footpaths around the garden were wet from an earlier shower, but all the plants in the garden, and even the lawn, seemed brighter and richer from their watering. Roy walked around the lawn until he reached a rose-bed and there he stopped to finger a rose and shake the water from its petals. It was white, with a faint yellow tinge near the edge of its petals. He looked at it for several minutes, absorbed by the perfection of its details, and then he left it, satisfied that it was too beautiful to pick from the bush. He moved on to a bed of geraniums and he saw the globules of water wedged in among their flowers like precious stones. He passed the privet hedge into the vegetable garden. There the peas were in rows, bushing around their hazel twigs. The runner beans looked small and fragile, as they started the long climb up the canes newly installed and fastened together into a long row. The potatoes were pushed up into neat bushes at the top of their ridges, and the onions, in their rich bed of compost, looked well, but did not show any prospects of the championship standards promised by the gardener. Roy saw all the detail of his garden with satisfaction, but with no pleasure; his thoughts were too serious. As he walked towards the greenhouse, along the bottom of the garden, by the rustling popular trees, he considered the George Turnbull situation.

Should he stick his neck out for George? After his failure with Cobba Green, dare he stick his neck out for George in front of Mr Pickersgill? How high was his standing now with Pickersgill? How high was Jenkins' standing with Pickersgill? Might it be true that George would be at a disadvantage with highly mechanised mining? If so, would it be better to make the break early and get a young fellow who could be trained to the job? In the greenhouse Roy sat on a bench and looked at the tomatoes, as the many questions spun around his brain. Every few minutes his thoughts focused on two people. He saw the cold, icy look of Reg Jenkins, and then he would see the short, grey hair and the bright eyes of George Turnbull. He could feel the callous coldness of the one, and the warmth and concern of the other.

Either I'm getting sentimental, or else I'm refusing to recognise a real man when I see one, he told himself in disgust. But Roy knew that he was faced with a difficult decision, and he concluded that a talk with George might be a good idea. He was aroused from his thoughts when he realised that his wife was calling him. He left the greenhouse and went to meet her.

'Two men have come,' Helen said. 'They look a strange pair. I hope you know them.'

'I'll come in and meet them and break the ice. I told the fellow down the pit that you were the one to talk to,' her husband replied.

★

Inside the house, Willie Carter was sitting upright in a chair, holding his trilby awkwardly on his knees. He was feeling very hot, and his starched collar was beginning to prickle his neck.

'I thought it was Mrs Dobson we were to talk to,' said Joe Horton. 'I wonder why she wanted to fetch her husband?'

'Aye, it is strange,' said Willie, and swallowed hard. As he heard footsteps nearing the room he stood up and turned towards the door. Roy Dobson entered in front of his wife. He looked at the two men and didn't recognise either of them.

'Let's see, it is?'

'Willie Carter, Mr Dobson.'

'That's it. Willie from 56s face. I didn't recognise you out of your pit clothes.'

'We do look a bit different at the pit, Mr Dobson.'

'And who is your friend? I don't recognise him either.'

'Oh, well you won't see him at Martins,' said Willie, smiling. 'This is Joe Horton. He's a farmer near Upthorpe.'

Roy Dobson shook hands with Joe Horton.

'Do sit down, please,' said Helen. 'And tell me all about this organ. I am completely in the dark.'

Willie glanced across at Joe, but Joe waved his hand.

'Nay, you do the talking, Willie,' said Joe. 'You've had most to do with this job, and you know most about it.'

Willie cleared his throat and began the story of the organ scheme. Helen Dobson was a good listener and, prompted by her interest and questions, Willie spilled all the facts, including a history of Upthorpe Chapel and some of its members, details of the old harmonium and Bertha Pearson, and the hopes that he held for his son, Peter. From time to time he wiped his forehead as he talked on and on. He had never been so impressed by a woman in his life, as he was with Helen Dobson. Her interest was so sincere that he could not stop himself talking.

'You must stay and have a cup of coffee with us,' said Helen, when, at last, Willie took a pause. She gave her husband a nod, and he went out to make the drinks.

'You'll not forget what we came for, Willie?' said Joe Horton.

'Well, I was leaving that part to you, Joe.' said Willie. 'You are better than me at persuading people to do things.'

Joe laughed out loud. 'He's told you everything but the thing we came about, Mrs Dobson, and now he wants me to do that for him.'

'Don't worry about that. We will be glad to make a donation to the organ fund.'

'It's not just a donation, Mrs Dobson,' said Joe, and he went on to explain the idea of the auction and the part they hoped Helen Dobson would play in it. He also explained that the original idea was to sell off organ parts, but now they were getting offers of other items to be auctioned off for the organ fund.

'I've never done anything like that before. But if you think that I can help you, I will have a try.'

'Oh, thank you very much, Mrs Dobson,' said Willie, his voice showing his relief and excitement.

Then Helen Dobson gave them a shock, as she announced her intentions on a more permanent basis.

'I have been considering my own church membership over the past few weeks. I've been a regular member of a Baptist church in Nottingham, for a number of years. It seems that it will be a long trip from Upthorpe to attend a Baptist church in this part of Yorkshire, and I do prefer to worship at the local church, if I can. So, if you will have me, I hope to attend your Methodist Chapel in Upthorpe.'

'You'll be very welcome, Mrs Dobson,' said Joe Horton, pleased with the news. 'And you'll get used to us Yorkshire folk and our ways, no doubt.'

The two men stayed on for another hour after they had drunk their coffee, and the Dobsons learned a lot about Upthorpe and its inhabitants, listening to Willie Carter and enjoying the slow, dry humour of Joe Horton.

As they were leaving, Willie was very effusive in his thanks to Mrs Dobson for her help, and for the coffee. He hummed softly to himself as they drove off in Joe's car.

'She's a lady, is Mrs Dobson, a lady,' he said. 'She was interested in what we had to tell her. You could feel it. I've never talked to anyone like her before.'

'Aye,' said Joe, very much impressed himself. 'She is a grand woman, there is no doubt, Willie. She will be a great help to the Chapel, if we can keep her.'

'She's a lady, Joe, a lady.'

Friday 3 July 1964

The telephone clicked as Helen Dobson answered it.

'Hello, is that Mrs Dobson?'

'Yes, this is Mrs Dobson speaking.'

'This is Sandra Green, Mrs Dobson. I hope you don't mind, but I would like a word with you about the babysitting next month.'

'Oh, yes. My husband said it would be all right. Is there some difficulty?'

'No, not really. It's just that I have a boyfriend now.' Her voice had a shy inflection. 'Nothing very serious, but he did want to take me out that night.'

'Oh dear,' said Helen.

'Don't worry, Mrs Dobson, I shall still be able to do the babysitting; I just wondered if you would mind if he came along with me for company?'

'Yes, I think that will be fine.'

'You needn't worry, Mrs Dobson, I'll make sure he goes home in good time before my bedtime. It was just that I didn't want to bring him along without asking you first. Some people are strict on these things.'

'I don't mind, Sandra. In fact, I shall feel a bit happier if you have a man to look after you for an hour or two, because this house is a bit isolated.'

'Oh, thank you very much, Mrs Dobson. We'll be along about five-thirty, as my Dad arranged. Goodbye.'

'Goodbye.' Helen replaced the receiver and returned from the hall to her husband in the sitting room.

'Who was that, love?' asked Roy.

'It was that girl, Sandra Green, wanting to know if she could bring her boyfriend along when she babysits for us. I said it would be all right. She sounds a nice girl. Is she?'

'Yes, she seemed a nice young woman when I met her at Cobba's house. She's a good-looking young woman as well.' He grinned at his wife.

In the telephone kiosk in the middle of Doncaster, Sandra Green replaced the receiver and pulled a face at Terry Lacey, who was wedged in besides her, breathing quietly lest his presence be detected over the telephone.

'I told you it would be easy to arrange. You can get anything if you ask for it the right way.'

'I must admit you sounded impressively innocent,' he replied with a grin.

'But I am innocent,' she said, with a shocked look on her face. 'Come on, give me a kiss before we go out.'

'What, here, in the middle of this busy street?'

'Yes, nobody knows us here.' She leaned her face against his, and again his head spun to the exciting touch of her lips and the intense smell of her perfume.

★

'Now, this is progress,' said Mike, as he looked down at the plan on the desk in front of himself, George and Roy. 'So they have accepted the layout to get into the Fuston seam as you put it forward, then?'

'They have asked for bigger roadways for more ventilation, but there are no real changes,' replied Roy. 'Mr Lacey brought the plan over this morning for me to sign it. As far as the scheme to convey the coal to the pit bottom, they are drawing that up into a Capital Project, but they hope to have it ready within the next week.'

'They have certainly moved faster than usual for the planning department,' continued Mike.

'How soon can we start on the mining works, Boss?' asked George.

'We need the other signatures on this plan first, but that should only take a few days if there are no major objections. You can make a start by sorting out the men to do the different jobs and getting the equipment together, George. You should be able to start the work within the next two weeks.' He turned to Mike. 'I would like you to do a detailed phasing of this entire work schedule for the Central Conveying Scheme, Mike, so that we know where each job fits into an overall programme. There will be a lot of extra work to do, but we need to keep the output on stream to get the pit into a better financial position.'

'Right you are. I'll do a phasing, Mr Dobson. Is there anything else?'

'No, you can go, Mike. But I want a word with George. Sit down a minute.'

Roy Dobson moved the plans to one side of his desk and he fingered his measuring scale nervously for a few minutes before he spoke.

'What do you feel about Martins Main now, George? Is there any sign of progress?'

'Certainly, Mr Dobson; I can feel a difference. We shall make the pit a success yet, I'm sure; especially when we get this new layout through.'

'These new plans are just one of the changes, George. There's a lot more to come. The real test for the pit will come when it has to cope with new mechanised production units. This is an entirely new method of mining, you can believe me. I have experience of mechanised coalfaces in Nottingham. It is much more machinery and fewer shovels and more horsepower. How do you feel, yourself, about learning your job all over again? getting used to steel panzer conveyors on the coalfaces, and different types of power loading-machines? When mechanisation is installed, it's a new world then, in the pits— all steel and nuts and bolts.'

'I reckon I've had a fair number of changes in my life in the pits already, so one more won't make much difference. It was all ponies and pit tubs when I started; there were no conveyors, then, and no coal-cutting machines, and not much shotfiring. It was sweat that won the coal in those days. These fellows would have a shock if they had to work like we did thirty years ago.'

'Oh, I know you have come through some changes, George, but mechanised mining is a big stride from where we are now at Martins. I just wondered if you felt too old to make another big change? Don't hesitate to tell me if that's the way you feel.'

George paused in surprise before he replied.

'Nay, Mister, you are not serious, are you? The pit is my life now, and especially this pit. I'm not ready for crying off yet. There is a lot of life left in George Turnbull, I can assure you. Anyway it's not the nuts and bolts that will get the coal out of this pit, or even your modern machines; it will be the men that work these new coalfaces that matter. And I know a lot about the fellows at this pit, and I still think I can lead them to get results with any sort of tackle you might bring here.'

'Yes, George, yes. I think you might be right. We have to get these men in the right frame of mind before we shall get any serious success here. Right then, George, off you go home for some dinner.'

George stood up to leave the office. He seemed more relaxed after Roy Dobson had accepted his view.

'Mind you, Boss, we still have some stupid buggers to deal with at this pit; young Gerry Moore for instance. He isn't a patch on his father. He's not fit for anything but supping ale in that club, and he cares nothing for his wife and kids. I told him today that if the pit depended on the likes of him, it wouldn't last long.'

'They are not all like him though, George,' replied Roy Dobson, smiling.

Somebody to handle the men; George Turnbull was right. That was what Martins Main needed now, and would always need. Roy was nearer to the answer to his problem, but he would need to prepare his case very carefully before the meeting next Thursday.

Sunday 5 July 1964

Roy Dobson parked the car in the drive outside his house. He had delivered the children safely to Sunday School at Upthorpe Methodist Chapel and he was anticipating a quiet hour with his Sunday paper before he fetched them back. Life was not so bad, after all, in Yorkshire. He whistled quietly to himself as he entered the house. He picked up the paper and went into the sitting room where Helen was reading a book by the window.

'Don't sit down, love. There's something wrong at the pit. George Turnbull rang. He's there now, and he wants you to ring him.'

'George was at the pit?' His voice sounded surprised. 'Something must be wrong; did he say what it was?'

'No. He said he was sorry to trouble you, but would you get in touch with him.'

The man in the lamp-room who answered the telephone said he would fetch George to the 'phone. Roy was left for two minutes searching for some clue as to what the trouble might be. He was relieved when he heard George's voice approaching the telephone.

'Mr Dobson?'

'Yes, George. What is it?'

'It is 56s coalface, Mister. Water has broken into the roof on the coalface and it's running down the face and flooding the main roadway.'

'Is it bad?'

'Pretty bad. It hasn't caused much roof trouble yet, but it's building up and it will soon stop the ventilation. I'm not happy about that. We shall get some methane forming quick if that happens. But I think I can beat it.'

'What have you organised so far? Can I do anything to help?'

'Let me tell you what I've already done. As soon as I spoke to the deputy underground, I realised that we needed to start pumping as soon as possible. The trouble is, we can't reach the water with the pump that we used in that district. I must admit, Mr Dobson, that I thought we had seen the last of any water on 56s district, and I left the pump behind the coalface. I need two hundred yards of pipes and the pump moving forward two hundred yards.'

'What about men for the job?'

'I've got that organised, now. I've been to the Club and dragged half a dozen of them out—Fred Moore and some of his mates. They were not very keen on leaving the blonde singer behind, and they are a bit worse for a pint or two, but they'll sober up sharp when they get down in three feet of water. I've got three of them for getting the pipes and three for getting the pump forward.'

'Do you need anything else, George?'

'No. There is a fitter down there and I've got some extra spanners. I'm changed now to go down with the men. I can sort this out. The only thing I could do with is the Sunday dinner. I was just going to sit down to it when the 'phone rang. It will keep warm, though, and I've got half an ounce of chewing tobacco to keep me going.'

'I think I'll come over to the pit in case anything else crops up.'

'You've no need to do that, Mr Dobson. You stay at home. There is no point in two of us being affected. I'll ring out to the lamp-room in an hour or two to let you know if there are any problems, and how we're getting on.'

'You sure you're all right, George?'

'Yes, of course, Boss. It's only a drop of water, after all, but doesn't it pick a bloody awkward time to show itself—Sunday lunchtime!' George gave a laugh to fit his remark.

'I'll be in the house all afternoon, so keep me informed, George.'

Roy put down the telephone and went into his sitting room. The room was alive with the freshness and cleanliness of the sun flooding in through the bay window, lighting a vase of multicoloured zinnias stippled against their background of green laurel leaves and spotlighting the bright floral curtains, the red carpet, the grey settee and making the whole room vibrant with an infinite wattage. In contrast, he could picture George walking with the men, five hundred yards below the sunshine, along the deserted mine roadways: silent, weird and horrific with all the machinery stationary and lifeless.

Their journey would be marked only by a flurry of dust along one branch of the latticework respiratory system of Martins Main. Throughout the afternoon, in the light fed by the sun's persistent burn, he disowned the brightness and the warmth, and his mind stayed with the men at their work. He felt their body heat grow as they buckled into their task, the sweat forming on the stripped arms and shoulders. He heard the curses at a nipped finger, the grunts at an unyielding obstacle, the heaving and the pushing to get the job done in time. He could sense the urging of George. They knew of no sunshine, these men, they gave it no thought. Their world was small, too small, hemmed into an arch of steel, slowly flooding with black, slimy water. Roy received no news for four-and-a-half hours. Then his telephone rang.

'Mr Turnbull has sent a message out of the pit that they have got the pump working, and that the water is under control. He's going forward into the water to lift the conveyor drive at the coalface, to save the electric motor.'

'Thank you. I'm relieved to hear that they have succeeded,' said Roy. 'Will you keep in touch with them and give me another ring when they are setting off for the surface? I want to come over and meet them.'

'Right you are, Mr Dobson.'

He timed his arrival at the pit just right. He had parked his car and gone up to his office, when he saw the shaft pulley wheels slowly start to revolve to lift the men up to the surface. He met them in the pit yard as they emerged from the cage into the bright, evening sunshine. They were soaked in dust and sweat, and several of them had been over their knees in the water so that their trousers hung down to the floor like black pipes.

'Right, lads; straight into the baths and put those clothes to dry. Then I want you to come back to my office. I've got a thirst quencher for you.'

The men hurried away, some of them obviously surprised at his offer. George paused to speak, but Roy Dobson waved him on his way. All his clothes were soaking wet, including his shirt and vest.

'Off you go to get those clothes off, George. Whatever happened? You look as though you've been swimming in it.'

'I nearly was swimming,' replied George, as they walked together towards the offices. 'I slipped down when I was trying to put a chain around the conveyor drive to lift it up. Some dizzy bugger had left a shovel on the floor there, and I put my foot on it. Never mind, we got the conveyor drive lifted and I don't think the motor is harmed. I'll have it checked to make sure, before morning.' George went for his shower some minutes later.

The men came into the office in a group. They looked different in their day clothes, and their faces were pink and flushed from the hot showers, but their eyes were rimmed in black where they had failed to remove all the coal dust from their eyelashes. They were shy and nervous about having a drink in the manager's office. Roy uncapped the bottles and poured the beer into glasses on his desk.

'We need this,' said one of the younger ones with a nervous laugh, as he took his glass.

'I wonder if we shall get water money for today?' said another. They all laughed, and the atmosphere was less strained. There was little conversation, and they were all refusing a second glass, when George entered.

'Is it good, Fred?' asked George, indicating the glass.

'Aye, it's not gone amiss,' replied Fred Moore. 'We'll be going then, now, and see if the dinner's ready, shall we, chaps?' They began to move towards the door.

'Yes, well thank you, lads. You've helped us out of a sticky corner,' said Roy, who felt he had to make some comment.

'We would have lost that coalface for a week or two, Fred, if you and your mates hadn't turned out for us,' said George.

The men left the office clattering down the stairs and when they reached the familiarity of the pit yard below, their tongues loosened and they laughed and discussed the afternoon freely as they walked off towards Martins Lane.

'I'll keep in touch tonight, and see that we get the water right down by morning,' said George Turnbull. 'Mind you, we shall have some pains with 56s tomorrow, getting the coal off after the water has seeped into everything.'

'Never mind about that, George, that's tomorrow's problem. You've sorted out today's problem, and that's good enough for me. Off you go now for that Sunday dinner; you must be ready for it,' said Roy.

'I am that; my stomach walls are meeting. Of course, I expect the dog will have enjoyed it by now!'

Chapter 5

It was another clear, bright day, and the headgear of Martins Main was silhouetted against a pale, blue-white horizon starkly visible to all the men as they approached the pit. In the pithead baths there was a one-way traffic of men changing into dirty, dusty clothes. Their two days of rest were a blurred and hazy memory. The pit yard had its usual muffled Monday morning look, all the men going down the mine, and only a few nightshift men coming up and going home. The wheels seemed reluctant to start after the weekend break, and the mine demanded a multitude of bodies sacrificed into its depths before it was willing to release the black gold. And the reluctance of the mine to release its product was particularly the case on 56s coalface that Monday morning.

There were great efforts of shoulders and arms and straining backs, but the slimy, seeping water made the conveyor belts slip, solidified the coal, weakened the roof and defied the efforts of George and his men. At the end of the shift their production of coal was minimal, and they all left the coalface admitting weariness and defeat.

When the statistical failure of 56s face to produce its output reached Region in the afternoon, Reg Jenkins reached for his telephone, eager to establish a guilty party and keen to have a victim.

'Why have they failed to fill the coal on 56s face?' His voice crisply demanded an answer from Roy.

'Well, as I told you this morning, Mr Jenkins, the water did do a lot of damage yesterday. And while we are lucky not to have lost the unit completely through flooding, I did anticipate some difficulties today. From the reports, I think everyone has tried their best in the circumstance.'

'Now then, Dobson lad, you are hiding other people with your excuses. You must look at the cause in the first place. Turnbull was at fault, and you know it. He should have had a pump range and a pump ready at 56s for that water. There has been water on that face before; it was bound to come back. Don't you accept that Turnbull is making excuses? He's gone too far this time. This will be a fine thing to report to Mr Pickersgill. He doesn't accept this sort of mistake from his management, you know.'

Roy Dobson hesitated to reply, wondering if Reg Jenkins had an audience in his office.

'I have checked with the surveyor and there is no evidence of water affecting the other faces near the position of 56s. I think it may be a stroke of bad luck we've had.'

'Don't talk of bad luck to me, Dobson lad. That is what they employ us for–to plan against bad luck. You're grasping at straws now. Turnbull is to blame; he should have been ready for some water. You can tell him from me that there had better be a bloody pump up with the coalface from now on.' Reg banged down the telephone. He was angry at the lost output, but quietly confident that he could use the incident as evidence when he met Pickersgill to ask for another undermanager.

George was late, that afternoon, going up to the manager's office. When he entered, Roy Dobson could see that his face had a weary look, and there was no sparkle in his eyes.

'Poor day, today, George.'

'Yes, Mr Dobson. Not good at all.'

'I'm afraid Mr Jenkins has been on the telephone about 56s. He's very upset; he says we should have had a pump up, ready for the water.'

'He's right, I suppose,' replied George.

'It's easy to be wise after the event; he's very good at that. We must make sure, George, that we don't get caught out with water again on 56s.'

'I'll see that a pump is always on the job, Mr Dobson.'

They discussed other parts of George's responsibilities. Roy threw out a whole range of searching questions. He was testing, probing and re-probing the quality of his undermanager. George did look tired. Maybe Reg Jenkins was right; maybe this man was getting old–too old to carry the detail of a big part of Martins Main. But the more Roy questioned, the more he was reassured as the answers rolled out. They weren't simple answers, but full details of the work being done, the men doing it, and a full summary of the short-term prospects and the changes that George had in mind.

'Off you go then, George,' he said at last. 'You must not miss your dinner today.'

Thursday 9 July 1964

'I can see some signs of progress at Martins Main, Dobson. How do you feel now that you have had time to get your eyesight?' asked Mr Pickersgill.

Roy moved uneasily in his chair. He felt an isolated unit in the meeting with the Region Personnel Manager, Reg Jenkins and Mr Pickersgill. He had found himself very nervous before the meeting. He wasn't sure how much it was George Turnbull who was on trial, and how much himself. He cleared his throat and licked his lips, to try to reply with a confident voice. Mr Pickersgill was fiddling with some papers in front of him and adjusting his spectacles; his eyes were not on Roy, but Mr Jenkins had a wide-eyed, hard look on his face, as he stared directly at his manager.

'I am hopeful, Mr Pickersgill, that the pit can be pulled round. We need to get some confidence into people at the pit and get everybody pulling with us. It won't be easy.' Roy's voice tailed off inconclusively.

'It's never easy, lad.' Mr Pickersgill inferred by his tone that the last remark was pointless and immature. Roy shuffled uneasily in his seat.

'Well, Reg, you asked for the meeting. What can we do to help you?' asked Pickersgill, turning to Reg Jenkins.

'You know my views on Martins Main, Sir,' he replied confidently. 'I have high hopes for the pit, not just sorting itself out, but becoming a highly profitable business unit. The main problem I see is a shortage of the right staff to work under Dobson. We must sort this out before we start mechanising the coalfaces. I know some of the young prospects in the Region, but not all of them, so I thought a meeting with yourself and Mr Watts would be the best way to get the matter cleared up. The main need is to get some young engineers settled in at the pit before we start the intensive mechanisation programme. But we must also strengthen the management staff.'

'Let's start with the engineers, first,' said Pickersgill. 'What have you in mind, Mr Watts?'

'I've looked through any possible candidates for Martins Main and, while there are several who would fit the bill, they're already settled in other pits. I think the Chief Engineer would have to be consulted before any transfers could be arranged.'

Mr Pickersgill called on his intercom for the Chief Engineer to join the meeting immediately. On his arrival, Reg put his case that Martins Main needed some extra engineers. When the Chief Engineer avoided a direct reply, and commented on the shortage of young men at other pits in the Region, Mr Pickersgill was sharp in his comments.

'Albert, you might as well realise that I am not going to have Martins Main as a thorn in my side for ever. The National Board delights in pointing to that pit as the weak link in my chain. They keep asking me what I am doing about it, and hinting at the lack of progress. Well, when the time is right I am going to flood Martins Main with machinery and equipment. I need some good young lads to look after that equipment and organise the engineering side. Have you got that?'

'Yes, Mr Pickersgill.'

'Right then, by tomorrow morning you pick out two lads, one electrical and one mechanical, and give their names to Mr Watts so that he can see them and arrange for their transfer to Martins Main.'

'Right, Mr Pickersgill.'

'And make sure that they are the best that you have, otherwise your department can expect some pressure if things don't go right.'

Roy Dobson listened with respect and awe. So this was the ruthless Mr Pickersgill, and this was the significance of Martins Main to him. It was his embarrassing problem—the problem other people could point to and the problem nobody else had sorted out. It was clearly the problem that he was determined would not beat him. So much so that he was prepared to become involved personally, even to the extent of giving direct instructions to senior members of his staff. In these circumstances could he be challenged by anyone? Should Roy accept Pickersgill's rulings to safeguard his own position? Dare he mention George Turnbull at all? His thoughts revolved inconclusively as the Chief Engineer left the room. Then he heard the critical question being asked. This was the moment. He would have to decide quickly.

'What are you ideas about the management changes then, Reg?'

'I think we need a new undermanager, Mr Pickersgill,' said Reg. 'George Turnbull has been at the pit all his life. He grew up in the village among the men, and he's too well known to them all. In fact, they call him by his first name. Things are too friendly between him and the men. I think you should find him a job at some small pit, where he can spend his last few years quietly. I'm not happy with him in the job now; goodness knows how he will cope in the future. We need a younger man, with wider horizons, who has seen other mining systems and has experience of the latest ideas.'

'How old is he?' asked Pickersgill. 'I've only met him once.'

Mr Watts provided a brief history of George Turnbull, reading from notes on his personal file.

'Yes, this can be arranged, Reg, but we can't do it overnight,' continued Pickersgill.

'I don't agree with Mr Jenkins on this matter, Sir,' said Roy, hurriedly.

The others looked at him.

'How do you mean, Dobson?' asked Pickersgill.

'I think George Turnbull should stay at Martins.'

'Well, go on. Give your reasons.'

'I agree that we need some extra management strength, and that a young man would be ideal to help with the installation of new equipment and trying new methods. But George Turnbull is vital to Martins Main. He is a good undermanager. I have studied him closely and checked his work. He is very thorough and he keeps his officials up to some high standards. In fact, I have never seen a better undermanager, Sir, and I want to keep him at Martins.'

Roy sounded very sincere, and as he looked up to find the eyes of the other three on him, he felt a strange relief that the moment was over, and that he had taken his stand beside George Turnbull.

'And what about him being local?' asked Mr Watts.

'It might be a disadvantage with some people, Mr Watts, but I think that George turns it to good advantage. He knows everybody, and he knows all their backgrounds. He understands them, and they can't hoodwink him like they would strangers. In fact, I know that the majority of the men respect him and will do anything for him. And you know, Sir, when we've put in all the new equipment and machines at Martins, we shall still need the men to work them. I think George has an important role to play in organising these men.'

The discussion continued for a while. Mr Jenkins stated his views bluntly, and showed no sign of changing his mind. Roy put his case carefully and sincerely, but without pressure, basing his arguments on examples he had seen of George Turnbull in action. He left Mr Pickersgill in no doubt that he saw himself and George Turnbull as a management team, not as two individuals in different levels of management. In the end, Roy had his way and he was sure he sensed some small respect from Mr Pickersgill for standing by his convictions, and his staff. It was agreed to send a specialist along to Martins Main to help with machine installations at a later date.

'Have you set up that meeting with Mr Lacey on Martins Main plans yet?' Mr Pickersgill spoke to his secretary on the intercom.

'Yes, Mr Pickergill. It's set for three o'clock tomorrow, in your office, after your lunch in Doncaster.' He flicked off the intercom.

'I want you to come to that meeting, Dobson. Mr Lacey has had a word with me and shown me the plans for developing the Fuston seam. He has also mentioned the conveyor scheme to take all the coal to the pit bottom. These represent big changes for Martins, and I have a few questions to ask before I sign up to such major developments and the capital costs that will be involved.'

'Right, Mr Pickersgill, I'll be there at the meeting,' said Roy, as he gathered up his notebook and put it in his attaché case.

★

'You seem quietly pleased with yourself tonight,' said Helen, as her husband entered the bedroom, humming to himself.

'Yes, things have gone right for a change,' he replied. He jumped into the bed beside her. 'I think George will be staying at Martins. I got my way at the meeting at Region this afternoon.'

'I told you not to worry, and to speak your mind. I knew it would work out all right.'

'You are a clever girl; you know all the answers. I have to go back and see Mr Pickersgill tomorrow, about the new pit plans. You'd better tell me how to approach that meeting.'

He lay close to her warm body. He touched her through her flimsy nightdress and, to his fingertips, her body rose nipple-hard, suddenly burning, while his own body stiffened in response.

'Prove to me that I am still a young bull then,' he whispered into her parted lips.

'Go, get yourself ready then. Quick.'

Saturday 25 July 1964

Sandra walked across the room to draw the curtains. She switched on the reading lamp on the table by the television set as she passed. It had been a long evening, as Mr and Mrs Dobson had left at six o'clock for their dinner-dance engagement, but everything had passed off well. She had played with the children, and then read them a story as they sat on her knee, before putting them to bed. Once in bed, they had gone off to sleep quite quickly. Her boyfriend, Terry, had pretended to study for an hour while she read a book, but the sight of her curled up on the settee had proved too big a distraction, and he had shut his files and leaned over and kissed her.

'You'll never pass to be a surveyor doing that,' she said

'What's the point in being a surveyor if you've missed all the pretty girls?' he replied.

★

Terry Lacey had grown up a lot in the short time he had known Sandra. His limited experience with girls had led him to doubt a lot of the stories told by his colleagues at the office. But now he was one of them. He had experience as well. He could nod in agreement now. He could laugh with the others, and he enjoyed it when they ragged him and tried to find out about his girlfriend.

'Does she let you have it regular, Terry? Or does she play hard to get?' one of his mates had asked at lunchtime on Friday. He had grinned back at them.

'He's got a bloody conceited look,' said one of the others. 'I'll bet she's a bombshell, and free with it. Where are you going tomorrow night, Terry? Let's be knowing, and then we can have a look at her.'

'Quiet night, tomorrow,' he replied shyly. 'We're going babysitting for some friends of hers.'

'Just think of it,' said one of his mates. 'Babysitting: kids in bed asleep; soft lights; comfortable settee; and she's taking you along with her. She's asking for it. You're in man. Get 'em down. Get in there. We shall want a report on Monday, shan't we, chaps?' They'd all laughed and slapped him on the back.

★

Terry looked across at Sandra as she collected the supper cups and plates onto a tray to take them into the kitchen. Her pink nylon dress was crumpled where she had been sitting curled up on the settee, but he could still see the shape of her lovely body. His desire to touch her and hold her rose up again, as it had done so many times during the last three hours. Would he ever reach satisfaction for his desire? He recalled again their kissing; the softness of her lips, the smoothness of her nylons to his touch, and the icy smoothness of bare flesh where they finished. But then there was the restraining hand – no argument, no scene, but a limit. She was in command all the time.

When she returned from the kitchen, she leaned over the back of the settee and looked down into his eyes.

'Time to go now, Terry; young girls like me need to have plenty of beauty sleep.'

'But it's only ten o'clock!' He must stall for time. His body ached to stay longer with her.

'I know it's early, but I have a lot to do before I go to bed. Doing my hair, creaming my face – you have no idea what troubles a young woman takes to make herself right for you men to see.'

'Well, if it's such a big job, you need some help.' He stood up. 'I told Mr Dobson I would see you were alright before I left. Now let me see, where do I start? I know, I'll follow the same process you did with the Dobson kids. I'll get the nightdress out. I'll fetch your case.'

He went out and fetched her case from the hall, where he had seen it. When he returned she was still leaning over the settee, smiling.

'Here we are.' He opened the case and took out a black, nylon nightdress – single layer and transparent. His hands shook as he laid it out over a chair. How long would she go on playing this game?

'Now, you take your clothes off,' he said very quietly.

She sauntered round to the front of the hearth.

'No, if you're doing the job, you might as well do it.' She turned her back for him to pull down the zip on her dress.

'You are a beauty, Sandra,' he whispered in her ear, as he nuzzled it.

'Watch the zip; it sticks, sometimes, half-way down,' she said, in a matter of fact tone.

The zip made a tearing sound as it opened and exposed a v-shape of skin crossed by neat, narrow straps. She raised her arms and stepped out of her dress. Dress off; underskirt off. She was like one of those postcards he had seen at work, but better. White bra, full and tight; white briefs, curving between her legs; and a white suspender belt clinging to her waist.

'You take the bra off, next. Then it's the nightdress on, and the pants, stockings and suspender belt follow from underneath.'

He moved close to her and tried to unfasten the bra. The smell of her body and the warmth of her flesh enveloped him. His fingers couldn't grip the small fastening.

'You're not used to hooks and eyes, the way you're fiddling there,' she said, as he failed to unlatch the bra. 'Let me do it.'

He stood back to watch. She slipped off the bra and bent forward to pick up her nightdress from the chair. He watched, dry-mouthed and breathing hard at the sight of her breasts hanging down. She removed the rest of her clothes. He had never seen a strip show. It was too much, too quickly. She stood before him, her nightdress shimmering, but through it he could see the curves, the salient points and the misty triangle of hair.

'And now the goodnight kiss,' she said.

He didn't move towards her; he couldn't move. She seemed so cool and controlled, in contrast to his trembling excitement.

'You are teasing me, aren't you,' he said. 'Trying to upset me and have a laugh at me. You are cruel, Sandra.'

She moved to him and pushed herself tight into his arms.

'No, Terry, no; I don't mean to be cruel.' She suddenly saw his reasons. 'I know I am a show-off. I know I've got a lovely body, and I want to show it off to you. But I don't mean to be cruel.' She sounded genuinely upset. 'I think a lot about you, Terry. I've never done anything like this with any other boy.'

'Oh, you are lovely, Sandra. I love you,' he said, as he gripped her to him. He could feel the curve of her body nestling to him, as his hand clasped her buttock. 'Don't try to explain, Sandra, it's not something you can put into words. I am the same; I can't put into words what I think about you: how you look; how you feel. I just can't tell you.'

She pushed him back, towards the settee.

'Lay down,' she said. 'Let me kiss you.'

While she kissed him, her hand fiddled with the buttons on his trousers, and then dived inside to search.

'What are you doing?' he whispered.

'Lay down, and relax. Give me your handkerchief.'

She knew what to do. She had secretly watched some boys doing it behind the toilets, when she was at school. But she wanted to see the explosion again, so she leaned over and, with her breasts touching his face, she turned her head to watch her moving hand. Rhythmic movements up and down. It had a strange soft-hardness to the touch. It was over quickly. His body tensed and arched, and he cried out beneath her.

'Sandra....oh love......oh.......'

As Terry Lacey drove home that night, his mind was plagued with a thousand visions of Sandra Green, and his body ached with contented pleasure. But that night, he knew for certain that this wonderful thing that had suddenly invaded his life, was there for keeps. It was his Sandra Green from now on; not a girl to talk about and boast about to his workmates, but his girl, to treasure, to trust, to scheme with, to have secrets with and to love more than all others. Terry Lacey thought he had grown up a lot, that Saturday night.

Chapter 6

A coal train hissed and steamed and jerked a line of full coal wagons out of the sidings at Martins Main. The regular members of the Enclosure looked out at the train, and beyond to the pulley wheels of the mine shaft that were furiously in motion.

'Makes you wonder who wants to buy coal, this weather,' said Charlie, taking off his flat cap and wiping his forehead. 'It's too hot for fires.'

'Let's hope that the hot weather lasts till the Feast,' said Cliff. 'There should be more money about this year. The pit's been doing better.'

The Feast was the local holiday taken in the middle of August, and interest in it had grown as the weather at the end of July had turned into hot sunshine throughout long, clear days. At Martins Main, the pit was running smoothly, as the men turned up for work and put in extra effort in Bull week – the week on which wages for their pay packet just prior to the holiday would be based. Roy was gaining a confidence about Martins Main that he had found elusive in his early months as manager. A comparison of the results for previous years showed the pit to be doing much better, and there were few troubles with the men and no signs of any disputes developing. Was it that Cobba was solving problems, rather than creating them? Was it that the men were turning over a new leaf? Or was it that Roy's direct style of management was paying off? Roy wasn't greatly concerned with the cause; his interest was in building on the improvement and securing the future for the pit. The project for central conveying in the Low Moor seam had been approved and, after full consultation with the men and lots of enthusiasm from Mike Darlow and George Turnbull, men had been redeployed to drive the new underground roadways and do the other work necessary to prepare the mine for the new conveyors. The work would take nine months, but Roy could see great improvements possible then, in output from the Benton seam. With mechanisation on the coalfaces as well, Martins Main could become a highly profitable pit.

'Nine months' hard work,' he kept telling his staff. 'And then we shall really start mining.' His enthusiasm had brushed off onto a lot of people at the pit, but in the Enclosure there were some sceptics.

'Show themselves up, do a lot of the men at Bull week,' said Albert. 'They do twice as much work as they ought to do, just for a few extra quid in the wage packet. Play into managements hands, the silly buggers.'

'That's not right, Albert,' said Cliff. 'The only time you get a true picture of a pit is at Bull week, when everybody is interested. The industry would be a lot better if they were all Bull weeks.'

'I reckon they've started to drive another roadway from the Benton seam to the Fuston seam,' said Charlie. 'Going to put belts in and then work the coal in the south west area. Have you heard anything?'

'They've started work on three shifts,' said Pat Milligan. 'They're going to get it ready as quickly as possible.'

'What's the attraction down there, I wonder,' said Albert. 'There's plenty of coal at Martins without working in that direction.'

'It's thick coal there,' replied Cliff. 'And it goes all the way out to Lucy Pit. My brother's lad is a shot-firer there.'

'They're also driving a roadway from the Benton seam up to the Low Moor seam,' said Charlie. 'What's that for?'

'It's part of the central conveying scheme,' replied Pat. 'It's a major scheme to convey all the coal to the pit bottom, with one loading point for the whole pit.'

'Is it an idea from this new-fangled manager?' asked Albert.

'No, definitely not,' replied Cliff. 'I remember George talking, about twelve months ago, about schemes to concentrate the workings. A lot of ideas were on the table when the new manager arrived. It's not the manager; George is behind these plans.'

'You still don't think much of this manager, Albert?' said Charlie, grinning.

'I don't think owt of him,' replied Albert, emphatically. 'He's a young, slimy character, and he's got something over Cobba Green, I'm sure of that. I can't get a bloody civil word out of Cobba, these days. He won't have owt to do with me. And that's not like Cobba. We were always close in the old days. I taught him a lot when he was younger. And I've led a few rag-ups and strikes for him when he wanted to cause trouble for management. But that's done with now; management are getting away with what they want, at Martins Main.'

Friday 14 August 1964

Cobba slipped his pay packet into his pocket after glancing at the nett pay figures at the bottom of the slip. He didn't care about the sidelong glances the pay clerk gave him. It was no business of anybody what he was paid. He was worth the extra money anyway, if the output figures were anything to go by. Martins Main was having its best results for years. Cobba had set about his role of management intermediary and pacifier by adopting a policy of non-involvement. He took up less of the detailed wage claims by individual men. These he left to his fellow union colleagues, especially Jimmy Bell, who got into deep water on several occasions, when he didn't have Cobba at his elbow in support. He brought forward no militant wage claims to challenge management, and he was appalled and disgusted at the lack of ideas from his union colleagues. When it came to pushing management ideas, he found that part easy. There had only been the Benton and Low Moor conveyor project, and everybody at the pit thought that was a good scheme, without Cobba having to emphasise his support. No, things had worked out rather better than he had hoped, and his pay packet was feeling the difference. He patted the envelope in his pocket as Jimmy approached him across the pit yard, with a workman at his heels.

'Just look here, Cobba, what George Turnbull has paid this fellow for a shift's work laying rail track,' said Jimmy, agitated. 'We are going in with this one, aren't we, Cobba? We can't let 'em get away with pay like this.'

'Well, I've had a message that the manager wants a word with me. I suppose it must be important; I'm on my way there, now. Thee go in with him, Jimmy, and see George Turnbull. And let me know how tha goes on.'

'Oh. Right, Cobba,' said Jimmy, dampened in his enthusiasm. 'Come on, lad. Let's get this sorted out straightaway.'

Cobba smiled to himself as he walked up the steps to the manager's office. Jimmy was on a hard case with that one; George never paid rates like that without good cause.

★

'You wanted to see me, Mr Dobson?' Cobba asked, when he was shown into the office where Roy was sitting at his desk, with a relaxed look on his face.

'Yes. It's nothing much, Cobba. I just wanted to show you the latest figures for the pit. You can see the difference in tonnage this year compared with last year, for the month of July, and the effect the improved tonnage has had on the pit's finances. Your help towards this is paying off.'

He pushed a sheet across the table, with the comparative figures for Cobba to look at. Cobba glanced at the figures casually, but his quick mind took in the financial column immediately. Martins Main was near to break-even, and only a few hundred tons extra per week would put the pit into a weekly break-even position.

'Aye, I suppose there is some improvement,' replied Cobba, as he pushed the sheet back. 'I reckon you'll not be satisfied until the pit is making a good profit, though'

'That's true, but it's no benefit to me personally, to make a profit. It will be a big advantage to all your men, though. This pit has a good living for everyone here for a lifetime. But I'm sure you know all this, Cobba. Let me tell you the other reason I wanted to have a word with you. I want to wish you a good holiday.'

'Oh, well thank you, Mr Dobson.' Cobba was somewhat surprised at this from the manager.

'There's certainly a holiday spirit about everywhere, today. You can feel it at the pit.'

'There's a lot of folks put money by all the year round to have a holiday at the Feast week.'

'Are you going away, Cobba?'

'We've nothing definite planned yet. Our Sandra is taking some time to make her mind up. I suppose we shall go off somewhere, for a few days.'

★

Sandra Green was having problems with her boyfriend. Terry had booked to go on holiday with his parents, starting in the middle of the Feast week, and Sandra wanted to be around in Upthorpe until he left. The trouble was that she had not told her father about Terry Lacey. She had dropped hints, but she didn't feel confident enough to expose him in flesh and blood to her father. She decided that it must wait until later in the year. However, her brother, David, provided the answer to her holiday problems, when he pointed out that Yorkshire had a County match in Leeds, starting on Saturday. She tackled her father at the first opportunity, when he came home from the pit.

'I'm not keen on rushing off straightaway, this holiday, Dad. Why don't you take our David to watch the cricket match in Leeds? I know you like to watch a cricket match. You could have three days there, and then we could maybe go off for a day or two later in the week?'

'That's a good idea, Sandra, I know our David would like that. Are you sure you'll be alright here, on your own? You could come with us?'

'No, thank you. I'll pack your sandwiches, but that's as far as I'm going, where cricket's concerned.'

'Alright, we'll do that then. But we'll have a day or two at the seaside later in the week. I want you to get some sun to that body of yours.'

'Don't you worry about my body,' replied Sandra, with a saucy nod. 'It's doing alright.'

Cobba grinned at her as she left the room with a wiggle of her bottom. He was proud of his daughter.

★

Peggy Moore finalised her holiday arrangements as her husband was putting on his shoes to go out to the Club.

'Have you got any plans for the holiday?' she asked him, diffidently. He had hardly spoken since he had come home from the pit with his pay packet.

'No,' he replied. 'I have no plans. How can you do owt with a couple of bloody little kids puking and shitting all over the place?'

'They are your kids as well as mine,' replied his wife, disturbed by his callousness.

Gerry Moore stood up and adjusted his tie in the mirror over the mantelpiece.

'Don't I know it. I can tell with the money in my pocket.' As he was going out of the house he added. 'I might be late tonight. Some of my mates are planning to go into Doncaster. I might hook on with them.'

Peggy Moore sat down, pale and weary and despairing. The heavy, sick feeling plucked at her stomach and her throat tickled with the desire to vomit. But she would not tell her husband.

'I'll never tell him,' she muttered to herself as she gazed at the hearth. 'I swear I'll not tell him. He'll have to see for himself.'

Her eldest son pulling at her apron broke her thoughts.

'Mammy look.' He held up a stubby thumb that had blood streaming down his hand from a gash he had just made on an old bean tin. His face had a shocked, surprised expression and big tears were forming in his eyes and running down his cheeks, cutting clean rivulets through the dirt on his face. She picked him up and clasped him to her. She put his thumb in her mouth and gripped the wound with her lips and tongue. The blood tasted strangely sweet, and although the little lad didn't know it, his tears, running onto her cheeks, calmed, comforted and reassured her.

Saturday 15 August 1964

Charlie and Albert were the first to arrive, at about a quarter past seven, but the others were all in position before eight o'clock. It was a recognised practice that the members of the Enclosure met early on the Feast Saturday morning, to see the holidaymakers leaving Martins Lane and the Upthorpe Estate for the different holiday resorts.

'Better weather this year than it was last,' said Albert, looking up at the sky, which was laced with pale, white, flimsy clouds filtering some of the sun's force.

'Bit chilly, though, for sea bathing,' added Charlie, as he hopped around the Enclosure seat.

'There's three there that won't feel the cold,' said Cliff, pointing at two young boys and a girl, walking with their parents from the bottom of Martins Lane.

The lads had bright, polished faces and their hair was parted and stuck into place with tap water. They wore their best clothes and walked carefully so as not to damage their new sandals. They carried raincoats over their arms and the elder boy swung along a small case, eager to show that it was not too heavy for him. The little girl, in a new dress, walked primly behind the boys, her head locked into position by two short, stubby, pigtails woven tightly to use all her available hair. Behind her, the parents carried the rest of the luggage, and their own worries; the mother wondered if she had packed enough clothes; the father wondered if he had enough money in his wallet, and if the digs they were going to would be as good as his mate at work had promised.

'Have you got the letter about the digs?' he asked his wife.

'Yes, I put it in my handbag.'

'I hope the place is alright. I've not been happy since my mate decided to go to that other address. Can't see why a fellow should want to change, if he knows a good lodging.'

'It's no use you wondering now. I only hope the kids behave themselves. Do you hear that?' she said, taking two quick steps forward so that she could poke the smallest lad with her umbrella. 'It's a posh place your Dad is taking us to, so it'll have to be best behaviour all the time. No being faddy at the table either. You eat what you're given and like it. We've paid a lot for this holiday, but if you don't behave, we'll not stop, we'll come back home.'

The little lad looked across the causeway at his brother, and smiled. They both knew that their mother always said this, but didn't mean it, really.

Other families too, along Martins Lane, were locking their doors, turning their cats and dogs loose to charity for a week, and making their way down to the bottom of Martins Lane where the buses were leaving for the various resorts on the east and west coasts.

From the Upthorpe Estate a few families in cars were making an early start to beat the traffic through York and Malton, or fight for an early place in the crush at Todmorden and Preston.

'Things are going smoothly,' said Cliff, as another bus pulled out of Martins Lane and turned off along the road for Doncaster and Skegness. As the bus pulled away, a taxi turned in off the main road and started checking the numbers on the doors, looking for number sixty.

★

Janet Hall and her husband were spending their holiday on a coach tour of the south coast and they were taking a taxi into Doncaster to join the coach. When the driver pulled up outside their house, he found the cases on the step labelled with the hotels and the tour number. Janet, in a pale-blue two-piece, with matching blouse, her hair set in place and her make-up immaculate, was standing at the door with her husband. He looked smart and well-scrubbed, in blue blazer and flannels, but a little ill at ease. His hands were his problem, and despite the attention of his wife for an hour the previous evening, they remained rough and corneous, the dust, grease and oil ingrained into the skin and finger nails, while one thumbnail remained a black, misshapen memento to a slipped chisel.

'You see to the cases and lock up, Bob, while I go along and say cheerio to Peggy,' said Janet to her husband. 'I'll not be a minute,' she added, as the taxi driver looked at his watch to suggest that he had other work lined up.

When she heard the clatter of Janet's high-heeled shoes on the yard outside her back door, Peggy Moore was swilling out her mouth at the sink, after another vomiting session. She quickly dried her mouth and pushed back her hair as she went to the door.

'Just wanted to say cheerio,' said Janet. 'We're off now. The taxi's here.'

'I hope you have a good time,' Peggy said, putting on a smile. 'And I like your new outfit—it suits you.'

Janet slapped her stomach.

'It's tighter than I thought it would be; I shall have to get a new roll-on. And look, Peggy, you take it easy a bit, this week. Let Gerry help with the kids for a change. You look real pale this morning; you could do with a rest. Aren't you feeling well?'

'I've had a poor night,' replied Peggy, covering up quickly. 'Our Tony has been awake a lot. He cut his thumb last night and it kept him awake.'

'Well, don't forget what I've said. And we'll send you a card to let you know how we're getting on.'

Janet turned and walked along Martins Lane to the taxi, nodding at one or two other women who were standing at their doors watching the activity.

After waving to the departing taxi, Peggy turned to go into her house to start her holiday – cooking, cleaning, washing up, feeding babies, washing baby clothes, and coping with a husband who had thick heads and hangovers. It promised a cycle, monotonous and continuous, forward into a future that held only one significant change – a terrifying and lonely ordeal promised for her in seven months' time.

★

By nine o'clock, the last of the departing holidaymakers were leaving Upthorpe, and the atmosphere in the Enclosure was one of satisfaction. They liked to see things go off according to plan, orderly and with no complications; and as the sun climbed higher into a clear sky, their thoughts might have been summarised by the blacksmith, who was examining the pulley wheels on the headgear at Martins Main. He was a regular at Upthorpe Methodist Church, and as he looked down on the village, with the traffic on the roads and a train steaming out of Upthorpe Station with its load for Blackpool, he murmured to the pulley wheels, himself and his God. 'Oh Lord, bless them all. Give them a safe journey and a happy holiday, and bring them back home refreshed and happy.'

But Albert Dunn had more mercenary thoughts. 'There's a lot of bloody money gone out of this district with them folks this morning.'

Monday 17 August 1964

Feast Week in Upthorpe was a strangely topsy-turvy affair. The people who were on holiday but had stayed at home, wanted to engender a holiday atmosphere, but the shopkeepers and the committee of Upthorpe Working Men's Club judged their Feast Week on the number of loaves sold and the number of pints of beer drunk. They saved their best offerings for the weekend when the holidaymakers would return with the tag ends of their holiday money to spend. So the holiday at home in Upthorpe could be a disappointing, half-hearted affair: a lost cricket match, because half of the first team were in Blackpool, nobody to play darts with in the Club, one randy bass singer for the Sunday night entertainment, and the usual warmed-up meat for lunch on Monday. However, for Willie Carter, the Feast Week provided the opportunity to clear up two of his major problems.

The first involved his son, Peter, who had just presented his father with a surprise ultimatum that he was finishing at school and going to work at the pit. He had completed his O-level exams at the local grammar school and Willie wanted the lad to wait for his exam results, and then stay on in the sixth form and go on to college. But Peter had refused to agree to this, and Willie had slowly been worn down.

'It's no use, Dad,' Peter had said. 'I'm not cut out to be a student. I might get through my O-levels but I shan't get very good marks, I know that now. I've no intention of carrying on wasting my time, and your money, and then failing to get anywhere. I'd rather pack up now and start on a job. In any case, I have my music to think about. I don't want to give that up. I think I can go a long way with that.'

So Willie decided to go up to the pit, tomorrow morning, to have a word with Mr Dobson, to see if he could help to set Peter on the right lines.

Tuesday 18 August 1964

'I wonder if you could spare us a few minutes of your time, Mr Dobson?' said Willie, twisting the neb of his flat cap. 'This is my lad, Peter. He plays the organ, you know – I mentioned it to you, I think. Well, he wants to leave school and get a job, and I'd like you to give us the benefit of your advice, if you will.'

Roy Dobson leaned back in his chair and looked at the two men; Peter young and at ease; his father nervous and without confidence, the product of an earlier age.

'I'll try to help, if I can,' he replied. 'But I don't normally deal with the recruitment side. The training officer looks after that, but of course he's away on holiday this week. What do you want to know?' he asked, looking at Peter.

Willie Carter nudged his son.

'Go on, Peter,' he said. 'Mr Dobson is being good enough to give up his time. Ask him the questions you have been on about.'

Peter needed no urging by his father; he spoke easily to Roy Dobson.

'I think I'm more suited to a trade, Mr Dobson, than a lot of studying. I'm good at fiddling and tinkering with things, and I was good at physics at school – that might help. I've taken O-levels in science subjects, and I think I'll get passes. I wondered what the prospects are now for electricians in the pits?'

'You can't go wrong there, lad. There is more electrical equipment going into pits every week, and my Electrical Engineer is always crying out that he is short of staff. I'll tell you what, you come up to the pit tomorrow morning and I'll arrange for the Electrical Engineer to show you some of the equipment we have at the pit top, and then we can arrange for you to start as an apprentice, if you're still interested.'

'Thank you very much, Mr Dobson,' replied Peter. 'That's very good of you.'

'It is that. I appreciate your help to get the lad fixed up, Mr Dobson.' said Willie. 'I don't know much about opportunities for craftsmen in the pits, and it has been worrying me since he said he wanted to leave school.'

'That's alright, Willie, but I hope that if he works here he will be more reliable than some of the young lads we have signed on recently.'

'Don't worry about that, Mr Dobson. I'll see to that myself,' replied Willie, to whom an alarm clock going off at four thirty in the morning was like a call from the Almighty.

*

Willie started to sort out his other problem with Joe Horton, later that evening, in one of the farm sheds where Joe was greasing his binding machine ready for the harvest.

'We've got to get the date sorted out for this organ fund social evening and auction, Joe,' said Willie, to Joe's backside as Joe reached for a grease nipple in the heart of the machine.

'Got any ideas, Willie?'

'Yes, I have, Joe. That's what I've come to talk to you about. As I see it, we've got to get it in at the end of September. Give folks the time to get over the holidays, and we must have it before the harvest weekend and before the women have their weekend at the end of October. They might get shirty if we get too near them.'

'That suits me, Willie. You make arrangements for the last week in September, if the others agree.' Joe Horton was preoccupied with the harvest on his farm.

Wednesday 19 August 1964

The holiday week, for Roy, was an opportunity to check all the plans for the mine reorganisation. He wanted to be sure that all the work to be done was in the programme, and that no overambitious performances had been included in the schedules. George was away on holiday, so Mike was in charge of the maintenance work being carried out at the pit. However, Roy had insisted that Mike should spend the whole day with him, going through the detailed schedules for the central conveying project. Mike and the Surveyor came into his office at nine o'clock, with a big bundle of plans under their arms. The Action Programme was impressive, with detailed bar charts for each job, showing when it was to start, how many weeks it would take, and which team of men had been allocated to the work. As some of the jobs had already started, some lines were coloured to show how much had been completed compared with the plan. In general, the work was up to programme, and in some cases, even in front of programme.

They spent all morning going through the information, and Roy continued to ask questions about the availability of machinery and equipment necessary to do the various jobs. Mike had all the answers. He knew the source of all the machinery and equipment, whether it was in other collieries, British Coal Executive workshops or with machinery manufacturers. By the early afternoon, Roy was satisfied that he was fully up to date with the present position of the central conveying programme. 'Well done, Mike Darlow', he murmured to himself, pleased that he had a mining engineer who could convert a concept into a detailed Action Programme. He felt very proud to be manager of Martins Main, and he decided that he could relax for the rest of the holiday, and spend some time with his family.

★

Earlier that morning, Cobba, with Sandra and David, was on the train to Scarborough. He'd booked them into the main hotel there for three nights, and he hoped that they could avoid the few people from Upthorpe who had also chosen Scarborough for their holiday. He didn't expect Sandra would want to sit on the beach, and he would try to take David off on walks in the nearby countryside. They'd enjoyed the cricket match in Leeds, but while the Yorkshire team were on top at the end of the first innings, the match had ended in a draw, through a stubborn second innings by their opponents.

Sandra had spent the weekend and Monday with Terry, before he went off with his family to Devon. They had travelled in his car into the countryside where they had walked and talked. Sandra had been careful not to get him too excited, as she wanted to test the sincerity of his feelings for her, before she introduced him to her father. She was planning to spend some time with David in Scarborough, and be the considerate, elder sister. She knew her Dad would enjoy a visit to the Spa on his own to listen to the Spa Orchestra. She was happy, and confident that life was going well now, for the Green family.

★

George Turnbull was sitting on the beach in Torquay, near the hotel where he always stayed because he knew his wife liked the food and the service. His thoughts occasionally strayed to Martins Main, and he wondered how the holiday maintenance work was progressing. He felt more confident than he had last year, with the state of the pit, and he had a growing respect for the management skills of Roy Dobson.

Thursday 20 August 1964

The holiday week, for Roy, changed drastically when he received a telephone call from Region. The call requested him to be present at nine o'clock on Friday morning, in Mr Pickersgill's office, and he was to bring with him the up-to-date position with the development of 57s coalface.

'What on earth is happening now?' he wondered. He couldn't ring for advice from Mr Jenkins, because he was away on holiday, and he would be on a hiding to nothing if he made any commitments in the absence of Reg. He got the plans from the Surveyor and took them home with him. He was in deep thought throughout the evening.

'What's the problem now?' asked Helen. 'I thought you said you were happy with the way things are going at the pit. You've spent all evening pouring over those plans. You are like a student swotting for an exam. And you're not very good company for a wife, either.'

He explained the telephone call and the puzzle of the subject. 57s coalface was not programmed for the next year, although George Turnbull had done some of the development work. It was a real mystery.

'Let it rest until tomorrow. You can't do anything else tonight. Come and sit here with me on the settee for five minutes.' He did as she asked, and she put her arms around him and gave him a hug. Helen had a way of knowing when her husband needed that special word, or action, from her, to calm him and build him up.

Friday 21 August 1964

Roy arrived early and took a seat in the waiting room outside Mr Pickersgill's office. Three other people, who he didn't recognise, joined him. All of them seemed a little tense.

'You can all go through, now.' Pickersgill's secretary gave Roy a brief smile.

In the office, the Chief Engineer for the Region and Mr Jones, the Regional Production Manager, were with Mr Pickersgill. Introductions were made of the other three people, who were in junior positions in the Mechanisation branch, the Supply and Contracts branch and the Planning branch. Mr Pickersgill emphasised the urgency and importance of the meeting, which he had decided to hold, even though several of the senior staff in the Region were away on holiday.

'We have a problem in the Region, that I want to sort out urgently, before it is taken out of my hands. A complete set of new mechanised coalface equipment is scheduled for delivery for Crompton pit, in our Region, in the near future. The coalface that was being developed to use the equipment, has hit a large fault and it's a write-off. Other Regions will gladly take over the equipment, but I want to keep it in my Region.'

'Let's get a few facts clear. When is the equipment to be delivered?' he asked.

'It should all be delivered by the fourth week in September, Sir. The powered supports will start to arrive during the second week of September.' The young man from the Supply and Contracts branch quoted confidently from a piece of paper in front of him.

'The machine for the coalface is in our Regional workshop now, Sir. It's a brand new trepanner.' The young engineer from the Mechanisation branch was very nervous.

Mr Pickersgill looked to the planner, who knew what was coming and stiffened in his seat.

'How bad is the fault on the Compton face development?'

'It's more than twice the seam thickness, Sir. I understand that there are some very disturbed roof conditions around the fault.'

'Was there no geological evidence of a fault in that area?'

'There is a fault in a similar position in another seam, but there is eighty yards vertical distance between the seams. I think it was assumed, Sir, that the fault would not pass through, but in fact it has got worse.' Pickersgill gave a cynical smile. 'Now we are getting at the truth. It sounds like wishful thinking by everyone who signed the plan for that coalface. You can't run a pit that way. Anyway, we will sort that out later. We can forget Crompton, that's for sure. Let's see if we have a way out at Martins Main. 57s coalface in the Benton seam has been suggested as a possible solution, Mr Dobson. What's the position there?'

Roy laid out his plan for 57s coalface.

'In our current plan, Mr Pickersgill, 57s coalface is needed in about a year's time, to replace 56s. But you can see that the opportunity was taken to drive the access roadways for 57s when the equipment and men were available. This has determined that the coal section there is thicker than normal, at around thirty-nine inches. There would need to be a bit of re-routing of the conveyors, but it could be sorted fairly easily. The only mining work of significance would be to open out the coalface.' He paused, as he did not want to present the planning change as an easy solution. Pickersgill had to define his requirements.

'Well, it does seem that Martins can offer us a get-out clause. How soon can you start the work of opening out the coalface, Mr Dobson? And bear in mind we need it as soon as possible?'

'We should be able to sort out the machines for that work during the first week after the holidays. If we deploy two teams of men, on three shifts, we should have the coalface ready for installation in about five weeks' time. We have been reorganising the manpower to undertake all the roadway drivage work for the Central Conveying project and I don't want to take the pressure off that work. So we will be a bit stretched for manpower, Mr Pickersgill.'

'Quite right,' replied Pickersgill, 'you must not delay the Central Conveying project, as that is vital for Martins. Is there any chance of using mining contractors on one of the development roadways, to supplement your manpower?'

'That would be a solution, but Martins union has always rejected the use of mining contractors. I can try to get them to change their views. They ought to change them, in recognition of all the money you are putting into the pit, Mr Pickersgill, but I am not sure they will.'

'You will have to raise that with them, Mr Dobson.'

'Yes, Mr Pickersgill.'

Pickersgill carried the meeting on for another hour, discussing detailed aspects of the coalface equipment and how it needed to be understood by everyone involved at the pit, so that 57s face delivered its designed output. He then issued instructions to the Planning branch that a coalface mechanisation project had to be prepared for 57s face, and signed by everyone as quickly as possible. The Mechanisation branch should organise to build up a length of the coalface equipment on the surface, so that it could be used to train the men who would work on the face; the pit had to draw up a detailed plan of how the coalface equipment would be installed; additional supervisory engineers had to be drafted in to Martins so that there was no delay in setting up the coalface. Pickersgill said that he would dictate a memo to his secretary on the actions agreed at the meeting, which would then be circulated throughout the Region. In summary, he considered that 57s face should be in full production before the end of November. He then declared the meeting closed.

As Roy started to drive back to Martins Main, his thoughts were supercharged. 'Bloody hell, what a fellow Pickersgill is! He certainly knows what he wants. And he has given me the baton to carry for the Region; I really am in the spotlight now. I wonder what Mr Jenkins will say to this change in plan? This is a major challenge to all of the team at Martins.'

★

Back at the pit, Roy decided that there was no time to loose. He called in Mike Darlow and explained the outcome of the meeting. They discussed the availability of manpower to do the face development. It would require transferring the best teams of men in the pit, for that type of work. The conveyors, machines and electrical equipment would have to be prepared and sent underground within a matter of days. This would require prompt action by the Mechanical and Electrical Engineers. There would need to be discussions with the union, informing them of the change in plans and the effects this would have on the pit. Roy decided that there was so much to do that he needed to have a meeting of his colliery management team on Sunday morning, before the pit started work on Monday after the holiday. He sent a note to all his management team, including those who were on holiday, informing them of the ten o'clock meeting. He signed all the notes himself, and as he did so, realised that his popularity with the wives of his staff might reduce significantly.

★

That evening, when Roy described to Helen the outcome of his meeting at Region, she was not impressed about the Sunday meeting. Helen had intended to start attending Upthorpe Methodist Church that day, and had hoped her husband would look after the children while she went. She hadn't told Roy of her plans, though, and when she had heard what he had to say, she decided to delay her start at the church for another week.

Monday 24 August 1964

'Well at least somebody is turning some coal,' commented Cyril Mann, as he observed the wheels turning on the coal shaft.

The members of the Enclosure had assembled to review the holiday week and assess the start-up of the pit after the holidays.

'The lads will have to get back to work to earn some cash. They were telling me that the price of a pint of beer has gone up in Blackpool, this year. They don't know what to charge in these holiday places.' Charlie emphasised his words as he marched around the Enclosure. 'At least the prices have not gone up at Upthorpe Welfare.'

'Don't count on that, Charlie,' said Albert. 'The committee there won't miss a trick if they think they can get away with a price increase.'

'I think Cobba will keep his eye on that, and stop any increases for as long as possible.'

'Tha's got a high opinion of Cobba, Charlie. Don't be so sure of him. I've been told that he went to Scarborough with his kids for three days and that they stayed in the best hotel in town. He seems to be going up in the world, does Cobba. I'm not happy with him.'

There was a pause, as the team didn't want Albert to get on his hobbyhorse of Cobba's handling of the union. Cliff decided to change the subject.

'I reckon Martins had a good run before the holidays, with the output up. I'll bet they nearly made a profit. This manager might be alright after all.'

'He was at the pit yesterday morning,' put in Pat Mulligan. 'All the management cars were parked at the pit. They must have been in a meeting, because they all left together just before one o'clock.'

'There must be something important going on, if they have to have a meeting on a Sunday before the pit gets back to work on the Monday,' said Cyril. 'We'll have to keep our ears close to the ground to find out what's cooking.'

'There's that Welsh bastard going to the pit,' said Albert, as Reg Jenkins' car swept into

Martins Lane. 'I'll bet he wasn't at the meeting yesterday.'

The Enclosure sensed that they were on the track of something significant on the first day after the holidays.

'How's old Walter?' asked Charlie. 'Has anybody seen him?'

'He's not well,' replied Cliff. 'I went to see him last Wednesday. His son took him out in the car, but they had to come back early as Walter was too ill to carry on. He's buggered. I doubt we'll ever see him here again.'

The Enclosure was quiet for a few minutes. They realised what Cliff was saying. They had to be prepared for the end of Walter.

★

Reg Jenkins swept into Roy's office.

'Did you have a good holiday, Mr Jenkins?' Roy wanted to test the water with his boss, before they got down to the detail of the meeting at Region.

'Yes, we had a good time. I didn't expect, though, to come back to find the plans for the pit turned upside down. Pickersgill called me into his office this morning for a quick talk.' He paused. 'It might be a good thing if you can pull it off, because the pit needs to get into mechanised coalfaces.' The conversation stopped as coffee was brought in. Roy had noted a positive hint that suggested he should not apologise for the decisions.

'You had better fill me in on how you plan to move forward.'

'We had a meeting of the management team yesterday morning, and agreed lots of actions, and everybody is busy today carrying out those actions.' Roy went on to explain that two teams of men, each team working three shifts, would start heading out 57s face as soon as the equipment was installed. He was satisfied that the men were the best team at the pit. A space on the colliery surface had been identified as suitable for the surface build of the face equipment. Mike was working with the Surveyor to prepare a detailed action programme for the development and installation at 57s. Roy indicated his expectation that the coalface could be in production by the end of November – which was the timetable set by Mr Pickersgill.

'You'll be bloody lucky to achieve that, in my opinion,' said Reg Jenkins. 'Martins Main has never achieved a challenge like this in the past. George Turnbull and his men will have to raise their game to get anywhere near that date.'

'You have to admit that we are only in the position to have this opportunity because George had driven the roadways for 57s well in advance of the programme.'

Reg made no comment. He discussed other aspects of the pit, and stayed on to have a sandwich lunch. Roy didn't raise with him the need to get the union to consider having outside contractors in to do some mining work for the Central Conveying project; he wanted time to think out his own approach to that subject, and he needed to talk with Cobba about a whole series of issues.

★

Peter Carter was amazed at how quickly his life had changed. His discussions with the Electrical Engineer had confirmed his decision to go for an apprenticeship. The Electrical Engineer arranged for him to be signed-on to start immediately after the holidays. He was to work in the surface electrical shop, helping the senior foreman, who was preparing electrical equipment to go underground.

Peter gathered that there was something of a panic on in the workshop, as they aimed to get machines checked and tested to go underground as quickly as possible. It was not a case of standing and watching; he was instructed how to make basic electrical connections, how to tighten the connecting bolts between sections of the machines, and then he observed how the machines were tested electrically. He was able to help as the machines were loaded and secured onto special vehicles for transport down the shaft and then forward to the underground workings. It seemed that everything was aimed at 57s development. Peter was thrilled; this was real work, and he got enthusiastically involved.

Late in the morning the Electrical Engineer came into the workshop to discuss progress with the senior foreman. He had a word with Peter, as he passed him.

'How's it going?'

'Very well, thank you,' Peter replied.

'You could not have started at a better time. We'll be very busy in here for the next two weeks, sorting out machines and electrical switchgear for some urgent underground developments. It will be a good breaking-in time before you go off to the underground training school. You'll not forget to enrol for the first year apprentice course at the Technical College in Doncaster, will you?'

'No, I'll do that next week, when the college is open for registration, Sir.' Peter was not sure how to address the Electrical Engineer, who was an experienced engineer in his early fifties. He decided that 'sir' was the safest way to show respect.

Peter had got a clear picture of his future: two weeks in the electrical shop; four weeks at the underground training school; then back to the pit, working under supervision, either on the surface or underground. If he got decent marks in his O-level exams, he might get day release for one day per week at the Technical College. That would speed up his studies towards an Ordinary National Certificate in electrical engineering. Life couldn't be better.

★

By mid-afternoon, Roy had completed discussions with members of his staff, and received updates on the pit performance during the dayshift, progress with aspects of the work for 57s development, and progress on the Central Conveying project. He decided to try a long shot to catch Cobba without his other union colleagues.

'Just see if Cobba is still at the pit, and if he is, ask him if can come up to my office,' he asked Gordon.

A few minutes later he got the reply he was hoping for.

'Cobba is in the union office, but his colleagues have left. He's on his way up to see you.'

Roy quickly got his thoughts together before Cobba came into the office.

'You wanted a word, Boss?'

'Yes, Cobba, there are a few things to talk about. But first, did you have a good holiday?'

'Yes, me and David had three days at Headingley, watching the cricket. Then we went off with our Sandra for a few days at the seaside. It was a change. There seems to be a lot of rumours going around the pit about some change in plans that have taken place during last week.'

'Yes, Cobba. We have been given an opportunity, and a challenge. I'll be having a meeting to brief you and your mates officially about the changes, probably tomorrow, but I wanted to fill you in, first.'

Roy spent ten minutes going over the meeting at Region, and the subsequent staff meeting, and the plans that were in place. He identified the manpower that was being switched from other parts of the pit, for 57s development. Cobba asked one or two questions, without sounding too enthusiastic. Roy decided to emphasise the opportunity for Martins from the new plans.

'It is a great opportunity for Martins, Cobba. It will get us a mechanised coalface much earlier than we anticipated, which will be good experience for everyone at the pit, before we go into the Fuston seam. But there are two problems that I anticipate. We're going to be tight for manpower, with all the men we're transferring onto 57s development and the Central Conveying project. We might be short of men to staff all the current coalfaces to turn coal each day. I'm not sure, yet, until all the changes are carried out, but that's my reaction. I'm reluctant for the output to drop. We were doing well before the holiday, and I would like to keep the output up to those levels.'

'You can't have everything, Boss. You want the penny and the bun,' replied Cobba, with a grin.

'There are ways that we can balance the books, Cobba, and I want to discuss them with you, on a confidential basis, to see what you think.'

'I'm listening, Boss, but my lips are sealed. You are not likely to get an answer from me today.'

'I don't expect that, Cobba, but let me explain. The first issue is something I have been looking at for the last month or two. The machines on all the coalfaces undercut the coal with a five-foot long cutter bar. In fact, we never get the planned depth of cut. It's usually two or three inches short. This reduces the wages earned by the workmen as they are paid by the volume of coal filled. Some pits I know have overcome this by increasing the length of the cutter bars on the machines, by three inches. Everything on the coalfaces stays the same, but the output goes up and so does the men's wages. That, to me, seems an easy change to make, and we could do this without making any fuss. What do you think?'

'It sounds very simple, but there could be problems. You'll have to make sure the shotfiring takes account of the extra coal.'

'I think I can avoid those problems. We would start with one coalface, and try it to make sure it worked alright, before moving on to the other faces. Anyway, just think about it, Cobba. We could introduce it as part of a standard repair programme for the cutter bars; we would just order them three inches longer, and slowly work our way around the coalfaces.' Roy was hinting that he was inclined to apply this change without telling anyone, except Cobba.

'I'll keep that move in my mind, but I won't own up to knowing about it,' said Cobba, who had got the idea.

'The other problem we have, is finding additional roadway drivage men for the Central Conveying project roadways. This is specialist work, and the solution often used is to engage outside contractors for specific new roadways. We have one roadway in the scheme that is ideal for an outside contractor.' Roy showed Cobba a plan of the roadway concerned. 'I understand that Martins has been against the use of outside contractors in the past; but we are in a new situation now, Cobba. Region has authorised the capital for the Central Conveying project and is going to authorise the capital for 57s coalface equipment. They are looking for Martins' union to take a more positive approach to this issue, which will contribute towards the success of the pit. How do you think this issue should be brought forward?'

'That is a difficult one, Boss. My union mates have got very fixed views on that subject. It will have to be a good case, for them to change their mind. You might have to sweeten the pill a bit, to get that through.'

'I'll not raise that at the meeting tomorrow, Cobba. I'll just concentrate on the new plans. I do, though, want us to sort out the outside contractors issue here, if we can. I don't want Mr Pickersgill getting involved. I know he's under pressure from Headquarters, to get Martins into a profitable basis, and I don't think they are giving him much time to show the improvements.'

'I guessed that, from what he said to me recently at a Yorkshire Welfare meeting.'

Cobba left the office. Roy Dobson reviewed his meeting. He'd made progress, but the contractors problem would be a difficult one to crack. Cobba had made the last point to let Roy know that he met Mr Pickersgill away from Martins. However he'd also indicated that he was aware of the pressure Mr Pickersgill was under.

★

When he got home that night Peter Carter was questioned by his father, who was pleased that his son was happy and enjoying the work.

'I might even get some overtime; there's a lot of equipment to get ready, and the foreman seemed pleased with what I've done today. He was staying on this afternoon to get some electrical switchgear ready. If he asks me to stay on with him tomorrow, I will. So don't worry if I'm late home.'

★

Janet Hall was having a cup of tea with Peggy Moore. It had got around to evening time before she had the chance to pay a visit after coming back from holiday. Bob and Janet had not got back from their tour of the south coast until Sunday evening. As well as unpacking, they had to get themselves organised for starting work the following morning; Bob was on the dayshift, so he had to get up at five o'clock, to be ready to go underground before six o'clock.

'We're back in the groove, now,' said Janet. 'The holiday seems a long way in the past, already. We were busy in the shop, today, and Bob had to do two hours' overtime. It seems they have a rush of work at Martins. Is it affecting Gerry?'

'No, I don't think so. He did go to work this morning, which was a bit of a surprise. He often misses the first shift after the holidays, on principle. Mind you, I was glad he went to work, because we need the money. He came home at the normal time, and he's popped round to see his mother; but I suppose he might call for a drink at the Club before he comes home.'

'Did you get a break at all, during the holiday?' Janet looked closely at Peggy's face.

'Not really.' Peggy cast her eyes down to look at her cup. 'I did take the kids round to see my mother, one afternoon, but they were restless, so we didn't stay long.'

Janet was concerned at the tired look in her friend's eyes, but she decided to change the subject.

'We need to fix up that visit to the Family Planning clinic that we talked about a few weeks ago. We should have fitted it in before the holidays, but we never got round to it. I'll sort out an appointment for you. I'll go with you but you will have to arrange Gerry to look after the kids for a couple of hours.' She stopped as Peggy burst into tears. 'What's the matter, Peggy?'

The sobbing continued, and then Peggy looked at her friend. 'It's too late, Janet,' she replied. An amazed look appeared on Janet's face.

'Oh no, Peggy, not again, and so soon? I can't believe it. What does Gerry say about the news?'

'I haven't told him, and I'm not going to. He'll have to wait until it's obvious,' replied Peggy, with feeling.

Janet went round the table and cradled Peggy in her arms. Her mind was in a whirl. What could she do? She had to help Peggy, before she was completely overcome by her family pressures and before it seriously affected her health.

'Let's talk about it, Peggy.' She took a chair at the side of Peggy, and took her hand. 'We must decide what we can do to help you. We have to get your strength up.'

'I don't know which way to turn. I've never felt so hopeless in all my life; I seem to have no strength to carry on. I know I'm letting the kids down; I'm not a good mother to them.' She burst into more tears.

'Come on, love, it's not hopeless. I'll help you all I can. The first thing we have to do is to talk to Gerry. He has to be involved, even if he doesn't want to be. Then we'll see your doctor. At least he should examine you to make sure you are alright physically. If nothing else, he should be able to give you a tonic to pep you up.' As Janet talked, she was beginning to think of things that could be done to help Peggy.

'Come on, wipe your eyes, and let us see a bit of a smile–like you did in the old days.'

Peggy wiped her eyes and tried to give a smile.

'You are so kind, Janet. You are the only hope I've got. It is difficult for me; I don't know what to say to Gerry. He's fed up with me, I can tell.'

'Don't worry about Gerry. I'm just popping back to have a word with Bob, and then I'll come back. Hopefully Gerry will be back by then, and I will help you talk it through with him.'

'He might not like you doing that.'

'I don't give a damn whether he likes it or not. He has to face the facts: that his wife has too much to do with the house, and two small kids, and another pregnancy. You need some help. Don't worry, I'll not shout at him. I want to help both of you sort things out. I'll be back shortly.' Janet left Peggy, and hurried down to her house, where Bob was thinking about getting his snap and clothes together for the next day's shift at Martins.

Janet filled him in on what she had found at the Moore's. He was shocked that Peggy was pregnant again, while his wife could not get pregnant despite all his efforts. He wasn't sure that Janet should go back again to be there when Gerry came home. Was it her business?

'Bob, let me make it clear to you. Peggy has been a friend of mine for years, and if she ever needed a friend, it's now. So you can settle in your mind that we, note we, are going to help Peggy Moore get out of the fix she's in at the present time.'

'Alright, Janet.'

When Janet returned to Peggy's, Gerry was not back, so she helped to do some washing-up, and then collected the kids' clothes and put them in the drawers, guided by Peggy. Janet was thinking of the things she had left to do at home before going to work in Doncaster in the morning. She would have to get up with Bob, to catch up after he'd gone to work. She was relieved when Gerry came in before ten o'clock; he had limited his drinking at the Club. He looked surprised to see Janet helping Peggy.

'What's up, Peg? I didn't expect to see Janet here.'

'We've been having a talk,' said Janet. 'And I have stopped on a bit, helping Peggy tidy up. She looked under the weather, to me, as if she needed some help.'

'Aye, she's not looked so good, lately.'

'Oh, you have noticed then, Gerry,' said Janet quickly. 'I think Peggy has something to tell you.' She looked across at Peggy.

Peggy took a deep breath, and then looked straight at Gerry.

'I'm afraid I'm pregnant again.'

'Oh, bloody hell. Not again. How did that happen?' Gerry sat in the chair and grabbed his head in his arms.

'Come off it, Gerry. You know the answer to that question,' said Janet. 'You can see that she is not well; I think she needs to see the doctor, to check if she is up to having another baby so quickly. And she needs a tonic to build her up. Don't you agree, Gerry?'

'Yes, I suppose you are right.'

'Well, I'll take her to the doctor, but you'll have to spend some time looking after the boys so that she can go. Do you understand, Gerry?'

'Aye, I've got the message.'

'I'm going now,' said Janet. 'I'll have a word with you from the shop tomorrow, to arrange to see the doctor.'

Peggy stood up and came over to the door.

'Thank you so much, Janet.'

'You get off to bed and get some rest. Good night, Gerry.'

'Night, Janet,' he replied from the chair.

As Janet walked back along Martins Lane, she reflected on the injustice of the world. Some people got more than they wanted, while some didn't get what they most desired.

Chapter 7

Tuesday 25 August 1964

The meeting with the union went on for two hours. Roy had plans pinned up on the wall, and he went in detail through the work to be done to develop 57s coalface. He explained the equipment for the coalface and showed photographs of the steel panzer conveyor, the trepanner coal-cutting machine and the powered supports. He was expecting lots of questions, but the reception was cool.

Roy then explained how the equipment would be installed, and how the coalface would operate. As the capacity of the conveying system could only handle one face at a time, it would mean that 56s face would fill coal on one shift, and 57s face on the other two shifts. This caused an immediate reaction from Jimmy Bell.

'Just a minute, Mr Dobson. Are you telling us that there will be three-shift coaling in the Benton seam when 57s face starts?'

'Yes, it's standard practice at mechanised mines to work three shifts on the coalfaces. It's the only way to justify the capital investment for the equipment. Usually the increased output requires coal-winding on three shifts.'

'We can't have that,' said Jimmy. 'That is a major change in the operations at Martins. We have not agreed to that at a union meeting. We will have to discuss this, Cobba, in the union.' Jimmy turned to Cobba, who did not react.

Roy decided to take a strong line on this.

'Come off it, Jimmy. You know that the mine is open for working throughout the twenty-four hours. It is management's responsibility to organise the operation of the mine for maximum efficiency and safety. Are you telling me that I must go back to Mr Pickersgill, and tell him that we don't want any mechanised faces at Martins because your union will not agree to three-shift working? You know what that will mean – the end of Martins straightaway.' Roy was cross, and it showed in the force that he gave to his words.

'Yes, I know, but you have not consulted us about the shift patterns,' said Jimmy, defensively.

'What the bloody hell do you think this meeting is about, Jimmy? I am consulting about all the issues that were only agreed after a meeting at Region on Friday. Since then we have been sorting out the equipment and manpower to carry out the plan. The objective is to have 57s face in production by the end of November. We want some help to achieve this, not obstruction and objections on issues that are not relevant.'

Cobba saw an opportunity to calm the meeting.

'Alright, Mr Dobson; we get the message. You will have help from the union to get these changes carried out. We want investment at Martins to upgrade the pit; but we will want to ensure that the men are protected, so that they do not lose out by the changes.'

'You know that you can rely on me, Cobba, to ensure that. If the pit is successful, the men will be better off. And you must remember that the mechanised faces will give safer working conditions. I hope safety is as important to the union as it is to the management.'

The meeting went on to identify the manpower that would be used on the work associated with 57s developments and installations. The union asked questions about the manpower, particularly those transferred from other parts of the pit. There were a few comments, but no objections, to particular names mentioned. At the end of the discussion, Cobba saw the chance to raise an important matter.

'With all these men moving onto development work, Mr Dobson, will you be able to keep the number of coaling shifts for the pit at the same level? If not, we can expect the output to reduce, I suppose.'

'That is an important point, Cobba. We will not know the answer to that until we have settled down, and all the men are in their new jobs. I don't want the output to drop, but we may lose the odd coaling shift on the coalfaces. You must also remember that we have the additional mining work associated with the Central Conveying project; not all those jobs are staffed at the present time. I will want to meet you and explain the implications, once they are all clear.' He was thankful that Cobba had given him a lead to that subject.

'There seems to be a lot of changes to sort out,' said Jimmy.

'There are, but that is what we are here for, Jimmy. If we are to get Martins sorted out, we have to make changes. These changes introduce new technology, and that is what the pit needs. So I am happy to face up to the reorganisation, as it should improve the pit performance significantly.'

'I think we realise the opportunity, Mr Dobson,' commented Cobba, as the meeting started to break up.

When the union people had left the meeting, Mike Darlow asked to see Roy, to update him on progress with the preparation work for 57s face.

'How did the meeting go with the union?' he asked.

'In the end, I think it went well. They annoyed me at first, by showing little interest in the coalface equipment. I suppose we can sort that out when we get the equipment built up on the surface. Then, when I told them the three-shift coaling pattern for 56s and 57s, Jimmy jumped in and more or less said that the union would not agree with that. He's a pillock.' Mike grinned at that comment.

'Jimmy always puts his foot in it. There's not much brain serving his tongue, Boss.'

'In fact, it worked out alright in the end. I got stuck in, and then Cobba calmed things down and said that the union would help with the changes, but he didn't want any of the men to lose out. I agreed to guarantee that. I also agreed to meet the union when we know what the impact of all the manpower changes will have on the number of face coaling shifts. It will give me a chance to raise the need for outside contractors; that will be an interesting meeting.'

After Mike had left, Roy rang his clerk in the outer office.

'Gordon, is George available?'

'No, Mr Dobson. He's not out of the pit yet. He has sent word that he is staying with a team of men who are getting some large conveyor equipment through to 57s development.'

Typical of George, thought Roy. If it's a tricky job, he wants to supervise the men himself, and he will stay with them to make sure they complete their work.

'Leave word for him to ring me at home this evening. I have to leave the pit soon, but I shall be in all evening.'

'Right, Mr Dobson.'

★

Peter Carter stayed two hours over time, and it meant that he was in a rush to get home, grab some tea, and then go on the bus to Leeds for his weekly organ lesson at the Parish Church. It wasn't the shortage of time, or the limited tea he was able to eat, that disturbed him, though; it was his hands. He had been helping to grease one of the machines for 57s' development, and the grease had penetrated his hands and fingernails. He scraped at his nails with his penknife, on the bus to Leeds, but the effect was to spread the grease, rather than remove it. What would his teacher say if he saw his hands? Would he be allowed to play the Parish Church organ, with fingernails in that state? Was it possible to work in the mining industry and be an organist?

His worries were unfounded when his teacher asked him why he was fifteen minutes late. When he apologised and then explained that he was now a workman at Martins Main pit, he faced more questions about the work he was doing and the career he aimed to follow as a mine electrician. To Peter's surprise, his teacher was full of praise and enthusiasm. He considered it was wonderful to have a career and to be a musician. A tough job in industry gave a person a realisation of what life was all about, he said, and then music gave access to another world. That other world of music was more wonderful and special because its availability was limited, so it had to be experienced to the full. His teacher went on to describe his own experiences, with male voice choirs and brass bands, where he had achieved amazing performances from amateur musicians performing from the heart. The discussions delayed the lesson by another fifteen minutes, but when Peter played the organ he was inspired, and achieved sounds he had never produced before. He completely forgot about the grease in his fingernails. That night, he made a major discovery in his life – he could be an electrician and an organist.

★

In the vestry at Upthorpe Methodist Church, the committee to raise funds for the new organ was in session. John Warwick was in the chair, and Willie Carter and Joe Horton were supported by the Minister's wife, Gwen Folds, who represented the ladies of the church. They had agreed the date for a faith supper and auction at the end of September. Helen Dobson had agreed to be the auctioneer, and they all thought that she would bring in quite an audience who would want to meet the colliery manager's wife. What they wanted, now, was something to auction; Willie had been a bit worried about this, as he had not been able to come up with any ideas.

'Have you any suggestions, Joe?' John Warwick asked Joe Horton, the farmer-member of the church.

'I've been thinking about that and I've got a couple of ideas. We need to make it worth a big bid; so, I've decided to offer a year's supply of eggs, and a year's supply of potatoes. I would deliver them as the winners need them. It could be a lot of eggs and a lot of potatoes, if the winners have big families.'

'It could indeed, Joe,' said Gwen. 'Those are very good offers.'

Joe's offers set the meeting on track. John Warwick said his father kept honeybees and he would arrange for several jars of honey to be available in display boxes. Gwen Folds said she would organise a cake stall with the other ladies of the church. Willie jumped at this, and promised that his wife would make some of her famous chocolate cake. Gwen Folds also said that she had a friend who did paintings, and she was sure she could persuade her to offer one for the auction. There was then a suggestion that there should be two paintings to auction – the second one, done by Gwen's friend, would be a painting of the organ when it was installed in Upthorpe chapel. It was quite a list, and Willie's fingers were aching as his notetaking tried to keep up with the discussion.

'We will have to see Mrs Dobson again, to let her know what is happening,' said Joe Horton.

'Yes, you're right, Joe. We'll have to arrange that,' replied Willie, feeling a bit apprehensive about another meeting with Helen.

'I think there is a chance that she might be transferring her membership to Upthorpe,' said Gwen. There was a stunned pause, and the three men looked at her.

'That would be wonderful news,' said John Warwick.

They all thought that the church was suddenly moving forward. John Warwick closed the meeting with a prayer that expressed this hope. They all said 'amen' at the end of the prayer, and felt the Spirit moving among them.

★

George Turnbull rang Roy, at eight o'clock, from the pit.

'You wanted a word with me, Boss?' said George.

'I wanted to let you know how my meeting on 57s had gone off with the union. But it's not urgent. What kept you underground this afternoon?'

'It was the big conveyor drive that has to go in for 57s face. It's a big piece and we had to get it through the conveyor servicing 56s face. We had to complete it or it would have stopped 56s filling coal tomorrow morning. I had some good lads with me, but they needed pushing to get the job completed. Anyway, it's done now, and I think we can get all the other equipment installed, ready to start 57s face-heading on Monday.'

'That's fine, George. You get off home now, and I'll see you tomorrow.'

'Right, Boss,' replied George, as he went to get a shower. He then rang his wife to tell her to warm up his dinner.

Wednesday 26 August 1964

Janet Hall entered the doctor's surgery with Peggy Moore. She linked arms with Peggy to help her to a seat, and they sat together. Peggy had been concerned at leaving Gerry with the children. She had hoped that they would both be asleep by the time they had to leave, but sleep seemed the last of the children's thoughts, even though they were both dressed in their night clothes. As they walked into Upthorpe, Janet told her not to worry about the children, and that Gerry had got to get used to doing his share of looking after them.

When their turn came, and they were called into the surgery, Janet felt that she had to explain her presence.

'Peggy is a long-term friend of mine, Doctor, and I have brought her along as she is not well and, as well as having two young children, she thinks she is pregnant again.'

'Right, let us have a look at you,' he replied.

He examined her and took her blood pressure. He confirmed that she was pregnant and he asked her if she was attending the baby clinic that he ran with the midwives. Peggy confessed that she had not felt well enough to attend the clinic over the past two months.

'You didn't tell me that, Peggy,' said Janet.

'In that case, someone in my team has slipped up. Your absence should have been noted, and you should have had a visit by a health visitor or myself. We'll put that right straightaway. I will arrange for you to have visits each week by a health visitor, until you are well enough to attend the weekly clinic. I will also give you a prescription for a tonic to build you up. We shall also be watching your blood pressure, and you will need to take tablets on a regular basis through the pregnancy.'

'Can I just ask one question, Doctor?' said Janet, treading carefully. 'Is Mrs Moore well enough to take on another pregnancy at this time?'

'It is my job, along with my staff, to ensure that she is well enough to get through her pregnancy. I am very conscious of the strain put on a person's health if, for any reason, a pregnancy is aborted. Obviously with two very young children and another pregnancy, there will be other aspects of Mrs Moore's way of life that will need adjusting, to reduce her workload. What about your husband, Mrs Moore, is he helpful about the house and with the children?'

'Well, he works on the coalface at Martins Main, and he's on dayshift and then afternoonshift, so it's not easy for him,' replied Peggy, making excuses that Janet didn't think were justified.

'We will make arrangements for some help around the house for Mrs Moore,' replied Janet, with no clear idea in her mind how that could be achieved.

'If you are still not well enough to attend the baby clinic in two weeks, I want you to come and see me again,' concluded the doctor.

★

When they had walked back to Martins Lane, Peggy was obviously very tired. Gerry was relieved to see them, as he was struggling with the children. The younger one, Michael, was in his cot, but wasn't asleep. The older one, Tony, was walking around the room with his teddy bear in his arms, touching anything that would move on the furniture.

'Come on, Tony, with Aunty Janet. Let me put you to bed, and I'll tell you a story.' Janet picked up the little lad, who went willingly to her. 'Don't you go out, Gerry, I won't be long. We have some serious things to discuss.' Gerry's idea of a quick release to the Club was thwarted, and he sat in the chair by the fire; Peggy sat on the other side of the fire. Janet returned from the children's bedroom after fifteen minutes, and all sounded quiet upstairs.

'Well, what have you told him, Peggy?' she asked.

'I've not said anything,' replied Peggy. 'I am not sure what to say.'

'Right then, Gerry, I will have to tell you what the doctor said. Peggy is pregnant, but we knew that anyway. She is also quite ill. Her blood pressure is too high, and she will have to take pills for that. He has given her a tonic to try and build her up. He's arranging for the health visitor to come to the house until such time as she is fit to go to the clinic. Did you know, Gerry, that she has not been going to the clinic for the past two months?'

'No, I don't know owt about the clinic.'

'No, I didn't know that either,' said Janet. 'But the main thing that the doctor said was that she has to have some help with the house. Peggy told him that you are on shifts at Martins, and that makes it difficult for you to help much. I think you will have to help more.' Janet spoke direct to Gerry. 'She is worn out, Gerry. She hardly had strength to walk back from the surgery in Upthorpe to Martins Lane. You have to do something to help. Do you know anybody who could do a few hours in the house each week?'

'Bloody hell, is it as bad as that?'

'Yes, it is, Gerry, it's serious.' Janet was determined to sort things out with Gerry.

'Well, happen our Jill might help a bit,' suggested Gerry. This brought Peggy into the conversation.

'That would be no help at all, Gerry. She's a real drip, and you know it. It would take me all day to follow up behind her, she's so untidy.'

'Alright, I was only trying to make a suggestion.' Gerry regarded that as the end of his contribution.

'Well, we'll have to think about that problem. For a start, Gerry, you will have to clean out the fire each morning, and empty the ashes and fill the coal. There's no way that Peggy can do any heavy lifting, like coal buckets. From now on you'll have to get up ten minutes earlier when you're on dayshift, to do that. That is what Bob does, to help me.'

Gerry gave a grunt, and decided that a few drinks in the Club might not be appropriate for that night. Janet agreed to pick up the prescriptions in Doncaster the next day, and as it was half-day closing, she would bring them over at lunchtime. She then left, feeling that some progress had been made, but that more was necessary.

★

In bed that night, when Janet was discussing with Bob the visit to the doctor, he made a good suggestion. He had a sister who was not married, and who might be able to help Peggy. Janet gave him a big kiss and a hug. She would break it to him later that they would probably be paying his sister for her work.

★

The day marked an upsurge in the development of 57s face.

One machine had started on Monday morning, and the other later in the day, but the men were negotiating a contract with George, and the men's price per yard advance was much higher than George's price. A compromise was reached late on Tuesday evening, and then the pace of work increased dramatically.

'They have done ten feet advance with both machines, this morning, Boss, and left everything in order for the other shifts to do the same,' George reported to Roy.

'That's good, George. If you can keep that sort of progress, the face will be developed in the next three weeks.'

'I knew that the buggers could do ten feet per shift, but they stuck out that five feet would be the best they could achieve.'

'Don't worry about that, George. They might earn very good money for the next three weeks, but if the face is ready a week early we will be the winners. I want us to show Mr Jenkins and Mr Pickersgill that we can rise to the challenge.'

Mike went onto the pit top to discuss where the powered supports should be unloaded, and he spoke with with the men who were to assemble the face equipment, telling them how it should be done. He had heard about the increased performance on the face-heading, and he realised that he might have to move all his plans for the training and installation work forward a week. He rang the Mechanisation team at Region to arrange delivery of the panzer conveyer as soon as possible.

★

Later in the afternoon, Reg Jenkins rang.

'I'm sending a fellow called Richard Wallace, to see you. Have you heard of him?'

'No, I don't think so, Mr Jenkins.'

'Well, I know him well. He runs a firm called UK Mining and Tunnelling. They do work in south Wales, but he wants to get a start in Yorkshire. I want you to show him the plans for the work you want doing by contractors for the Central Conveying Scheme. He has a machine available to put on the job straightaway, which is an advantage.' Roy Dobson's heart missed a beat.

'But, Mr Jenkins, I have not got an agreement with the union to use outside contractors. In fact, I'm meeting them tomorrow to try to get their agreement. There is no way that

105

I can see any contractor at the pit now. If I do that the union will never agree to change their position.'

'Well, that's alright. See him after you have met the union. In any case, we shall be seeing him on Friday night, and we can discuss it then. He's invited the two of us, with our wives, to go out to dinner with him, at a hotel in Derbyshire. It will be a dinner, followed by dancing. I'll let you know the details when he confirms the arrangements. It will allow our wives to get to know each other.' Reg rang off. Roy stormed round the office. The last thing he wanted was to get an agreement for outside contractors, and then be landed with an unknown Welsh company, when there were contractors in Yorkshire, with proven expertise, who operated internationally. Damn Reg Jenkins! And he didn't know what Helen would have to say about the invitation.

★

After they had finished tea, Roy decided to raise the issue of Friday night.

'What are your plans for Friday night, Helen?'

'I was hoping to have a quiet night at home with my husband, without 'phone calls from the pit, if that's possible.'

'Well, Mr Jenkins rang this afternoon, and he wants us to join him, and his wife, with a contractor he knows from Wales. It will be a dinner, followed by dancing, at a hotel in Derbyshire. He's going to confirm the details when he knows. I don't really want to go, but I don't want to cross Reg at the present time, either.'

'We'll need a babysitter, for starters.'

'I can fix that tonight. I shall see Cobba at the Welfare meeting; I'm sure he can arrange for Sandra for to do that.'

'Well, if we have to go, I suppose we may as well try to enjoy it.' Helen was being her usual considerate self, thought Roy, thankfully.

★

The Welfare meeting took its normal format: there was discussion on beer sales, income from the one-armed bandits and profits from the bingo; there was evaluation of the success, or otherwise, of the artists that had been hired, and the usual pressure on the entertainment officer to improve his performance by hiring better acts; there were odd details of poor behaviour by members, but nothing sufficiently serious that might require the committee to consider banning a person from being a member of the Club.

At the end of the meeting, Cobba asked to have a word with Roy, and they went through into Cobba's office while the other committee members gathered up their papers in the conference room and proceeded down to the bar.

'I need a word with you as well, Cobba,' said Roy, explaining the need for a babysitter on Friday night. Cobba said he would fix it and get Sandra to ring Mrs Dobson to confirm the arrangements.

'What do you want to discuss, Cobba?' asked Roy.

'I wanted to have a word about tomorrow's meeting on contractors, if you don't mind.'

'I'm glad to discuss any thoughts you might have on that subject.'

'Well, Boss, I think there are two issues that will need resolving. Firstly, some of these contracting firms insist that their men are not members of any union. We will not accept that at Martins. The firms only do it so that they can push the men around as they like. We need them to be members of our union branch. We won't get involved in their pay, but we will represent them on safety matters.'

'I don't see that as a problem; I'm sure that I can make that a condition in the contract tender document.'

'The other problem is Jimmy Bell. I need Jimmy to be sold on this change so that he puts it to the union meeting, not me. I can back Jimmy up, but if I put the case and there is some pressure from the floor, there is always the risk that Jimmy will change sides, and put the case against the motion. So you have to sort Jimmy out.'

'How do you suggest that I do that, Cobba?'

'I understand that Jimmy would welcome some extra cash, to sort out some family problems he's encountering. I think this could be done by appointing Jimmy as the workman's inspector for that part of the pit. We could argue that the union is so concerned that this work is carried out successfully, that we are keeping an eye on it. Jimmy could do a couple of underground visits each week and those underground shifts could qualify for the extra pay. It would also keep him out of the scene, and let me sort out any problems that might arise with 57s face.

'I can buy that, Cobba; but how do we get to that solution at the meeting tomorrow?'

'Leave that to me, Boss. I'll speak to Jimmy, and we'll feed in ideas at the right time. Think on, though, that we will have to put on a performance so that the other members of the union team, in the end, think that they are the winners.'

Roy Dobson drove home with a tingle of excitement. If he could pull off an agreement with the union to have outside contractors, he would really have scored a major victory. He would have to consider the Welsh problem later.

Thursday 27 August 1964

The meeting with the union started at eleven o'clock, and Roy noted that the union team was larger than usual. Cobba was not risking any of the union committee missing the meeting and not being party to the final decisions. Roy had Mike at the meeting, and he had his secretary, Gordon, there to take minutes.

Mike did a presentation, with plans, on the roadway in question. It would become the main conveyor roadway for the pit, carrying the coal from all the seams to a loading point in the pit bottom where the coal would be loaded into tubs to be wound up the shaft. The roadway was five hundred yards long, through old seam workings, and was completed by eighty yards of cross-measure drivage into the pit bottom. He explained that it would be independent of other workings at Martins. The dirt would be loaded into pit tubs and hauled up an old roadway to the pit bottom. The tubs would be taken to the surface up the non-coal-winding shaft. They would be tipped on the surface and the dirt taken straight onto the mine tip, so that it did not get mixed with the coal. It was therefore an ideal job to be done by outside contractors, as they would effectively be independent of the rest of the mine.

Cobba replied from the union point of view.

'Mr Dobson, your plan sounds sensible, but we have men at Martins who I'm sure could do that work.' There were nods from the union men round the table.

'In fact, Cobba, we do not have men at Martins who can be spared to do that work. If we redeploy men to that work we will have to stop one of the production faces. We would then have colliers without a job. Roadway tunnelling is specialist work, and all our experienced men are in use. We have to have that roadway driven, to allow the conveyors to be installed for the changeover at holiday week next year.'

This involved further explanations by Mike about the Central Conveying Scheme.

'Surely you can find enough men from around the pit?' said Jimmy.

'Jimmy, we have scraped around everywhere to carry out 57s development work. Which coalface do you suggest that we stop, Jimmy?' asked Roy.

'I'm not falling for that one. It's your job to run the pit.'

'I accept that, Jimmy, and you can take my word for it that we have spent a lot of time on this. We do not want to stop a coalface and have the pit output dropping, and a lot of colliers without a fixed job. I know that would cause labour problems for you, and me.'

'That is a fair point,' said Cobba. 'None of us want men losing regular jobs and losing money.' The union team agreed with that. Cobba continued. 'But we hear all sorts of problems from outside contractors at other pits.'

'That's right,' said Jimmy. 'They seem to do what they want. They brag about what they earn. They get weekend work when they want. And they look down on our union men.'

There was a whole series of examples quoted by the union men of problems with contractors at various pits in Yorkshire.

'You can understand, Boss, why our union is against the idea of contractors, when you hear stories like those,' said Cobba.

'I do understand, Cobba. But it's not like that at all pits, I can assure you, from my experience. The big advantage of contractors is that they move on when they've finished the contract. We do not want contractors at Martins full-time. When this job is done, we want them out. We will have enough Martins men for all the jobs, when we get this Central Conveying Scheme completed.'

There were further suggestions that once contractors got in at a pit they were kept on full-time. After another round of examples from the union men, Roy entered the discussion again.

'My view is that those examples reflect bad management. I can guarantee that we would let a contract for this work, and it would specify a termination date in the contract.'

This led to a further protracted discussion about the form of contract. Both Roy and

Mike were able to answer detailed questions from their experience. Time was passing, and they did not seem to be getting anywhere.

'We have heard all the arguments, and examples that have been quoted about using outside contractors, Boss, but you have not put forward any information, so far, to suggest that we should change the decision of this union branch to oppose the use of outside contractors,' said Cobba.

'Well said, Cobba,' said one of the union team.

'What made you take that decision?' asked Roy.

'We were told that if we had outside contractors, they would not be members of our union, and we would have nothing to do with them,' replied Cobba. 'And that is just not acceptable.'

'You are right, Cobba,' said one of his supporters.

'You see, Boss, if anything happens to one of those men, if they have an accident, it is us, as union officials, who become involved. We have responsibilities for the safety of this pit, just as you have in management.'

There was a pause, and the union team looked at Roy. He decided to play his first card.

'I agree entirely with your view, Cobba,' he said. There was surprise on the faces of the union team.

'How can you sort it out though, Boss?' asked Cobba.

'I will make a condition in the contract that the contractor's men have to be members of Martins Main union.'

There were some surprised looks between the union men. Roy decided to play an extra card.

'If you chaps agree, I will get Gordon to organise some tea and sandwiches from the canteen. I think we all need a break.' There were mumbles of agreement, and Gordon left the office. There was general chatting between the union men, but Roy kept away from Cobba. He said that he was going out for a few minutes with Mike, to check on the pit performance during the morning.

When they were in Roy's office, Mike asked the question.

'Are you sure that you can make it a condition of the contract that the contractors men have to be in the Martins union?'

'I have no choice now, have I? If we get an agreement, I don't see anyone at Region objecting to that clause.' Roy sounded more confident than he felt.

Back in the conference room, they joined the union men in having a sandwich. The atmosphere in the room seemed more relaxed.

When the meeting resumed, there was a discussion on how it would work with the contractor's men being members of the union. Cobba summed it up.

'So what you are saying, Mr Dobson, is that the men would be members of our branch of the union. Everything to do with their pay and organisation would be between them and the contractor, but we would deal with them on safety issues.'

'That's right, Cobba. I would have to spell out that arrangement at the contract meeting, so that everyone understands how it would work. At least you would benefit, with more union subs into your funds.'

'Yes, that would be helpful to the union. But how are you going to ensure that they operate safely and to the right standards?'

'I've been thinking about that, Cobba. Basically, management and the union,' he emphasised the last three words, 'are going to have to keep an eye on the contract and the work done. What I have in mind is to nominate a workman's inspector, for that part of the pit, who will visit the site regularly, say twice a week. As the union needs to be satisfied that everything is being done properly, I suggest that it should be a union man who has that job. What do you think?'

There were general murmurs of agreement among the union team. They were looking at each other to try to guess who would be the nominated person.

'I think it should be Jimmy, if you all agree,' said Roy. 'I know Jimmy has plenty on, but I am sure he is respected at the pit, and will do a good job for Martins, and for the union. How are you fixed, Jimmy?'

'If you want me to do that job, I will take it on, Mr Dobson.' Jimmy seemed to stretch up two inches in his seat. His other colleagues could not disagree with the proposal.

The meeting went on for another short discussion of procedure. Roy would circulate the minutes of the meeting. The minutes would include an agreement by the union to take this issue to a general meeting, with a recommendation that outside contractors should be used for the Central Conveying Scheme.

When Mike got back to his office he sat in his chair and pondered for a few minutes. 'How does this fellow do it?' he said to himself.

★

Later that afternoon, Mr Jenkins rang up.

'The arrangements for tomorrow night are sorted now. It's a long trip to Derbyshire, so I've got a driver from Region, with one of their cars. We'll travel together, and I'll pick you up at six o'clock. Is that alright?'

'Yes, that's very good, Mr Jenkins.'

'How did the meeting with the union go?'

'It was a long slog, but I think we might be alright. They are taking it to a union general meeting, with a recommendation to agree to use outside contractors on the Central Conveying Scheme. I had to agree a few concessions, but it should be acceptable to everyone.'

'That's good news,' said Reg, as he rang off.

★

Roy decided to brief his wife on the dinner dance arrangements as soon as he got home.

'We'll be travelling in style, tomorrow night,' he began. 'You will have to dress the part, like nobility.'

'Just what do you mean, Roy?' asked his wife, with a grin.

'Mr Jenkins has arranged a driver and a car from Region, to drive us to the dinner in Derbyshire, and we will be picked up at six o'clock. I'll have to make sure I'm home with enough time to get changed.'

'If it's as early as that, I'll have to ring Sandra, and ask her to be here a bit earlier than we'd agreed. I've arranged to have my hair done during the afternoon, but I've not yet decided what to wear. If it's fairly posh, I could wear my long, blue, satin skirt, with the white blouse. But the blouse has a plunging neck line that is a bit revealing. What do you think?'

'I certainly like that blouse. It might be a bit teasing for Reg, but I'm sure his wife will keep him in order.'

★

Helen rang Sandra, and arranged for her to be picked up by Roy so that she was there before six o'clock.

'Will your boyfriend be coming as well?' asked Helen.

'He's arranged to play football with his mates from work. He wanted to cancel the football to babysit, but I insisted he get the exercise. We're going out in Doncaster, on Saturday, so we shall get one night out together this weekend.' Sandra didn't tell Helen that she'd told Terry that she didn't want a repeat of the goodnight striptease that had happened last time she stayed overnight.

Friday 28 August 1964

The Enclosure had been treated to the sight of lorry loads of equipment arriving each day for 57s face – lorry loads of powered supports and face panzer equipment. But today surpassed the previous days in providing a spectacle for the Enclosure members. They gazed down as one lorry, with a bright-red machine fastened onto the lorry bed, turned into Martins Lane. The machine was more than twelve feet long and looked like no other type of machine used in mining. It had an augur at each end, a turret-cutting disc in the centre and a control panel that jutted out of the side of the machine. They didn't yet know it as a trepanner.

'That looks like some machine,' said Cyril. 'It'll require a good machine-man to drive it,' he added, implying that, as an ex–winding-engineman, he was an authority on driving complex engines.

'There's some quantity of bloody equipment on these new mechanised coalfaces,' said Albert. 'I hope the union knows what they're doing backing all this fancy tackle.'

'This is the way the pits have to go, Albert,' said Cliff. 'That machine will load what twenty or thirty men would fill in a shift, and there'll be no blasting of the coal. It's far more efficient.'

'That's alright, Cliff, but it must be costing a packet for all that equipment made of steel,' said Albert.

The members of the Enclosure looked at each other to see who would provide a figure of the cost; but they all had blank faces.

★

Mike was discussing with Roy the surface build-up of the face equipment, now that all the components had arrived.

'We'll get it all built on the surface over the next two weeks, Boss, so that it's available for training the men. This means that we'll have to agree, with the union, the men for both shifts on the face by that time.'

'That should be achievable. I've agreed with George that the face-heading men can work tomorrow morning as an extra shift. At the rate they're going, the coalface should be completed in a week. If we can achieve that position we shall be in front of our programme.'

'I've another suggestion for you to consider, Boss,' said Mike. 'Why don't we use the weekend at the end of the training week to have the equipment in working order so that other men from the pit, and anyone from Upthorpe, could see a demonstration of the system? It would be a bit of good publicity for the pit, and the local paper could get some photographs to go with their write-up.'

'That is a dammed good idea,' replied Roy. 'I'll have a word with the local paper when we've got agreement to have an open demonstration. You'll have to fence-off the area, for safety and security, and we'll have management on site for the day. We did a similar build-up and invited the press at my last pit in the Midlands, and it worked well. I'll have to make sure Cobba and his mates are in agreement. By the way, Mike, I shall be out tonight with Mr Jenkins, so can you keep an eye on the pit. I'll leave the telephone number of where we are with the babysitter, in case there's a real emergency.'

'That's okay, Boss. I'll keep in touch with the pit.'

★

The car pulled up at the house on time, and the driver jumped out to open the door for Roy and Helen. Sandra was standing at the front door, with John, the youngest child, in her arms and Robert at her side, as they waved goodbye to their parents.

Reg Jenkins was sitting in the front seat, and his wife was in the back. Roy and Helen squeezed into the back with Mrs Jenkins, who introduced herself as Polly. Helen was relieved to see that Polly was also wearing a long skirt. Reg apologised that the car was a Granada and not a Jaguar, as he had planned, and explained that Mr Pickersgill was using the Jaguar as his car was being repaired. The conversation throughout the journey was an exchange of family details: both families had two children, but the Jenkins children were at university; how the Jenkins family were reacting to life in Yorkshire; the options for shopping and entertainment. There was no mention of mines and mining issues and Roy was relieved at that.

At the hotel they were met by Richard Wallace, a Welshman with a heavily-lined face and flowing white hair. He introduced his wife, Denise, who was obviously much younger than him. As Helen and Polly went to the cloakroom to leave their coats, Polly explained to Helen that Denise was Richard's third wife and had been his secretary. When they returned to the lounge they joined Denise, who was sitting away from the men. Denise was tall, with long black hair and a full figure, and she oozed the confidence of a secretary who was secure in the knowledge that she was in charge of the office, and also knew how to organise and manipulate her Boss to his advantage.

The three men sat together and Reg wasted no time in moving the discussions to the mining business. He asked Richard Wallace how his business was performing in Wales. The answer was vague: the company had regular work at several pits, but there seemed to be a reluctance to use outside contractors more widely in the coalfield. That was behind his plan to seek contracts in the major Midlands coalfields.

'We certainly need outside contractors in Yorkshire, to introduce new methods, and to break the restrictive practices by some of the trade unions,' said Reg.

'My company has a reputation for doing that,' replied Richard. 'We have a hire-and-fire policy; if a man doesn't work to our standards, he's out. And we don't have any truck with the trade unions. I've some good shift bosses who know how to push men for performance for the full shift. The shift boss's pay, as well as the workmen's pay, depends on the results.'

'We need that at Martins,' said Reg.

'What's the position on outside contractors at Martins?' asked Richard.

Roy Dobson decided that he should introduce a note of caution.

'I have had meetings with the union, and made some progress, but they need to get a decision at a union general meeting to change their policy on outside contractors. It won't be easy. And there's always the possibility of them coming back with some conditions that are unacceptable to the management.'

'You have to win this one, Roy, if we are to get Martins turned round,' said Reg.

'I am aware of that, Mr Jenkins. We are making a lot of changes at Martins at the moment, and the men and the unions are being positive. We've selected a roadway drivage that is ideal to be done by contractors, as it will be essentially separated from the rest of the pit. So there should be little interaction between the contractor's workmen and Martins' men. It's that aspect that upsets the union at many pits in Yorkshire.'

'An arrangement like that will be ideal for us,' put in Richard.

'I'll be in touch with you as soon as we know the outcome of the union meeting,' said Reg.

'I would appreciate that,' said Richard.

That was not the only discussion of mining matters, however. Denise Wallace talked freely in the ladies' corner about her husband and his company.

'Richard is a wonderful example of a self-made man. He started in the pits as a workman and then became a charge-man over a team of men. He then realised that he could organise and lead a company, so he set up UK Mining and Tunnelling. It was a struggle at first, but he stuck at it, and he has regular contract work at several pits now. He has also got some work in tunnelling for the water authority in Wales. Of course, when a fellow is successful, some people who knew him when he was a workman are jealous of his wealth, and try to pull him down. That's where he needs me to keep him going and encourage him to expand the company. You must have experienced jealousy of your success?' she added, turning to Polly.

'Yes, we saw it a bit when we were in Wales, but now we're in Yorkshire, Reg just does his own thing and he doesn't care what people think of him.' Polly gave a dismissive wave of her hand. Helen didn't join in the conversation.

The discussions then turned to descriptions by Denise of the wealth of her husband: a large house in Wales; another property in France, and a boat in Cardiff Bay. She spoke freely and easily, with no signs of any boasting. She was proud to be the wife of Richard Wallace.

The menu was excellent and no one had difficulty selecting items they fancied. They were attended by the head waiter, who had been primed by Denise that his attention to their clients was essential. The wine was of the best quality, and flowed freely. At the end of the meal, Roy was relaxed and he smiled across at his wife, who looked charming in her outfit, and definitely not outdone by the very expensive 'designer' dress worn by Denise. He decided that he could stand a little more of this pampering, after his intensive hard work at Martins Main.

A six-piece band had been playing quietly during the meal, but when couples started to dance they upped the tempo and the volume. Roy was surprised when Denise made the first move.

'Come on, Roy, I need a dance to shake the food down,' she said. Roy had no choice but to lead her to the floor.

He took her in his arms in what he thought was the correct hold, but was shocked that she moved so close that her body was wedged to his and their faces were almost cheek-to-cheek. She was a very good dancer and she followed his lead with ease.

'I understand that you have a great future in the mining industry?' she murmured in his ear.

'Oh, I'm not sure of that,' he replied with a smile. 'I am really just starting in colliery management. Martins Main is a real challenge; I'll have to make a success of that pit before I have a future.'

'Don't talk yourself down. You have to look after yourself in this world. Nobody else will do it for you.'

Roy noticed that Reg was dancing with Helen, and holding her closer than he expected. He knew that he must dance next with Helen, to escape further attention by Denise, though he had to admit that dancing with Denise was one of the best dances he'd experienced for a long time.

The next dance was a waltz, so he took Helen onto the dance floor. They talked over the event so far, agreeing that the meal had been very good. Denise, who she thought was honest and straightforward, impressed Helen. However, she had already realised that Denise had real power over her husband.

'Your boss has got wandering hands,' she said.

'How do you mean?'

'Well, I've never had so much of my body explored in one dance!' replied Helen with a smile. 'His hands are never still. He's stroked my bottom, and thighs, and he must know every piece of underwear I'm wearing underneath. He dances quite well, but he moves his partner towards him and away from him all the time; I've never danced with a partner like him,' she laughed. 'He managed to get a good look at my plunging neck line as well!'

'It's all in the line of business,' said Roy, with a grin. His wife squeezed his hand.

They all danced with different partners through the evening, but Richard preferred to sit and talk through some of the more energetic dances. Near the end of the evening, Roy had a slow foxtrot with Denise. She danced even closer on this occasion, with her thighs and bust rubbing against his body. Her cheek was next to his, and she took the opportunity to whisper in his ear.

'I hope that we will get other opportunities to meet in the future, Roy. I've really enjoyed meeting you and your wife. Doing business with Richard will be very much to your advantage.'

Roy was speechless at this, but dancing with Denise Wallace excited him. He had never in his life had a dancing partner like her.

At the end of the dancing, in the early hours of the morning, there were kisses all round between Richard and Denise and their guests at the entrance to the hotel, where the driver was waiting with the car doors open.

The drive back was quiet, but Reg summed up the trip.

'That was a good night out. Richard and Denise are a great couple who know how to entertain. We'll have to make sure that they get established with some business in Yorkshire.'

Roy did not know how to reply to that.

★

When Roy and Helen were back at home and Helen had checked the children, they sat together in the lounge.

'Well, that was a real eye-opener,' said Roy. 'Reg Jenkins has a reputation for enjoying the good life with lavish entertainment; but that was very special. I wonder if he has other firms who treat him to nights out like that?'

'I think it's very likely,' replied Helen. 'I got the impression, though, that Richard Wallace was a tired man without driving ambition, but that Denise seemed to fill the gap. And from what I saw she was a very intimate dancer...'

'She was indeed,' replied Roy. 'She danced close so that she could whisper in my ear that doing business with Richard would be to my advantage. I don't know what that means.'

'She is certainly a smart woman who knows how to show off her body.'

Roy put his arm around Helen.

'Never mind talking about Denise. Let me tell you that you looked ravishing tonight, and I was proud to have you with me. I would rather have you than a dozen women like Denise.' He gave her a squeeze and a kiss.

'If you are hinting at a grand finale to the night out, you can forget it.' Helen spoke with a smile as she pushed him away. 'I'm too tired, so save it for tomorrow.' She stood up to go to bed.

Saturday 29 August 1964

Janet went round to see Peggy mid-morning. Her first job was to apologise that she hadn't been round earlier in the week.

'I never remember a week like it,' she told Peggy. 'Bob has been working overtime every day. They seem to be made out with fitting work at Martins. In the shop we have had one girl off all week, and loads of new stock to sort out. I haven't had a minute to catch my breath. Thank goodness this is my Saturday off. But never mind about me, how are you feeling, Peggy?'

'I'm getting by. But I still feel weak and tired, and I haven't got past the morning sickness yet. The health visitor has been and she arranged for the doctor to call yesterday. He says he's still not happy about my blood pressure and he wants me to go to the surgery to see him next Thursday.'

'Is it the evening surgery?' asked Janet. Peggy nodded. 'Right then, I'll go with you for company. Is Gerry on dayshift?' Peggy nodded again. 'Well he can look after the kids then. How did you get on with Bob's sister? Did she turn up as we arranged? I was thinking about her.'

'Oh, yes,' replied Peggy, and she brightened up a little. 'She came two afternoons and she was great. The kids took to her and I dread to think what state the house would be in now if she hadn't been here.' Then Peggy's face changed to a worried frown. 'But there is a problem, Janet.'

'Oh, what's that?' asked Janet, fearful that the arrangement was falling apart so soon.

'Well, I asked her what I owed her and she said it had all been sorted. What did she mean?'

'Don't you worry your head about that, Peggy; Bob has done a deal with his sister. It's a sort of family agreement; you won't have to pay her anything. But don't tell Gerry that. Let him increase your allowance as though you are paying.'

'Oh, Janet, what can I say?'

'Don't say anything; let's have a cup of tea.' Janet stood up and went to put the kettle on.

Talking over tea, Janet learned that Gerry was filling the coal and taking the ashes out, and generally being a bit more helpful at home. However, he'd drawn the line short of considering taking the kids out at all. He couldn't risk being seen wheeling a pram like a proud father – that would destroy his image at the pit and at the Club.

★

Sandra and Terry enjoyed their night out, dancing in Doncaster. They had a few drinks, but they concentrated on improving their dancing together. Sandra saw one of her friends and had a quick word, but she stuck close to Terry. He nodded to one of his colleagues from work, who gave Sandra a thorough appraisal for reporting to the rest of the office on Monday morning, but Terry managed to avoid any introductions.

As Terry had the car, they were able to stay until the last dance, and when they arrived back in Upthorpe it was after midnight. Terry stopped the car and leaned over, pulling Sandra into a cuddle. She was willing at first, but as Terry's hands wandered and her short dress was soon around her waist, she became concerned. She clamped her legs together and pushed him away.

'No, Terry, stop that. I'm not comfortable cramped here in the car. Anyway, it's time I was in the house; I don't want my Dad coming out to investigate.'

'If you're not comfortable in the car, you should have let me babysit with you last night,' said Terry, who was getting frustrated.

'That's a grand thing to say. Is that all you're interested in, Terry Lacey? Having me to grope so that you can satisfy your sexual passions?' Sandra's voice cracked. She moved over towards the door and straightened her dress. 'I had hoped for better behaviour than that. I thought that you might really like me, and respect me.'

'Sandra….' But he was too late. She was out of the car. The door banged shut and Sandra went into the house without a look back.

Sunday 30 August 1964

Sandra had a word with her Dad before he went off to his union committee meeting.

'Dad, if a young man called Terry rings up to have a word with me today, tell him that I'm not available. I won't answer the 'phone if it rings while you're out this morning.'

'What's the matter, lass; have you had a tiff?'

'Sort of, Dad. Nothing serious though, but I don't want to talk about it at the moment.'

★

The 'phone rang twice as Sandra prepared the Sunday lunch, but she didn't answer it, and she made sure that her brother didn't come through from his bedroom to answer it either.

There was another call in the early evening, and this time Cobba answered it and followed Sandra's instructions.

'Who is that speaking?' Cobba asked. When he got the reply he said, 'I'm afraid she's not available; I think she may have gone out with one of her girlfriends.' He winked across at Sandra.

★

Peter Carter was playing the harmonium for the evening service at Upthorpe Methodist Church, in place of the regular organist. He'd selected several pieces to play before the start of the service, while the congregation were finding their places. The organ voluntaries demonstrated Peter's skills, and required the old harmonium to produce sounds it had never made with the regular organist. In the middle of one of the voluntaries, he noted a disturbance in the congregation. Willie, his father, was showing a tall, distinctive-looking lady to a place in one of the pews, and this was causing murmurs and whispering among the regular worshippers.

Helen Dobson took her place and bowed her head in prayer. It was her first visit to the church and she felt exposed and lonely. She hoped this would be the exception, and that her regular attendance would provide her with the spiritual peace and inspiration she had found in her previous places of worship.

Helen had told her husband that she wanted to attend the evening service, and he had agreed to drive her to the church, and to pick her up after the service. There had been some banter during the short drive there.

'Have you a lot of sins to confess?' asked Roy, with a grin.

'Not as many as you, after the way you danced with Denise Wallace the other night,' she said. 'Asking for forgiveness for you, and also for Reg Jenkins, will leave me little time for any prayers for myself this week!'

As she thought of this remark while sitting in church, she felt ashamed of her trite comments, which seemed to reduce her faith to a shallow level. She need not have worried; her faith would be revived by the service.

The service was conducted by Reverend James Folds, whose wife, Gwen, was also in the congregation. The hymns, the readings and the prayers were all presented by James in a quiet, non-dramatic way, but clearly came from a person of very sincere faith. His style of preaching was to mix humorous stories from everyday life with a message that was clear and concise, and based on the Bible. His concluding comment was delivered after a long pause.

'There is nothing, nothing in this world, to compare with a life walked every day in the company of the Lord Jesus Christ.'

There were one or two spoken 'amens' in the congregation, and Helen felt a sense of relief that she was back again in the presence of the Spirit of the Living God.

At the end of the service, Helen Dobson was the centre of attraction. Willie took her to meet James and Gwen Folds. John Warwick shook her hand, as did farmer Joe Horton. Others too, whose names she could not remember, had a word with her. It took her fifteen minutes to escape to Roy, who was waiting patiently in the car outside.

'I thought they were keeping you in for detention!' he said, as she settled in the car.

'No, there were just a lot of introductions. They were all very welcoming.' There was a pause, and then she decided she must add some more. 'It was a beautiful service and just what I needed. I feel that I can settle at that church, Roy.'

Helen was quiet on the drive home, and Roy knew that she had renewed an essential part of her life and that no words from him were required.

Chapter 8

Wednesday 2 September 1964

It was a proving to be a good week for Roy. The pit was performing well, and the output from all parts of the pit was up to budget. Reg Jenkins had announced on Tuesday that he would pay a visit the following day to see the progress on 57s development. He was surprised at the progress being made, and George Turnbull had used the time since learning of the visit until now to ensure that everything was tidy and in order.

Roy Dobson and Reg Jenkins crawled up to where two men were working in the face-heading. The men were dressed just in shorts and knee-pads, and their bodies were coated in sweat and coal dust as they loaded coal onto the conveyor.

Reg enthused at the thickness of the coal seam, and the potential output from the mechanised coalface and Roy complimented the men on their progress. They replied that they were trying to achieve more yardage than the other team doing the rest of the face-heading. Roy also raised with them the need to have experienced machine drivers for the trepanner on the mechanised face, and they appeared interested.

The visit to the other face development team was equally successful.

Back in the office, Reg noted the progress and then worked out that there was a possibility of having the mechanised coalface ready earlier than the current action programme had anticipated. Roy explained the progress with the equipment build-up on the surface, and his idea to have an open day to show off the equipment to the rest of the pit and to the public. As they were using only part of the equipment on the surface, this wouldn't delay the installation underground. Mr Jenkins approved of the plan for an open day. Having got that approval, Roy realised that it might be possible to get the mechanised face into production earlier than planned.

Reg asked about the date of the union meeting about outside contractors. Roy explained that the date was not yet fixed and that he didn't wish to push Cobba on the issue. He thought Cobba was planning to get the motion moved by Jimmy Bell, rather than himself, and Reg saw the sense of that.

Thursday 3 September 1964

Janet linked arms with Peggy and they walked slowly down to the Upthorpe surgery. Peggy seemed to be walking even slower than she did on their last visit to the doctor.

In the consulting room, the doctor gave Peggy a full examination and asked her lots of questions about her symptoms and her tiredness. Janet explained the change in the domestic arrangements for Peggy, but expressed her concern that Peggy didn't seem to be improving much.

The doctor said that as far as he could tell the baby was progressing normally, but that he would change the tablets to try to get better control of Peggy's blood pressure. He said that it was not going to be an easy pregnancy, and Peggy needed to rest as much as possible. It would most likely be necessary for the delivery to take place in the hospital, so that Peggy and the baby had the best possible expertise and care available. Peggy looked surprised at this.

As they walked slowly back to Martins Lane, Janet told Peggy not to worry about the hospital. It would be no problem, she said, and she would think about the arrangements for the other two children and Gerry. Peggy squeezed Janet's arm.

'What can I say, Janet?'

'I keep telling you, Peggy, you don't have to say anything.'

Friday 11 September 1964

The Enclosure was in session, and there were important topics to discuss. Cyril reported from his old mates in the winding houses that they were winding more coal at the pit than they had done for a long time.

'This manager seems to be getting a response from the men,' said Cliff. 'I understand that they will complete the opening out of 57s coalface within the next few days. It will be all hands on deck, getting the equipment installed then.'

'There are some new starters in the management team – a new assistant mechanical engineer and an assistant electrical engineer.' The Enclosure members were impressed by this information from Pat Mulligan.

'What the pit used to have was mining men; now they are all engineers, but they don't know how to mine coal. They can only keep the machines running,' said Albert.

'That's the secret of getting coal,' said Cliff. 'In the future it will be machines that mine the coal, not men with shovels. Keeping the machines running will be vital.'

'I'll believe that when I see it,' replied Albert, with a sarcastic comment. 'Bloody engineers.'

'I've heard that next Saturday the new equipment for 57s face will be working on the surface, and all the men at the pit, and the public, will be able to go and see it,' said Pat.

'How did you get to know that?' asked Charlie. Pat just shrugged his shoulders. 'If that's the case, we shall all have to go, as a team.' They all nodded in agreement.

'There's something bloody fishy going on in the union,' said Albert. 'They've called a special union meeting for a week on Sunday morning, in the Club, but no bugger knows why. I suspect that Cobba is up to his tricks again, although Jimmy is keeping his mouth shut. He usually spills the beans, but not this time.'

'It's probably about 57s face,' said Cliff. 'It'll be a major issue – staffing a mechanised coalface rather than a hand-filled unit.'

'No, it's not that,' replied Albert. 'That was sorted out with the manager last week. They've picked men from all parts of the pit, and they're having training sessions during next week. There is so much happening at Martins at the moment that I reckon that the manager just does what he bloody wants, and no bugger in the union asks any questions.' One or two of the Enclosure team thought that might be why the pit was doing better, but they didn't comment.

Saturday 12 September 1964

It had taken two weeks for Terry to establish contact with Sandra. She was never available for his 'phone calls, so he'd written to her. His letter was full of apologies for his behaviour, and he asked to meet with Sandra for him to talk things through with her. In the end, she agreed to meet him again, for a night out in Doncaster. This time it was different: he'd booked a table at a hotel for the evening dinner and dance. Sandra had bought a new dress for the occasion, and some new perfume. The dress was short and flared, and showed off her legs. And she knew that if she spun round too quickly when dancing, she would show off more than her legs. When she got into the car she set the rules for the evening.

'Terry, I do not want any discussions about our tiff; it's over now. I want us to behave as though it had never happened. We're out to have a pleasant evening together. Is that alright for you?'

'Definitely alright by me,' replied Terry. He was relieved, as he had been rehearsing for days what he would say to Sandra, and he was not sure he had got the words right. His fear was that she might take offence, and end their relationship completely. He reached over and touched her hand as he drove off.

The dinner was a success, and the dancing to the hotel trio was traditional ballroom dances, with only two excursions into rock and roll. Terry and Sandra were definitely the youngest couple there, and they were surprised at the abandon with which some of the senior citizens tackled the rock and roll numbers. In these dances Sandra tried to protect her modesty, by keeping one hand down by her side, but it was only partially effective. She was glad that she was wearing new nylon knickers.

When Terry got the bill Sandra took a five-pound note out of her handbag and passed it over to him. He tried to push it back.

'No, Sandra, it's my treat.'

'No, Terry, it's our treat. I get a good allowance for the housekeeping, so you'll take that towards the bill.'

'Thank you very much.' Terry was not sure that he had said the right words.

Back in Upthorpe, there was a cuddle, but it was carefully cautious from Terry, and very relaxed as far as Sandra was concerned. Then she dropped her bombshell.

'I want to go on seeing you, Terry, but I want you to meet my Dad and my brother. I'll talk to Dad and suggest that you come over to have a meal with us. I'll have to check when Dad is available, because he's always attending meetings for the union, or the Club, or the Council. Will you accept an invitation, Terry?'

'Oh yes, Sandra. Just let me know when you can arrange it. Will I be seeing you again soon?'

'I'll give you a ring. This next week looks very busy for our family: there's an open night at school for David, and I know that Dad has several meetings. We've not planned who's doing what, yet, so I'll ring you when things are sorted out.'

Sandra got out of the car, but left behind the aroma of her perfume, and a young man who was excited by the evening, but not sure what his parents would say about him going to Sandra's house for a meal. It was moving the relationship up a gear, and they might not approve.

Monday 21 September 1964

Peter Carter got home at nine-thirty from his evening class at Doncaster Technical College. He was tired and wanted to get to bed, as he was on the dayshift at Martins the next morning. He was enjoying the work underground, working under the close personal supervision of an electrician, and the Technical College course was well within his academic capabilities. It was just that there seemed to be so much to fit in to his time. When he got into the house his father was waiting for him, all excited.

'Peter, you will not believe the news I have for you. At the church council meeting tonight, the decision about the organ was finalised. Joe Horton said he would lend the church the money to buy the organ, and that he would see to the transport of it, from Pontefract to Upthorpe, in his trailer. John Warwick is arranging the builder to alter the seating at the front of the church, in the choir seats, to make a place for the organ. The builder will also manufacture the plinth to fit on the back wall, to carry the organ pipes. The work will start immediately after the Harvest weekend. What do you think to that?' Willie paused for breath.

'That's great, Dad,' replied Peter, but he didn't stay to prolong the conversation. He started getting his things together for the next morning. It would be wonderful to have the bigger organ to play in Upthorpe, but would he have time to practise? And what if they asked him to play the organ at all the services?

★

Roy was discussing the coming weekend with Helen.

'It's going to be a big weekend. We have the open day with the equipment for 57s face on display for the public to see; the local paper is coming to take photographs and get reactions, and there's a possibility of the local television people dropping in. Then on Sunday morning, Cobba is holding the special union general meeting on the use of outside contractors at Martins. If both events go off well, then things are really looking up.'

'Just a minute,' said Helen, 'you are only talking about your side of things. Remember that it's a special weekend at the church, too. There's the supper and auction on Saturday night, and I want your support at that, and you had better have your wallet handy. I've been to see the gifts being auctioned; there's a good variety of things, but there is a special one that is really a promise. The artist who has presented a painting to be auctioned is also going to do a painting of the new organ when it's installed in the church. I think you should bid for that. There might be no interest in it from Upthorpe people.'

'It's going to be tricky for me to get away from the pit on Saturday, if the press and television arrive late,' said Roy.

'I don't think that will be a problem. If they are coming at all, they'll be early. Pressmen don't like to be working on a Saturday afternoon. I've arranged for Sandra to look after the boys on Saturday evening, so you can't use them as an excuse. Oh, and I've agreed to read the lesson at the Sunday evening service; but I'll excuse you attending that, provided you take me in the car and pick me up after.'

'You seem to have got everything carefully planned, and no doubt I will have to fit in,' replied Roy with a grin.

Saturday 26 September 1964

The Enclosure team met at the pit gates at ten o'clock. Cliff had his walking stick and wore his trilby, as he wanted to demonstrate that he was knowledgeable about these mining systems; he expected to have to answer some questions from his Enclosure colleagues.

Mike was on the scene and he was keen that the public stayed behind the cordoned-off demonstration area. There were only a few miners observing the equipment operated by a team of five men. One man drove the trepanner; one man watched the cable that fed power to the machine and three men rammed the panzer conveyor over and then lowered and advanced the supports. When the machine reached the end of the mock face the supports were lowered and pushed back to their original position, the panzer conveyor was pulled back and the trepanner moved the opposite way along the coalface.

Charlie was excited to see how the coalface equipment worked. He was moving along with the machine and he was most impressed. He came back to Cliff with two questions.

'How much coal does it produce, Cliff?'

'It should cut about a twenty-seven inch deep web,' replied Cliff. 'That's about a ton of coal for every four feet the machine moves along the coalface.'

'Wow! That is going some. How are these supports powered?' he asked.

Again Cliff gave the answer. 'It's a hydraulic circuit.' He pointed to the end of the layout, to a pump that was pumping the hydraulic fluid into the system. 'You can see the pump there; it feeds a pressure line through those hoses to the supports. Any unwanted fluid passes into a return line, back to the fluid tank.'

'Bloody clever,' said Charlie.

'That panzer conveyor makes a lot of noise when it's running,' said Cyril.

'I understand that when it's loaded with coal it's much quieter,' said Cliff.

The Enclosure team discussed various aspects of the operations and were fascinated watching the machine move from end to end.

★

More and more people were coming to the site. Workmen were bringing their children as a Saturday treat. One or two men, who were in the 57s team, brought their wives, to show them which jobs they would be doing on the coalface. One wife summed it up after a few minutes.

'It looks bloody simple to me. You only have to pull a few handles; it's like pulling pints in the bar. I thought you said mining was hard work?' Her husband wondered if he had done the right thing bringing her to the open day.

★

Roy came down and had a few words with the men operating the equipment. They seemed to be confident that they could work the system. His appearance created some interest in the Enclosure team, as it was the first time they had got a close-up view of him. Albert gave his views of the manager to his colleagues.

'I must say, he looks to know his job and at least he talks to the men. Mind, it might just be a show for us; he might be a clever bugger in his office.' He looked across the pit yard. 'Bloody hell, there's Cobba coming with his lass. I didn't expect to see him.'

Sandra picked her way carefully across the pit yard in her high heels, but she was dressed in a sensible coat and trousers. Cobba spoke to the men who were watching the demonstration and then he concentrated on explaining the operations to Sandra. He nodded to Albert, but didn't stop to speak to him. Nor did he speak to Roy as, at that moment, a television van drove into the pit yard. There was excitement all round as one of the local TV presenters got out of the van and went over to Mike and Roy. The TV producer wanted to plan some shots of the equipment working and agree the ideal place to do a short interview with Roy. The men working the equipment were persuaded to go to the lamp-room and get cap-lamps, to increase the authenticity of the shots. The arrival of the local newspaper photographer further increased the excitement, and he wanted some shots of the children watching the demonstration. He prevailed upon Roy to let him take a photograph of a ten-year-old lad, dressed in a pit helmet, with his hand on the trepanner controls. Nothing sells local papers better than shots of children, thought Roy.

Cobba moved away with Sandra. He had no wish to be interviewed by either the local newspaper reporter or the television people. There was the risk of having to field some question about union business, and that was to be avoided at all costs during this weekend.

News of the TV van spread along Martins Lane and the crowd increased, but by lunchtime the film was in the can and, as the TV team disappeared, the crowd dispersed and it seemed a natural end to the open day.

Roy arranged for Mike to wind things down, ensure that all the power was switched off and that security was on site to ensure that there were no unauthorised visitors during the rest of the day.

'There'll be nothing for them to see, Boss,' said Mike. 'I've arranged a team of surface men to load up the panzer drives and get them down the shaft this afternoon. The trepanner will be transported to the fitting shop this afternoon to be stripped down for transport underground tomorrow.'

'I think this morning has achieved what we wanted,' said Roy, hoping that his interview with the television reporter would come over well. 'You've done a good job, Mike, with this surface build, and the training programme, as well as the open day.'

'Thanks, Boss,' said Mike, pleased that his efforts were recognised by his manager.

★

At lunchtime, Roy adopted a casual approach to Helen's questions. Yes, the open day had been a success, and he had no need to go back to the pit during the afternoon.

'Did the TV team turn up?' she asked.

'Yes. And the photographer from the local paper.'

'I told you they would come in the morning.' Helen was pleased with her correct forecast.

'What time do we have to be at the church tonight?' asked Roy.

'The auction starts at seven o'clock, so I want to be there at least fifteen minutes before that. I don't want to be rushed, but I don't want to be so early that everybody starts talking to me. Why do you ask?' Helen was detecting something unusual in the question.

'I would like to see the local TV news, to see if they put anything on about the open day.'

'Why, were you on the film?' asked Helen with a quizzical look.

'As a matter of fact I did do an interview with the local TV presenter.'

'Wow! Did you hear, kids? Your dad will be appearing on TV.' Helen moved over and gave Roy a hug.

Robert and John stopped eating their lunch and looked at Roy in amazement.

'Will you really be on TV, Daddy?'

'Yes, if they decide to include the bit I recorded.'

★

The local TV news was on at six o'clock. Usually it concentrated on the local football results, with a little splattering of news. This week there must have been a shortage of news because they ran the Martins Main open day as the lead item. The equipment was shown operating; there was a shot of the crowd watching, and they used Roy's interview in full, at the end. It was a first appearance on TV for Roy and he felt satisfied that he'd answered the questions reasonably well and had sounded confident about the future of Martins Main.

Sandra had arrived to babysit just before the news started, so she joined the whole family watching the programme.

'Well done,' said Helen, 'You came over as a confident young manager. I'm proud of you.' She went over and gave Roy a kiss before rushing upstairs to complete getting ready for the church auction.

'It was very interesting to see the equipment working on the pit top,' said Sandra. 'I went up with my Dad and he explained it to me. We didn't stay after the TV van arrived; Dad isn't keen on publicity.'

'Yes, I saw you, Sandra, but I was too busy to come over. Mind you, I think your Dad would not have thanked me for talking to him, with all the public around.'

Sandra gave Roy a smile, and gathered the two children to take them upstairs to their playroom, where she could read to them and play games before bedtime. Roy waved goodnight to the kids and admired the back view of Sandra in her tight skirt. He also considered her a very mature young woman.

★

In the schoolroom of Upthorpe Methodist Church Roy hoped to stay in the background, but it was obvious that a lot of the people there had seen the TV news programme. There was a lot of whispering and nodding in his direction and he was relieved when Joe Horton came over and introduced himself. Helen had told Roy about the farmer and Roy immediately knew who he was and asked him about his farm. Joe liked the interest being shown in him, and he sat by Roy and talked about the harvest and the farm business.

'It's very good of Mrs Dobson to act as auctioneer tonight,' said Joe. 'It has certainly brought some extra people in from Doncaster and Wakefield. And they also have you here as a TV personality, as well,' said Joe with a grin.

In good Methodist tradition, the evening started with a hymn and a prayer led by Reverend Folds. Then he gave a brief progress report on the organ project, concluding with the information that work would start in two days' time adapting the church and then installing the organ.

James Folds introduced Helen, as the wife of the colliery general manager at Martins Main, and mentioned that he too was present tonight, and he noted that Roy had been on the local TV news. Roy slid a little lower in his seat, embarrassed by his fame. The evening was then passed over to Helen. Roy hoped she would cope.

He need not have worried.

Helen explained that she had never run an auction before, so she would explain how she would go about it. People had a list of items to be auctioned but she would not necessarily be following the numbers on the list. The auction would be in three parts: the first group would be general items; the second group would be the toys and games for children, and she hoped that the children would bid themselves, with guidance by their parents. The final group would include the major items. Each item would be held up and she would quote its number.

'Now remember,' said Helen, 'I will be looking for any sign that you are bidding. If you scratch your ear or tap your nose I shall take it as a bid – so watch what you're doing! We have a lot to get through before we can have supper.'

The auction got away to a fast start, with some keen bidding that responded to Helen's encouragement. There were many bargains. Willie was holding up the items for the audience to see and Peter had the job of recording the successful bidders and the prices. After twenty minutes the first batch was finished and over forty pounds had been raised. Helen paused for a drink of water.

'Now for the children's items,' she said. 'We will take this slowly so that none of you miss out on any item that you fancy.' There was a scattering of children around the hall, most of them sitting on their parents' knees.

Slowly the children got the idea, and the books and toys were sold for good, bargain prices. The last two items were a large doll, fully dressed in a luxurious outfit, and a bright red racing car in its box. In both cases there were several children competing, with the blessing of their parents.

The doll got to over eight pounds and there were just two bidders left. Both the girls adopted the same routine. If their bid was topped, they would look up to their parent and, if they got a nod they would increase the bid. It was a wonderful game as far as they were concerned. In the end, it was a visitor from Wakefield who won it, for nine pounds fifteen shillings.

With the car it was more serious, because the fathers, with the encouragement of the boys, did the bidding. It ended as a contest between two parents. There was laughter round the hall when one of the fathers hesitated. His son shouted out so that everyone could hear him. 'Come on, Dad, you're going to miss it.' The father couldn't risk another outburst from his son, so he got the car for ten pounds, two shillings and sixpence.

The final section included the major items. Joe Horton's year's supply of potatoes was the first item.

'This is a big offer, especially for a large family,' said Helen.

'It will be an even bigger offer if the winner owns a fish and chip shop!' called out a young man at the back of the hall. There were peals of laughter. The bidding got going and there was wide interest. In the end it fetched fifteen pounds.

'Now for the eggs,' said Helen. 'A year's supply of fresh farm eggs; what a wonderful offer.'

'And they are all free range,' put in Joe.

'I think I'll have a go at this,' whispered Roy to Joe.

After the bidding had gone on a while Roy put in a higher bid.

'Oh, there is a bid from a gentleman I know,' said Helen. 'I think he is after me making more chocolate cakes with fresh eggs.'

Roy eventually succeeded and his year's supply of fresh eggs cost him sixteen pounds five shillings. He had no idea if he had got a bargain, or paid over the top, but he was happy that he had supported his wife.

Two visitors from Doncaster contested the painting. They seemed to know the value of the painting and pushed the price up by ten shillings each bid. There was absolute silence in the hall as the bidding went over twenty pounds. It was finally sold for twenty-three pounds.

'Now the final offer for auction – and we have nothing to show you. The artist who did the last painting has agreed to do a painting of the new organ when it is installed in the church.'

'Can I have a starting bid please,' said Helen. There was a pause and she was dreading no interest, when Roy bid ten pounds. That started the bidding, with the two experts from Doncaster and Roy bidding against each other. In the end, Roy was successful with a bid of twenty-one pounds.

Helen thanked everyone for their support and she was relieved that her ordeal was over. The minister thanked her profusely and said that the total figure raised in the auction would be announced at the end of the supper, when the figures had all been added up.

There was then a bustle as ladies appeared from the kitchen and everyone moved out of the way as the men set up long tables down the hall and the ladies loaded them with sandwiches, home-made cakes and trifles for the supper. Helen and Roy sat with James and Gwen Folds and enjoyed each others' company. There was laughter all round when Joe delivered a dozen eggs to Helen at the table.

'Laid for you specially, this afternoon, Mrs Dobson,' he said.

In the car going home Roy looked across at his wife.

'You were wonderful tonight,' he said. 'I didn't know you had it in you to work an audience like that. It was a good total from the auction, at over two hundred pounds.'

'I didn't know you had it in you to perform on TV,' she answered with a grin. 'Thanks for your support, Roy. There are some good folk here in Yorkshire. I think we'll be alright here.'

Sunday 27 September 1964

Sandra was watching the clock and checking the Sunday lunch in the oven. She always cooked a joint of meat on a Sunday, with vegetables and Yorkshire pudding, but she never put the puddings in the oven until her Dad came home. He could never forecast when a union meeting would end. This week he had been more uncertain than usual and he had told Sandra not to expect him before two o'clock. When he came in the door she gave him a careful look to see if he appeared tired or stressed, because she intended to have a talk with him during the afternoon.

'Did the meeting go alright, Dad?' she asked, as she put the Yorkshire puddings in the top of the oven and turned the power up. She put the onion gravy on the stove to warm it up.

'Yes, we sort of got the agreement we wanted, with a bit of a struggle. That dinner smells good; what joint is it today? Do I need the carvers?'

'It's pork and, yes, you'll need the carvers. It will be about ten minutes, if you want to go and get a wash. Tell our David to come down for his dinner. He's been in his bedroom for the last three hours; I hope he's been doing his homework.'

Cobba went upstairs to wash his hands and when he came down he'd put on his old cardigan. Sandra took this to indicate that he was spending the rest of the day at home, probably with a book and his radio.

Both Cobba and David heaped up their plates and ate well, and David even had a second helping of the treacle pudding and custard that was the dessert. Sandra was pleased to see her efforts appreciated by her two men, but her portions were much smaller, in the interests of keeping her figure.

'We've not had a chance to discuss the parents' evening I went to on Thursday night at David's school,' said Sandra.

'How do they treat you?' asked David. 'You must look so different to all the other parents. One of my mates has a father who's nearly sixty.'

'I have no problem,' replied Sandra. 'I explained that your Dad couldn't come because he had a council meeting, so they dealt with me like any other parent. They know the set-up in our family now, anyway.'

'What did the different teachers say about our David?' asked Cobba. 'That's what we need to know.'

'It was generally a good report. There were no complaints about his work; he's good at sport and he's expected to play for the school teams at both football and cricket in the next year or so. He will need to work harder at his maths and science to get good O-level results, though.'

'Why is that, David?' asked Cobba.

'It's the maths teacher we have that puts me off. He's always wittering on about things and he never explains the principles right. It should be better next year because we'll get a different teacher.'

'Next year might be an improvement, David,' said Cobba. 'But you mustn't put all your eggs in that basket. Try to improve this year. If you don't understand something, have a word with me or our Sandra.'

'I doubt if our Sandra can help me,' said David.

'You might be surprised, young man. If I can't help you, then I might know somebody who can,' Sandra replied, with an air of confidence.

'Who do you know? Have you got some boyfriend, or something?'

'As a matter of fact, I do have a friend and he's working in a surveyor's office and studying to be a qualified surveyor.'

'He should be pretty good at maths then,' said Cobba.

That was the end of the conversation, and David went back up to his bedroom. Sandra cleared the table and did the washing-up. When she'd finished she went into the sitting room, where Cobba was reading a book and listening to music on the radio. This was Sandra's opportunity to talk to her Dad.

'Dad, I want to ask you something,' she said in a way that got Cobba's attention right away.

'What is it, lass? Is something worrying you?' he asked, as he put his book down.

'No, it's nothing to worry about, Dad; but I do have a sort of boyfriend. We get on alright together most of the time, but I want you to meet him and see what you think of him. I wondered if you think it would be a good idea to invite him over for a meal some time? Maybe he could also meet our David and see if he can help him with his maths problems. What do you think?'

'That's fine by me. You could make it a Sunday lunch, but not next week, because I have the regular union meeting then. Fix it up and let me know. I take it he's the fellow that you had the tiff with when you wouldn't talk on the 'phone. Is that all sorted out now?'

'Yes, that's all sorted. I'll invite him to Sunday lunch in a few weeks' time, when it suits you.'

'If you cook a meal like we had today, he'll realise what a catch you are,' replied Cobba, with a grin. He stood up and gave his daughter a hug.

Monday 28 September 1964

Roy arrived at the pit hoping that the new week would bring more good news for him. He had not received any communications from Cobba, and he did not want to appear concerned to know the outcome of the special union meeting; he would bide his time and contact Cobba later in the morning. When he entered the office, his secretary, Gordon, was waiting with important news.

'I have just had a message from Mr Franks, the Mines Inspector, saying that he's coming to the pit this morning, and that he wants to do an underground inspection.'

'Damn; that means I will have to alter my plans. Did he say where he wants to go?'

'Not exactly, but he was asking questions about 57s face. I think he wants to go there,' replied Gordon, who was usually right with these predictions. 'I will arrange lunch for you, and do the usual, for the inspector,' he concluded. 'The usual' was to arrange for his car to be cleaned and his car boot filled with a bag of firewood.

'Yes, do the usual, Gordon; we want to keep him sweet. We don't want a bad report about 57s development. You'd better get George on the 'phone, and then I'll speak to Mike, who is probably at 57s supervising the installation work.'

Roy spoke to both men, emphasising that he expected the visit to be to 57s coalface. He wanted arrangements made for the man-riding train to be available in the pit bottom when he went underground, so that they could travel to 57s face without any waiting. Also, they must check that the plan of the support system was posted, showing the transition from the wooden supports to the powered supports. Then he had to sit and wait. Mines inspectors, in Roy's experience, ranged from mischief-makers, who set out to cause trouble and show their power, to genuine mining engineers who tried to work with colliery staff to encourage good practice. He had not met Mr Franks, so he did not know which category he fell into.

In fact, Mr Franks had a laid-back approach. His cup of coffee, which he had on arrival, lasted over half an hour, as he reminisced about his time in Northumberland as a colliery manager and his time in Lancashire as an inspector. He had been posted in Yorkshire for only two months, and this was his first visit to Martins. He confessed that he had heard some disparaging reports within the inspectorate about Martins. Roy decided not to discuss these views, but he emphasised the need for them to go underground as soon as possible to avoid the main shift changeover.

George Turnbull met them at the end of the man-riding roadway and led them to 57s face. He had already travelled the route and given instructions to the men, some of whom gave George a look that said, is that OK, Boss? George usually gave a nod of approval.

The visit went well, and 57s was a hive of activity. The panzer conveyor was installed, and several fitters were working on an extra drive unit. Thirty of the powered supports were installed and a team of men were placing them in position as they were hauled down a special track along the coalface. There were also electricians installing the electrical equipment in the main roadway of the face. The inspector and Roy spoke to each set of men, and the men answered questions put to them. There was no sign of anyone stopping work because the inspector was present. Peter Carter was with the electricians and when he was asked a question by the inspector he explained that he was under close personal supervision and he indicated that the person supervising him was by his side. Roy nodded to Peter, and he was pleased that the lad had given a very proper definition of his status. Peter was obviously working hard because he was sweating profusely as he pulled heavy cables into position.

When they caught up with Mike he was overseeing the men transporting the powered supports to the coalface. After the introductions, the inspector asked questions about the layout of 57s face and its relation to the rest of the pit. Mike took some chalk from his pocket and proceeded to sketch the pit layout on a piece of conveyor belting laid at the side of the roadway. This was how Mike explained a lot of the questions he was asked when travelling underground. He also illustrated the Central Conveying Scheme and how that would significantly improve the efficiency of Martins. There was a long discussion about this before the four of them set out to go out of the pit.

'The mechanisation programme and the major scheme do not give me the impression of a failing pit,' said Mr Franks. 'The stories about Martins must have been wrong, or there are big changes taking place.'

'There are certainly big changes taking place,' put in Mike, before Roy could give his answer.

As a result of the leisurely progress of the tour and the many discussions with the men, it was after two o'clock when the men returned to the surface. After a shower, a sandwich lunch and final discussions, it was nearly four o'clock when Mr Franks left the pit.

As soon as the inspector had left, Roy asked Gordon to come into his office.

'Have you seen anything of Cobba today, Gordon?'

'Yes, he called in the office this morning after you had gone underground with the inspector, but he didn't leave any message,' replied Gordon.

'I wonder if he's still at the pit?' said Roy.

'I doubt it, Boss. He's usually left by this time, unless he has a meeting here.'

Roy pondered for a moment. 'Have you heard anything on the bush telegraph about the union meeting yesterday, Gordon?' he asked.

'Not a whisper, Boss. And Cobba didn't ask to see you. Do you want me to get him on the 'phone at home?'

'I don't like to ring him at home; he'll think we've had a serious accident. But I do need to check something with him before I ring Mr Jenkins tomorrow morning. Just try his home.' Gordon went out and shortly afterwards Roy's 'phone rang.

'Cobba for you, Boss.'

'Put him through, Gordon.' The 'phone clicked.

'Cobba here. You wanted a word with me?'

'Yes, Cobba. I'm sorry I've been tied up with the Mines Inspector all day and couldn't see you. How did the union meeting go yesterday?'

There was a pause, and Cobba didn't reply immediately; he was wary of listening ears on the pit 'phone.

'We need a meeting, Boss. I'll have to talk to you.'

'Right, Cobba, I can arrange that. Are you available tonight?'

'I'm not involved in any meetings tonight,' replied Cobba, cautiously.

'I'll be in touch,' replied Roy.

Roy cleared his desk and left the pit to go home earlier than usual. At home, he described his day to Helen and explained the frustration at not being able to meet the union. He put his plan to her.

'I feel something did not go right at the union meeting yesterday, and I need to meet Cobba tonight. I want you to drop me off at Cobba's house at about eight o'clock; it should be getting dark by then. I'll ring you when I've finished and you can drive round and pick me up. I don't want anybody to see my car parked outside Cobba's house, or it will start tongues wagging.'

'This sounds a bit like a cloak-and-dagger mystery. Is that a part of a wife's role in supporting her colliery manager?'

'It certainly is, and I shall wear my flat cap as a disguise,' replied Roy. And he wasn't joking.

★

Sandra opened the door as soon as Roy knocked.

'Good evening, Mr Dobson,' she said, as she closed the door. 'Dad is in the front room. Can I get you a drink and a piece of my cherry cake?'

'That would be great, Sandra. I think I need a coffee.'

After the small talk, Roy got down to business.

'So you had problems, Cobba?'

'Yes and no. It was all a farce, really. You noted that I brought most of the union committee in to the meeting with you. I did not include one fellow, Luke Marwin, because he was on nightshift and he's an awkward bugger at times. Well, he decided to lead the men who are dead against outside contractors. He trotted out the old arguments: they want the work for Martins' men; Martins' men are as good as any contractors; they don't care if a coalface has to come out of production and some men lose regular jobs – all the usual stuff. Jimmy tried, with me, to put the other arguments, but the meeting wasn't swayed. When we put forward your assurances about the contractors' men having to be members of the union, and the union having responsibility for the safety of the work done by the contractors, Luke Marwin said he did not believe us; he was adamant that we were trying to con the meeting. He insisted that he wanted to be in a meeting with you to hear those promises. I agreed to arrange a meeting and we did then get a motion agreed that if Luke Marwin was convinced on the promises given by you, then the matter would be dealt with at the next union meeting. It should be easier to get it passed then. I think you will have to sweeten Luke a bit. You might suggest that he does the odd workmen's inspection, with Jimmy? That should change his mind.'

While this report was being presented, Sandra brought in the tea and cake, which she placed on a small table in front of the two men. She poured out her father's tea, and then asked Roy if he took milk and sugar in his coffee.

'Am I allowed another piece of cake?' asked Cobba, with a grin.

'Only as a special treat,' said Sandra. 'You must try this, Mr Dobson; it's one of my specialities.'

'I will, Sandra, but I don't want you to tell my wife that you've been feeding me with cherry cake. She doesn't agree with nibbles after our evening meal.' Sandra gave him a big smile with a hint of a wink.

'Well, I think we can sort this out, Cobba,' Roy said. 'You see me, with Jimmy, tomorrow morning and we'll arrange the meeting when you can bring along Luke Marwin. In the meantime I will get some work done on the competitive tender document so that I can quote the conditions from it. That should answer any questions raised from the floor at your meeting. When will that take place? '

'Next Sunday,' replied Cobba. 'There should be fewer members there, as they don't like two meetings in two weeks.'

The rest of the evening was spent discussing the inspector's visit and the progress with 57s installation. Roy asked Sandra to ring and ask Helen to come and pick him up. As he left the house, wearing his flat cap, he looked more like a rent collector than a colliery manager.

Tuesday 29 September 1964

Roy spent the day trying to sort out the issue of outside contractors. He agreed to see the union committee on Thursday afternoon, and Cobba assured him that Luke Marwin would be at the meeting. He'd arranged with the contracting department at Region to send a member of staff over for discussions with him so that they could make a start preparing the tender document for the outside contractors to drive the roadway for the Central Conveying Scheme. The discussions took all afternoon and Roy was careful to ensure the clause on union membership was included. The young man from Region was surprised at this.

'We don't usually have that clause in, with outside contractors,' said the Regional man. 'In fact, it is almost always the other way round; some managers want to be sure that the contractor's men will definitely not be members of the union.'

'It's a special situation at Martins,' replied Roy. 'This contract will work better with that arrangement.' He hoped that the young man would not highlight this back at Region.

So far, Mr Jenkins had not asked him any questions about the outcome of the union meeting, and Roy had avoided telling him the latest position. The weekly output at Martins had been higher than normal and this seemed to avoid detailed questioning from Mr Jenkins.

Thursday 1 October 1964

The meeting with the union committee passed off with no problems. Luke Marwin was polite when asking Roy questions, and seemed a little overawed by being at a meeting in the manager's office. Roy decided that Cobba had been working on Luke, so he treated him with sympathetic respect, emphasising that his aim as colliery manager was to achieve the best arrangements for everyone at the pit. From that approach it was easy to suggest that Luke should accompany Jimmy on some of the safety visits to the Central Conveying Scheme roadway. Luke took the bait willingly, and said he would support the motion at the union meeting on Sunday. Roy decided that he now had a positive answer to give if he was asked any questions about the use of outside contractors. He rang the Regional contracts office and ascertained that the tender documents would be available at the pit the following Tuesday.

Friday 2 October 1964

Janet Hall was visiting Peggy, and they discussed Martins Main and the changes taking place there.

'Bob is working overtime nearly every day, and also Saturdays and Sundays. It's this new mechanised coalface. Everybody seems to be rushing to get it into production. At least his pay packet is bigger than it has ever been. Bob thinks he might be a shift fitter on the face.'

'Gerry's going to have a job on that face, as well,' said Peggy. 'From what he said, his Dad had a word with George Turnbull and asked that Gerry should have the job of cableman on the face. Gerry said that the job would be to watch the loop of the power cable for the coal-cutting machine as it moves along the coalface. He says it'll be easier than filling coal every day.'

'He should be pleased with that.'

'Yes, but the trouble is that he will have to work three shifts.'

'I know, Bob said he would have to work all three shifts as well. It seems as if when they put in these new machines they have to work them every shift. We'll have to have hot water bottles in bed instead of our husbands!' They both had a laugh.

'I think Gerry's Dad was fed up with Gerry always being behind the other colliers on the face, and having to be helped to fill all his coal. I'll bet he thought that having Gerry on an easier job would save him some problems.'

Peggy was looking a little better, but she was still not strong enough to take the older two children to the clinic, so the health visitor came each week to the house. The house was looking cleaner and tidier, and that was making Peggy more cheerful. Janet had also started doing shopping for the Moore household, on a weekly basis. Peggy prepared the list and Janet insisted that Gerry handed over some money before she did the shop in Doncaster. Gerry was glad to pay up rather than having to do the shopping himself. His visits to the Club had also been reduced. One night in the Club he had been happily talking at the bar when one of his mates spoke up.

'I saw thy wife in t' doctors last week, Gerry. She looked buggered. What's tha been doing to her? Tha should be at home looking after her, not swilling theeself in t' Club.' Gerry was speechless at that remark. He did not enjoy his next pint.

★

Sandra rang Terry and asked him to lunch on Sunday, as agreed with her father, and he accepted the invitation. She also suggested that they should take advantage of the warm autumn weather and have a walk along the banks of the river Don this coming Sunday afternoon.

Sunday 4 October 1964

Sandra was in a happy mood; her father had come home from his union meeting with a smile on his face.

'You look happy,' Sandra said.

'Yes, it was a short meeting today, and we got the answer we wanted. Mr Dobson should be happy now,' Cobba replied.

Sandra served the Sunday lunch as quickly as she could.

'I'm being picked up in twenty minutes, and we're going for a walk in Doncaster, along the river bank. So I'll leave the washing-up until I get back, if that's alright, Dad?'

'Yes. You get off while there's still some sunshine left.'

Sandra had dressed in trousers and a warm coat, and she wore walking shoes. Terry had a slight limp from an injury at football the day before. He should have rested his bruise, but he didn't want to disappoint Sandra, so he masked his limp as much as possible.

★

Terry and Sandra held hands as they walked along, and there were other walkers, both old and young, taking some exercise and enjoying the fresh air. Sandra was feeling quite mature and comfortable, like many of the others they passed on the walk.

Are you going to accept the invitation to come to lunch, Terry?' she asked. 'You've never given me a clear answer, and I need to know how many I'm cooking for.'

'I'm sure I will be there. We do normally have a family Sunday lunch, and Mum likes me to be there when Grandma is invited, but I'll sort it out, Sandra, never fear.' Sandra was not too happy with his reply.

As dusk fell early, they had to shorten the walk and re-trace their steps back to the car, but it had been a pleasant afternoon.

★

Terry did indeed have problems with both his parents when he announced that he was invited out to Sunday lunch in Upthorpe.

'Who do you know in Upthorpe?' his mother asked.

'It's just a girl that I met in Doncaster, when I was out dancing.'

'What's her name?' asked his Dad.

'Sandra Green,' he replied, feeling the pressure building.

'What does she do?' asked his mother.

'She looks after her father and her brother. Her mother died nearly two years ago,' he replied.

'Her father is not the union president at Martins Main, is he?' asked his father.

'I think he might be,' replied Terry.

'Come on, lad. What are you thinking about?' His father's voice was raised, reflecting his concern. 'Surely you are not settling for the daughter of a trade union man? Cobba Green is known throughout Yorkshire as a left-wing militant union leader. You have not let her get her teeth into you, I hope?' said Ralph Lacey.

'After all we have spent on your education, and setting you up with good prospects in a job, we expected to see you pick a girl of your own class.' His mother had a catch in her voice and Terry hoped she was not going to cry. He realised he had to defend Sandra.

'She's a very nice girl,' Terry started. 'She was at grammar school and would have gone on to the sixth form, but when her mother died she had to take over the family. She's in charge of running the house, and she does all the shopping and cooking and cleaning.

She actually wants me to go so that I can have a word with her brother, who needs a bit of help with his O-level maths course.'

'I was going to invite your Grandma, next Sunday. I don't think you should go,' said his mother.

'But I've already accepted the invitation, so I've got to go. If you don't believe what I say about her, why don't you invite her to visit us? I'm sure you'll be impressed by her.'

'We are certainly not at that stage,' said Terry's father, with a note of finality to the discussion. But he didn't actually forbid Terry from accepting the invitation, so Terry left the room with relief.

★

A little later, Terry went to the nearest telephone box to ring Sandra. After some small talk he confirmed that he was looking forward to having lunch with them on a Sunday, as he had agreed. Sandra asked that he come prepared to help her brother with some of his algebra maths studies. After the conversation ended, she turned her thoughts to the menu she should prepare for the lunch, and the need to have a cherry cake, in case Terry stayed on to have tea as well.

★

Helen attended the evening service at Upthorpe Methodist Church. There were more people there than usual, as they all wanted to see the progress with the new organ installation. The main change since last week was that the pipes for the organ had been installed and secured to the plinth on the back wall of the church. The plinth was painted with the dark-oak colour of the organ, and the pipes had been cleaned and looked like new. The layout of the church had a completely new appearance. The well for the organ itself was cleaned out and installing the organ was the main objective for the coming week.

Reverend Folds took the service. His theme was 'growing in grace' and he ended his sermon by indicating the new organ.

'We are witnessing within this church a wonderful example of growing in grace taking place before our eyes. It is involving change. The church has had to be altered to accept the new organ. It involves hard work and skill. There has been a lot of hard work and sweat already gone into making the change, and there will be more to come. It involves vision. There was great vision in the decision to bring this organ to Upthorpe. There was also respect and admiration for the past, in the wish to preserve a wonderful instrument bought by our Methodist forefathers in Pontefract. These are the essential features of growing in grace: accepting the need for change; working hard to make it happen; having a vision for what we are aiming for, while preserving the heritage of our past. And what will be the outcome of this growing in grace?' He paused. 'It will be the magnificent sound of great music sent forth from this church to the glory of our God. Amen.'

Peter Carter was sitting with his father. He looked across and saw tears running down his father's face. He reached his father's hand and grasped it. Willie held on to his son's hand. He was full of praise to God that his son was with him to share his moment of supreme joy.

Helen had also noted the emotion experienced by Willie at the end of the sermon. By the end of the service, when the final hymn had been sung and the benediction given, Willie had recovered his composure, but Helen still went over to him. She held his hand and gave him a hug and bent down to whisper in his ear.

'That was an emotional end to the sermon, Willie. The spirit was moving in this church tonight; I also felt it. God bless you, Willie.'

'Oh, thank you, Mrs Dobson,' said Willie. He could say no more, but when he was walking home with Peter he added the rest of his thoughts.

'Mrs Dobson is a lady, Peter; but she might also be an angel.'

Chapter 9

Monday 2 November 1964

George Turnbull was crawling through 57s face for another look at the equipment. He had visited the coalface each day and studied all the different parts of the mechanised system. He had operated the powered supports; he had assisted the fitters coupling the panzer chain; he had observed the build-up of the trepanner, but he decided that he would leave the driving of that machine to the experts. He was determined to be as familiar with the mechanised face as he was with the conventional hand-filled face.

George had also discussed with Mike Darlow the face-end operations, where there would be the largest number of men. There would be two teams cutting and filling coal to prepare the stables for the trepanner at each end of the coalface. There would also be two teams excavating the roadways that would follow the coalface and allow access for the workmen and materials. George realised that the output would be dependent more on the face-end operations than on the coal-cutting machine. He suggested to Roy that it would be more efficient to carry out one shift of the roadway drivage operations on the non-coaling shift.

His body ached so much from scrambling through the powered supports and he wished his body was the slimmer version of George, as he was twenty years ago. But he was full of confidence and he passed this on to the installation workers. After detailed discussions with Mike, George knew that it would be possible to have the coalface in production two weeks earlier than the action programme, and that that would be one in the eye for Reg Jenkins. His wife had asked probing questions as to why he had had to go underground on Saturday and Sunday, but George had assured her that it would not be a regular practice once the face was operational.

★

In the afternoon, Reg Jenkins came to see Roy for a discussion on the latest position at Martins. He explained that there had been major problems at one of his other pits, with water breaking in from some old workings and flooding two coalfaces, and that was the reason he had not been able to spend time at Martins. Roy was sympathetic to the other pit's problems and asked if they needed any help from Martins, but apparently they had all the pumps and staff they needed.

Roy outlined the up-to-date position on 57s face. The installation was nearing completion and they expected to start up the face later in the week. If everything worked satisfactory, he planned to have one full shift on the coalface next Monday, and introduce the second shift the following Monday.

'They have done well with the installation,' said Reg. High praise indeed, thought Roy.

'George and Mike have done an excellent job,' said Roy. 'They have both been underground the last two weekends keeping up the momentum. I am very pleased by their performance. We also had a good visit by the mines inspector to 57s. The other piece of good news is that the union have accepted that we can use outside contractors on the Central Conveying roadway. I've been in touch with the Regional contracts section and the tender document will be ready tomorrow.'

'Now that is good news. I'll have a look at that, and we will have to agree which companies we put on the tender list.'

This was a somewhat changed Reg Jenkins, Roy thought. He was less belligerent in his approach and seemed more sympathetic to the progress at Martins. However Roy decided not to push his luck and didn't raise the matter of the special conditions he'd insisted upon in the tender document.

★

The trustees of Upthorpe Methodist Church were holding a special meeting to decide how to mark the completion of the organ installation. It was estimated that the organ would be available for use in three weeks time, although it would be undergoing testing and sounding before that date.

'We have a great opportunity to have a special event on the Saturday evening, when people can hear the organ and we can also raise some more money towards the costs,' said John Warwick. 'But I must emphasise that the giving to this project has been magnificent. The auction gave the lead, but all the other ideas and events have now taken the total to just short of five hundred pounds. So the special event should be a celebration first, and a fund raiser second.'

'I agree,' said Reverend Folds, who was chairing the meeting. 'Has anyone any suggestions to make?'

'We need a very good organist to show us what the instrument can do,' said Willie. 'Our Peter still has lessons with the organist of Leeds Parish Church, and if the special event is on a Saturday night, maybe he could be persuaded to give a recital?'

'That is a great idea, Willie. Can we leave it to your Peter to ask him and make the arrangements?' said James Folds.

'That is ideal for the organ, but we need other performers as well, to attract a big audience,' said Joe Horton. 'Could we invite some soloists, or even a choir, to also perform?'

'We're now making it into a major event, which is ideal, but we have only three weeks to make all the arrangements,' said John Warwick.

The Church Council decided to aim high. One member was appointed to approach a male voice choir, from a mine near Pontefract, to see if they would perform; another member knew a soprano who appeared in local concerts and musicals, and was to approach her; the ladies agreed to provide refreshments in the schoolroom after the concert; and Reverend Folds agreed to act as chairman for the evening and to introduce the performers. It was then decided that it would be an all-ticket occasion, and that the partition at the side of the church would be opened to allow extra seating so that the audience could reach one hundred and ninety. To make sure that the programme was balanced, Reverend Folds, with help from Peter Carter, was asked to approach all the performers to coordinate their contributions.

At the end of a long meeting, Willie rushed home to talk to Peter, but he found that his son was in bed as he was on dayshift the following day. Willie knew that Peter had been working hard with his supervisor, helping to get 57s face ready for production, and everyone was under pressure now to complete the job. He would have to see Peter in the morning when they both went off to the pit.

Tuesday 3 November 1964

Roy had a meeting with George and Mike, to review 57s installation.

'We are really at the last push now, Boss. All the equipment is at the coalface and it's a case of powering-up everything and testing it,' said Mike.

'That's right, Mr Dobson, but the whole district of 57s needs a good tidy up,' said George. 'I intend to spend tomorrow sorting out the transport system and sending anything that we don't need out of the pit. When we start turning coal we want the whole of 57s district to look as though it belongs to somebody.'

'I agree, George,' said Roy. 'If the mining standards are right, we'll get the output up to the right level. What do you propose then, Mike?'

'Well, we could start cutting coal tomorrow, but I think that we should wait until Thursday. It would be better to arrange a team to take the first cut off on the afternoon shift. 56s coalface is on dayshift this week, and the conveyors and loading point will not handle output from both faces. We could arrange the men to come in at midday before the main afternoon shift. We'll have an expert trepanner driver from the machinery manufacturer available to give our drivers extra training and guidance for the first week, and so we could arrange for him to come on at that time with the men.'

'Right, we'll do that. Are you happy with those arrangements, George?'

'Yes, Mr Dobson, by then I will have the district fully prepared for production. I'll sort out with Mike which men we'll use on that shift and get them organised.'

'We'll only need a part-team,' said Mike. 'We can work the face-ends on the other shifts.'

'That suits me,' said Roy. 'I have to go to Region on Thursday morning to meet with Mr Jenkins to decide which contractors will be on the tender list for the Central Conveying Scheme. If I get it sorted out in reasonable time, I'll probably go underground in the afternoon to see how 57s face performs. It's going to be an important day for Martins.'

'Yes, Boss, but please don't bring Mr Jenkins down the pit with you,' said George. 'Give us a week or two to get everybody up to speed before you bring any visitors.'

'I'll do that, George,' replied Roy with a grin.

Thursday 5 November 1964

In Mr Jenkins' office, the Head of the Contracts Section brought in copies of the tender documents for the Central Conveyor roadway; he gave copies to Roy Dobson and Mr Jenkins.

'This seems an ideal job for outside contractors,' said Reg Jenkins. 'Mr Dobson has isolated the job from the rest of the pit operations and it should be possible to manage the work so that the contractors have to deliver what they promise. Which member of your management team will have direct control of the work, Mr Dobson?'

'I plan to let Mike Darlow have control of this contract. He is Assistant Manager, but I have been impressed with his performance during the last two months. He understands the importance of this part of the Central Conveying Scheme as he had a significant input into its design.'

'I agree,' said Reg. 'Young Darlow will make a good undermanager in the next year or two.'

'The only thing we have to decide, then, is which contractors we put on the tender list,' said the Head of Contracts Section. 'I think we need three, as a minimum, to get a competitive price. We could offer it to the usual big three of the Yorkshire coalfield, if you agree? That's what's been happening with other contracts in the Region during the last six months, and I don't think any of them are overloaded with work at the present time.'

'I agree with having three on the tender list, but I think we should stir the pot a bit,' said Reg Jenkins. 'We can have Cento from Doncaster, and Tyson, the German contractor who was done some good work in the Region recently. Then I think we should put UK Mining and Tunnelling on the tender list. They are a Welsh contractor and I know that they can do a quality job.'

'I don't know the firm,' said the Head of Contracts. 'They have not done any work in the Region, so far. We will have to check their financial strength, but I can arrange that if you like, Mr Jenkins.'

'Yes, you run the rule over them straightaway. But I know that you'll not find any problems on that score; I've worked with them in Wales for several years. Do you agree with my proposal, Mr Dobson?'

'I am just happy that we can use outside contractors on the job, and I would expect that any of the firms should be able to perform to our requirements. However there is some urgency to get the contract let and get the winner on site as quickly as possible; we need them established on site and driving at full speed before Christmas.'

'I'll limit the time to return their proposals, and I'll set a start date on site of 1st December,' said the Head of Contracts.

'Is there anything you can do at the pit, to speed up the start of operations when they are on-site?' asked Reg Jenkins.

'We will be onto that next week, when we get 57s mechanised face away. I intend to switch Mike onto that scheme. We can get the conveyor in ready and make sure the loading point works. The haulage system to the pit bottom is still in running order but we'll check it out.' Roy, thinking on his feet, realised that he would have to leave George to run 57s face and get Mike focused on the Central Conveying Scheme.

After a few general comments, he left the office to drive back to the pit. He knew that he would be in time to go underground with the team going to start up 57s face, if he had a quick lunch. He asked Mr Jenkins' secretary, Rita, to ring Gordon and tell him to have a sandwich ready for when he got back to Martins, as he needed to go underground with the afternoonshift. She gave him a strange look.

'You must be keen, Mr Dobson, to be going underground on the afternoon shift,' Rita said.

'There is something special to see at Martins today, Rita. And remember, one picture is worth a thousand words.' Rita was impressed with his keenness.

★

Back at Martins, Roy eat his sandwich and spoke on the telephone to George, who was underground.

'I'm coming down with the men to 57s, George. Is everything ready to start up?'

'Yes, I think everything's ready. Mike is staying with the machine and will see you there. I am going off to the loading point at the end of the conveyor circuit. We have a scratch team there this afternoon and I don't want any slip-up there stopping the flow of coal. When I am happy that the loading point and the tub haulage system to the pit bottom are working alright, I'll come and join you at 57s. I want to see that machine cutting coal,' replied George.

'That's fine, George, I'll see you later.'

★

Roy changed into his pit clothes in the private bathroom next to his office. He was excited by this visit underground. Equipped with his knee-pads, safety helmet with a cap-lamp and his silver-coloured oil-lamp, he felt dressed for his role as the professional mining engineer and manger of the mine.

As he went down the stairs into the pit yard and towards the man-riding shaft, the men waiting to go underground were surprised to see the pit manager, but they suddenly realised that he was heading for the same place underground as them. They surged forward to the shaft side. The banksman signalled three, for man-riding, to the winding engineman and to the onsetter in the pit bottom. The safety gates on the cage were locked in position and the men moved into the cage; Roy took the last place. There was not the usual banter, as the manager was with them, but the ride was at the usual speed as far as the winding engineman was concerned. The initial acceleration, with full steam power, gave the sensation, even to regular travellers, that they were in free-fall. When the brakes were applied, near the bottom of the shaft, there was the sensation that they were moving back up towards the surface.

It was a small team of men, compared with a normal shift, but in the pit bottom Roy saw how the men were deployed to the various jobs and given clear instructions by the official. When they all moved off to the man-riding train, Roy went with them, and sat at the front with the guard. He used his strong spotlight to identify the standard of the rail track and the roadway supports along the route. The walk from the end of the man-rider to the coalface was nearly half a mile. All the men went to the end of the face where the trepanner was installed. When they reached the coalface they took off their coats and hung them in the roadway and stripped down to their working dress – generally trousers, a vest and knee-pads. Some had a drink of water before they went onto the coalface, as they would be on their knees for a few hours before they had a chance for a bite and another drink.

Mike came off the face to talk to Roy.

'I think we're all set, Boss. We've run the machine; we'll have some supports to move after they've cut twenty yards, to push the conveyor over at this end, but after that it should be straight going to the other end of the face. I'll stay behind the machine to sort that out.'

'Right, you do that, Mike. I'm going to go down the coalface in front of the machine, to see how it performs.'

Roy crawled onto the coalface and squeezed past the machine driver until he was several yards in front of the machine. He then listened to the communications, mainly by Mike, to get the whole system rolling. When the panzer conveyor started running, the driver from the manufacturer started the trepanner and set it hauling forward. The augur head cut into the coal and formed a core of coal. This core hit breaker picks on the augur and lumps of coal were scooped onto the panzer conveyor. With the coal from the other cutting elements on the machine, it formed an impressive flow of coal on the panzer. Roy moved further down the coalface, away from the machine. He noted that the company driver was talking to the Martins driver and explaining to him what he was doing to control the machine. After about fifteen minutes the conveyor stopped and so did the trepanner. The message was passed to Roy that they were changing supports and ramming over the panzer conveyor at that end of the coalface. After ten minutes the panzer started again and the coal loading recommenced. Roy Dobson was thrilled to see the coal being produced. It was a triumph of engineering and he was proud to be a part of it. Looking back up the face he could see that as well as the panzer being rammed over behind the machine, the supports were also being pulled over and set in their new positions. It was a flowing system, just as it had been on the surface mock-up, but now there was over a ton of coal per minute being produced.

Roy then saw that it was the Martins man who was driving the trepanner, and the company man was watching carefully how he performed. Encouraged by the expert driver, he increased the speed of the machine and the flow of coal increased. Roy looked down the coalface and he saw a bright light moving towards him. It was George and he was sweating profusely.

'Is everything in order at the loading point, George?'

'Yes, Boss. The deputy on duty there is an expert on the transport system, and I have told him to stay there all this shift to supervise the lads. He'll be better than me. How is it going?'

'It's going very well, George. Just look at that scene! It is the most thrilling picture in coal mining; a machine smoothly moving along and coal pouring onto the panzer conveyor. And look at the size of the coal! There will be a lot of top-size coal from this coalface, and it will get the best prices in the market. I think this is my best day at Martins so far.'

'It certainly is a grand sight, Boss. We shall just have to keep this machine going up and down this coalface until it becomes dizzy,' said George, with a grin.

They moved along in front of the machine until they were near the middle of the coalface.

'I think we should let the machine pass us now, and see how things are looking behind, as the supports are moved over.'

'Yes, Boss, but I want to talk to the lads as we go through. We will be relying on them as a team from next week. There are some good lads, but one or two that need to lift their game.'

When the man ramming the conveyor into its new position got to them, Roy noticed that he was looking back along the coalface to see that the panzer conveyor was in a straight line. He saw that Roy was looking at him.

'I've been told to keep the panzer in a straight line, if I can,' he explained to Roy.

'You're doing a great job. Just because these panzer conveyors will bend, it does not mean that we want the coalface to have bends in it. A straight coalface always has better roof conditions, and the equipment runs more efficiently. Keep it up.'

As the man moved away from them George came close to Roy.

'He's a young fellow, but he is a first-class workman. He can be relied upon to do a good job,' said George.

They decided to crawl back to where the machine started. When they came to the workman who was following the loop of the power cable for the trepanner, George changed his approach.

'Gerry Moore, I've listened to thy father and given thee the best job on this face. Tha keeps thy bloody eyes and thee hands on that cable every minute of the shift. If that cable gets damaged and it is thy fault, watch out, because tha will have me to answer to. Tha doesn't realise what a lucky fellow tha are. And tha can get used to the idea of coming to work every shift each week. Does tha hear me?' said George, raising his voice.

'Yes, I hear thee,' said Gerry. He was pleased to have this job, but he did not want to say so to George Turnbull.

★

Roy went out of the pit with Mike and George. George had given clear instructions to the deputy in charge of 57s on what they should do to get the trepanner through to the end of the coalface and, if possible, started on the next cut. He wanted a report from him on the telephone when he got out of the pit.

'Come into the office for a few minutes,' said Roy when they got to the pit top. In the office, he produced three bottles of beer, which was a welcome drink, especially to George and Mike who had both been underground since early morning.

'I'm very pleased with what you have both achieved on 57s face. The speed of the development and the efficiency of the installation will not go unnoticed at Region. I know we have to get the teams settled in over the next two weeks, and we will have to negotiate a contract for the face. But as I see it we could have a real winner, here, that could raise Martins into profitability. But we do have other issues to face. We need to prepare for outside contractors to do the Central Conveying Scheme drivage. What I propose, Mike, is that you take over that scheme in total from next week. We have to get the work done ready for the changeover during the holiday next August. So don't arrange any holidays for that week, Mike,' Roy, added with a grin.

'That's fine by me, Boss,' said Mike. 'What about the Fuston seam developments?'

'I realise you have been keeping an eye on them, Mike, but I think George will have to take over those developments, as well as his production faces. The Fuston seam is defined as a part of George's area of responsibility anyway.'

'I appreciate the help that Mike has given me over the last three months, but you can leave it to me, Boss,' said George. 'If you can keep the men cooperating as they have done over the last few weeks, I think we will be alright.'

'I intend to see if I can get a newly-qualified young fellow to do some running about for you, George. We need someone with some motivation and a pair of young legs who can get around your part of the pit and sort out problems before they arise. Anyway, it's late and you guys have had a long day. Off you go and get some rest at home. That's what I intend to do.'

Sunday 8 November 1964

Sandra Green was watching the clock and checking her preparations for Sunday dinner. Her father had popped out to the Club, but had promised to be back at one o'clock sharp. He noticed, before he went, that the house was looking pristine, after Sandra had spent Friday in a hectic bustle of cleaning and polishing. She had lectured her brother David, and her father, that any untidiness was forbidden until after Sunday. She had also told David that he had the chance on Sunday to get advice on any maths problems that were worrying him. She hoped that Terry would be able to demonstrate his mathematical prowess.

It was a traditional Sunday dinner of roast beef, with Yorkshire puddings, roast potatoes, carrots and peas, with onion gravy; the dessert was apple crumble and custard. Everything was under control, so she decided to go upstairs and get changed. Her outfit for the day was a new, cream blouse, a brown skirt and a new pair of low-heeled shoes. She had a new apron that she would wear for the final few minutes of cooking before the start of the meal. Upstairs, she put her head into her brother's room and reminded him that he had to appear downstairs when the visitor arrived and that he should wear some smart trousers and a tie. And, she told him, she didn't want him making any cocky remarks about her and boyfriends. He said that he would behave himself. What he did not tell her about were the firm instructions he had already been given by his father about his conduct.

★

Cobba arrived back home fifteen minutes earlier than he'd promised, to be sure that he was there for Terry's arrival. He'd met Terry's father, who had the reputation of being a good mining engineer but not one with a long-term future in modern mines. He wondered if the son would be similar to his father; and why Terry had opted for another career, rather than the mining industry?

When there was a knock at the front door Sandra was the first to react.

'I'll go,' she shouted.

She opened the door to Terry. He was looking quite smart and he had a small bunch of flowers in his hand, which he held out to Sandra.

'Thank you, Terry,' she said, giving him a quick peck on the cheek. 'Come in and let me introduce you. Dinner will be ready in a few minutes.'

She put the flowers on a table in the entrance hall and took him through to the front room.

'Dad, this is my friend, Terry. You look after him while I finish the cooking.'

They shook hands. Terry was obviously quite nervous.

'I am very pleased to meet you, Mr Green,' he said.

'Come and sit down, lad. I hope you've got a good appetite; our Sandra cooks us some fine meals. This is our David,' he added, as David came into the room. David sat down quickly in the nearest chair. He had no wish to shake hands with Sandra's fellow, and he was not looking forward to discussing his maths problems in the afternoon, but he knew Sandra would insist on him having a session with Terry.

'Sandra says that you play football,' said Cobba, in an attempt to open up a conversation.

'Yes, I play for a local club in section two of the Doncaster league. It's a bit rough in that league, but we are doing quite well. We're fourth in the league now, after we won yesterday.'

'Our David is keen on football and is doing quite well in his school team. Tell him, David.'

'I play in the Colts team, and I've played twice for the second team.'

'That's good,' said Terry. 'You should get into the school first team when you are in the sixth form.'

'The school expect him to be in the first team at both soccer and cricket,' said Cobba, with a sense of pride.

'So, what are you going to do in the sixth form? Have you decided?' asked Terry.

'I'm not sure. We've not discussed it yet,' replied David.

'As far as I am concerned he is going to go into the sixth form. Our Sandra would have done well at school and could have gone on to university if she had been able to continue, but she gave it up when her mother died. There is nothing stopping our David going as far as he wants with his education. What did you study in the sixth form, Terry?' asked Cobba, trying to appear interested but really aiming to test his visitor.

'Well, I did one year in the sixth form but I decided that I didn't fancy an academic career. I was lucky because my Dad was able to get me signed-on with a company of surveyors. I hope to get qualified as a surveyor and then complete the RICS exams. I've passed one year, but there are four more to go. If I can pass the RICS, then there will be plenty of options in property and estate management.'

The discussion ended when Sandra called her Dad.

'Dad, come and carve the meat, please, while I put the other dishes on the table. You can all come through now.'

★

Sandra put hot plates out on the four place-settings and carried the dishes of vegetables from the kitchen. She was delighted to see that the Yorkshire puddings had risen well and were holding their shape and not sinking. She showed Terry to the right place so as to leave the family sitting in their normal places. Cobba came in with a plate piled with slices of steaming-hot beef.

'That was a lovely piece of beef, Sandra. It carved as tender as chicken. Come on, all of you, help yourselves.'

Terry had a good plate of food, but not in the same league as David and Cobba. He smiled at Sandra, which was really to acknowledge that it was a far better meal than he would have had at home, and the company was better than being with his Grandma. Terry did have another slice of meat, but not a full second helping like David. They enjoyed the apple crumble with thick and creamy custard. Sandra felt that her efforts had been successful. She said she would serve a cup of tea in the front room after she had washed up. Terry agreed to help her, which he thought might get him out of further questioning from her father, but Cobba gave him a friendly caution.

'Be bloody careful, lad, in that kitchen. It's our Sandra's territory, and she has strict rules about what anybody is allowed to do in there,' he said with a laugh.

'Go on, Dad. Who d'you think you're kidding?'

However, Sandra gave Terry clear instructions that he should wipe, while she did the washing; he was instructed where to stack the crockery and cutlery, which she would put away later. He came very close to her as she dipped her hands in the soapy water of the bowl.

'It was a wonderful meal, Sandra,' he whispered. 'And it's great to be able to help you in the kitchen.' He leaned over and kissed the side of her cheek.

'Don't get distracted,' she said, with a smile. 'This is work, not play.'

After they'd finished the washing-up and all was cleared away, Sandra prepared a pot of tea and put it along with the crockery onto a tray. Terry carried the tray through into the front room.

'That's what I like,' said Cobba 'a nice cup of tea after a good Sunday dinner.'

They had their tea and there was some more discussion about the weather and Terry's next game of football the following Saturday. That gave Sandra the opportunity to suggest that David should take Terry up to his bedroom and have a session on mathematics. David knew that he had no choice, so he stood up and led Terry upstairs.

★

When Sandra had cleared the tea things away she joined her father in the front room.

'What are your plans for this afternoon, Sandra?' asked her Dad.

'We haven't made any. I think Terry ought to go home by tea-time so that he can see his Grandma, who will be at their house this afternoon. When they've finished upstairs I'll show Terry the rest of the house, and see what his plans are. We'll probably have a piece of cherry cake and another cup of tea, and then he can go.'

'It's up to you, Sandra.' Cobba settled down to read the Sunday paper.

★

The session between David and Terry lasted well over an hour. David had prepared several issues that he needed to understand better, to gain confidence for his exams. They were mainly about calculus and statistics. Terry treated the questions seriously and, using David's textbooks, went through the principles and explained them, firstly to refresh his own memory, and then to try to help David's understanding. David found Terry easy to talk to and his explanations clearer than those given by his teacher at school. When they'd finished, he begrudgingly admitted that his sister had actually picked a useful boyfriend. They went back downstairs.

'Come on, Terry, before you settle down I'll show you the rest of the house,' said Sandra. As she started up the stairs she added. 'You've seen David's room, but you might as well see the rest upstairs, particularly the biggest room, which happens to be my bedroom.'

Terry asked to be excused, to visit the toilet in the bathroom, and he was impressed by the modern bathroom suite and tiles in a peach colour.

'This is Dad's bedroom, but you can see that it's mainly his library.' Sandra just opened the door and Terry was surprised to see shelves filled with books along two walls.

'And this is my bedroom,' she said, as she walked into the front bedroom. 'Dad insisted that I had this room after my mother died, and he allowed me to have new furniture and decorate it to my taste.' There was a dressing-table in the bay window, a large wardrobe and a three-quarter-sized bed. The curtains were pink, with a pelmet made of the same material that matched the drapes on the bed. The bed was topped by a beautiful white eiderdown. The fitted carpet had an elaborate pattern, with pink as its main colour, but at the side of the bed was a fluffy, white rug.

'It's a very beautiful room, Sandra – a real credit to your skill in home design.' Terry was genuinely impressed, especially when he compared it to the dark-brown colours favoured by his mother.

'Thank you, Terry.' Sandra moved close to him and gave him a kiss. Terry put his arms round her and pulled her to him. He gave her a full kiss on the mouth and he felt the thrill of her body close to him. Sandra broke away.

'That's enough,' she said. 'We don't want any evil thoughts downstairs about what we are doing up here on our own. Anyway, I think you should go back home soon, Terry, so that you can see your Grandma.'

'Must I do that?'

'Yes, I think you should.'

This settled the decision, which Sandra announced when they got back downstairs. They all had another cup of tea, with a piece of cherry cake. David thanked Terry for his help with the maths questions. Cobba said he had been pleased to meet Terry and that he hoped they would meet again. Sandra went out with Terry to his car.

'Thank you for coming, Terry. I hope that you've seen that we do have nice houses in Upthorpe, and that we do eat good food,' she said with a grin.

'You can say that, for sure. Thank you very much for inviting me, Sandra. Dinner was great. When can I see you again?'

'I'll give you a ring,' she replied and she walked away without giving him another kiss that might be observed by the neighbours.

★

Back in the front room, Cobba was on his own as David had retreated to his bedroom.

'What do you think of him, Dad?' asked Sandra.

'He seems alright, lass, but it's early days yet. His folks will think they are a cut above us, living where they do in Doncaster. You'll have to see how it goes. But just be careful.'

'I will, Dad. I think he was impressed by the dinner and the house, particularly the design of my bedroom.'

Sandra knew that her Dad was reserving his judgement on Terry.

Monday 9 November 1964

'Has 57s started up alright, George? I know that they left the machine in-cut, ready for a good start, when they finished on Friday afternoon.' Roy was in his office before eight o'clock and was asking George about the staffing and start-up in his part of the pit.

'They must be cutting OK, Boss, because there's plenty of coal reaching the loading point. The men were asking me what they are going to be paid for these shifts, before the contract for the face is agreed. I told them to get stuck in and we would make sure they were well paid. They might not go flat-out though until they know what 'well paid' means.

Have you agreed anything with the union about this, Boss?'

'Not yet, George, but I will get on to it today. I hope that they will do two cuts of the face this morning, even if it needs a bit of overtime to complete the second cut. If they do that then I will feel inclined to be generous, but I will have a word with Cobba some time today.'

★

Roy arranged to see Cobba later in the morning. He wanted to discuss several issues with him. He signed all the statutory reports that required the manager's signature, and then when Reg Jenkins rang he reported the results for the pit for last week and updated the position on 57s for him. Reg asked an important question.

'If 57s face is a success, can you handle the coal at the loading point, and transport it to the pit bottom fast enough to keep the face going?'

'That is a good question, Mr Jenkins. We have to train additional men on that haulage system, but George says he has some good officials available to use there. We could give the Benton seam priority over the Low Moor seam, with the allocation of empty tubs in the pit bottom. But I don't want to do that until we have tried to squeeze a better performance from the coal-winding shaft and all the underground haulage systems. We don't want to gain in the Benton seam only to lose in the Low Moor seam.'

'I agree with that approach, but we must get the potential from 57s face. I want to get more mechanisation systems for the pit, but I can only do that if the results are there to justify the additional capital expenditure.'

'Right, Mr Jenkins, I know what you are aiming for.'

★

During the next hour, Roy was conscious of the coal-winding shaft operating. He could hear the steam exhaust puffing out like a railway engine as each wind was accelerated away, and then when the cage landed he could hear the rattles as the full tubs were pushed out of the cage by empty ones being loaded. Each deck of the cage carried three half-ton tubs, which gave a payload of three tons for each wind. When the Central Conveying Scheme was commissioned there would be two specially-designed tubs per deck, but each one would carry one ton. That would increase the payload to four tons per wind. The challenge was to increase the output with the existing system for the next nine months.

★

Cobba came into the office in the middle of the morning.

'You wanted a word with me, Boss?'

'Yes, Cobba, there are a few things I need to discuss with you.'

'Do I need my mates? I can get hold of Jimmy in a few minutes.'

'No, Cobba. You can brief them after we've talked. Firstly, we need to sort out the pay for 57s face until we get a contract with them. Now, as you know, these contracts are

153

negotiated with the Industrial Relations Department at Region. They will not want to do that until the face is fully manned and settled down. So that will be at least three weeks. We have one shift this week and the second production team will start next Monday. The men are getting used to the equipment and the method of working. They are doing well, so far, and the surface training has certainly helped. I'm hoping that they will get two cuts off this morning, even if they have to do a bit of overtime.'

'You can't expect them to do that sort of performance for some fall-back rate, Boss.'

'I know that, Cobba. I am prepared to pay them a good wage if they can get two cuts each shift this week. What do you suggest?'

'Well, the best wages are earned by 40s face in the Morley seam. They have good conditions and they always complete their task. You could pay them 40s average wage.'

'I could do that, Cobba. It will only apply to the face men. I suppose the men driving the roadways on 57s face can be paid to the contracts for roadway drivage in the rest of the Benton seam.'

'That might not be straightforward, Boss. The roadway drivage is usually on a separate shift from the coal production. Now they will both be taking place at the same time. That might cause some problems.'

'I accept that, Cobba, but I think we should try that. Can you have a word with 57s face team and suggest that you might be able to get that sort of agreement – if they get the performance right during this settling-in period?'

'I'll have a go, and let you know how I get on.'

'The next thing I want to say is that I have put Mike Darlow on full-time responsibility for the Central Conveying Scheme. This is essential to achieve the changeover next year during the holiday week. This means that George is also taking over the Fuston seam development as well as the Benton seam production.'

'That should be no problem for us. What's the position with the outside contractors job?'

'I wanted to fill you in on that as well. We agreed to go out to tender to three contractors. The tenders have to be returned in two weeks and we would expect the winner to be on the job by the middle of November. And the union membership clause is in the tender document, as I described it to you,' added Roy with emphasis.

'That's good,' said Cobba.

'Mike Darlow is getting the conveyors, power supply and all the services onto the job during the next few weeks, so that they can start operating as soon as they are on site.'

Cobba left the manager to go and talk to Jimmy and arrange for them to see 57s men when they came out of the pit. The men were an hour late coming to the surface as they had stayed on to complete the second cut under George's supervision. Martins Main had had a good Monday morning's coal production.

Tuesday 10 November 1964

Peter Carter was at Leeds Parish Church having his weekly organ lesson. When they paused for a break he decided to ask Dr Sloan, his teacher, about the concert to celebrate the new organ at Upthorpe Methodist Church. Dr Sloan consulted his diary and said he would love to attend and play the organ. Peter explained the plans for the concert.

'It's to be a mixed concert: hopefully there will be a male voice choir, and a soprano soloist, and there will be a supper afterwards. So the idea is for a few items from each performer. The minister is chairing the event, so it will no doubt start with a hymn and probably end with one.'

'That sounds really good. What I'll do is pick out a few organ solos that are varied in style and fairly short. They should also show what the organ can do. I have another suggestion, though. We could have your lesson at the church on the week of the concert, and then I can play the items for you to hear them. Then you can tell me what you think of my choices.'

'I'm sure they'll be ideal, and it would be nice for you to try the organ and to show me how to get the best out of it.'

When Peter arrived home there was a message that the minister, Reverend Folds, would call to see him about the concert the following night. Peter was pleased that he had sorted out his part of the concert.

Wednesday 11 November 1964

James Folds was very excited when he arrived at the Carters' house. Peter explained that his father was on afternoonshift and would not be home until later.

'The concert is developing into something rather special, Peter,' said James. 'The conductor of the male voice choir rang me up and explained that the soprano soloist who we've approached, and who has promised to appear, has performed on several occasions at concerts with the choir. They have some items of music that have been arranged especially for the soloist and the choir to sing together. He says that they are very effective, and he wonders if we would like them in the programme.'

'I think that we would!' replied Peter.

'I told him that we must have them in the programme. But it goes further than that; he is suggesting that the choir rehearses that week in the church, along with the soprano soloist. It will give them a chance to sort out their seating arrangements and they will be able to test the acoustics. They'll have their rehearsal next Thursday night, which will be alright as far as the church is concerned. In one piece they will want to use the organ as well as the piano. I thought that you would be willing to play the organ for them, at the rehearsal, and at the concert. Can you be available for the Thursday night?'

Peter said he would and also explained that Dr Sloan, the organ soloist, would be at the church to try his pieces on the Tuesday evening of that week.

'The other exciting thing is that the choir will want a significant number of tickets for their followers. So it's hopefully going to be a sell-out.'

As Peter saw him to the door, James Folds turned to him and squeezed his arm.

'Thank you for all that you are doing for the church with your music, Peter. May the Lord bless you.'

Peter walked back into the house feeling that the new organ at Upthorpe Church was weaving some strange magic over him, lifting his life into new experiences.

Chapter 10

Monday 16 November 1964

It was a chilly morning when the team met at the Enclosure, but the conversation was very positive.

'They wound more coal last week than Martins has done for years and years,' said Cyril. 'And they are winding like bloody hell this morning,' he concluded, looking across to the coal-winding shaft.

'I fancy that they are on three shifts now, in the Benton seam,' said Charlie. 'I'll bet some of those fellows on 56s face will not feel like filling a stint of coal in the middle of the night; I never had to work nightshift when I was filling coal.'

'It was all pit tubs and pit ponies when you were filling coal, Charlie,' said Albert.

'Yes, but we had to know how to get the coal in them days. There was no cutting and shotfiring then. It was a skilled job.'

'Bollocks,' said Albert.

'It's going to affect everyone at Martins,' said Cliff. 'I understand that they have switched some of the deputies around so that they have experienced officials to supervise getting the coal from the loading point in the Benton seam to the pit bottom.'

'It's all bloody change with this manager,' said Albert. 'I'm amazed how he gets away with it. They cut ten strips on 57s face last week with that new machine, and they have got no contract yet. The silly buggers will have a right job negotiating a contract now they have shown what they can do. If I had been there, I would have told them to go slow until we had sorted the contract out.'

'I understand that Cobba negotiated a special rate with the manager,' said Pat. 'Anyway, the men were happy with the rate they got paid.'

'I'm told that this fellow will pay well if men work hard and give their best,' said Cliff.

'The lads who opened out 57s face certainly got some top wages,' said George. 'I saw a pay slip in the Club from one of that team, and it made my eyes water.'

'I wonder what this manager will try next?' said Albert.

'They are out to tender for contractors to drive a trunk roadway for some conveyor scheme,' said Pat.

'Bloody hell, what is Cobba doing,' said Albert. 'We won't be able to recognise Martins if this carries on.'

'But if the pit is a success and the men earn good money, what's wrong with that?' said Cliff.

'It won't last,' replied Albert. 'It's an illusion. I've heard it all before; it doesn't work. When things are going well, the managers get their orders from above, and then they have to have their pound of flesh so they start making cuts and saving money. The result is that the men are worse off and they have to do more work than ever. You can't work with management, you have to fight them. That's the union's job.'

'I don't think we are ever going to change you, Albert,' said Cliff.

'You bloody well aren't,' said Albert, and he marched off.

★

Over breakfast, Helen took the opportunity to have a word with her husband about the concert for Upthorpe Methodist Church's new organ.

'Roy, there's the opening event to commission the organ at the church, on Saturday. I think that it may be a good evening, with organ solos, a male voice choir from Pontefract and a soprano soloist. Gwen Folds was telling me that the tickets are going very well and it's sure to be a sell-out, so we'll have to decide what we are going to do.'

'Are you wanting to go?' asked Roy.

'Certainly, I think we should go. But I've had another thought. Why don't you invite your mother to come for the weekend, and then she can go with us? She's not visited us in Yorkshire, yet, and I am sure she would like to see her grandchildren again.'

'That's a thought. I've been thinking that I haven't been in touch with her as much as I should. When I ring her up I'm always telling her how busy I am with the pit. She always says that she is alright, but I sometimes think she would just say that anyway. How will we get her here?'

'You could see if your sister would like to come as well, and she could bring her. But come on, Roy; think about it. She is your mother; she deserves the best from you. You can have a few hours off from the pit and go down to Nottingham in the car for her on Saturday morning, and take her back on Sunday evening.' Helen was quite forceful in her suggestion and Roy felt suitably admonished.

'You're so right; I'll ring her tonight.'

★

Mrs Dobson senior was flattered by the invitation to stay with her son, and gladly accepted. She explained that she would be on her own, as Roy's sister would be in Manchester on Saturday. Helen ordered tickets for the concert at church and arranged for Sandra to babysit for Saturday evening. Sandra asked if she could bring her boyfriend along and Helen agreed.

Tuesday 17 November 1964

Janet delivered the weekly shopping to Peggy, and they had both unpacked it and put it away in the pantry. Peggy was now looking more obviously pregnant, but her face had more colour and her eyes were brighter. They sat down to have a chat.

'How's Gerry getting on with the nightshift?' she asked.

'So far, he seems OK. He's having a nap now, before he gets ready for the pit. I don't think he likes nightshift, because the kids are noisy on a morning when he wants to sleep.' She leaned over and whispered to Janet, 'And he can't fit his drinking time in at the Club,' she said, with a smile.

'We have that to face next week,' said Janet. 'Bob is fitter on the other shift to Gerry and he's on afternoons this week. He seems to have to do overtime most shifts, with maintenance work on the machines. Of course, I won't disturb him when he wants to sleep during the day, because I'll be at work. There is one thing, though, with all this shift work,' she added with a grin. 'There's no chance of me getting pregnant. We're always passing one another either going to work, or coming back from work. There's no chance for a bit of slap and tickle.' They both had a laugh, and then they heard Gerry coming down the stairs.

'The kids haven't woken you, have they, Gerry?' said Peggy, wondering if she had missed them crying.

'No, I can't bloody sleep. It's a stupid shift is bloody nightshift. You're eating at daft times, working at daft times and trying to sleep during the daytime.'

'You'll get used to it, and then you'll be on dayshift again next week,' said Peggy.

'Have you got everything you need for going to work?' asked Janet.

'I'm not going yet. I don't need to get to the pit until half past nine. There are some of the team get there before nine, and they're there talking about the job, and checking what the previous shift has done and where the machine is. Bugger that for a lark. I spend enough time at the pit without doing any extra time. I'll just need to put up some snap.'

'I'll get that for you,' said Janet, jumping up from the table. 'What is there to put in his sandwiches tonight, Peggy?'

'There's some dripping in the pantry,' replied Peggy. 'He usually takes that. He has four slices and you will have to squeeze them a bit to fit them in his snap tin.' Janet wrapped the sandwiches and fitted them in the snap tin but she pushed in a chocolate biscuit as a surprise for Gerry. She often tried to fit in surprises for Bob when she put his snap up for him.

Janet left them shortly afterwards, to prepare some supper for Bob when he got home. She'd arranged to take Peggy to the doctor again, early the next week, for another check-up.

Thursday 19 November 1964

Peter was in the church with the minister, James Folds. They had come early to be there when the members of the male voice choir and the soprano soloist arrived. James had also been there on Tuesday evening when Peter was having his lesson, and when his teacher, Dr Sloan, was practising his organ solos for Saturday's concert. They had both been pleased at the sounds produced by the organ when played by Dr Sloan, and mesmerised by his playing of the Bach Toccata and Fugue which was to form the finale of his recital.

The members of the choir arrived in several cars. They popped their heads round the door and when they saw that the conductor had not yet arrived they went back outside, some of them for a cigarette. When the conductor arrived he was accompanied by the soprano soloist. The conductor was a young man who clearly had a magnetic personality as far as the choir members were concerned. They all gathered at the front of the church and waited until he instructed them where they should sit. They answered for members of the choir who could not attend the rehearsal but who would be present at the concert, and seating places were left for them. The choir members were dressed in casual clothes and it was obvious that some of them had worked underground that day, as they had eyes blackened by traces of coal dust.

The conductor introduced himself to James Folds, and shook hands with Peter when James introduced him as the organist. James and Peter went and sat in the congregation seats with the soprano soloist, while the conductor set up his music stand and addressed the choir.

'We'll just loosen up the voices with a couple of pieces before we get down to rehearsing the items for Saturday,' he said. 'It's not very suitable for a church, but let's have a run through Up with the Jolly Roger.'

There were about thirty-five members in the choir and they filled the choir stalls, which were a full row along the back of the church and seats flanked down either side of the organ. After the opening chords from the piano they began to sing with power in all the parts and complete confidence in the notes. With the final bars of the Jolly Roger, encouraged by the conductor, they reached a fortissimo with the first tenors hitting a top-A with such certainty that the other parts could sing flat out without drowning the tenors. Peter stared at the choir and was amazed at the sound made by an unlikely-looking collection of casually-dressed men.

'Bravo,' said the soprano soloist, and she waved at the choir. They smiled at her, satisfied that they were singing well and grateful for the support.

'Just for contrast, we'll sing Deep Harmony,' said the conductor. 'Don't forget, the second verse is a tenor solo with the choir humming in the background; the third verse pianissimo; and then the final verse with all the power you can give, but watch me for the flow of the words.'

The choir sang the hymn unaccompanied, and they leaned slightly towards the conductor, with their eyes fixed on his moving hands. The tenor singing the second verse solo was on the front row, and had a beautiful voice made more effective by the humming of the choir, which blended in perfect harmony, but rose and fell in volume at the direction of the conductor, interpreting the words. The third verse was a whisper, but every word was clear and the harmony was perfect. In the final verse there was a series of breaks to match the words. 'Then shall I see, (break) and hear, (break) and know all I desired or wished below; (break) and every power find sweet employ (break) in that eternal world of joy.' The word 'joy' had a sustained emphasis that depicted the wonder of the eternal world. James Folds was deeply moved.

'That was truly inspiring,' he said out loud, and quite openly. 'I hope you'll sing that for an encore, on Saturday.'

'The acoustics are very good,' said the conductor. 'We'll enjoy singing here, I can assure you.' Then he clapped his hands. 'Now, let us get down to work.' He called the soprano forward.

'We need to practise your main collaboration with the choir while we are all here. I want to hear the effect of using the organ in the final chorus of The Holy City.

The Holy City was a very popular solo by Stephen Adams, which Doris Arnold had arranged for male voice choirs. It had been adapted so that the first verse was a solo and then the choir joined in the chorus. The soprano soloist created a sense of mystery with the first phrase: 'Last night I lay a-sleeping, there came a dream so fair.' When the choir began the chorus there was a shock of power and strength. 'Jerusalem, Jerusalem, Sing for the night is o'er'. In the second verse, the choir hummed as a background for the soloist, and then the soloist sang the chorus. In the third verse, the soloist sang out with great power and in the final chorus, the organ was to join in with the piano, the choir and the soloist. As Peter followed the music towards the final chorus he was full of tension; he had to come in exactly to the tempo of the conductor. He wiped his hands down his trousers to make sure they were not sticky. He hit the chords of introduction to the final chorus and was surprised at the sound when the choir and the soloist joined in; it was very inspiring and reached a dramatic climax in the final notes. At the end, the conductor spoke. 'This will certainly wake up anybody in the audience who's having forty winks on Saturday night. I want to do the last verse again. First tenors, remember I want you to go up on the last note of all. The soloist will have the high notes on the word 'ever' but you will have the highest note on the last word 'more'. Bass and baritones, you can give me all the power you can on those last few bars. Peter, the organ was excellent. You noted that I was taking the final chorus slightly slower. We want you to give it all that you have at the end, but remember that your entry will be the one thing that will stir up all the singers to make the last chorus something special. Right, everybody, we'll take the last verse and the final chorus.'

This time Peter was more confident of his role, and he made some adjustments to the organ to produce more power. It was a wonderful sound.

That is exactly right, Peter,' said the conductor, and his applause to Peter was joined by applause from the choir.

Peter sat with James Folds through the rest of the rehearsal, and he anticipated the thrill of performing to a packed audience; he'd have to make sure he kept his nerves under control. Reverend Folds explained that there would be a hymn at the start of the evening, and one at the end, and that he would like to have the added support of the choir to lead the audience in the singing. Hymn books were passed around and Peter went back on the organ to play O, for a Thousand Tongues to Sing and Love Divine, All Loves Excelling – both Charles Wesley hymns. The conductor rehearsed Love Divine to make sure that the men were singing the correct male voice parts, which added to the magnificence of the tune.

'We're in for something very special, on Saturday,' said James Folds, as he locked up the church and said goodnight to Peter.

Saturday 21 November 1964

The Dobson family had a busy day. Robert and John spent some time showing their grandmother around the house and garden, and enjoyed chatting to her. Roy then dragged his mother off, with the children, in the car to see the surrounding countryside. As they returned up Martins Lane, Roy stopped the car short of the pit yard and gave his mother a summary of the basic facts about the pit. After a few minutes there was a comment from the back seat.

'He's always talking about the pit, Grandma,' said Robert. 'As well as spending all day there, he gets lots of 'phone calls from the pit and he has to go out to meetings at night. Mummy says that he's married to the pit.'

'But I'm sure he is a good manager for the pit,' said his grandmother. 'I think when you grow up, and get a job, you will work hard just like your father.'

'Mummy has said that to us as well,' said Robert and John, in unison.

★

Helen had been making two cakes that she had promised towards the refreshments for the concert. She had also rushed around to tidy up the house, ready for Sandra and Terry who were babysitting. She also prepared them some sandwiches for supper. After tea she finalised the arrangements with Roy.

'We need to go early, as I have to take these cakes. And I understand that it's a sell-out, so we have to be early to get a good seat.' Then she added, as a guilty confession. 'I did, though, have a quiet word with Willie, last Sunday, and asked him to keep three seats for us, so that we could be together.'

'I'm sure Willie will look after us,' said Roy.

★

Sandra and Terry arrived early, so there was no problem for the Dobsons getting to the church in good time. There was a crowd of people going into the church, including some who had come with the choir. True to expectations, Willie went to meet Roy, with his mother and Helen, as soon as they entered the church, and guided them to some ideal seats in the middle of the audience.

'Very glad to see you, Mr Dobson,' he said. 'I'm glad you could come to this concert. It's a big night for our church, and also for our Peter.'

'Thank you, Willie,' said Roy. He noted that Willie was dressed in his best suit, and there was perspiration on his brow as he rushed around making sure that each row was filled up with people. In the end, every seat in the church, and in the extension, was taken, and a few extra chairs were squeezed in for some late-comers.

The choir filed in to their seats, looking very smart in black suits. Peter realised that there were over forty people in the choir for the concert. Then the choir conductor led in the soprano soloist, who was wearing a startling, long, white dress. Reverend Folds followed them and took his place in the pulpit. He welcomed the performers and the audience and pointed to the organ, which he also welcomed to the church.

'We are going to start and finish this concert with a hymn,' he explained. 'Both the hymns are by Charles Wesley. Now, we have not got a thousand people here tonight, but we have some fine singers, so it is appropriate to start with O, for a Thousand Tongues to Sing. Ladies, you will have to try very hard tonight to hold your own against all these male voices. We will be singing to the tune Lydia.'

Peter played two lines of the tune for introduction, while everyone stood up to sing. It was a fine sound, with the choir putting in the male harmonies. As he needed more power from the organ to lead the singing, he adjusted the stops. After the hymn, there was a short prayer by Reverend Folds.

'Lord, we have gathered here tonight to share in a feast of music. We will hear for the first time this organ that has been brought here to enhance the worship in this church. We are glad that music offers so many opportunities for people to play various instruments and also to sing using their voices. We thank you for music in all its forms, and particularly tonight we will experience the wonder of musical harmonies when a choir combine and sing together. All this music we present to your praise and glory. Amen.'

The concert proceeded with the different performers presenting their items. The soloist demonstrated her singing power as she stood at the front, although some of her solos were very quiet and full of feeling. The organ solos showed the range of the organ, again with soft and loud pieces. The choir had a mixture of male voice pieces, from boisterous marching songs to quiet love songs, and they sang one test piece from a competition in Wales that the choir had won. The final item on the organ was the Bach Toccata and Fugue. This was a triumph of fingers and feet, and on the final chords there was an outburst of applause. Dr Sloan left the organ and stood in the centre of the church, taking the applause. He bowed several times, but the clapping continued so he had to give more bows. Peter slipped into the organ seat for the final item by the choir and soloist. James Folds introduced it as The Holy City and said it had been arranged for the choir and the soloist. He didn't mention the organ.

The soloist sang the first verse, and Peter sensed the reaction of the audience when the choir joined in with the chorus. When the third verse was finished, the organ joined the piano with the introductory bars to the last chorus. Then they were off. The singing was far more powerful than at the rehearsal and it reached a dramatic crescendo on the last chord. Before the conductor had ended the singing there was an outburst of applause, and a man near the front stood up and shouted out 'bravo, bravo'. The rest of the audience then rose to their feet and gave the choir and soloist a standing ovation. Peter had never been so thrilled in all his life. Then the conductor beckoned Peter to the front of the church and applauded him, and he had to take a series of bows. The choir were clapping him as well, so he turned and bowed to them. He couldn't see his father, but felt that he had justified the support he had received from his father for his training. Helen, though, did see Willie, standing at the side of the church, and she saw his face full of smiles. He was also wiping tears from his eyes.

Reverend Folds suggested the audience remain on their feet and the concert ended with everyone singing Love Divine, All Loves Excelling to the tune Blaenwern. It was another musical climax, with the male voice choir singing the last two lines of each verse with the harmonies that took them to the top of their vocal ranges, and they lifted the singing to an unbelievable level of intensity. Peter had the organ at full power for the last verse, and a shiver ran down his spine when the whole audience sang the last two lines, 'Till we cast our crowns before Thee, lost in wonder, love, and praise.'

Reverend Folds closed the concert by thanking the choir, the organist and the audience, and then invited them to join in refreshments.

The audience drifted into the schoolroom, and all the talk was of an amazing evening. Never had Upthorpe Methodist Church had such an inspiring event. It was a squeeze to get everybody in the schoolroom, and people moved into other rooms when they had got their tea and cake. Roy's mother said she had really enjoyed her trip to Yorkshire and that she would never forget the concert as long as she lived. Helen had a quick word with Willie, but when Peter came into the schoolroom she made her way over to him. She gave him a big hug and congratulated him on his performance on the organ. Peter was thrilled, and somewhat taken aback, to be given a hug by the colliery manager's wife.

★

It had also been an unforgettable evening for Sandra and Terry. The evening had begun with Sandra, in her usual, efficient way, putting the boys to bed. She talked to them about their Grandma and then read them a story. They were clearly very tired, and when she went back to check them fifteen minutes later, they were both fast asleep, with every indication of staying that way through the night.

'I don't think we shall hear anything from them, tonight,' said Sandra. 'What do you want to do now, Terry?'

'That's a silly question, Sandra, and you know it,' he replied. 'I want to give you a long kiss and hold your body in my arms.'

'Well then, come and join me on this settee.'

Terry gave her a long look, to check that she really did want him to join her. He went over and took her gently in his arms. She grasped him around his neck and kissed him fiercely. Within a matter of minutes they were both aroused and gasping and whispering to each other. With his right hand Terry undid the buttons on her blouse, and he was able to stroke her breasts through her bra. He got no objections to this, and when Sandra slipped her left hand from behind his neck and stroked his chest and stomach, he willed her to feel lower at the swelled-up member in his trousers. He moved his hand from her breasts and stroked her legs, pushing up her dress and exposing her stocking-tops and bare thighs.

Sandra moved away from the kissing, and looked into his eyes.

'You are turning me on, Terry. You can touch me down there if you like. But do be gentle.' She moved lower and, as he renewed the kissing, he looked down to see her open her legs to reveal her pink knickers and the mound of her passion between her legs.

'Oh, Sandra, you are so beautiful,' he said. 'And you have a wonderful, exciting body. I want to excite you even more.' He stroked between her legs, and he felt her gasp with pleasure. 'You are so ready, Sandra,' he whispered, as he felt the dampness through her knickers. He stroked her more and more. Then he slipped off the settee and kneeled on the floor. He slowly pulled her down so that she was laid on the settee with her legs spread wide.

'Take them off,' whispered Sandra, and she arched her back so that Terry could pull down her knickers. She kicked them off onto the floor, along with her shoes. Terry kissed her and she clasped him round his neck while his finger slowly parted her and then went inside. He knew that this was his turn to forget about himself and give her a sexual experience to remember.

'Just relax, Sandra. I'll be gentle and try not to hurt you.'

'You are being gentle, Terry, and you're not hurting me,' she said softly, as she gasped for breath. 'Keep moving your finger and let it go in and out.' She arched her body slightly, as Terry started a slow in–and–out movement.

'Oh, Terry, that is a wonderful feeling, keep going.' She gasped and closed her eyes, and she started little thrusts towards his finger. Terry watched in amazement at the sight of her body movements and he heard her gasping for breath as she moved a bit faster.

'Oh, Terry, keep with me. Do it a bit faster. Oh…. Oh…. Oh….' Terry felt the convulsion and change in her body. He wondered what he had done, and he was relieved when she gasped. 'Stop, stop. That is enough. I can't take any more.' She reached up and pulled his head down and gave him a long kiss. After a few moments, when her breathing had returned to normal, she stood up and pushed Terry down on the settee.

'It's your turn now, Terry,' she said. She started to unfasten the belt on his trousers. 'I'm not going to grapple around. You saw me uncovered, so I want to see him in all his glory.'

She pulled down Terry's trousers and left them on the floor near her knickers, after extracting a handkerchief from the pocket. When she pulled down his underpants she was surprised to see the size of his member. It was thick and long, with a purple head and a tight sack at its base.

'He is big, Terry,' she said. She cradled his sack and then remembered an earlier discussion she had had with her friend Pauline, about blowjobs and oral sex. Pauline had said that she didn't think she would ever be able to do it. Sandra's reply had been that she was sure Pauline would be able to do it if she had a fellow who deserved it. Did Terry deserve it? She thought that he probably did. She bent down and kissed the end and then took the crown into her mouth and flicked it with her tongue. Terry squirmed with pleasure and reached out his hands to Sandra's head.

'Sandra, you are an absolute darling,' he whispered.

Sandra decided she had done enough with her mouth, so she lifted up her head and stroked Terry using both her hands. She knew he could not last long. She threw the handkerchief over just before he burst open and spurted his seed, which kept coming, and coming.

'That was a big load, Terry. Keep still; I need another handkerchief,' She wiped her hands and his subsiding member.

After they had both adjusted their clothes and Sandra had replaced her disturbed make-up, they had a quick tidy-up in the sitting room, and then went for tea and sandwiches in the kitchen. While they were washing up the pots, Terry asked a question.

'Do you think that Mrs Dobson would approve of what we did tonight?' he asked.

'She's a nice lady, Terry, and very religious. I don't want her to suspect anything; so watch what you say and how you look when they return.'

★

When the Dobsons returned, Sandra reported that the children had been very tired and even had difficulty staying awake for their story. She'd checked them in the last half hour, and they were still in the same positions as they had been when they went to sleep. So, they had had a quiet evening, she said.

'Oh, thank you very much, Sandra,' said Helen, as she saw them to the door. 'We've had a wonderful evening at the church, and a concert that we will never forget.' She slipped an envelope into Sandra's hand.

'Thank you very much, Mrs Dobson,' said Sandra. 'We've been glad to help you, and thank you for the sandwiches and cake for supper.'

In the car, taking Sandra home, Terry could not resist a comment.

'An evening like that – and you get paid for it!' he said.

'Don't you be cheeky, Terry Lacey. Remember, I don't need to have an assistant for my babysitting commitments.'

Monday 23 November 1964

It was mid-morning when Roy put the telephone down after he had arranged the contract meeting for 57s face. It would take place on Friday morning, at the end of the third week of production. He was generally satisfied with the progress on the coalface. After ten strips on the first week, they'd managed sixteen strips on the second, but this was on two-shifts production. The new team starting that week had had a few technical problems initially, but they'd got better as the week went on.

This third week had 57s face on afternoonshift and nightshift, with 56s face on dayshift. Roy was concerned that the tempo on 57s face might reduce when the men had less senior management involvement. He felt the vulnerability of multi-shift working on his management control. Martins' performance was improving and last week's output was the highest for two years. How could he keep the output going up? The next hurdle was agreeing the contract for 57s face. A successful contract, that was accepted by the men and gave them a real incentive to improve performance, would be the next move to provide a surge in the life of Martins Main. He had to ensure that an agreement was reached at the meeting on Friday. He needed to talk to Cobba, and he wanted it to be a casual chat. Might it be possible after the welfare meeting on Tuesday evening? He looked at his diary. He had an accountability meeting at Region in three weeks' time to review the pit's financial results. If 57s face was performing well, if the weekly output was even higher than last week and if the outside contract for the Central Conveying Scheme was settled, then he should have a good story to report. That was his objective.

Tuesday 24 November 1964

Roy was at the Upthorpe Club meeting. The meeting had been routine until the agenda got to 'Any Other Business'. One of the committee asked to discuss the brewery that had the contract to provide all the beer and spirits for the Club.

'What's wrong with the beer?' asked Cobba, who had clearly not heard of any problems.

'Oh, there's nothing wrong with the beer,' replied the questioner. 'It's the financial arrangements that I think we should discuss. I have been checking at other clubs around this part of Yorkshire and I understand that the barrelage at other clubs is a good bit higher than this one. That can't be right, as we have a bigger trade than many other clubs; we should have the best barrelage.' Barrelage was the discount per barrel, given by the brewery in recognition of their exclusive deal with the club. It was well known that the discount was used to pay the expenses of the club committee members, and that the higher the discount, the higher the committee expenses.

Cobba quickly entered the discussion to offset the nods of agreement from some other committee members.

'We have the best beer in Yorkshire at this Club, and we want it to stay that way. The brewery gives us a good service and I am not prepared to go begging to them for a bigger barrelage. We all get a good rate of expenses at this Club and we have no right to be greedy,' he concluded.

The committee man who had raised the issue was shocked by Cobba's reaction, and didn't know what to say.

'I propose that this matter is left until we negotiate the next year's contract with the brewery,' said Cobba.

There were nods around the table at this, and the matter was closed. The meeting ended shortly afterwards.

'Can I have a few minutes with you in the office, Boss?' said Cobba to Roy Dobson. 'There's something I want to discuss.'

'Alright; I'd welcome a few minutes on our own.'

When they were in the office, with the door firmly closed, Cobba opened the conversation.

'That bugger who raised the barrelage is the laziest sod on the committee. If there is any hand-out he's always there; if there's any work to do he's always missing. I am going to make sure that the barrelage is raised with the brewery when I choose, not at a time that he thinks it should be raised. If he is involved he will go bragging in the community that he was the one who got any increase. Sorry about that, Boss, but I can't stand idle fellows who are always after anything they can get for nothing.'

'I agree with you, Cobba. I'll back you when you want to have discussions with the brewery.'

'What I wanted to discuss with you, Boss, is an issue with the Home Coal scheme. We have three lorries and they can just about keep up with deliveries, unless we have heavy snow or very bad weather. Now, two of my best men are going to pack up in the near future and I am going to have to make changes. As you know, at the present time all the coal has to be hand-loaded out of railway wagons into the lorries. I noticed last week that you have installed a small bunker that they can drive under and fill up by opening a chute at the bottom of the bunker.'

'Yes, Cobba. We've put that in to load coal that's going to schools and industrial boilers. It holds the one-inch to half-inch size.'

'What I could do with, Boss, is a similar small bunker for the Home Coal, without any shovelling. With that arrangement I could deliver all the coal with two lorries instead of three.'

'I'll look into that, Cobba. It might be possible, but what's in it for me?'

'Well, I would never agree that I suggested this, but there might be a slight change in the size of coal for the Home Coal. At the present time, the agreement is for three-inch to two-inch size. If the Home Coal had some two-inch to one-inch mixed in, I wouldn't object. It would give you more large coal for sale in the commercial markets, and there's always a shortage of that size.'

'Now you're talking, Cobba. If it was one third of the smaller size in the Home Coal mix, I think I could get the money to install a bunker with a conveyor from the Coal Preparation plant. I'll get onto this, Cobba, straightaway. Leave it to me.'

'Thanks, Boss. I will have to sell it as a system to guarantee deliveries of Home Coal on time. The union should back it as they are always getting someone complaining if the coal is delivered late.' Cobba seemed to relax as though that was the end of the discussions, so Roy moved in quickly.

'There is one more thing I would like, Cobba. Are we going to be able to get a contract agreement settled on Friday for 57s face?'

'It won't be easy, Boss, because this is the first mechanised face at Martins, and the Region negotiators have a reputation of insisting on some very high standard performances for these faces. If the standard is too high then there's no incentive for the lads to push for extra strips.'

'I'm aware of your worries, Cobba. But there are other ways of ensuring that the men have a real incentive to increase performance and see the result in increased wages. In the

Midlands we had certain ways of safeguarding the incentives by the way the contract was specified.'

'I'm not familiar with this type of contract, so you'd better give me a few tips, Boss,'

'One important factor is the depth of advance by the trepanner for each cut. In theory, it should be about twenty-seven-inches, but in reality the average advance is less than that, and can be as low as twenty-four-inches. It's important to keep the face line straight, and the men have been trained to do that. Sometimes, in order to keep the face line straight, the panzer conveyor has to be held back in parts of the face, and it can be argued that this causes the average advance to be less than the theoretical advance. Another factor that can help is the number of men in the team. We have staffed the team very tightly at Martins. This is alright if conditions are very good, but if there is extra work cleaning up around the powered supports, or behind the panzer conveyor, an extra man would be required. If that man is included in the team contract and the face runs without him from time to time, then the earnings will increase. If these two factors were established in the contract, then I'm satisfied that the standard performance should be two completed strips per shift. I don't think Region would accept any standard less than that. If the teams achieved twenty strips per week they would have a good wage; if they could get one or two strips extra per week, then they would be on a significantly higher wage.'

'I hear what you say, Boss, and I think I can make a case to get a fair contract. I will bring a chargeman from 57s to the meeting. He will be able to bring out some of the points you've made.'

'I'll appear very surprised if these issues are raised, but I'll do my best to get a fair contract,' concluded Roy.

He had a quick drink with the men at the bar and then went home. He was hopeful that Friday's meeting would reach a conclusion.

Friday 27 November 1964

Roy had two meetings this morning. The first one was with his engineers and the Coal Preparation Manager, to sort out the arrangements for the Home Coal bunker. He had discussed this with Mr Jenkins on Wednesday morning and the Region Group Manager had agreed to the proposal straightaway, as it would give the pit more large coal for the commercial markets. The site for the bunker was readily agreed, and its size settled at one hundred tons. The discussion with the engineers then revolved around how to get the right mixture of coal from the Coal Preparation plant. The solution was to have chutes that could be swung into position and then adjusted to take the required amounts of three-inch and two-inch coal, whenever the bunker required filling.

'Right then, that's agreed,' said Roy. 'I want the work done as soon as possible.' He turned to the Mechanical Engineer. 'I suppose you'll be getting the bunker made by an engineering firm?'

'Actually, I was going to use our own blacksmiths, Mr Dobson. We have the steel for the framework, and plenty of plate for the bunker sides. We will need to purchase a powered door for the bottom of the bunker, but I thought it would be quicker and cheaper to do the job with our own men.'

'I agree to do it with your men if it's organised to happen quickly.'

'I would expect to have it operational in a couple of weeks,' replied the Mechanical Engineer.

'We've already discussed this scheme, Mr Dobson, and we have certainly got all the electrical gear we need to do the job,' offered the Electrical Engineer.

'My plan is to have the bunker full each morning, and I would think that a hundred tons will be enough for a day's work for the Home Coal lads,' said the Coal Preparation Manager.

Roy closed the meeting and he was certain that he had delivered a good deal for Cobba – and in a short timescale.

★

At the beginning of the second meeting the union team was very wary of the Regional Negotiator. He was negotiating contracts every day, around the Region, and tended to talk down to the Martins men. Roy decided to get down to the specifics for the coalface.

'We are setting a contract here for the men on the coalface. We've agreed that the men driving the roadways will operate to the seam contract for roadway drivage. You can confirm that that is the position for 57s face, can't you, Cobba?'

'Yes, Mr Dobson, the men have agreed to that.'

'That is a little unusual,' said the Regional Negotiator. 'We usually establish a contract covering all the men on the coalface, which includes the roadway drivage men.'

'Well, as 57s face can only work two shifts, one of the shifts for roadway drivage will be on the non-coaling shift. This will help them to carry out their work without any interference from the coal production operations. They have accepted this arrangement,' said Roy. 'I think we should consider the manning of the face team.'

This was tabled and the Regional Negotiator said that the numbers looked about right.

'I am not sure about that,' said the chargeman, who was sitting alongside Cobba. 'It's a small team on 57s. You know that you have kept the manpower tight, Mr Dobson. What we have found over the last three weeks is that when there is extra work to do on the face, the team gets behind and the trepanner has to slow down or stop. I think that there should be an extra man on the face, who is flexible and can concentrate on any problems. In fact, if you are keen to get the maximum performance, the flexible man should be the chargeman, who can get stuck in anywhere to keep the job going.'

'The chargeman is specified as a job on some contracts,' said the Regional Negotiator.

'Well, I can accept the chargeman as an additional job in the team,' said Roy. 'I certainly want 57s face to be a winner through good teamwork and organisation.'

So the team size was agreed. It only remained to agree the performance to be achieved each shift. The Regional Negotiator said that the working time at the coalface for 57s men indicated that a performance of more than two strips per shift should be achieved. This was immediately rejected by the union team as too high. After half an hour of argument, with various views expressed by all parties, it was agreed that the standard should be two strips per shift.

The discussion then concentrated on the depth of each cut. The Regional Negotiator insisted that at other installations in the Region, on similar coalfaces, the contracts had a depth of cut of twenty-seven inches. This was contested by the chargeman and the union team as far too high. Many reasons were advanced for why it should be lower, and the union team insisted that the only figure they would accept was twenty-four inches. After a long discussion, Cobba asked Roy a direct question.

'Mr Dobson, you know that the advance so far on 57s has not been anywhere near twenty-seven inches. Can you tell us what the figure has been?'

'I think we'll have a short adjournment, and I'll check the records to see what the average advance has been since the face started,' replied Roy.

The union team left the meeting and Roy sent for the workbook for 57s coalface to assess the number of shears recorded, and the total advance of the coalface, since the start. He was not sure what the figure would be, but he was aware that some of the shears had not obtained a full cut. A clerk brought in the workbook and Roy asked him to work out the figures. After a number of calculations and checks on the figures, he reported that the average advance had been slightly less than twenty-five inches. The Regional Negotiator suggested that there needed to be a review of the method of operation of the equipment to try to increase this figure. Roy stressed with him the importance of reaching an agreement on the contract, and said that he would ask the union to agree an advance for each strip of twenty-five inches.

The union team was called back in and Roy put the calculations from the 57s workbook onto the blackboard in the conference room. The union team spoke strongly that their concerns had been proved right, and this indicated that the twenty-seven inches put forward by the Regional Negotiator was an attempt to con them into an unfair contract.

Roy tried to calm down the arguments and emphasised that he wanted a contract that was fair to all parties. He said he was prepared to settle for an advance of twenty-five inches for each strip in the contract. If that could be agreed, the contract could be finalised and signed. He was sure that the men on 57s would be able to earn good money and produce the coal that the pit needed.

'That's fine, Mr Dobson,' said Cobba. 'But will he agree to that?' he added, pointing at the Regional Negotiator.

'If Mr Dobson is in agreement, I will recommend that it is approved,' replied the Regional Negotiator. 'I must add that I think you have got a lower standard of performance than applies in other pits in the Region.'

'Bugger the other pits in the Region,' said Jimmy. 'We want a contract that is right for Martins' men.'

After the union team had left the office, Roy spent a few minutes seeking to appease the Regional Negotiator regarding the advance per strip. He suggested that the management would work on trying to achieve a higher figure. The aim then would be to use the average that had been obtained over a long period of experience in any future contracts. The Regional Negotiator accepted that this was a sound argument.

Roy felt that he had achieved a good contract, and that 57s men would have the right incentive to produce coal and earn good money.

Tuesday 1 December 1964

Roy Dobson was on his way to the Regional office to meet with Reg Jenkins and the Contracts Branch Manager to select the winning contractor for the Central Conveying Scheme drivage. This was the last issue he needed to sort out before his accountability meeting with Mr Pickersgill. 57s coalface was working to the new contract, and was marginally exceeding the performance set in that contract. The output was such that it was putting strain on the coal handling system. Hauling the loaded pit tubs from the loading point to the pit bottom was the limiting factor. Roy had suggested to George Turnbull that he spend some time on the haulage system, to try to increase its capacity, even if it required arranging overtime between shifts, so that 57s face was not delayed by haulage stoppages. Roy didn't want men complaining that they were being prevented from producing more tonnage.

In the meeting, the Contracts Branch Manager presented a summary of the three tender submissions. This showed that the highest price was from Cento, but that they gave an earlier completion date for the work. Tyson gave the lowest cost, but their completion date was the latest, and they had not specified what machine they would provide. UK Mining and Tunnelling was a slightly higher cost than Tyson, but they had a machine readily available to do the job.

'You have to make a choice, Mr Jenkins, as any of the three could be selected,' said the Contracts Manager.

'I would like to get UK Mining and Tunnelling onto a job, to bring more competition into Yorkshire,' said Reg Jenkins. 'But I have to admit that this job is critical to Martins, and it must be finished for the holiday week next year. It might be a risk to let the job to them, as they have to set up a local organisation. What do you think, Mr Dobson?'

'I share your fear of offering the contract to a company who has to set up from scratch,' replied Roy. 'It's going to be a challenge to complete the job in good time to allow us to install the conveyors; the sooner it's finished, the better. Therefore I am attracted to the Cento bid.'

'I thought you might say that,' said Reg. He looked at the Contracts Branch Manager. 'Is there any other job in the Region that needs contractors, where we could try UK Mining and Tunnelling?'

The Contracts Branch Manager paused before he answered that question.

'Well, I have been approached informally by the manager at one of your other pits, Mr Jenkins, enquiring about the possibility of outside contractors for a job that he wants doing urgently.'

Reg had a stern look on his face at that statement. 'Right, that settles it, as far as this meeting is concerned,' he said. 'We'll offer this contract at Martins to Cento. But I want you to make sure you draw up the paperwork so that they understand that we will be watching that they stick to their finishing date. We will discuss the other matter outside this meeting.'

'How soon will Cento get the confirmation?' asked Roy.

'We'll get it in the post today,' replied the Contracts Branch Manager.

Roy left the meeting satisfied that he had got what he wanted. He wasn't sure that the other colliery manager would escape a bollocking from Reg Jenkins for approaching the Contracts Branch Manager without going through him. Indirectly, though, Roy thought he could claim that he had helped UK Mining and Tunnelling to get a start in Yorkshire.

★

When Roy got back to the pit he made a call to the General Manager of Cento. When he was put through, after the formalities, he gave the news.

'I am ringing you because I'm led to believe that you will be getting a letter from Region tomorrow. It could be good news for you.'

'I am very pleased to hear that, Mr Dobson,' replied the General Manager.

'What I would like is to arrange for the engineer who will be in charge of the contract to visit Martins in two days' time, so that we can discuss the start date for men being on site, and the way the work will be organised.'

'We will arrange that, Mr Dobson, and make our plans as a matter of urgency.'

'Yes, there is a sense of urgency,' continued Roy. 'I have a very important accountability meeting at Region next week. I want to be able to report, then, that the work on the Central Conveyor Scheme drivage is underway. A report there of a very prompt start to the work will reflect very well on Cento, I think you will agree?'

'I do agree, Mr Dobson. The matter will have my personal attention.'

Thursday 3 December 1964

The Cento General Manger arrived at Martins Main and introduced to Roy and Mike Darlow the young fellow who was to be the Cento Site Manager. After a discussion, the four of them went underground and saw the place prepared for the start of the roadway and the other installations that Mike had arranged. The site was ready for the job to start.

In the office, as they had a sandwich lunch, the General Manager expressed his surprise at the way the job had been set up.

'We often go to start on contracts and find that nobody has done any planning or organised the facilities. We spend the first week chasing up folks at the pit to give us the tackle they were supposed to have provided. Then they wonder why there is a delay on the project.'

'We cannot stand a delay,' said Roy. 'The main reason you got the contract was because you gave us the earliest finishing date. We shall do all we can to ensure you achieve that date.'

Before they left the pit, and after a few 'phone calls, the Cento staff confirmed that they would deliver to site a tunnelling machine on Friday afternoon, and working tools and equipment for the men. Mike said he would have everything taken underground over the weekend so that the Cento men could start assembling it on Monday morning. Cento would have a small team on each shift on Monday, to build the machine. They would have the full complement of men on site later in the week, to commence tunnelling. Roy Dobson was satisfied that the Central Conveying Scheme drivage was off to an early start, and he was confident that Mike would keep it moving.

Friday 4 December 1964

It was a cold, windy morning, and the team at the Enclosure were well wrapped-up with scarves and gloves. They kept moving about to keep their feet from freezing.

'Where's Cliff?' asked Charlie. 'He's usually here well before this time. Is there something wrong with him?'

'He was alright last night, when I saw him in the Club,' said Albert. 'Bloody hell, but there was some drinking going on there last night; I reckon that 57s men are earning some good money now. Some of them were flashing it around.'

'They must be doing well,' said Cyril. 'The pit was winding coal on every nightshift last week, and George was spending a lot of his time on the Benton seam haulage system to try to keep the face going. My mates say they have never wound as much coal.'

'They cut three shears on one shift, on 57s face,' said Pat. 'Now that earns them real money.'

'They're also going to wind the dirt from some drivage or other up the number two shaft,' said Albert.

'That dirt will be from the mining contractor's job,' said Pat Mulligan.

A lorry with Cento painted on its side turned into Martins Lane.

'There you are, that's the company who got the job,' said Pat.

'Well, I am amazed at what this manager can get away with,' said Albert. 'Cobba must have given up as a union man. He's lying down and letting the fellow walk on him.'

'Oh, I don't know about that,' said Cyril. 'I had some coal delivered last week and the driver told me that they have got a new bunker under the screens and they just have to drive the lorries under and open a chute. No more shovelling. We should get our Home Coal delivered without any waiting this winter. I reckon Cobba is looking after himself, and the men, if he can pull off deals like that.'

'I hadn't heard that,' said Albert.

'There's Cliff, coming now,' said Charlie, and he went a few strides out of the Enclosure to meet Cliff.

There were gruff words of welcome to Cliff, and questions about his late arrival.

'I've been delayed. I'm afraid I have some sad news for you.' The Enclosure was suddenly very quiet. 'Walter White passed away yesterday morning. I called to see his sister; she's going to let me know when the funeral is.'

'Poor sod,' said Albert. 'His lungs have been buggered for years. How old was he, Cliff? D'you know?

'Yes, I asked his sister. He was sixty, three weeks ago.'

'He looked eighty,' said Cyril. 'And he has been ill for years.'

'He never had much of a life,' said Albert. 'He never married and he lived with his mother until she died, and then he's lodged with his sister. The poor bugger. The pit got him with the dust. I'll bet all those wealthy folks in the new houses down there don't think about Walter giving his life for the coal they burn.'

'I think we should go to the funeral,' said Cliff. 'It will be at the Methodist church.'

There were murmurs of agreement, but the team were not looking forward to going to church to follow Walter's coffin. The news subdued the discussions that morning, and with the cold wind blowing, it was a short session before they went back to their homes and the warmth of their own coal fires.

Chapter 11

Thursday 10 December 1964

The five men from the Enclosure stood in one pew of the Methodist church, along with eight more, as Walter White's coffin was carried down the aisle and placed on a stand at the front.

Reverend Folds looked at the small number which made up the congregation. He was saddened that a life in Upthorpe could raise only a dozen people to attend his funeral. He was relieved that his wife, Gwen, was there to lead the singing, and he was glad that there were only two hymns in the service. Bertha Pearson, the assistant organist, was playing, and she showed her fear of the new organ by playing all the time on one manual, with no foot pedals and many of the notes omitted.

When he spoke of Walter, James Folds gave a brief resumé of his life as a miner. He also described him as the faithful and loyal son to his mother, while she lived on as a widow. He then referred to his disability from the dust in the mines, which eventually took his life. However he also explained that Walter's sister had confirmed that he had never complained about his health, and that he was patient to the end. James Folds concluded his review of Walter White's life with the following words.

'Walter White was a quiet man, who never had a bad word for anyone. He did his best, whatever he had to do, and he never complained when life was hard and cruel to him. Some folk might think that Walter was a 'nobody', a man of no consequence. But the more I have learned about him over this last week, the more I have realised that, in his quiet way, he always served his family, his friends, and his community, faultlessly to the best of his ability. We can all be thankful for a humble life selflessly lived. When Walter passes over to the other side he will be welcomed with three words. 'Well done, Walter.' Amen.' Even Albert had a lump in his throat.

As they stood together by the church gate, Albert summed up his feelings.

'That parson was right, when you think about it. Walter hurt nobody in his life. The poor bugger deserved better than he got, I'm sorry to say.' The others nodded in agreement.

★

Roy gathered up the thick file of papers that he had been going through at home the previous night. Today was his accountability meeting at Region, with Mr Pickersgill and his senior team. Roy had put on a suit, and a white shirt with a new tie that Helen had bought him. She went over to him and gave him a tight hug and a kiss.

'Don't worry, Roy. You'll be alright. Martins Main is doing much better; you have a good story to tell. I think you are a very good manager; just tell them that.'

'Just think about me at eleven o'clock – that is when I am due in.'

'I'll think of you all day, my love,' she replied.

★

As Roy drove to the pit, he reviewed the situation at Martins. Output had been up in the last few weeks; the results from all the hand-filled coalfaces were improving, as the programme of extending the cutter jibs was nearing completion; 57s face was exceeding its standard, but there were some delays due to stoppages on the haulage system to the pit bottom; the work on the Central Conveying Scheme was progressing, and they were up to programme including the outside contractor's drivage; there had been no disputes for the last three months; the market for the coal was good and Martins was not having to stock coal like some other pits; the financial results were better on a week-by-week basis, although the pit would still lose money for the full financial year. It was generally a good story, but he had to have other cards to play to produce even better results. When the Central Conveying Scheme was completed he had to be able to fill the increased capacity in the coal shaft to get the pit operating with significant profit margins. He needed another mechanised coalface. Dare he suggest this at the meeting?

★

The accountability meeting was to take place in the Regional Director's office and Roy had to wait in the same office where he had waited for his appointment interview. At least he was now known to Mr Pickersgill's secretary. He reflected that a lot had happened since that interview.

'How are you enjoying life at Martins Main now, Mr Dobson?' Diane asked, with a friendly smile.

'Life is a challenge, with limited time for enjoyment,' he replied.

'But you are doing better now, I understand.'

'Yes, the recent results are better, but we still have a long way to go. Does Mr Pickersgill always use his office for accountabilities?'

'Yes, he does. He likes his office and I think it puts the rest of his team on their guard more than they would be if he held accountability meetings in one of the conference rooms. And he has me here to keep things organised. It's a long day, doing all Mr Jenkins' pits.'

Five minutes later, the door opened and a colliery manager came out. He closed the door behind him and then wiped his brow.

'That was a torrid time,' he said. 'No matter how you get yourself ready for these meetings, that Finance Director always raises some figures to grumble about. He's a sour old sod. He certainly got out of bed on the wrong side this morning.'

'He's always like that,' replied Diane. 'It's his Scottish upbringing coming out.' She went into the office to collect some coffee cups. Roy realised that he had never met the Finance Director. His heart missed a beat or two.

'You can go in now, Mr Dobson.' Diane gave him a smile as she held the door open for him.

Roy went in and took the chair at the side of Mr Jenkins, who was sitting at a small table facing the large desk of Norman Pickersgill. Others were sitting at the side of Mr Pickersgill's desk. It was quite clear that the accountability was between the colliery manager and Mr Pickersgill; the others were there to listen, and contribute when they were asked.

'Good morning, Mr Dobson. This is your first accountability meeting. We excused you from the previous meeting, which would have been about someone else's management. But now we have the chance to review three months of your stewardship. We can then discuss the prospects for the future at Martins.'

The next fifteen minutes were taken up with reviewing the brief which had been prepared about the pit's performance and financial results for the three months to the end of September. The results were disappointing, it was said, and the financial loss for the year was significant. Roy was able to explain that it had been a period of reorganisation and installation of the first mechanised coalface at the pit. The Finance Director pointed out that the overtime levels at the pit were higher than the Regional average figures, and he asked why that was. Roy explained that he had used overtime to get 57s coalface into production two weeks earlier than planned, and that this had paid off in the last few weeks.

'Can you quantify the pay-off?' asked Pickersgill.

'The pit has made money on a week-by-week basis during the last five weeks,' replied Roy. 'I appreciate that those results are over a short-time base and that the financial results for the year will be a significant loss, but it does give me hope that Martins can become a profitable pit.'

'I wish I shared your optimism,' said the Finance Director.

'Just a minute,' said Pickersgill, with an angry look at the Finance Director. 'Let the young man tell us more about how he sees the future.' Roy took a deep breath and decided to state his views.

'Well, I think the challenge is to get Martins' men to believe that the pit can be successful. We are making progress; there have been no disputes over the last six months, and industrial relations issues are being resolved without rag-ups. The men have taken to the first mechanised face, and that has lifted the output to higher levels than the pit has seen for years. We have outside contractors doing work for the Central Conveying Scheme; that is on programme for the changeover during the holiday week next year. When that takes place there will be big jobs savings throughout the pit. But more importantly, the shaft capacity will be lifted by one third. It would be an ideal time to introduce a second mechanised coalface to fill that shaft capacity.' Roy paused for breath. He was helped out by Reg Jenkins.

'I agree with Mr Dobson, Sir,' he said. 'A second mechanised face, in September next year, would set the pit up to be really successful.'

'Well, why can't you have another mechanised face?' asked Mr Pickersgill. 'Is there one in the programme?'

'Not at the moment, Sir,' said Roy. 'We have been waiting to see how 57s coalface performed. Not only has the face done well, but we are able to sell all the coal produced at Martins and we have increased the percentage of large coal available for the market. We could get the next face in the Benton seam ready in time for production in September.'

'Mr Jenkins, I want you to sort out to have another set of equipment available for a further mechanised face for Martins.'

'I will do that, Mr Pickersgill,' replied Reg Jenkins.

'And I want you, Mr Dobson, to organise the development of the next coalface in the Benton seam to be ready for production in September next year.'

'Yes, Mr Pickersgill, I will make sure of that.'

'Is there anything else you want to raise?'

'There is just one issue that will affect the long-term success of Martins. We have agreed that the pit should exploit a large area of the Fuston seam in the medium term. This seam is over six-feet thick and has a rock roof. We have now installed a conveyor system into the seam to develop it. I have looked at the conditions again in the last week and I want to discuss the implications with Mr Jenkins. I think that the best way to work the seam could be to drive roadways out, taking the seam and two-feet of the floor, and then retreat the coalfaces back. This method would leave the rock roof in place, and that would make the roadway drivage much easier. I understand that there are some retreat coalfaces being worked at other pits in Yorkshire, and I would like to visit them and check their designs for the roadways and for the coalfaces.'

'I am sure that Mr Jenkins can arrange that. So in summary, I feel that there is a faint ray of hope at Martins. There are opportunities in the near future for the pit to be financially successful and plans are in place to increase the overall output and efficiency of the pit when the Central Conveying Scheme is completed. You have made progress in the few months that you have been at Martins, Mr Dobson. You know more than anybody else that there is still a long way to go. I am pleased with the progress you have made, so keep up the good work and keep the improved results coming. Off you go.'

'Thank you, Mr Pickersgill,' replied Roy, as he prepared to gather up his papers and leave the room.

'How was it?' asked Diane, when he emerged from the office.

'Not too bad. He did acknowledge that we had made some progress, which was nice to know. I'd better get back to Martins, before he changes his mind!' said Roy with a grin as he headed for the door.

'Don't you worry, he'll not do that.'

★

That evening, when he walked into the house, Helen gave Roy a questioning look, and repeated the same question Norman Pickersgill's secretary had used earlier: 'How was it?'

'It was much better than I dared hope. There is no doubt that Mr Pickersgill knows what is going on in his pits. He realised that we had made progress, and he said he was pleased with what I had done. He agreed that we could have another mechanised coalface, next September. He just wants me to keep the improvement going. I have never had praise like that before.'

'I told you that you are a good manager, Roy. I'm proud of you. You can tell Mr Pickersgill that you are a good husband as well.' She put her arms around his neck and gave him a long kiss. It was the prelude to a passionate session of love-making later that night, initiated by Helen, and dominated by her. Roy went to sleep physically exhausted and satisfied, and deeply thankful that he had a wife who inspired him and supported him, in his fascinating life as a colliery manager.

Friday 11 December 1964

Janet Hall was discussing Christmas presents with Peggy.

Peggy was looking very pregnant and when she moved around the kitchen she had to hang on to the table and chairs. While she hadn't had any serious set-back to the pregnancy, her doctor and the health visitors were keeping an eye on her every few days to check her blood pressure and her general health. Janet realised that she would have to do the shopping for the Christmas presents for the children, as there was no chance of Peggy going anywhere to shop for Christmas. It was still two months before her confinement, but Janet was confident that she had everything under control, and she even noted that Gerry now accepted her input to the family.

By the end of the evening Janet had a list of things to buy for the kids, and something for Gerry. She stayed until Gerry came in from the afternoon shift, when she served up the supper that Peggy had prepared for him.

'Have you had a good shift, Gerry?' Janet asked, as she filled his plate with a stew.

'As a matter of fact, we have; we completed three shears today. Why do you ask? Are you interested?'

'Of course I'm interested. Bob always tell me how his shift has performed. I know that the more coal you cut, the bigger the wages. I assume that you have seen some extra money these last few weeks, Peggy?'

'Yes, I have,' said Peggy. 'Gerry has given me more for housekeeping and some extra to spend for Christmas. It's not money that's the problem now; it's me. If only I felt fitter, so that I could do more in the house and for the kids.'

'Peggy, I've told you not to worry. Between me and Gerry we will sort everything out. That's right, isn't it, Gerry?'

'Yes, I keep telling her to rest and do what the doctor tells her,' said Gerry.

'There you are, Peggy, straight from the horse's mouth. You just do as Gerry says. I'll pop in tomorrow night when I've done the weekly shop.'

Janet knew that she was on a mission. It wasn't a chore; she accepted that it was an additional part of her life. She didn't know where it would end, but she was sure that she was filling a need, even keeping this family afloat. Bob also accepted that what she was doing was right, and there was no more talk of trying to start a family as far as he was concerned.

Monday 14 December 1964

Roy was sitting in his office making lists in a notebook. It was the start of Bull week, when the men earned the wages they would draw when they finished for the Christmas holidays. He was not going underground because there was a buzz at the pit. He felt it was better for him to stand back and let whatever it was happen. There was negligible absenteeism, and every job was being done to achieve maximum performance and maximum earnings. He could hear the steam engine at the coal shaft going flat-out and when he checked his watch he noted that they were continuing to wind coal through the snap-time break. Presumably George Turnbull had come to some arrangement with the men to snap each other off one at a time in the pit bottom to keep the shaft winding, and the same arrangement was applying on the surface.

Roy needed to have his thoughts down on paper for the evening event he had arranged for the office staff. He had agreed with Cobba for the pit to have the back room in the Club. There would be a free bar, and the stewardess at the Club was providing refreshments. She had a reputation for catering with good plain food that absorbed alcohol and encouraged the guests to drink more. Roy was confident that his staff would not abuse the free drink and food, but he wanted to talk to them, firstly, to thank them for their efforts since he became manager, but, more importantly, to inspire them with his view of the future of Martins as he saw it.

The review of the latest results at Martins was easy. The output was up, absenteeism was down, there had been no disputes for the last six months, all the output was being sold and there was a demand for more, quality coal, the average earnings for the men were higher than last year and the pit was making a profit on a weekly basis.

The future was what mattered. Roy had to give enough information to keep his team in the picture, but not imply that he had all the answers. There was the Central Conveying Scheme and the efficiencies that would follow, but there would need to be significant redeployment of the men saved. That was not without its complications. There was also the question of a bunker for the coal in the pit bottom. There was nothing in the Scheme to cover that, and it was impractical to expect the coal to arrive in the pit bottom at the same rate that the shaft would wind it. He had his own ideas of how to solve the problem without major capital spending. But was this the right time to explain his ideas? He decided not to use the Christmas event to cover that subject; instead he would wait to play that card with his key staff later. There was to be another mechanised coalface in the Benton seam. Again there would need to be transfers of men onto that face from other parts of the pit. The whole management team needed to work together to solve that issue like they had done with 57s face. And then there was the development of the Fuston seam. He had visited other mines in Yorkshire with retreat coalfaces. The results were impressive, but some of the mines had specialist tunnelling equipment to drive the roadways. There was no chance of Martins getting that type of equipment until its results were on a sound financial basis and the pit was regarded as a certainty to give a good return on any investment. They would have to use conventional cut-and-fill methods to drive the roadways. He would explain his plans for the Fuston seam as he intended to staff-up two teams for this work after the holidays. He would like to use the teams of men who had opened out 57s face, as they could be relied upon to get good results.

The final job to be done on that evening was to hand out letters to the members of staff showing them the review of their performance for the year, and their annual salary for the coming year. Roy had undertaken discussions with the Personnel Department at Region, and was satisfied that several members of staff would receive higher increases than the average. No one had been selected for a zero increase. The few members of staff whose abilities and commitment Roy doubted had been given the benefit of the doubt; but he would sort them out during the next year.

He decided to draft out his final comments that he would memorise before the event. 'My time at Martins has been challenging in many ways, but I have had the support of you all as a willing team. We have made progress. We have achieved successes. We are slowly turning this great ship called Martins Main around. We are not on the right course yet, but we are getting there. I know that there are more challenges facing us for the coming year. Some we know about, and there will be others that we don't know about. But I think that we have to be confident in our ability as a team, and know that if we continue to work together, we can sort out all the challenges thrown at us. So I want to wish you all a wonderful Christmas, and encourage you to take inspiration from the successes that we have achieved. And when you come back after the holiday, you can rely on me to be trying my best as your colliery manager. I hope I can rely on you all to be trying your best in your jobs. And now I've got a blue letter for you all, showing you your salary for next year.'

Roy was satisfied with his final draft, so he took out his diary to check his commitments up to the Christmas holiday. As well as the evening with his staff, there was an evening children's party at the Club for children of Club members. He felt he should put in an appearance at that event. There were two other evening engagements: he had been invited by Mr Pickersgill to a dinner dance at a hotel on the outskirts of Doncaster. Information about this was scarce, as it was a new event that had not taken place the previous year. The organisation seemed to revolve around Diane, Mr Pickersgill's Secretary. Roy had accepted the invitation, and Helen had bought a new evening dress in Sheffield. The dress was knee-length, in midnight-blue satin and Helen had found some high-heeled shoes in matching blue. When she tried the dress on for Roy, and did a twirl, he thought she looked stunning. The final event was on New Year's Eve. Reg Jenkins had told him to put it in his diary and he would give him the details later when they were finalised. Roy wondered if it would be another evening with UK Mining and Tunnelling. For a moment his mind strayed to thinking about dancing with Denise Wallace.

Friday 18 December 1964

The Enclosure was fully staffed and there was a positive flavour to the discussion.

'The manager was in the Club last night, for the children's party,' said Charlie 'I don't remember that ever happening before.'

'Nor do I,' said Cliff. 'I think this fellow has more to him than we thought when he first came to Martins. Do you agree, Albert?'

'Well, I have to say that he seems to have some good points. But it's early days yet. We'll have to see how he's performing in another six months.'

'He's certainly getting some coal out,' said Cyril. 'I had a talk with my mates in the winding house yesterday. They gave me the figures of coal wound up to that time, and this week could be a record for Martins if they keep going today. And they certainly seem to be going flat out now.' He looked at his watch. 'They're winding through snap again this morning.'

'They've started to develop 58s face and I understand that they're getting another set of mechanised equipment, like 57s face,' said Pat Mulligan. '58s should be in production after the summer holiday next year.'

'Well, by that time, each cage will carry four big tubs each, with over a ton of coal in them,' said Cyril. 'That is a big increase in shaft capacity. My mates say that they will have no difficulty in winding the extra coal if the engineer keeps the steam pressure up.'

'There's something going to happen in the Fuston seam, too' said Cliff. 'George is in charge of that now. He's installed conveyors, but what they are going to do is not clear.'

'There are bloody millions of tons in that seam,' said Albert. 'But no pit has had any good results working that seam so far. It has a thick sandstone rock roof that is very hard to work. I hope this fellow knows what he's doing.'

'The manager has been to look at other pits in Yorkshire working retreat faces,' said Charlie. 'But I don't think they were working the Fuston seam. If they go for retreat faces they'll have to drive the roadways first, and then retreat the coalfaces back.'

A lorry loaded with two white-tracked machines turned into Martins Lane. No one in the Enclosure had seen anything like them before. Even Cliff had no suggestion to offer.

★

Roy was in his office when there was a call from his Mechanical Engineer to say that the loading-machines had arrived.

'Unload them near the fitting shop, and I will come down to see them when I've finished my meeting with the union.'

'Right you are, Mr Dobson.'

Cobba had asked to see Roy. He had not stated the reason, and Roy was intrigued to know what Cobba wanted. He hoped that it was nothing to do with Sandra, who was staying the night while he and Helen went to the Regional dinner dance in Doncaster.

'What can I do for you, Cobba?'

'I hope you can spare an hour on Tuesday night, Boss. It concerns the issue of barrelage that was raised at the Club a month ago. I have arranged a meeting with the brewery rep to come and see us on Tuesday evening. I haven't informed the committee, but I would like you there. If we both meet the brewery rep, and we both give the committee the facts at the next meeting, they'll not dare challenge us.'

'Yes, I'll come, Cobba. Will it be hard bargaining?'

'No, I don't expect any problems. But I didn't want that greedy bugger sticking his mouth into the discussions. The brewery rep is a straight fellow; he knows what's going on at other clubs, with other brewery companies, and he'll make sure we get a good deal.'

'By the way, how's the Home Coal set-up working, Cobba?'

'I was going to mention that, Boss. It's first-class. The Coal Preparation team leave the bunker full at the start of each day and the lads just fill up and deliver the orders. We are right up to date and there are no complaints on deliveries. As you know, we are running with one less lorry and the lads are happy. There is the odd grumble when one load gets more than its fair share of the smaller coal, but we just ignore them. How are you getting on with your new gardener?' With the changeover of the Home Coal system, Cobba had suggested that one of his men would make a good gardener for Roy. The existing gardener was nearing sixty-five and wanted to retire. So the changes were agreed and everybody was happy.

'He seems to have settled in, and he's top side of the job,' replied Roy.

'Dennis Gates is also a bloody good driver,' said Cobba.

'I'm already on to that one, Cobba. He's driving us tomorrow night to a function in Doncaster. I might see you then, when I pick up Sandra for another of her babysitting jobs. She'll be staying the night, as we have no idea when the function will finish. It seems to have been organised by Mr Pickersgill, and he has got us all guessing.'

'That's one of his games – to keep his staff guessing,' replied Cobba with a grin, as he left the office.

★

Roy went down to the Mechanical Engineer's office and then he and the enginner went to see the two machines that had been delivered.

'It's years since I saw one of these machines in use,' said Roy. 'I found that they were on stock in the North East Region. They were glad to get rid of them.'

The loading-machines consisted of a central chassis that contained an electric motor. The machine was moved by tank-like tracks on either side of the chassis, which were powered by hydraulic motors. The front of the machine had an angled blade that scraped the floor. At each side of the blade was a paddle that rotated and fed any debris onto a central chain conveyor that ran over the top of the chassis and onto a swivel jib behind the machine.

'I've never worked with this type of machine before,' said the Mechanical Engineer. Roy ignored his cool response.

'I think they will be ideal for our application. I want to use them in the Fuston seam developments. What you need to do is get some of your fitters on a day's training course on these machines at the workshops. You also need to get some sets of drawings. If they work as I think they will, we will have a lot of work for them. They might be an old design, but we will need them to be reliable.'

Roy felt he had partly solved the method of mechanising the Fuston developments.

Saturday 19 December 1964

As he drove over to pick up Sandra, Roy was feeling in a relaxed and happy mood. He had been to the pit that morning and seen the estimated results for the week. It was a record output for Martins, as far as he could ascertain. That was the ideal card to have up his sleeve at the social event in Doncaster.

Sandra was ready and carried a little case out to the car as soon as Roy drove up. Sandra got in the front next to him.

'Good evening, Mr Dobson. Are you looking forward to your evening out?' she asked.

'Yes, I am, Sandra, but there has to be a note of caution when it's the Big Boss who is organising the event. You never know when you will be asked a tricky question. It pays not to drink too much, and to keep your wits about you.'

'That's not my idea of a good night out,' replied Sandra.

When they arrived at the Dobsons' house they got out of the car and the gardener, Dennis Gates, turned the car round ready for leaving. Roy noted he was wearing a white shirt and a dark suit. He was not going to be shown up by the regular chauffeurs who would be around.

In the house, the kids were waiting expectantly for Sandra.

'They're excited at having Aunty Sandra to look after them again,' said Helen, who was ready to leave.

'Oh, Mrs Dobson, you look stunning in that dress,' said Sandra, as she paused to take a good look at the full outfit. 'I hope you have a wonderful evening. I'll look after everything here.'

'Thank you so much,' said Helen, as she left with Roy, feeling that she could enjoy the evening knowing that Sandra was in charge.

★

When they got to the hotel it was clear that a big event was taking place and there were many cars dropping people off at the entrance. Roy had arranged for his driver to go back home to Upthorpe and to return to the hotel for one o'clock in the morning.

Helen took Roy's arm as they entered the large bar area where waitresses were moving around with trays full of glasses of champagne or orange juice. Roy noted that Helen took a glass of champagne and not her usual orange juice. The ballroom was adjacent to the bar area and there was a large display board at the entrance showing the table layout and a list of names for each table. There were sixteen tables around the sides of the room, with a dance area in the middle. Each table had ten seats. There was a stage laid out for an eight-piece dance band. Roy left Helen and went over to check the seating plan. He came back with a shocked look on his face.

'You will not believe this, Helen. We are on Mr Pickersgill's table.'

'That's fine by me,' she replied, with a smile. 'Who else is on that table?'

'Reg Jenkins, the General Manager of Cento, and I think the other will be Pickersgill's secretary. It seems that there's a rep from the different machinery companies and contractors on each table. That's an unusual arrangement. I'm not sure I'm looking forward to this evening,' Roy shook his head. He looked around the room and saw that most of the colliery managers were present, with some senior staff from the Region. It was a select assembly from the Number Two Yorkshire Region of the coal industry.

★

When dinner was called it was easy for Roy and Helen to find the way to their table. What they then found was that the wives were separated from their husbands. Norman Pickersgill had Helen on one side and the Cento General Manager's wife on the other. Roy had Mrs Pickersgill on one side and Pickersgill's secretary, Diane, on the other. When everyone had arrived at the table there were introductions all round. The man accompanying Diane was introduced as her husband, Paul, but he looked an unlikely husband for the sophisticated Diane. More like a farmer than an executive, Roy thought.

There was a microphone in front of Mr Pickersgill's place. When all the guests had found their places, the head waiter called for order 'for Mr Norman Pickersgill, Regional General Manager, to address the assembly.' There was an immediate hush throughout the dining room and, at a signal from the head waiter, all his staff quietly left the room. Pickersgill spoke with his usual quiet voice, but the amplification system ensured that everyone could hear him.

'This is an unusual event,' he began. 'I know that everyone in the coal industry is ready for a break and some relaxation over the Christmas period. Anyone who works for me will definitely have been working hard. I think I can see some of the wives nodding their heads.' He paused and there was a titter of agreement and smiles all round. 'But it is not just people who work for the British Coal Executive who have been working hard. The industry is a partnership between the Coal Executive and the mining equipment manufacturers and the mining contractors. We are all dependent on each other and we have to work together. If we get our partnership right we will have a successful coal industry in the UK, but our suppliers will also be able to develop an export business which will be very much to their advantage.'

'So I decided to try to bring representatives of all parts of our industry together at this event tonight. It was not difficult to get the invitations to our suppliers accepted, and they volunteered to contribute to the cost of the evening.' Another pause and there were more smiles. 'Now, technical discussions are not banned altogether tonight, and I have no doubt there will be some sales pitches, but please remember that we have the table seating plan. This means that any orders from pits in the New Year will be checked against the seating plan to see if any supplier has abused their position.'

'One final point I would like to share with you all: an event like this takes a lot of organising. Most of that organisation has been done by my secretary, Diane, in addition to all the other work I give her.' He indicated to Diane to stand up, which she did, to loud applause.

'Finally, I want to wish you all a pleasant evening and a happy Christmas. Would you all please be upstanding now for grace, which will be given tonight by the lady on my left, Mrs Helen Dobson.' He slid the microphone over to Helen who waited until the shuffling of chairs had stopped and the dining room was totally quiet. Roy looked across at his wife. Her eyes were tightly closed and then she spoke with a clear voice.

'For good food and the fellowship of friends and colleagues, we give you thanks this night, O Lord, Amen.' There were some more 'amens' whispered around the room.

The meal was good quality Christmas food, and the service excellent. Roy noticed that the head waiter made sure that Mr Pickersgill's table had assiduous attention. During the meal he learned more about Diane, and he thought it might stand him in good stead in the future. He also found out that the General Manager of Cento, with his family, had spent several years on mining contracts overseas, and his wife certainly knew what it was like to bring up a young family in the wilds of Africa.

★

When the dancing started, Roy took the opportunity to take Helen onto the dance floor. He wanted to know the answer to the question of the grace.

'When did you know that you were to give the grace?' he asked her.

'It was almost the first thing Norman asked me after we sat down at the table,' she replied. 'He said that he knew I was a practising Christian, and he thought that it was right that a person of true faith should say grace. What could I say? I just took a deep breath and did my best. I think it was alright, because Norman squeezed my hand when we sat down and he thanked me.' Roy drew her very close. He was more thrilled with Helen than he had been with the output figures.

'You were wonderful, darling. Everyone can see what a fortunate man I am, to have a wife like you,' he whispered in her ear.

They exchanged partners for the dances and Helen had one slow waltz with Mr Pickersgill, although he only came up to her shoulders. Reg Jenkins danced with her, but his exploration of her body was less evident than on the previous occasion. Helen wondered if he was wary now because he was aware of her religious beliefs. Denise

Wallace came over from a table at the other side of the room and, after a few minutes of talking, suggested to Roy that they should dance. It was a slow foxtrot, and although she danced close to him, he was not as excited as last time. She did, though, say something of interest to him.

'I understand that indirectly you had a hand in the company getting a start in Yorkshire,' she said.

'Oh, I'm not sure about that,' he answered.

'Yes, you did. And we might get a chance to discuss it some more on New Year's Eve?'

'I'm looking forward to that,' said Roy, as though he knew what the arrangements were.

Near the end of the dance, she surprised him with a last remark.

'You have a truly remarkable wife, Roy. In one sentence tonight she told everyone in the hall a lot about her faith and her personality. I have immense respect for her.'

'So have I,' said Roy, feeling incredibly proud.

★

Roy got a few minutes, towards the end of the evening, sitting and talking with Mr Pickersgill. In answer to some general questions he used the opportunity to report on the excellent results for the Bull week at Martins. Pickersgill's reply was something to remember.

'That is good news, Roy. I thought we had made the right choice when we picked you for Martins. After tonight, I know for certain that we made the right choice. You have a great advantage over many other managers. Every successful manager needs the encouragement and support of a good wife. It was a pleasure to meet your wife tonight; she is a beautiful woman, but she is also a person of great sincerity and strong beliefs. She told me about some of her experiences as a nursing sister in Nottingham. You have to have some strength of character to do that sort of work. You're a very fortunate man, Roy. You must look after her.'

'I will indeed, Sir.' Roy felt that he must say something else. 'It has been a very successful event tonight, Mr Pickersgill. Thank you for inviting us. I complimented Diane on her organisation and she appeared pleased with the way the whole evening has turned out.'

★

When they were back home, and Helen had checked that the children were fast asleep, they decided to have a cup of tea before going to bed. As they sat together, Roy took Helen's hand and looked into her eyes.

'Mrs Dobson, you had an accountability meeting tonight, and you passed with flying colours. Mr Pickersgill said the kindest words about you that you could ever imagine, and he told me I must look after you. I will my darling.' He leaned over and kissed her.

'I am what I am, Roy. He did talk to me a lot and asked me many questions. I told him the truth, as I see it. As you know, I have always needed my faith to get me through the challenges of life.'

Thursday 31 December 1964

Bob Hall was sitting in the kitchen, reading the paper, when the door opened and Janet came bustling in.

'I'm sorry to have taken so long, love, but Peggy is not too good tonight, so I stopped and put the kids to bed. I think they've enjoyed the presents over Christmas, and Gerry has spent some time with them.'

'How are you going to cope when Peggy has to go into hospital?' asked Bob, who was concerned at the amount of time Janet was spending with Peggy.

'Oh, don't worry, Bob. I'll think of some way to fit everything in. Your sister might be able to give us a bit more time. Peggy is going to arrange for her mother to have one of the kids, but she can't manage both of them. It's supposed to be another six weeks before the baby is due, but Peggy looks very pregnant, and she is quite weak. I wouldn't be surprised if the doctor sends her into hospital before the end of January.'

'Look, Janet, you can't do everything. You might have to have a few weeks off work. Why don't you try to arrange to have a month off? Explain the circumstances. They'll understand. If they don't agree, just pack the job in. We can manage on my money now; I have plenty of chances for overtime. I just don't want you to wear yourself out completely. There is me, as well as Peggy and the kids, who depend on you.'

'That was a long speech for you, Bob. I can assure you that I'm sorting everything out. But I do appreciate your support. Poor Peggy is on her own tonight as Gerry has gone to the Club to let the New Year in. But you are here for me. I am so lucky.' She went and gave him a big kiss. She then decided to wear one of her sexy nightdresses to encourage Bob to let the New Year in. He deserved it.

Chapter 12

Saturday 2 January 1965

Roy was sitting alone in the lounge, while Helen and the kids were upstairs in the playroom testing some of their Christmas games. He had been to the pit at lunchtime to check the reports with Mike, who was in charge. The inspections had not reported any serious change in conditions, the ventilation was normal and all the water was pumped out. Roy had insisted that there should be minimum cover over Christmas and New Year, so that the staff could have a real break. In the year ahead there would be so much to do to get Martins on course.

Roy reflected on the past two weeks. His evening meeting with his staff, at the Club, had gone well and he had been asked some good questions, which suggested that a number of the staff were as keen as he was to see Martins improved. In contrast, the meeting at the Club with Cobba and the brewery rep had been a farce. Cobba had briefed Roy on the sort of figure that he considered reasonable for the barrelage but, within five minutes of the meeting starting, the rep had offered a significantly higher figure. Cobba could not bring himself to refuse the offer, so the rest of the meeting was spent chatting about the alcohol trade. Cobba had an offer of barrelage that would surprise the committee and put them in front of the other local clubs, and the rep went away very happy to have the contract for another year.

The New Year's Eve event then filled Roy's thoughts. It had been at a hotel in Leeds, with the Jenkins and the Wallaces. It was equally as up-market as the previous dinner dance hosted by Richard Wallace, in Derbyshire, and Denise was even pushier about the company and their hopes for the future in Yorkshire. But somehow Roy was a little wary of Denise and her provocative dancing. He'd particularly enjoyed dancing with Helen, showing her off as his prize possession. Possibly he wasn't in the mood for corporate entertaining, after the time spent with the family. Their first Christmas in the house had worked very well, and it had been wonderful to see and hear the excitement of the boys opening their presents. Helen had triumphed again.

What were his priorities when the pit went back to work in the morning? Firstly, he must encourage his staff to get the momentum back into operations, like it had been before the holidays. It wouldn't be easy, though. The men were always reluctant to return to work after Christmas; it was a long haul to the Easter break, and there were the dark nights and winter cold to meet them when they came back to the surface after their shifts underground. Secondly, Roy must sort out the developments in the Fuston seam. The staff had been interested in the thoughts he expressed at the staff meeting about the opportunities for retreat working, but George Turnbull had not been too confident when Roy had discussed the method of driving the roadways. He needed to get down on the job with George, and also talk to the workmen. He wondered whether it would be a good idea to seek advice from Reg Jenkins. Thirdly, he had to keep his eye on the progress with the Central Conveying Scheme. The mining work was up to programme, but he would need to hold meetings with the engineers to ensure that all the equipment for the project was on order. Fourthly, he must talk to the Surveyor and get him to draw the layout that he had in mind for a roadway bunker in the pit bottom. He was sure this could be made to work, but it would need some good engineering. Finally, he planned to spend more time with his finance officer. He knew that there must be costs that could be saved at the pit. His finance officer, Jeff Briggs, was new to the pit and he came with many years' experience in the wages offices in the Region. He always approached Roy with great caution, as though he was afraid to disturb him with financial matters. Probably the best way to tackle this would be to have a regular weekly meeting with him. Little did Jeff Briggs know it, but the New Year would be a new experience for him, when he would be encouraged to use all his financial experience to influence the decisions of the colliery manager.

With these thoughts going around in his head, Roy Dobson closed his eyes and fell asleep. Helen found him still sleeping there when she came back downstairs to get the tea ready. She moved about quietly in the kitchen to let her husband continue his nap. He was obviously feeling the effects of a late night out, but the notes on his lap suggested that he had been preparing himself for the pit tomorrow.

Wednesday 13 January 1965

Roy was underground in the Fuston seam developments, accompanied by Reg Jenkins. George Turbull and the development men were at work in the roadway. The seam was fully exposed and two feet of the floor dirt had been taken up. The roadway was twelve feet wide and the total height was eight feet and a few inches.

'This is the size of roadway that we think we need, Mr Jenkins,' said Roy. 'It will allow us to have a thirty-six-inch wide conveyor belt and a track to get any supplies up to the coalface.'

'That looks about right to me,' said Reg. But his main interest was to examine the coal seam. 'Just look at that bloody seam section. If we can't make a name for ourselves working a seam like that, we all want sacking. What do you think, Mr Turnbull?'

'I agree with you, Mr Jenkins; it looks a good prospect. But we need to agree a method of driving these roadways.'

'That is the issue we are trying to reason out,' said Roy. 'We have a coal-cutter to undercut the coal ready for shotfiring, and we have a loading-machine to load out the debris. The trouble is the floor dirt. As the men have pointed out, it's difficult to fire shots in the floor dirt at the same time as firing shots in the coal. One suggestion is to just work the coal seam for a stretch, say thirty yards, setting temporary supports; and then come back and shotfire the floor dirt and load that out and set the final supports.'

'I can see the problem,' said Mr Jenkins. 'It's an unusual system. Setting the supports twice is also inefficient. This sandstone roof is so strong that there is no need to set any supports at all, but the inspector will insist on a clearly-explained support system. What are you planning for the supports, Mr Dobson?'

'There will be a twelve-foot long, six-inch by five-inch steel girder in the roof, with wooden props at each end. These will be spaced at four-feet centres along the roadway,' replied Roy. 'I suppose we could use hydraulic props set to the roof girders when we take the coal out, and replace them with the wooden props when we have taken up the floor dirt?' Roy looked across at the workmen. 'What do you think to that as a solution?'

'We've talked about that, Boss.'

'I do think that we should work the coal out first and then come back to get up the floor dirt. This loading-machine will soon shift either the coal or the dirt. It's a lot easier than shovelling.'

'What do you think, Mr Turnbull?' asked Roy.

'I think we shall have to work the coal and then come back to lift up the floor dirt,' replied George. 'We'll have to work out the best distance to go forward in the coal before coming back. It will affect the number of belt extensions.'

'Don't worry about that,' said one of the workmen. 'This loading-machine will pull the belt in and push it back. We can fix the extension of the belt without any trouble, George.' Reg Jenkins gave Roy a look of disgust at the workmen addressing George Turnbull by his first name.

'Right, we all agree on the method of working,' said Roy looking around at the workmen. 'I'll go and get the Surveyor to draw up the detailed support rules for extracting the coal and getting up the floor dirt. We have to get the support system right. This seam is the future of Martins.'

'You fellows are not development men like you used to be,' said Mr Jenkins. 'You are production men. There will be eight tons of coal for every yard advance that you make. That is a lot of output. These two headings should be capable of over six hundred tons per week, Mr Dobson. Can you lads give us that sort of output?'

'We'll have a go, Boss, if the price is right,' replied one of the men.

'You know the contract will be right,' replied Roy. 'You made good money developing 57s face, I seem to remember.'

'Not bad, Boss, but it didn't last long enough.'

'Ah well, this will be different,' replied Roy. 'You have a thousand yards to go in these roadways. That should keep you busy for a few weeks, or even a few months.' The men grinned at Roy's humour.

Tuesday 9 February 1965

It was a crisp cold morning, with a biting wind blowing around the Enclosure.

'I was told in the Club last night that they have got the developments going now in the Fuston seam. They're driving the roadways out towards the boundary, and they'll retreat the coalfaces back,' said Charlie. 'What do you know about retreat faces, Cliff?'

'Working coal from the boundary back towards the pit bottom has always been recommended as a good method. You leave the problems behind you. But the old mine owners couldn't wait to get the roadways driven to the boundary. They needed the money. So they worked from the pit bottom to the boundary.'

'The rumour is that it's different now, with the mechanised coalfaces,' said Charlie. 'If they have all the roadways driven they just go up and down with the coal-cutting machine, like a bacon slicer. It's a doddle. They just have to shorten the conveyor and let everything fall in behind them.'

'I have heard that some pits are doing well with retreat faces,' said Cliff. 'But some have had ventilation problems, and I think it gets more difficult to keep the roadways open if the workings are at depth.'

'There's no easy bloody method of mining,' put in Albert. 'Don't believe all that the Welfare Club mining engineers tell you, Charlie. They're spinning a tale.'

'It's not gossips that I got that from, Albert. The manager was in the Club last night and he was talking at the bar. Apparently they are driving about thirty yards per week in each of the roadways in the Fuston seam now. The manager said that is giving over five hundred tons of extra output each week.'

'Somebody is doing well,' said Cyril. 'Both shafts are going flat-out.'

'This manager is certainly making a difference. You must agree, Albert. Martins Main has not had a run like this for years and years,' said Cliff.

'Don't you all get conned. I heard last week that the manager has a session with his new finance officer each week, to go into the finance side of things,' replied Albert. 'I told you what would happen. If things are going well he will start clipping away at costs – a bit here, a bit there. This fellow is out to make a name for himself. He wants to have some big profits from Martins. Then he can get promoted. He'll leave it for somebody else to sort out the problems. Colliery managers are all the same.'

'I think that is a bit hard on the fellow, Albert,' said Cliff. 'I've heard some good comments about him. He will talk to workmen and officials, and get their views on jobs. I heard that he stood up for George Turnbull when somebody at Region was trying to shove George out. You have to have guts to stand up to your bosses for one of your own staff.'

'That would be that Welsh bastard,' said Albert. 'I know he has had a go at George a few times.'

'It's George's part of the pit that's getting the extra coal, now,' said Cliff. 'I knew he would be successful if he had the right manager.'

'I've heard that the engineers are shitting themselves at the thought of all the work they have to do in the summer holiday this year, to change to the Central Conveying system,' said Pat.

'It'll be a big job,' said Cliff, 'I'll grant you that. But the manager has put Mike Darlow in charge of that project. He gives people a clear picture of what he wants them to do, then lets them get on with it. That's the way to manage. I heard that he had a meeting with all his staff at the Club just before Christmas. He actually thanked them for the support they had given him while he had been at Martins.'

'That's a bloody first for a colliery manager, in my experience,' said Albert.

'Also, he told them what he wanted them to concentrate on for this coming year. They got some free drinks and free snap, but he marked their cards for this year. I think he will turn out to be a good manager,' concluded Cliff.

'I'm still not convinced,' replied Albert.

An ambulance pulled into Martins Lane. The Enclosure team watched it in silence. An ambulance going to the pit usually meant a serious accident, but on this occasion it stopped at a house along Martins Lane. The medics went into the house and returned assisting a heavily pregnant woman into the ambulance.

'I wonder who that is?' said Charlie. 'At least it isn't an accident at the pit.'

★

Janet went back into the house after the ambulance had left. The two boys were sitting together in a chair by the fire. The older one, Tony, had his arm round his brother, Michael, who was sucking his thumb. They both looked worried at their mother leaving them to go into hospital. Janet had arranged to have two weeks off from her work in Doncaster to help with the children through this period. They had agreed that she would keep both the boys together in their own home rather than splitting them up with one going to Peggy's mother. Looking at their faces she realised that she had to take the boys' minds off their mother.

'Come on, Tony, we'll take Michael out for a walk in his pram. It's a bit cold, but we'll wrap him up in some warm clothes and then put the hood of the pram up. You go and get your coat and a scarf and your cap and some gloves; we must keep you warm.' Tony shuffled off the chair.

'He smells, Aunty Janet,' he announced as he went upstairs for his clothes.

'Right, Tony, I'll change his nappy before we go.' Michael was eighteen months old, but not yet potty-trained, despite his older brother setting him an example.

When they were ready, they left the house and turned along Martins Lane towards the pit. Janet planned to walk to the pit gates and then return to her house to give the boys a drink and some lunch.

When the doctor had decided that Peggy should go into hospital, Janet had put her plan into action. She would look after the children either at her house or at their own. The boys would sleep at their own house. She would sleep at her own home each night, taking over from the boys' father when he went to the pit. Gerry had seen George Turnbull and got permission to work regularly on the dayshift until Peggy was out of hospital. He would not be able to have his regular job, but would be a spare man going anywhere where there was a vacancy. This arrangement meant that Gerry would have to look after the children through the night, and Janet intended that he would also have to visit Peggy each evening in the hospital. He would have little chance for visits to the Club. She would compensate him by having a cooked meal ready for him every afternoon when he got home from the pit. Bob, who was continuing to work on the three-shift cycle, would have to fit in where he could, but at least he would have Janet in bed with him for two weeks out of the three.

Along the road to the pit there was a lot of traffic making a noise and throwing up dust. Janet was surprised at the number of lorries taking coal from the pit. When they got to the pit entrance, the boys were able to watch the colliery loco taking a run of loaded coal wagons down the loop to the main line. Back at Janet's house the boys seemed to be settling down as they had sandwiches and drinks of milk for their lunch. Bob was with them as he was on the afternoon shift. When Bob left for the pit, Janet and the boys went back to Peggy's house to get a meal ready for when Gerry came home.

★

From the start of the new year, Roy had adopted a new pattern to his work as manager at Martins. He tried to do underground visits on three days each week, and he liked to do an underground trip each Monday. On one day, usually Tuesday, he concentrated on administration, with meetings on finance, planning and provisioning in the morning; in the afternoon he held a meeting with his mining staff. He was now better informed on the financial performance of Martins, and able to identify where he needed more support from members of his staff for the control of costs.

Jeff Briggs had raised two issues as possible cost savings. Firstly he'd identified that the steel support costs in the Low Moor seam were higher than in the other seams. Roy found that the spacing of supports had traditionally been at three feet in the Low Moor seam, while the other seams had a spacing of three feet six inches or four feet. He adjusted the spacing to three feet six inches, and this represented a twelve percent cost saving on steel supports in the Low Moor seam. Jeff Briggs had also mentioned the question of manning levels at the pit. With the application of the Central Conveying Scheme later in the year, there would be significant manpower savings. In anticipation of this, he suggested that there should be an immediate ban on any recruitment. In the meantime, all wastage through retirement, dismissals or workmen leaving would give a reduction in the wages cost for the pit. Roy agreed this, and put it to the staff as his proposal. They weren't happy, and suggested it might affect operations in the short term, but Roy decided that the numbers would not be significant, and he was sure there was enough slack in the system.

With his Surveyor, Roy had plans prepared for a roadway bunker. The roadway would be fifty yards in length and fourteen feet wide and twelve feet high. A conveyor in the centre of the roadway, at roof level, would carry the coal into the bunker, and a movable scraper would plough the coal off into the bunker. A panzer conveyor in the side of the roadway, which was set below the floor level, would feed the coal back to the main conveying system. Steel plates from the floor to near the roof of the roadway would retain the coal from the panzer conveyor. The bottom sections of these plates would act as powered doors that could be raised to release the stocked coal onto the panzer conveyor. It was estimated that the bunker would hold up to four hundred tons of coal. When the detailed plans were complete Roy had tabled them at a staff meeting. The concept was discussed and the site of the bunker roadway was agreed. However, Roy accepted that the bunker roadway could not be driven and the equipment installed in time for the pit holiday changeover. It would have to be a priority job immediately after the holidays. The Mechanical Engineer suggested some refinements to the design that would make the bunker more effective, but he was very relieved that it would be commissioned after the completion of the Central Conveying Scheme.

Thursday 11 February 1965

Visiting Peggy in the hospital in Doncaster was not an easy trip; it involved a bus journey from Upthorpe to Doncaster, and then another short bus journey to the hospital. Gerry had gone the first day after Peggy was admitted, and was very noncommittal about her condition when he returned.

Janet had arranged to go today, while Gerry stayed to look after the boys. When she found the ward and the doors were opened for the visitors to go in, Janet saw that Peggy was laid down in the bed, but she wasn't asleep.

'Now then, Peggy, how are you feeling?' said Janet, trying to sound cheerful. Peggy was thrilled to see her and she asked Janet to help her sit up. When she was settled Janet adjusted the pillows to make her more comfortable.

'I am so glad to see you. It's so good of you to come and see me, Janet. How are the boys?'

'The boys are fine, Peggy. Don't worry about them. What is more important is how are you feeling?'

'I don't know, really. They keep coming and examining me, then they take samples, and they are always bringing me pills. I don't know what is going to happen. After the examinations the doctors have a discussion at the end of the bed, but they don't tell me what they have decided. I feel so low, Janet. I wish it was all over.'

'Don't you worry about anything, Peggy. Just relax and try to get your strength up. I'll have a word with the Ward Sister before I go, and see if I can find out when they are going to induce the birth. I gathered from your own doctor that you might have to stay for a while until they are sure that it is right for you and the baby to go home. Are you short of anything? I gave Gerry some fruit juice to bring last night.'

'Yes, he brought that. He didn't say much. I suppose it's difficult for him working and then worrying about the kids. He's not used to it.'

'Gerry's alright. We now have a regular routine that's working well. He looks after the boys during the night, and I go round to them when he goes off to the pit in the morning. If anything happens in the night, he knows he can come to our house and knock me up.

I have to get used to the idea of getting up every morning at five o'clock, though,' Janet added with a laugh.

'I wish I could see the boys, but they don't seem to allow it. I miss them so much.'

'They might let us bring them when you have had the baby.'

'Do the boys ask about me?'

'Of course they do. I talk to them each day about you, and why you are in hospital. They want you to get better.'

'I wish I could,' said Peggy with a sigh. Janet held Peggy's hand to try to cheer her up. Janet thought how worried she would be if she was ill in hospital and didn't know what was happening.

Janet stayed for another half-hour and then she had to leave to catch the bus back into Doncaster. She had a word with the Ward Sister and explained that she had been visiting Peggy, and how she was looking after the family. The nurse was very kind and asked about the other children. She couldn't tell Janet any firm plans about the birth, but she emphasised that they needed to improve Peggy's condition and build up her strength. Janet went away with the feeling that Peggy's case was more serious than she had appreciated.

Sunday 14 February 1965

Gerry had dutifully visited Peggy on Friday and Saturday, so Janet persuaded Bob to go along with her for a change for Peggy. Bob was very shy, being in the ladies ward, and he left all the talking to Janet. There was little obvious change in Peggy's condition, and there didn't appear to be any firm plans of when the birth would take place.

'I think we'll have to get used to our current arrangements for a while,' said Janet, on the bus going back to Upthorpe.

'Will you be alright on your own, this next week? I'm on nightshift,' said Bob.

'Of course I'll be alright. You've been on nightshift before. The only bit we'll have to organise is sorting you out when you get home; I shall be with the boys. The trouble is, I never know if you will be staying on overtime.'

'I can try and avoid the overtime, if it makes it easier for you.'

'No, you carry on as normal. I shall be around. It's just that I don't know where I'll be. At least I'll not be going to work at the shop every day; I'll try and treat it as a holiday.'

'Some holiday!' said Bob.

Tuesday 16 February 1965

At ten minutes past eleven, Gerry Moore was killed in a roof-fall on 56s coalface. Roy Dobson was in his office, having discussions with Jeff Briggs, when his telephone rang. He was annoyed at being disturbed, and it showed in his voice as he answered.

'What is it, Gordon? I didn't want disturbing.'

'I think it's serious, Boss. George needs an urgent word with you.' He put the call through.

'We have a bad accident on 56s, Boss. It's a fall of roof. The fellow who is buried is Gerry Moore. His Dad is on the job trying to get him out. It sounds very bad. I'll go up the face and have a look and then I'll come back to fill you in.' George Turnbull was gasping for breath. He had obviously been running to get to the coalface.

'Right, George, I'll keep my 'phone clear to take a call from you.' He looked at Jeff Briggs. 'We'll have to leave it today, Jeff. It sounds as though we have a major problem.'

★

Roy had been involved in accidents before in his career, but he had not had to handle a fatal accident during the time he had been a colliery manager. His heart was thumping as he walked around the office thinking of all he would have to do if it was a fatal accident: tell the next of kin; inform the unions; bring in the police; inform the Mines Inspectorate; arrange to have a plan made of the accident site; and he would have to try to keep the rest of the pit working to protect the compensation for the widow. He would also have to go underground with the Mines Inspector, to check the site for himself. Then there would be the funeral. Some managers never considered going to the funeral, but he was not sure. He had to show respect for the man who had lost his life. Then the death would have to be considered in the coroner's court and the colliery manager would have to appear. His thoughts went into other aspects of the accident, until his 'phone rang again. It was George.

'He's gone, Boss. They have got to him, but it's too late. It's a massive wedge of rock that's come down. It's taken the supports that were set with it, and the wooden pit props are broken and laid beside the body. It's broken off to a shiny break in the roof, like a fault. It will take a while to get the lad out, as they'll have to break up the rock. I will go back to them and come out with body. Naturally, his Dad is very upset, and I want to keep my eye on him.'

'Right, George, you do that.'

'There's something else, Boss, that makes this a very bad case. His wife is in hospital. She's expecting a kid very soon, but she's not well and there might be complications. I agreed that the lad could work dayshift so that he could visit her in hospital. He's usually on 57s face. He has two very young kids, and a neighbour is looking after them. She's a friend of the family. It needs someone like her to go to the hospital and break the news to his wife. Don't just let anyone go, Boss.'

'Leave that to me, George. I'll put everything in motion and I'll see you when you get out of the pit.' He put the 'phone down and went to the door of his office.

'Gordon, put a call out for Cobba Green, and ask him to come to my office straightaway. But first get my wife on the 'phone; I need to talk to her.'

'Right, Mr Dobson.'

Back at his desk, he was gathering his thoughts when Helen was put through to him.

'What is it, Roy?' she said. 'You don't usually ring me in the daytime.'

'I'm afraid it's the one thing that a colliery manager dreads: we have had a man killed underground this morning.'

'Oh, Roy, I am so sorry for you,' said Helen, with sadness in her voice.

'It's a complicated situation, and I need you to help me, love. The man has switched shifts because his wife is in hospital expecting a child anytime, but she's not well and there could be complications. They have two other small kids and a neighbour is looking after them. She's a close friend and I think she is the best person to break the news to his wife at the hospital; I don't want to leave it to the police. What I am going to arrange is to send you my car, to take you to get Sandra Green. If she will look after the two kids, then you and this neighbour can go to the hospital to speak to the wife. I want you to do it quickly, before word gets out of the pit and rumours start spreading down Martins Lane. Cobba is here now, so I'll get him to ring Sandra.'

'I'll do my best, Roy,' and she rang off.

Roy explained to Cobba what had happened and asked him to ring Sandra to see if she would help by looking after the two Moore children. Cobba got through straightaway and told Sandra to get ready to be picked up. While that was happening, Roy went into the outer office and told Gordon to arrange for one of the drivers from the garage to take Roy's car to his house to pick up Mrs Dobson and drive her for the rest of the day.

'This is going to be a bad day for those two little bairns,' said Cobba. 'He's not been much of a dad to them, but he was better than not having a dad at all.'

Roy's heart missed a beat when he contemplated his own two sons facing a future without him.

★

Underground, Peter Carter was rushing to 56s face with his supervisor, who was an experienced first aid man. They were carrying a box of first aid equipment and they collected a stretcher when they neared the coalface. When they got to the scene, George saw them and went over.

'You won't be able to help him, I'm afraid. But stay until they get him out, and then you can clean him up a bit and load him onto the stretcher. We'll need some young arms to help to carry him to the man-riding train; it's a long walk, and the lad might not be very big, but he will get heavy before we get him out.'

Peter took his turn as four men at a time carried the stretcher. They had taken Gerry's helmet off and wiped his face to remove some blood and some of the dirt before they laid him on the stretcher. Then they covered him completely with a blanket so that the body was not visible. It was a silent procession, with the carriers sweating and stumbling along. George was at the front, and arranged for obstacles to be moved and doors opened to get the party through. Fred Moore insisted in taking his turn to carry his son. Those behind remembered the earlier scene: the cries for help; the rush of men to the fall; the heaving and straining to move the fallen rock; then the sight of the crushed and twisted body when they got to it. Through it all, they had witnessed Fred Moore using all his experience and strength to try to get to his son before it was too late. They were all haunted by the look of despair on Fred's face when he had to accept that he had failed. And they all realised that it could be one of them now laid lifeless on the stretcher. When they reached the man-riding train, Peter was helping to carry the stretcher and he was sweating profusely and gasping for breath. There was a team of men sitting on the train, talking and joking as they waited for it to go to the pit bottom. They probably didn't know about the accident, but that didn't worry George Turnbull when he got to them.

'Get off your bloody arses and show a bit of respect,' he shouted. The men quickly jumped off and stood at the side of the roadway as the stretcher was placed on the special carriage designed to carry it safely. There was a complete and ominous silence among the men. When he was satisfied that everything was ready, George gave the order.

'Right, let him go,' he shouted to the guard, who signalled to the engine-man, and the train started on its way to the pit bottom. When the man-riding train reached the pit bottom, Peter hung back, but George beckoned him to come forward.

'Take one of the positions, lad. I want to keep his Dad away from the stretcher. I don't want him carrying it through the pit bottom and certainly not on the surface up to the first aid room. I'll look after Fred.'

So Peter, with his supervisor and two of the face team from 56s, carried the stretcher to the shaft side, watched by all the pit bottom men, in silence. In the cage they didn't put the stretcher on the floor, but kept hold of it and wedged themselves to the side of the cage. On the surface there was a full shift of men waiting to go underground, and Cobba Green was in among them encouraging them to go to work. As they carried the stretcher through the yard and up to the first aid room, some men took off their helmets and bowed their heads. Peter's young body had been physically tested by this unusual task, but he felt strangely privileged to have played a part in the last journey of Gerry Moore.

★

Helen Dobson got into the car while trying to gather her thoughts. She'd spent a few minutes in prayer in her bedroom, seeking help from the Holy Spirit to guide her through the next few hours. She had also rung her husband at the pit and found out the address of the Moores, and the name and address of the neighbour.

'Thank you for helping out, Sandra,' said Helen. 'This is going to be a very difficult mission and it will be a great shock for a lot of people. I think for the time being we will have to keep it from the little boys, whatever happens. So just keep them busy and try to distract them from asking where their father is.'

'I'll do that, Mrs Dobson. I've brought some toys with me that might help.'

'The first thing is to get this neighbour, Janet Hall, away from the kids to break it to her. It will be a great shock for her. Then we have to get the kids settled with you, so that she and I can go to the hospital. I'm not sure where we shall find Janet: she might be at her own home or she might be at the Moores' house. At least I know the numbers of both houses.'

There was no answer when they knocked at the door of the Moores' house so they went to Janet Hall's. In answer to the knocking, Janet opened the door.

'Janet, I'm Helen Dobson, the wife of the manager of the mine. He has asked me to come and see you. Can I come in?'

'Yes, please do,' replied Janet, as she opened the door wide. The two boys were eating lunch at the table and they looked up at the two unknown women entering the room.

'Hello, boys,' said Helen. 'You carry on with your lunch while I have a quick word with…' she paused. 'Is it Aunty Janet?'

'Yes, it's Aunty Janet,' replied Tony.

Helen pointed to the door leading through to the front room. Janet nodded.

'You carry on with your lunch, I'll be back in a few minutes,' said Janet. The three women went through into the front room.

'This is Sandra Green who is going to help us. I think you should sit down, Janet,' said Helen, speaking very quietly. 'I don't want the boys to hear anything.' Janet sat on the edge of the settee. She looked worried. Helen took a deep breath.

'I'm afraid it's very bad news. There has been an accident at the pit, and Gerry has been killed.'

'Oh no,' cried Janet, and clasped her head in her hands. Helen sat down beside her and took her in her arms.

'Just relax, Janet. I am here to help. Try not to get too upset. We don't want to tell the boys at this stage, so we don't want them to see you in tears.'

Janet started to pull herself together. 'Let me explain what we have to do,' said Helen. 'We, that is you and me, have to go to the hospital and tell their mother and help to look after her. Sandra will stay here and look after the boys. So the first thing you have to do is tell the boys that you have to go off with me, and introduce them to Sandra.'

'Well, my husband is in bed because he is on nightshift, so my first job is to wake him up and tell him the news; he'll be able to help with the boys. Then I'll sort the boys out.' She wiped her eyes and went into the kitchen.

'I'm just going to wake up Uncle Bob, and then I'll be back down,' she called to the boys.

★

During the next twenty minutes, Janet changed her clothes, got Bob to wake up and appear somewhat bleary-eyed in the kitchen, introduced the boys to Sandra and told them a plausible story that she had to go off with Mrs Dobson but that they would be looked after by Uncle Bob and Sandra. They took the bait and she gave them a hug as she left. She was relieved that they didn't ask when their father would be coming home.

★

In the car, Helen discussed with Janet what they should do at the hospital. They needed to talk to the Ward Sister and explain the position to her, and they might have to see a doctor who could give an assessment of the impact on Peggy. The doctors may decide to sedate her, said Helen, but they felt it would be better if they could stay and support Peggy.

'I don't think I will be able to tell her, Mrs Dobson,' said Janet. 'When I think of the implications for Peggy, I am near to tears now. Just imagine: two little boys under three years old and a baby; it's just hopeless for her.' Janet took her hanky out of her pocket and wiped her eyes. Helen's reply was an attempt to get her relationship with Janet and Peggy right.

'Don't call me Mrs Dobson, Janet. My name is Helen.' She held Janet's hand. 'I want Peggy to know me as Helen, and also as a friend. I will tell her the news after you have introduced me. But we must be prepared to talk to her and try to answer her questions; she has to know that she is not on her own. You are a friend that she can trust; there will be other people, who will become friends, who will help her, I can assure you of that, Janet. We have to surround Peggy with people who she can trust.'

★

When the car pulled into the hospital car park, Janet realised how much more convenient it was than travelling on the buses. At the ward, they discussed the position with the Ward Sister. She explained that such tragic news would be traumatic for Peggy in her present state. She put a call through for the consultant to come down to the ward. Helen briefed him on the circumstances.

'We don't want Peggy to hear about Gerry's death in some other way,' Helen said. 'There will be press coverage of the accident and someone visiting tonight might start talking in the ward. We want to tell her ourselves, and stay with her; we're not going to leave her to suffer on her own. We know that she will need answers to lots of questions. We have to let her know that she will have support from all sorts of people in this tragedy.'

'I think that we will have to induce the birth in the next few days,' said the consultant. 'I don't want to give her more drugs because of this news. What she will need is as much comfort and support as you can organise.'

'We will see to that,' said Helen. Janet was not sure how Helen was going to deliver that promise.

'I suggest you go ahead and tell her the sad news. The nurses will monitor her and if she is too distressed we will sedate her, but I would prefer not to do that.'

'Thank you,' said Helen. 'We will do all we can to help her.' The Ward Sister went to see what the position was on the ward. She came back and reported that Peggy was just finishing lunch, and that now might be a suitable time for Helen and Janet to see her. When they approached her bed, Peggy looked at them with surprise.

'What brought you here, Janet, at this time?' she asked.

'We wanted to see you. Have you finished with your lunch tray?' Janet asked. When Peggy nodded, Janet busied herself moving the tray off the bed. The Ward Sister removed the tray and partially closed the curtains around the bed so that there was an element of privacy. Janet went to sit at one side of the bed and Helen went to the chair at the other side. They both leaned over so that they could speak to Peggy privately without raising their voices.

'This is Helen Dobson, who has come with me. Her husband is the manager of Martins Main.' Janet stopped talking abruptly and looked across to Helen, who took Peggy's hand in hers.

'We need to talk to you, Peggy. We're here to help you and support you. We hope we can give you strength to be very brave.'

Helen clasped Peggy's hands in both her hands. Peggy had a puzzled expression on her face as she looked straight into Helen's eyes. Helen held her eye contact and she was sure that Peggy had no idea of the nature of the news.

'I am afraid it is bad news.' She paused, but Peggy continued with her puzzled look. 'There has been an accident at the pit and Gerry has been tragically killed.' Peggy let out a gasp and a loud yell of despair, as she pulled her hands free of Helen's hold and clasped her head. Helen sat on the edge of the bed and put her arms around Peggy and comforted her as she wept freely. After a few minutes, Peggy calmed a little and then looked at Janet with a troubled expression.

'What are we going to do?' she asked. Helen answered for her, when she realised that Janet was near to tears.

'We are going to sort out your problems,' said Helen. 'That is why we are here. Janet is doing a wonderful job with the boys and she will carry on. Just relax as best you can and then tell us what you want to know.'

Peggy spent several minutes weeping and looking at her two visitors. She was obviously thinking of what the news meant. Then she looked directly at Helen.

'How did it happen? Did he suffer a lot?'

'I don't know, but I will in a few minutes,' replied Helen. 'I will go and telephone my husband and then I will come back and tell you. You stay here, Janet, and remember any other matters that Peggy raises that we have to sort out.' Janet nodded. Some moments later, when Helen had left, Janet spoke to Peggy.

'Helen is a very kind woman. I hadn't met her before, but she's told me that she will arrange a lot of help for you. I think we can trust her.'

When Helen returned after about ten minutes, Peggy was still tearful, but she was talking to Janet.

'I just caught my husband as he was getting ready to go underground with the Mines Inspector. The accident happened on 56s coalface, and it was a roof fall. Gerry's dad was there, and he organised the rescue with the other men. But it was a large fall of rock that knocked out the roof supports. Gerry was dead when they reached him, and my husband thinks, from the reports, that he would have been killed instantly. So he did not suffer.'

'That's a relief,' said Peggy.

'Peggy is wondering about the funeral,' said Janet. 'She does not get on with Gerry's parents and she would not want them to take over.'

'Well, I think that you should decide what you want for the funeral, Peggy. I can ask the minister at Upthorpe Methodist Church to look after those arrangements. I was going to ask him and his wife to visit you in any case. They are experienced at supporting people battling with bereavements. I don't think you'll be able to attend the funeral, Peggy. You will have a baby by then, and the priority will be to get you and the baby fit and well.'

'Oh, but I want to be there; I want to be there with the boys.'

'We will have to wait and see how things work out,' said Janet. 'Bob will be there with me and I am sure that there will be plenty of other people there. The men at the pit usually support their mates when there has been a fatality.'

'There will also be a lot of people there from the church,' said Helen. 'I have no doubt that Willie Carter will be there, because he works on 56s coalface. And there will be management from the pit there. You have no need to worry about the funeral, Peggy. Gerry will be put to rest with all the respect that he deserves.'

'Peggy is worried about the house,' said Janet. 'Will she be thrown out on the street?'

'The British Coal Executive does not do things like that,' said Helen. 'They have compensation awards for fatal accidents and they will look after you. My husband will keep his eye on that side of things. I've heard him talk about other, similar, cases.'

'How can we tell the boys?' asked Peggy.

'That is the difficult one to answer,' said Helen. 'We need to do it, but we want them to be settled as much as possible before we tell them. As Janet will be very busy with all sorts of arrangements, I suggest we get Sandra Green to help looking after the boys. She's looking after them now, and I am sure they'll like her. She babysits for me when we have to go out on an evening, and my boys get on very well with her. I know they are a lot older than yours, but she seems to have a natural way with children. Don't you agree, Janet?'

'Yes, I am sure that would be a help, if she could do it.'

'I'm sure I can arrange that,' said Helen. 'I want to go now and have a word with James Folds and his wife, Gwen. He's the minister at Upthorpe Methodist Church and they're wonderful people.' Helen left to go to the 'phone again. While she was away, Peggy raised another problem.

'I do so miss the boys,' she said. 'Do you think they will let me see them?'

'It will be difficult to get the hospital to agree,' replied Janet. 'They seem to be against kids visiting patients in hospital, but we'll discuss it with Helen. She may be able to pull some strings, if you think it will give you a boost.'

When Helen returned she announced that the minister and his wife would be coming to visit Peggy straightaway.

★

James and Gwen Folds arrived half an hour later. Helen introduced them and, after a short period, left them talking to Peggy, who was slowly beginning to relax.

★

Back in Martins Lane, Helen arranged for Sandra Green to be with the boys each day for the next week, which would allow Janet to spend time with Peggy in the hospital and sort out other domestic matters. Helen also arranged for Sandra to take over from the gardener in looking after Robert and John that evening, so that she could go back to the hospital to stay with Peggy. She prepared a meal for the family and then rang Roy at the pit, but he was still underground. She left word with Gordon to arrange for Roy to get a lift home, as she was taking the car to go back to the hospital.

★

Roy Dobson and the Mines Inspector arrived back at the surface in the early evening. When he got the message from his wife, Roy was thankful that Helen was doing all she could to comfort the person who had most to lose as a result of the accident. The inspector's visit underground, to the site of the fatality, confirmed that it was a genuine accident. The statements by the men and officials on 56s face had indicated there was no contributing failure on the part of Gerry Moore. He had set supports as required and these had been pushed out by the fall of roof. George Turnbull had summed up the position to Roy on the surface, prior to them going underground with the inspector.

'Gerry Moore was not the best of workmen, but I have to say, Boss, that on this occasion he could not be faulted. He had set the supports that were required, but it was a bloody big stone that came down, with no warning. The poor bugger.' George was depressed by the death of one of his workmen.

'Don't take it to heart, George; it is not your fault. Tragically these accidents do happen. I'll speak to you when I get out of the pit with the inspector.'

The Mines Inspector confirmed the statements from everyone involved. The roof was competent and well supported, except at the accident site, where the large stone had fallen and knocked out the wooden supports and killed Gerry Moore. It was another fatality recorded under the category of 'falls of roof'.

★

When Roy got home, using a van from the garage, he was surprised to see Sandra, who was busy preparing the children for bed.

'I'd better take you home first, Sandra,' said Roy.

'There's no need to do that, Mr Dobson. I have told my dad that I will probably be here late. I will get you your dinner and then I'll finish putting the boys to bed. I hope you don't mind, but I had some dinner with the children. It is a very tragic day for Mrs Moore.'

'It is indeed, Sandra. These are the days that one dreads, as a colliery manager.'

'I can understand that.'

Sandra brought out the meal that she was keeping hot in the oven, put it on the table and left Roy to serve himself, while she went upstairs to put the children to bed. When she came back down, Roy looked across at her.

'Are the boys settled?' he asked.

'Yes, I think they'll be asleep in no time.'

'Good,' said Roy, with a sigh. 'I don't think I'm up to talking to them tonight. I keep thinking about those two poor kids who have lost their father today; I wonder how they're feeling?'

'They don't know yet what has happened. Mrs Dobson thought we should not tell them today, when Janet and everyone were upset, but we shall probably have to break it to them tomorrow.'

★

Helen stayed at the hospital well after visiting time was over. She held Peggy's hands, and talked to her about how matters could be resolved and what help was available. Reverend Folds was sorting out the arrangements for the funeral and he had contacted a funeral director. He'd said he would come to the hospital tomorrow to see Peggy and discuss details about the funeral service. Eventually Peggy raised the one issue that was worrying her most.

'I do wish that I could see my boys. I ought to be the one to tell them about their dad. I don't want them to hold it against me that I didn't tell them the truth about their father.'

'I'll see the Ward Sister and try to arrange to bring the boys in tomorrow,' replied Helen. 'You keep your spirits up and if any of the staff here mention the boys, tell them that you just want a few minutes with them. They might agree to it if they think it won't upset you any further.'

Helen went to see the Ward Sister and explained the position. She persuaded her to agree that if Peggy was reasonably settled tomorrow afternoon, then Helen could bring the boys to see their mother for a few minutes. Helen didn't tell Peggy this, but she said she would see her in the morning.

Peggy Moore settled down to sleep. It had been a traumatic day, and there were lots of problems facing her in the future, but she was strangely at peace. She had never in her life had such help from people she had never met before. She remembered two moments in particular: just before Gwen and James Folds had left her they were both holding her hands and then James had said a prayer:

'Lord in your great mercy, bless Peggy and empower her with your strength. In this time, when great troubles are facing her, give her your peace.'

When Helen had left, she also had held her hand.

'God bless you, Peggy. I will hold you in my prayers, tonight.'

★

Back home, Helen held Roy in a close hug, as they stood together in the kitchen.

'I am so sorry for what you have had to suffer today, darling,' said Helen. 'I know it must have been the worst day in your life as a manager.'

'Helen, you have been such a strength and help. You have been doing the worst part of all in this tragedy. How is his wife now?'

'She's being very brave. James and Gwen Folds were a great help, and they are sorting out the funeral arrangements. The trickiest part of all is tomorrow; Peggy wants to tell the boys about their father. I have more or less sorted it out with the Ward Sister that I can take the boys in for a few minutes, tomorrow afternoon. I think she is right to try to do it, but it will be a great struggle for her. I need to go and say my prayers now.'

'Yes, you do that, Helen.' Roy usually held back and let Helen go secretly to her prayers, but on this occasion he wanted to encourage her. On this night, a lot of people required the additional strength of answered prayers – not least himself.

Wednesday 17 February 1965

Helen went to the hospital mid-morning. She arrived when the Consultant was doing his ward round, so she had to wait outside until he had finished. When he came out, he recognised Helen and went to have a word with her.

'Mrs Moore seems to be bearing up well to the bad news,' he said. 'Your support for her is paying off. We will watch her for any delayed shock during the next twenty-four hours.'

'We are trying to spend as much time as possible with her, and when she raises a problem we are trying to provide a solution.'

'Well done, keep up the good work,' said the Consultant, as he left her. Helen had decided not to raise the visit of the boys with him, in case he banned the idea.

Peggy seemed glad to see Helen, and she talked about several matters to do with the funeral that she would discuss with James Folds when he came later in the morning. Helen assured her that the boys were being well looked after, and she asked Peggy if there was anything she needed. Peggy was hesitant at first, but then she confessed that she wanted a clean nightdress. Helen promised to organise this.

*

After leaving the hospital, Helen went straight into Doncaster and bought two new nightdresses for Peggy. She went to Janet's house and parked the car outside. Tony and Michael were there, and Sandra was playing with them, while Janet was washing some of the boys' clothes. The youngsters looked up at her when she walked into the room.

'Good morning, everyone,' Helen said. Janet and Sandra gave her a welcoming smile, but the boys were silent.

'I have a big surprise for you. I'm coming back this afternoon with the car to pick you all up and we are all going for a ride. I want you all to be dressed up, because we're going to the hospital to see your mummy. She will want to see that you are being good and that you are helping Aunty Janet and Aunty Sandra to look after you.'

'We are being good,' replied Tony.

'I know you are, and that is why the doctors are letting you go to see your mother. You want to make her feel better, don't you?'

'Yes,' said Tony.

'I think you should come as well, Sandra, so that you can help with Michael. They might not let us all go onto the ward together, but we will see. I want to get there after two o'clock, when the afternoon Ward Sister is in charge but before visiting time which starts at three o'clock.'

'We'll organise a bit of lunch, now,' said Janet. 'And then we'll go to the other house, because the boys' clothes are mainly there.'

'I'll help to get the lunch, then.' Sandra seemed to be working with Janet as a team.

'Right, I'll leave you to it, and pick you up at the Moores' house this afternoon.'

Helen left to go home for some lunch herself.

★

In the afternoon, when she picked them up, Helen noticed that both the boys looked smart in their best clothes, with shining, washed faces. Tony was excited by the ride in the car. It was a first for him, and he watched with interest as Helen drove the car. As they entered the hospital they were a conspicuous group: Sandra was carrying Michael, Tony was walking along holding Janet's hand, and Helen was carrying the parcel she had made up of the two nightdresses for Peggy. They went into the Ward Sister's office. The children were quiet and subdued by the strange surroundings.

'How is she, this afternoon?' asked Helen.

'She seems quite calm and my colleague on duty this morning was surprised how well she is bearing up.'

'I would like to go and see her for a minute or two, first,' said Helen. 'If she's ready, we'll take the boys in for a few minutes. It's really Tony that I think she will want to talk to.'

'I'll go with you, and we'll draw the curtains round the bed for some privacy,' said the Ward Sister.

★

'I'm back,' said Helen, as she stood at the side of the bed and held Peggy's hand. 'I've brought you the nightdresses that you need; I'll put them in your locker.'

'You are kind,' said Peggy. She tried to sit up, and the nurse helped her and made her comfortable, before she drew the curtains around the bed.

'Why has she drawn the curtains?' asked Peggy.

'She wants us to have a bit of privacy,' replied Helen. 'I hope the other ladies in the ward are not envious of you having so many visitors.'

'I don't think they mind. They know about the accident and some of them have come and said how sorry they are for me. You have all been very kind. The minister and his wife came again this morning, and we talked some more about the funeral. I don't know how to thank you.'

'You don't have to thank us; we all want to help you. Are you feeling up to some more visitors? We have a surprise for you.'

'Who else is coming?' asked Peggy.

Helen didn't answer, but went through the gap in the curtain and out to the office. The party went down the ward: Janet in front, holding Tony's hand; and Helen carrying Michael. Sandra stayed in the office, with instructions to come to the bed in ten minutes, in case Michael was restless. As they went through the gap in the curtain Peggy gasped with shock and delight.

'Oh, my boys!' She put out her arms to hold Michael and give him a cuddle. She motioned to Tony to come and sit beside her on the bed and she put an arm around his shoulder.

'What a wonderful surprise! How glad I am to see you.'

'We came in a car,' said Tony.

'Did you?' said Peggy. 'That must have been exciting.'

'Yes, it was.'

Michael was turning around from the cuddle and sucking his thumb. He wasn't comfortable, and Janet saw this and took him in her arms.

'They are both being very good boys,' she said. 'And they are helping me to look after them. And they have a new friend, now, and you like her, don't you, Tony?'

'Who is that?' asked Peggy, looking at Janet and Helen.

'Aunty Sandra,' said Tony. Helen quickly explained who Sandra was, and what she was doing. Then she went and fetched Sandra and introduced her to Peggy.

'They are two lovely boys,' said Sandra. 'It's a pleasure to be with them. We play a lot of games and have fun.'

'Lots of fun,' said Tony.

Michael reached out for Sandra, and she took him from Janet and said she would take him outside, as he was not comfortable in the hospital. This gave the opportunity for Peggy to concentrate on Tony. Janet wiped her eyes with her handkerchief; she was dreading the next few minutes.

'I'm glad you are being a good boy, Tony,' said Peggy. 'I need you to help me with Michael and we will soon have another baby to look after. What do you think to that?'

'It's OK,' said Tony.

'There is another thing, Tony.' Peggy paused, trying to think of the right words to explain what had happened. She took a deep breath and held on to Tony's hands. 'We won't have Dad around any more. He has had an accident in the pit and he was killed.' Peggy waited for a reaction. Tony was thinking about what he had been told.

'Not ever, any more?' he said.

'Not ever, Tony,' said Peggy, and she clung hold of his hands.

'But we'll still have Uncle Bob,' said Tony. Janet burst into tears and fled through the gap in the curtain. Peggy did not know what to say, and a tear ran down her cheek.

'Yes, you will still have Uncle Bob,' said Helen. 'You can be sure of that.' Tony held his mother's hand and looked at Helen. She was not sure how much he understood, but he seemed calm.

'You have been a very brave little boy,' said Helen. 'You've made your mother feel better, and she is so pleased to have seen that you and Michael are being good boys while she is in hospital. Give your mother a kiss, now, as we must go back to your house. You can sit in the front seat of the car going back, so that you can see how I drive it.'

Tony gave his mother a brief kiss and jumped down off the bed and held Helen's hand.

'Thank you for coming to see me, Tony,' said Peggy. 'I will try to get better so that I can come home to be with you soon.' She gave Helen a smile of relief. Helen promised to come and see her the next day.

Saturday 20 February 1965

Peggy gave birth to a little girl, who weighed seven pounds and ten ounces. The baby was quite healthy, and not apparently affected in any way by the traumas influencing Peggy's life. Peggy herself was so relieved to have completed her pregnancy successfully, but she was very weak and knew that she would still be in hospital on the day of the funeral.

Monday 22 February 1965

Helen realised that the funeral arrangements would have to be finalised by Janet and herself. She'd visited Peggy every day in hospital, and gone over the arrangements that she'd made. She'd seen Gerry's mother and father, and asked them to walk behind the coffin. Janet and Bob would take Tony to the service, and they would sit on the front row, but would not go on to the burial. They decided that those attending would be invited back to the Methodist Church schoolroom afterwards, where refreshments would be provided; Gwen Folds arranged this part with the ladies of the church. Sandra would look after Michael, and would bring him to the reception. The wreath on the coffin would be from Peggy, Tony, Michael and the little girl, who was to be called Dawn.

Helen spent some time with James Folds, going through the service details. She agreed to read the lesson, which was to be the twenty-third psalm. Peter Carter was to play the organ, and the hymns were to be well-known and reflect hope in the future rather than the despair of death. James Folds had been to see Roy and George Turnbull, so that he could have full details about the accident. He was determined to emphasise the bravery of Peggy, and the wonder of the new baby girl. The new baby would never know her father, but James was sure that many friends, in the best tradition of mining communities, would welcome her.

Tuesday 23 February 1965

The funeral went according to plan. The church was full, and Willie Carter had the difficult task of fitting everyone in and reserving the front seats for the family. Roy Dobson, George Turnbull and several members of the management team from Martins Main went to the service. Cobba Green was there with Jimmy Bell, and there were several men from both 56s and 57s coalfaces. Fred Moore and his wife were dressed in black, and appeared utterly desolate; at the burial they stood by the grave and wept openly as they cast dirt onto the coffin of their son. Helen persuaded them to go back to the reception, and both George and Roy spoke to Fred to try to offer him support and give him some hope for the future.

At the reception, Sandra carried Michael around, and showed him to lots of people. He was happy to smile at them, but there was no way that he was going to leave Sandra's arms. Tony stuck closely to 'Uncle Bob' but he did enjoy a few sandwiches and some cake.

★

When Helen got back home in the evening she went over the day's events as she spoke to Roy.

'We've managed to work our way through the difficult early part of this tragedy; but we've still to seek a final solution. Even with all the help we can provide, I don't think Peggy can bring up those three children on her own. It's not just a money problem; it's the continual drudgery that will get her down.'

'I have no solution to offer you,' replied Roy. 'That is the real tragedy of these situations. As Cobba said to me when the accident happened: Gerry was not much of a dad, but he was better than no dad at all.'

'I will have to pray about it.' And Helen went upstairs to do just that.

Chapter 13

Tuesday 2 March 1965

It was exactly a week after the funeral, when Peggy came home to Martins Lane from the hospital. She smiled as she carried her daughter, Dawn, into the house. The place was clean and tidy, with flowers in a vase on the table. Janet was there, with the two boys, to welcome her. Tony looked at the little bundle that Peggy placed in a cot by the table, and said, 'She's only tiny.' He then walked away back to his toys.

'She will grow until she is as big as you,' said Janet.

'No, I'll always be bigger than her,' he replied.

Peggy clearly needed to rest and gain her strength. Janet had agreed to keep the two boys at her house, to let Peggy concentrate on the baby. She had notified the shop that she would not be able to return to work for some time. The boys were happy with the arrangement. They also enjoyed the time that Sandra spent with them on several days, playing games and taking them out for walks.

Helen wondered if this could develop into a permanent solution. She visited Peggy on most days and got Janet to arrange for Bob's sister to spend more days each week cleaning for Peggy and helping with the baby. Helen also encouraged Sandra to drop in and spend some time with Peggy. Sandra jumped at this opportunity, and delighted in helping with Dawn at feeding-time and at bath-time. Peggy had never enjoyed such help and friendship. When Cobba Green and Jimmy Bell called to discuss the financial payments that she would receive following the fatality, she took it as just another part of the support that was being given to her.

Wednesday 31 March 1965

Peggy had been at home for about a month and Helen thought it was time to review the situation.

'You are looking so much better, Peggy, and it's so good that you can enjoy the baby without being under pressure with the boys as well.'

'I know. I was dreading coming home, but it has been wonderful. I do feel so much better. I don't know what I would have done without Janet.'

'Janet has looked after the boys as if they were her own,' said Helen. And the boys have certainly benefited by having Uncle Bob to talk to. I am sure it's helped them to get over the loss of their dad.'

'But what are we going to do in the future?'

'That is up to you, Peggy. You need to think about it. It would be possible to have Janet and Bob as a part of a permanent solution for the boys. They wanted children of their own, as you know, but haven't been able to manage it. They are an extraordinary, loving couple, and they are giving the boys everything that you could wish them to have.' Helen carefully watched Peggy's face, to gauge her reaction.

'I know what you are suggesting,' replied Peggy, with her head bent down so that she did not look at Helen. 'But I don't want to lose the boys altogether.'

'You would never lose them, Peggy; you would always be a part of their life. Janet and Bob would make sure of that.'

★

Helen discussed her views with Roy that night. He knew, when he came home from the pit, that she had something on her mind. When their boys had gone to bed and they were sitting together on the settee, Roy asked Helen to open up.

'Mrs Dobson, I feel that you have something important on your mind tonight. Is it some problem that you would like to share with your husband?'

'Is it as obvious as that, Roy? Actually I would like your advice on something. It's rather important and affects several people. I've been discussing the future with Peggy Moore. She is improving in health so much, now that she has only the baby to look after. Since she came out of hospital, life has been much better than she ever dared hope. She sees that the boys are very happy with Janet and Bob. I took a bit of a gamble and suggested to her that it might be a good solution for the two boys to stay with Janet and Bob on a permanent basis. I think Peggy might agree with this. I feel a bit exposed getting involved like this. What do you think?'

'Do you mean that Janet and Bob should adopt the boys?'

'Well, I suppose that's another way of saying it. I've not considered the mechanism to make it happen; I've not even spoken to Janet and Bob, yet. I was trying to see if Peggy was open to a solution, and I think she might be.'

'You are certainly in at the deep end, now,' replied Roy. 'The next step will be to have a talk with Bob and Janet, I would think.'

'I'll try to do that tomorrow. I think Bob is on dayshift, so he should be at home tomorrow evening. If it can be a possible solution, there will also be a need to talk to the boys. Michael is too young to understand, but Tony is a shrewd little lad. Mind you, Michael is developing fast, and Sandra has taught him to say a few words, now.'

'Just take it one step at a time,' replied Roy. 'But don't try to rush it. I'll be interested in keeping up with your progress.'

'There's such a lot to raise in my prayers, tonight. I need a lot of guidance to get the right answer.' She stood up and left Roy. He realised that it was going to be a long prayer session tonight.

Thursday 1 April 1965

It was near the end of the dayshift when the trepanner on 57s coalface refused to move forward or backwards. All the cutting elements were working, but the machine refused to move. As fitter on the coalface, Bob Hall inspected the trepanner. The problem must be in the hydraulic section of the machine: it could be shortage of oil, but he checked, and that was not the cause; he tested some of the valves to make sure they were not sticking; he then realised that there must be a major failure of the hydraulic section and that would mean changing it. The hydraulic section was the biggest component of the machine, and to change it meant splitting the machine into three parts, removing the old hydraulic section and getting a new one into place, and then a major machine re-build. As the trepanner was on the coalface twenty yards from the main roadway, it was a challenging job in cramped conditions where there were restrictions on the space for the craftsmen to work.

Roy Dobson was in his office when George called on the pit 'phone.

'We have a major breakdown, Boss. The hydraulic section of the trepanner has failed on 57s face. The engineer is arranging to get a replacement from Region. He's sending extra fitters onto the face to strip the machine down. I've persuaded the dayshift fitter to stay on a double shift, and I've fixed up some men to help him. I've got other men starting to prepare a track up from the main roadway to get the old section out and the new one in. It's a bugger, Boss. They'd done two shears and were starting on the third; the breakdown will lose us two to three shifts' production from 57s face. I thought we were going to have the best week's output since Christmas, but now we're buggered.'

'George, don't get frustrated. We have to organise the repair as quickly as possible. You sort the job out down there. I'll follow up the arrangements for the new section, and get it on its way down the pit. I'll also check with the Mechanical Engineer that he has organised the best fitters and engineering supervision on 57s for the next twenty-four hours.'

★

Roy left the pit in the early evening, when the new section was loaded up and ready to go down the shaft. A team of men were waiting for it in the pit bottom, to transport it to 57s face. On the coalface, the trepanner was split and they hoped to have the old haulage section pulled off the coalface, out of the way, by the time the new one arrived. George had sent for some snap and he was staying underground until the old section was off the coalface. There was a chance that 57s face would be able to produce some coal on the dayshift the following day, if there was no problem with the re-build during the night. Roy was pleased with progress.

★

When Roy got home, Helen had returned from her visit to talk to Bob and Janet and she told him that Bob had not been at home.

'I'm sorry that you have been frustrated,' he said. 'We have a major breakdown on 57s face and Bob Hall is doing a double shift to get the repair started.'

'Oh, we ladies can manage without you unreliable men!' replied Helen. 'I've been able to have a confidential talk with Janet. She admitted that she was dreading the boys going back to Peggy; she couldn't imagine how much she would miss them. I don't think that she had considered a permanent arrangement, but now I am sure that she is willing to consider it, if Peggy is positive. As far as Bob is concerned, I get the impression that he will do whatever Janet wants to do. So I'm making progress. How are things at the pit?'

'A bit like you – things are moving forward. With a good run during the nightshift we should be coaling again sometime tomorrow morning.'

That night Helen's prayers were dominated by expressions of humble thankfulness and requests for guidance to all those involved. She determined to speak to James and Gwen Folds, and seek their help and advice to achieve a solution for Peggy and her family.

★

The boys were asleep in bed, and Janet was dozing in front of the fire, when Bob came in at ten o'clock. He was obviously exhausted, and so much so that he ate only a part of his dinner that Janet had warmed up. He desperately needed to get some sleep before the alarm went off at five o'clock the next morning. Janet decided that she would wait to discuss the future of their family with Bob once his life was back to normal.

Friday 2 April 1965

At the pit, Bob found a note on his lamp, telling him to go straight to the fitting shop. There he picked up a hydraulic hose that was needed on 57s face for the trepanner. He was told that the re-build was almost complete but that a hose had been damaged and there was no spare underground. Fortunately it was an external hose, but it required a contortionist to get to one of the connections. Although Bob was only working on the machine for an hour to fit the hose and then assist in filling the machine with oil, he was covered in sweat and grease by the time he had finished. It was a great relief when the trepanner was started up and it hauled normally in both directions.

★

When he saw the machine operating again, George briefed the men on his immediate plans.

'Now lads, I want us to try to catch up some of the output we've lost. I want you to stay on overtime until the afternoonshift gets here. Is that OK?'

There were nods from some of the men and the machine driver increased the speed of the machine and the whole coalface operation went full-speed ahead. When the afternoonshift arrived, the dayshift had just completed their second shear. George spoke to the men taking over, and encouraged them to try to gain back some more of the lost production. They said they would try their best. This was a new attitude, thought George, and he went to have a word with Roy.

'We've had a good run this morning, Boss, and completed two shears. The afternoonshift team are going to try to gain back some more of the lost coal.'

'That is good news, George. Well done. Are you coming out now?'

'It's not as straightforward as that, Boss. I'm going to the loading point, to keep things going there for an hour or two. We need the maximum number of tubs from the pit bottom to the Benton seam this afternoon, to keep 57s face going flat out. Can you have a word with the pit bottom, Boss?'

'I'll do that George, and I'll keep my eye on the coal-winding shaft. If you can get three more shears off 57s coalface this afternoon, we shall have the best day's output at Martins for a very long time.'

Roy Dobson had a thrilling feeling, which he had never had before at Martins. The pit was on song. The breakdown at 57s had been sorted quickly and the men were going flat out to recover the lost output. That message would get round the rest of the pit and every team would lift their game. It was the attitude that every colliery manager wanted to create: a positive, willing workforce that expected to succeed. He stayed at the pit until George came out at six o'clock, and then went to talk to him.

'You've had two long days, George, but boy, have they been successful! You've coaxed out of your men a magnificent performance, to get the machine repaired and then the desire to recover the lost coal. You might have lifted the attitudes of Martins men to a new level.'

'I have to admit, Boss, that the atmosphere on 57s has been different today; I hope it'll stay that way.'

'It will not just be 57s face, George. The change could spread around the rest of the pit. I know it won't be the end of our problems, but I would rather have the problems of success, than the problems of failure. Go and get yourself bathed, George, and get off home. And have an easier day tomorrow!'

Roy went home very happy with the way things were progressing at Martins Main.

★

Helen was waiting for Roy when he got home.

'I've been to see Janet, this afternoon. What are you doing with your men at Martins? Bob stayed on overtime again today, after doing a double shift yesterday!' Roy explained what had happened, and the good reaction that had come from the men. He hoped that these were the signs of a much improved attitude for the whole mine.

'Well, I've had a good day too! Bob was very tired, but Janet spoke to him about the boys and he has raised no objections to them staying, if Peggy wants that to happen. I also went to see James and Gwen. They think it's a good plan, for the benefit of everyone, if Peggy is happy. They did suggest, though, that it might be wise to carry on with the present arrangement for the next six months, or even a year, before considering adoption.'

'That sounds like a good idea,' said Roy.

'Another thing that is likely to happen is a christening. Peggy has spoken to James and asked about having the baby baptised at church. I think it will just be the baby for now, though I doubt if the boys have been baptised. There's no doubt that James and Gwen have been a great help to Peggy; they've given her a bit of confidence in herself, and some hope for the future. I almost dare to think that I can see the solution to Peggy's problems.'

'I almost dare to think that I can see the solutions to Martins Main's problems.' He gave Helen a kiss and a cuddle.

'We are very fortunate to have problems that have solutions,' replied Helen.

★

Peter Carter came home from his organ lesson in Leeds with his mind in a bit of a whirl. Dr Sloan had asked Peter a rather searching question.

'How far do you want to take your organ playing, Peter?' he'd asked at the end of the lesson.

'I'm not sure I understand what you mean, Dr Sloan. I suppose I want to improve as much as I can.' His voice trailed away. He hadn't prepared an answer to such a searching question.

'Well, you see, Peter, I think that you could become a very good organ player, in the future. It would require hard work, but I am sure you would cope with that. It would also require more study of music and passing exams; but again, I am confident that you have the intelligence to pass the written exams. If your playing continues to develop, you should be able to pass the practical skills examinations, as well.' Dr Sloan paused, and gave Peter time to consider what he was saying.

'I do want to progress with the organ. But I'm studying at the Technical College for my electrical qualifications, as well as working at the pit. I have a busy life as it is, without taking on another challenge. How much of a commitment would the exams be?'

'The Royal College of Organists organise the exams, which are conducted each year. Like all bodies carrying out examinations and issuing certificates, they have different levels. The lowest level is the certificate, which if you pass, allows you to put CertRCO after your name. The next level is Associateship Diploma, and the letters become ARCO. The highest grade is Fellowship Diploma, and the letters are FRCO. You see, Peter, I think you need an objective to be aiming at. I'm confident that if we focus on the RCO exams, you could be taking the certificate grade within the next twelve months. Go away and think about it; we can discuss it further next week.'

'I'll do that, Dr Sloan. I'd better discuss it with my parents, as well. It's a big opportunity; I need to know that they would support me.'

'Right, Peter. I'm sure your parents will support you. They've been very good to help you to get to where you are now.'

Going home on the bus, Peter turned over the issues in his mind. Could he fit in more study and organ practice? Was it possible to run his electrical career alongside an organ career? It didn't seem to leave much time for other things in his life. At the pit he heard

3124223

---

the talk by his mates of their adventures with girlfriends. Some of his workmates had sporting activities for their pastime. He had no time for sport, and he had little contact with girls, except at the church. The girls that interested him there were at the grammar school, and led a very different life to his at the pit. But there was the attraction of having letters after his name; that would certainly appeal to his father. By the time he got home to Upthorpe, he'd decided to put to his father Dr Sloan's idea as a clear plan, not something open for discussion and decision.

When Willie heard of the plan, he couldn't contain his enthusiasm and pride. He couldn't wait to tell James Folds that Peter was being recommended by his teacher to take the Royal College of Organists exams to get letters after his name.

Saturday 24 April 1965

Sandra and Terry were spending the day in Scarborough. The weather had been fine – and much better than during last week's Easter holiday weekend – and in the afternoon's warm sunshine they'd decided to have a dip in the sea. Sandra had brought a large towel and, with it wrapped around her, she changed from her clothes into a new, bright-yellow bikini. She bundled up her clothes and put them on her deckchair and stood up for Terry to admire her. It wasn't just Terry on the beach that admired her. She looked stunning. The bikini bottom was brief, and helped to display her long legs; the bikini top showed the size of her bust and, with her hair tied back and a smile on her face, she looked the picture of a healthy and happy young woman. Terry also changed under the towel, and they spent nearly an hour splashing and swimming in the sea.

Sandra realised that it would not be easy to dry herself under the towel and get dressed into her normal clothes. So she employed Terry to hold the ends of the towel tightly round her neck and ensure that it did not fall down to reveal her to everyone on the beach. When she was engaged in the tricky process of pulling on her knickers and her bra, Terry couldn't resist saying, 'I'll bet I could raise a bob or two, from some of these fellows around here, if I let the towel drop now.'

'It would be the end of our relationship if you try that one, Terry Lacey,' replied Sandra, with a laugh.

★

The trip to Scarborough had been her concession to Terry's complaints that she was not available as much as she used to be. With her commitments to her father and brother, and the time she spent with Peggy and Dawn, along with her babysitting for Bob and Janet as well as for Mr and Mrs Dobson, she had a very full diary. She was fascinated to be involved in all these people's lives, and she was learning so much about babies and children. She really felt she was maturing. Those things had to have priority over nights out with Terry; he would get the benefit of her experience later.

★

After they'd had tea in a café on the beach, they headed home. It was when they were near Sherburn-in-Elmet that Terry turned off the road, onto a track that led into a wood, and parked the car. The light was fading and he switched off the car headlights.

'Why are we stopping here?' asked Sandra. 'I was going to suggest that you had a drink at our house when you dropped me off at home.'

'We can do that as well, but I have wanted to hold you in my arms all day. And when I saw you in your bikini on the beach, I really ached inside. You have no idea what you do to me, Sandra.'

'You're a softy, Terry,' replied Sandra, ruffling his hair. 'Come on then, we can have a cuddle, but I don't want you to get sexy; this is not the place. And I am not going to start doing contortions in a car to satisfy your desires.'

It was a hectic twenty minutes, with lots of touching and kissing. Sandra had to admit that Terry aroused her, and she knew that she certainly aroused him without even trying. In the end she pushed him away.

'We must stop now, Terry. If it goes any further it might be classed as rape, and you wouldn't want that, would you?' Terry was shocked by that remark.

'What do you mean by that, Sandra?'

'I don't want you forcing me to have sex with you, Terry. When we get to have sex together I want it to be a beautiful experience that we both want. And it will have to be at the right time, and in the right place. This is neither the time nor the place.'

Sandra straightened her clothes and re-applied her make-up. Terry drove her home, but he was subdued and quiet. He realised he could have spoilt her day. He did, though, stay and have a cup of tea with Sandra and her father. He was a little reassured when Sandra walked with him to his car and gave him a quick kiss and said, 'Thank you for a wonderful day out, Terry.'

Tuesday 27 April 1965

Roy was visiting the Fuston seam developments with George Turnbull. The two roadways had settled down to doing a reasonable performance of thirty yards of completed roadway per week. Mining the coal seam and setting the temporary supports was easy, and was done quickly, but the second part of the process, of going back with all the equipment and getting up the floor dirt and setting the final supports, was taking far more time than expected.

'The finished roadway certainly looks good, George,' said Roy, as he looked along a length of the completed roadway which had the conveyor on one side, suspended from the roof supports, and on the other side a rail track for getting supplies up to the workmen. A flexible hose, two feet in diameter, was suspended over the conveyor, which carried a flow of air up to the working position to dilute the methane gas and provide air for the workmen. The flow of air back along the roadway was slow and, as a result, the temperature was higher than was normal on the coalfaces at the mine. George knelt down and wiped the sweat from his face.

'The bloody trouble is, Boss, that this two foot of floor that we are getting up has a six-inch hard layer of stone in it. It's right in the middle, and it's very difficult to drill the boreholes through it. The lads will explain it to you. They have to drill through the hard layer because it's that which needs the explosives to break it up. If they don't put enough boreholes in, the hard layer ends up as big slabs, which the men have to break up with hammers before they load it onto the conveyors.'

'I can see that band of rock in the side of the roadway, George. It looks like fine-grained sandstone. We have to take it up, to get to the height of roadway we need. Let's go in to the working face and talk to the men.'

Before they moved off there was the sound and shockwave of an explosive charge being fired. As they walked forward, a cloud of dust and explosive fumes came to meet them. When they reached the working face, the men were inspecting the results of the shotfiring. The coalface was broken up and heaved forward for a depth of over six feet.

'Are you ready to load that out, now?' said Roy to the two men. The deputy who had fired the round of shots stood by the men.

'This is the easy part, Boss,' replied one of the men. 'This loader will soon shift that heap of coal as fast as the conveyor will take it. We can usually do two rounds each shift; it's getting the floor up that's the problem.'

'Mr Turnbull has been explaining that to me,' said Roy. 'That is why I've come to have a look. The finished road is what we need for the retreat face. The standard of work looks good.'

'When we started we thought that we would need just a few shots to loosen the floor, and that the loading-machine would break up the dirt suitable for loading on the conveyor,' another worker said. 'In fact, we have to pepper the floor dirt with shot holes to break that hard layer. And it's a bugger drilling through that rock band for each borehole.'

'We're working to a cycle of taking the coal out for about thirty yards and then pulling everything back. Then they take the floor dirt up and set the permanent supports,' said George. 'We expected the last part of the cycle to be easy, but it's taking as long as getting the coal out.'

'This floor dirt is stopping us earning some good money at the end of the week,' said one of the men. 'We need to try something a bit different.'

'OK,' said Roy. 'I'll arrange to get a representative from the explosives company to come down and see if we are using the right explosive. He might recommend something a bit stronger that will crack the hard band. He's also an expert at drilling patterns, so you'll be able to explain to him that you want to have to drill as few holes as possible. We'll sort out something to speed up the extraction of the floor dirt. Let's go and have a look at the other roadway, now, Mr Turnbull.'

'If you're going to visit them, you'll see the problem,' said the deputy. 'They're working on the floor dirt today.'

'They might ask you to drill a few holes in the floor!' said one of the men, with a wink and a grin to his mate. 'That'll encourage you to find a solution mighty quick.'

'Don't thee be cheeky,' said George. 'The Boss has come here today to try and help you.'

'I'll see what I can do,' said Roy. 'I know that we can make some improvements.'

As they were walking back along the roadway, the conveyor soon passed them with a full load of coal on it.

'That's a wonderful sight,' said George, pointing to the conveyor 'That loading-machine soon fills out the coal. The men have got used to it and they can make it talk.'

'That's as it should be, George'

When they visited the other roadway the men were drilling boreholes in the floor. They demonstrated how difficult it was drilling through the hard rock band, and they showed how the drill bits were being blunted very quickly. Roy explained his intentions, and the men were pleased that their problem was understood.

★

When Roy got out of the pit, he rang the explosives company and explained the problem in detail. He got the company to send a representative to the pit the next day to undertake an inspection. He suggested that George should meet the explosives representative and accompany him into the Fuston seam roadways, and then they should both come to his office for a meeting in the afternoon.

Wednesday 28 April 1965

At ten o'clock Roy met with Jeff Briggs, the finance officer. He produced the figures covering the first three months of the year for Martins. These would be the subject of Roy's next accountability meeting at Region, which was scheduled in the near future. Martins had made a profit for the three months, but it was not as large as Roy had hoped for. Jeff had been given a long list of detailed questions that Roy needed answers for. This information would let Roy answer any questions that may arise at the accountability meeting. He was determined to show that he had a full knowledge of the financial figures for the pit, as well as the latest operational position. It was a long time since Martins had shown a profit over a three-month period, but that did not mean that Roy could expect an easy passage.

★

The meeting in the afternoon with the explosives representative was a revelation to Roy and George. The young man approached the problem with caution, but with new ideas.

'I can understand why you are working the roadways like you are, Mr Dobson, but it does involve a lot of double work, setting the supports twice and withdrawing the equipment to take the floor dirt up.'

'Are you suggesting that we take the coal and the floor dirt out at the same time?' asked Roy, somewhat surprised at the suggestion.

'I think it is an option, Mr Dobson,' the young man replied. 'We could make some adjustment to the explosives to help break the floor dirt up with the present method, but the real difficulty is drilling the shot holes, and the only way to help with that would be to introduce compressed air drills. That's a further complication to the operations.'

'How would you suggest we work the coal and the floor dirt as a combined operation?' asked George Turnbull, who was also puzzled by the suggestion.

'You could mount the coal-cutter on a frame, and undercut the coal seam as you are doing now. Then drill the coal seam as you are currently doing, but also drill the floor dirt. These holes in the floor dirt could be drilled just underneath the hard rock band. The holes would be easy to drill and we could arrange a pattern of holes and explosives that would break up the hard band of rock. Then you would fill out the coal and dirt for the full excavation and set the final supports. To fire a full round you would need permission from the Mines Inspectorate, but they have given permission in similar cases and I can let you have details of these.'

'Well, that seems a good suggestion, George,' said Roy. 'What do you think?'

'I'm all for it, Boss, if we can get permission. It'll simplify the operation a great deal.'

Roy thanked the explosives representative and asked him for a detailed report on which he could base his discussions with the Mines Inspectorate.

'When we have sorted this out, George, we'll need to have the men in to a training session, so that they understand exactly how the work has to be organised. If the Mines Inspectorate gives permission, they will pay us a few visits to check that everything is being done to the right standard.'

'I think the lads will be glad to operate it as a single-pass operation, if it avoids drilling through that rock band,' said George.

★

Helen was checking that everything was in order for her visitors. She had arranged an afternoon meeting, at three o'clock, convenient for Bob who was on dayshift. Helen hoped that there would be no problems that would keep him at the pit. Sandra was looking after the three children, so that Peggy was free to concentrate on the proceedings. James and Gwen would be there, and Helen hoped that they would lead the discussion. She had the kettle heated, and cups and saucers laid out for tea; she'd baked a sandwich cake and filled it with jam and cream. She wanted everyone to be relaxed, so there was no tension in the discussions. She knew that this was the day when Peggy had to make some big decisions.

A lot had happened over the last ten weeks: baby Dawn was thriving, and giving out toothless smiles quite freely, especially to Sandra, who spent many afternoons with Peggy and the baby; Peggy, too, was thriving and putting on weight, despite breastfeeding the baby; the two boys were happy with life at their temporary home with Bob and Janet;

Michael was now potty-trained and starting to talk; Tony was playing the older brother role and accepting responsibility beyond his years.

Peggy had made several approaches to Tony to discuss the possibility of both the boys staying with Bob and Janet. His answers had somewhat shocked her with their directness and simplicity. On one occasion he had replied, 'That's OK.' Another time, he'd said, 'That's fine by me.' Peggy wondered where he had learned such an expression. Janet had explained that it was a stock answer from Bob, to any suggestion made by her.

★

When her visitors arrived, Helen served the refreshments. She was pleased that Bob had two pieces of cake and appeared quite relaxed. When everyone had finished, Janet and Helen cleared the table. Helen then looked across at James Folds, silently signalling that it was time to get down to business.

'I would like us to start with a word of prayer,' said James. All heads were bowed and a strange silence filled the room. The ticking of the clock on the sideboard was deafening.

'Oh Lord, we come before you now, seeking your continued presence as we try to look to the future of Peggy and her family. We are confident that you will guide us in our discussions, because over the past two months, your Holy Spirit has been continually with us, so that this tragedy has not destroyed Peggy and her children. Your love for little children is assured, and we want Peggy's children to be happy and thrilled with life. We want to hear them laughing and full of joy. We thank you, Lord, that Janet and Bob have come forward and offered their lives to serve these children. Peggy, Janet, and Bob deserve that supreme happiness that comes from seeing children grow in a family and develop into young people and adults that are blessed by you. We especially hold before you Peggy, whose bravery and courage has amazed us all. Give her the strength to make the right decisions for herself and for her children, as we consider the future. Amen.'

Janet was wiping tears from her eyes, and Helen had a lump in her throat. However Helen felt that she should say a few words.

'I have to say that my prayers ever since Gerry's death have been filled with you, Peggy, and the children,' she said. 'I hoped that we could find a solution that gave you all a future that was full of hope and promise. In my opinion, Bob and Janet have provided that opportunity.'

'Janet and Bob, you should have the first chance to tell us how you feel,' said James Folds. 'You have had an opportunity to look after these boys. You know what the challenge is in terms of work, but more importantly, in the every day commitment to provide love and nourishment.'

Bob looked across at Janet, as much as to say that she must do the talking.

'What can I say?' said Janet, with a wave of her hand. 'The boys have been wonderful to look after, and very brave about the loss of their father. We have tried to give them all the love and care that they need, but we have not aimed to take anything from Peggy. Can I just say something else?'

'You can, indeed,' said James. Janet took a deep breath and then continued.

'When we decided that we would like to have children, we had ideas of what it would be like. And we were both very sad when we found out that it was probable that we would never be able to have any children of our own. But now we know that our ideas were all wrong. It's not possible to understand how wonderful it is to have children as part of the family until you have had them about the house continuously, every day – the things they say; the questions they ask; the cuddles they need; the challenges they bring. But then there are the goodnight hugs they give us and their smiles of appreciation.' Janet paused, with her thoughts overpowering her words. She spoke through a great sigh. 'Peggy, you can have them back, because they are yours, but we shall miss them more than we can ever explain.'

'Thank you, Janet,' said James. 'We all know that no one could have given those boys a better home during this period than you and Bob. Can we hear from you now, Peggy?'

'I have little to say,' said Peggy, in a quiet voice. 'I shall never forget the shock and panic that I suffered when I heard of the accident and Gerry's death. How was I going to look after the two boys and the baby? I wasn't sure the baby would even be born, after all the stress. You all told me that help would be provided, and you certainly made sure it was. I am very thankful to you all. I'll never be able to repay you.' She paused.

'You have nothing to repay,' said Helen. 'Seeing you and the baby both growing in health and strength is everything that we all wish to see. It's more than a repayment for what we have been able to do to help you.'

'Janet has been my friend since we were teenagers, and she has stood by me through all my troubles,' continued Peggy. 'Without her, I would definitely have gone under on several occasions. It's a lot to ask, but I would like her and Bob to continue to have the two boys. I can see that the boys are happy, and I want them to stay that way. Janet and Bob, I can trust you to do what is right for them, and bring them up far better than I could on my own. I hope that I'm not being selfish but, with the boys settled, I think that I will be able to bring up Dawn on my own, and give her a good life and a secure future.'

Peggy stood up and went over to Janet. They hugged each other and tears streamed down their faces. Everyone else got to their feet, and there were handshakes and hugs all round.

There was some further debate, and they agreed to wait another six months before Janet and Bob started proceedings to adopt the two boys. Peggy would keep seeing the boys, and there would be no problem with her being referred to by them as 'mother'. The boys called Bob and Janet 'Uncle Bob' and 'Aunty Janet' and it was considered best to continue with this.

After another cup of tea, and more cake, James Folds said a prayer of praise and gratitude at the outcome of the meeting.

Thursday 6 May 1965

Roy had spent several hours in discussions with the Mines Inspectorate in an attempt to get them to agree to a system of shotfiring such that the Fuston seam developments could work the coal seam and the floor dirt as a single-pass operation. There had been an underground visit by a specialist inspector, who had recognised the need for a change in the method of working; there had also been discussions with the trade unions, to ensure their support.

When the letter of exemption came, with its detailed definitions and descriptions of how the work was to be carried out, Roy arranged a briefing meeting with all the workmen and officials involved. It lasted for some two hours and he had to answer lots of questions from the workmen and officials. He was confident that everyone knew exactly how the operations should be carried out. He concluded the meeting with a final comment.

'We now have the co-operation of the Mines Inspectorate to allow us to work these roadways with a better mining system. They have given us exemptions under the Coal Mines Act to allow us to do this. They are relying on us to carry out the work exactly to the conditions of the exemption. They will no doubt be coming to visit us to make sure that we are complying. I am relying on you lads to not let me, and them, down. When they come, I hope that they will see a mining operation to the very best standards – that they can talk about as an example when they visit other pits.'

'You can rely on us, Boss. We'll not let you down,' replied one of the miners.

Friday 21 May 1965

The new system had been in operation for two weeks when Roy got the telephone call to inform him of the first inspection. The Mines Inspector, Mr Franks, had paid two previous visits to Martins, and on neither occasion had he raised any major issues from what he had seen. Roy was greatly relieved that this visit was even better. Operations were being carried out in both roadways when they got to them. The supports were set according to the plans that were posted at the entrance to the roadway; everything was tidy along the completed roadway, and the whole roadway was covered with a layer of stone dust; the ventilation system was up-to-date, and there was no methane in any place where the inspector tested; in the two roadways they saw different parts of the cycle – in one, the men were setting supports; and in the other they were loading out the coal and dirt.

Over lunch, Mr Franks recapped on his visit.

'You have a very good mining system in that seam, Mr Dobson,' he said. 'The standard of work is excellent and a credit to the men and management of the pit. You might have a gold mine in that seam when you get the coalfaces working. Have you a lot of coal to work in the Fuston seam?'

'Yes, there is a lot,' replied Roy. 'I'll ask the Surveyor to bring the plans in, so that you can see the extent of the workings, if you like.'

The Surveyor brought the plans and one of them showed the limited areas worked at surrounding pits.

'It's surprising, with a seam section of over six feet, that so little has been worked so far,' said Mr Franks.

The Surveyor explained that the rock roof had made driving roadways very difficult, and at some pits there had been incidents of sudden weighting of the sandstone roof that had destroyed the supports.

'We're aware of some of the history of difficulties,' replied Roy. 'That is why we have gone for retreat coalfaces. Modern mining roof supports are very different to the wooden pit props of the old days.'

'That's true,' said Mr Franks.

Roy also discussed with the inspector the latest information about the circumstances surrounding the explosion at Cambrian Colliery in Clybach Vale in South Wales, which had occurred earlier in the week. The deaths of thirty-one miners had resulted from the explosion. It was another tragedy circulating around the coal industry.

The inspector left the pit with a clean car and a bag of sticks in his boot, and an easy report to write. It had been one of his better days. Roy, also, was satisfied that it had been a good day. His immediate priority was to delve into the progress with the Central Conveying Scheme.

Tuesday 25 May 1965

Roy had asked Gordon to organise a special meeting with his key staff, insisting that everyone must be present. When the staff were assembled in the conference room there were puzzled looks on their faces.

'This will be a short meeting,' Roy began, 'but it is an important one. When I go to the accountability meeting next week there will be some important issues discussed about Martins. We have a good story to tell because, as you know, Martins made a financial profit over the first quarter of this year. No one remembers when that last happened. But Mr Pickersgill and his team are not interested in the past; they want to know about the future. We have to deliver two objectives by the end of the August holiday. One, we have to have 58s coalface ready for production, and, two, we have to have the Central Conveying Scheme completed, so that we are loading the coal in the pit bottom. This is a great challenge to us all.' There were nods of agreement.

'I'll explain how we are going to do this. Firstly, we are all, as a management team, going to be working through the August holiday. Some of you may be able to take a break at Whit, in a week's time, but in general, holidays will have to wait until September.'

'Secondly,' he went on, 'we are going to have a series of sessions when we go through Mike's detailed action programme, which lists everything that has to be done to complete the Central Conveying Scheme. In those meetings we will try to tease out anything that we can do before the holiday break, and who will do it. If any job has been left out, this will be the time to have it included.'

'Thirdly, we will identify how long each job will take, and who is going to do it, and who is going to supervise it. Then it will be your job to ensure that you have the right men available through the holiday period. If we need to call in extra men or extra supervision, we need to know now. I hope that you'll be able to carry this project through with Martins men; it's their pit and they are probably more reliable than outsiders. So you will not be pleasing me if you ask for lots of contractors to do the work. If the men are leaning towards taking their holidays at the normal week, suggest to them that the weather is forecast to be bad in August.' Roy got a few smiles from his last comment.

Friday 28 May 1965

Over three days, Roy and Mike had held separate sessions with all the staff that would be involved in completing the Central Conveying Scheme on schedule. At the end of these briefings, Roy knew more about the scheme than anybody else. He also had a list of agreed actions to bring the work forward. Most important of these was to organise the building of the trunk conveyor in the new roadway, as soon as Cento had finished driving it. Also, it had been decided to alter the current track in the pit bottom, so that the new loading point could be constructed along with the conveyor drive. It would make current operations in the pit bottom more constricted, but that would be a price worth paying to complete that part of the project work early. These decisions caused a host of issues with machinery manufacturers, requiring delivery dates to be brought forward.

Roy had had a separate session with his undermanager, regarding 58s mechanised coalface. George was confident that the mining work for 58s would be completed by the end of June. Roy agreed that they should aim to complete the installation in July, so that all the pit resources could focus on the Conveying Scheme during the pit holidays. George had been given permission to work weekends to achieve that objective.

Roy went home with his mind saturated with details and decisions involving the project work. He also had lots of documents from Jeff Briggs, with financial information that might be relevant at his forthcoming accountability meeting. He was going to have a busy weekend. In all the excitment of work, he had forgotten another important event happening that weekend.

★

When Roy staggered into the house with his overflowing briefcase in one hand and several folders in the other, Helen gave him a questioning look.

'I hope all that luggage doesn't mean you're intending to spend this weekend buried in pit papers?'

'It's my accountability next Wednesday, and I have a lot to swot up,' replied Roy.

'Well, you won't get much done on Sunday; it's the christening on the morning, and you have to be there. Had you forgotten?'

'Oh, I'm afraid it had slipped my mind,' replied Roy, with an apologetic look on his face.

'You can't have been concentrating at all, then, when you've been at home during this last week. You've obviously not noticed all the baking I've been doing, ready for the christening party coming back here for a sandwich after the service.' Helen adopted a rather militant role. 'You'll be able to make up to me by being a good host when they get back here. We will not, however, expect you to change Dawn's nappy. That should be a relief for you,' Helen said, with a smile that lightened the atmosphere. Roy put down his papers and went over and gave Helen a kiss.

'I'm sorry, love; I have been preoccupied with the pit during this last week. I know that this weekend is an important time for you. You have done wonders to rescue the Moore family from tragedy. I'll not let you down on Sunday, especially now I know that I shall not be on nappy-changing duty.'

Saturday 29 May 1965

While they were having their morning cup of coffee, Helen told her husband about the arrangements for the christening.

'James Folds is going to make the christening the focal point of the tomorrow's morning service. He usually has christenings as an extra, after the end of the service, but this one will be different. So the organisation is a little complex, however I think everything is now in place. Peggy has asked Sandra to be a godparent, as well as us two, with Bob and Janet. Tony and Michael will be there and they'll be able to go to the front with Bob and Janet, but Michael may not want to do that. Sandra has persuaded her friend, Pauline, to be there to look after Michael. Pauline has been with Sandra to the Hall's and made friends with Michael. In case there are any complications, Gwen Folds is going to sit with us so that she can help Pauline. Your job is to get us all there on time. We will take our two boys up first, with Sandra and me. You'll then have to nip to Martins Lane to pick up Bob and Janet and their two boys, along with Peggy and the baby. It'll be a bit of a squeeze, but I'm sure your car is big enough to get them all in. After the service your job is to do two trips to get us all back here. James Folds might help, with the spare seats in his car.'

'You seem to have thought of everything,' said Roy.

'I am hoping that the Good Lord will keep his eye on Martins Main so that there are no emergencies to distract you tomorrow. One last thing: there is a response to a question for the godparents in the christening part of the service. The response is 'With God's help we will.' Don't mumble the answer; I shall say it out loud and clear, and I have had a word with Sandra for her to do the same. I don't like it when people mumble, as though they are not sure if they mean it. I know, Roy, that you can speak loud and clear when it's something to do with the pit; this reply could be more important for little Dawn than anything to do with the pit.'

Sunday 30 May 1965

The morning was fine and sunny, and Roy delivered his second car-load to the church fifteen minutes before the start of the service. Helen met them and suggested that they stay outside in the sunshine, as Willie had reserved the front row of seats for them. She admired how smart Tony and Michael looked, and was impressed that they seemed to understand that they were to behave in church. Peggy was dressed in a new, pale-blue coat and skirt over a darker blue blouse. Her hair was swept up and her make-up discreet. She was obviously nervous, but Helen was surprised by how much improved she looked. She went over and had a look at Dawn, who was fast asleep in Peggy's arms.

'Let Sandra have her for a few minutes, Peggy, to give you a rest.' Sandra took Dawn, with the confidence of someone who was experienced at doing that task. So smooth was the changeover that Dawn didn't even wake up.

'Just relax, Peggy,' said Helen. 'Don't worry about anything; James Folds is very good on these occasions.'

When they went into the church they saw that it was almost full. The children of the Sunday School were also in the congregation, prior to going off to their classes.

James Folds opened the service with a few words to set the scene.

'Six weeks ago, on Easter Sunday, we celebrated the resurrection of our Lord and Saviour, Jesus Christ. Today we celebrate a new life born into our community. We shall take the christening part of our service after the first hymn, so that the Sunday School pupils can share it with us.'

After the first hymn, Reverend Folds called the christening party out to the front. Bob held Tony's hand and Janet had Michael in her arms. They stood on one side of Peggy; Helen and Roy, with Sandra, stood on the other side. Some of the Sunday School children gathered by the communion rail for a better look at the proceedings.

The minister spoke informally of the place of children in the ministry of Jesus, and of the long tradition of babies at the start of their lives being brought into the church. He took the baby from Peggy who, in a clear voice, named her as Dawn. Dawn was awake by now, and when he touched her forehead three times with the water, she blinked but didn't cry. James then put the three questions to Peggy on her responsibilities in bringing up her baby. On each occasion, with a clear but soft voice, she answered, 'With God's help, I will.' This contrasted with the reply from the godparents, which was loud and clear: 'With God's help, we will.'

James then faced the congregation and lifted up Dawn so that they could all see her. Her eyes were open and she looked out into the church.

'I want you all to look at little Dawn. She has come into the world with an apparent disadvantage. She was born a few days after her father was killed in the mine. She will never know her father. There will always be a gap in her life. It is our task to fill that gap. We have to make sure that she is not at a disadvantage. She needs love and friendship; she needs friends who play with her and make her smile; she needs people who will give her confidence and hope. Her mother will give her all these things to the best of her ability, but Dawn needs help from the people of Upthorpe, and especially from this church. Will you, in this church, take little Dawn in your arms and give her your love? But most of all, will you maintain this church as a witness to our Lord and Saviour, so that little Dawn is held in the arms of Jesus and so that the power of the Holy Spirit guides her throughout her life?' There was a loud response of 'With God's help, we will.' The minister walked down the aisle and showed the baby to the congregation. Some members held out their hands to touch the child as she passed, and there were whispers of 'God Bless you, little one.'

The christening party returned to their pew, and Peggy cuddled Dawn. She bent down to kiss the baby's head. Helen squeezed Roy's hand and she turned and gave him a big smile. The children left for the Sunday School and James deliberately kept the rest of the service short. He spoke briefly on the wonder of children and how their innocence and trust was an example to grown-ups. In the prayers, he prayed openly for Dawn, and for Peggy. He also prayed for Tony and Michael, and their new life with Bob and Janet. At the end of the service there was a queue of church members wanting to speak to Peggy and admire the baby. While this was going on, Roy took Helen, with Sandra and Pauline, back to the house and then returned for the rest. James took Peggy, and Robert and John Dobson, in his car, so Roy ended up with Bob and Janet and the two boys to complete the party. In the car, Tony found his tongue.

'I've been in this car before,' he said.

'When was that?' asked Roy, in all innocence.

'When we went to the hospital,' replied Tony.

★

Helen had everything organised when Roy arrived back at the house. She had a low table set up for her boys and Tony and Michael. Janet was serving them small sandwiches, followed by jelly. Peggy went upstairs to feed the baby and Sandra helped her. The grown-ups had larger sandwiches, with pies and sausage rolls, and there were cakes and trifle to follow. Pauline was organised to serve tea or coffee, and orange juice to the boys. Roy realised that he was surplus to requirements for domestic duties, so he decided to be a good host and talk to his guests. He tackled Bob first, who had a plateful of sandwiches.

'How is life on 57s coalface now, Bob?'

'Alright, Mr Dobson, just now,' he replied. 'But George has told me that he'll want me on 58s face when they get to the installation work. He says that he expects to install it quicker than 57s, now that we know all about the equipment. Also, the Mechanical Engineer has asked me to be available for the holiday week, to work on the Central Conveying Scheme installation.'

'Well, that's great for you, Bob,' said Roy. 'You are in big demand at Martins. That is what we need – experienced craftsmen. Have you agreed to work during the holidays?'

'I've discussed it with Janet, and she agrees that we'll take a holiday in September, after the schools are back. Tony won't be starting school until next year, so it's no problem. So

I'll be putting my name down to work during the holiday week.'

'Excellent, Bob,' said Roy. 'Enjoy your lunch. I'll have a chat with James and Gwen.' The Folds were on their own, in the corner of the room. Roy went over to them.

'Roy, we just want you to know what a wonderful role Helen has played in supporting Peggy and finding a long-term solution to the family's problems,' said Gwen, in a quiet voice so that Helen couldn't hear her over the other noise in the room.

'She is an inspirational Christian in all that she does,' added James.

'She is full of praise for your involvement,' said Roy. 'She's told me, on several occasions, that it was your support that gave her the confidence to carry on and do what she thought was right.'

Peggy had come back downstairs without the baby, and Helen was helping her to get a plate of sandwiches. She brought Peggy over to Roy and the Folds.

'The baby is asleep on the bed in the spare room, so Peggy can have a bite in peace. Pauline is taking the boys upstairs now to play with the toys. She'll keep an eye on the baby, so that Sandra can come down and eat too,' said Helen, setting the scene. 'I've brought Peggy across to make an introduction. She knows Gwen and James very well, but she has never met my husband. So there you are, Peggy, this is Roy.' Peggy looked around to put her plate down so that she could shake hands, but Roy put his arm round her shoulder.

'No formalities, Peggy,' he said. 'We may not have met, but I feel I know you very well, from all that I have heard from Helen. I'm glad to see you looking well. I'm a great admirer of you, and the way that you have faced the tragedy of losing Gerry. You have been very brave and I think today marks another step forward.'

'Thank you, Mr Dobson,' replied Peggy. 'Yes, today was another step forward. It was a wonderful service, and all the people at the church were very kind.' She looked across at James. 'Thank you, James.'

'Don't thank me, Peggy. Little Dawn and you made that service. It is what worship needs – real situations and real people. The church thrives on examples of where there has been tragedy, and pain and despair, but where the story continues with people rallying round, throwing in love and hard work, opening doors so that the love of God and the power of the Holy Spirit brings renewed life and hope. Believe me, nobody who was at that service this morning will ever forget it. Little Dawn will not remember the service, but she had the starring role when I took her through the church and showed her to the congregation.'

Roy realised that Helen's respect for James Folds was well-founded.

Monday 31 May 1965

Mr Jenkins rang Roy early in the morning. When they'd covered the results for the previous week, and Roy had answered some other questions about the pit, Reg made a surprise announcement.

'I want to come over this afternoon and have a session with you about the accountability meeting. There are some things you need to know. I'll be there about two o'clock. Sort out your diary so that you are free, and tell Gordon we don't want to be disturbed.'

'Right, Mr Jenkins I'll arrange that.' He cancelled his planned underground visit, and then spent the morning sorting out his papers for the accountability. It was so unlike Mr Jenkins to arrange such a meeting that Roy could only think that it meant there was a serious problem somewhere.

★

Reg arrived on time, and he declined a drink. He sat with Roy at the large conference table in the office. Roy had laid out all his accountability papers in readiness. Reg came straight to the point.

'Pickersgill has been to London, with the other Regional Chairman, and there has been some tough talking about the performance of the industry. As a result of this, he has been as fierce as hell at the accountability meetings so far. He was so mad at the excuses of one colliery manager, that he's shifted him and downgraded him to be a deputy manager at another pit. You'll be hearing about that in a few days. So you cannot expect an easy ride on Wednesday, even if your results are better than Martins has achieved for many years.'

'Forewarned is forearmed,' replied Roy.

There followed an hour of discussions about the financial figures for the first quarter. Roy explained all the answers he had for the variances from the budget. Certain factors they decided to play down, but one they decided to emphasise.

'One advantage with Martins is that there's a ready market for all your coal,' said Reg. 'You must mention that.'

'We have also raised the percentage of large coal. The deal we made on the Home Coal with Cobba is releasing more large coal into the market.'

'That is an important plus; you must work that into the discussion somehow. If the last three months is reasonable, it will be the future that Pickersgill will focus on.'

Roy gave a detailed account of all that he had arranged about 58s coalface.

'I agree with your plan to install 58s face before the holiday, using overtime,' said Reg. 'But don't make any reference to overtime. Just say that the face will be ready before the holiday.'

Roy explained the plan to have all the management team on duty over the holidays to complete the changeover with the conveyor scheme.

'You must get that in,' said Reg.

Roy spent half an hour outlining his recent discussions with his staff. The plans for the Central Conveying Scheme were then discussed. Roy explained that the trunk roadway, driven by Cento, should be completed before the end of the month, and that one week should see the roadway cleaned up and the temporary conveyor system removed. He explained that the two conveyor drives would be installed by colliery staff, but that he would need additional men to build the conveyor structure. The Cento men were excellent miners at developing roadways, he said, but they would not necessarily be the right men for installing the conveyor structure. He did wonder if UK Mining and Tunnelling might be able to do that work.

'Leave that to me,' said Reg. 'I'll have a word with Richard Wallace, and get him to come and inspect the roadway when Cento have finished. It may be better to pay them on a day-works basis, but I am sure they'll be able to provide some suitable men.'

'They will have an incentive to give us value for money, because I could need outside contractors for other work in the future,' said Roy.

Roy tabled the layout plan for that pit bottom bunker, with the Surveyor's detailed drawings of how it would work. Mr Jenkins thought the proposal was sound, but again he insisted that it should not be raised at the accountability meeting.

The Fuston seam developments were the next topic for discussion. Roy reported that the new method of working had increased the advance to thirty-five yards per week for each roadway, and that this was giving a weekly output from the seam of six hundred tons of coal. The Fuston seam developments could give an output of about a thousand tons per week, after the holidays, if an additional team of men was deployed.

'This Fuston seam should not be raised at the accountability meeting. Pickersgill might want to know the start-up date for the first retreat coalface, though. Have you got a date for that?'

'I'm not keen to give an early date,' replied Roy. 'There's a lot to resolve on the face design, and it will be a big installation. I think we should suggest February next year.'

'I can back that,' said Reg. 'There are some new designs of shearers being discussed, and they might be ideal for the Fuston seam faces. The priority for Martins is clear: we have to get this conveyor scheme completed, and 57s and 58s coalfaces into full production. That should set Martins up for the future. The picture here is much better than most pits, but Pickersgill wants more pits improving like Martins, to get the Regional results up to the right level.'

★

When Reg Jenkins left, Roy was exhausted, but he sat down at his desk and made a list of things he had to raise at the accountability meeting. Then, in block capitals, he listed those matters that he must not raise.

He decided to get back to the real world of operations. He buzzed his secretary.

'What is happening in the pit, Gordon?'

'Not too good, Boss. There's been a derailment of tubs on the Benton seam haulage system. It happened just after Mr Jenkins came. George has gone back down the pit. He sent a message about half an hour ago to say that they have got the pit tubs sorted out and they are now re-laying the damaged track. I expect to hear from him anytime now.'

'That will mean 57s coalface will have lost about half their shift,' said Roy looking at his watch. 'That is a blow, at the start of the week.'

Tuesday 1 June 1965

The Enclosure was in session and had been discussing cricket, with Cliff giving his considered views on the Yorkshire team players, some of whom he had met when he was umpiring in the Yorkshire League.

A lorry turned slowly into Martins Lane, and the team had a good look at its load of three large pit tubs, obviously new from the manufacturers.

'They must be the first delivery of the new tubs for winding the coal at the number one shaft,' said George. 'They do look bloody big, compared with the old ones. I hear that there will be two new cages for the shaft as well. My mates tell me that it will be one hell of a job during the holiday week. As well as changing the two cages, there are some fabrications to alter at the shaft top, as the cages are three inches longer than the old ones. Apparently the tipplers which empty the coal out near the shaft side will take the new tubs with minor modifications, as they will tip one of the new tubs instead of two of the old ones.'

'I think that all the management team will be working the holiday week,' said Pat. 'The Manager has said no one can have holidays until September.'

'He certainly puts his foot down, does this fellow,' said Charlie. 'And he is getting some coal out. The lads on the pit top are talking about the increase in coal trains leaving the pit, and there is more coal going away by lorry.'

'The prospects must be good for Martins,' commented Cliff. 'The pit is selling all its coal and not having to stock any, like some other local pits. With the increase in shaft capacity, and another mechanised coalface, it's difficult to calculate how much the output might increase.'

'Don't count your chickens too soon,' said Albert. 'The pit has had a good run lately. This manager will not get everything his own way; I'm sure the union will have some problems for him, before long. Mind you, I have lost faith in Cobba and Jimmy to take on the management; they seem to be happy that the pit is doing well.'

'They should be happy,' said Cliff. 'There's a lot more money coming out of Martins every pay day.'

'There's certainly more beer being drunk in the Club,' put in Charlie. 'They've taken on another girl at the bar, after there were complaints from members who had to wait too long to get served.'

Another lorry, this one carrying a load of powered supports for 58s mechanised face, turned into Martins Lane.

'Bloody hell,' said Albert. 'There's some money going into this pit. This manager must have a supporter at Region putting the money up. I hope they know what they are doing.'

★

On the evening before an accountability meeting Roy would normally spend time looking through his papers, but he decided to attend the meeting of the Welfare Committee at the Club. He thought it might give him a chance to talk with Cobba about one or two pit issues.

The meeting covered the normal business very quickly, so that two extra items on the agenda could be discussed. Business was good; the takings were up; there were more people using the Club; the entertainment acts were pulling in the crowds, and the one-armed bandits had never taken so much money.

They then moved on to the extra agenda items. Firstly, there was the new barrelage rate. Cobba spoke on this matter, and there was keen interest from the committee.

'We have now received the cheque for the barrelage for the first quarter of this year, and the treasurer will have put it in the bank,' said Cobba. 'I have not raised it before with this committee, because I wanted to ensure that we got it, but, with Mr Dobson, I met the brewery rep just before the end of last year and agreed a rate with him. The new rate, with the increased consumption in the Club, means that we will be able to increase the expenses paid to committee members by ten per cent compared with last year. You'll realise that this will place this Club's committee members at significantly higher expense rates than other clubs around here.'

There were comments of approval all round.

'Would you like to say a few words, Mr Dobson?' asked Cobba. Roy responded to the script, as already agreed with Cobba.

'We are very fortunate to have this agreement with the brewery company. I know you all work hard to make this a successful club, but I think you should agree that these rates are treated as confidential information. I shall be very disappointed if anyone discloses them outside this room.'

'I'll go further than that, Mr Dobson,' said Cobba quite forcibly. 'If it is proved that someone has disclosed these figures, I think that they should not continue as a member of this committee, or of the Club.' There were nods from the committee, although some felt that it was rather a harsh approach.

The final item was to go through the detailed arrangements for the children's trip to Scarborough, on Saturday next week. It was open for all children under ten, from families of Club members, and there could be one adult for each two children. There had been a record number of applications and this meant there would be six buses instead of the five they'd had the previous year. A committee member was identified to be in charge of each bus, and it was his responsibility to ensure that no one was left behind at each stopping point. Roy thought that this was a sensible way to spend a significant part of the profits from the one-armed bandits.

As the meeting broke up, Roy asked Cobba if they could have a few minutes in the office to discuss one or two pit matters.

'What is it, Mr Dobson?' asked Cobba.

'It's really a minor change on the Central Conveying Scheme. As you know, Cento has done a good job, and they should have the roadway completed and cleaned up by the end of this month. It was always our plan to get them to install the conveyor structure under the contract. However, the men that they have are top rate men, so the rate they will charge will be too high. I plan to get another contractor to take on the job with more appropriate men, which should save us some money. We want to get those conveyors running before the holiday. Martins engineers will build the conveyor drives, but we need the others to build the conveyor structure.'

'I'm not sure about that, Boss,' replied Cobba, shaking his head. 'What will Jimmy have to say?'

'I don't think Jimmy should complain. We'll keep him doing his workmen's inspection role. It will be essential to keep safety issues up-front during the next phase.'

'That should help. Jimmy has been going around saying that the reason the job's gone so well is because he's been involved. Any bugger who believes that must have a slate off!'

'Just let Jimmy keep thinking he's important, while we get the job done. Will you have a word with him? I'm at an accountability meeting, tomorrow, and I know that Mr Pickersgill will be asking questions about that scheme. It's so important to have everything working by the end of the holiday.'

'I'll try and fix it, Boss.'

Roy left straightaway, but Cobba declined a lift, as he wanted to put in an appearance at the bar.

Wednesday 2 June 1965

The accountability meeting was at two o'clock, so Roy presumed that his was the first one of the afternoon session. He hoped that Mr Pickersgill had enjoyed his lunch and was in a good mood. Roy had no appetite, so he'd just had one sandwich. He arrived early, and entered Diane's office.

'How are you, Diane?' he asked.

'I'm fine, Mr Dobson. That is more than can be said for some of the colliery managers.'

'Oh dear; I hope that I'm not the next one to be slaughtered.'

'I think you will be alright.' She gave him a smile.

When Roy was called in, he got the impression that there were some rather ragged people around the table, as a result of the morning meetings.

'Well, it's a change to have a pit that is showing progress,' began Mr Pickersgill. 'So the good weekly results before Christmas have been maintained for a full quarter?'

'Yes, Sir, we are beginning to see some signs of consistency. But there is more to come.'

They went through the figures, and Roy was able to give reasons for the variances. On the marketing side, he explained how the Home Coal deal with Cobba had increased the large coal available for the commercial market. This was noted. On the wages front, he explained how he had stopped all recruitment, so that the jobs saved from the Central Conveying Scheme would reflect in real wages cost savings. He had to accept that the overtime costs were too high, but he hoped to resolve that when the major changes were completed at the pit holiday. He emphasised that the whole management team would be on duty over the holiday period to complete the changeover. That, too, was noted. The meeting also accepted that the use of outside contractors had been a success. Roy gave assurances that 58s coalface would commence production after the holidays. This would fill the additional shaft capacity, he explained, and allow the output to increase. There was no mention of the Fuston seam.

Mr Pickersgill summed up the meeting.

'We have seen some progress, which is beginning to reflect in the financial figures. There is potential for further increases in output and improved profitability. Of course, Mr Dobson, you have to accept that if Martins is to be a front-running pit in Yorkshire, there is still a long, long way to go. You'll have to lift your sights even higher, and take the pit upwards with you. It's still a great challenge.' Pickersgill looked him in the eye. Roy felt the need to reply.

'I will be seeking to take the pit up to its full potential, Mr Pickersgill. I think we are only at the start.'

'Off you go, then.'

Roy wondered what comments were made after he had left the room. He gave Diane a smile as he passed through her office. 'You were right; it wasn't too bad. But Mr Pickersgill is good at setting his staff higher targets when he sends them away.'

'He always has been good at that,' she replied.

Chapter 14

Monday 7 June 1965

Roy had arranged to take Richard Wallace down the pit to look at the new roadway that was ready for installation of the conveyors. They were met by Mike Darlow. After the introductions, they walked along the new roadway.

'Cento men have certainly done a good job, Boss, and they have cleaned the roadway up perfectly for the installation work,' said Mike, who was proud of the finished work.

'I agree, Mike. I shall be happy when you've got the conveyors running along the road, and then we can really get the pit moving.' Roy was feeling the pressure. There were so many things to do before the end of the pit holiday week, that he was restless to start ticking some of them off as completed before the holiday started.

Following the visit underground, and discussions in the office, Richard Wallace agreed to provide four men each shift, one of which would be a craftsman. They agreed where the build-up should start. Mike Darlow considered that each shift should be able to build up forty yards of the conveyor structure. He would arrange for loads of that length of structure to be available on trams each shift, at the entrance to the roadway. The men's task would be to transport it onto the site and build it up, and then return the empty trams back to the entrance to the roadway. The same haulage rope would be in use for transporting sections of the conveyer drives into position for build-up. So there would need to be co-operation with the colliery staff. Mike would arbitrate on priorities.

Richard Wallace said he would provide the men within two days after he had received the purchase order for the work. Roy said he would instruct Region to give this their urgent attention. Actually, he intended to speak to Mr Jenkins to get pressure applied.

Mike Darlow stayed on to have a talk with Roy.

'It's going to be tough, Boss, to get everything supplied into the pit in the next two months. The coalfaces are moving forward at full speed; and the Fuston developments have speeded up. As well as the equipment we need for the conveying scheme, there's all the equipment for 58s face installation. I just wonder if there is enough rolling stock at the pit to handle everything? The lads on the surface are willing, but if they have no trams to load they can't deliver the orders.'

'What do you suggest, Mike?'

'Well, I think we can do two things. Firstly, we want to have a purge throughout the pit to get every empty vehicle sent to the pit top on a daily basis; in some districts they are lazy at organising this. Secondly, it might be a good idea to have an additional crane on the surface. We only have one at the moment, and it's often called away to unload goods delivered to the pit, when it should be loading equipment to go underground.'

'Those are two good points, Mike. I'll tackle the vehicles underground tomorrow. I've had to do this at a previous pit.'

He called for the Surveyor to come to his office. 'I have an urgent job for all your team. I want a vehicle survey of the whole pit, tomorrow morning. I need to know whether the vehicles are full or empty, and where they are going. I'd like that information available in my office tomorrow afternoon, when I have my management meeting. We'll have to turn round our rolling stock much faster in the next few weeks.'

'Right, Mr Dobson,' replied the Surveyor, who was not used to urgent requests like that.

Roy then rang the Mechanical Engineer and told him to find a small crane from another pit, and sort out a driver for it. Delays were arising in getting materials into the pit. He had his major theme ready for the management meeting the next day.

Tuesday 8 June 1965

When the management team entered Roy's office, they were surprised to see a young man sitting next to Roy. They all had notebooks and plans that they thought might be relevant to the discussions. As Roy looked around the table, he detected that some staff had worried looks on their faces, and this didn't fill him with confidence. He opened the meeting with an introduction.

'Firstly, let me introduce to you an additional member of our team. Jim Lord is a graduate mining engineer who is nearing the completion of the Graduate Training scheme, before he takes his Mine Manager's Certificate exam. He's with me for three months, and I have promised him that, in that time, we will broaden his experience more than he can contemplate. He's not here to look and listen, he's here to help make things happen.' There were nods of welcome.

'We are now entering two very critical months of change at Martins,' continued Roy. 'We have to keep the output flowing, but we also have to start making changes. Firstly, we need to transfer some men over to install 58s face, and train them to operate it. These men will come from the Morley seam, and I shall be discussing with the union over the next week who we are taking. The plan that I've discussed with George, is to put one or two men from the Morley seam into 57s teams; they will get used to operating the face equipment. The men they replace will go onto 58s installation, because they know how to install the equipment.'

'The next issue we have to face is a logistics problem. With all the equipment to go underground for the Central Conveying Scheme and for 58s installation, along with the normal supplies for the pit, we could easily fail to deliver the total supplies required, unless we make changes. The first change is to chase out every empty vehicle parked up around the pit. I have the result of a vehicle survey done this morning by the surveyors.' Roy started to pass copies round the table. 'You'll see that I have marked, in red, where empty rolling stock is parked up. I don't want any reasons or excuses, just get them out. From now on, equipment and supplies must be unloaded immediately they arrive at their destination and the empty vehicles returned to the surface. You will all have to brief your staff of this change in policy. We are altering the pit top arrangements to give more capacity for handling supplies there.' He looked across at the Mechanical Engineer.

'An additional crane will be delivered on Thursday, Mr Dobson, and we have a surface-man who is trained to operate it.'

'So, the problems will not be on the surface,' said Roy. 'Can we now turn to other matters? Are there any delivery problems with the equipment?'

The Mechanical Engineer responded, 'The new pit tubs are being delivered and they will take up quite a space on the surface to store them. The two new cages, though, will not be delivered until the end of July. We would have preferred them on site earlier. The major problem is the work we have to do in the pit bottom, and on the surface, to fit the new cages. In discussions we've decided that the best way will be to put in a temporary platform across the full shaft at the surface, just below the landing level. This will make the job much easier, but it will mean that the shaft is not available.'

'But that will limit the number of men that we can have in the pit,' said Roy, who was surprised at this new issue.

'I realise that, Boss, but with this method we can do the job in two days. If we work off the cages it will take much longer, as we can only do one side of the shaft at a time. If you can get an exemption for us to use burning and welding equipment in the pit bottom as well, we think we can do all the structural changes at the shaft top and shaft bottom in two days.'

'Can you make those two days the Saturday and Sunday when the holiday starts?' asked Roy.

'Yes, I would prefer to do that, to get that part of the changeover out of the way.'

'Right, we'll do that. It means we'll have limited manpower available for other work on those two days. You'll have to ensure priority for these jobs on those two days, Mike,' said Roy. Mike made a note in his book.

'I have another suggestion, Mr Dobson,' said the Mechanical Engineer. 'We have agreed to take out a piece of the pit bottom track, to start work on the new loading point. If we can take out a further hundred and fifty yards of that track, we could build the whole of the conveyor that feeds the loading point. This will be a big advantage for us. The pit bottom seems to be managing pretty well, so far, without that length of track.'

'Mike, will you look at this?' said Roy. 'I'm keen to do anything that will allow us get additional work done before the holidays.'

'Right, Mr Dobson,' said Mike.

After further discussions of other details, Roy ended the meeting, but asked George to stay behind, with Jim Lord.

'I need to talk to you a minute, George,' said Roy. 'I always intended to put Mike back with you to cover the installation of 58s face, but I've had second thoughts. We need to keep him on the Central Conveying Scheme. My guts tell me that we'll have some surprises from our engineers before the job is complete.'

'I agree with you there, Boss.'

'So, I want you to take Jim under your wing for the next two months. He can concentrate on 58s installation, and he will also be able to do some leg-work for you around your patch. Also, I shall want him to spend some time with me, particularly when I have my sessions with Jeff Briggs, on the pit finances.'

'Right, Boss, I'll look after him. Come on, lad. Where are your pit clothes? You might as well get changed in my bathroom.'

'They're in my car, Mr Turnbull,' replied Jim.

'Now let's get one thing straight, for a start: my name is George. Everybody at the pit calls me George, so you can do the same.'

Roy thought Jim would gain some significant experience over the next three months at Martins Main; and a dose of George Turnbull would be a good first course.

Sunday 13 June 1965

Peter was playing an organ solo after Sunday evening's Pentecost service. It was a new piece he had been studying with his teacher. The congregation were having their usual gossip to each other, but several stopped talking and listened to the organ. The fingering was fast and furious, and it ended with a loud, triumphant final chord.

'Well done, Peter; that sounded magnificent,' said James Folds. 'Is that a new item from your repertoire?'

'Yes, I've been studying some new works with my teacher.' Peter closed the organ and came out into the church.

He went across to join his father, who was talking to Helen Dobson.

'That was fine playing, Peter,' said Helen. 'You seem to be getting better and better.'

'Thank you very much, Mrs Dobson. By the way, can I give you a message for Mr Dobson? I hope you don't mind.'

'No, I don't mind, Peter. What is it?'

'Can you tell him that I've passed all my exams for the first year of my electrical course? He set me on the way to be an electrician.'

Willie was standing proudly by, smiling. 'Go on, Peter, tell Mrs Dobson the full story.'

Peter hesitated with embarrassment.

'I got the highest marks of anybody on the course, and won a prize.'

'Congratulations. I'll tell him as soon as I see him. I know he'll be delighted. You are becoming a very busy young man now, Peter, and, it seems, a very successful one.' Helen gave him a warm smile.

Saturday 19 June 1965

The Enclosure was fully staffed, and on duty very early. They were observing the assembly and departure of the children's Club trip to Scarborough. It started with the families walking along Martins Lane towards the Club. It was clear that some fathers had been coerced by their wives to go to the starting point as bag-carriers. Some bags seemed somewhat excessive in size, for a day-trip, but they contained toy spades and buckets for playing on the sand, and multiple changes of clothing in case of accidents. There was also food for lunch in some instances, to avoid any spending for meals in cafés. The sound of last minute instructions to the children drifted up to the Enclosure.

'Just remember, stay with your mother all the time; no wandering off with your mates. Your mother has enough to think about with the little one,' from a worried father.

'This is your last chance to go on this trip; if you behave like you did last year, that'll be the end of these trips,' from a mother who was not looking forward to the day.

As the departure time got nearer, the stragglers appeared, rushing along the road and dragging their kids along in a hurry. One woman with two kids was in a panic, and clearly blamed her husband.

'You carry the lad. We are going to have to run to get there,' she said. 'I bloody told you we should have got up earlier. It's always the same with you – a last-minute rush.'

She need not have worried. The Committee had decided to have a list of people for each bus. Unfortunately, however, they had not got duplicates of the lists, so each person had to visit each of the six committee-men to check if they were on his list, until they found their name. Just to add to the confusion, the committee-men were working with bus numbers one to six, but the buses were designated by big letters A to F on their windscreens. One woman was dragging two kids along looking for bus number three.

'I can't find number three bus,' she was shouting out.

'You need bus C,' she was told.

'Which silly buggers have set that up? They're just trying to confuse us!'

The buses departed fifteen minutes late. There was one woman and child on nobody's list. She was adamant that she'd booked places, and she named the committee-man who had arranged it for her. She was squeezed onto the last bus.

As the convoy of buses appeared onto the main road and turned towards Pontefract, the Enclosure team wished them well for the day.

'I didn't see any sign of Gerry Moore's kids going on the trip,' said Charlie.

'You wouldn't expect to,' said Pat. 'The two boys are continuing to live with Bob Hall and his wife. Gerry's wife is on her own with the baby.'

There were surprised looks from the team.

'Is that going to be a permanent arrangement?' asked Albert.

'Nobody knows,' replied Pat. 'The manager's wife spent a lot of time with Gerry's wife after the accident; she might know the answer.'

'She did a good job then,' said Cliff. 'I saw Mrs Moore wheeling the baby out the other day. She looks a changed woman – a lot healthier and a lot smarter.'

'I should think she's better off now; Gerry was a poor tool of a husband. Best of luck to her, I say,' said Albert.

Cyril Mann wanted to brief the team on changes affecting the shafts.

'They're taking advantage of this weekend to prepare the coal-winding shaft for the changes to the landing decks at the pit top,' he said. 'That's why number one shaft is stood. They're drilling into the shaft wall and putting in some brackets so that they can fit a platform to work from. They want to do that work on the first two days of the summer holidays.'

'They seem to be trying to get as many jobs as possible done before the holiday, which makes sense,' said Cliff. 'But it'll be a challenge to get all the coal to the pit bottom for after the holiday.'

'It's a bloody major change for the pit,' said Albert. 'The end of the Morley seam coalfaces; a new face in the Low Moor seam; and another mechanised face in the Benton seam. No bugger will know where to go after the holiday. There will be a lot of other men without a job, with the closure of the haulage roads. They will all need sorting out. This manager is a real glutton for punishment.'

'He's spending all his time every day going into the detailed work programme, to check that everything is going to plan,' said Cliff. 'He might just pull it off.'

Monday 21 June 1965

'What a difference a year makes,' thought Peter Carter, as he went in to the Electrical Engineer's office. Peter confirmed with the Electrical Engineer that he had finished his day-release course at Doncaster Technical College and would now be working at the pit full-time.

'Right, Peter, I have the ideal job for you, and you'll be able to do regular dayshifts. I want you to take charge of installing the signalling system along all the new conveyors. I'll give you a young lad as a mate, and when the electrical connections are made to the conveyor motors, you'll be working with a foreman. There is a signal box every forty yards, fastened to the side of the conveyor structure, and a pull-wire stretched between the boxes. Have you worked on these signals already?'

'Yes, I helped to install them on 57s conveyors last year.'

'Just one other thing you need to know. We have sent a load of boxes and cables down in a pit tub. Your first job is to empty it and leave the tub where it can be transported out of the pit. There's a desperate need to get empty rolling stock out of the pit as there's so much equipment to go underground at the moment. The first conveyor for you to start on is the new one being installed in the new roadway up to the pit bottom in the Low Moor seam.'

Peter went into the electrical shop to collect his tool bag, and meet the young lad who was to work with him. He spoke to the assistant electrical engineer who was responsible for installing the electrics for the conveyor drives, and was told of the plans for the installations.

'If you get ahead with your work, you'll be able to help us a bit, Peter,' said the assistant engineer. 'We have a lot on.'

Peter was very happy. He was known, now, among the electricians and had a reputation for working hard. The pay was good and, with the overtime, he'd accumulated a healthy balance in the building society. By contrast, last year at this time he'd had no firm plans, and his father was encouraging him to stay on at school. It had been a good year. He went over to the shaft side with his new mate.

Later that morning, when Peter was coupling up another box to the side of the conveyor, while his mate ran out the cable, he saw someone with a bright light and an oil-lamp walking along the roadway. It was Roy Dobson, accompanied by Mike Darlow.

'Good morning, Mr Dobson,' said Peter.

'Hello, Peter. They've got you involved, then,' said Roy.

'Yes, the two of us have the job of installing all the signals along the new conveyors. We've only started today, but it shouldn't take us too long. The fittings are straightforward.'

'You are certainly making a tidy job.' Roy looked along at the boxes clamped to the conveyor structure and the cables retained neatly in pigtails. 'Keep going; there's quite a lot to do. By the way, I was glad to hear that you've done well with your studies,' he added.

'Thank you, Mr Dobson.'

When Roy and Mike had gone further along the roadway, his mate came up to Peter.

'Do you know the colliery manager?' he asked.

'Yes, I suppose I do. I've met him a few times.'

'Bloody hell; I wouldn't dare speak to the colliery manager. He's an important fellow.'

Monday 28 June 1965

It seemed to Roy that he was entering a period of regular meetings with the union. There were so many changes in the deployment of manpower, that would be fully applied after the holiday, that he had to take them one at a time. His first meeting was to agree which men were to be transferred from the Morley seam. The meeting started with a question of policy.

'Are you sure, Boss, that you are right to be shutting the Morley seam?' asked Jimmy. 'I know that you've explained it to us before, but there is coal left on the two coalfaces and the men have worked there for years.'

'I hear what you say, Jimmy, but those workings are the furthest from the pit bottom and there is no way we can link them into the central conveying system. In any case, we need the men to staff-up the additional coalface in the Low Moor seam, and for 58s mechanised face.'

'I understand where Jimmy is coming from,' said Cobba. 'It just seems that most of the men at the pit will have a different job after the holiday. Can we cope with it?'

'I think we can, Cobba. It's my intention that we will agree most of the changes over the next few weeks, so that the men know where they will be working, and what shift they will be on, after the holiday. We'll meet every few days to sort out the changes one step at a time.'

It was agreed that eighteen men would be taken from one coalface in the Morley seam and split between installation work on 58s face and production on 57s. The coalface in the Morley seam would be worked on partial production, according to the availability of manpower. Because attendance was generally better in the run-up to holidays, Roy hoped the loss of output would be minimal.

Thursday 1 July 1965

At the second meeting of the week between Roy Dobson and the union, it was agreed to take all the men on the other Morley coalface, as a block, onto the extra coalface in the Low Moor seam. It wasn't an easy solution, because it was giving the Morley men priority over the Low Moor men who had been expecting a regular place on the new coalface. Roy had argued that a block move would avoid confusion, and keep the Morley team together, and this view eventually won the day. Cobba agreed to get a list of the Low Moor men who would be disappointed, and he would then see them individually. Roy suggested that Cobba could assure them that he had a guarantee from the colliery manager that they would have a regular job within a few months.

Friday 2 July 1965

For a third time, Roy met with the union. This meeting was to concentrate on the pit bottom loading point and the tub circuit from the shaft to the loading point. This would be on a three-shift cycle. The two men at the loading point were critical; they had to ensure that the tubs were full and that any spillage was cleaned up, so that nothing stopped the conveyors. There were experienced men from loading points around the pit, but they would not have handled anything like the rate of coal-loading that they would face in the pit bottom. Roy selected the best men available. The rest of the men around the circuit would be made up of the current men in the pit bottom, who were expert at coupling and moving full, and empty, tubs.

Roy explained the circuit to the union men. When the empty tubs left the cage they would be coupled as two tubs from each deck. They would gravitate down to an escalator chain that would lift them up so that they would gravitate round to the loading point. When they left the escalator they would be coupled so that a set of about sixteen tubs made up a run for the two hundred yards to the loader. There were two tracks, so that a stock of empty tubs could be held until the loading rate exceeded the winding rate, and then these tubs could be fed into the system. In the same way, it was a double track of about two hundred yards from the loading point to the shaft side, so that one track would stock full tubs if the loading point was beating the shaft. Managing the flow of tubs and stocking the coal was an essential part of the organisation. There would be a pit bottom deputy on each shift, to supervise the operation. Roy expected the shaft to do sixty winds to the hour, which would be about two hundred and fifty tons per hour. There were two hundred and twenty of the new tubs, so effectively there was a stocking capacity of about a hundred and ninety tons.

'Will that be enough, Boss?' asked Cobba.

'I can tell you, definitely, that it will not be enough. We have a plan to provide some bunker capacity, in addition to the tubs. But there is no way we can fit in that work for the holiday changeover; it will be a priority job after the holiday, and I'll explain that to you then.'

Wednesday 7 July 1965

Roy Dobson called the union in to office to discuss staffing-up the number two shaft in the pit bottom, which was to handle all the materials and equipment going into the pit. It wasn't ideal, to take all the materials that way, because it was the up-cast shaft taking the air out of the pit. This meant that most of the vehicles would have to pass through ventilation doors around the pit bottom before getting onto the haulage roads to take them into the workings. At management meetings there had been discussions about taking vehicles down the coal shaft at dedicated times during the day, but Roy had overruled that idea. He wanted nothing to interfere with the coal-winding shaft. His sights were set higher than his staff's on the potential output levels for Martins Main.

Cobba asked to discuss the manning on the surface, including the Coal Preparation plant.

'I realise that you will be winding coal on three shifts,' he said. 'But will you also be washing on three shifts? Some of our lads in the washer say that they need time to do maintenance of the equipment. There are no washer operators on the nightshift anyway. What do you think?'

'I'm waiting to see how things go with the Coal Prep plant,' replied Roy. 'We can stock some coal on the nightshift. I expect the plant to start up at six o'clock in the morning, to wash the stocked coal, and it should wash continuously through to the end of the afternoonshift. That will allow maintenance on the nightshift, as happens now. If the output goes up significantly, then we'll have to arrange to put on some additional washing time. There are other options, like sending some coal to another pit to wash, but I don't want to do that, because there is a demand in the market for all the coal we can produce.'

'We don't want to depend on someone else, Boss. We want to treat all the coal here,' concluded Cobba.

Friday 9 July 1965

Janet and Peggy, with the three children, made their weekly trip to the Welfare playing fields. In one corner, the Club had constructed a children's play area. There were swings and slides and other fixed attractions. The boys ran from one to another, while baby Dawn sat up in her pram and watched. Janet and Peggy pushed the boys as required, and sorted out any arguments, while at the same time they discussed the gossip of Martins Lane and the changing circumstances of the two families. Tony was also keen to kick a football around and there was plenty of room for that. He wasn't impressed with Janet as a football player, compared with his Uncle Bob.

'Have you managed to arrange with Bob for us to have a trip to Doncaster, yet, Janet?' asked Peggy.

'There's no chance, Peggy. Bob is working all the hours that there are. He's installing another mechanised face, 58s, and they're trying to get it ready before the start of the holiday. He's then going to work on the big conveyor scheme through the holidays. He says that the scheme is a bit behind programme, so there will be lots of overtime to get the job finished.'

'You must never see him.'

'Oh, I do see him, and no matter when he gets home, he has his time with the boys. I never dreamed that he would be as good with them as he is.'

'At least he must be earning a big wage packet.'

'You can say that again; he's never earned as much as he is now. This mechanisation at Martins has certainly been a wage booster for the craftsmen. How are you for money now, Peggy?'

'I'm alright; I've sorted out what I'm getting each week, and we can live on that. I've told Bob's sister that I can manage without her, now that I'm fit again. I still owe you for all that she has done for me. She was the first bit of help that gave me hope.'

'That's all been settled, Peggy, so you can forget it. In fact, she's going to help me for one afternoon each week, now. The problem is, I don't know when Bob will come home, so I can't plan anything. I just fill his snap tin as full as I can, to try to keep him going. He always says, 'I'll see you when I see you' when he leaves for the pit.'

'Of course, Sandra still keeps popping in. She's a bit of company, and she's very good with Dawn. Helen calls about once a week. I don't know how she is coping; she tells me her husband is at the pit every day of the week, and underground most days. He seems to be under a lot of pressure at the moment.'

'It might sound impressive, but I don't think it's any fun being a colliery manager,' replied Janet.

'He's a nice fellow, though,' said Peggy.

Wednesday 4 August 1965

The pit was producing well – particularly so as it was Bull week. There were just seven more working days to go before the holiday and Roy was underground with Mr Jenkins. They were on 58s face because Reg Jenkins wanted to see the progress with the installation. They crawled through the coalface to where the powered supports were being installed. George Turnbull was there, with the three men who were turning each support into position as it was sent down the face on a haulage rope. The support was fastened to the panzer conveyor and then the hydraulics hoses were coupled in and the support set, and any temporary wooden supports removed.

'Good morning, Mr Turnbull,' said Reg. 'How are things going?'

'We are not doing too bad, Mr Jenkins,' replied George. 'As you can see, the panzer conveyor is installed and they are fitting the drives at each end. This is the fifteenth powered support, but we will speed up now, as these lads have got the idea. There's a lot of work to do in the main roadway, as you will see when you get there, but the craftsmen are working on the electrical and mechanical build-up. The trepanner has not arrived at the pit, yet, so that will be the last job.'

'You should be able to get the face ready by the holiday, anyway?' said Reg.

'Yes, we'll do that, I'm sure,' replied George.

'We are going to walk the route of the new conveyors on the way out to the pit bottom.' said Roy.

★

They followed the conveyors that carried the coal from 56s, 57s and 58s coalfaces in the Benton seam. They reached a junction, where the coal from the Fuston seam developments loaded on to the belts.

'This is where the new conveying system starts,' said Roy. 'The first conveyor takes the coal up this roadway to the Low Moor seam. As you can see, one job for the holidays is to pull the tail end of the new conveyor into place and remove the conveyor that goes to the Benton seam loading point. All the way to the pit bottom the conveyors are forty-two inches wide.'

'They should be able to carry some coal!' said Reg.

They walked up the roadway to the Low Moor seam. The conveyor drive was partly built and two fitters were working on it. The electrical control panels were in place near the drive, but no electricians were working on them. Roy made a mental note of this. They then followed the new conveyor line that was being installed in the Cento roadway. After four hundred yards they came to the intermediate conveyor drive. Again, two fitters were building the drive and connecting it to the tail end of the next conveyor. The electrical control panels were on site, but not coupled to the drive. Further up, they came to a team of men, supervised by an electrical engineer, who were laying out the main power cable and tying it up to the roadway supports. This was the power supply for the intermediate conveyor. As they moved forward, Roy noted that all the conveyor signalling boxes and cables were in place. At least that part of the work was completed, he thought.

When they reached the end of the Cento roadway, a further big conveyor drive was being installed, but this drive was elevated in to the roof of the roadway. It delivered onto a conveyor in a roadway, at ninety degrees to the Cento roadway, that went the last hundred and fifty yards to the loading point. That conveyor structure was elevated onto a steel platform to allow the pit tubs to run under the conveyor to the loading point. There was a lot of activity in this area, but clearly a lot of work still to do.

'Well, we have seen the plan and the conveyor structure being built, but we have not seen one yard of conveyor belt in place,' said Reg. 'You have some work to do, young man, to get this lot sorted by the end of the holiday.'

'I know that's what it looks like, but I'm sure we'll get there,' said Roy.

★

After a sandwich lunch, and when Mr Jenkins had left, Roy had a call from the Mechanical Engineer, who wanted to see him, with Mike. Roy guessed that it would be bad news.

'I need to have some additional fitters, Boss. I'm afraid we're falling behind with the build-up of these conveyor drives. I could do with at least four extra craftsmen on each shift.'

'I've been looking at the phasing, and we definitely need some extra strength, Boss,' said Mike.

'Where do we get them from? We're a bit late asking for help so near the holidays.'

'I didn't think we would need any help, Boss, but our fitters are not familiar with these big conveyors,' said the Mechanical Engineer. 'Most of them have never built one before; they are spending too much time looking at the drawings.'

'Do you think we can get some help from the conveyor manufacturer?' asked Mike. 'One or two of their engineers, who are familiar with these drives, would help.'

'I'll follow that up,' said Roy. 'You see if you can get help from the Regional Workshops. If they have no one, you'll have to go to one of the local companies who provide craftsmen.'

'I think I know one local company who will help us, Boss. I know they have some good craftsmen available,' said the Mechanical Engineer.

'Well, get on to them, and sort it out,' replied Roy, somewhat annoyed at this developing situation.

Roy quickly arranged for two engineers from the conveyor manufacturers to come the next day. He informed the Mechanical Engineer to meet them, and instructed that each of them should have one of the conveyor drives as their responsibility. He was beginning to question the planning of jobs by the Mechanical Engineer, so he decided to ask him another question.

'We have all these new pit tubs on the surface; have you run any of them on the tracks to see if they are the right wheel gauge?'

'No, Boss, not yet,' was the reply.

'Well, can I suggest that you set someone onto that this weekend?' said Roy. 'They should also be checked in the surface tipplers, to see what modifications have to be done there.'

'Right. I'll arrange that, Mr Dobson,' the Mechanical Engineer replied.

'We need to get any checks done now, to avoid us having last minute surprises,' Roy said.

★

When Roy got home that night, he was clearly on edge, and Helen noticed it immediately.

'You seemed to be stressed, tonight. Are there problems at Martins?'

'Yes, there are. Reg Jenkins has been underground today. He thinks that we're facing a big challenge to get the major scheme completed for the end of the holiday, and I wasn't impressed by some of the progress over the last few days. I think one or two of the staff are beginning to panic; I hope they don't crack up altogether.'

'Do they need some help?'

'Well, one of them has asked for additional engineers today, and we've sorted some out for him. What gets me cross is that they don't think enough about the total project and plan what can be done in advance. Lots of the work can be done and equipment checked before we get to the holiday. They just tackle jobs in sequence. If we get near the end, and some equipment doesn't fit, it'll be a shock. It's the possibility of a last-minute shock that is worrying me.'

'Come here, Mr Manager,' said Helen. She gave him a hug and a big kiss. 'Sit with your wife and relax for a few minutes.' Roy did as he was told by his wife. After she had chatted to him about family matters, and church events, he felt more relaxed and calmer. Helen had worked her usual magic on him.

Monday 9 August 1965

The Enclosure members were discussing the state of the pit.

'They had a good Bull week for output,' said Cyril. 'My mates gave me the figures of tubs wound for last week, and the Manager should be happy.'

'I understand that he's not concentrating on the output at the moment,' said Cliff. 'They're struggling to get the conveyors running for the changeover at the end of the holiday.'

'You all know how many lorry-loads of conveyor belting have been delivered to the pit over the last few weeks,' said Albert. 'But not one roll has gone underground yet. There must be some problems.'

'They've got some experts from the conveyor manufacturers to help,' said Pat.

'Some extra craftsmen from a local company are now working underground,' said Charlie. 'Or so I was informed at the Club last night. They're also asking for more men to volunteer to work during the holidays.'

'I told you not to get too confident about this manager. He's bitten off more than he can chew, with this changeover,' said Albert. 'He might end up with a pit full of men on the first day after the holidays, and if the new conveyors are not running, there is no way that the men can fill any coal. That could be the end of him.'

'I hope that they can get the changeover finished,' said Cliff. 'Just think of the pit then. Two faces in the Low Moor seam filling coal on dayshift and the other two faces filling coal on the afternoonshift. Then in the Benton seam there will be 56s face filling coal on either days or afternoonshifts. Then there will be 57s and 58s faces filling coal on all three shifts. If they are all performing well, that will be well over three thousand tons per day. Martins has never done an output like that.'

'I am told they have orders for every ton that they can produce,' said Pat. 'Even though it's summer, there have been lorries coming from the Midlands to fetch the large house coal.'

A large lorry turned into Martins Lane and the team looked down on its load.

'That must be the trepanner for 58s face,' said Charlie. 'That should have been at the pit two weeks ago. They were saying in the Club last night that George has been hopping mad at the delay, as he wants to get the installation completed this week. He might have a chance now, if they get it straight down the pit,'

An hour later another two lorries turned into Martins Lane.

'At last!' said Cyril Mann. 'They're the two new cages for the number one shaft. They should have been delivered weeks ago. It's to be hoped that they fit, when they're installed in the shaft.'

★

Peter Carter was working with two electricians and the assistant electrical engineer, coupling up the signalling system and putting power on to the two motors of the intermediate conveyor drive in the Cento roadway. The fitters had filled the gearbox with oil and released the unit to the electrical engineers. They put the power on and signalled the motor to start. The audible warning sounded, and the motor started, and the driving drums for the conveyor revolved. There was relief that everything was working. When they applied the same procedure to the second motor, however, there was no response. The electricians began a series of checks, but after they proved positive on the signals, and on the circuits to the motor, a senior electrician voiced his conclusion.

'It all points to the fucking motor,' he said. 'They must have sent us a dud. Go and get the Mega tester from the pit bottom, and we'll test the motor.' Peter went hurrying off to the electrician's cabin in the pit bottom. He came rushing back thirty minutes later, flowing in sweat, carrying the heavy-duty testing machine.

The electrical engineers got to work applying a series of tests on the motor windings.

There was an earthing fault in the windings.

'Damn and blast the people who cleared this motor from the workshops,' said the senior electrician. 'After all that we have done, we're now going to have to dismantle this motor from the conveyor.'

The assistant electrical engineer rang the surface to report the urgent need for another motor. The message got to Roy within minutes. He couldn't believe the news.

'How can we have got a dud motor?' he asked the Electrical Engineer.

'I don't know, Boss, but we have no option but to change it,' was the reply. 'In the meantime, the conveyor will run on one motor to allow the installation of the belting, when the rest of the drive is completed. I will get onto Region to get another new motor. The lads are dismantling the old motor from the drive. We'll have it checked and find out how it cleared the testing procedure.'

'I wonder what else can happen to delay this scheme?' thought Roy.

Friday 13 August 1965

In the afternoon, while the majority of the men were drawing their Bull week wages and their holiday pay, and thinking of their holidays at the seaside, Roy was reviewing, with members of his staff, the position of the pit. He agreed with George to take only one shear off 57s face on the nightshift, with the small team that was likely to be available, and to leave the face secure for the holidays. 58s installation was complete, but there had not been any chance to take a shear off before the holiday.

The three conveyor drives from the Benton seam to the pit bottom were complete, and the drives powered-up, including the replacement motor on the intermediate drive, but none of the new conveyor belting had been installed. There was more work to do on the pit bottom drive to the new loading point, and that, too, would need the conveyor belting installed as the last job.

'I want you to take charge of installing the conveyor belting on the conveyor from the Benton seam up to the Low Moor seam, George. You'll not be able to start until Monday morning, as we can only have limited men in the pit over the weekend due to the number one shaft modifications.'

'Right, Boss, I'll sort that out. But I want to do it my way,' replied George.

'Which way is that?' asked Roy.

'I remember a few years ago we were installing a new conveyor in a steep roadway like this one, when we had an accident. The men were manually pulling some new belting onto the conveyor when it got away from them and ran to the bottom of the roadway. One man was injured with a broken leg and crush injuries when the belting trapped him as it piled up around him. It could have been worse. This job is even more difficult, with this heavy duty belting which is wider than any we have in the pit. My method will be to take the narrower belting from the Benton seam loader belt, which is now redundant, and thread that onto the new belt structure and through the drive. We can then mount the rolls of new belt behind the drive and use the power to pull the old belt off and feed the new belt in. With luck, the changeover will be done in one shift. There's only five hundred yards of belt involved. I'll have a word with the engineers to provide the reels that we'll need, and arrange to set the conveyor to slow speed.'

'I'll leave that with you, George, and we'll see how it goes.'

★

Roy agreed with Mike the priorities for the weekend: they were to concentrate on the shaft modifications, and use any additional craftsmen to work on the loading point and the conveyor feeding it. Mike explained that this was slow work because each section of the conveyor was elevated above the tub track. It was important for that conveyor to be right, as any problems could interfere with the tub track and stop the pit.

'There are so many design features that we cannot test until the system is working,' said Roy.

'I agree, Boss,' said Mike. 'But I am still hopeful that we'll get a run of coal through the system before the end of the holiday.'

'I wish I was confident that we'll achieve that,' replied Roy. 'But there seems to me to be so much still to do, and I'm dreading any more hiccups.

Chapter 15

Saturday 14 August 1965

It was the first day of the holiday. Those going away had left Upthorpe. The limited number of men at work at the mine was concentrated at the number one shaft. The Mines Inspector arrived at ten o'clock to see the shaft operations. After discussions in the office, Roy went with him to the shaft top. The Mechanical Engineer was on the job, supervising the cutting and welding. Roy noted, with satisfaction, that all the safety equipment was on site, ready to tackle any fire that might arise from the cutting.

'How is it going?' Roy asked the Engineer.

'Very well, Mr Dobson. We have cut the metal back and all we have to do now is weld on some guide plates to act as receivers for the cage. Then that will be this level done. The upper level will be easier. This platform has made it a much more efficient operation.'

'How is the pit bottom progressing?' asked Roy.

'My deputy is down there now, and he reported to me half an hour ago. They have no problems for access and they have completed all the cutting; they're welding on new guide plates. They should finish later today. When we've finished up here, we'll remove the platform. I have the shafts-men lined up tomorrow morning to change the cages. As you can see, we have the new cages ready.' He pointed to the two new cages standing on bogies in the building near the shaft. Roy knew that the new pit tubs had been tried in the cages earlier in the week, and that they fitted satisfactorily.

Roy then went underground with the Mines Inspector. They saw that the work at the shaft side was well advanced, and noted again that the safety equipment was on display. They followed the tub route around the pit bottom. When they came to the loading point and the conveyor feeding it, there was a flurry of activity assembling equipment at various points. The Mines Inspector asked how many men were working in the pit.

'There are no men in any part of the pit now, other than these in the pit bottom,' explained Roy. 'The limit is thirty and that is the number at work. We might be two over,' he added with a grin. 'But those two are you and me. I did not bring two men out of the pit to let us go in, as I was confident that we would not be too long. We're on a tight schedule to get this changeover done, so we need every man working flat out.'

The inspector made no comment. He was happy with the safety procedures in place, and that the exemption would not exceed the two days stated. He left to go to his golf course; he was going to fit in an extra round that he hadn't planned.

Tuesday 17 August 1965

Sandra and Terry were in the Yorkshire Dales, taking a long walk. Sandra had arranged a packed lunch of salad sandwiches and home-made chocolate cake, and Terry had borrowed an ordnance survey map and planned a ten-mile circular walk. The weather was ideal, with intermittent sunshine and little wind. They decided to have lunch at the highest point of the walk, where there was a splendid view.

'That was a smashing lunch, Sandra; I really like your cooking and baking.'

'Is that all you like?'

Terry reached across and took her hand. 'You know that I like a lot more about you!' Terry squeezed her hand. Sandra turned serious.

'Terry, can I ask you a question?'

'Yes, of course you can. What is it, Sandra'

'I'm wondering about our future, Terry. We keep going out together; we keep doing the same things. But what is the future of our relationship? I feel that we're just drifting.' Sandra had a catch in her voice and her head was bowed, suggesting that she might start crying.

'Sandra, you know I love you,' said Terry, wanting to cheer her up. 'I want us to have the whole of the future together. Come on, Sandra, don't be sad.' He moved over and put his arms around her.

'I hear what you say, Terry, but something doesn't seem quite right. I've not met your family yet and we've been seeing each other for well over a year now. What does that mean?'

Terry had to think quickly. 'You know what it is with parents,' he said. Terry was quickly trying to make light of the question. 'They treat us all like kids, and don't want us to grow up.'

'My father is not like that, Terry. He has trusted me to run his house and help to look after his son; he treats me as a grown-up. And Helen Dobson treated me as a grown-up, when she asked me to support her as she was trying to rescue Peggy Moore and her family, after Gerry was killed. Peggy was keen that I should be a godparent to Dawn – that's a grown-up responsibility. I think the real truth is that your parents don't want to see me. They don't want me to be a part of your life. I suppose they hope that when you're away on holiday with them, you'll meet someone else, and forget about me.'

'Don't say that, Sandra,' Terry said quite forcefully. 'You're seeing problems that are not there. Come on, we mustn't get morbid. Let's finish the walk.'

Terry stood up and started collecting their things together and putting them in the knapsack that he was carrying. When Sandra stood up, Terry took her arm as they set off. He didn't know what more to say. Sandra had hit the nail on the head.

Terry's mother had said exactly what Sandra had guessed she had – that she hoped he would meet a suitable girl when they were on holiday in Cornwall. His attempts to get Sandra invited to meet his parents had been greeted by a blank refusal from both his father and his mother. He didn't know what to do next to change their views. One option would be to leave home, but he had a good relationship in the family, and his life was subsidised by his father. Leaving home was not an option, and he suspected that his parents knew this.

They enjoyed the rest of the walk, and the subject of their relationship wasn't raised again. When Terry dropped her off at home, Sandra leaned over and gave him a long kiss, and thanked him for the day out. She had the next ten days on her own to think about things, as Terry was going to Cornwall, tomorrow, with his parents.

Cobba had decided not to go off to the seaside, as he was concerned that there might be issues at the pit that needed him. He'd told Roy that he would be around, and would call in at the pit towards the end of the week.

★

After lunch, Roy was reviewing progress with his undermanager.

'The belt from the Benton seam to the Low Moor is completed, Boss, and we have given it a good run,' said George. 'The new belt ran in a treat, this morning, and we've got all the old conveyor belting onto reels. What's next?'

'I think you should move on to the next conveyor, George,' said Roy. 'Mike is doing the belt from the pit bottom down to the intermediate conveyor. He's using the haulage rope to pull the new belting into place. I think they have now got about half the belt on.'

'If I am on that job, Boss, I would prefer to use my method. I have five hundred yards of old belting available. I'll get the afternoonshift to go into the Morley seam and load up another five hundred yards of belting from the conveyors that are now redundant. If we can get the old belt run out onto the new conveyor tomorrow, then we should be able to get the new belt up and running on Thursday.'

'If you can achieve that, George, it will be great.'

'How's the rest of the job going, Boss?'

'We're beginning to see results. The new cages are installed in the shaft, and they've been given a good run. They've loaded some of the new tubs into the cages, and that has worked fine. The last job to be finished will be the pit bottom conveyor and the loading point, but they should be ready by Saturday. We'll see how things look on Friday, and then we'll consider if we can run some coal through the system to check for any snags.' Roy was beginning to feel a bit more confident that everything would be finished by the end of the holiday.

Friday 20 August 1965

Sandra was helping Peggy give Dawn a bath and change her into clothes suitable for going out in the pram. Sandra planned to call and see Janet, and then take Dawn for a walk down into Upthorpe, to her own home. When they'd finished dressing Dawn, Sandra explained where she was going.

'That's fine by me, Sandra,' said Peggy. 'You have everything that you might need to deal with her. It gives me a chance to have a couple of hours cleaning the house. I've never had so much free time to fit in all the housework. I might even do a bit of baking.'

When Sandra called in at Janet's house, the situation was not quite so straightforward. The boys were playing, but Michael was in a fractious mood and kept interfering with Tony's toys; Janet was trying to do some washing, but had to keep breaking off to calm things down between the boys.

'How are things, Janet?' asked Sandra, as she entered the house with Dawn in her arms. The boys came over to hold Dawn's hands.

'It could be a bit better, now that you've come; there's been some rivalry around this morning, but we'll get over it.'

'How's Bob getting on this week?' asked Sandra. 'I know that they're very busy at the pit. Dad decided not to go away on holiday, as he thought there might be some problems to sort out. I think he'll be going to the pit this afternoon.'

'Bob has lived at the pit these last four weeks; he just comes home to eat and sleep, and then he goes off again. He's spent less time with the boys than he's ever done. I'm hoping that he'll have more free time after the holiday.'

'I think there are a lot more people hoping for that,' said Sandra. 'I spoke to Helen earlier this week, and she's the same as you; she hardly sees her husband, who spends all his time sorting out problems at the pit. They're hoping to have a holiday away, in September.'

'We're planning the same, but Bob will not arrange the time off until he's sure that things are settling down.'

Sandra stayed for about half an hour, playing with the boys, allowing Janet to get on with her work. When she went home, Cobba was reading the paper, and her brother was upstairs in his room.

'I've brought you a new visitor,' she announced, as she walked into the house carrying Dawn. 'She's my goddaughter, and she's a beauty.' She bounced Dawn up and down in her arms. Dawn responded with happy smiles and coos of delight.

Cobba watched the baby with some interest.

'So, this is Gerry Moore's little lass? She seems to be thriving, and appears to be quite happy with you, Sandra.'

'I see her a lot, as I keep visiting Peggy, so I would expect her to be happy with me. Not only is Dawn doing well, but Peggy now looks like a new woman. You would not credit the difference from the way she was when I first met her in the hospital at the time of the accident. Here, Dad, you hold Dawn while I make us a cup of coffee.'

She placed Dawn in Cobba's arms and the baby looked into his face without any bother. Cobba was reminded of the days when he had held Sandra the same way. So much had changed for him and his children since those days. He was proud of the way Sandra had grown into a mature woman.

When the coffee was ready, Sandra brought it into the room, with some biscuits. David came down from his room in answer to Sandra's call. He took one look at the baby.

'Are we operating as a baby clinic now?' he said.

'This is not just any baby, David; this is my goddaughter and she's very special. Do you want a turn at cuddling her?'

'Not likely. I don't want to have anything to do with babies.'

'You'll change. You'll find out that there's more to life than football and cricket.'

★

Roy was in conference with George and Mike. All the conveyors had been run, except the one to the loading point in the pit bottom.

'They should complete that later this afternoon, Boss,' said Mike. 'We'll be able to run empty tubs around the circuit tomorrow morning.'

'That will be a start,' said Roy, 'but the system will only be proved when we run coal through it. At many of these transfer points there will be chutes to adjust and deflection plates to alter when they're handling a flow of coal. I feel that we should try to run some coal through the system before Monday morning.'

'I agree, Boss,' said George Turnbull. 'We need to run some coal. It's not just the conveyors, it's all the pit bottom circuit that needs the bugs sorting out. I suggest we get a skeleton team in on Sunday morning and take a shear off 58s coalface. It wouldn't be a full-depth shear, but it would give us about a hundred tons of coal. It would also set up the face for a full cut on Monday morning. Why don't you let me get half a dozen men, including a trepanner driver, and some men to staff-up the belt line? We'd also need a few of the regulars in the pit bottom. It would cost a bit in overtime, but it would be a bloody good investment for getting some coal on Monday.' George had the bit between his teeth.

'Would you need to have word with the union?' asked Mike.

'It's nothing to do with them,' said George. 'We're only commissioning the system; it's part of the project.'

'Yes, George,' said Roy, 'but as Cobba is likely to call in this afternoon, I can tell him what we're organising. Off you go, George, and sort out the men you need.'

★

Later in the afternoon, Cobba came into Roy's office to see what the latest position was with the conveyor project. Roy brought him up to date, itemising the difficulties that had arisen, and the additional men that had been required to get the job completed. He gave the finishing time for the work to be tomorrow afternoon. In order to prove the whole system, he explained what was organised for Sunday morning. Cobba said he had no objection to this, and he confirmed that he would be at the pit for the start of the dayshift on Monday morning.

★

Roy spent some time reviewing the last three weeks of the project. He realised that his engineers were good at the engineering but bloody awful at reviewing the total project to establish priorities. Mike had done a good job at phasing the project work, but thank God he had retained George as the practical operator. George's input had made a real difference during the holiday week. Finally he knew that Norman Pickersgill was getting value for money with his deal with Cobba Green.

Sunday 22 August 1965

At first light Roy looked across at the clock at the side of his bed. It showed five o'clock. He carefully slipped out of bed, but Helen detected his movement.

'Where are you going, Roy?'

'I'm going to the pit. I want to be there to see the conveyor system in operation when we run some coal through it. George has organised a team of men to cut some coal. This will prove if we have got the installation right. We don't want to find problems tomorrow morning.'

'I was hoping that you were getting up to fetch me a cup of tea.'

'I'll bring you some tea before I go.' Roy realised that he must humour Helen, after all the time he had spent at the pit over the last few weeks.

When he took her a tray with teapot, cup and saucer, and a plate of biscuits, she was sitting up in bed, and he could see the shape of her body through her thin nightdress.

'Thank you very much, Roy. This is a nice surprise.' She gave him a provocative look. 'Are you sure that you wouldn't like to crawl back into bed and share this with me?'

'Helen Dobson, you are a temptress,' replied Roy. 'You can be sure that if everything works as it should, I shall be back to exploit your offers.' She leaned over and gave him a kiss.

'I look forward to being exploited,' she whispered in his ear.

★

Roy, changed into his pit clothes and descended to the pit bottom. George had gone forward to 58s coalface, with some men, and Mike had gone to the intermediate conveyor in the Cento roadway. Roy decided to stay at the loading point. He didn't recognise the two men there.

'So, what do you think of the new system?' Roy asked the older man.

'It should be alright, Boss, when it all gets run in,' he replied.

'Have you been on a loading point before?' Roy asked.

'We were on the Morley seam loading point. The two of us have filled many thousands of tubs over the years. Mind you, these tubs look big, compared with the old ones. I have to say, though, that I haven't yet grasped the idea of filling all the coal for the pit at this one loader. It will certainly be a bit hectic when it's at full flow. Have you got enough storage for when the loading point is beating the winding rate at the shaft?'

'No, we haven't got sufficient stocking capacity. We know that we've got that problem to sort out. Initially there are extra tubs for stocking, but we intend to create an extra few hundred tons of storage in a roadway bunker.'

The telephone rang at the side of the loader.

'Pit bottom loading point,' said the man, and he listened to the message. 'Right,' he replied as he looked across at Roy. 'They've started cutting on the coalface, and they want the conveyors running.'

It took twenty-seven minutes for the coal to arrive at the loading point. Roy watched as the man let the tub fill up and then he pulled the lever and the tub moved forward onto its back axle. He then topped up the tub so that it was full, without the coal overflowing. He pulled the handle and let the full tub move forward and the following tub move under the loader. A piece of conveyor belt fixed at the bottom of the chute flicked between the tubs to avoid any spillage between them. When there was a line of ten full tubs, another workman from the pit bottom team released the full tubs and let them roll forward to the pit bottom. Without the pull of the full tubs, the tub under the loader was slow at moving forward, and the loader man's mate had to force the empties forward.

'Put some water on the rails,' the loader man shouted to his mate. The lad took a drum of water and dipped a wooden stick into it. At the bottom of the stick was nailed some rags, and it was these that he used to wet the rails. As soon as three tubs were filled, the weight of the full tubs pulled the empties through the loader. Roy realised that there was experience and skill in the loader operators, but that this would be tested when the full output was being loaded.

He left the loading point and moved along the conveyor. He saw that the conveyor was riding in the centre of the belt structure and there was no spillage. At the transfer point from the first conveyor in the Cento roadway, there was some spillage and the man there was cleaning it up and putting it into the tubs as they passed him. Roy made a mental note to get the engineer to check the centralising plates at that transfer point. He went around the rest of the circuit and he saw another of the pit bottom team putting water of the rails to get the empty tubs to run better.

Roy went back out of the pit and watched the operations in the tippler house. When the tubs were pushed off the cage, they were uncoupled so that they could be tippled, one at a time, in the two tipplers. He was surprised at the amount of coal in each tub.

When he was back in his office he got a report from George that they had completed one shear and left the trepanner in cut, ready for the Monday morning shift. Mike reported that there was some minor work to do on the centralising plates on the conveyors and that he'd organise this before the morning.

Roy sat back and smiled. 'We've done it,' he said to himself. 'We have really done it! Now it will be possible to go for significantly higher tonnages at Martins.'

Monday 23 August 1965

'Well, they're winding coal,' said Cyril Mann to his Enclosure colleagues. 'Not at the full rate, but some coal is coming out of the pit. They must have completed the new conveyor scheme.'

The Enclosure team had been on duty by nine o'clock, with their attention focussed on the mine.

'They took a cut off one of the mechanised faces yesterday morning, and ran the whole system,' said Pat. The team looked at him.

'I thought that we might be seeing a pit on an extra day's holiday while they finished off,' said Cliff. 'Of course there are lots of changes for the men, now that the Morley seam is finished. So it'll take a day or two to get everybody settled down.'

'Last night, they were talking in the Club, saying that the manager has been at the pit every day, pushing things along. He certainly gets stuck in,' said Charlie.

'From all the talk of problems before the holiday, I think they've done well to get the conveyors running and the changes made to the shaft,' said Cliff. 'What do you think, Albert?'

Albert grunted before he replied. 'I'm surprised to see the pit working this morning. Mind you, we'll have to wait and see if the scheme gives the results they're expecting. I'll bet Cobba didn't know that they were cutting coal yesterday morning.'

'He probably did, because he was at the pit on Friday afternoon,' said Pat.

They all looked at Pat, and then turned their attention to the pit. Cliff took his pocketwatch out and measured the winding time for each draw.

'What times are you getting, Cliff? I don't think they're up to full speed,' said Cyril.

'It's just over one minute per wind. At that rate it's over two hundred tons per hour.'

'Bloody hell,' said Albert. 'Is it as high as that?'

They all looked at Albert. Was he really getting interested in the output of the pit!

★

While the Enclosure was meeting, Roy Dobson was underground, and back at the loading point. From his office he'd rung Reg Jenkins and reported that the conveyors were running and that the pit was winding coal. He also told him of the trial run on the Sunday morning. There had been a pause at the other end of the 'phone.

'Well, I must say that you have done well to complete it. After what I saw underground before the holiday, I didn't think you stood much chance of finishing everything for this morning.'

Roy described the redeployment of all the men, and his view that it would take a few days for everything to settle down. When he put the 'phone down he'd hoped that Reg Jenkins would brief Mr Pickersgill on the success at Martins.

★

At the loading point it was the same two men who had been there on Sunday morning.

Roy nodded to the men and noted that they had filled quite a few tubs that had then been wound up to the surface. Roy watched as the rate of coal flow increased, such that the loader man was pulling his handle every few seconds and the number of full tubs stretched to the shaft. The pit bottom deputy arranged for the extra tubs to go into the stocking track, and eventually that was full, too, and there were no empty tubs behind the loader. The conveyors were stopped. This was what Roy wanted to see. He decided to go to the shaft side and observe the winding operation. When he got there the onsetter spoke to him.

'There must be some problem at the pit top, Boss. There's a pause every wind, after we have rung the cage clear, before it sets off.'

Roy decided to go out of the pit at the other shaft, to see what the problem was. On the surface he went across to the coal shaft and asked the banksman if there was a problem.

'There's a problem with the rail levels on the top deck, Boss. It is very hard for the man to push on the empty tubs, and that's delaying us.'

'Have you told the engineer?'

'Yes, Boss, and he's had a look at it. He's sending the fitters to put some thin packers under the rails.'

Roy went up onto the top deck, and he could see the problem. There was a small step between the rail level on the pit top and the rail level in the cage. It was a real struggle for the man to get the empty tubs to enter the cage and so shove the full tubs out; he was working flat out, and sweating profusely. Roy got the Mechanical Engineer on the 'phone.

'Send two of your big lads up here. The conveyors are stood, underground, and the fellow here needs some help. When will the fitters be here to put the packers in?'

'They should be up there in about ten minutes. They're making packers of various sizes. They should be able to fit them while the shaft is operating.'

A couple of minutes later, two big young lads from the blacksmith's shop rushed up onto the top deck. They got their shoulders behind the tubs as though they were in a rugby scrum, and the empty tubs bounced up the step and pushed the full tubs out. The winding rate increased. Then the fitters came and started hammering in the packing pieces around the track, to gently lift the rails.

Roy spoke to the two lads from the blacksmith's shop and told them to carry on for a bit to give the man on the top deck a rest and allow him to get his snap. To keep the shaft running through snap-time the men went in turn to have their break.

Roy went back to the bottom deck, where he could see the full cycle and hear the shaft signals. When the cage arrived at the pit top, it was higher than the deck level. The banksman pulled a lever, which pushed the stops that held it in position out from under the cage, and the winding engine-man lowered the cage onto these. The empty tubs were loaded and the full ones released to enter the tippler house. When the top deck was loaded and the empty tubs locked in place, the man signalled the banksman that all was ready. Then the onsetter signalled to the banksman and to the winder. The banksman signalled to the winder to lift the cage up from the stops, which he immediately withdrew, and then he signalled the cage away and it plunged into the shaft. There was a rhythmical flow to the cycle that was fascinating to watch, and the skill of the banksman working his levers and signals was like a batsman at the crease.

After lunch, Roy spoke to George Turnbull, who was disturbed by the delays on the conveyor belts. Roy explained the problems on the pit top and assured George that things would improve.

'That might be true, Boss, but we will get much higher tonnages than we did this morning.'

'What we have to do, George, is spread the load. There was no coal to the pit bottom loader until seven o'clock this morning. We need one of your mechanised faces to go underground at five o'clock, to give some early coal to the shaft. Will you have a word with the men, and I'll mention it to Cobba? It doesn't need to be the full team, just enough men to work the power loader.'

'I'll do that, Boss. I think I'll try 57s men. They have the bit between their teeth, and they're keen to keep their money up, even though they are now on three shifts.'

★

It was not a brilliant day at Martins, but before the Enclosure team left their post, they had recorded that the shaft had wound sixty winds in one hour.

'Bloody hell,' said Albert. 'That's some coal to wind in one hour.'

Tuesday 24 August 1965

At nine o'clock Roy had a meeting with Jeff Briggs, to discuss the financial effects of the project work over the holidays. The number of shifts worked was higher than he had hoped, but at least the work was completed. They identified the opportunity to save costs by reusing equipment from the Morley seam instead of buying new. Salvage teams were established to load up the equipment. They also agreed to do a manpower survey to check where all the men were after the redeployments around the pit. The total manpower at the pit had declined over the past few months, as no recruitment had taken place to replace wastage and Jeff had figures that suggested there could be further opportunities to lower the manpower in the future.

Roy was confident that the shaft capacity could be higher than the four tons per wind that was quoted in the financial information for the project. He'd set up a recording system, so that his secretary kept a log of the number of winds each hour through the day. In his office he was aware of the activity at the coal shaft, as he could hear the thump of the tubs as they were changed in the cages. He noticed that the thumps were louder than they had been with the smaller tubs. That sound was followed by the pulse of the steam engines when the cages were in transit through the shaft. It was a continual sequence of sounds that was a barometer for the health of the pit.

★

With the initial reports of success with the project, Helen Dobson had decreed that they should go out to dinner tonight. She'd told Roy that she would make all the arrangements, including asking the gardener to drive the car. All Roy had to do was get home from the pit in reasonable time. He was thinking about this commitment when the 'phone rang in his office.

★

'Mr Pickersgill's secretary on the 'phone, Boss,' said Gordon. 'I'll put her through.'

'I have Mr Pickersgill for you, Mr Dobson.'

Norman Pickergill's squeaky voice came on the line. 'I just wanted to say that I am pleased to hear that you have completed the conveyor scheme and that the pit is working normally. What are the prospects for increased tonnage, now?'

'They are much improved, Sir. The shaft capacity is one third greater than it was, and the conveying system is settling down. We've made major changes in the deployment of the manpower, and they are all finding their new places in the organisation.'

'What about the second mechanised coalface? How is that performing?'

'That's on three shifts, Sir. So far we have had four shears from the coalface, which is one shear per shift. That has moved the coalface forward into new ground. I hope that we will see them doubling that performance in the near future. We're also adjusting shift times for the teams, to spread the coal flow to the pit bottom over as many hours of the three shifts as possible. Cobba has been helpful in agreeing these changes. We need this to work, as the peak coal flow to the pit bottom loader is faster than the shaft can wind, and we have only about a hundred and eighty tons of storage in the tub circuit.'

'Can you increase the storage capacity?'

'Yes, Sir. I've had initial discussions with Mr Jenkins and we have a plan to install a roadway bunker in the pit bottom. We'll be tackling that as soon as possible.'

'Good. Well, remember what I said at the last accountability meeting; I want you to lift your sights to new levels for Martins. You have made a good start, which I appreciate. I hope to come over to the pit, some day soon, to see the new shaft system, and then we can talk about the future.'

'I look forward to that, Sir. Thank you very much.'

Roy was thrilled that the big chief had heard of the success of his team at Martins, and that he'd taken the trouble to ring him. He was a little apprehensive of an underground visit from Mr Pickersgill, however, but he was more worried about the discussions afterwards. Would Roy's idea of the future optimum performance of Martins coincide with that of the Regional Director? He knew it was a difficult question to answer.

★

Helen was getting changed when Roy arrived home somewhat earlier than she had anticipated. She'd been undecided on what to wear: the problem hinged around what underwear to choose. Roy always bought her underwear for Christmas and for her birthday. He usually presented her with the gift in the confines of their bedroom, as he considered it unsuitable to be on display in front of the boys. He gave her another present, of perfume, when the children handed over their presents. This was an occasion when Helen thought it appropriate to wear one of his sexy purchases. The choice lay between a pale-blue set, and the latest purchase, a black set. In the end, she opted for the black set of bra, suspender belt and knickers. Over these, she wore a bright-red satin blouse and a knee-length black skirt. The skirt showed off her legs and was complemented by black stockings and black high-heeled shoes. She checked her stocking seams for straightness and, before putting on her blouse and skirt, she admired herself in the full-length mirror. Roy bought faithfully to her size, but on this occasion Helen did feel tightly contained, but her heart skipped a beat when she realised how provocative she looked. By the time Roy came into the bedroom she was fully dressed and sitting at the dressing table, finishing her make-up. Roy didn't seem to notice her appearance, and immediately gave her his news.

'Guess what, Helen? Just before I left the pit, Mr Pickersgill rang up and said how pleased he was that we'd completed the conveyor scheme and got the pit working immediately after the holidays. What do you think to that?'

'I think he knows a good manager when he sees one. Did you tell him that your wife has been an widow for four weeks, and that is why she is taking him out to dinner tonight, to celebrate the end of her hibernation?'

'No, I didn't tell him that. I couldn't, because I still don't know where we're going. He would think I was a right mug to let my wife organise a night out without me making any input!' Roy paused, and then gave his wife a close inspection. 'You look very smart tonight, dear. What do you want me to wear?'

'I assumed you would insist on wearing your pit clothes, but if you've left them at the pit, then I think you should wear a suit – a dark one.'

★

While Roy was getting changed, Dennis Gates went to fetch Sandra, who was babysitting, but not staying the night. When she came in, Helen was ready to leave and had a short, red coat over her outfit. Sandra paid her the usual compliment, but this time with especial emphasis.

'Oh, Mrs Dobson, how do you do it? You look absolutely beautiful tonight. You are a very lucky man, Mr Dobson,' Sandra said, giving Roy a long look.

'I know I'm very lucky, Sandra, but I notice you don't compliment me on my appearance! I hope my wife doesn't look so attractive that she leaves me to go off with some other young fellow who picks her up when we're out tonight?'

'I am sure there is no danger of that,' said Sandra, and she went in to the two boys who were waiting for her.

★

In the back of the car, Roy was holding Helen's hand. The driver clearly knew where to go, as he drove off without saying anything to Helen. When they arrived at the country house hotel on the outskirts of Pontefract, Helen was welcomed by the head waiter. He confirmed that he'd reserved a table for her, in a quiet corner of the dining room.

The evening was utterly and completely relaxing. There were one or two faces that Roy vaguely recognised from the coal industry, but they were in the main part of the dining room, and well away from Helen's choice of table. Helen talked to him about the children, family relatives, a possible holiday abroad, Upthorpe Methodist Church, Peggy and Dawn, Janet and the two boys, and even the possibility of a trip to the seaside next weekend, but never once did she let the conversation refer to Martins Main.

The meal was very good, but the portions too large for both of them. When they'd finished the dessert, Helen reached under the table and took Roy's hand. She looked straight into his eyes.

'I am very proud of you, Roy,' she said, 'And I love you very much. I wanted to have a treat for just the two of us, so that we could fall in love again.'

'Oh, Helen,' Roy had a lump in his throat. 'It has been a wonderful treat. We've never fallen out of love; I still feel like I did in those early days, when we were first married.' He leaned over the table so that he could whisper to her. 'I could take you out of here and make mad, passionate love to you, I want you so much.'

'You can, Roy. But wait until we get home!'

★

Roy paid the bill and left the waiter a sizeable tip. The car was waiting outside, and as they drove home he sat close to Helen, who rested her head on his shoulder. He held her hand and gently stroked her thigh, feeling the suspender through her skirt. When they arrived home they walked into the sitting room, arm-in-arm. Sandra was about ready to leave, but she gave them a quizzical look, as she could see emotion in their faces. Helen went to the door with Sandra.

'Has it been a good night, Mrs Dobson?'

'It has been truly magical, Sandra. Thank you for making it possible for us to go out without worrying about the children.' She slipped an envelope into Sandra's hand.

'Thank you, Mrs Dobson,' she said. 'But you have no need to pay me. I'm happy just to come and look after the children.'

★

Back in the sitting room, Helen went over to Roy and gave him a kiss.

'Just give me five minutes, Roy, and then come up. Think on – no more than five minutes. No switching on the television, or ringing the pit!'

'I promise. I'll have difficulty waiting the five minutes.'

He visited the downstairs bathroom to clean his teeth, and then went up into the bedroom. Helen was not in bed, but standing in the middle of the room in her dressing gown.

'I've checked the children, and they're fast asleep. Close the door quietly. I haven't got into bed because I wanted to show you what your wife has been wearing tonight.' She let the dressing gown fall to the floor, and stood there in her bra, suspender belt, knickers and stockings. Roy gasped at the sight. Helen knew that she shocked him – and thrilled him.

'You look ravishing, Helen. Come here, let me hold you.' He took her in his arms.

'I want you, Roy,' she whispered, as she began to loosen his tie. 'Get your clothes off, quickly.'

Roy started to undress. When Helen appeared as though she was going to take her underwear off, he put his hand up.

'Don't touch anything, Helen; that's my job. Just lay on the bed.'

Roy lay on the bed beside her, naked and aroused. They kissed and stroked each other. Roy removed Helen's bra so that he could kiss her breasts; then he stroked her thighs and, when her legs parted, he touched her and felt the moisture through her knickers.

'I'm taking your knickers off, but nothing else,' he whispered in her ear, as he slipped them down her legs and Helen kicked them off.

'There's no time for anything else; I can't wait any longer. Come and take me, Roy.'

Helen took hold of him and, as he knelt over her and between her open legs, she guided his member into her. Helen always did this when they made love, and Roy never failed to be thrilled by this sign of her love for him. They fell into the rhythm of their lovemaking and both sighed and gasped at the pleasure. Roy looked across to see their reflections in the dressing table mirror, and he saw her legs, in their black stockings, clasped around his back.

'Come on, Helen, I can't hold out much longer,' he said.

'I am with you, darling. Oh, Roy, Roy,' she cried out as they both reached climax together.

They lay clasped together for several minutes, panting and getting their breath back. Then Helen raised herself up beside Roy.

'That was wonderful, Roy. But I'm a greedy girl tonight, and I feel naughty; I want him again. Do you think he can manage another session, if I encourage him?'

She took hold of Roy's member, and slowly brought it to another erection. Then she knelt over Roy and he watched as she placed it in her open, welcoming wetness and lowered herself so that it was totally inside her. Helen then leaned back and straightened her back and Roy's body tensed as he felt the depth of her. It was Helen's game, this time, and Roy watched as she rose up and down, sometimes with her hands on his chest, and other times with her hands clasped at the back of her neck. All the time he could see her breasts moving up and down with her strokes, and there was a look of ultimate pleasure on her face from the deep penetration. In the end, she cried out and Roy shot his sperm into her once again.

Some time later, after they had settled down again, Helen got out of bed and went to the bathroom. When she returned, she put on her nightdress, but didn't remove her suspender belt and stockings. Before she went to sleep, she whispered to him, 'We've never had a night like this, Roy. Even on our honeymoon it was never as good as tonight. We'll remember tonight as long as we live. Sleep well, darling.'

Wednesday 25 August 1965

Roy had indeed slept well. However, in his office at the pit at eight-thirty, his concentration was broken as memories of the previous night kept flashing before his eyes. Then his secretary came into the office, and the pit problems took over.

'Cobba wants a word with you, Boss,' said Gordon. 'Shall I ask him to come up?'

'Yes, Gordon. Is he on his own, or will Jimmy be with him?'

'I think he'll be on his own, but I think the union team might be getting a bit restless.'

A few minutes later, Cobba came into the office.

'Good morning, Cobba. What can I do for you?'

'There are a few things brewing, Boss. My team is pestering to have a meeting, and I think we should have one as soon as possible.'

'I've got no problem with that, Cobba, but tell me what it's about.'

'Basically, it's all the changes that have taken place. There are too many men from the Morley seam who have not got regular jobs yet. They're used to having regular jobs, and they were some of the best-paid men at the pit, so they are asking a lot of questions. Then the pit-top men are not happy, as their arrangements have been changed. The lads at the shaft side are working through snap, and it appears that it might be a regular set-up. They're arguing for some extra money. Jimmy is dancing up and down, and one or two of the militants are leaning on him. It looks a bit ominous, Boss.'

'Right, Cobba, I don't want issues to fester. I'll alter my diary for this afternoon so that we can meet at two o'clock. Is that alright for you?'

'Yes, Boss, I'll sort out my team.'

★

Roy got to work to find out the background to these problems. He contacted Jeff Briggs, and asked him to find out how many men from the Morley seam didn't have regular jobs; he brought in the Coal Prep manager to find out about the changes affecting the surface men; and he discussed with the Mechanical Engineer the shaft operations and the need to wind coal through snap-time.

The findings were interesting. There were more men from the Morley seam identified without regular jobs than he'd expected, and he would have to place them in regular jobs very soon. The only options were the pit bottom bunker drivage, and an additional development team in the Fuston seam. The pit bottom bunker had not yet received signed planning approval, so he might have to get around that somehow.

On the pit top, his questioning eventually found the answer. The timing of the afternoon shift for the surface men was from two o'clock to ten o'clock. With the low pit outputs over the last few years, the practice had developed of allowing the afternoonshift to start at one o'clock and then men had been allowed to finish when coal washing was completed. So in fact, they had been finishing at about eight o'clock. It was one of those customs and practices that had crept in to Martins Main that had been of no consequence, as it didn't affect the pit operations. However, now it did affect the pit operations, so it must be put right.

With regards to winding through snap-time, Roy felt that it would be helpful to have it formalised on the dayshift, but it should not always be necessary on the afternoonshift. However, he had to ensure that the pit bottom was staffed to wind coal up to ten o'clock, if needed. There must be adjustments there, as he wanted coal to be washed to the end of the afternoonshift, so that coal stocked on the nightshift was only the minimum amount.

In the short time available, Roy put his thinking cap on to find answers. He decided to take Mike and Jeff with him to the union meeting.

★

The union team came into the office for the meeting at two o'clock as planned—Cobba and Jimmy, and two other members of the committee. Roy welcomed them and then explained why he was supported by Jeff Birggs and Mike Darlow.

'I just want to say a few words, before we start the meeting, and discuss the items you want to bring up. I think you all realise that Martins has undergone a major change over these last few weeks. The additional mechanised coalface, and the Central Conveying Scheme, has updated Martins so that it can compete with the modern pits in the coal industry. I want to pay tribute to the work done by my management team, and by the workmen and craftsmen of Martins. Now, I do accept that it has involved a major change for many of the men at Martins, and we have to sort out any problems that this might have caused. It's early days yet, and we have not got everybody settled down, but if there are any issues to sort out, we need to know about them.' Roy paused, so Jimmy jumped in.

'You talk as though there are only minor things to sort out,' he said. 'The pit is all upset. These last three days, since the holidays, the lads have been queuing up to see me.' He looked across at his colleagues. 'If you don't act fast, we'll not be able to stop the lads walking out on strike.'

'Come on, Jimmy,' replied Roy. 'We don't want threats of strikes. We've not had them for months, so there's no need to talk like that.' Roy detected that this was the old Jimmy flexing his muscles. 'Let's discuss the issues one at a time.'

'I agree with that, Boss,' said Cobba. 'Let's start with the Morley seam men. There are too many of them without a regular job. You are surely not saying you want to get rid of these men? They have been some of the best men at Martins.'

'Getting rid of these men is the last thing I want, Cobba,' replied Roy. 'I have to admit there are more of them without regular jobs than I'd expected. We have two jobs to staff-up. One is an additional team of development men in the Fuston seam, the other is the pit bottom bunker drivage and installation. This is a specialist job, because it's a big excavation. The problem is that I do not have a signed plan, yet, for either of these jobs. They will be covered at a planning meeting at Region in two weeks' time.'

'I hope you're not hinting at the pit bottom bunker work being done by outside contractors?' said Jimmy. 'There is no chance of that, with all these spare men. That will definitely cause a walk out.'

'I agree with Jimmy,' said Cobba. 'I know that there are men from the Morley seam who are quite capable of doing that job, and some of them are without regular work.'

Roy looked across at Mike, who gave him a nod of agreement.

'Right, Cobba,' replied Roy. 'You deal with Mike, and get teams for that work on three shifts. You can also discuss the additional development team in the Fuston seam with George Turnbull. We'll start those jobs after the meeting at Region.'

'But we can't wait that long, Boss,' said Cobba. 'Surely you can let them start getting the jobs set up with equipment. If they do a few yards of excavation before the plan is signed, does it matter?'

'I hear what you say, Cobba, and I'll make arrangements for the work to start. That should sort out the Morley men.'

'I don't think that will be enough regular jobs,' said Jimmy. 'It will help, but there will still be some good men left in the market.'

'There are other development work jobs to be filled very soon. George will be starting to develop the next coalface in the Benton seam, for a start. So that will need some additional men. You have to show a bit of patience, Jimmy. It is only the third day after the holidays; we need a bit of time to settle down.'

'Our lads don't have any patience,' said Jimmy. 'And I agree with them.' He looked round at his mates.

'We'll talk to George about 59s face developments as well, Boss,' said Cobba, trying to calm down the atmosphere.

'What is the next problem?' said Roy.

'We need to go back to the custom and practice for the afternoonshift in the Coal Preparation plant,' said Jimmy. 'This is a clear case of somebody interfering with the way the pit operates.'

'I don't understand what you mean, Jimmy,' said Roy. 'Can you explain it to me?' He saw Cobba look across at Jimmy, as if to warn him.

'There has been an agreement for years that the afternoon shift in the Coal Prep plant started at one o'clock and finished when coal-washing for that shift stopped,' began Jimmy.

'Who made this agreement?' asked Roy. 'What is the shift length for surface-men?'

'Come on, Boss,' said Jimmy, grinning. 'You know that the shift length is eight hours, on the surface. I don't know who made the arrangement, but I know it's operated for years.'

'Well, let me tell you, Jimmy, that the washer is now required to operate from six o'clock in the morning until ten o'clock at night, each day. That means that the dayshift men will work from six o'clock to two o'clock, and the afternoonshift will work from two o'clock to ten o'clock. And if you look at the small print of the agreement for surface-men, it says that the shift length is eight hours, plus twenty minutes for snap-time. If there has been a custom at Martins, in the past, for the afternoonshift to work a short shift, it will now have to be put right.'

'We can't accept that, Mr Dobson,' said Jimmy. 'There is such a thing as custom and practice. These lads are very upset; it's a major change to their lives, having to work through to ten o'clock at night. You can't just change it.'

'Jimmy, I have changed it. They know what their shift times are, and they will have to work to those times.'

'Oh, I can see we're going to have trouble, here,' said Jimmy, shaking his head. 'These lads will go on strike if you don't concede that they can continue at their old times.'

'That is up to them; and it's up to you, as a union. If you want to fight that case, you know what to do.'

'Leave it now, Jimmy,' said Cobba. 'We'll have to discuss it. The next problem is the pit bottom men, Boss, and winding through snap-time. They have a really tough job, now, to keep the pit going, and they want to know what they will get paid.'

'I've spent some time with those lads, and I'm impressed with their skill and their hard work. I think we will want to run through snap-time on the dayshift as a regular practice, so I will pay them overtime for that.'

'Right,' said Cobba. 'We have got something, then. What about the afternoonshift, Boss?'

'I want us to be winding coal if it is still coming to the pit bottom until ten o'clock at night. I also agree with the pit bottom and loader men starting the afternoonshift at half past one, to take off the dayshift men. If they have to wind through snap, I will pay them like the dayshift, and I will also pay them overtime if they stay on to wind coal through to ten o'clock at night.'

'That seems fair,' said Cobba. 'We can accept that.'

'Is there anything else?' asked Roy.

'There is one more thing,' said Jimmy. 'The lads are playing hell about the pit turning coal on the Sunday morning at the end of the holiday. We never agreed to that.'

'We did not turn coal for the fun of it,' said Roy, who did not want to involve Cobba. 'Some of us lived at the pit over the holiday. It was always our intention to run coal to prove the system, as the last item on the project. If it had been on the Friday at the end of the holiday you would not have known about it. But we were running late and the pit bottom belt was not finished until Saturday afternoon.'

'What did you learn from the Sunday morning?' said Jimmy.

Mike Darlow jumped in. 'There were a lot of adjustments made to chutes and guide plates on the Sunday nightshift. It was well worth the exercise on Sunday morning to show us the problems, and it certainly avoided a lot of delays on Monday morning.'

'We did not need to ask you for permission to try a system and to make sure that it was in a safe working order,' said Roy, looking hard at Jimmy.

The meeting broke up, and the union team left. Roy realised that he would probably get a chance to have a word with Cobba at the Welfare Club committee meeting later that evening.

★

Once the Club Committee's business had been dealt with, Cobba and Roy went to the office at the back of the Club.

'Jimmy seemed to have gone back to his old ways, this afternoon, Cobba. Why has he changed?' asked Roy.

'Just think for a minute, Boss. You know why he's changed; he's lost his extra cash, now that the conveyor scheme has finished. He's feeling the pinch; he needs another sweetener.'

'I've got an answer to that,' said Roy. 'After the meeting with you this afternoon, we evaluated the option of forming a salvage team to withdraw all the spare equipment from the Morley seam roadways. There are thousands of yards of roadways, with good supports, rail track, electric cable and conveyor belt structure. If we get a team organised to do the job efficiently, we can save thousands of pounds of materials costs for the pit over the next six months. Just come and see me, with Jimmy. We can use some of the spare Morley men, too, and, if you ask me, I might agree to Jimmy having an inspection job on that work.'

'That might keep him quiet for a few months,' said Cobba. 'I'll let him sweat a bit with the Coal Prep men. There is no way we can win that one and, if the Region team get involved, they'll wipe the floor with us.'

'I agree, Cobba.'

Roy reckoned that his time at the Welfare Club meetings had some pay-offs.

Chapter 16

Saturday 28 August 1965

Peggy walked along Martins Lane to see Janet and Bob and the two boys, who were going away for a week's holiday at Scarborough. She had agreed to lock up after they'd gone, and also look after the house while they were away.

'I'm here, Janet,' she called, as she entered the house, carrying Dawn in her arms. 'Are you all ready?' She looked at the two boys and saw that Tony was carrying a small case, while Michael had a bucket and spade in his hand. They both looked smart.

'We're going on a train,' said Tony.

'That will be exciting,' said Peggy.

'I think we have got everything we'll need,' said Janet. 'It's all been a bit of a rush, with Bob only arranging three days ago to have next week off. It was lucky that we had an address for a boarding house there, and that they had a 'phone. I was always using the 'phone at work, but it felt strange ringing up for myself. Bob, just go outside, love, and watch for the taxi coming.' Bob went outside and Michael followed him, walking carefully down the steps.

'We're living it up a bit, having a taxi into Doncaster,' said Janet.

'You're doing right,' said Peggy. 'Bob needs a bit of luxury after the way he's been working these last few months.'

'Yes, but he's nervous about it; he's asked me to pay the taxi driver. I only hope that the weather is good so that we can get on the sands and let the lads have a good time. Oh, isn't Dawn growing up quickly.' Janet walked over and took Dawn's hand, and she was rewarded with a big smile. 'You will have to think about going with us next year, Peggy.'

'That's some thought,' said Peggy. 'But things will have to change a lot for me to be in a position to even consider it. I do hope, though, that you have a good holiday, Janet. If anybody deserves a holiday this year, it's you.'

'The taxi's coming,' said Bob, as he came into the kitchen and picked up the two large suitcases.

Janet grabbed her shopping bag and handbag, and looked around to see that there was nothing left behind. She gave Peggy a hug and a kiss, as she went past her. Outside, Peggy watched as they loaded up the taxi, and she saw that Janet sat in the front with the driver, and Bob sat in the middle of the back seat with one boy on each side of him. She gave them a wave and then went and locked the door and went back home.

★

Peggy thought about what Janet had said. Had she been seriously suggesting that they all went on holiday together next year? What would have to change for Peggy to be able to go with them? She would have to have more money for a start; she would also need to have a bikini, like Janet. She laughed at the idea of having a bikini. She was not jealous of them going on holiday, because she was happy with her life now and delighted to be able to concentrate on bringing up Dawn, who was the light of her life.

She sat down and cuddled Dawn, who relaxed and then went off into a deep sleep. 'How lucky I am,' thought Peggy.

Monday 30 August 1965

Roy was checking the output figures before he rang Mr Jenkins. The best weekly performance before the holiday had been twelve and a half thousand tons saleable. The pit had now exceeded fourteen thousand tons saleable for the week – not a bad result, considering it was the first week back after the holiday, and all the changes that had been made within the production faces in the pit and re-deployment of so many of the men. But Roy knew that it should be much higher. He had to get 58s face onto a contract, and he had to ensure that all the Low Moor coalfaces produced each day of the week. He did some calculations and estimated that if all the coalfaces gave a par performance, there could be an additional three and a half thousand tons for the week. To be producing above seventeen thousand tons per week was a massive increase on the best that Martins had ever done and, on that basis, the pit would certainly be highly profitable. He decided to keep his calculations secret to himself, because there were issues to resolve before they could handle that amount of coal up the shafts and through the Coal Preparation plant.

'How did the pit perform last week?' Mr Jenkins did not sound to be in a good mood.

Roy made a cautious reply. 'We ended up with just over fourteen thousand tons saleable. Considering all the changes at the pit, and the men getting used to their new jobs, I am reasonably satisfied.'

'I want you to come to my office, this afternoon. There are some things we need to discuss. Make it for three o'clock; I'll be free by then.'

'Right, Mr Jenkins, I'll arrange to be there on time.'

Roy sat at his desk wondering what could be behind the meeting. Something was upsetting Reg Jenkins. What was he going to bring up this afternoon? Did he know that Mr Pickersgill was thinking about visiting the pit? Had Reg made some promises about Martins to Pickersgill? Roy decided not to go underground, but set to work preparing a list of the issues he wanted to bring up at the meeting.

When Roy entered Rita's office, next to Reg Jenkins' office at Region, she was banging away at her typewriter, with a grim look on her face. She pointed to Reg's office, and whispered to Roy.

'He's in a bloody awful mood. I don't know why, but nothing is right for him today. I think his wife must have put him in the spare bedroom.'

Reverting to her normal voice, she announced that Roy was there, and showed him through. Roy sat opposite Reg Jenkins, who was writing at a pad on his desk.

'Will we see an improvement this week?' Reg asked bluntly.

'Yes, I think so, Mr Jenkins. There are things we can do to improve the performance.'

'Such as?'

'I want to get 58s coalface onto a contract. As the face equipment is identical to 57s I'd like to use the same contract for both faces. It seems logical as a part of the team is made up of men from 57s.'

'Have you discussed it with the Regional Negotiator?'

'Not yet; we did not get on too well with him, when we were negotiating 57s face contract.'

'Ring him up, and tell him what you propose. Those buggers are always delaying settlements. What I want to sort out with you is your plan for the pit bottom roadway bunker.'

'We do need that as soon as possible; we can't even keep the belts running continuously with the present output, so with more output, the delays will get bigger.'

'Have you got detailed drawings of your plans?'

'Yes, I intend to table them at the planning meeting, next week.'

'I want them to put to UK Mining and Tunnelling, so that they can put in a price for that job. They've been pushed out of a job at one of my other pits.'

'We can't do that, Mr Jenkins,' replied Roy, with a shocked look on his face. 'We have manned that job up with Morley seam-men and they're setting up to begin drivage today.'

'I didn't know you were going to do it with your own men; you didn't tell me.' Reg was obviously very cross.

'When we got all the men sorted out, we had more spare than we expected, and the union came making all sorts of threats from the Morley seam-men. We used some men for that job, and then others for an extra development team in the Fuston seam.'

'That's fucked it, then,' said Reg, and he threw his pencil down on the desk. 'Are you sure they can do that job? It's specialist work.'

'Yes, I am assured they are good men and will do a good job,' said Roy, hoping that he was right. 'We've had a tricky week, on the industrial relations front. The Coal Prep men are threatening to go on strike because we have altered their shift times. Jimmy Bell was behind that one. We've also had to recognise the need to spread the coal-winding time in the pit bottom and pit top; I think that's sorted. At the present time we're not washing any coal on nightshift, but we may need to introduce a part-shift of washing in the near future.' He decided not to mention his aim to sweeten Jimmy.

'Are there any other specialist mining jobs coming up in the near future?'

'Not really, Mr Jenkins. We're focussed now on concentrating every man possible onto production work. We have had enough project work to last us a year or two.'

'What about the planning meeting, next week? Pickersgill has been putting pressure on Lacey to check that colliery plans include an element of growth. He's adamant that the pits must either grow or be wiped out. The Region results are being ruined by the improvements of some pits, like Martins, being cancelled out by declining pits.' Reg did not spell it out, but Roy thought that Mr Pickersgill was leaning on Reg about the performance of some of his other pits.

'At the planning meeting, we need to get agreement to the plan for the pit bottom bunker. We also need the layout in the Fuston seam approved. This shows the start date for the first coalface in February next year,' Roy went on.

'It needs discussions on a design for that face, as soon as possible,' said Reg 'They've introduced a ranging drum shearer for trial in some pits. The cutting drum is on an arm that ranges up and down, which means that the machine cuts the coal with a double pass, cutting the top-coal on the first pass, and then lifting up the bottom-coal on the second pass. We'll not get one of these shearers unless we start nagging now.'

'The Fuston seam will be the next big move at Martins. It should allow the output to show a significant increase. I suspect that the limit will be the winding and washing capacity. I've heard rumours that Mr Pickersgill might pay us a visit, to go underground. Have you heard anything?'

'He doesn't go on pit visits very often, but you might come into the frame. He has commented about the progress at Martins, in Regional meetings. If he does do a visit, you'll have to be clued up about everything to do with the pit. He has the habit of getting a manager in a corner, and encouraging him to make promises that he has no chance of keeping. He's a bugger at that technique, and then he gets on to Regional staff if it doesn't happen.'

'If he comes, would it be a good idea to get him to consider a ranging drum shearer for the Fuston seam?'

'You can try; if he backs the idea, you'll stand a better chance of getting one.'

The meeting went on to other matters. Roy was also asked his opinions on Jim Lord, the graduate trainee. He gave a positive reply, and said that he'd be glad to keep him in a regular appointment.

The mood of Reg Jenkins had not improved, Roy thought, as he left his office.

★

When Roy got back to the pit, he decided to ring the Regional Negotiator about the contract for 58s mechanised face. He used his meeting with Mr Jenkins as the springboard to make his suggestion for the same contract on both faces.

'I've been in a meeting with Mr Jenkins, at Region, today, and he's pressing me to get 58s face up to full output as soon as possible. There's no problem as far as conditions are concerned, but we need to get them onto a contract.'

'Yes, I am aware that we need to negotiate a contract. But, as you know, we like to wait at least two weeks to get everyone used to the mining system before we undertake the negotiations.'

'With respect, that is not necessary. 58s face has identical equipment to 57s face. Also we have split up 57s men so that they are the core men on 58s face, and we've replaced them with new men on 57s. So both faces are identical. This was the strategy laid down by Mr Pickersgill when he instructed us to go for a second mechanised face. What I think we should do is apply the existing contract to both faces. I think I can persuade the union to agree to that, and we can apply it from tomorrow.'

'I don't think we can do that,' replied the Negotiator. 'We'd like to review how the 57s contract has worked, and see if any aspects of it need to be altered. There's nothing to be gained by rushing the system.'

'Are you sure about that?' said Roy, his voice giving the impression of disbelief. 'It's possible that Mr Pickersgill is coming on a pit visit in the very near future. I don't want to have to explain to him that we've been delayed settling the contract on 58s face, because of your procedures. I will have to tell him of my proposals, which have the blessing of Mr Jenkins. Are you sure about your ruling?' Roy noted that there was a delay in the reply.

'I suppose that this is an unusual situation, with two faces identical in design, and men on the new face who have worked on the old one. I'll think about it.'

'Can you give me a ring first thing in the morning? The union are coming to see me in the morning and they're pushing me on this issue. If you give me the green light, then I think I could get it all settled tomorrow, and then the men will put the accelerator down. I know that Region would like that.'

'I'll ring you first thing tomorrow morning.'

'Thank you,' replied Roy. He asked Gordon to get Cobba to come and see him.

★

When Cobba came in to his office, Roy agreed the plot with him. 'I want you to come and see me tomorrow, Cobba, and push me to agree that the contract for 58s face should be identical to that for 57s. If the Regional Negotiator analyses the way 57s contract has worked out he'll probably want to increase the advance per shear in the contract for 58s, which will reduce the wage levels. Mr Jenkins supports the need to get 58s settled down as soon as possible. If you agree that we apply the same contract on both faces, we can get it all sorted out tomorrow. That ought to get the pit settled down.'

'I hear what you say, Boss. My mates might not think you are doing us a favour, though; you'll have to sell it to them.'

'I'll do that, Cobba.'

★

Roy Dobson sat with his wife, that evening, planning just how he would sell the idea to Cobba and his team. He made notes on the way he would approach the discussion, and the arguments he would make. He also rang George at home, and explained what he was attempting. George gave him some additional points to help his case.

'You seem very involved, tonight, with the pit,' said Helen. 'Are you engaged in some conspiracy?'

'Yes, you could call it a conspiracy. I'm playing a hand of cards that does include some bluffing. If I pull it off, it will be an advantage to everybody at Martins, but it won't be easy to convince some of the union team. I need a 'phone call in the morning to give me the green light, first.'

'I wish you luck with your scheme and I hope you don't get your fingers burnt, because I never knew you were any good at card playing.'

Tuesday 31 August 1965

Roy got the 'phone call from the Regional Negotiator at ten-thirty. It was a reluctant agreement, Roy explained when the union team met with him, and he suggested that, if he got their agreement, all that was needed was one copy of the contract that was headed 57s and 58s faces. The Negotiator agreed that this was a good idea.

The meeting with the union lasted for an hour, and Roy arranged sandwiches for them when they'd finally agreed to his proposal. Jimmy had pushed for some improved terms, but Cobba shut him up, as there was the risk of having worse terms for both faces. They agreed that the contract should be applied from that afternoonshift. Cobba met the men before they went underground and told them the news.

Roy monitored the performance of 58s coalface, and the team had clearly moved into a higher gear. He arranged for the shaft to wind through snap, and both 57s face and 58s face completed two shears for that shift. It was a very good afternoonshift for Martins Main.

Saturday 4 September 1965

The Dobson family were travelling to Nottingham, to see Roy's mother. They'd left mid-morning, after Roy had received the output figures. He was pleased that the pit had produced over sixteen and a half thousand tons saleable. There had been a significant increase from 58s face, but 57s had also increased its results, compared with the previous week. When he looked at the analysis of the figures he realised that there was still more to come.

Roy found his mother in good spirits, and glad to see her grandchildren. Roy and Helen went for a walk alone around his childhood haunts, and enjoyed the time together away from the telephone and the pit.

★

Janet and Bob, with the two boys, travelled back from Scarborough. Peggy had lit a fire to warm up the house, and she was waiting for them when they arrived, with the kettle boiling ready to make a cup of tea.

'Oh, you shouldn't have bothered,' said Janet. 'But I must say that I'm looking forward to a proper cup of tea; other folk don't make tea like we do in Upthorpe!'

'How was the holiday?' asked Peggy, while Bob started bringing in the cases.

'It was wonderful. The weather has been good, so that we could go on the sands every day.'

'We built sandcastles,' said Tony.

'That would be fun,' said Peggy.

'Sea, sea,' said Michael.

'He's learnt a new word!' said Janet, with pride.

'Did you go in the sea?' Peggy asked the boys.

'I went in deep,' said Tony.

'Bob went in deep, with Tony, and kept lifting him up when the waves came. I stayed on the edge with Michael, but he liked paddling. Bob said I looked good in my bikini.' Janet laughed at this, and Peggy also giggled.

Peggy poured the tea, and gave the boys some milk, with a biscuit.

'Come on, Bob, and have a cuppa,' said Janet. 'I'll sort out the unpacking later, when the boys have gone to bed. How have you been, Peggy?'

'I've been fine. Sandra came up one day, and then Mrs Dobson called. She was going into Doncaster, and asked me if I wanted to go. We left Dawn with Sandra, so I was able to have a look at the shops. Helen insisted that we had lunch there so it was a nice day out.'

'Did you buy anything?'

'I did splash out a bit. I'll show you when you come round.'

★

Sandra and Terry went to a dance in a ballroom in Leeds. It was their first trip out after Terry's holiday in Cornwall. Terry was keen to renew his relationship with Sandra, and when he rang to arrange the night out, he was happy when she'd agreed. He'd rung off before there were any discussions about his holiday.

When they were settled in the car on the way to Leeds, Sandra started to ask questions.

'Was it a good holiday then, in Cornwall?'

'It was alright, but my mother and father are not the most adventurous people to be with on a holiday. They enjoy eating in the hotel rather than going out to shows.'

'Why do you go with them then, Terry? We could have had some days out together in Yorkshire, during the holiday.'

'You're right, Sandra. I think I'll make changes for next year.'

'Are you saying that there were no other young people in the hotel for you to mix with?'

'Yes, there were some younger people that I got to know over the holiday. The hotel had a small band that played for dancing each night. But the girls were nowhere near as good as you at dancing, Sandra. That's why I suggested this night out in Leeds.'

Terry hoped that the interrogation was over. Sandra wondered if the girls who were not so good at dancing offered other allurements to charm a single young man on holiday with his parents. She decided not to ask any more questions, but to just enjoy the night out.

Sandra was wearing a smart knee-length taffeta dress that showed off her figure and her legs. During the evening she noted the many appraising looks in her direction, by young men, and jealous young women, as she danced around the ballroom. Terry was delighted to have Sandra in his arms, and his escapades with young women in Cornwall were relegated to a farcical memory. They stayed on to the end of the dance, when Sandra allowed him to hold her very close for the last waltz.

As Terry dropped her at home in Upthorpe, she allowed him some deep kissing, but no groping. They both felt their relationship was back on track.

Thursday 16 September 1965

It was approaching harvest festival time at Upthorpe Methodist Church. Reverend Folds had approached Helen Dobson to discuss some new ideas for the services. There would be the usual opportunity for the children to bring gifts of fruit and vegetables, to be received at the morning service, but he wanted the theme to be widened to cover the harvest of coal from the mine. Would Helen ask her husband, he'd wondered, whether he could provide a large lump of coal to be on display?

When Helen had put this to Roy, he'd asked how big a piece she wanted.

'As big as possible,' was her reply.

'I'll see what I can do.'

Roy spoke to George Turnbull.

'We are to feature at the harvest festival at Upthorpe Methodist Church, next week, George. They want to display a large lump of coal on a table at the front of the church. My wife says we should provide as big a lump as possible. I suggest you give the job to Willie Carter, and tell him to carve out a large lump from 56s coalface. Tell him to put it on a tram and send it out of the pit marked for my office. That should avoid it getting into the coal washer.'

'I'll see to it, Boss,' said George.

Friday 17 September 1965

George rang Roy and asked him to come down into the pit yard. There, strapped on a tram, was a large lump of solid coal. It was nearly three-foot long, two-foot wide and over one-foot thick; it weighed well over a hundredweight.

'It will have to be a bloody good table to carry that weight, Boss,' said George.

'They'll need some good miners to lift it onto the table,' agreed Roy. 'How did they get a piece that big?'

'It was Willie who used his skill at hand-getting,' said George. 'I'm told that he took several sharp pick blades to the coalface. He must have spent a long time, to under-cut the seam by hand, and then trim the coal so that it parted from the roof. I suppose Willie will have arranged some help to lift it; I'll have a word with him. I suggest we send it to the church strapped to the tram.'

'They usually auction off the harvest produce,' said Roy. 'Whoever bids for that will need a big hammer to break it up before he takes it away from the church!'

Sunday 26 September 1965

Roy was persuaded to make one of his rare attendances at the harvest festival evening service, because Helen was reading one of the lessons. The front of the church was weighed down with two tables full of fruit and vegetables. However pride of place, in the centre, was the lump of coal. It was on a table covered with a white cloth. It had been cleaned and polished so that it was shiny black. Roy looked at it with pride as, to him, it represented the success of his pit.

Reverend Folds gave a sermon that ranged far and wide on the theme of harvest, concluding with the following.

'Today, we have rightly celebrated the wonderful harvest that we have received: the harvest of fruit and vegetables from the gardens; the harvest of cereals and meat from the farms; and the harvest of coal from the mines. All these are gifts from God. We do not know of famine in Upthorpe, we are not affected by war, like many parts of the world. We are truly privileged, and that is why we need to give thanks at harvest time. But so many of us take it for granted, and many of us grumble and ask for more. We have all these fruits because of the hard work of the many workers who toil every day to provide us with the goods and services that make our life so good. We thank God for all the hard work of these people. Some of them we see at work, as we travel around, but some we never see. Underground, at Martins Main, there is another world. It stretches for miles and miles from the mine site. It is an underground world, working to extract the coal to keep us warm and feed the schools, the hospitals and the gas industry. But it costs more than sweat. Earlier this year we met in this church for the funeral service of Gerry Moore, who lost his life while working in the mine. We mourned the loss of a young life. Later, we had the privilege of his daughter, Dawn, being baptised here. Dawn never even saw her father. We have to enfold that little girl in the arms of this church, with love, so that her life blossoms to her own harvest in the future. May the guidance of God be with all who work in the mines, and every day may He lead those with responsibilities for management to make the right decisions as they plan and operate the mines to harvest the coal. Amen'

At the end of the sermon, Roy believed that Martins had benefited from some divine support over the last year. As he bent his head, with his eyes closed for the final prayers, he felt Helen press his hand. Whether she knew his thoughts, or she was just thanking him for joining her at the service, he wasn't sure.

Tuesday 19 October 1965

Martins Main had had several good weeks and the weekly production had stayed above seventeen thousand tons. At the planning meeting, Roy had got agreement for the pit bottom bunker roadway and the layout for the Fuston seam. Mr Jenkins seemed to be busy at his other pits, and didn't visit Martins, so Roy was able to manage the mine in his own way. He did his underground visits, encouraging the men in a positive way; he reviewed the financial results each week, and he was impressed with the reduction in overall costs, despite the tonnage increasing. The cost-saving was mainly due to the re-use of salvage equipment from the Morley seam. The wages costs per ton also reduced, as the overall number of shifts worked went down, a few men left the pit for work elsewhere and overtime levels were reduced. It all looked very good, and Roy was feeling more confident that his strategy was working. Then he had a telephone call from Region.

'Mr Dobson, this is Diane, in Mr Pickersgill's office.'

'How are you, Diane?' said Roy, immediately wondering why she was ringing him.

'I am fine, but I have a message from Mr Pickersgill for you. He has rung me from London, where he is at meetings for two days. He says he will visit the pit on Thursday morning, to go underground, and then he plans to have discussions with you over lunch in the office. He expects to get to the pit for about nine-thirty.'

'Thank you, Diane. What does he like for lunch?' asked Roy. He was aware that a good pit visit, followed by an inappropriate lunch for VIPs, had resulted in disaster for some colliery managers.

'He likes simple salad sandwiches, as he's trying to lose a bit of weight. He has a sweet tooth, though, and he likes a dessert to finish off. His favourite is black forest gateau or lemon meringue pie, neither of which is any good for his weight,' she laughed.

'Thank you very much, Diane,' replied Roy. 'I will try to keep him happy, both underground and over lunch. Did he say where he wants to go, underground?'

'He didn't say, but I know he has been talking a lot about your new conveying scheme and pit bottom loading. He keeps telling people what a difference that has made to the pit.'

'Thanks, Diane. Is there anything else?'

'I will arrange for his pit clothes to come over tomorrow, so that they can be laid out to get aired.'

Roy immediately got Gordon on the 'phone and asked him to send George and Mike up to his office.

*

'We have thirty-six hours to make sure the pit is ready for an underground visit by Mr

Pickersgill, and I think he will be coming on his own, without Mr Jenkins,' Roy told his undermanager and assistant manager.

'Where does he want to go, Boss?' asked George.

'The favourite is to see the pit bottom and the conveyors, but he might want to go to a coalface. So my plan is to be ready for a visit to either. You sort out 58s coalface, George. Is it a good team on dayshift this week?'

'Yes, they'll be alright, Boss. I'll see to the district looking top-class and tidy. I was there this morning and it already looks pretty good. There's plenty of stone dust available, so I will get some of it spread this afternoon. Leave that to me.'

'Mike, I want you to concentrate on the pit bottom and the conveyor roads. They'll need a thorough stone dusting. If anything stands still for two minutes, cover it with stone dust. He will probably also want to see the new bunker roadway in the pit bottom, so you'll have to make sure that it's well supported, and that the men are working flat out when the visit's taking place. I hate to have to take visitors to see something and then find that the men are all sitting around having their snap.'

'I'll see to that, Boss,' said Mike.

'I think you should be around the pit bottom on Thursday morning, Mike, to try to keep things rolling. Of course, he might see a stoppage of the conveyors, if the faces are doing well, but that is why we need the pit bottom bunker, so I can explain that to him. I'll rearrange my diary so that I can have a visit to the pit bottom and the conveyors tomorrow morning, just to check for myself. I don't want you to get everybody in the pit in a panic, but it is important for us all that we impress him and show that Martins is a different pit now.'

★

Thus began a full day of briefing people on what Roy wanted them to do. He instructed that his bathroom should be thoroughly cleaned, and Mr Pickersgill's pit clothes laid out ready for him to put on. He briefed the canteen manageress on the food he required. He instructed her how he wanted her to bring it into his office, when he asked for it, and how she was to lay it out on a separate table, which should have a cloth and place settings. He suggested that she should be dressed appropriately.

'Don't you worry, Mr Dobson,' she said. 'I've been on a training course, and I know just how to dress for these occasions.'

Roy had Jeff Briggs in his office, and asked him for all the latest financial figures which he could take home to brief himself, so that he could answer any financial questions. He told the Surveyor to be ready to bring in the detailed plans for the underground pit bottom bunker, if they were required.

Wednesday 20 October 1965

Roy's underground visit took three hours, and he spoke to all the men he came across.

He noted that the whole pit bottom, and the conveyor roadways, were cleaned up and almost sparkled with a thick layer of stone dust.

Roy's last task was to talk to Cobba about the visit.

'I suggest that it would be a good idea, Cobba, if Jimmy was underground tomorrow. The last thing we want is for him to be around with a team of men who think they have a problem, when Mr Pickersgill is visiting the pit.'

'I'll fix that, Boss. Do you want me to get lost, as well?'

'No, Cobba,' replied Roy. 'That is the last thing I would suggest. It's possible that he might want a word with you, so I think you should be where Gordon can get hold of you quickly. From what Pickersgill's secretary said, he wants to talk about Martins over lunch, and that may be more important than the underground trip. She says he's already broadcasting the benefits the pit has obtained from the conveying scheme project.'

'That's right, Boss. I heard him talking about Martins, at one of the Yorkshire Welfare meetings. I kept quiet, but it was nice to hear what he thought.'

★

Roy spent all the evening studying the financial figures for the pit and committing the key ones to memory. He was poor company for Helen; during the night she woke up on several occasions and found Roy checking some more papers he had taken to bed with him.

Thursday 21 October 1965

'That's him,' said Pat. 'He has a chauffeur to drive him around. He always sits in the back, reading reports and making notes.'

The team in the Enclosure were observing the pit, and they were the first to see Mr Pickersgill's car driving along Martins Lane.

'It will be a tough day for the manager,' said Cliff. 'Pickersgill has a right reputation for grilling managers when he goes on pit visits.'

'He's been known to sack one or two, if he's not satisfied with what he sees,' confirmed Charlie. 'They were talking in the Club last night, saying that the manager has been underground and that everything is spick and span in the pit bottom and the conveyor roads. They reckon that there's been hundreds of bags of stone dust spread.'

'You would think he'd be satisfied with the output the pit is getting, now?' said Cliff.

'Don't you kid yourself,' said Albert. 'These fellows are never satisfied. They always want more. I keep telling you, they want blood.'

'Well they are winding at full speed, this morning,' said Cyril. 'Somebody is producing some coal. And they have been winding through snap every afternoon so far this week.'

'They've not been able to wash all the coal this week, on the two shifts,' said Pat. 'They've stocked some unwashed coal in railway wagons in the sidings. They'll have to wash it on nightshift, or send it to another pit to be washed.'

'That must mean they are doing better this week than last week,' said Charlie.

'You could be right, Charlie,' said Cliff.

★

Roy Dobson was sitting in his office, drinking a coffee with Mr Pickersgill, as they talked. He'd been impressed with the dress of the canteen manageress who had served them: she was wearing a black skirt and a white blouse, and high-heeled shoes, showing off her black stockings. Roy wasn't sure what her perfume was, but it smelled expensive.

Mr Pickersgill did not seem to be in a hurry to go underground, and he wasn't asking any questions about the pit, or its results. He asked about Helen, and he wanted to know details about Roy's children. Roy explained that his elder son, Robert, had started at the local school, and seemed very happy there. His younger son, James, who was two years younger than Robert, was pestering Helen to allow him to start school as soon as possible. He asked about the house and the garden, and said how pleased his wife had been with the vegetables that Roy's gardener had been sending to his office.

'I am sure that there will be some more vegetables in your car when you leave today, Sir,' said Roy, who was pleased that he had arranged that little detail.

'I think I would like to see the pit bottom arrangements, and the new conveyors,' said Mr Pickersgill as they were getting changed.

'I suggest that we look at the pit top arrangements first, before we go underground,' said Roy. He managed to get a message to Gordon, so that he could let the number one shaft know to be ready to expect them. The number one shaft was the coal-winding shaft at Martins.

They went to the shaft side and watched all the operations working to their normal cycle. It was noisy, so conversation was not easy, but Roy was able to explain, from the information on the board at the shaft side, that they had wound at a rate of sixty winds per hour from the start of the shift. This represented about a thousand tons of raw coal produced so far that morning. They then went into the tippler house. This was adjacent to the shaft and was the place where the coal was tipped from the pit tubs onto conveyors to transport it to the Coal Preparation plant. They saw the two tipplers rotating, and Mr Pickersgill commented about the amount of large coal in the tubs. It all looked very efficient. Roy hoped that the picture would be the same underground.

They then went across to the number two shaft, which was used to transport all the men and materials into the mine. When they got to that shaft side, there were some men waiting to go underground, and the shaft was stationary. The banksman had a worried look on his face.

'What's the problem?' asked Roy.

'They've had a tub with a broken axle that got jammed in the cage,' replied the banksman. 'They've got a chain on it, and the're pulling it off the cage. We should only be a minute or two.'

Was this an omen? thought Roy. However, before he started to explain the position to Mr Pickersgill, the signal came from the pit bottom that the shaft could be used for man-riding. Gates were fixed on the cage so that the men were transported safely. In the pit bottom they saw the offending tub pulled to the side to let them through.

At the loading point, they met Mike Darlow. Roy introduced him to his visitor. The flow of coal over the loader was heavy, and the operator was pulling the handle every few seconds to release the full tubs.

'They're sending it thick and fast, this morning, Boss,' Mike shouted across. Roy saw the full tubs in the extra track, and he knew that they were being filled faster than the shaft could wind. Within a few minutes there were no empties behind the loading point, and the conveyors had to be stopped. The loading point man and his mate grabbed a drink of water while they had chance.

'We'll have to wait until we get two runs of empties before we start up, to give us a chance of a reasonable run before we have to stop again,' said the loading point man. They could hear a run of empties approaching the loading point, but it was another four minutes before the second run arrived and they were able to start up the conveyors.

Roy walked on, with Mr Pickersgill, and explained how they had staggered the shift times on the coalfaces to spread the load. He then asked Mike to lead the way to the team driving the roadway for the pit bottom bunker. The three men in the roadway were on a platform, drilling holes with two boring machines for a round of shots. The roadway was fully supported, and looked large and impressive.

'This is a top priority job for us, Mr Pickersgill,' said Roy. 'When it's installed it will hold about four hundred tons, and this should avoid any stoppages for the loading point.'

Mr Pickersgill asked questions about the design, and Mike got out his chalk and drew sketches on a metal sheet in the roadway. Pickersgill was impressed, and asked more questions.

'I'll get the Surveyor to bring in the detailed drawings this afternoon, but Mike has given you the basis of the bunker operation,' said Roy.

They moved on to the conveyors in the Cento roadway, and Roy was pleased to see a steady load of coal, and there was only one more stoppage of the conveyors during the two hours they were underground. Roy was also pleased to see that there were no men along the roadway, only a man at the intermediate conveyor drive. When they reached the end of the Cento roadway, Mike again drew a sketch of the conveyors, showing the connection to the Low Moor seam, the connection to the Fuston seam developments, and then the connection to the Benton seam.

'Well, the conveying scheme has certainly made a difference to the pit, and it looks to be a good installation that can handle a lot of coal. We'll discuss the potential, when we get out of the pit,' said Mr Pickersgill. Roy took this to indicate that there was another big challenge to come over lunch.

Mike left them to go to another part of the pit, while Roy led the way through to the man-riding train that was waiting for them. They rode to the pit bottom alone, on the man-rider, and Roy was glad that they'd missed the main shift change, when there would have been a full load of men going to the pit bottom. The visit could not have gone much better, he thought.

When they had showered, Roy Dobson and Norman Pickergsill came back into Roy's office, and the table was laid out for lunch, just as Roy had requested.

Roy had a stock of various drinks in his cupboard, just in case alcohol was required, but Mr Pickergsill requested a cup of tea. As if by magic, the canteen manageress entered the room, with a tray carrying a pot of newly-mashed tea and a china tea-service. While they were drinking the tea, Roy was interrogated about the recent results for the pit. He gave the details that he'd memorised, illustrating the output trends with details of the financial results. He realised that Mr Pickergsill was evaluating the information, and comparing it with the figures that Martins had achieved in the past.

'So, on a week-by-week basis, you are getting results that have not been achieved before at Martins for a sustained period?' he said.

'That's correct, Sir,' said Roy. 'As you saw this morning, we are filling the shaft through periods of the day, but the peak load is causing some delays. We should overcome those delays when we get the pit bottom bunker.'

'When do you expect to get the roadway bunker completed and in operation?'

'Well, I would expect the excavation to be completed in another four weeks,' replied Roy.

'What about the installation of the equipment? Is that organised?'

'We've kept that in-house, Sir. The Mechanical Engineer has all the steel plate that he needs, and he's started manufacturing the girders that are fixed to the roadway supports. Once the excavation has been completed, you can rely on us giving top priority to the installation of the equipment.'

'So, when the bunker is operational, you can expect to see a further increase in weekly output?'

'I think the increase will be marginal, because there are other factors that will come into play. We're expecting a small geological fault to pass through one of the Low Moor faces in a few weeks time. It may have little effect on performance, but it might lose us some output. I see the bunker allowing us to maintain the current levels of output on a reliable basis.'

'I think we should have some lunch,' said Mr Pickersgill.

Roy asked for the refreshments, and the canteen manageress brought them in and laid them out on the table.

'That looks very appetising,' Roy said to her.

'Thank you, Sir,' she replied. 'Would you like me to serve you some fresh tea?'

'Yes, that would be a good idea.' He was impressed with the manageress.

They began to eat the freshly-made salad sandwiches, which were delicately prepared from fresh, thinly sliced brown, and white, bread. When the canteen manageress brought in a fresh pot of tea, she removed the used cups, and replaced them with clean ones.

'If you will tell me when you are ready, I will bring in the desserts,' she said.

When they'd had their fill of the sandwiches, the manageress returned with a plate of black forest gateau and a plate of lemon meringue pie, both of which were cut into sizeable wedge-shaped pieces.

'Oh, you are a naughty woman, tempting me with desserts like these,' said Mr Pickersgill, with a laugh.

'I am sure that you deserve a nice dessert, after your underground visit, Sir,' she replied, in no way showing any shyness.

Norman Pickersgill had some of each of the sweets, and Roy joined him.

'Do you always eat like this?' he asked.

'I can assure you that this is a one-off,' replied Roy. 'It's the first time I have used her to cater, but I was told that she knows her job, and she is well respected as the canteen manageress.'

When the meal was finished and the table cleared, Norman Pickersgill indicated that he wanted to spend some time looking at the underground plans for the pit. The Surveyor brought in the plans and left them with Roy. They started by examining the detailed drawings of the pit bottom bunker, which won Pickersgill's approval as a good local initiative. Then they moved on to the plans for the Low Moor seam, and the projected fault on one of the coalfaces was clearly shown. The layout of future faces showed that there were several more years of life in that seam. In the Benton seam, the positions of the three operating faces were shown, along with the availability of more coalfaces in the same block of coal.

Finally, Roy rolled out the plans for the Fuston seam. It showed the up-to-date position of the three development roadways that were being driven, and the layout of the coalfaces.

'This is the future of Martins,' said Roy. 'You can see how large the reserves are. Each coalface will be worked as a retreat face and, with a seam over six-feet thick, the potential output is very high.'

'One coalface could give you all the output for the pit,' said Norman Pickersgill. 'Have you considered this?'

'I have considered the implications, Sir, but I've not yet identified anything on paper. I do not want any rumours getting out about major change in plans, but I am anticipating some changes. For example we are not recruiting any men at the present time, so the total manpower is declining. We will need to wash coal on three shifts, so we might need to increase the surface manpower a little. When the Fuston seam goes into production we will reduce the number of faces in the Low Moor seam, by at least one. So I am thinking about changes in the pit when the Fuston seam comes on stream. However we have not agreed the design of the Fuston seam coalfaces yet.'

'Are there issues to resolve for the design?'

'There are two issues, Sir, which I've been discussing with Mr Jenkins. Firstly, it's a strong, sandstone roof for the seam, so the powered supports will need to be very strong. Secondly, Mr Jenkins thinks that this might be an ideal application for the new design of shearer, the one that has the cutting drum on a ranging arm. With one of these machines, we could cut the top-coal with one pass through the face, and then lift the bottom-coal on the way back. It would be a simple design, with one machine on the coalface, and it should produce some large coal when lifting the bottom-coal.' Roy paused for breath. Pickersgill was making calculations in his notebook.

'When will the Fuston seam face be in production?'

'We think we can get it in production by February next year, but that assumes that the coalface equipment can be available by that date.'

'What do you think the weekly output will be then?' Roy knew this was the killer question. He paused before answering.

'I think we could reach between nineteen and twenty thousand tons per week, Sir.'

'But think of the output that the Fuston face should give you! I think you should set your sights on at least twenty-two thousand tons per week. That should be your potential in tonnage, and that would give some excellent financial results.' Norman Pickersgill gave Roy a hard look. This was his instruction. Roy decided he had to make a reply.

'I can assure you, Mr Pickersgill, that I have the team who can achieve the potential for this pit. When we get the Fuston face design resolved, we'll ensure that we exploit the opportunities that it gives us. We have done that with the mechanised faces in the Benton seam, and we'll seek to do the same with the mechanised faces in the Fuston seam.'

'Well, you know now what you are aiming for. I will check my diary and come and have a look at the developments in the Fuston seam. It sounds like a real opportunity. I'll get the people at Region to give some thought to the face design. Will Cobba be around? I think I would like a word with him.

'Yes, I'll get him to come up,' replied Roy.

When Roy had set Gordon off to get Cobba, he thought he should clear his position.

'Will you want me to leave you with Cobba, Sir?' he asked.

'Good gracious, no. I have nothing to say to Cobba that I wouldn't want you to hear.' Two minutes later, Cobba came into the office.

'I've had an interesting visit underground and I'm pleased to see that the new conveying scheme has improved the performance of the pit, in the way it was designed to do. Mr Dobson has filled me in on the plans for the pit in the near future. He needs the pit bottom bunker as soon as possible. Then it will be introducing the output from the face in the Fuston seam. It all looks a lot different from the position that Martins was in eighteen months ago. How do you see things, Cobba?'

'The position of the pit is much better, Mr Pickersgill,' replied Cobba. 'But I wouldn't want you to think that everything is calm and straightforward. There are still some men here who would welcome a chance to stir up trouble. In general, the men are getting better pay now, so that does help, but we keep having our little problems to sort out.'

'I appreciate that, Cobba, but you are good at sorting out these issues without strikes now,' said Mr Pickersgill.

'We do our best,' said Cobba. Roy admired the way Cobba justified his contribution to the operations and so made sure that Norman Pickersgill did not think he was getting his pay for doing nothing.

After a few more minutes of general talk, Cobba left. Then Mr Pickersgill thanked Roy for the visit and went down into the pit yard, where his car was waiting. Roy accompanied him to the car and waved him goodbye as the car drove away.

★

Back in his office, Roy sat down to gather his thoughts. He was exhausted, but he reflected on the day's events. It had been a good visit, and he must thank his team for the effort they'd put in. But the visit underground had not been the prime objective of Norman Pickersgill coming to Martins. Roy was sure that the real purpose had been to lay down the objectives for Martins, in the discussions after lunch – twenty-two thousand tons saleable per week; four thousand four hundred tons saleable per day. Nobody at Martins had ever dreamed of such a tonnage. Everything at the pit would have to be operating flat out to achieve that. It was a major challenge for everybody, but the man who had to organise it, and deliver it, was Roy himself. He now had a clear objective to aim for, but it was an objective that he couldn't share at this stage with any of his staff. It was a lonely life being a colliery manager.

Friday 22 October 1965

The next afternoon, Mr Jenkins came to Martins to have a talk with Roy.

'The Boss had a good visit yesterday,' he said. 'He had a talk with me this morning. He wants me to go underground with him when he comes to see the Fuston seam. He should fit it in within the next week or two. He's given Jones a real bollocking, because he didn't know anything about the Fuston seam, and the coalface designs. He's got his teeth into the Regional Production team now. They're scared to death whenever he goes underground.'

'I don't think I said anything out of place,' said Roy, hoping that he was not getting the blame for setting up the Regional Production team for the wrath of the Regional Director.

'No, you did what you should do,' replied Reg. 'You look after your pit; that's your job. There are lots of folk around the Region aware that Martins has shown what it can do with new technology. They are bound to be a bit jealous.'

They discussed the pit position, for a while, and then Reg left, with instructions that Roy was to set up the developments in the Fuston seam for the visit of Mr Pickersgill.

★

Helen Dobson greeted her husband with three brochures for overseas holidays, as a surprise.

'I have brought you these to consider,' she said. 'We talked about the possibility of an overseas holiday. These are to the Canary Islands, where they get sunshine all the year round. So all you have to do is pick a week when you can leave the pit behind, and we can go. We can keep Robert off school for one week, and it will do both him and John good to get some sunshine.'

'I'll look at them,' replied Roy, with some hesitation. 'But I'll have to try to plan it for when nothing of great importance is happening at Martins.'

'If that's your criterion you'll never get away,' said Helen. 'Remember that there is no such thing as an indispensable man; even Roy Dobson can be spared for one week from Martins Main!'

'I'll look through them in the next day or two.'

'That isn't good enough,' replied Helen, with a slightly sharper tone to her voice. 'Your job tonight, after you have had your tea, is to study these brochures and select three alternatives. I want to be able to go to the travel agent tomorrow and check if there are hotel vacancies and suitable flights. We want to go before Christmas – in other words in about six weeks. If you like, I'll ring Mr Pickersgill and arrange your holiday leave with him. We'll need to be back by the time of the regional dinner dance, if he's having one this year. I'll make it a condition of me saying grace, that he lets you have a holiday abroad for one week.'

'You have no need to contact Mr Pickersgill. He's coming to the pit sometime in the next two weeks. Once he has been, there's no reason why we can't have a holiday.'

Roy did some mental calculations on events: he wanted to be on duty to see the commissioning of the pit bottom bunker; and he wanted to be on duty for the Bull week before the Christmas holidays. With luck, the first event should take place before his holiday, and the second would be after his return. He spent the evening going through the brochures and selecting hotels that looked suitable for the children. Helen took his list, with a brief comment.

'I'll sort it out,' she said.

Saturday 23 October 1965

When he came home, Roy was presented with the fruits of Helen's discussion with the travel agent.

'There you are,' she said, 'It's all arranged. We go in five weeks' time to Puerto de la Cruz, in Tenerife, and we fly from Gatwick, on a charter flight.'

'That was quick!' replied Roy. 'Did you have any problems?'

'There were no problems,' said Helen. 'Particularly if you have the money readily available – which you have, Roy Dobson, because you spend so much time at the pit that you have no time to spend your money. So I am helping you to do just that,' she added, with a smile, and gave him a cuddle. Roy realised that his wife was taking the initiative in their family life again.

'There's another thing I want to discuss with you,' continued Helen. 'I took Peggy into

Doncaster with me today, so that she could do a bit of shopping. Both Peggy and Dawn really enjoyed the trip. Peggy's obviously feeling much fitter now. She said that she thinks she should consider having a part-time job. She's discussed this with Janet, and Sandra, and they've both offered to look after Dawn when she's working. The extra money would help give her more independence. Have you any part-time jobs at the pit? Peggy is bright; she went to school with Janet and did quite well academically, until she left. She only worked for a short time before she got hooked up with Gerry, and the rest, as we know, is history.'

Roy paused before he replied. 'The only places where we employ women are in the canteen, and in the wages office. They do bring in extra help on Thursdays and Fridays, for the wages office. They sort out the cash, which is brought to the pit on Thursday, and set up the pay packets. Then they pay them out to the men on Friday. We do the wages at Martins for two other small pits, as well, so it's a pretty big operation. It's a bit like working in a bank, because there's a lot of money around. The doors of the wages office are sealed, and locked, so that no one can go in when the money is there, and there are guards on duty outside. I suppose I could have a word with the Group Wages Officer who's in charge. He's a very strict, ex-military man, and all his staff fear making a mistake. His wrath reduces the young girls to tears. I suppose Peggy could handle a strong manger?'

'I'm sure Peggy wouldn't let him down. A two-day job would be ideal for her. Can you have a word with him please?'

Monday 25 October 1965

Roy Dobson spoke to the Group Wages Officer and found that he was in the process of recruiting two more part-time staff due to vacancies caused by girls going off with pregnancies. He agreed to interview Peggy.

Roy gave the news to Helen, who arranged for Janet and herself to have a session with Peggy to brief her on how to appear at the interview. They advised how she should be dressed, and some of the questions she would be asked. They encouraged her to explain her position, as a widow from the fatal accident to Gerry, and her wish to be able to earn some extra money for her household. Peggy accepted the advice and eagerly awaited a letter inviting her to an interview. She was excited, but not nervous about the prospect of an interview. This could be a good opportunity for her – another one that had come from the support and friendship of Helen Dobson. She was determined not to let herself down at an interview, for her own sake, as well as for Helen's sake.

Chapter 17

Tuesday 2 November 1965

Roy Dobson had set himself a clear objective to achieve before he went off on holiday: he must get the pit bottom roadway bunker operational. He approached this by having a meeting with the Mechanical Engineer, during which he found that the manufacture of the steel girders and plates was well advanced, and that all the other equipment was already at the pit. Now, all that was required was to install the equipment as quickly as possible. Roy decided that the job would be staffed with workmen and craftsmen on three shifts, with an engineer in charge of each shift. Mike would have responsibility for arranging the transport of the equipment onto the site. Roy decided to make Jim Lord, his graduate trainee, in charge of the installation. This would be a real test of the young man's ability, before he completed his time with Roy.

As soon as the excavation was complete, the plan was put into operation, but Roy was distracted by the visit of Mr Pickersgill to the Fuston seam roadways. However, the visit was very successful, and Roy allowed Reg Jenkins to have a major role in the visit, which he fulfilled very well. He expressed his view that a seam of that section should allow major tonnages to be achieved from the coalfaces. Pickersgill had agreed with him and, after minimal discussions underground, had stated that he would ensure that the coalface had the best powered roof supports available, and one of the new ranging drum shearers for the coal-getting machine. This was all that Roy and Reg had wanted to hear, so tension about the visit had reduced.

The lunch was on the same basis as the previous lunch for the Regional General Manager, with variations in the menu, but the same excellent service by the canteen manageress. Mr Pickersgill addressed her as an old friend, and appeared very relaxed. Roy was relieved that there were no discussions about the potential objectives for the pit, which he'd kept to himself without briefing Reg Jenkins.

★

When he got home, Roy was greeted by a smiling Helen, who couldn't wait for his news of the visit by Mr Pickersgill before telling him her news.

'You are a genius, Roy Dobson,' she said. 'Peggy got a letter this morning, telling her that she has to go to the pit to be signed-on for a job in the wages office. She'll start working Thursdays and Fridays from next week. She walked all the way here, with Dawn in the pram, to tell me. She's over the moon. She clung onto me in tears, she was so happy. I also cried. When I compare the desperate state she was in, when Gerry was killed, with the way she is now, I can only fall on my knees and thank the Lord for answering my prayers.'

Roy took her in his arms and hugged her. She clung to him as tears flowed down her face. She pulled herself free and looked at him.

'I'm so sorry, love,' she said. 'I should have asked you first. How did your visit go?'

'Don't worry about me,' Roy replied. 'Our visit went very well, and Mr Pickersgill is going to arrange the face equipment that we need for the Fuston seam coalfaces. But I think your news is the more important. Peggy is a life saved, and you played the main part in arranging it. Have you told James Folds?'

'Yes, I rang him and told him. He's going round to see her tonight, with Gwen. He was very pleased. He said this is an example of the healing spirit of the Living God at work.'

Wednesday 3 November 1965

The Enclosure was in session, and the discussion reviewed the news about the pit.

'The talk in the Club last night was about the Regional General Manager going to see the roadways in the Fuston seam yesterday,' said Charlie.

'How did it go?' asked Cliff.

'The lads said it seemed to go well,' replied Charlie. 'Reg Jenkins was there, too, and he's pushing for some new equipment for the coalfaces.'

'It worries me when that Welsh bastard is getting involved with the pit,' said Albert. 'It might be a thick seam of coal, but no pit has made a success of working it yet. I keep telling you, I have my fears about that seam.'

'Yes, but the new methods of mining, and the new equipment should make a big difference to working conditions,' said Cliff.

'That's the second visit that the Regional fellow has made underground in a few weeks,' said Charlie. 'He seems to be getting involved more than he does at his other pits.'

'I've heard that the success of Martins is having an important effect on the results of the Region,' said Cliff. 'Pickersgill is known as a shrewd fellow, and he probably realises that if Martins can do very well, he can show a big improvement in the Region.'

'He's the fellow who picked this manager for the pit,' said Pat. 'He's tough on any manager who doesn't perform; he's demoted two, this year.'

'Where do you get all this information, Pat?' asked Charlie.

'I have my contacts, Charlie,' replied Pat.

Tuesday 9 November 1965

Roy focussed on progress with the installation of the pit bottom bunker. He realised that it would be ready in less than two weeks after Mr Pickersgill's visit. The visit had immediately generated major activity in the Regional Production department: there were visits underground to the Fuston seam by senior people involved in the design of coalface equipment. They'd been back to see Roy, a few days later, with detailed drawings on the coalface designs, showing the powered roof supports which would each have six legs that yielded under a load of forty tons. This meant that each powered support would carry a load of two hundred and forty tons. This compared with the one hundred and fifty tons carried by each powered support on the Benton seam's mechanised faces. Also, Roy was impressed by the special supports that would fit across the roadways. These had long roof beams that passed over the panzer conveyor, and had two additional legs. These beams were designed to hold the roadway roof supports in place while the coalface moved under them. They were taller than the coalface supports, to fit the eight-foot height of the roadways. They could take a total load of three hundred and twenty tons, and looked enormous.

The power loader was a two hundred-horse power shearer, which would have a ranging arm that carried the cutting drum. The drum was forty-eight-inch diameter, and would cut a twenty-seven-inch deep web. It would cut the top forty-eight inches of the seam on the first pass through the coalface and then, on the way back, lift up the remaining floor-coal.

Roy felt satisfied that the designs used the best equipment available on the market at that time. However, when the Regional team had come back with the completed submission, to seek financial authority for the face design, Roy was shocked to see the total cost. He'd signed the submission, on the basis that the potential of the Fuston seam coalfaces would recover that cost over a relative short timescale. Reg Jenkins confirmed to Roy the next day that he had countersigned the submission, with no qualms. He regarded it as a sound investment.

Saturday 13 November 1965

After her first two days' work in the wages office, Peggy went over to see Janet. Sandra had looked after Dawn for the two days, so Janet had not heard from Peggy.

'How did you get on, Peggy?' asked Janet, as soon as Peggy had taken a seat in the kitchen.

'It was fine, Janet,' replied Peggy. 'Everyone was very kind and helpful – even the man in charge, who is supposed to be very fierce. There are thousands of pounds delivered every Thursday and it all has to be checked and accounted for; then it's put into the wage packets, and the amount of money in the packets checked, to balance with the amount delivered from the bank. We can't go home on a Thursday night until everything is accounted for, and the wage packets are locked away in a big safe.'

'Did they let you get involved?' asked Janet.

'Oh, yes. I got better at counting out the money as the day went on, and I filled some of the wage packets. Yesterday they let me serve the wages to the men, who came to collect their pay packets from one of the windows. You have to be sure that it's the right man who comes to the window; he has to give his name and his check number. It's very complicated if a man wants his wages collected by his wife, or somebody else. When that happened at my window I let someone else cover for me; I suppose I shall learn how to handle those situations in the future.'

'Did you enjoy it?' asked Janet.

'To be honest, Janet, there was so much going on that the time passed quickly. I was so excited that I could only eat part of the lunch that I'd taken each day. I feel so relieved that I've got through the first two days. Sandra said Dawn was quite happy with her, so I don't feel guilty at having a job.'

'You mustn't feel guilty at all, Peggy. It's the best thing that could have happened for you. At least you only have to walk along Martins Lane to get to work. It makes a big difference, compared with having to travel into Doncaster. That journey added an hour-and-a-half to my working day.'

'I know what you mean, Janet. I realise I am so lucky to have a friend in Helen Dobson. I know that it was her husband who made the enquiries about the job and set up the interview. I'm determined not to let him down. I'm sure I'll get a lot faster at counting the money when I've had more practice. I hope the people always stay as friendly as they were this week. I don't want them to pity me, I just want them to help me to get better at the job.'

'I'm sure they'll do that,' said Janet.

'Where are the boys?' asked Peggy, looking around; they usually appeared when they heard her voice.

'Oh, they've gone off with Bob,' said Janet. 'He's taken them for a walk and a run around on the playing fields. It's the first Saturday that Bob has not been working, for weeks. Let's have a cup of tea and a chat until they get back. You might as well stay to see the boys. And they will want to see Dawn. Tony often talks to Michael about her, and about you being in the hospital when she was born.'

Sunday 14 November 1965

Everything was completed with the installation of the pit bottom bunker, but the special deflection chute had to be installed over a weekend. Roy went underground to watch that part of the installation. It was an imposing chute, power-operated to feed the coal onto the pit bottom loader belt or, at the operation of a handle that energised two rams, divert the coal onto the bunker conveyor. Roy watched the operation several times and was impressed. He realised that the man on duty at that transfer point would have to be slick at pressing the handle to operate the rams. He was also pleased to note that the Electrical Engineer had rigged up a loudspeaker system from the pit bottom loading point, so that the operator there could warn the man at the transfer point when the loader belt was going to be stopped.

Monday 15 November 1965

Roy spoke to Mr Jenkins and discussed the previous week's production, which was just over seventeen thousand two hundred tons. He reported that the pit bottom bunker was operational and that men were deployed to work it on the three shifts. He also explained that they planned to start washing coal each night, in the Coal Preparation plant, after snap-time and that this would give an extra half-shift of washing each day. He explained that there were over two and half thousand tons of raw coal in railway wagons that needed washing. This would be in addition to any extra output that came from better running time for the conveyors by using the pit bottom bunker.

After the 'phone call, Roy went underground to spend the morning in the pit bottom, and he knew, as soon as he got to the loading point, that there would be a need for the new bunker. There was a heavy load of coal, and full pit tubs were on both tracks towards the shaft.

'How are you doing?' he shouted to the loading man.

'We've already had one stoppage here, waiting for empties,' the man shouted back. 'I told him we would be stopping the belt, and I assume he put coal into the bunker.' Roy nodded, and immediately headed for the bunker roadway. Jim Lord was there, and they both climbed up onto the gantry and went to the man who was operating the plough. They looked down, and could see that about five yards of the bunker had coal in it.

'It worked alright, Mr Dobson,' said Jim. 'I was with the transfer point attendant when he got the message that they were going to stop the loader belt. He just operated the diversion chute straightaway, and put the coal into the bunker. This might be the best way to operate, because it avoids any spillage during the time that the chute's moving.'

'Just keep your eye on the system, and when you're happy about the best way to work it, we can give instructions to all the shifts to do it that way,' said Roy.

★

Roy went out of the pit and got the morning's results. It was clear that there had been minimal belt stoppages and that the coalfaces had increased their performance. The pit bottom bunker had done its job. The next thing to check would be the performance of the Coal Preparation plant, to see if the throughput there had similarly increased. He would only know that with tomorrow morning's results. He was also reassured when he spoke to George in the afternoon.

'We noticed the difference, Boss,' said George. 'There was a better run with the belts. It will make a difference by the end of the week, with 57s and 58s. The lads were talking about seeing more money in their wage packets from now on.'

'That is what we want, George,' said Roy. He now felt that he could really look forward to that holiday in the Spanish sunshine in a fortnight's time.

Friday 19 November 1965

Gordon delivered to Roy the week's figures, and Roy was pleased to see that the saleable tonnage for the pit was seventeen thousand one hundred tons. But that wasn't the true figure, he knew, because there was still over five hundred tons of unwashed coal left in the railway wagons, despite running the washer for several hours each nightshift. No credit for that unwashed coal was included in the saleable output figure. This would be included in the saleable tonnage for the following week, provided the coal was washed. He was glad that this was in reserve, because the geological fault had just entered the face run of the Low Moor coalface. The roof conditions were difficult in the fault area, and this could be expected to reduce the output from that face. However, Roy was satisfied that, with the pit bottom bunker working, it should still be possible to produce over seventeen thousand tons from the mine each week. The financial results from that tonnage would show a significant profit per ton. He'd never dared, yet, to consider turning that profit into a percentage of the total income for the pit. He did some calculations now, and arrived at a figure of twenty-three percent. Surely that was too high? He would ask Jeff Briggs to check the figures at their session next Tuesday. If the figure was right, it would place Martins very near the top of the Regional league of profit-making pits.

★

When he got home, Helen had some news for him about the church.

'On Sunday, there's a special service in the evening. James Folds has asked me to play a part in it. There are seven young people who will be accepted into membership of the Methodist Church, and one of them is Peter Carter. So, I think you should be with me at that service. James wants me to say a few words of welcome to the seven, and then present each of them with a Bible, which will remind them of this special day in their life.'

'Yes, I'll come with you,' replied Roy. 'Have you decided what you will say to the young people?'

'Not yet,' Helen replied. 'I was only asked this morning, and it needs a lot of thinking about. It's a big challenge, to try to say a few words that the young people will remember, maybe for the rest of their lives.'

'I am sure you'll think of something suitable.'

Saturday 20 November 1965

Sandra Green had been out to the cinema in Doncaster, with Terry. Their relationship had continued, but they had been limited in opportunities to go out together, because of their various commitments. Sandra had decided that she could not accept any invitations on Thursday or Friday nights, after her full days of looking after Dawn while Peggy was at work. She'd agreed with Peggy that Janet's offer to have Dawn should only be used as a last resort, as Janet had enough on her plate, looking after the two boys. Terry had night schools on two evenings each week, and he had his football training on another night. Terry had mentioned to Sandra that he needed to give more time to his studies for the RICS exams, which he was finding academically tough-going, compared with some of his colleagues at the surveyor's office. On Saturdays, and occasionally on Sundays, he also had football fixtures. On this particular Saturday night they'd enjoyed the film, and Terry was driving Sandra home in his car.

'There's something I want to discuss with you, Sandra,' he said, as they drove along.

'I'm all ears,' replied Sandra, who was feeling relaxed and contented.

'The firm have issued the details this week of their Christmas event. It's a dinner and dance, on the Saturday before the Christmas weekend. I'd like to take you with me to the event, Sandra.'

'That would be very nice, Terry. Do I have to decide straightaway?'

'There's some urgency, because they want to know the names of all the guests going with members of staff,' replied Terry.

'I've agreed to babysit for Mr and Mrs Dobson, for their Christmas do, and they've not told me the details, yet. I'll ask Mrs Dobson if she has the date. She's going away next week, so I'll ask her tomorrow.'

'There's something else happening that weekend. My mother and father are going down to London for the weekend, and taking my Grandma with them. They wanted me to go, but I insisted that I had to attend the company Christmas function. It means that there'll be no one at our house that night, so you could stay there overnight.'

'Oh, I am not sure about that, Terry,' replied Sandra. 'Has your mother agreed to me staying?'

'No, I've not mentioned it to her,' said Terry. 'But it would be much more convenient. We can get a taxi back from the hotel to our place, then I can take you back home in the morning, when we've both sobered up a bit. Some of the staff book a room at the hotel where the function is held, but I don't want to do that.'

'I'll let you know, when I've sorted things out with Mrs Dobson,' said Sandra. However she was slightly concerned to learn that Terry had not mentioned his planned arrangements to his mother.

Sunday 21 November 1965

The service, during which the seven young people were to be accepted as members at Upthorpe Methodist Church, was well attended. It was organised by Reverend Folds in such a way as to incorporate all the seven youngsters in some part of the service. Two of the girls sang a duet; another girl sang a solo; Peter Carter played an organ solo; one boy gave a moving testimony, describing how he came into the church; and the other two read lessons.

James Folds brought them all out to stand behind the communion rail, facing the congregation. He spoke to the congregation.

'Please, look at this wonderful sight,' he said. 'There is nothing more wonderful in the life of a Methodist minister than to see a team of young people offering themselves to the Lord, and to their church. They have their lives before them, but they are brave enough now to make the most important decision of their life. They are putting their future into the hands of Jesus. He will never let them down. Now, I want Mrs Dobson to come forward and say a few words.'

Helen left her seat and went to the front. She stood at one side, so that she could speak to the young people and to the congregation at the same time. On a table beside her were the seven Bibles.

'I rejoice with all the members of this congregation in welcoming you into membership of this church. You are joining a great company of believers who have gone before you in the history of the Methodist church. Many of them were humble souls, but they kept the faith in far harder times than we face today. Their reward for a life of faith and service was to be promoted to glory. They have left us wonderful examples to follow.'

She paused, and looked at the congregation. There were smiles of pride and hope, and there were some tears of joy. She looked across, then, and spoke directly to the young people.

'You all have every right to face the future with hope. Some of you will go on to university, and will achieve senior positions in industry or in public life; some of you will work in local businesses or trades, but you too will still have the satisfaction of doing a job well, whatever you do; some of you might end up as housewives and mothers, like me, and you will know the responsibility of looking after a family. Whatever you do, and wherever you go in the world, keep hold of your faith. I am going to give you all a Bible, which you can keep to remind you of this day. I hope you will read it. There are many words and statements in the Bible to give you strength and hope when life is hard. There are also comments about life and its challenges. One of my favourites is found in chapter ten of St Luke's gospel. It's the story of the Good Samaritan. Read this, because you will need to remember it. Wherever you are in the world, you will see opportunities to help people in trouble. You will see many examples of people who pass by on the other side. For them, to help is inconvenient; they have no time; it's someone else's responsibility; or their status in life is too important for them to get their hands dirty. But for you, it should always be a privilege to be a Good Samaritan. There may be times, also, when you will need a Good Samaritan to help you out of your troubles and when the help you expect is not forthcoming – when people pass you by; when your friends are absent. But don't despair. In the hands of Jesus, you will never be alone, and the Holy Spirit will lift you up and give you strength. And remember, there is no greater Good Samaritan than Jesus Himself.'

Helen then walked along the row, giving each new member a Bible. She shook their hands, and spoke a few words to each of them in turn. The seven then took Holy Communion, as a team. After that, the whole congregation went to the front and took the bread and wine, which James Folds proclaimed was freely available for everyone. Helen took Roy's arm and led him to the front, and he knelt at the communion rail by her side.

The service ended with the hymn, Love Divine, All Loves Excelling, to the tune Blaenwern. James Folds announced the hymn with these words: 'This hymn, by Charles Wesley, was made for an occasion like this. Let me quote a few lines from each verse.

In the first verse the affirmation of Jesus:

Jesu, Thou art all compassion,
Pure, unbounded love Thou art;
Visit us with Thy salvation,
Enter every trembling heart.

Then, in the second verse, there is our commitment:

Thee we would be always blessing,
Serve Thee as Thy hosts above,
Pray, and praise Thee, without ceasing,
Glory in Thy perfect love.

In the last verse, there is a picture of our journey's end:

Changed from glory into glory,
Till in heaven we take our place,
Till we cast our crowns before Thee,
Lost in wonder, love, and praise.

★

Peter Carter played the organ at full volume and there was an atmosphere of great joy throughout the church. After the final prayers, people were shaking hands with each other and everyone knew that they had been a part of an evangelical service that they would never forget. The seven young people were all treated to words of welcome and admiration with hugs and kisses. Even Peter Carter was embraced by ladies that he had never considered to have any passion in their lives. He treasured most, though, the embrace from Helen Dobson. Everyone then went into the schoolroom for tea and cakes. Roy spoke to Willie Carter, who was overcome with excitement, after the service and his son's progress in life.

'You have a son of great talent, and a very wonderful young man, Willie,' said Roy. 'You must be really proud of him.' Willie had a smile on his face, and tears in his eyes.

'Oh, Mr Dobson, I can't tell you how proud I am of my Peter. I never dreamed that he would turn out to be such a son as he is. I am so fortunate.' He moved nearer to Roy, looked him in the eye and spoke very softly: 'Mr Dobson, I am not the only one who is very fortunate, there is also yourself. I said it to Joe Norton, last year, and I will say it to you now. Mrs Dobson, your wife, is an angel. There is no other way to describe her. I have never met a woman like her.'

'Yes, Willie, she's very special,' replied Roy as they shook hands.

Monday 22 November 1965

Sandra rang Terry in his office at work. She had never tried to contact him at his home, even though he'd given her his home number.

'Terry Lacey here; what can I do to help you?'

'It's me, Sandra. I've spoken to Mrs Dobson, and their Christmas event is on the Friday night this year, before yours on the Saturday. So I'm able to accept your invitation.'

'That's great, Sandra,' replied Terry. 'Sorry for the way I answered the 'phone; it was my answer to a telephone call from a client. Not that I get many calls from clients. It's nice to hear from you, Sandra. What are you doing today?'

'I'm busy with housework, and then I have some baking to do. Because I have Dawn all day on Thursday and Friday, I have to plan my work here, now. I have two men to look after, you know, and they demand very high standards.'

'I hope you'll remember the third man in your life, and look after him to the same high standards,' replied Terry. 'But not with cleaning and baking,' he added with a laugh.

'I don't know what you mean,' replied Sandra, also laughing. Her tone altered. 'But Terry, I don't think I'll be able to stay at your house, after your company evening. I shall be staying overnight at the Dobson's the night before, and I don't want to stay with you if your parents aren't there.'

'Don't worry about that now; I'll sort it out with you nearer the time,' Terry replied. 'Oh, I have to go now, somebody is waiting for me at my drawing board. Bye, Sandra.'

'Goodbye, Terry.' Terry was being evasive about this event, thought Sandra, and she wondered what she was letting herself in for.

Monday 6 December 1965

Roy was in his office on the first morning back after his holiday. He was tanned from the Spanish sunshine, and feeling fit after the amount of swimming he'd done in the hotel pool. It has been a very acceptable family holiday for the children, who had enjoyed the hotel facilities so much that they were exhausted by the evening and had gone to bed early. This had allowed Roy and Helen to have a leisurely evening meal together, in the hotel. They'd done some touring of the island, but had decided that the children were not best amused by time spent in a car, or on a bus, seeing the views and sights. One excursion, into the shops of Puerto de la Cruz, had been a definite turn-off for the boys, so the majority of the week was spent using the hotel's excellent facilities.

In Roy's absence, the pit had performed well, and Mike Darlow was pleased to report that the weekly output had just touched eighteen thousand tons saleable. But there had been problems with the fault on the Low Moor coalface and this was going to continue for about the next two months. There were three weeks left before the Christmas break, and next week would be the Bull week. Roy had done some rough calculations, and he considered that there was the possibility of topping the nineteen thousand tons saleable output in the Bull week, if everything clicked together. That was his objective, and Roy thought it would be a nice result to mention to Mr Pickersgill at the Regional Christmas event. He arranged a series of discussions with his staff, and probed how they could achieve the extra tonnage required. They identified special work to set up the coalfaces, and the Fuston seam developments, on the weekend before the Bull week. The outcome was in the hands of the gods, but Roy had done his best to get everybody motivated to achieve the nineteen thousand tons-objective.

On the financial side, Roy was pleased to see figures from Jeff Briggs that showed profit margins were very good at the present tonnages, and it was clear that the pit would make a profit for the year overall. The washing on nightshift had reduced the stock of unwashed coal, but there was still about two hundred tons waiting to be washed. Any further increase in output would require a new approach, and a new market. He needed to discuss the marketing situation with someone at Region, to see if there were any opportunities.

The one piece of information waiting for him, on his return from holiday, was the delivery dates for the equipment for the first Fuston seam coalface. The scheme had been approved quickly, but there was a waiting list for both the powered supports and for the ranging drum shearer. They would be delivered at the end of February, but it had been agreed to have a surface build-up for training purposes. This would mean that the coalface could not start production until the end of March. This took the heat off the Fuston seam developments, and gave the opportunity to get everything else up to a high standard in the seam, before the start of production. The Fuston seam was too important to be rushed, and the pit was able to continue making a positive financial contribution in the meantime.

★

Cobba came to see Roy in the afternoon. He looked a bit down in the dumps.

'Have you had a good holiday, Boss?' Cobba asked.

'Yes, Cobba, it could not have been better. The hotel was good, the weather was excellent and the kids loved it. Mrs Dobson and myself had a good time as well. And I've come back to see that the pit is not doing too bad, either.'

'I need to have a word with you about the Welfare Club,' said Cobba. 'I'm pretty sure that we have a problem.'

'That's a surprise, Cobba,' replied Roy. 'I thought everything was in good shape, from the results that have been tabled at the Committee meetings.'

'The results are very good, by most standards, but I think someone has had their fingers in the till. The Secretary had a word with me. He'd checked the figures for bar takings, last year compared with this year. We've sold more beer this year, but the bar takings are only achieving the same figures. If anything, the margins should be higher, so something's missing.'

'What have you done so far about this, Cobba?' asked Roy.

'I've spent some time with the Secretary, at the Club, over this last week, watching the operations at the bar. Neither of us saw any of the girls doing anything suspicious. Last

Saturday we went through the daily bar totals, and they just don't add up. It suggests that the Club Steward has been pocketing some money and adjusting the totals to cover the deficit.'

'I thought he was a reliable fellow?' said Roy.

'He was supposed to be reformed. He got the job because his wife is the best part of the partnership. She's very good at catering for events, and the Club has made money from her efforts. He's always had a weakness for the horses and I think that could be the problem. The manager of the betting shop did tell me, in confidence, that he has been betting a good bit more, during the last six months.'

'Where do we go from here then, Cobba?' asked Roy.

'We'll have to interview him, and I could do with your help. I don't want to see him with any other member of the Committee. There's always a chance that one of them could be involved, although I don't think they are. Their chance to fiddle is with the bingo; they don't get involved with the bar takings.'

'If we can get him to confess, that will be the best solution, without bringing the police into the Club,' said Roy. 'But he'll have to go.'

'That's the difficult part. It'll be a terrible blow for his wife. They'll lose the house that they have, alongside the Club. It's not a Christmas present anyone would want to receive. They've two teenaged kids as well. He's just a silly bugger who doesn't realise how lucky he is.'

'You let me know when you want me, Cobba. It'll be a rotten job, but we have to do it. That's why they have trustees for these Clubs.'

'I'll be in touch, Boss,' replied Cobba, and he left the office. Having had this problem presented to him, Roy lost some of the good feeling gained from his holiday.

Monday 13 December 1965

It was the first morning of Bull week, and the Enclosure team were in full session, but the discussions were not about the pit operations.

'The Club was all talk, last night, about the Steward,' said Charlie. 'He's gone. Apparently Cobba, Mr Dobson and the Club Secretary met him on Saturday morning. He must have been helping himself to some of the bar takings. Anyway, they had enough information to make him confess before they called the police in. So he's gone and is looking for a job.'

'What a silly fool, to lose a job like that,' said Cliff.

'It's a bloody sight easier being Steward at the Club rather than filling a stint of coal,' said Albert.

'There'll be no chance of him getting a job at the pit, because they're not signing anyone on, now,' said Pat.

'Is that right, Pat?' asked Charlie.

'They've not signed anyone on since last Whitsuntide,' replied Pat.

'I wonder why that is?' said Albert.

'It must be something to do with starting coaling in the Fuston seam,' said Cliff. 'They'll not be able to run all the current coalfaces when the Fuston face gets away. I understand that it will not take many men to staff that face, because it's a retreat face. All the roadways will be driven, so all they have to do is cut the coal and move the supports over.'

'Well, they can't get much more coal out of the pit, according to my mates,' said Cyril. 'The pit is winding coal now on three shifts, and the Coal Prep plant is washing coal all day and most of the night. The pit is nearly full. They're doing very well, but one thing is certain: you can't get a quart in a pint pot, as far as winding coal is concerned.'

'I suppose they'll be advertising for a new Steward for the Club?' said Albert.

'I'm not sure about that,' said Charlie. 'The rumour going round last night is that his wife has been kept on. She was certainly in the Club last night. Whether it's temporary, till they get someone else, I don't know. They might appoint someone to look after the cellar, and do the heavy work, and let her be in charge.'

'She's a bloody good hostess,' said Albert. 'I think her husband only got the Steward's job in the first place, because she came with him.'

'She will be in charge,' said Pat. 'They've appointed a young fellow from Martins Lane to do the heavy work. He's the young fellow who has a damaged foot and who couldn't get a job at the pit. I think he's been asking Cobba to help him get a job. He's strong enough, and he should do what he's told.'

'It might work out alright, then,' said Cliff.

'I'll bet she could belt him for being such a fool,' said Albert. 'He'll be lucky if she doesn't kick him out.'

'She might keep him because of the two kids,' said Charlie.

'Well, it's Bull week. What output do you think they'll get this week?' asked Cliff, changing the conversation back to their normal subject matter.

'They surely can't get any more than in the last two weeks?' said Albert.

'I think the manager wants to get a figure of nineteen thousand tons saleable, now that he's back from his holidays,' suggested Cliff.

'Bloody hell, that fellow's never satisfied,' said Albert.

★

Roy reviewed the Club issue as he got changed to go underground. He was satisfied that they'd arrived at the right solution for the Welfare Club. It had been his suggestion to keep the wife on as Steward, and provide her with some help. Cobba had taken up the suggestion immediately, and they sent for her to come round to the Club, while they waited. She was obviously shocked at what her husband had just told her and, initially, she appeared fearful that they were going to accuse her of some misconduct, too. When they explained what they were planning, she was palpably relieved. The whole catastrophe that had been hanging over her was removed. She was ready to offer guarantees as to her conduct, and assure the Committee that her husband would not be seen anywhere near the premises. They'd explained that her husband had been given a lifetime ban, and would not be able to enter the Club, under any circumstances. He'd obviously not communicated that fact to his wife.

Roy had laid out his plans to go underground for the first four days of the Bull week. He wanted the men to see that he was leading them from the front. He was with them at the point of production, encouraging them to achieve the best possible outcome – for their pay packets, and for the pit output. As he went around the pit, he used the underground 'phones to ring his office to keep up to date with the performance of the coal-winding shaft, the stock of coal in the pit bottom bunker, and the position of the trepanners on 57s and 58s coalfaces. By late afternoon it was apparent that there was a competition underway between the two mechanised faces, to see which one could cut the most coal.

Wednesday 15 December 1965

Roy was told that both 57s and 58s coalfaces had completed fourteen shears so far this week, but 57s face had started its fifteenth shear half an hour in front of 58s. The output for the first two days of this Bull week was estimated at eight thousand six hundred tons – a rate higher than the required daily tonnage to achieve the weekly output of nineteen thousand tons.

'They really have the bit between their teeth, on both faces, Boss,' reported George Turnbull. 'I've agreed to some overtime between shifts, to push the face-end work forward, so that there are no hold-ups there to stop the trepanners.'

'That's good, George,' replied Roy, who saw that there was a real possibility of achieving his objective.

Roy was also regularly checking on the throughput of the Coal Preparation plant. It was not managing to wash all the coal that was being wound up the shaft. He'd decided, with the Mechanical Engineer and the Coal Preparation manager, to staff-up the washer throughout the twenty-four hours starting on Wednesday morning. If at all possible, he didn't want any stock of unwashed coal at the end of the week. It was a gamble, reducing the maintenance for three days, as it could result in a breakdown, but Roy decided it was a risk worth taking.

Friday 17 December 1965

By the time Roy went home to get changed for the Regional dinner dance, he was confident that the output for the week would be more than nineteen thousand tons. He wouldn't agree to the figure being much higher than nineteen thousand tons: if it was significantly higher, then he would hold some back for the following week; he didn't want Mr Pickersgill lifting his objectives to new levels.

★

The evening dinner dance was of a similar format to the previous year, and at the same hotel. Roy and Helen were on the same top table again, but there were different guests. Roy was surprised to see that the Regional Finance Director was on the table, and it was his wife who was sitting on one side of Roy, and Mr Pickersgill's secretary, Diane, on the other side. The Finance Director's wife was a bubbly young woman, much younger than her husband, and a complete contrast to her husband's dour, sinister manner. When Roy commented on this to Diane, she whispered to him. 'She's his second wife, who he picked up on a rebound from the divorce when his first wife left him. Wait until you see her on the dance floor. She loves rock and roll, and will put on a real display when she's had a few drinks.'

Mr Pickersgill was more positive in his speech this year, when he commented on the Regional results. Roy got the impression that the Region was moving up the national league on financial performance. Helen again said the grace, in response the Mr Pickersgill's invitation. There was silence throughout the dining room, and all heads were bowed as she gave a completely different prayer to the last time.

The dancing was to a different band to the previous year – a young team who played with more zip and rhythm than the conventional hotel dance band. Roy took the opportunity to dance early on with the Finance Director's wife, before she was powered with alcohol. He was glad he did this, because when the band played rock and roll later on, she danced with her husband, who swung her around in twists and twirls that had other dancers stopping to watch, and younger men thrilled by her display of underwear. After the dance they got a round of applause, and the Finance Director came to sit with Roy, to get his breath back.

'I've been watching your financial results,' he commented to Roy. 'There seems to be some impressive figures, and they appear to be on a solid base across the board. I'm beginning to think that Martins will make a profit for the year. I hope that you're not going to disappoint me at the final hurdle?'

'I am sure that we will not disappoint you,' replied Roy. 'Martins will make a profit for the year.' Roy was surprised to note a tone of approval from the one person at Region whom he thought would always be against him.

It was later that Roy got the opportunity to talk with Mr Pickersgill for a few minutes, and he was able to tell him that the results for the Bull week would be another record for Martins. He got a reply that he didn't anticipate.

'I expected that you would be bringing good news to this event, like you did last year,' said Mr Pickersgill, with a smile. 'That is the second reason why I had you on my table; the main reason was so that I could spend another evening with your wife.'

Roy did not tell his wife about this conversation. When they arrived home, as soon as Helen had gone upstairs, he rang the pit and found out where the trepanners were on 57s and 58s faces, and the number of tubs filled at the loading point at the end of the afternoon shift. He went upstairs into the bedroom with a smile on his face. He knew that a major success had been achieved by Martins Main — his pit. It was the same sense of achievement which compared with the highest sporting moments: scoring the winning goal in a cup match, or hitting a century in a cricket match. Roy Dobson had risen to the upper echelons of colliery managers.

Saturday 18 December 1965

Roy drove Sandra home and relinquished her from her babysitting duties, after she'd spent the night at the Dobson house. He reported briefly to her on the regional event, and Sandra told him about the company Christmas dinner dance in Doncaster, that she was to attend later with her boyfriend. Roy wished her a very happy evening.

It was to be an evening that Sandra would remember for the rest of her life.

★

Janet Hall took advantage of Bob taking the boys out to the playing fields to call on Peggy. Dawn was crawling around the floor as Peggy was hand-washing some clothes in the sink.

'How are things, Peggy? Are you getting used to the job?'

'I'm fine, Janet,' replied Peggy, with a smile. 'I seem to have picked up the different operations alright, but they say that next week will be the big one. There will be all the earnings from Bull week to pay. One of the girls says that the men are always in a rush to get their pay. I suppose they want to get home to sort out the Christmas presents. So we'll have to be careful not to make a mistake and give them the wrong wage packet.'

'I think some of them will have other ideas what to spend their money on, rather than Christmas presents,' replied Janet, with a smile.

'You're right, Janet. I should have known that from my own experience.'

'Oh, I didn't mean to remind you of that,' said Janet, concerned that she had opened up old memories for Peggy.

'It's fine, Janet. I think about the old days, with Gerry, from time to time, but more often than not, I keep pinching myself to check that I'm not in a dream. I just cannot believe how life has improved for me and this little bundle here.' She picked up Dawn and gave her a cuddle.

'There's no reason why you shouldn't continue to have a happy and enjoyable life,' said Janet. 'I did hope to have a word with you about the future. Bob and I have been talking, and Bob thinks that we should now consider moving on to the next stage, and starting procedures to adopt the boys. But we need to be sure that you're happy with that happening, Peggy.'

'Bob is right, Janet,' Peggy replied. 'The boys are happy; I've never seen them so settled and full of fun. I made my decision months ago that they were in the right place with you, and nothing has happened to make me change my mind. They are yours, Janet. You might as well get it all made legal. I'm all for it. What will you have to do?'

'It's not just us, Peggy. You will have to be involved, to register your agreement. I think the first move will be to see a solicitor. I'm going to talk to Helen, to get her advice.'

'You let me know when you need me, but don't forget that I'm working two days each week now, and I don't want to take any time off. Sandra is doing a great job, looking after Dawn on the two days. She won't take any pay from me, Janet. Will you have a word with her about that?'

'Peggy, just forget it. Sandra's not short of money, and I think she'll be upset if you force it on her. Her father's not short of a few pounds, if the rumours are right.'

Janet went away from Peggy's feeling very happy with the discussion. She would talk to Bob, now, and they would make decisions about proceeding to adopt the boys. She had been worrying that Peggy might have changed her mind.

★

Terry picked Sandra up at her home, in his car. She was dressed in travelling clothes, and she placed her long evening dress in the car, carefully, so that it wouldn't get creased. She carried a small case containing her other clothes and make-up. Sandra was determined to make an impression with Terry's senior staff. When they arrived at Terry's home, Sandra was impressed by the size of the house and the garden. It was her first visit. Terry led her upstairs into a spare bedroom that was near the bathroom. She had thirty minutes to get changed and into her new dress. Terry went into his own bedroom, to change into his evening dress. He asked her if she would need any help, but she assured him that she was quite happy on her own, and that she would see him downstairs when she was ready.

★

Terry was waiting in the hall when she came down the stairs. He gasped at her appearance. She looked stunning in her long, dark-blue, evening dress with a halter-neck. It was shaped to her figure, and showed off her bust and her narrow waist. Its length was just short of the floor, so that her matching blue shoes could be seen. But the most remarkable change was her hair, which was pinned up so that her face was fully in view. Her make-up also matched the dress; her eye-shadow was a matching blue, and her lipstick was a strong, deep-red shade, tinged with blue.

'You look staggering, Sandra,' he said. He moved towards her, but Sandra put her hands up.

'Just for looking; I don't want anything smudged before the start of the evening.'

Terry did not get a second chance, because the taxi drew up at the door.

★

At the hotel, the Managing Director was on hand, with the manager of Terry's office, to welcome guests before they went through into the dining room where there was a free bar at one end. Quite a few people were settled at the bar, and there was a queue waiting to be welcomed. Terry was aware that Sandra was getting quite a few looks, as she stood with him. He introduced Sandra as his friend and guest. The managing director was very polite, but Terry's boss asked Sandra a few questions and held her hand longer than he should have done. He was obviously surprised that Terry could bring such a good-looking partner.

As they went to the bar, Terry was greeted by some of his colleagues from the Doncaster office, who gave him nods and winks. Sandra noticed some of these looks, and hoped that Terry had not been talking about her. As she surveyed the room, she saw that some of the wives of the older men had made only limited efforts to dress for the occasion: a lot of them wore short dresses, and their hairstyles and make-up reflected a casual approach to the event. However Sandra was pleased to note that there were some other ladies there who were wearing long dresses and had adorned themselves with sparking jewellery and diamonds. She relaxed then, when she realised that she hadn't misjudged the style of the function.

There were six tables of ten people, and Terry was pleased that he was on the table with the Managing Director and that there was only one other person from his office on that table. That person was a nosy guy, who was always stoking up the office gossip. He wasn't particularly friendly, so Terry decided that he would have to make sure that he didn't get an opportunity for a dance with Sandra.

★

The evening followed the usual format: traditional Christmas food; a speech about the company; exhortations to the staff for more effort; compliments to the ladies; and toasts to the Queen and the company. At the conclusion of the formal part of the evening, there was a dash to the bar by some of the men, who wanted to drink with their colleagues. They left their wives, who only saw each other at this time of year, to chat in groups. Sandra wondered if she would be left on her own, but soon the managing director's wife came to chat with her. As soon as the band started to play, Terry took Sandra onto the dancefloor, and they danced a quickstep with more skill and flourishes than most of the other dancers. They intended to sit out the next dance, which was a waltz, but Sandra was invited to dance by the Managing Director, so Terry felt that he should return the compliment by dancing with his wife. The evening continued with the usual range of dances, and Sandra managed a break when she went to repair her make-up. When she returned to the table, Terry's manager was talking to Terry. As soon as the next dance was called, the manager asked Sandra for the dance, which was a slow foxtrot. He was a good dancer and held Sandra very close, leading her around the floor with some fancy footwork. His intention was to put on a display so that he didn't need to bother with small talk while they were dancing. This suited Sandra, but she was conscious of quite a few in the hall watching them.

In the next dance, with Terry, he commented on her dance with his boss.

'Bloody hell, Sandra. That was some performance you put on, with the Boss. You had quite a few spectators watching the two of you. I didn't think you could dance so well.'

'I was just following him, Terry; he's a good dancer. I was being a good girl and following the man. I hope it wasn't too obvious, and looked as though I was showing off?'

'You've done a great job, Sandra. He even came and had a chat with me,' said Terry. 'I don't think he would have done that if I'd not had you as a partner.'

★

When it came to the last waltz, Terry asked Sandra if she'd enjoyed the evening.

'I've enjoyed it very much, Terry. I think I've drunk too much, although there are others who will have thicker heads than me, tomorrow morning. My only problem is my feet, which are really aching. I wish I'd worn these shoes before tonight, to break them in.' In the taxi, going back to Terry's home, she took her shoes off, to rest her feet.

★

In the house, Terry set the lights low in the sitting room, and pulled Sandra to him on the settee. He kissed her passionately.

'I've been desperate to do that all night, Sandra,' he said. 'You were the best looking woman in the room. There were fellows there who would have offered a small fortune to have you tonight, Sandra.'

'I'm not for sale, Terry. I'm free,' she replied. Whether it was that last remark that gave Terry the green light, she never did know, but there followed an avalanche of mutual passion. Clothes were pulled off and thrown around the floor; there was kissing, and stroking, and finger penetration, with each of them gasping and encouraging the other.

'You are so ripe, Sandra,' he whispered to her. Then he moved so that he was kneeling over her and between her legs. He took her hand, which was holding him, and guided it in a clear direction. Then she realised that he was inside her. It was a strange experience, with a little pain, but then she knew that she was losing her virginity.

'Terry,' she gasped. 'I hope you know what you are doing. You've not taken precautions.'

'Don't worry, Sandra. I'll pull out. Just relax.'

He moved up and down, over her, and she didn't resist his movements. Then he let out a gasp and pulled out, but not in time. Sandra felt the wetness on her stomach and thighs. While Terry gasped with pleasure, she struggled out from beneath him and rushed to the bathroom to wash herself.

When she came back downstairs, wearing a dressing gown, she was crying.

'Terry, we should not have done that. I didn't want it to be a forced job, in the heat of alcohol and passion. I don't know what I wanted, but not that. I want to go home, Terry. There is no way I can stay here, now.'

'Don't be upset, Sandra. You were wonderful. It'll be alright. I don't think I'm sober enough to drive you home.'

'Go and put the kettle on, and make some strong black coffee for both of us. We'll drink the coffee, and then in half an hour we'll drive to Upthorpe. I'll make sure that you drive slowly. I'm going to get dressed to go home. I'm so sad with what's happened, Terry.'

★

Terry drove her home, slowly, as she requested, but she was softly crying all the time. There were no embraces when she got home. She gathered up her dress and her case, and left the car. Terry had achieved his objective, but not with the outcome he'd hoped. Sandra had been the belle of the ball, but he had blown it. He'd lost her, he thought.

Sunday 19 December 1965

Sandra got up early and inspected her face to ensure that there was little evidence of her tears. Cobba asked her his usual question.

'Was it a good do last night, Sandra?'

'It was well organised,' replied Sandra. 'The bosses of the company were there, and I danced with the Managing Director, and with Terry's boss. The new dress looked fine. Terry's boss was a very good dancer, and I was able to show off a bit when he was leading me in a slow foxtrot. A few of the crowd thought we were doing a demonstration dance.'

'I thought you weren't going to come home until this morning?'

'I decided to come straight back, after I got changed at Terry's. I just didn't want to be away a second night,' she replied.

Cobba gave her a searching look, but Sandra deliberately avoided eye contact with him. She spent the morning concentrating on her household duties.

Friday 24 December 1965

Roy came home feeling very satisfied with life. When he was sitting in the lounge, with Helen, he produced an envelope from his pocket, and gave Helen a blue letter.

'Just look at that,' he said. 'Norman Pickersgill certainly pays for success. That annual increment is about twice the average in the Region.'

'Well done, Roy,' said Helen, as she looked at the figures. 'You have to admit that you have put the effort in for it. Do you think he's paying a bit for me saying grace for him at the regional Christmas event?'

'He certainly likes to have you at his table,' replied Roy, without elaborating on why he was making that comment.

'Does it mean that I can go on a spending spree in the January sales?'

'I'm not sure about that,' replied Roy, turning quite serious. 'I've been thinking that we need to make plans about educating the boys. I want them to go to good secondary schools after they've passed the eleven–plus. We might need to have some money available, if they have to go to a direct grant school.'

'Now that does surprise me,' replied Helen. 'You've never mentioned that before. I assumed you would want them to go to the local schools, like you did.'

'The world is changing. They'll need degrees to get on in any career when they are grown–up. I was lucky; I squeezed into my university education through a back door.

That will not be the way to go, in the future.'

'I understand, Roy. I won't spend the extra money each month. I have no interest in the sales, anyway. I thought we had been building up our savings, over this past year?'

'You are quite right. We have grown our savings. It's not expensive to live in this Coal Executive house, and we get a lot of free vegetables from the garden.' Roy gave a laugh. 'Of course, Mr Pickersgill gets some free vegetables from time to time, too. I wonder if he allowed for the vegetables in calculating the annual increment?'

Chapter 18

New Year, 1966

Roy returned to Martins Main keen to continue the good results from recent weeks. His staff consultation session had been more positive than the previous year's, and he was sure that his team were beginning to believe in success. He'd enjoyed Christmas with his family, and the visit to his mother in Nottingham had gone well.

★

Peggy Moore was looking forward to returning to work in the wages office at Martins. Dawn was making good progress, and Peggy was very pleased with the way she was growing up.

Janet Hall had taken an opportunity to talk to Helen about proceeding with the adoption of Tony and Michael. Helen was relieved that Peggy was still positive about the change, and she felt that this could be a great success for everyone involved. She'd briefed James and Gwen Folds, who were also very supportive of the move.

★

Cobba Green had spent some extra time at the Club over the Christmas break, keeping his eye on the new Steward. She'd performed particularly well with the children's party, and other special events, over the holiday period. When he'd checked the takings, they were significantly up on the previous year. This reflected well on the new Steward, but was helped also by the large increase in earnings by the men at Martins. Cobba got positive comments from some of the men about the pit, which he had never had before. Also, the financial results of the Home Coal scheme had improved after having a full year with the new bunker in operation. Cobba allowed himself an increase in expenses from the scheme, as payment for his initiative.

★

Willie Carter also thought that life was looking good. His son was doing well with his organ studies, and he would take the first part of the Royal Society of Organists exams in the spring. Everyone who heard Peter playing his organ voluntaries in church commented on how well he was playing. Willie was confident that Peter would pass the exams. Also, Willie was thrilled that the congregation of Upthorpe Methodist Church was growing, because the atmosphere in the services was uplifting, due to the ministry of James Folds.

★

Since his company Christmas party, Terry Lacey had only seen Sandra for a few minutes, when he called round to give her a Christmas present. She'd exchanged a present with him, at his car, but there had been no conversation, and no suggestion of meeting over the holidays. Terry wondered if Sandra regarded their relationship as permanently damaged. However, he'd been whisked along by family commitments, so had given little more thought to the matter. Sandra had been fully involved in the Christmas agenda, too, with cooking and baking for her Dad and her brother. She was determined to give them everything they required. When the New Year came, she began to worry; she was sure that her period was late. The dreaded thought of the consequences began to torment her. Whatever would happen, if she were pregnant?

Wednesday 19 January 1966

It was a squeeze in the solicitor's office: Bob and Janet were there, along with Peggy; Helen Dobson and James Folds had agreed to go along, as Bob and Janet were worried about dealing with the solicitor. The first task for the solicitor was to find out the names of everybody, and their role in the case. Helen realised his problem, so she gave him a summary of the events surrounding the fatal accident to Gerry, and the efforts that had taken place to help Peggy in her bereavement. She went on to outline how the temporary solution, of Janet and Bob looking after Tony and Michael, had extended in time until it became evident that it could be a permanent solution. James Folds emphasised that there had been full consultation, throughout, to make sure that Peggy was in agreement with the arrangements. The solicitor made notes, and asked questions, until he had a clear picture of the facts. He asked Peggy a number of questions, to satisfy himself that there had been no pressure on her to agree to the adoption. When he was satisfied that he had all the necessary information, Helen asked him what happened next.

'There are several possible routes,' he replied. 'But I would recommend that the case is presented to the County Court, for a Judge to review the case and sign the documents approving the adoption. This normally takes the form of a visit by the parties to the Judge's chambers, when he can see all the people involved and ask any questions he needs answering. That would be you, Mrs Moore, Mr and Mrs Hall, and of course the two boys concerned. It might help to have the baby, Dawn, there, as well, so that he can see that she will be a benefiting party to this adoption.'

In answer to a question about the timescale, the solicitor replied that it should all be settled in the next three months. It was only after they'd left the meeting that Helen realised they should have found out about the costs. She didn't want Bob and Janet to be presented with a large legal bill that they were not prepared for. She decided to try to find out about the costs from another source, in case she had to organise some financial support.

Helen drove Peggy, Bob and Janet back to Upthorpe. They called to pick up the three children from Sandra's house. She'd kept the three of them occupied, but she was relieved to see the parents arrive, and gladly handed over the children, along with their toys and luggage.

'I didn't think Sandra looked her normal self, today,' said Janet, as they drove to Martins Lane.

'No, she looked a little bit off-colour,' replied Peggy. 'Maybe she's been living it up, over the holidays. But I can't manage without Sandra, now. She's the one who makes it possible for me to have my job.'

'We don't want anything to stop that, Peggy,' said Helen, with a smile.

Thursday 3 February 1966

Sandra decided that she needed to meet with Terry, so she rang him at work. He answered the 'phone with his usual 'client answer', but when he found it was Sandra, his voice became more interested. She made an effort to sound as normal as she could.

'I just thought we should get together, now that all the holidays are over,' she said.

'That's great, Sandra,' Terry replied. 'Can you do tomorrow night? We can at least go to the pictures.'

'I'd prefer Saturday night. I never know when I'll be free on Fridays, as Peggy has to stay until all the wages are cleared.'

'Right, we'll make it Saturday,' said Terry. 'I'm playing football, if the pitch isn't frozen. I'll come and pick you up at about six o'clock, and we'll go in to Doncaster.'

'That'll be fine, Terry. See you then.' Sandra put the 'phone down. She was glad that she'd made the arrangements to meet Terry, but she now had to think about what to say to him. If her period hadn't come by Saturday, the prospects were desperate. What would Terry's reaction be?

★

Roy Dobson was considering his options for change. The overall manpower at the pit was declining by a few men each week; all the jobs at the pit were manned, but there would soon be a demand for manpower to install the first coalface in the Fuston seam. He didn't want to use the teams developing the roadways in the Fuston seam for the installation work, as it was essential to keep those teams preparing the roadways for the future coalfaces. The teams on salvage work, in the Morley seam, were having a major impact on lowering the materials costs for the pit, so he didn't want to stop that work and there was enough equipment there to keep the men busy for at least another year. One option was to stop the coalface in the Low Moor seam, which was being affected by a fault. He looked at the figures for output from the face, and the number of shifts being deployed. It was by far the least efficient coalface at Martins.

Roy did an underground visit to the Low Moor coalface to see the conditions. In the zone affected by the fault there was water dripping from the roof like a rain shower. The immediate roof, where the fault displacement showed, was made up of very soft clay-like material, which fell down as the coal was extracted. The resulting roof cavity had to be filled by a matrix of additional wooden supports. The men working there were wet through and often kneeling in two inches of water. There were indications that the displacement of the fault was increasing, and that the length of the coalface affected was also increasing. Roy spoke encouragingly to the men, and sympathised with the conditions. He realised that they were being compensated for working in the water, but really the position was verging on the unacceptable. By the time he'd finished his visit his mind was made up. He arranged a meeting with the union.

Friday 4 February 1966

Roy had arranged to meet with Cobba and his union colleagues, but he took them by surprise when he declared that the meeting was about the Low Moor seam. He explained that he'd visited the coalface and was very impressed by the efforts of the men, but that he'd decided to stop the coalface and commence salvage operations. Cobba realised that the decision had long-term consequences for that part of the pit.

'I understand that the conditions are very bad, Boss,' said Cobba. 'We've been encouraging the lads to persevere, to try to get the coalface through the fault and to safeguard the future of that part of the pit. The other two coalfaces in the Low Moor seam will be affected in the future by the same fault. What will happen to them?'

'I am aware of that issue, Cobba. The next coalface will reach the projected fault position in about six months. We will obviously see what the conditions are like when we get there. The other coalface will reach the fault during the next eighteen months. Of course by then we will have output from the Fuston seam, so there will be less requirements from the Low Moor seam.'

'I understand that, Boss,' replied Cobba, 'but you seem to be putting all your eggs in the Fuston seam and the Benton seam. Is that too risky for a pit this size?'

'I know that it appears a major change in policy,' replied Roy. 'But if you go into the Midlands, where pits are fully mechanised, you'll find that the result of mechanisation is to concentrate the workings into a lower number of coalfaces, operating in fewer seams. It's a natural consequence. We're very fortunate to have been able to introduce mechanised mining into Martins as quickly as we have done, due to the Region giving us some preferential treatment. I must add that I think we've deserved that treatment, given the results we've produced.'

'It all seems a bit fishy, to me,' said Jimmy. 'I think you're trying to get rid of some men. What will these lads in the Low Moor do, if the face is closed?'

'They'll be needed to salvage the face equipment, and then they'll be redeployed to install the Fuston face equipment, which should be available in two months' time. That will be a big job, as the equipment is heavy-duty, compared with the Benton seam equipment.'

'So you'll have a job for these lads?' said Jimmy. 'We can tell them that as a firm promise?'

'Yes, you can tell them that those are our plans,' replied Roy. 'As far as the overall manpower at the pit is concerned, it's dropping by a few men each week, but we can handle that. It's certainly not my policy to actively run the manpower down.'

'You will tell us if there is any change in that policy?' said Cobba. 'As you know, there are pits now being shut in other parts of the country, due to the overall reduction in the demand for coal.'

'We are not affected by this reduced demand, so far, Cobba. Our sales are taking just about all our output and our house coal is a preferred product. You'll see extra lorries along Martins Lane, fetching that large coal, which is going to markets well outside Yorkshire.'

'But the washer is struggling to keep up now, Boss,' said Cobba. 'The lads tell us that they're worried that the maintenance time has been reduced, and that there's a bigger risk of more breakdowns. How are you going to tackle that? I know you can wind more coal out of the pit, but I don't think you'll be able to wash it all. What about when the Fuston coalface starts?'

'I agree, Cobba, that we could do with more capacity in the washer. I have a meeting with the marketing department from Region, next week, to see if they have any ideas that might help us.'

Roy felt pleased that he had achieved his objective of gaining flexibility in his manpower. However, it was clear that Cobba was wise to his overall policy for concentration of the workings, and of the effect that this would have on the manpower for the pit.

Saturday 5 February 1966

Terry picked up Sandra at her house, as arranged. When his car drew up, she appeared at the door. She'd taken great care to dress smartly, and used a large quantity of cosmetics and perfume. The objective was to disguise the feeling of nausea that was affecting her. She was sure that she was pregnant, but she wanted to appear at her best. She leaned over and gave Terry a kiss, when she took the seat beside him. He was thrilled by her approach and he thought that his fears of a permanent split with Sandra had been wrong.

During the journey to Doncaster, conversation flowed easily, as they discussed what they'd each been doing over the holidays.

They enjoyed the film – *Paradise, Hawaiian Style*, starring Elvis Presley – and during it, they held hands and snuggled close together. When they got back into the car, Sandra decided it was time for her to talk with Terry about what was on her mind.

'Don't drive off straightaway, Terry; I'd like us to have a talk,' said Sandra, taking his hand and squeezing it. 'I have something to tell you.'

'Go on, Sandra. I'm all ears.' She paused for a moment. She'd been rehearsing how she would break the news to Terry, but she still wasn't confident that she'd got the right words.

'We have something important to sort out between us, Terry. I'm afraid that I'm pregnant.' Terry pulled his hand away from her, and gasped.

'You can't be, Sandra,' he said. Thoughts were flashing through his mind: what would his parents say? They were dead against his friendship with Sandra, and his mother was always making harsh comments such as 'I hope you're not going out with that girl again', and 'When will you have some sense and get a girl of your own class that we can accept'. He realised that he was in real trouble.

'Terry, it's true. I've not been to the doctor yet, but I know that he'll confirm it. You know when it happened, so you shouldn't be shocked.'

'But it should not have happened,' he persisted. 'I pulled out. Are you really sure, Sandra?'

'Terry, I am sure. It's no use denying it. We have to decide what we do now.'

'I don't know what to do. It's a hopeless situation,' he said, holding his head in his hands.

'I hope you're not going to leave me to sort it out on my own,' said Sandra, taking account of Terry's reaction. 'I want us to work this out, together.'

'I need time to think it over,' he replied. 'I'll take you home now, and we'll have a talk in a day or two.'

He started the car and drove off towards Upthorpe. They were both stony-faced during the drive and neither of them spoke. When Sandra was ready to get out of the car, she felt she had to say something.

'I'm a bit disappointed with your reaction, Terry. I thought you would have been more supportive, after all the time we've been together.' She started to cry.

'I'm in shock, Sandra. I need time to think what to do. It'll take me a day, or two. I'll ring you.'

Sandra got out of the car and dried her eyes. She didn't want her father to see her in tears. She didn't know how she was going to break the news to him. The night out had made it clear to Sandra that Terry had shown no immediate inclination to assure her that their relationship should proceed to a permanent one. Her life, which had appeared so positive and secure, was about to be turned upside-down.

Tuesday 8 February 1966

The Regional Marketing Manager chaired the meeting, in his office. Reg Jenkins and Roy Dobson were there from Martins, and the Regional Coal Preparation Manager was also in attendance.

'Mr Jenkins, you have asked for this meeting about marketing policy for Martins Main. Can you please outline the issues?' The Regional Marketing Manager was a former civil servant, who had come directly into this position in the mining industry. These appointments were made when it was realised that coal would need to be actively sold, rather than just distributed – the position that had prevailed throughout the War and until the late-1950s.

'Martins is being mechanised, and it has succeeded in increasing its production, with additional shaft capacity,' began Mr Jenkins. 'Later this year, it will be starting another mechanised coalface, in the Fuston seam, which is over six-feet thick. That coalface will be a retreat face, so the potential for tonnage is massive. I know that Mr Dobson will be able to wind more coal, but the washer is now at full capacity. We need to examine the markets that the pit can supply in the future. We also need to decide what we can do to increase the throughput of the washer. I should also add that Mr Pickersgill is keen that this pit should not be restrained in any way; he believes that it is the one pit in the region that can increase its performance the most.'

'I am aware of Mr Pickersgill's views,' said the Regional Marketing Manager. 'At the current time, we have buyers for all the coal produced at the pit, in a range of markets: the industrial market, the gas market, the house coal market, and some coal is going into a blend for coking. The only market that Martins is not servicing, at the present time, is the electricity generation market. This will be the growth market for the future, as the Generating Board are planning a number of new power stations. Can we have the views of the Coal Preparation department?'

'Well, Sir, the Coal Preparation plant at Martins is definitely working flat out. It's producing reliable, quality products and it's the preferred supplier for some of its customers. It would not be easy to increase the capacity of the plant without a major rebuild, which would not be feasible in the short-term. It seems to me that we have two options. We could transport the coal across the region, to another Coal Preparation plant that is under-utilised. This would reduce the profitability of the pit, as there would be the transport costs of moving the raw coal to the other pit. Alternatively, we could devise a scheme to produce a blend of coal for the electricity market. This might be quite easy. We would have to screen out some minus-one-inch raw coal, which would then be blended with washed products, to give the required ash content for the power station. Taking out some of the raw coal would reduce the load on the washer.'

'I am sure we could obtain orders in the electricity market, provided the coal is easy to handle. They will not take coal with a high moisture content. What are you views, Mr Jenkins?'

'I am all for the second option; washing at another pit is a last resort.'

'How much could you provide on a daily basis?' asked the Marketing Manager. 'And would it be for rail transport, or lorry?'

'If it's to be worthwhile, we ought to make it a significant quantity,' put in Reg Jenkins. 'I would say at least one thousand tons per day. That will leave Martins with plenty of coal for its other markets.'

'We can make the amount as high as you like,' said the Coal Preparation Manager. 'It will depend on the screen area that we provide, and the dryness of the raw coal. If you agree, I'll get someone out to the pit to draw up plans for a simple modification to the plant. It might be advantageous to put the blended product into a bunker that can be loaded-out either into lorries or into railway wagons.'

'If you can arrange that, it would give us a bigger choice of power stations,' said the Regional Marketing Manager. 'Are you happy with this approach, Mr Dobson?'

'Yes, indeed, Sir. We will do anything we can at the pit to resolve this issue, to give us more capacity when the Fuston coalface starts.'

Roy left the meeting thinking how easy it had been. He'd got what he wanted, without any arguing. It was another example of the power of Mr Pickersgill to guide the making of decisions. It was fine if his power was in your favour, but it must be hell if it was against you, Roy thought.

★

Terry had rung and arranged to see Sandra tonight. He picked her up in the car, and they drove out to a secluded parking area on the outskirts of Doncaster. Sandra was very quiet during the drive, and she was trying to decide, from Terry's silent approach, what his answer would be. When the car was parked, neither of them spoke for what seemed like minutes. Sandra decided to break the silence.

'Well, Terry, you've had time to think. What do you think we should do?'

'It's a very difficult situation,' he replied. 'I don't see how we could get married. Have you considered any other approach?'

'What do you mean by that, Terry?'

'Well, have you thought about getting rid of the pregnancy?'

'I've not given any thought to that as a solution, and I do not intend to go down that route. So you can rule that out of your thinking.'

'I'm sorry, Sandra, but it's just that I thought it would be the best way to sort out our present position, for everyone involved.'

'So you favour a solution that does not face up to the responsibility for what we have done? I always feared that might be the trouble with you, Terry. You want the pleasure, without the responsibility.'

'It's not that, Sandra. It's just not the right time for us to go to the next stage of our relationship.'

'Why do you rule out us getting married?'

'Well, my parents wouldn't agree to it, I'm sure.'

'Have you told them, then?'

'Good Lord, no. They would have a fit. I dare not think about what they would say, or do. You know that I've been trying to get them to meet you, and get to know you.'

'Well, you haven't tried very hard, Terry. We've been going out for nearly two years, now, and I still haven't met your family.'

'It's not easy, Sandra. They have very fixed views about some things.'

'Like I'm not good enough for you, I suppose. Well, I think that you should tell them the position that we're in. You can also tell them that I intend to have the baby. That will focus their minds.'

'That will certainly put the cat among the pigeons. Are you sure you want me to do that?'

'Of course I'm sure. It's me that you've been courting; I'm sure that we could make a good partnership if we get together. By the sound of it, your parents will never be satisfied, no matter who you choose as a partner. You want to remember that, Terry.'

'I know that what you say makes sense, Sandra, but I didn't want us to have to fight to establish our relationship with our families. I hoped that we could do it without trouble.'

'Terry, you have to face the fact that we now have trouble, and lots of it. There is a little baby starting to grow inside me, and I'm determined to fight for the best outcome for that baby. I think that the best outcome would be for the two of us to accept our responsibilities, and work together to provide a home for the child. I'll do that in any case. Whatever your parents think, this baby is going to affect them, and your family.'

Terry agreed to talk to his parents and then to see Sandra again, later in the week.

As they parked outside her house and she leaned over to give him a kiss, Sandra had the parting shot.

'This is not a new situation, Terry. It's happened to couples before us, and they've sorted themselves out. Just remember that it needs both of us, to do what is right. We're both grown-ups, Terry. You're a man, now; you have to be brave and strong, and act as a man, and show some guts. I'll be thinking about you.' Sandra got out of the car and saw that Terry was downcast as he drove away. She wasn't sure that he had taken on board what she'd said.

Wednesday 9 February 1966

'They're winding flat out again,' said Cyril Mann, as he looked across from the Enclosure to the mine shafts. 'It seems like the pit is carrying on where it left off before Christmas.'

'I've heard that the pit made a sizable profit for the full year,' said Cliff. 'Although I think it might be a rumour, because it usually takes longer than this to get the annual results.'

'They were talking about it at the Club, last night,' said Charlie. 'I think Cobba has dropped a hint, and he seems to know everything these days. The manager has stopped the Low Moor face that had a fault on it. Apparently the men were working in water, and he reckons that they don't need that coalface, anyway.'

'I'll bet Cobba has accepted that, as usual,' said Albert. 'He just goes along with anything the manager says. I don't understand him. They seem to be putting their faith in this Fuston seam, and you all know what I think about that.'

Thursday 10 February 1966

The Mechanical Engineer and the Coal Preparation Manager were in Roy's office, looking at the sketch plans showing the modifications to the washer.

'It's not a difficult job, to screen out the raw coal, Boss,' said the Mechanical Engineer, pointing to the plan. 'And we have just got room to fit in a conveyor to take that product through the Coal Prep plant. We're going to screen from just one of the tippler belts, and the holes in the screen will be just over one inch in diameter. That should give us plenty of raw coal. The difficult bit will be to get the washed coal for the blend. This shows the choice of three washed products so that we have flexibility what to use, depending on the other orders for the pit. It means three extra conveyors in the plant, feeding onto the power station conveyor. It'll look a bit messy, but it will allow us to have flexibility.'

'We need that,' said Roy. 'We want to be able to make this change to help the washer throughput, but we need to keep as much washed coal as possible going into the high-priced markets.'

'I'm sure we can achieve that, Boss,' said the Coal Preparation Manager. 'I think we should only scalp off the raw coal on the dayshifts and afternoonshifts. We'll get plenty of coal to give us a thousand tons a day for the power station order, and we can make sure the quality is right.'

'The region is drawing up a contract to get a company to make the bunker and install it,' said the Mechanical Engineer. 'We've found a rail track that's free, and I'll arrange to build up a road so that lorries can also load-out at the new bunker.' At the meeting, yesterday, we agreed to aim for completion in six weeks.'

Roy was pleased that another obstacle to the future capacity of Martins Main had been eliminated. Thank you very much Mr Pickersgill, he said to himself.

★

Terry Lacey decided to bite the bullet with his parents. The three of them were together in the lounge, and the television wasn't switched on, as his father had been working on some letters.

'I need to have a word with you both, if you don't mind,' he said.

'What is it, Terry?' said his mother. 'You seem to have been preoccupied with something over the last few days.'

'Yes, I am worried about a problem,' he replied.

'Is it about work?' his mother asked. She was in one of her motherly moods – keen to help her son as though he was still a schoolboy.

'No, it's not about work. It's more serious than anything to do with work.'

He paused, before he continued after taking a deep breath. 'I'm afraid I have to tell you that Sandra is pregnant.'

His father reacted first. 'You bloody fool,' he said. 'After all that we have said to you about that girl. I knew she was after getting you snared. I just don't believe it.'

'I thought you had cooled off with her,' said his mother. 'You haven't been seeing her as much as you used to do. I'd hoped it was all going to end.'

'It's true that we've not seen each other as much as we used to do. She's been busy looking after a baby for one of her friends, and you know that I've been busy with my studying.'

'I suppose that looking after a baby has got her broody,' said Mrs Lacey. 'Did you not realise that?'

'No, it wasn't like that at all,' said Terry. 'You've not met her, Mother; she's a very responsible person.'

'When did it happen?' asked his father.

'After the company Christmas event,' replied Terry.

'Where did it happen?' asked his father.

'It was when we called back here for her to get changed.'

'In our own house, when we were away! I can't bear to think about it,' said Terry's mother, as she started to weep.

'This is just unbelievable,' said his father. 'Has it been a regular practice, having sex together?'

'No, it was the first time,' replied Terry. 'It just happened. We'd had a good time, and plenty to drink, which might have contributed to us losing control.'

'I'll bet your firm thought she was a hussy, on show with you?' said his mother.

'No, no. It was not like that at all. She was one of the smartest women there, and she danced with my boss and he was very impressed with her.' Terry was desperate to try to defend Sandra as much as he could. 'You haven't met her, Mother, so you can't judge her.'

'And I don't want to meet her!' replied his mother. 'I always dreaded that this might happen. What will our friends think? She has ruined your life.'

'Let us not reach too many conclusions,' said Ralph Lacey. 'What have you said to her? Is she sure she's pregnant? Has she seen her doctor?'

'She hasn't seen her doctor, yet, but she is quite sure she's pregnant. She's having morning sickness, which is not like her. I've not made any promises to her, at this stage,' said Terry. 'But she is determined to have the baby, and she wants me to support her.'

'Supporting her is one thing,' said his father, 'But marrying her is something very different. I think you have got to go back to her and say that you will not marry her, under any circumstances. You have your career to think about, and your family. Then let's see what she does.'

'I did tell her that I thought we were not ready for marriage yet, but she thinks we should accept the responsibility for what we've done, and sort it out together,' said Terry.

'Oh dear, I will not sleep a wink tonight,' said Mrs Lacey. 'To think of all that we have done for you, and you have let a young woman trick you into ruining us all.' The tears started to flow. Mr Lacey went over and comforted his wife.

'You go and lie down, love,' he said. 'Let me talk this through with Terry.' He led her to the bottom of the stairs.

When he got back to his chair Ralph Lacey assumed an attitude of superiority, giving responsible parental advice.

'Just think on, Terry, you have to stand back from this now, and be firm. You can see what you have done to your mother. Your aim is to find a solution that keeps the baby from being common knowledge, and linked to you. That way we might be able to avoid major damage to the family. It will probably cost us some money to get a private solution. She may have to go away for the birth, but that can be arranged. It's been arranged in cases like this, in the past.'

Terry was shocked at his father's approach. He didn't rate his chance of achieving such a solution.

'But, Dad, there's no way of keeping it private, like you want. Sandra is well known in Upthorpe, and she's friendly with the manager's wife and lots of people. Her father is also a powerful person, as you know.' He paused and looked at his father, with despair on his face. 'I'll see Sandra again, and I know what you want. But I think you have set me an impossible task.'

Terry Lacey was beginning to realise the magnitude of his problem.

Friday 11 February 1966

Mike Darlow was with Roy in his office, talking about general pit matters. When they reached the end of their discussion, Mike asked to raise another matter.

'I would like a bit of advice, Boss. There's a colliery manager's job advertised in the Region. I'm very happy working with you at Martins, but I feel that I ought to apply for it. What do you think?'

'Certainly, you should apply for the job. And I will help you all I can to prepare for the interview. You should get an interview, because Martins is now held in higher regard by the Regional senior staff than it used to be.'

'Thank you, Boss, I do appreciate your support. I've certainly learned a lot during the last eighteen months, working for you. It makes me feel much more confident now, and I feel I can accept the responsibility of being a colliery manager.'

'The most important thing for you to get to grips with is the financial aspects of running a pit. The technical side you can deal with quite easily; the financial aspects are more difficult. Jeff Briggs is getting together the brief for my accountability meeting in a few weeks' time. Fill in your application form and, if you like, I'll go through it and see if I can suggest any amendments, to make it more attractive. Then I'll let you have a copy of my brief so that you are fully up to date with the financial figures for Martins. You'll have to treat the information confidentially, because there are statistics and financial implications in that brief that I would not like to become public knowledge. You'll realise, in the future, that when you have a successful business operation showing a high level of profitability, there's the risk that it can act as a de-motivator for some of your employees, so the figures have to be expressed very carefully.'

'Thank you, Mr Dobson, I appreciate your help.'

Roy realised that he would have to think about getting a suitable replacement, as Mike could well get the job. He could do worse than try to get Jim Lord back to the pit. He'd shown himself to be keen, and hard-working, with a good brain that could see how to organise a job. He needed to check where Jim was placed in the Region and what he was doing.

Saturday 12 February 1966

'I'm going out with Terry again, tonight, Dad,' said Sandra. 'He's picking me up. I'll take a front door key, but I don't expect to be back late.'

'I have a meeting with the Secretary at the Club tonight, so there'll only be David at home,' said Cobba.

'I'll see you in the morning then,' said Sandra.

Terry picked her up and they drove to the same parking place as earlier in the week. Again, there was no discussion during the drive, but this time Terry started the talking when he'd parked the car.

'I've thought things through, and discussed it with my parents, Sandra, and I think I know what we should do. I know that you'll be disappointed, but I've decided that there is no way that I can marry you. That's the first thing I want to say.'

'Well, Terry, that's not bad for starters. No doubt your parents are backing you in that position. You're quite happy to desert me and leave the problem to me.'

'It's not like that, Sandra. We're just not ready for marriage – you know that. I can't support you and the baby if we get married. I have to get more qualifications before my salary will go up to a realistic level to support a family. You must accept that.'

'Terry, I am not worried about the finances and economics of the future at this stage. I want this baby to have a father when it's born; I want a husband beside me through this pregnancy; I want a husband to share the joy of the baby when it's born. Can't you see that you have a role in this, and that it's more than just providing the money?'

'But you will want money, Sandra, and my family are prepared to help with that.'

'I'll bet they are. And what do they want in return for the financial support? Do they want me to go into a convent until the baby is born, so that I'm out of the way?'

'Not exactly that, Sandra, but it will be easier for you if you can escape the exposure of your condition in Upthorpe, with all the gossip about you. I'm sure something can be arranged.'

'Terry, I'll make my position clear to you. I am not leaving Upthorpe. I have my responsibilities to my father and my brother and I will carry on caring for them. I have friends in Upthorpe, who I know will support me. I'm saddened that this has happened as it has, but I am going to do everything I possibly can for this baby. I want to bring it into the world, and provide it with all the love and care that it deserves. If I have to do it on my own, I will. But I shall not hide the fact that you are the father. You might escape some of the public contempt by living in Doncaster, but you will certainly have it on your conscience.'

'Sandra, I do want to help you, but I just don't see that I can marry you.'

'Don't you have any feelings for the baby? Don't you see that it's a wonderful thing to happen to us? Have you no feelings for sharing this adventure with me? I'm sure that we could develop a very successful marriage, Terry.'

'I hear what you say, Sandra, but you are asking too much from me. It's more than I can give.'

'You can't escape your involvement, Terry. You might walk away and leave me, but your responsibility will stay with you. What will you say to your boss at work when he finds out? What will be the attitude of your mates in the office?'

'Don't go on, Sandra. It's been hard for me to make the decision, but I think it's the right one.'

'You'd better drive me back to Upthorpe, then, Terry. I know where you stand. I know now that I am on my own and I'll have to plan accordingly. It's a great disappointment. I did like you, Terry, and I was sure that we had a future together. I do wonder, even now, how much it's your decision and how much it's a case of your parents deciding for you.'

Terry could not argue with that assessment, so he made no reply. He started the car and they drove back to Upthorpe in silence. Sandra had a resigned look on her face. She was determined not to cry, and to show Terry that she would be strong. As she prepared to get out of the car, she had a final comment.

'I suppose that we should say goodbye, if that's the end of our friendship, but I'm not sure we are at that stage yet.'

Terry kept his head down, and said nothing. He had to admire the way that Sandra had put forward her views. She was a woman with much strength of character.

When he got home he reported to his father on the discussions that had taken place. Clearly, the options for privacy, that his father had specified, would not be achieved. His father summed up the situation with one sentence.

'Just sit tight, Terry, and see what happens, and don't talk about it to your mother.'

Sandra, on the other hand, decided to have another day reflecting on her position, before she broke the news to her father.

★

Peter Carter had now received from Dr Sloan a range of music that would prepare him for his first examinations for the Royal Society of Organists. He'd arranged with James Folds that he could practise on the church organ during afternoons when there was nothing taking place in the building. This was convenient when he finished on the dayshift with no overtime. His work at the pit was getting more interesting, and as his experience grew, he was able to take on more responsible electrical work. He'd be glad when he'd completed his current academic year at college, when he would get his first certificate as an electrician. That would mean he could tackle work on electrical equipment, up to certain voltages, without supervision.

Peter was playing the organ, and repeating the tricky parts of some of the pieces until he had them right, when Gwen Folds came into the church to see to the flowers. Peter stopped playing when Gwen came to arrange the flowers in a vase on the table behind the communion rail.

'Don't stop for me, Peter,' she said. 'I like to hear you playing the organ.'

'It's not really playing, today,' replied Peter. 'I'm practising the difficult bits in some new music that Dr Sloan has given me to prepare for my first organ exams later in the year. It'll be very boring for you, hearing the same few bars played over and over until I think I've got them right.'

'You carry on, Peter, but don't ask me to judge when you've got them right. They all sound right to me. Can I ask you something, while you're not playing?'

'Certainly you can,' replied Peter, who liked Gwen Folds.

'James was thinking about asking you to do a favour for him. I'll ask you, to save him the trouble. He's been invited to preach, one Sunday, in a big Methodist church in Birmingham. The church has a wonderful pipe organ, but they've lost two organists who have died during the last year, and he understands that they now have to manage with a person who has limited experience. He'd like to arrange that you go with him, for the day, to play at the services and also to play some extra voluntaries. Do you think you could do that?'

'Yes, I would like to go with him,' replied Peter. 'It's an advantage for me to get experience playing on different organs. They all have their own characteristics, and you have to get used to them, but I would do my best.'

'That's great. I'll tell him that you have agreed. It's months away, but he'll give you the date.'

Peter went back to his practising. He hoped that the date didn't clash with when there was some extra weekend work on at the pit. He'd been pleased to see the size of his wage packet when he'd done a weekend shift, and his building society account continued to grow nicely.

Monday 14 February 1966

Sandra decided to catch her father for a talk, immediately after David had gone off to school. She knew that Cobba had some flexibility in the time he was needed at the pit.

'Can we have a talk, Dad, before you go to work? There's something I need to discuss with you.'

She went into the front room, and her father followed her.

'Now then, lass, what is it? I've thought you've looked a bit off-colour, lately.'

'I've not been feeling too good on a morning,' replied Sandra. 'But there is a reason for it. I'm sorry, Dad, but I have to tell you that I'm now quite sure that I'm pregnant.'

'I take it the fellow is young Terry?'

'Yes, Dad. It happened after his firm's Christmas dinner and dance. We'd really enjoyed the evening, and we got carried away when we got back to his house. I didn't want him to do what he did, and it had never happened before. But he didn't take precautions, so now we have the consequences. I really am sorry.' Sandra was trying to hold back her tears.

'Don't get upset, Sandra. What does Terry say about it?'

'We've had several discussions, Dad. He doesn't want to marry me; he thinks we're not ready. His parents have always been against him going out with me. He hasn't said so, but I know that because they've never agreed to meet me. I believe that Terry really has tried to get them to accept me, but I'm sure that they're putting pressure on him not to accept any responsibility for what's happened.'

'Does he think he can just walk away, and leave you on your own?'

'He did talk about them being prepared to provide some money, but they would want me to go away to have the baby.'

'The bloody cheek of it! They must think we are primitive natives.'

'Don't get cross, Dad. I've made it clear that I'm staying in Upthorpe, to look after you and David. I'm having the baby here. I shall get support from my friends here, and I shall make it clear who is the father. So they can't expect to escape any involvement in the matter.'

'What do you really think of the lad?' asked Cobba. 'He seemed alright when you brought him here, but I hardly know him, really.'

'Honestly, Dad, I think he's a nice young fellow. I really thought we could make a good team together. I'm sure that I could help him to do what he wants to do. I know that his parents have dominated him. I told him that it was doubtful, from what I've heard, if he'll ever find a partner who his mother likes.'

'And could you accept him, even now, when he has rejected you.'

'Yes, I could,' replied Sandra. 'But I would want us to live here, with you. I don't think I could consider living with his parents.'

'There's no way I would agree to you being subject to them. You'll be alright, lass, I'll see to that. I think you should go to see the doctor before too long. I'll think about the position. I don't think we should tell our David, yet. Let me know if Terry comes up with any other suggestions.'

'I'm so sorry, Dad. I didn't want to worry you with something like this. But I want the baby, I'm determined to do what is best for it – with or without Terry.'

'I'm sure you are, Sandra.'

Sandra felt a great sense of relief. She thought she'd been honest about her feelings for Terry and the explanation of how it had happened had been truthful. Her father hadn't criticised her and he was obviously going to support her. She suspected that he might want to do something in the short-term, but she couldn't think what that might be. A visit to the doctor would have to wait, but she might want to explain her position to Helen and Janet before too long. Sandra got down to her daily chores in the house, and she noticed that she didn't feel quite so queasy now.

★

Roy spent the morning underground, with George Turnbull, viewing the Fuston seam development roadways. When they'd travelled over five hundred yards along the first roadway, they paused to have a rest and a talk.

'These roadways are standing very well, George. The conditions should be ideal on the coalface. We should be able to produce plenty of coal.'

'There's no movement at all, Boss. The conditions are almost too good to be true. I've never seen a seam with roof conditions as good as these. In another two weeks, we should've completed the first roadway to the boundary. Then we have only the coalface to develop.'

'We will need to open out the coalface just taking the coal section. It should be a very quick job to open out the two hundred and twenty yards through to the other roadway.'

'The lads are looking forward to that. This team wants to have that job because they think they can complete it in three weeks. They are hoping to make some big money in that time.'

'That will be in good time, because the coalface equipment won't be delivered for another seven weeks. If we can keep the other faces going well, I think we should not rush the installation, but do it right and be prepared to start the production in this seam soon after the Easter holidays.'

'I think you might get some pressure from Mr Jenkins to start it as soon as possible,' said George. 'He's setting high hopes from this seam.'

'You could be right. I'll have to keep my eye on him.'

When Roy got out of the pit there was a message that Cobba wanted a word with him. His visit underground had gone well, and the coalfaces had produced good results that morning, so Roy was in a relaxed state.

'Did he say what it was about, Gordon?' Roy asked.

'No, Boss; he seemed to want to keep it to himself.'

'I'll see him after I've got changed and had a bite of lunch. It doesn't sound to be urgent.'

★

About an hour later, Cobba came into the office.

'Now then, Cobba, what can I do for you?' asked Roy.

'I need a bit of help, Mr Dobson.'

Roy sat up and paid attention. It was rare for Cobba to address him by his name. 'It's not about the pit, it's a private matter and, if you don't mind, I would prefer not to discuss it in detail with you at this stage.' Cobba paused, so Roy reassured him.

'That's fine by me, Cobba. How can I help?'

'I need to have a chat with Mr Pickersgill. There's a Yorkshire Area Welfare meeting on Thursday. If he's going to that meeting, I could probably do it after the meeting, if I can get him on his own. If he's not going to the meeting, I'll have to see him somewhere else, or in his office. Have you any way that you can check if he'll be at the meeting?'

'I'm sure I can get the answer to your question, Cobba. I have a good relationship with his secretary, Diane; I'll give her a ring now'

'Hello, Diane, it's Roy Dobson here, with a question for you. Is Mr Pickersgill going to the Yorkshire Area Welfare meeting on Thursday? I'll tell you later why I want to know the answer.'

'I'll check the diary.'

In a few moments, Diane gave Roy the reply. 'Yes, he's going to the meeting, but he's planning to come back to Region to collect some papers, as he's going to London the next morning.'

'Thank you, Diane. Just a minute, please.' Roy put his hand over the 'phone and asked Cobba if he should tell her that he wanted to talk to him. Cobba nodded in the affirmative.

'Could you leave a note for Mr Pickersgill, saying that Cobba Green would like a few minutes after the meeting to discuss a private matter with him, if possible?'

'Yes, I will do that, Mr Dobson.'

'Thank you very much, Diane. Goodbye'

'I appreciate that very much, Boss,' said Cobba.

He made his exit without any further discussions about the private matter, or indeed pit business.

Now that is very interesting, thought Roy. He had never seen Cobba taking that approach before. And why would he want to talk to Norman Pickersgill about a private matter?

Chapter 19

Thursday 17 February 1966

The Yorkshire Area Welfare meeting followed its normal format. There was the usual competition for the allocation of finance from the coal industry social and welfare fund, to finance projects in the mining communities. It was clear, from some schemes that were awarded grants, that there had been deals done among members of the committee to support each other's projects. One extra item raised by Mr Pickersgill, at the end of the meeting, caused some additional concern and discussion. He pointed out that there had been a change in other parts of the country, where significant numbers of pit closures had left the welfare schemes in some communities operational, even after the local pit had closed. Without the flow of wages from the pit, the welfare schemes needed to be managed with care, financially. He'd suggested that the same circumstances might arise, in the future, in the Yorkshire coalfield.

At the end of the meeting, Cobba drifted across the room so that he was near Norman Pickersgill, who was in conversation with another Regional Director. He gave Cobba a nod and, as soon as he was free, he came towards him.

'You wanted a word, Cobba,' he said. 'Come this way; let's find a room where we can have a chat in private.' It was clear that Pickersgill knew his way around, because they went down a corridor and into a small office that was not in use.

'I see that Martins is doing quite well, Cobba,' he said. 'But my message said that you wanted to discuss a private matter.'

'Yes, it's a private matter, Mr Pickersgill, and I am very grateful to have the chance to discuss it with you. It concerns my daughter. She's nearly twenty, now, and she has looked after my son and me since her mother died over three years ago. She's a smart young woman, and I am proud of the way that she gave up her education, and prospects in life, to look after the family. She's also active in helping other people in the Upthorpe community, and if you want to get an opinion of her, other than from a biased father, you could talk to Mrs Dobson who knows her very well.'

'Sandra has had a friendship, for nearly two years, with the son of one of your senior staff. The boyfriend's name is Terry Lacey. I've met him, as Sandra brought him over to have lunch with us, and he's often called in when they were going out together. He seems a reasonable young man, and he's training to be a surveyor, in an office in Doncaster.'

'I have had some concern for a while that she has never been invited to visit his family, and it has now become clear that they do not consider her good enough for their son. Well, after attending a Christmas function for Terry's firm, they got carried away, and now she's pregnant. She's going to have the baby, and she wants to do the best she can for it. She will get all my support in doing that, but I'm afraid that Terry has told her he will not marry her, and I am sure his parents are pushing him. The thing that got me really upset, Mr Pickersgill, is that the lad suggested to her that they – presumably his family – would give her financial support, but that they would want her to go away to have the baby, so that there's no local publicity. I won't tell you what I think of that approach, and of the people who are behind it.'

'No, I can well understand your feelings, Cobba. What does your daughter feel about this lad, now?'

'I would not be here talking to you, Mr Pickersgill, if she had not given me the answer to that question,' said Cobba. 'She is quite clear that she still thinks a lot about the lad, and she is sure that they could make a good team together. Our Sandra would be good for him, I am sure, and she would encourage him to get on in life. There's no way that she would want to live with the Lacey's, and I can fully understand that. But that isn't a problem; they could certainly move into my house, for a start.'

'Like you, Cobba, I detest people who think they are in a different class, and look down on other people. Your daughter sounds to be a fine young woman who is prepared to accept her responsibilities in life. I will think about this matter, Cobba, and I may be able to help.'

'Thank you very much, Mr Pickersgill.'

'Keep up the good work at Martins, Cobba.'

'Yes, I will, Mr Pickersgill.'

★

Helen Dobson was surprised to get a 'phone call, late that afternoon, from Norman Pickersgill.

'Mrs Dobson, I wonder if you can help me. I have been briefed today, about a young woman called Sandra Green. I think you know her. Have you seen her recently?'

'Yes, I was with her for a few minutes last week. She was looking after three children to help a friend of ours.'

'Is she a responsible young woman?'

'She is a very sensible and mature young woman, Mr Pickersgill. She's been a great help to me, and several other people in Upthorpe. She babysits for my boys, and they love her. I don't know what the issue is, but I cannot speak too highly of her.'

'Thank you very much, Mrs Dobson. I think you should have a talk to her as soon as you can.'

'I will do that, Mr Pickersgill.'

Now what was that all about, thought Helen. She would go to see Sandra tomorrow morning. She decided to see Sandra before she mentioned the 'phone call to her husband.

Friday 18 February 1966

Sandra was surprised when she answered the door and saw Helen Dobson standing there.

'Good morning, Sandra,' said Helen. 'I was out this way and I thought I would drop in. We haven't had a chance for a chat, for several weeks.'

'Do come in, Helen,' said Sandra. 'Have you time to have a coffee?'

'Yes, that would be very nice.'

Sandra led her into the sitting room, which was neat and tidy, and she went to make the coffee. When she brought the drinks in, she sat down opposite Helen. She realised that she had not made up her face, so she would look a little pale. Helen noticed this, and used it as a starting point.

'It was good of you to look after the three children, when we went to the solicitor's office the other week. It was very helpful, but Janet said she thought you looked off-colour that day.'

'I was a bit under the weather, then. Peggy told me last Friday that it was a successful meeting with the solicitor.'

'Yes, it was a very good meeting. I think that the adoption will go through in the next few months.'

'Oh, that is great news,' replied Sandra. She didn't know whether to tell Helen her news, as she had not yet planned in her mind what to say.

'You're still not looking very well, Sandra. Is something wrong with you?' asked Helen.

Sandra decided that she might as well confide in Helen.

'I wouldn't say that there is anything wrong, exactly, but something has changed.' Sandra paused and looked at Helen. 'I did plan to come and see you, and tell you of my situation.'

There was a long pause and Sandra had a catch in her voice when she continued. 'I'm afraid that I'm pregnant, Helen. I hope that you're not angry with me. It happened after the company function that I went to with my boyfriend, Terry, just before Christmas. We got carried away, I'm afraid, and went too far. It was the first time, and I didn't want it to happen that way, but now we have to face the consequences.'

'Sandra, I am not angry with you at all. I am your friend, and I will do all I can to help and support you. How does Terry feel about the news?'

'That's the real problem that I have to sort out right now. Terry has said that he cannot marry me. His parents have never agreed to meet me; they don't think I'm good enough for him. It was the first time I had been to their house, when it happened, and he only took me to get changed there because his parents were away. He did say that they would offer me some financial support, but that they would want me to go away to have the baby, so that there was no local publicity. That really upset my Dad, when I told him,' said Sandra, with an attempt at a smile.

'I'm not surprised,' said Helen. 'There's no reason for you to leave Upthorpe. You know you have plenty of support here. I'm surprised that Terry has not stood up to his parents, and told them what he wants to do.'

'I think they have always had a strong hold over him,' replied Sandra. 'I'm sure that we could make a good marriage if we worked together. I must say that I'm disappointed that he hasn't tried a bit harder to get them to change their position. I've not altogether given up hope that everything is lost between me and Terry. I don't hold it against him, what's happened so far.'

The discussion went on for a while, and Helen left Sandra in no doubt that she was not alone in her troubles. Sandra was clear that she would continue to look after Dawn, for Peggy, on two days each week, and do any other babysitting that was required. She also agreed that Helen should tell Janet and Peggy about her position, but tell them to keep it confidential. Helen also agreed to go to the doctor's surgery with Sandra, when she thought it was the right time to go.

★

It was late afternoon, when Norman Pickersgill had a meeting with Terry's father, the Region Planning Manager, in his office. He had Mr Lacey's personal staff file open on his desk. Mr Lacey had his notebook with him, ready to take notes of the mining issues that his boss might want him to follow up. He had no idea what those issues might be.

'Mr Lacey, I have been looking through your file history. You've had a varied career in the mining industry; some would say that you have had a very successful career.'

'Yes, I think so. Thank you very much, Mr Pickersgill,' replied Mr Lacey.

'I note that you are a Fellow of the Institution of Mining Engineers, and that you've served on their Council.'

'Yes, that is true, Mr Pickersgill. I was on the Council for seven years.'

'There is also a note, here, that you are a Freemason. Is that true?'

'Yes it is, Sir.'

'So you will be active in doing your bit in the community?'

'We do try to make a difference with our initiatives, Sir.'

'So, you must be a man of some status in your local community in that part of Doncaster?'

'Yes, I think I can claim to have the respect of my friends around Doncaster.'

'Your life must be very good, then. A good, well-paid job, a recognised position in the coal industry, an active Freemason and a prominent position of some importance in the local community. There must be nothing, then, for you to worry about.'

'No, I am very fortunate, Sir,' replied Mr Lacey, with a self-confident smile.

'Well, that puzzles me,' said Norman Pickersgill. He paused, and ran his hand through his dishevelled hair, before he continued. 'I am under the impression that you have a major problem in your family. From what you have just said, you don't appear to think that it is a problem. I understand that your son has got a young woman pregnant, and that he has walked away from the situation and left her on her own. What do you say to that?'

'I did not think you would want to discuss that, Sir.' Ralph Lacey was completely shocked by the change in direction of the discussion. His hands were shaking and he did not know what to say.

'Why should I not want to know about your son's problem? Do you think he has done the right thing by this girl?'

'I am not sure, Sir.'

'Did you advise him on the matter?'

'Yes, we did discuss it, Sir.'

'So you are a party to the decision?'

'I suppose you could say that.'

'So, this person who works in a senior position for me, who is a pillar of the industry, and a notable person in the community, has encouraged his son not to accept his responsibilities. Mr Lacey, I do not like hypocrites: people who appear to be examples to the community, but who walk away when something happens to disturb their way of life.'

Mr Lacey was gripping the arms of his chair, and sweating so much that the perspiration was now showing on his brow.

'Tell me, what is wrong with this girl? Have you met her?'

'No, we have not met her, Sir. We do not know her.'

'How long has your son been going out with her?'

'I am not sure, Sir.'

'Would it be nearly two years?'

'It could be, Sir.'

'So you have decided that she is not good enough for your son, yet you have made no attempt to get to know her?'

There was no comment from Mr Lacey. He was literally tongue-tied. He dared not open his mouth. During the pause, Norman Pickersgill kept his eyes fixed on Mr Lacey.

'I suggest that you go home and have another think about this issue over the weekend, and then see me again on Monday. Remember what I said: I do not have hypocrites working for me. With the contraction taking place elsewhere in the coal industry, I will have no difficulty in replacing you. If you are released from your job and take early retirement, you will then be able to spend all your time doing good deeds in the community.' He closed the file on his desk. 'Good afternoon, Mr Lacey.'

Sunday 20 February 1966

Sandra was sitting in the front room, with her father, after clearing up after the family Sunday lunch. The telephone rang and Cobba went to answer it.

'Yes, she's in,' he replied. 'I'll get her for you.'

'It's for you Sandra.'

'Who is it?' she asked, as she went out into the hall to the 'phone.

'A young fellow,' Cobba said.

'Hello, Sandra here,' she said. When she heard the voice of Terry, she listened carefully. He wanted to come and see her, as soon as possible.

'Well, I'm at home, and not planning to go out anywhere,' she said. 'Come over this afternoon.' Back in the sitting room, she looked at her father. 'Terry wants to come over to talk to me as soon as possible. I wonder why?'

'He's probably seen sense, and changed his views,' said Cobba. 'You'd better see him in here, on your own to start with, but then I will have a word with you both.'

★

Terry arrived at Upthorpe within half an hour. It was a long afternoon stretching through tea-time and into the evening. Terry explained that there had been long discussions between his parents on Friday night, and all day Saturday, culminating in them changing their views and backing a marriage between Terry and Sandra.

Terry's first concern was to find out if Sandra would have him back. He said it was important that his mother and father knew the answer to this question as soon as possible. When Sandra stated that she had always wanted them both to be together sorting out their future, Terry asked if he could telephone his parents to tell them that news.

From then on, guided by Cobba, they'd agreed that they would live with him, that Sandra would carry on running the household, and that Cobba, would pay all the household running costs.

'So you'll be able to save all your income towards your future. Not a bad deal for you, Terry, I reckon,' Cobba concluded. Terry thanked him profusely.

'Don't forget to tell your mother and father what the deal is,' said Cobba. He hoped that they might feel inclined to match it financially.

There then followed discussion about the wedding.

'You are not living over the brush handle,' said Cobba. Terry didn't know what the phrase meant, so Cobba explained that it was a local expression for two people living together but not married.

Initially there was talk about a small, civil ceremony at the Registry Office in Doncaster Town Hall. Cobba wasn't in favour of that approach. The matter was resolved after Sandra had 'phoned Helen Dobson and explained to her the changed situation. Sandra asked whether Helen thought James Folds would be prepared to officiate at a wedding at the Methodist church. Helen agreed to speak with Reverend Folds, and she felt sure there would be no problem. Helen also suggested that it would possible to have a reception in the church schoolroom, after the wedding, which she would be glad to organise. She explained that it would be better than going to a hotel, but that there couldn't be any alcoholic drinks. That would be a good thing as far as she was concerned, stated Sandra.

There followed a lot of discussions between Cobba, Sandra and Terry about a date for the wedding, and all the trimmings like bridesmaids, best man and who should be invited. Sandra made copious notes, which she said she would finalise when she'd met with Helen and sought her advice. Cobba listened to the discussion, but made few comments. He was impressed with the way Sandra took the lead and showed her skill at planning her life. Terry was getting a prize, he thought.

It had got around to nearly nine o'clock when Terry raised the final point of the evening. He insisted that it was essential that Sandra met his parents. They'd changed their position, he said, and he wanted them committed to the marriage.

'They want to meet you, Sandra, they really do. They've changed their position completely. The sooner it takes place, the better,' insisted Terry.

'I'm not sure I can meet them straightaway, Terry.' But Cobba put in a few words of wisdom.

'You have to go to meet them as soon as possible, Sandra, love,' he said. 'The meeting won't get any easier by delaying it. In any case, you want to show them that their son is getting a bargain for a wife. Once they get to know you really well, I'm sure they'll respect you, like other people in Upthorpe do.'

This led to another 'phone call, by Terry, to his parents. The outcome was that Terry would take Sandra to have a meal with them on Tuesday evening, at their house.

There was another call, from Helen, to say that Reverend Folds would be very happy to take the wedding at Upthorpe Methodist Church. Sandra agreed to see Helen on Monday to go through all they had discussed on this most dramatic of Sundays.

★

Helen decided to fill the gaps in for her husband, that night, before they went to bed.

'I had a strange 'phone call from Mr Pickersgill last week,' she said. 'He asked me about Sandra Green. He said someone had been talking to him about her, and he wondered what I thought of her. So I told him the truth and said what a fine young woman she is. He suggested that I ought to get in touch with her. So I called to see her on Friday morning. It was then that she told me that she was pregnant and that her boyfriend wouldn't marry her. She was upset, but determined to have the baby and do the best she could for it.'

'That's interesting news,' said Roy. 'I helped to set up a meeting between Cobba and Norman Pickersgill, early last week. Cobba would not discuss the details with me, but said it was a private matter.'

'Well, the outcome of 'phone calls from Sandra today is that there has been an about-face by Terry's parents, and they are agreeing to the marriage, which I think is good news. Also, the wedding will take place at Upthorpe Methodist Church, and the reception will be in the schoolroom afterwards. So, I shall be busy with that, and no doubt we will be invited to the wedding.'

'I see the hand of Mr Pickersgill somewhere behind this,' said Roy. 'Cobba is a very clever fellow. He knows where the power is, and how to switch it on.'

Roy also thought to himself that this success for Cobba, at the hand of Norman Pickersgill, should mean that Cobba would remain committed to his supportive role for the future success of Martins Main.

Monday 21 February 1966

Monday was a frenetic day for Roy at Martins Main. One of the cutter sections on the trepanner on 57s face failed, on the dayshift, and required a replacement. Then, on the afternoonshift, on 58s coalface, a motor on the face panzer conveyor failed and had to be replaced. This meant that both coalfaces lost two shifts' production for the day. The coal flow to the pit bottom was very slow and there was no need to use of the pit bottom bunker.

Roy spoke with his engineers to try to establish why the maintenance work over the weekend had not identified the possibility of these failures. With his accountability meeting scheduled for the following week, Roy had wanted to achieve a very good tonnage this week, so was annoyed with the breakdowns.

★

After lunch time, Mike Darlow was keen to report to Roy that he'd got an interview for the manager's post he'd applied for. Roy promised to spend some time with him tomorrow, to brief him on the finances of Martins and help to prepare him for the interview. Mike looked a bit downcast at the twenty-four hour delay, but Roy realised that the rest of the day would be filled with sorting out the pit's breakdowns, and he did not want to divert his attention from that.

★

It was also a very busy day for Sandra Green. She spent the morning, and part of the afternoon, with Helen Dobson, sorting out the arrangements for the wedding. By the end, she had a long list of decisions that had been made, and also a list of things that she had to do to allow other decisions to be made.

★

When Sandra and Cobba were sitting down to their evening meal, Sandra told him her view on the day.

'Helen could not have been more helpful, Dad, if she had been my mother.'

'She was probably more helpful to you than your mother would ever have been.'

'I discussed with her my worries about meeting Mr and Mrs Lacey. I think she gave me some good advice on that, too. She told me to be relaxed and to act as I normally do. She told me to remember that it's them that got things wrong, and the best way to make them realise their mistake is to pretend that it never happened. I think I'll try that.'

'You do that, Sandra,' replied Cobba. 'I think that's very good advice.'

Tuesday 22 February 1966

Roy was was pleased with the speed with which the repairs on both 57s and 58s had been completed. He also admired the pressure being applied, by George, to recover some of the lost tonnage by the end of the week.

★

By the afternoon, Sandra's positive approach regarding Terry's parents was wilting, and there were fearful feelings in the pit of her stomach. She couldn't pinpoint the cause of these feelings – whether it was belated morning sickness, or simply a fear of meeting the Laceys. She concentrated on writing out all the decisions that she'd agreed, which she could put to them as information, and a list of all the questions she wanted to ask them. She was determined that they should not get bogged down in small talk. The dress style that she settled on for the visit was a white blouse and a knee-length black skirt, with black stockings and shoes. She put her hair up, so that her face was fully displayed, but she was cautious with her make-up, using only enough to give some colour to her cheeks, but her eye-shadow and lipstick were restrained.

★

As they were driving to Doncaster, Terry gave Sandra some additional information.

'They haven't told me what happened, but when Dad came home from the office on Friday, he was in a right state. He didn't eat any tea and he was with my mother all Friday night, and all day Saturday, in some detailed discussions. I kept out of the way as I thought it was something to do with his work. It was a surprise to me when they called me in, late on Saturday night, and said that they had reviewed the situation and decided that we should get married. I suggested that you might not agree to it, after the way I'd behaved.'

'Ah, well you see, Terry,' replied Sandra. 'I didn't close the door completely. I hoped that there might be a change of view, by you, and your parents. I told my dad that. But let's be clear, Terry, we don't discuss it any more. It's in the past, and we'll forget about what was said and what happened. Let's only talk about the future, from now on. I shall take that approach when talking to your parents, tonight.' And she did just that from the moment Terry introduced her to them.

'I'm very pleased to meet you, Mr Lacey, and you too, Mrs Lacey,' Sandra said as she shook hands with them. 'So much has happened since Terry came to see me on Sunday, that we have a lot to talk about. I will also need some help from you, in arranging the wedding.' As Terry took her coat, she extracted her lists from her pocket, to have them with her. 'You can see that there is so much for us to discuss that I have made lists, so that we don't forget anything.'

Mrs Lacey was taken aback by Sandra's approach. She was relieved that there seemed to be no need for any of the apologetic words that her husband had rehearsed, so she suggested that they went straight in to dinner and Sandra helped her carry the food through to the dining room.

Over the chicken casserole Sandra said that it was vital for her to continue to keep house for her father and brother, so Terry would move in with them. There was no question of them living anywhere else until well into the future. She mentioned that her father would finance all the running costs of the house, so that 'the new Laceys', as she described herself and Terry, could accumulate savings for the future. She also explained how she was involved with her friends in Upthorpe, and described her connections with Janet Hall and the boys, and with Peggy Moore and baby Dawn. She described her close friendship with Helen Dobson. She said she would leave the discussion about the wedding arrangements until after dinner.

When the meal was over, Sandra helped Mrs Lacey to clear the table, and move things to the kitchen.

Sandra took a deep breath as they walked into the lounge, as she recalled the scene that had caused her to become pregnant. Immediately, though, she took out her lists and concentrated on the wedding arrangements.

The Laceys didn't question anything that had been decided. They did debate the possible choices for a young bridesmaid from among their relatives. The girl would walk and stand alongside Tony Moore, who was to be a page-boy, and they would be marshalled by Sandra's friend, Pauline, who would be chief bridesmaid. There was also discussion about who should be invited to the wedding by the Laceys. When Sandra reminded them that there would be no alcohol at the reception, it seemed to rule out some possible guests. At the end of all the discussions, Ralph Lacey raised the question of a honeymoon, but Sandra said she had not considered one. Mr Lacey saw his opportunity and said he thought a few days away would be essential for the newly-married couple. He suggested a short holiday, in a hotel he knew in Torquay, and he offered to pay for it. Sandra thanked him for his offer, and said that she would finalise the dates to fit in with her commitments to childminding on Thursdays and Fridays.

The goodbyes at the end of the evening were much less strained than the introductions at the start of the evening.

★

When Terry pulled up at the Green's house in Upthorpe, Sandra leaned over and gave him a passionate kiss.

'Do you realise, Terry, that in three weeks' time we will be newly married as 'the young Laceys'. I'm really looking forward to that time. Goodnight, darling.'

★

Back in Doncaster, Mrs Lacey said that she'd been impressed by the way Sandra was organising things. She hoped, though, that Sandra would not dominate Terry all the time.

'But that is what you have done, dear,' said her husband. 'He's used to it. I could argue that he needs it. I have to admit that she impressed me much more than I thought she would.'

He had reported to Mr Pickersgill the change in their decision. Would he need to tell him that he was very impressed with Sandra Green? He decided that this would not be desirable, as it would emphasise and exacerbate his initial decisions and so reflect badly on him.

Tuesday 1 March 1966

Four days of intensive study of the report and accounts on the full year results for Martins Main, in preparation for his accountability meeting, had left Roy feeling like an inflated sponge, with facts and figures filling his brain.

The meeting followed the normal format, and there were no contentious questions asked, but still Roy didn't relax.

There was a question on the manpower figures for the pit. Roy explained how he was not recruiting any new men at all, including young trainees. The Personnel Manager had intervened on this subject.

'You might not be able to stick rigidly to that, as we will be under pressure from the Government to take school leavers in the summer. There will be a figure that the Region has to take, and it will be shared out among all the pits.'

'That is typical of your department in London, to agree some stupid figure with the Government, without realising what effect it will have on operations in the field,' said Norman Pickersgill. The Personnel Manager wished that he had kept his mouth shut.

The meeting continued, and then Pickersgill focussed on the future prospects.

'What can we expect during this year then, Mr Dobson?'

'We are running output around seventeen to nineteen thousand tons per week, and this is showing a healthy profit margin as we are able to use a lot of salvaged materials. We're in the process of removing a capacity problem in the Coal Preparation plant, which will allow us to have a product for the power station market. A significant part of that product will be screened-off raw coal, which will be sweetened by washed products. We'll retain the flexibility for washed products, to allow us to fulfil all our orders for high-priced sales. It should increase the total throughput of the plant by up to a thousand tons per day, and be operational by the end of next month.'

'That will be a significant modification,' commented Mr Pickersgill. 'Will it avoid the need to send any coal to other pits for washing?'

'That is what we are expecting, Sir.'

'What about the Fuston seam?'

'The development roadways for the first coalface will be completed in the next two weeks. We're awaiting delivery of the powered supports and the shearer. The conditions of the roadways look excellent, and they haven't changed from the way they were when you saw them, Sir.'

'When are you expecting to start full production?'

'We think we should be in full production after the Easter holidays, if the equipment deliveries are made to the latest dates we've been given. There's been about two weeks of slippage for the deliveries in the last two months.'

'And what about the output when the Fuston seam is in production?'

'It will certainly increase to twenty thousand tons per week. We're aiming to keep the output at that figure as we reduce the output from the Low Moor seam, and eventually to concentrate all the production from the Benton seam and the Fuston seam. When we have achieved that concentration we'll have a surplus of manpower, unless the wastage rate increases to about eight men per week.'

'There you are,' said Mr Pickersgill, looking across at the Personnel Manager. 'We have a manager who is planning to increase the output from his pit and at the same time reduce his manpower to increase his profitability. And your department will dream up a policy that will force him to take manpower that he doesn't want. Stick to your plan, Mr Dobson, and if anyone tries to divert you from it, just let me know. Off you go.'

'Thank you, Mr Pickersgill.'

★

Roy was very relieved at the outcome of his accountability meeting. His one cause for caution was that he now had a good number of potential enemies at Region, who had felt the sting of Mr Pickersgill over issues relating to Martins Main. He would be alright as long as Norman Pickersgill remained in charge.

Wednesday 2 March 1966

Sandra had begun a period of hectic activity, as she finalised arrangements for the wedding. She visited Doncaster, with Helen, to purchase the wedding dress and the dresses for the bridesmaids. Sandra was determined not to wear a white dress, and she was pleased when they found a long dress, in ivory satin, that needed few alterations. The bridesmaids' dresses were in pale blue.

Janet and Sandra had enjoyed agreeing the outfit for Tony. He was to wear a blazer, with long trousers in dark blue, with a white shirt and a tie that matched the bridesmaids' dresses. They'd explained to him his important role of looking after the ring, which he had to produce from his pocket at the right time and hand it to the best man. Tony took on board all the fuss with a calm approach: so calm, in fact, that Janet wondered if he had really understood what they'd told him.

Now that all the details for the reception catering were finalised, Helen prevailed upon Sandra to agree a change in her approach to the honeymoon. Helen insisted that she would look after Dawn on the Thursday of the week after the wedding. This would allow the honeymooners to stay in Torquay from Sunday through to Thursday. For the Saturday night they booked into a hotel in Nottingham, which meant that they could leave the wedding reception in Upthorpe in the early evening. As well as signalling the end of the wedding, their departure would allow the church to be changed over, ready for its Sunday use, which was one of Helen's worries.

Sandra was keeping Terry informed of all the detailed plans, but decided not to tell him about the wedding dress. Terry passed on the information to his parents, who were suitably impressed with the effectiveness of Sandra's organisational skills. They weren't aware of the input of Helen Dobson.

Cobba Green was fully aware of the part Helen was playing, though, and thought this was a very fortunate benefit for his family. He agreed with all that Sandra proposed, and she in turn felt her father was very laid back about the costs of the wedding.

Monday 7 March 1966

It was a cold, crisp morning and the Enclosure team was on duty. The pit was winding coal at its usual fast rate, which caused no comment any more from Cyril. The discussion centred around two other issues.

A lorry, loaded with sections of steel structure, turned into Martins Lane and proceeded to the pit.

'That looks like the new bunker that's being installed to hold the coal for the power station market,' said Cliff. The Enclosure then discussed the scheme to produce a power station product, and Cliff explained the method being used, in answer to questions from his colleagues.

'Mike Darlow has got the manager's job at another pit in the Region, and will be leaving,' said Pat Mulligan.

'I hadn't heard that,' said Charlie. 'And I was in the Club last night.'

'The Club doesn't get to know everything first,' said Cliff. 'I suppose it was inevitable for him to get promoted, after his part in the success of Martins. I wonder who the manager will get to replace him?'

'It'll be Jim Lord,' said Pat. 'He did a spell at Martins as a graduate trainee. The Manager was impressed with him, so he's got him back.'

'He seems to get his own way, does the manager,' said Cliff.

'You're bloody telling me,' said Albert.

★

In the afternoon, Cobba asked to see Roy. It was the beginning of the wedding week, and Roy regarded the wedding as the right subject with which to open his discussion with Cobba.

'Now then, Cobba, how are the preparations going for the wedding? A lot of people regard it as the most important event this week.'

'I think everything is now organised,' replied Cobba. 'I must say, Boss, how much I appreciate what your wife has done to help Sandra get things sorted. Our Sandra is a good organiser, but she needed the guidance of your wife to give her confidence to make the right decisions.'

'That's fine, Cobba. Helen wants to do anything she can to help. She thinks a lot of your Sandra, you know. She has appreciated all that Sandra has done to help her, particularly with Gerry Moore's wife and the kids. Helen thinks that the adoption should be finalised before too long.'

'Well, Peggy Moore looks like a new woman, now. She paid me my wages at the window last week and she seemed to be full of confidence. It was a tragedy, but if Gerry was still alive and her husband, he would never have done anything much for his wife and kids, I'm afraid to say.'

'What did you want to discuss with me, Cobba?'

'It's something that I have heard is smouldering at the moment, but it may cause us problems. The majority of winding enginemen in Yorkshire are in a separate union, and they are buggers for ploughing their own furrow and causing trouble when we least expect it. I understand that they've been asking for additions to their basic rates, because they're claiming that their differentials have altered, compared with other surface rates. Now, what they have done in the past is introduce a go-slow, which knackers up everybody else's wages. It also reduces the output from the pit by about seventy percent.'

'I've not heard anything about that, and I've not been approached by the winding enginemen,' replied Roy.

'You are not likely to be involved, as their rates are finalised on a coalfield basis,' said Cobba.

'Is there anything we can do?' asked Roy.

'Not really, but there is one thing you should know, and that's why I wanted to talk to you. One of the winding enginemen at this pit is in our union, not with the other winders. This has happened at a few pits, over this last year or two, to try to reduce the risk of more disputes. I expect that the other winders here will put pressure on him to support them, if they introduce a go-slow, and if he sticks with us they'll probably send him to Coventry. What I suggest is that I have a talk to him to see if he's getting any pressure. I'll let him know that our union will support him. There might be a time when you will need to talk to him, to tell him he has the support of management.'

'I'll certainly do that, Cobba. You just keep me in the picture, if this develops.'

'There is another thing you might want to consider. He winds at the number two shaft at the present time. You might want to move him to the coal-winding shaft if there is some form of action. At least we would then have one shift where we could wind some coal at full speed. If I remember right, the last time they were on go-slow they only did about one wind every five minutes. It was completely frustrating for everyone at the pit.'

'Thanks for telling me about this issue, Cobba. It's the last thing we want, now the pit's settling down. If I don't see you again this week, I'll see you in the church, on Saturday,' said Roy with a grin.

'Yes, that will be a challenge for me. I'll have to be on my best behaviour,' Cobba added, smiling.

Saturday 12 March 1966

The wedding day dawned bright and clear, with plenty of sunshine after a frosty start. Helen Dobson was at the church with the flower ladies, arranging two large displays for the front of the church. They also had small posies of flowers clipped to the end of each pew. In the schoolroom, tables were laid out with thick white tablecloths, and small bowls of flowers were spaced along these tables. Following last minute discussions with Sandra and Terry, Helen placed name cards on all the tables. There was some mixing of the different families, but care was taken to avoid any possible cliques developing. Helen and Roy had agreed to sit with Mr and Mrs Lacey and their 'posh friends'. Peggy and Dawn were at the end of one long table, near the door to enable them to do a quick exit if Dawn started to create a disturbance. Janet and Bob, with the two boys, were with them. Helen had insisted that Peter Carter and his father were invited to the reception, and they were in a group of church members. Reverend Folds and his wife Gwen, at their request, were placed among guests from the Lacey family, so that they could make them welcome. Helen surveyed the scene when they were finished, and she was happy that the schoolroom looked warm and welcoming, fit for any newly-married couple.

In the kitchen, other church ladies were laying out the food that had been provided by a catering bakery from Doncaster. The many piled-up plates of meat and pies, and the garnishes of salads, were supplemented with large plates of freshly-baked bread and teacakes. The volume of food provided suggested that the seventy guests might struggle to clear the tables for the first course. Then there were individual trifles to be served as a sweet. In good Methodist tradition, the meal would be lubricated by the continual provision of tea, served from jumbo-sized metal teapots. Two ladies were nominated to circulate throughout the meal with tea, so that nobody suffered from the slightest thirst. Small glasses were provided on each place-setting, to drink the toasts in non-alcoholic wine. Helen went into the kitchen and greeted the ladies as they draped cloths over the piled-up tables to protect the food until the afternoon. In their bright floral aprons, and nets protecting their hairstyles, they presented an impressive team who knew what they were doing and would not welcome any interference. Helen smiled and beat a hasty retreat.

★

Sandra was steeping herself in a hot bath, before lunch. Her morning sickness had passed for the day, but she had made only a light lunch for herself and her dad. Her brother David was playing football for his school, in an away fixture at the far side of Pontefract. He'd assured Sandra that he would get home in time to be at the church for the wedding, at three o'clock. Sandra had insisted that all his clothes for the wedding were laid out on his bed before he went to the match. She'd checked her honeymoon case to ensure it had all the things that she'd bought specially for the holiday, and wondered what Terry would think about her new nightdress and new, provocative underwear. Her going-away outfit was laid out on the bed, and her wedding dress was hung up, resplendent, behind the door.

The bride-to-be hoped that the wedding would be a success, even though it depended on a lot of voluntary help. Roy had insisted that he would provide the car, and Dennis, his gardener, as driver. Terry had organised one of his mates from work to be the photographer, but there would be no posed photographs, just a series of shots throughout the ceremony and the reception. Terry had picked one of his football team to be the best man, and Sandra had some fears that his speech might include some inappropriate stories, especially for a reception held in a church. Cobba had been quiet over the last few days, but he had bought a new, dark-blue suit for the wedding.

★

Peter Carter had decided to play organ voluntaries for thirty minutes before the wedding. He chose a range of music, including an arrangement of popular songs, jazzed-up, that would normally be played on the organ in a cinema, or in the ballroom in Blackpool. His experimentation with the stops of the organ in the church resulted in a sound similar to a cinema organ. It certainly caught the attention of the congregation. He followed this with classical organ music, where his skill and expertise surprised the Lacey family, who did not expect such professionalism in a local church. Peter's father, Willie, was acting as steward, and guiding people to the appropriate side of the church. He was bursting to say that it was his son playing the organ.

★

Just before three o'clock, the bridesmaids and the page-boy assembled in the porch to wait for the bride. Janet was there, with Tony, keeping him calm and reminding him of his role with the ring. He kept putting his hand in his pocket, to check that it was there. Helen was also there, as she wanted to see that Sandra was comfortable with her dress and veil before she went down the aisle. She was surprised to see that there were many children and adults waiting outside to see the bride. When Sandra stepped out of the car there were several comments from the crowd saying how wonderful she looked. It was the same when she walked down the aisle, accompanied by her father. The congregation looked across and saw a beautiful young woman walking calmly down the aisle, on the arm of her father, smiling and full of confidence. When she reached the front, she smiled at James Folds, who welcomed her, and then when Terry joined her, she gave him a reassuring smile as he gasped at the way she looked.

The ceremony proceeded without a hitch. There was a titter from the congregation as Tony moved forward and held out the ring box for the best man and said in a loud voice, 'The ring'. When James Folds asked who was giving the bride away, Cobba answered with a clear voice that could be heard around the church: 'I do.'

While the key members of the wedding party were in the vestry, signing the documents, Peter entertained the congregation with some excellent organ playing. His skill and choice of music was such that conversations were suspended to listen to the music, something that Helen Dobson said she had never witnessed in a wedding ceremony before.

Afterwards, the bride and groom walked back up the aisle, out of the church and round into the schoolroom. As there were no outside photographs, the guests were welcomed to the reception by the bride and groom, with Cobba and Mr and Mrs Lacey in the foyer of the schoolroom. As the guests passed into the hall they milled about looking for their seats. When everyone had passed into the hall, Reverend Folds called the assembly to order and asked them to welcome Mr and Mrs Terry Lacey. There was loud applause as Terry and Sandra took their places at the top-table. The best man asked Reverend Folds to say grace, and everyone stood up. James Folds waited until there was absolute silence, and then raised his arms.

'Dear Lord, we are privileged to be here today, to share in the wedding of Sandra and Terry. We have witnessed the start of a new family, and we pray your blessing on that family. Now we are all going to share a feast, and we thank you for the food and fellowship we shall have together. We pray that Sandra and Terry will have a continual feast in their future life together, over the years, a feast of true love and close companionship. We ask this prayer in the name of Jesus. Amen.'

It was a friendly occasion and lots of introductions were made between the Upthorpe people and the Lacey's friends from Doncaster. There was some serious eating, which was much enjoyed. The ladies in the kitchen reviewed the food that was returned and nodded to each other as they noted that their forecast of a surplus had been right. The remains were carefully placed in boxes, to be shared between the kitchen team. They also divided up the cake, when it had been cut, into more pieces than was necessary, so that again there was a surplus that was consigned to the boxes.

The speeches were short, and the best man told stories about Terry that were funny, without being naughty. At the end of the formalities, Sandra and Terry circulated among the guests. When Sandra got near her Upthorpe friends, Dawn reached up to be held by Sandra. During the rest of her tour, Sandra carried Dawn around the room and introduced her to people from Doncaster and persuaded Dawn to give them smiles. Even Mrs Lacey had to comment on Sandra's obvious baby-handling skills.

There was a gap while Sandra went home to get changed, and then she came back with Terry, to say goodbye. The whole party went outside to wave them off. Roy Dobson noticed that Sandra's last act was to hug her father and thank him for the wedding, before she got into Terry's car. It was a long hug and, when they broke up, Roy saw that the tough Cobba was reduced to a tear or two. He went over to him.

'Come on, Cobba,' he said. 'You're coming back to our place tonight, for an hour or two.'

Cobba didn't object and got into Roy's car. Roy left Helen to sort out the church while he looked after Cobba with a few drinks - this time of an alcoholic variety. Helen was later taken home by James Folds, who then insisted on taking Cobba home. When they'd gone, Helen said that she had so much to be thankful for that she went upstairs straightaway to say her prayers.

★

On arriving at the hotel in Nottingham, Sandra had set the scene.

'I want us to make love together as it should be, Terry; both of us giving everything to the other, so that we can fulfil all our desires. It should be alright for a while, as far as I am concerned, but you will have to be careful not to disturb this little lump inside me. In a few months' we'll have to adapt what we do, to take account of my fat belly, but we'll meet that when we get there. You'll also have to accept that I'm likely to be feeling sick in a morning for the next few weeks.'

Thursday 17 March 1966

Driving up the A1, on the way back from the honeymoon, Terry was wondering about life in his new home, with Cobba Green. He was a bit frightened by the man who had a reputation as a militant union official. He'd quizzed Sandra about how their married life would work out in Upthorpe, and Sandra had been reassuring and had played down her father's reputation.

'There is one thing we will have to change though, Terry,' she said. 'We will have to be less noisy when we make love. That is, unless we can arrange to do it when my dad and David are not in the house. You have to admit that we have both been carried away during the last few days, and have cried out when we've climaxed.' She leaned over and squeezed his leg. 'It's been a memorable honeymoon, though,' she added.

'I'll certainly never forget it,' replied Terry.

Their honeymoon had been a passionate affair, and not only at night. Terry recalled the lunchtime when he had seen Sandra in her sexy underwear when she was getting changed to go out. He'd grabbed her.

'Let's put off lunch, Sandra,' he'd said, as he dragged her towards the bed.

'Terry Lacey, are you never satisfied? You must be getting something in your diet that is going straight to your balls.' She didn't resist, though, as Terry turned her over so that she was kneeling on the bed and he pulled off her knickers. Terry cried out, on that occasion, as he came. Sandra was pleased for him, but her statement was more prosaic.

'You'll have to wait a bit longer for your lunch, Terry, as I want another shower now.'

★

Cobba was pleased to see them, when they got back to Upthorpe. He had ensured that the house was tidy, and that there was plenty of food in the pantry.

Sandra immediately took charge. She organised the washing after they had unpacked; she instructed Terry to bring the rest of his clothes and belongings over from Doncaster; she discussed with her father some additional storage space for their things; and Sandra made it clear to Terry that he should go back to work the next day, as she would be busy looking after Dawn, so she did not want him around. The Greens and the Laceys were now linked as a family.

Chapter 20

Friday 18 March 1966

A large lorry, full of small coal, moved slowly along Martins Lane.

'That looks to me like the new power station coal,' said Cliff. 'It's obviously mixed sizes, and mainly small coal. Have they got the new system working?'

'I know that they were working on commissioning the bunker and the conveyors over the past weekend,' said Cyril.

'I think it must be the power station coal, then,' said Cliff. 'It'll be interesting to see how much goes out by road.'

'Don't forget that they can load railway wagons from the same bunker,' said Cyril.

Shortly after the coal lorry had joined the main road, to head for one of the power stations, a lorry turned into Martins Lane with its load of four large, white powered supports.

'Bloody hell. Just look at them!' said Albert. 'What are they for? They look mighty big.'

'They could be the first powered supports for the Fuston seam,' said Cliff. 'They do look big compared with the supports for the Benton seam, though. Of course, they're much stronger, as well as being suitable for the thicker seam section.'

'Just compare that with the wooden pit props we used to use,' said Albert. 'It's a new world, this mechanised mining.'

'I wonder if they'll build some up on the pit top, like they did for the first Benton seam face?' asked Charlie.

'They've prepared an area on the pit top to do that, and to train the men,' replied Pat.

'I wonder if they'll open the place up, so that the public can see them, like they did last time?' said Charlie.

'I think they should,' said Cliff. 'You'll have to suggest it to the manager, when he's in the Club, Charlie. He does put in an appearance from time to time, I believe.'

'I wouldn't dare speak to him, though.'

'Well, suggest it to Cobba, when you see him in the Club,' said Cliff. 'He'll be able to fix it with the manager.'

'That's true,' said Albert. 'I reckon Cobba might as well be on the management, now. He always seems to be in the office, having talks with the manager. I don't know what they'll be dreaming up next.'

'The manager went to the wedding of Cobba's lass, last week,' said Pat. 'And they used the manager's car as the wedding car.'

'They were talking in the Club, last night, about the wedding,' said Charlie. 'It all seemed to be arranged in a bit of a rush. Somebody said that they'd seen Sandra in the doctor's surgery, with the manager's wife. One fellow wanted to bet that she's in the pudding club.'

'She's still living with Cobba, and her husband has moved in there,' said Pat.

'We'll have to watch what we say about her, or else we might get the wrong side of both Cobba and the manager,' said Cliff.

'There could be trouble with the winding enginemen, before long,' said Cyril.

'Why, what's the problem there?' said Cliff.

'My mates tell me that they've been trying to get a new agreement for Yorkshire to lift the pay of the winding enginemen. They argue that it's dropped behind other surface wages. The lads are getting restless as they don't seem to be getting anywhere.'

'What can they do about it?' asked Charlie.

'They're thinking about starting a go-slow,' replied Cyril. 'We had to do it in the past, and it did focus the thinking of the bosses, when they saw how much coal they were losing. Mind you, it was not popular with the other men at the pit, who also lost a lot of money.'

'That would test the manager, to see if he could get out of that one,' said Albert.

★

Roy was having a couple of hours on the surface as he had to go to a meeting of managers at Region in the afternoon. He'd spent most of his time in the Coal Preparation plant, observing the effectiveness of the raw coal screen and the blending of the washed products to make the power station product. He'd seen the loading of a lorry with fifteen tons from the bunker in only two minutes. They were expecting about ten lorry loads to leave the pit that day. There was every chance that the bunker would be full by the end of the afternoonshift. The first reactions from the power stations had been good, and the ash content had been twelve point five per cent, which was actually a bit too clean.

The Mechanical Engineer came to tell Roy that the first of the powered supports had been delivered for the Fuston coalface. Together they went over to see them unloaded, and Roy decided to use the first twenty chocks delivered to form the coalface part of the surface build. They would need the special chocks for the face-ends to complete the surface demonstration site. He put in a call to his newly-appointed Assistant Manager Jim Lord, underground, to tell him that the surface build and the training programme would be his responsibility. Roy would discuss it in detail with him later in the afternoon, when he got back from the Regional meeting.

★

In fact, Roy didn't get back to the pit that day, as he was called into Reg Jenkins' office for a talk after the managers' meeting.

The managers' meeting had been called mainly to brief all the colliery managers on the potential dispute with the winding enginemen. There was a long presentation showing the background to the dispute and demonstrating that the claim was unsound as the winding enginemen covered all shifts at the weekend and their overtime was very high.

Their average earnings compared favourably with many underground men, and their surface rate was therefore not relevant. The Region, along with the rest of the pits in Yorkshire, would resist the claim, on the basis that it would probably lead to other claims if it were granted. Some colliery managers raised the question of weekend work for these men. Custom and practice was for the winding enginemen to work out their own rotas and, as a result, they covered every shaft on every shift over the weekend. However, many shafts were not in use on some shifts during the weekend, so surely that practice should be stopped? The Regional Personnel Manager did not agree with this suggestion. This was not the time to precipitate another issue that could inflame the dispute and might lead to a total strike, he argued. There was to be a survey of the pits that had winding enginemen who weren't in the Yorkshire Winders Association – there were only twenty-six of these men, so it was felt that the impact wouldn't be significant.

The expectation was that there would be a go-slow in the near future, if no agreement was reached. What action could the colliery managers take against the men operating a go-slow? The Personnel Manager didn't have any clear advice. He suggested that the position would be reviewed if and when a go-slow took place, and then Region would advise on coordinated action. This comment was not well received by some of the colliery managers. One of the older managers, who had experienced a previous go-slow had very strong views.

'Don't you realise that these bastards have done this before. It upsets all the men at the pit and it takes months to get everybody settled down again. What we ought to do is to tell them that if they don't work normally, then they can bugger off. Then we should use anybody who can operate the winders and train up some new people. Most of our engineers have their papers authorising them to operate the engines. There are also the engineers who do the statutory testing of the winding engines. If we brought them all into play, we could cover a lot of the pits. I'll bet if we took that approach it would bring these buggers to their senses.'

The Personnel Manager would not agree to any pit taking such initiatives at the outset of the industrial action.

★

Later, in Reg Jenkins office, they discussed the meeting.

'That Personnel Manager is as weak as piss,' said Reg.

'I agree,' replied Roy Dobson. 'As colliery managers, all that we got out of the meeting is what we can't do. We certainly got no guidance on how to resolve the industrial action.'

'The trouble is that this matter is being handled at Yorkshire level, by a team that is seeking to get an agreement without a dispute. Pickersgill is not involved in the team and he's reluctant to take any action that exposes him to blame if a dispute does take place. It's just like laying down to be raped.' Reg Jenkins uttered the last sentence as his secretary, Rita, was entering the room with pot of tea.

'Mr Jenkins, I heard that!' she said. 'What do you know about rape?'

'Not a lot, Rita. What's your experience of rape?'

'Don't be cheeky. I don't think you should talk about such things in front of an innocent man like Mr Dobson.'

'Thank you, Rita, for looking after my welfare,' said Roy.

They discussed the present position at Martins, and Reg showed his frustration at the likelihood of the pit being thrown out of gear by industrial action from a small number of workmen who were really quite well paid. Roy decided to investigate what the winding enginemen at Martins were getting paid, and how it was split between normal time and overtime.

Saturday 19 March 1966

Janet Hall opened the imposing-looking letter from the solicitor's office. It included details of the meeting that had been fixed for the parties to meet the County Court Judge, in his chambers in York. It was to be on Wednesday 13 April, in the afternoon. She immediately took the letter and went round to see Peggy.

'Have you got one of these letters, Peggy?' asked Janet, holding up her copy.

'Yes, I have. But I've not dared open it yet.'

'It's nothing to worry about,' said Janet. 'It just contains the details of our meeting with the Judge, to finalise the adoption. You're not having second thoughts, are you, Peggy?'

'No, certainly not. I just had the thought that there might be some problems and the solicitor was writing to tell us about them. That was why I didn't open the letter straightaway.' She opened her letter and read the information.

'Well, that won't cause me any problems with my job,' said Peggy. 'I'm always doing a mental calculation when anything comes up, to make sure that it doesn't affect me on Thursdays and Fridays.'

'We'll have to decide how we're going to travel to York, and who should go,' said Janet. 'We may decide to take Sandra, who is so good at looking after Dawn. She might not be keen to go, as she's starting to show her pregnancy. But I have no doubt that the Judge will want to ask you a lot of questions, to be sure that you're certain about the adoption. If Sandra can keep Dawn amused, it will be a lot easier for you to concentrate. But that's for you to consider, Peggy.'

'It's not easy to get to York, from here,' said Peggy. 'So transport will be a problem.'

'Don't you worry about that,' said Janet. 'I'll have a word with Helen. She's played such an important role in all this that I think we should have her with us. I know that Bob will agree with that. If she goes, I'm sure she will take some of us in her car. Sandra's having driving lessons from Terry, so that she can drive his car. I don't know when she's taking her driving test, but it may be before this date. If not, she may insist on Terry having a day off work to drive her to York, if she's in the party. So transport may not be a problem at all.'

'I saw Sandra yesterday,' said Peggy. 'She's full of beans again, now. The morning sickness is finished and she says Terry has settled in with them at Upthorpe. Sandra has been over, occasionally, to see the Laceys, in Doncaster, and relationships there are on a stable footing. She says that she's pushing Terry with his studies, as she wants him to keep up with his exams. The doctor seems happy with the pregnancy, and she is so pleased with the help she's receiving from Helen. Aren't we all lucky to have Helen as a friend?'

Tuesday 22 March 1966

Roy gave Jeff Briggs the task of investigating the split of the winders' wages and he decided to have a morning visiting the winding engine houses. The magnificent steam winding engines impressed him. They glistened in their green colours and there was a huge hiss of steam as the pistons moved through the cylinders. A greaser was moving around the engine, oiling parts and replenishing grease in containers. Housed in a separate cabin was the engineman who reacted to the signals and pushed the levers around to control the direction of travel of the cages, and their speed. The engineman appeared to be working in a semi-automatic state, but his skill came into play when he applied the brakes so that the cages landed, at speed, precisely to a marker on the large diameter drum that held the winding ropes. Roy had to admit that it was a magnificent system. He went into the cabin and spoke to the engineman.

'It's a fine engine. It must be a thrill for you to drive it,' he said.

'Yes, it's a good engine,' replied the winding engineman. 'You get used to it, though, and I have to admit I've operated this engine for many hours with my mind thinking I was on Blackpool sands.'

'You'd make a fortune if you had an engine like this giving rides on Blackpool sands,' replied Roy. He didn't comment about the pending overtime ban, but he moved to the other engine house, where the engineman was the one in Cobba's union. Roy introduced himself and asked how things were for him.

'I'd be happier if we were not going to be involved in the go-slow,' he replied. 'But from what I hear, it seems almost certain now there will be some form of industrial action.'

'Are you being pressurised to take part?' asked Roy.

'Not yet, but I do keep getting sly looks. I think that there'll be some pressure when the action starts.'

'Well, if there is, then I want to know. The management will stand by you. I'm sure that Cobba's team will also look after you.'

'That's nice to know, but it might not be here where the pressure is put on. It's more likely to be at home. I worry about the kids being affected at school.'

'You must let me know if that happens. We might want you to move over onto the coal-winding shaft, to allow us to wind normally on at least one shift each day.'

'That would certainly cause some reaction. But I have worked on that engine on some weeks. Both the engines are identical, anyway.'

'I'll keep in touch with you, and let you know what our plans are,' said Roy, as he left the engine house.

★

Roy then went on to see the steam-raising plant and he was joined by the Mechanical Engineer. There were two chain grate boilers, and one on stand-by. Two men were attending these and loading coal into the hoppers that fed a steady stream of coal onto chain grates. They were also responsible for clearing away the ash that was tipped off the chains at the end of the burning cycle.

'This is a tough job,' Roy said to his engineer.

'Yes, Boss, it is. These lads earn their corn, and they operate in this part of the pit top that nobody sees. They have to maintain the high steam pressure to keep the winding engines going flat out. We also have a steam compressor producing compressed air for the blacksmith's shop. If we were using compressed air underground, we'd have to have the third boiler in use, and that would put us under real strain.'

'I don't foresee us having to use compressed air underground in any big way,' replied Roy. 'Some pits are converting to electric winding engines which are more efficient and save costs.'

'Electric winding engines are certainly less of a problem to us mechanical engineers, but these steam engines are wonderful to see, and they give a real sense of power. They'll do everything we ask them to do for Martins, I'm confident of that.'

'Well, we expect to be challenged to wind more coal when we get the Fuston seam into production,' said Roy.

★

Roy decided that his day had been worthwhile, as now he was very familiar with the system that might be affected by a winders dispute.

Wednesday 23 March 1966

The Enclosure was in session when two important deliveries were made. The first one was a lorry with just two powered supports on it.

'Just look at that load,' said Albert. 'Those buggers are massive, and look how many props they have on them.'

'Ah, they are what the pit has been waiting for,' said Cliff. 'They're the special supports that go in the Fuston seam roadways. That is why they're so tall. Each one of those supports will take a total load of over three hundred tons. They should be able to finish the coalface build-up on the surface now, and then we'll be able to see how the whole system works.'

'The new coal-cutting machine hasn't come yet,' said Charlie. 'They'll need that for the training on the surface.'

'You spoke too soon,' said Albert, as a lorry turned into Martins Lane. Its load was a single machine, fully built-up: the ranging drum shearer. 'That machine looks to be a big bugger, as well.'

'It's a new type,' said Cliff. 'It cuts part of the coal seam moving one way and then lifts up the bottom-coal as it travels back. I want to see how it looks on the surface training demonstration. It's been cleverly designed so that it can raise and lower the cutting disc. There are some very clever engineers in the mining industry, now.'

'The industry used to be made up of clever miners, who used their skill to get the coal; now it's clever engineers who build machines to cut the coal. They'll never be as good as first-class miners,' said Albert.

'The trouble in the past was that there were a lot of second-class miners, as well as the first-class ones,' said Cliff. 'They weren't very good at getting the coal. You have to accept, Albert, that the mechanised faces at Martins have made a lot of difference to the pit's results.'

'The pit is making a very good profit every week now, I've been told,' said Pat.

'Yes, but how much is all this mechanised equipment costing?' said Albert. 'I'll bet they don't count those costs in the weekly figures.'

'Oh, yes they do,' said Pat. 'They include so much each week in the accounts to cover the cost of all the equipment at the pit. I was told that, with all the costs included, Martins is now printing money; its profits are so high.'

'Well, we'll be able to see how this new system will work in the Fuston seam when they have the surface training sessions,' said Charlie.

'Who fixed that, Charlie?' asked Cyril.

'I had a word with Cobba, like you suggested. He said he would fix it. So it will be on show to the public on a Saturday morning, like it was last time.'

'We'll all have to go as a team,' suggested Cliff.

The Enclosure passed that motion unanimously.

★

Helen had made her sitting room available for a meeting of the parties to the adoption procedures, in order to discuss their visit to the Judge. Janet and Bob were there, with Peggy. The three children were there as well, but Sandra had escorted them into the playroom, with their own toys and those of Robert and John.

Helen started the discussion. Her first job was to emphasise that it would not be a formal occasion with the Judge dressed in his robes. The aim was for it to be a friendly chat, with questions from the Judge to convince him that adoption was the best solution for all parties. Peggy wanted to know if she should discuss the death of Gerry. She was encouraged to raise this, as it had been the one incident that had changed her life completely. Helen also thought she should report on the way she had been able to take on a part-time job, which had given her some additional income and more independence.

Bob said he thought Helen should be present, as it was her influence that had provided support for Peggy at the time of the accident. He also reminded everybody that it was

Helen's suggestion that the boys should continue to stay with him and Janet on a permanent basis.

There was much debate about how the children should be briefed about the meeting. Janet was given the job of talking to Tony, as he was likely to be the spokesman for both himself and Michael. After his performance at Sandra's wedding, she was confident that his apparent indifference to any instructions was just a cover, and that he could be relied upon to play his part.

After quite a long discussion about the wishes of the boys, there was confidence that the boys would not suggest that they wanted to go back to live with Peggy.

'I love them to bits,' said Peggy. 'But there is no way that I could give them a life like they are getting with Bob and Janet.'

'Don't even talk about it, please,' said Janet. 'It would break my heart to lose them now.' She took out her handkerchief to wipe her eyes. Bob stood up and went over to Janet and put his arm around her. He realised that until the adoption was finalised, Janet would be on edge as she had so much to lose. Helen also recognised this problem and resolved to make some visits to Janet before the meeting with the Judge. Helen also agreed to contact the solicitor, to tell him the names of those who would be visiting the Judge, so that he knew whom to expect.

Sandra was persuaded to be a member of the party, so that she could look after Dawn if she was restless in the meeting.

'My driving test is next week,' said Sandra. 'So I have an additional incentive to pass, so that I can drive to York. I'll be able to take Peggy and Dawn with me. If I fail, Terry will have to take half a day off work to drive us.'

★

Reports on the discussions with the winding enginemen had continued to come to the colliery managers from Region. Several of these reports indicated hopes that a solution to the dispute was imminent, and this raised everyone's hopes. Reports on local television and radio had tended to contradict these hopes, though, and it was from the media that Roy learned that the go-slow was to begin at the start of the Bull week before Easter. Roy rang Cobba when he heard the news.

'Have you heard about the winders' go-slow, Cobba?' Roy asked.

'I certainly have, Boss. I told you what they would do. They're a set of bastards. They have deliberately picked a start date that will upset all the men, and ruin their earnings for the Easter holidays. We shall have some tricky problems to watch. I can think of a few Martins' men that might be inclined to threaten the winding enginemen with a good thrashing.'

'I wouldn't mind if the winding enginemen actually had a case, but there is no way they are underpaid,' replied Roy. 'I will show you what they are earning at Martins, next time you're in the office. I'm certainly going to review their overtime when we get back to normal.'

Thursday 24 March 1966

When it was clear that negotiations were pointless there was a further meeting of colliery managers at Region, but this time the meeting was chaired by Norman Pickersgill. Whether he'd made the choice to take a proactive approach to the industrial action, or whether there was a new policy decision from London, from the start of the meeting it was clear that decisions were to be made. Colliery managers were instructed to meet the winding enginemen and warn them that they were in breach of their agreement if they introduced a go-slow. If they didn't call off the action at the end of the first week, alternative arrangements would be made to cover the pits. In the meantime every person who had been trained as a winding engineman would spend time on the engines to familiarise themselves with the operations. Other engineers and specialists throughout the Region, who might be suitable for the job, would be put into training. Also, the enginemen who were not in the winders' union would be deployed to best advantage for production at the pits.

★

Immediately he got back to the pit, Roy contacted the Mechanical Engineer and told him to arrange a meeting straightaway with the enginemen. All of them would be invited to the meeting, but the coal shaft would be kept in operation by using the non–union engineman on that shaft during the meeting. This was a way of letting them know what would happen if they introduced industrial action. The meeting was set for nine o'clock the next morning.

Friday 25 March 1966

The meeting was attended by the five enginemen who were in the union, but they also brought with them an official of their association. Roy was supported by the Mechanical Engineer and Jeff Briggs, his finance man.

After the introductions, Roy opened the meeting.

'I understand that you are to impose a go-slow from next Monday morning. I have three things to say to you. Firstly, I do not think that there is any need for it at Martins. Jeff will give you a list of the earnings of the five of you, expressed on an annual basis, and then shown on a weekly basis.' Jeff gave out copies of this information. 'You will see that your earnings are higher than many underground men. I appreciate that you have put the time in for those earnings. When we have analysed the time you've been working, we can see that there are opportunities to reduce that, particularly at weekends. We will introduce these changes after the Easter holidays.'

'Secondly, I want to give you notice that we will be using the engineman who is not in your union to wind at the coal shaft during the dispute.'

'And thirdly, from now on, we will be training other members of staff to operate the winders. If the go-slow is not resolved over the first week, we will use these other trained members of staff to operate the engines and keep the mine working as near to normal as possible.'

'Oh, we're trying to be clever, are we?' said the union official, who was a burly fellow and keen to show his strength to his members.

'No, I'm not trying to be clever,' interposed Roy, who was determined to focus his arguments to his own winding enginemen. 'I am stating facts, and telling you what is going to happen. I am not in the business of playing politics with people's livelihoods.' He'd heard that the union man had ambitions to become a Labour Party MP.

'Let me tell you that if you use other people on these engines you will be in danger of having a full-blown strike,' said the union official.

'I can use anyone I like on those engines, once I am sure they are competent,' replied Roy. 'I have to sign the legal document that allows them to operate on those engines. No doubt your lads here have got copies of their approval to be enginemen. I am surprised that you're talking about a full-blown strike; I've not heard any of my enginemen talking about a strike?' The winding enginemen nodded to this.

'I am suggesting to you that what you are talking about is a risk of causing a strike,' said the union man. He was a bit wary of taking a positive line, now, in his arguments. 'We've not heard other pits in Yorkshire taking your line,' he added.

'Well, you might be hearing from other managers,' said Roy.

'We have put our case, which covers every pit in Yorkshire, for a special increase in the rate, and we have taken the view that we're being fobbed off; so we have to take action.'

'It could be that it's not a strong case, as the figures for earnings at Martins show,' said Roy.

'Our view is that we do have a strong case, and we intend to pursue it,' said the union man, looking for support from his members. They weren't looking at him though, but at the papers they'd been given.

'You've certainly focussed attention on your members,' said Roy. 'As colliery managers, we need to be reminded, from time to time, to put the spotlight on some detailed element of our operations. We usually find that we can improve our efficiency and reduce our costs. I've been happy with the way our enginemen operate, and they've helped to increase the results from Martins. However, I will now need to consider how they're organised in the future.'

'You're just bluffing, to frighten our lads,' said the union man, almost mocking Roy.

'Don't you be deceived,' replied Roy, very firmly. 'Have a word with your lads outside this meeting. I think they will tell you that Roy Dobson does not bluff. When he says he will do something, he does it. I don't think there is any need to extend this meeting, Gentlemen. Your union has made an unfortunate decision, and I have told you what we will do as a result of that decision.'

The men left the meeting and Roy got the impression that his enginemen were not happy with the outcome. They might also be wondering how they had been led into the present position, he thought.

The Mechanical Engineer stayed behind and told Roy that they had three members of staff who were trained to operate the engines and could start immediately. There were two other engineers who could be trained, and he was confident they would soon be able to fill any manning void. He also noted that Jim Lord wanted to train, and from his experience driving other forms of steam engines, it was thought he might make a very competent operator. Roy agreed that training should start for the three extra potential operators straightaway. He rang Reg Jenkins and told him about the meeting.

The immediate objective for Martins was to complete the surface build-up of the Fuston seam equipment. That would allow the rest of the week, before the start of the industrial action, for surface training of the Fuston workmen. Roy had agreed to Cobba's suggestion that the equipment should be available on the Saturday morning for the public to see a demonstration.

Saturday 26 March 1966

It was a bright, breezy morning when the Enclosure team visited the training build-up for the Fuston seam coalface. It was fifty yards long, with the roadways set up at either end with supports just like the real ones underground. The ranging drum shearer was mounted on the panzer conveyor and the powered supports and the panzer conveyor could be operated.

'Now we should be able to see how it works,' said Cliff.

The machine operator set the machine off to move as if along the coalface. He had the shearer disc set in a high position, as though he was cutting the top-coal. The cutting disc was shrouded with a cowl that was designed to force the coal onto the panzer conveyor. The team walked alongside, observing how one workman pushed out a fore-pole from each powered roof support canopy, which provided support to the roof immediately behind the shearer.

'That's a neat way of getting some early support to the roof,' said Cliff.

'They seem to have thought of everything, with this design,' said Charlie.

When they reached the end of the run, and the shearer was parked on the panzer conveyor across the roadway, the shearer driver operated the hydraulic arm and lowered the shearer disc down to floor level. Another workman hung a chain on the cowl, and as the shearer started to move back along the coalface the cowl swung over until it was immediately behind the disc and it could be clearly seen then how it would force the coal onto the panzer conveyor.

'That's bloody good,' said Albert.

As the shearer moved along the coalface, two workmen followed, ramming the panzer conveyor over and then pulling in the powered supports. As the supports were pulled over, the fore-pole automatically retracted into the canopy of each support. When the machine reached the other roadway, only the shearer disc was exposed into the roadway, the rest of the machine was along the coalface. The Enclosure team watched as the disc was raised and the cowl again swung over. A wooden roof support was taken out and the steel girder was held up by the special roadway supports. Then the machine was rammed over, ready for it to start a new run.

'Come on, Cliff, do some mental calculations,' said Charlie. 'How much coal will that machine produce for each run up and down the Fuston seam coalface?'

'Well, let me think,' replied Cliff. 'Let me think a bit.' He paused to do some mental maths. 'It must be over three hundred tons for each trip up and down the coalface.'

'Bloody hell,' exclaimed Albert. 'If they work it three shifts each day that will be more coal than Martins used to produce from eight or nine hand-filled coalfaces.'

'They'll never be able to wind all that coal, as well as the other faces at Martins,' said Cyril Mann.

'They'll be cutting down on the number of faces in the Low Moor seam,' said Cliff.

'The Fuston face will be worked by men from the Low Moor seam,' said Charlie. 'There were some of them in the Club, last night, and they were bragging that they will produce more coal than the Benton mechanised faces.'

'Look who's here now,' said Cyril. 'Cobba has come for a look, and he's brought his lass and her husband.'

'They're still talking in the Club about her being pregnant,' said Charlie. 'But you can't see it from what she's wearing this morning. I'd better go over and have a word with Cobba, because he fixed this demonstration.' Charlie left his mates and walked over to chat with Cobba. He stayed with him a few minutes and listened in as Cobba explained the mining system to Terry and Sandra.

'I'm not going over to speak to Cobba,' said Albert. 'He never has time for a word with me, these days.'

★

Jim Lord had been practising on one of the winding engines, but at midday he came across and closed the demonstration. A team of craftsmen started to strip the equipment down, to start getting it underground that afternoon. Jim wanted to complete the installation of the Fuston coalface before the Easter holidays.

There had been quite a few men from Upthorpe and the surrounding villages, accompanied by their children and the occasional wife, visiting the demonstration. But the numbers had not been on the scale of the Benton seam event, which had benefited from the TV cameras. Roy had banned any publicity. He didn't want any questions to answer about the proposed industrial action by the winder enginemen.

★

Cobba, Sandra and Terry had another engagement that afternoon. David Green had been spotted by a scout from Doncaster Rovers football club, when he was playing for his school's First XI. Although he was two years younger than most of the school team, he'd played a pivotal role in them beating one of their rival schools. It had resulted in him being interviewed, and then attending some special training sessions. He'd been selected to play in the right-half position for the Doncaster Boys team against Stoke Boys team.

Cobba was proud to sit in the stand and, although there was only a small crowd of several hundred present, he considered it a special day for his son. Terry was teaching Sandra about many facets of the game, as it progressed, and he was impressed by David's positional play and his through-passes to the forwards. Sandra was vocal whenever David was involved in the play, and she stood up and cheered when Doncaster scored their two goals. It was a tense finish to the match, as Stoke scored a goal back and put Doncaster under severe pressure in the last ten minutes of the match. David got a big cheer when he cleared the ball off the Doncaster goal line in the last two minutes of the match when their goalkeeper was beaten.

'That should get him a mention in the press report on the game,' said Cobba. 'We'll have to make sure we get a copy of the local paper, Sandra. He's had a good game, so we might have to keep a folder with press cuttings about his sporting achievements.'

'I'll certainly see to that, Dad,' replied Sandra. She clung on to Terry's arm as they walked back to his car. She was happy for David, but she was generally very happy with life. She got into the driving seat of the car to get more practice before her test.

Monday 28 March 1966

There was a strange, unreal atmosphere at Martins Main on the Monday morning of the Easter Bull week. Nobody knew what was going to happen. Roy had arrived at the pit at five o'clock, and was in consultation with George Turnbull. He ensured that the non-union engineman was on the coal shaft for the dayshift.

'Essentially, George, it's business as usual this morning, so tell everybody to get stuck in. I'm going to the man-riding shaft to try to make sure we get everybody into the pit on time.'

He went into the engine house and stood looking over the safety rail that went round the engine. He could hear the signals to the winding engineman, and he could see the reaction to those signals. It appeared that there was no delay in his responses; the men were getting underground at the normal rate. He waved to the engineman and then went back to his office. The coal shaft started winding normally at six o'clock, clearing some stock coal from the previous Friday night. As he was satisfied that the pit was effectively operating normally, he went home to have some breakfast with the family. It was a pleasant surprise for Helen.

★

When Roy returned to his office at eight o'clock, the figures showed that the coal shaft was lifting near-normal tonnages. He rang Reg Jenkins, who was pleased to hear the good news about Martins. Apparently, the news from some of the other pits was much worse, with little coal being produced and frustration for the officials and workmen underground.

Roy decided that he would spend the morning in the pit bottom to try to ensure that the maximum tonnage possible was raised to the pit top on that shift. At midday he got a call from Gordon to say that there would be problems on the afternoon shift, as the engineman for the coal shaft had sent in a sick note. Roy immediately came out of the pit. This was an interesting challenge. None of the enginemen would work any overtime during the dispute, so it was theoretically impossible to let anyone go underground during the afternoon shift. Roy put a call through to Mr Jenkins.

'We have an interesting position, at Martins, for this afternoon.' He explained the situation. 'My view is that this is an unacceptable position, and that we should apply alternative resources. I have staff who are authorised to operate the winding engines, and I'm inclined to deploy them. If the regular enginemen object to this action, and withdraw their labour completely, we will then cover the shafts entirely with other staff. I will meet the regular enginemen and explain to them why we have to use other people to operate the engines. What I need is clearance to do what I've suggested.'

'Leave that to me, and I will get back to you,' replied Reg. 'This fellow of yours might have played into our hands.' Roy hoped he would get an early reply.

It only took half an hour.

'You go ahead as you have outlined,' said Reg. 'I discussed the situation with the Personnel Manager; he hummed and muttered that it was unusual, and he didn't want to make a decision, so in the end I told him to forget it and that I was going to speak to Norman Pickersgill. Pickersgill was quite clear. The Manager has responsibility for managing the pit safely, which includes regular inspections on all shifts. Whether your engineman is sick, or swinging the lead, it doesn't matter. He's not there and you have to operate the pit. Fuck 'em. Let's see how they get out of that one.'

'I'll get onto it straightaway, Mr Jenkins. I'll contact you later in the afternoon, to tell you how we're getting on.'

He rang the Mechanical Engineer and told him to get some extra snap, as he'd be winding at the coal shaft during the afternoon shift. He asked Gordon to send for Cobba.

★

'The pit has operated as normal this morning, Cobba, and I think that the men will be brought to the surface at the end of their shifts without any delay. We have a new development this afternoon, though.' He explained the position to Cobba, and stated the solution he'd arranged.

'So that means we shall be operating nearly as normal this afternoon, as well?' said Cobba.

'It does indeed, Cobba. I could hope that we might have the same solution on the nightshift, but that would be too much to expect.'

'I'll bet that their association will be hopping mad at the engineman who's put in a sick note. I know who it is; he's not much bottle for any trouble. He's not blessed with much brain, either, to use a sick note on the first day of an industrial action.'

★

Roy went across to the number two shaft enginehouse and saw the two enginemen at the shift changeover. He explained what had happened, and what he'd arranged, and why he had no option, as colliery manager, but to take the decisions he had. They were obviously concerned, and said they would have to speak to their association. Roy responded that he understood this, and that he'd like to know how they got on. He told them he'd be in his office.

★

About half an hour later, he got a call from the association representative who had been in the meeting at Martins.

'So, you have been able to play your cards very early at Martins?' His voice was cynical.

'I think it is one of your members who has played an early card,' corrected Roy.

'Well, you might find that it will be a different story, tomorrow.'

'I would be surprised if he will be cured so quickly. The sick note he sent to the pit this morning is for one week, and what he is suffering from is not usually subject to miracle cures. I have it here in front of me. In fact, I would be staggered if he gets back to work before the Easter holidays.' There was silence at the other end of the line.

'Fucking hell. I'll be in touch with you later, when we get things sorted out.'

'That's fine by me,' replied Roy.

He rang Mr Jenkins and told him of the discussion with the association representative.

★

On the nightshift, Roy went to the pit and saw the two union enginemen on duty. He got an understanding that at the man-riding shaft, the men would get into the pit, and out of the pit, at their normal times. As far as the coal shaft was concerned, he was told that the engineman would limit his performance to twelve winds per hour, instead of a figure of around sixty. He would also stop for his snap-time. Roy said that such a performance was entirely unreasonable and declared that if the score was less than two hundred winds for the shift then he would reserve the right to adjust his wage rate. The engineman confirmed that he heard what Roy had said. He didn't withdraw his labour, however, which was an outcome Roy would have welcomed.

George was livid at this approach, but Roy sought to calm him down.

'All your men can do, George, is fill the bunkers in the pit bottom, as well as sending out what the shaft winds. After all, Martins will have done about two-thirds of its normal daily output, and that is likely to be better than any other pit in the region.'

Tuesday 29 March 1966

The daily results for all the pits in the region were faxed to every pit at eight o'clock. The data clearly showed which pits had been able to deploy non-association enginemen, but no pit had obtained tonnages anywhere near that of Martins. After speaking to the Mechanical Engineer, Roy modified arrangements for the rest of the week. On the afternoon shift, at the coal shaft, he would use two members of staff on a four-hour spell each.

★

By the end of the day Roy had demonstrated that two of the newly-trained staff were by far the best operators. Jim Lord was a natural, and achieved winding rates as good as the regular enginemen. A deputy electrical engineer was very nearly as good, and was only about two winds per hour behind Jim. Roy therefore was able to have a plan of action if he had to run the engines with his own staff.

Thurday 31 March 1966

Discussions and publicity about the dispute were ongoing. The association had been speaking of unsafe practices and of novices being used on the engines. They stopped that, however, after a press visit to Martins, where photographs were taken of Jim Lord operating the engine. Jim made a comment, which was quoted in the newspapers, that driving a car through Doncaster traffic was much more challenging.

★

This morning Mr Pickersgill had called another meeting with all the managers. Each manager had to provide information of how they would run their mines if the association enginemen withdrew their labour completely.

Roy reported that he would be able to operate nearly as normal, using his own staff. This shocked some other managers. Their projections were much worse, with only enough resources to cover the pit for inspections, and no production. Mr Pickersgill then put up two display boards: one showed the people available from Region, and the other showed the pit requirements. Martins Main, and one other mine, were rubbed off the sheet, as they were self-sufficient. The Regional staff were deployed according to a ranking of pits that could produce most coal. In the end, two pits got no help at all and had to face a partial shut-down. Instructions were given that all the association enginemen had to be told on Friday that if they didn't perform normally next Monday morning they would be deemed to be on strike, and their places would be taken by other staff.

Friday 1 April 1966

Roy spoke to his four association enginemen on Friday morning. The results of the general election were being announced and it indicated that Harold Wilson and the Labour Party would have a significant majority. Roy wondered if this would have an impact on his meeting with the association enginemen, but they were not supported by their representative on this occasion. He took a very supportive line with them, and emphasised that he was sorry that they had been led into this situation.

'As you are aware,' Roy said, 'Martins can operate normally using other staff, without your services. I shall take this action as it's the only way to avoid this dispute causing bitterness towards you by the men losing wages due to your action.'

One of the enginemen responded. 'We hear what you say, Boss. We didn't want to be involved with this issue, and we certainly don't like the idea of the rest of the men at the pit being against us. There should be a general meeting of our association this weekend. What the outcome will be is not clear.'

'I hope you'll let me know what happens at that meeting,' said Roy, and they agreed to communicate it to him.

Sunday 3 April 1966

It was at three o'clock in the afternoon when Roy got the 'phone call. The winding enginemen's association meeting had not been unanimous, but it had agreed to continue the action.

A spokesman for the association appeared on local television and radio, stressing the validity of their claim, and asking the other workman at the pits to support them by not going to work.

Roy made sure that word got round Upthorpe, via the Club, that the pit would be working normally tomorrow morning. He spoke by 'phone to all his senior staff, confirming who would be operating on which winding engine, on each shift through the week, and thanked them for their cooperation.

It would be another early start for Roy in the morning.

Thursday 7 April 1966

It had been another good week for Martins Main. With the coal shaft manned by the non-association engineman, Jim Lord and the deputy electrical engineer, the output each day had been normal, at over three and half thousand tons saleable. This gave a weekly output of nearly sixteen thousand tons for the four days of the working week up to the Good Friday holiday. As well as the good tonnage result, George had spent his time on the Fuston face installation, in place of Jim Lord. Late in the afternoon he'd reported to Roy that they would be able to start taking the first shear off the coalface after the holidays.

Friday 8 April 1966, Good Friday

Despite the industrial dispute, the daily output at the Region's pits was higher than in the previous week, and was increasing. An advert in the local press on Wednesday evening had asked for applications to train as winding enginemen and this may also have had an impact, but the association were holding a general meeting, despite it being Good Friday.

They agreed to resume normal working on the following Wednesday, after the Easter holidays. There was a general feeling around the Region that Norman Pickersgill had contributed significantly to overcoming this dispute, by his positive action. A report came back to Roy from a discussion among some of the managers in the region.

'That bugger, Dobson, always seems to get his name up in lights at the front during these disputes. He's either bloody good, or fucking lucky.'

Wednesday 13 April 1966

The Judge opened his room for discussion of the Moore boys' adoption case. He was dressed in a collar and tie, and a waistcoat. His blue striped shirt had its sleeves held in place by arm-bands; there were no signs of his wig and legal attire. To his party of visitors, he looked like a family man. He'd arranged enough seats for all those attending and he shook hands with them all as they entered, including the two boys and Dawn. He then took his easy chair in the middle of the room and surveyed the half-circle of people around him. He had a file on his knee. He realised who Peggy was, because she had Dawn sitting on her knee; he recognised Bob and Janet, as they each had a boy at the side of their chair. The other person must be Mrs Dobson.

'You can see that this is a very informal occasion,' he began. 'I am required to talk to you to satisfy myself that it's appropriate for me to sign the documents approving the adoption of Tony and Michael. I am advised that it would help me if I asked Mrs Dobson to set the scene. I understand that you have been involved with all these people here, through a difficult period in their lives, Mrs Dobson.' He looked across at Helen. She had not anticipated this, but she was pleased to be able to speak to the Judge.'

'Your Honour, you see here two ladies who became friends at school and have fortunately stayed friends into adulthood. This friendship was helped by them living a few houses apart, on Martins Lane, in Upthorpe, when they were married. However, their lives have followed different paths. Peggy became married first, to a mineworker, and she was immediately blessed with two boys, at the start of her marriage. Janet later married a craftsman at the mine, but they were not blessed with any children. This meant that Janet pursued her job, in a shop in Doncaster, while Bob was a fitter at the mine. It would be fair to say that in financial terms, Bob and Janet were financially much better-off than Peggy and her husband, Gerry. But that did not stop the continuing friendship of Janet and Peggy. When Peggy became pregnant again, she was in very poor health and, to get her through that pregnancy, Janet became more than a friend, helping her in many different ways.'

Peggy nodded at this and looked across at Janet, who had her eyes cast down. Janet felt embarrassed by what Helen was saying.

'The hospital decided that Peggy should have the last days of her confinement under their care. To make this possible, Janet got special leave from her job and looked after Tony and Michael full-time. Peggy's husband, Gerry, arranged to change shifts, so that he could visit his wife in hospital. He was tragically killed in a roof fall at the mine, before the baby was born. My husband, who is manager of the mine, asked me to get involved, as it was clear that Peggy would be facing immense pressures. Janet and myself, along with others, did all we could to give Peggy the strength to pull through. Peggy was very brave and trusted in what we were trying to do for her.'

This time Janet looked across at Peggy, who had her eyes cast down.

'When Peggy came out of hospital she was very weak and needed to get her strength back, so Janet gave up her job and the boys stayed with her and Bob. We all realised that Peggy was benefiting from the arrangement, so Peggy and all of us agreed to let it continue for a matter of months, until a final decision could be made. That decision was made a couple of months ago, when we discussed with the solicitor the possibility of moving to the adoption of the boys by Bob and Janet. That is why we are here today, your Honour.'

'Thank you very much for that summary, Mrs Dobson. It was much more informative than the words in my brief.' He looked directly at Peggy. 'You have been very fortunate, Mrs Moore, to have had support in your time of greatest need.'

'I have been very fortunate, your Honour,' replied Peggy.

'You look very well now, Mrs Moore. Have you fully recovered from the weakness and illness of your last pregnancy?'

'Yes, your Honour. My health is now very good, and it's unbelievable compared with what it was twelve months ago. I'm now able to work two days each week, in the wages office of the mine, and that has given me confidence and additional income.'

'Your daughter, Dawn, seems to be thriving.'

'She is indeed, and she's over a year old now. She's full of life, and I think we shall see her getting restless, before long.' Dawn was starting to climb up onto Peggy's shoulders.

'Your Honour, we have a contingency for Dawn outside,' said Helen. 'She has a great friend who looks after her two days each week when Peggy is working. If you agree, we can let Dawn have a walk outside.' The Judge nodded, and Helen took Dawn outside to find Sandra. When Dawn saw Sandra she immediately climbed into her arms with delight on her face.

'Is Dawn isolated from her brothers?' the Judge asked. Peggy looked across at Janet, who decided to reply to that question.

'No, she sees her brothers often,' replied Janet. 'And we try to let them have a run around together at least once each week, if the weather is suitable.'

'So you like to see your sister and play with her?' The Judge directed this at Tony.

'Yes, she can walk now, but she falls down when she tries to run,' he replied.

'Do you pick her up when she falls?'

'Yes, lots of times,' replied Tony. 'But she can't play football, yet.'

'No, I would not expect her to play football yet. Do you go to school and play football there?'

Tony looked across at Janet.

'No school now, but later this year. We play football with Uncle Bob.'

'So you like living with Uncle Bob?' said the Judge.

'Yes, it's great,' replied Tony. 'Lots of fun.' Bob smiled and Janet wiped her eyes.

'And are you happy, Michael?'

'Yes, great and good,' he replied, his eyes sparkling.

'That seems pretty conclusive,' said the Judge.

The dialogue continued. Janet explained how they intended to use the terms Uncle Bob and Aunty Janet, so that Peggy would always be 'mother' and how they hoped to keep both families close together. Bob was asked questions about his job and he explained how his earnings had grown, with all the mechanisation at the pit. Helen explained how Dawn had been baptised at the Methodist church and how her godparents and the church supported her. There was also comment about the full names that the boys would take. They were to be named Tony Moore-Hall and Michael Moore-Hall, as a way of recognising the two families involved. The Judge noted that this was in his brief and he discussed it with both families and then accepted that it was a reasonable arrangement that would need to be incorporated into their birth certificates.

At the prompting of the Judge, Peggy and Janet had the last words.

'I love them to bits, your Honour,' said Peggy. 'But there is no way that I could give them a life like they are getting with Bob and Janet.'

'They are two wonderful boys, your Honour,' said Janet. 'It would break my heart to lose them now.'

The Judge looked at one or two comments in his papers and decided there was no need to continue the deliberation. He summed up his findings.

'This has been a wonderful case, of an arrangement forged out of a tragedy, that has benefited all parties, and I feel it is right to legalise the position. You will receive the documentation from me shortly.'

They all shook the Judge's hand as they left, and in the corridor outside there were hugs and tears. Tony brought them all back to earth.

'Why are you crying, Aunty Janet and Mummy?' he asked.

'Because we are both very happy,' they replied.

★

The Enclosure resumed their morning meetings following a break for Easter. The weather was fine and sunny, and the gardeners of Upthorpe had started setting their gardens and allotments with vegetables.

'Not much of an incentive to start back underground, with weather like this,' said Albert.

'There'll be some interest in the start of the Fuston face, though,' said Cliff.

Albert changed the subject with a grin on his face. 'Your mates back at work now, Cyril?'

'Yes, they called off the action last Friday,' replied Cyril, who did not really want to discuss the dispute.

'It didn't affect Martins, much, anyway,' said Pat. 'The pit produced more coal than any other pit in the Region, and I'll bet it made a profit on both weeks.'

'They say that young Jim Lord was a natural, and that he pulled as much coal as your experts, Cyril,' said Charlie.

'So I heard,' replied Cyril.

'The only people who lost money were your mates, Cyril,' said Cliff.

'Serves your association right,' said Albert. 'They couldn't organise their way out of a paper bag. When we had a bloody dispute, everybody knew what they had to do. If one of our key men had fallen ill we would have carried him to the pit on a stretcher, to make sure he was on duty. When the regular engineman went sick, he played right into management's hands.'

'This manager doesn't miss a chance like that,' said Cliff. 'I'll bet he got some stars on his card at Region for the way he handled the dispute.'

'He's going to look at the weekend rota for enginemen as well,' said Pat.

'I reckon you lost that match, six bloody nil, Cyril,' said Albert, with a laugh.

Chapter 21

Thursday 14 April 1966

Roy had delayed the official start of the Fuston seam coalface until next Monday because of the disturbance of the go-slow by the enginemen. Yesterday George had completed the final details of the installation and tried the power to all the equipment, so it was decided to take the first cut off today.

An operator from the shearer manufacturer was on the coalface to support the machine driver. Roy got to the coalface in mid-morning, and as he passed along the conveyors there was a flow of coal, but it wasn't as big a load as he'd expected.

'This coal is bloody hard, Boss,' said the undermanager, when he met Roy at the coalface. 'We've checked the load on the shearer and it's using its full two hundred horsepower, but the machine is only going slowly through the coalface.'

'I've had this with some coalfaces before, George,' replied Roy. 'There will be no weight on the coal from the strata yet. We'll see how the machine goes on the return trip when it's just lifting up the bottom-coal.' They walked through the coalface and saw the machine land at the other roadway and then start its run back. It was a different story, on that run, and the machine moved much faster and filled the panzer conveyor with coal. The men operating the supports couldn't keep up with the machine, and there were the usual teething problems with the hydraulic equipment. It was decided to leave the face ready for Friday morning.

Roy asked the shearer operator from the manufacturer what he thought of the system.

'It should be a very successful coalface, Mr Dobson. The test for the shearer drivers will be to keep the picks cutting just below the rock roof. The roof is abrasive sandstone, so if the shearer disk cuts into it, the machine will become overloaded and the cutter picks will be ruined. The trouble is that there's no marker band in the coal seam to guide them. It might get easier when there's some weight on the coalface because then the coal may come away from the roof naturally.'

'We'll take account of your advice,' replied Roy, 'and brief the shearer drivers accordingly.'

It looked as though the Fuston coalface might have its own special challenges, thought Roy. In view of the need to make sure that the shearer drivers were very careful in the way that they operated the ranging arm of the machine, Roy decide to operate the coalface on just two shifts for the first week. He discussed this with Mr Jenkins.

'Training the shearer drivers with the ranging drum shearer will be critical in the Fuston seam, Mr Jenkins,' reported Roy. 'I've studied technical papers on some applications of this type of machine, where the drivers got the extraction section wrong and created havoc with face conditions. We cannot afford for this to happen at Martins. If they cut into the sandstone roof they'll ruin the cutter picks and also probably damage the machine with shock loads. So I'm taking the view that we need a steady start, on two shifts, where quality of output from the Fuston seam is more important than quantity.'

'How long will you be before you show an increase in tonnage for the pit?' asked Reg Jenkins.

'I would expect to see a small increase straightaway, to around nineteen thousand tons saleable per week,' replied Roy. 'That should be followed, in a few weeks' time, to the maximum level of above twenty thousand tons per week. I don't think we can wind any more than that figure, unless marketing department sell more coal into the power station market. I would expect to show a continued high profit level, though, as we'll be using salvaged equipment from the Low Moor seam now, as well as from the Morley seam.'

'It should be a good picture for the accountability meeting on the first quarter's results, then?' probed Reg.

'Yes, I'm quite pleased because we made money in the last week before Easter, when we had only four days' output. We also made money on the first week of the go-slow, thanks very much to the sudden illness of the engineman.'

'Has he recovered?'

'Yes, he's back at work. Cobba has spoken to him and complimented him on the timing of his incapacity which was worth thousands of pounds in the pay packets of the men at Martins. Cobba said he smiled as though he had done the right thing. I'll bet his association could throttle him.'

'I'll have to come and visit the Fuston face before the accountability meeting,' said Reg Jenkins, at the end of their discussions. Roy hoped that he would give them at least a week or two, to get things settled down.

Saturday 16 April 1966

Roy was in his office, discussing the pit with George Turnbull and Jim Lord. The results for the past three days, since the return after Easter, had been good for the pit, and the output was just over eleven and a half thousand tons. The Fuston face had contributed one and a half thousand tons to that figure. They were to continue for another week on two shifts, to let the men get familiar with the system. The men were happy because it avoided them going onto the nightshift.

'It's still the same on the Fuston face,' reported Jim. 'Hard cutting, and none of the roof has collapsed behind the powered supports. So there's a large, open space there. 'Surely it must collapse soon.'

'I think it might take some time yet,' replied Roy. 'It's a thick bed of sandstone and it's very strong. It must be forming a bridge across the cavity. It'll be a big bang when it does cave in.'

'There's no load on the powered supports, Boss,' put in George. 'I'll bet we could lower them all off and not a bit of roof would fall. It's uncanny; I've never experienced anything like it.'

'You'll know when something is going to happen, because the powered supports will start taking the load,' advised Roy.

'While you're both here, there's another thing I want to discuss with you. I'm looking at the phasing of the coalfaces for the future, next Tuesday, and I want you there, Jim, to help with the exercise,' said Roy. 'There'll also be the Surveyor and Jeff Briggs there.'

'What's the problem, Boss?' asked George.

'I don't know, George; that's why I'm undertaking the exercise. But there are some factors that will affect us. We'll have gaps in the output when we have to move the powered supports from 57s face to 59s face. There'll also be gaps when we have to transfer the supports from one face to another in the Fuston seam. Then there will also be an end to 56s face and the last faces in the Low Moor seam. Do we need to keep one hand-filled coalface, as a stand-by? If we were to get two face changeovers at the same time, we'd be in right trouble. I suppose it comes under the title of 'catastrophe planning', or working out an insurance policy for the pit.'

'I am sure we need to check these risks, Boss,' said George. 'It's alright for young Jim, here; he's only seen Martins when things are doing well. I've lived through times, here when it was all contingency planning – a rush to get out of one problem only to be faced with another one. We need to avoid problems, not solve them. You have a chance to do that now, Boss, because nobody is breathing down your neck.'

'That's right, George. But Region has some high expectations, now, for what Martins can do. There's one change for next week: we have an order from the power stations for one coal train each day, of nine hundred tons, and there will be some lorry loads to go out each afternoon, to a different power station. It shows that the marketing department thinks they can rely on us.'

Sunday 17 April 1966

Helen was keen to talk to Roy. 'I've some very exciting news for you, Roy. Gwen Folds had a word with me tonight, after the service. She went to see Janet and the boys last week and two things happened. The first is that the boys will start attending Sunday School. Tony has made friends with a young lad who goes, and he's decided to go, and take Michael with him. The second thing is that Janet asked Gwen about having the boys baptised at the church. James is keen to do it and he'll probably make it a part of the Whit Sunday afternoon service. This is the annual Sunday School anniversary service for the children, when they sing special hymns and say poems and lead the service. I think it's wonderful news and you must put it in your diary – it's the thirteenth of May.'

'I'll do that,' said Roy. 'How will we be involved?'

'As far as the baptism is concerned, I wouldn't be surprised if we were asked to be godparents. But I also think that we should offer to put on sandwiches here, afterwards, for those closely involved. We did it after Dawn was christened, and I think we should do the same for Tony and Michael.'

'I agree,' said Roy. 'We might go into christening receptions on a regular basis. There could be Sandra's baby to follow. I don't think we'll be able to offer a reception for all the christenings at your church, though.'

'You are a clever clogs, Roy Dobson,' said Helen, as she gave him a thump on his backside as she walked past him. 'But I do love you.'

Tuesday 19 April 1966

Roy spent most of the day on Tuesday working with the Surveyor and Jeff Briggs, preparing an action programme for all the coalfaces at the pit. Jim worked out the tonnages and the Surveyor scaled off onto the working plans when each coalface would reach its finishing line. They started with the Benton seam.

'There we are; there's the first problem,' said Jim, pointing to the plan. '57s and 56s coalfaces will reach their finishing lines at about the same time.'

'This is what this exercise is all about,' said Roy.

They then phased the three remaining coalfaces in the Low Moor seam and evaluated the options of either working up to the fault, or working through it.

They then moved on to do projections for the Fuston seam.

'How do we define the performance for the Fuston seam?' asked Jim. 'If the coalface was going flat out it could produce nearly fifteen thousand tons per week, but we know that we can't handle that coal with what we're getting from the rest of the pit.'

'I've been thinking about that,' said Roy. 'I have an alternative approach. We should leave the rest of the pit doing current performances and let the Fuston seam produce the balance, up to the potential output up the shaft. With the power station coal order being at least a thousand tons per day we might reach an output figure of twenty-two thousand tons per week.'

'That will put the Fuston seam at about five thousand tons per week, for the time being, Boss,' said Jim.

'I'll settle for that,' said Roy.

'It'll give some remarkable financial figures, if the output is anywhere near that twenty-two thousand tons,' said Jeff Briggs.

'The winding engines will have to be on top-song, to get that amount of coal out in one week,' said Jim.

'We might even have to get you back winding on the number one shaft!' said Roy, with a grin at the young man he highly respected.

Saturday 23 April 1966

Roy had spent much of his time during the preceding week in the Coal Preparation plant, checking that the rate of production of the power station product was satisfactory for the orders. He detected that the slow cutting of the shearer on the Fuston face was producing a lot of small coal that was being screened-out for the raw coal element of the power station blend. Even though the shaft was winding flat out, there were periods of the day when the pit bottom bunker was full and the loading point had to stand idle. Also, the Fuston seam was only cutting three shears per day, which was less than a thousand tons. At the end of the week the total output for the pit was just over twenty-one thousand tons. There was a problem to think about: there were too many production units for the capacity of the shafts.

The review of the conditions on the Fuston coalface was discussed again by Roy and George, at their regular Saturday morning progress meeting.

'There's still no break in the sandstone roof behind the coalface, Boss. It's a massive cavity now. I think the floor is taking some pressure, now, and it's lifting slightly to start filling the void. I have never seen anything like it, Boss. One positive thing is that the shearer drivers are getting good at cutting just below the roof. In fact, one of them must be a painter, he's able to just tickle the roof line without doing more than making a mark in it.'

'This sandstone roof is a new experience for me too,' replied Roy. 'I'm sure the roof will have to break some time, but the longer it takes, the bigger will be the bang when it happens.'

'What are you going to do about the number of production faces, Boss?' asked George. 'The lads on the Benton coalfaces are saying that we're back to square one now, with belt stoppages reducing their chances of earning more money. I think some of it's exaggerated, because they're able to work the face-ends while the belts are stood. But this week, both 57s and 58s are each a couple of shears down on their best performances.'

'It's a difficult problem to solve for the short-term,' replied Roy. 'It we stop the three hand-filled faces I'll have to declare that we have at least a hundred men surplus to requirements. The union has always said it was my aim to get rid of a lot of men from the pit, and I have denied that that was my aim. We know that there will be times when we need cover from the hand-filled faces – when we're doing face-to-face transfers of equipment, for example – and there will be at least one of them every year, and sometimes two. At the moment I intend to just man the Fuston face on two shifts until we have normal roof conditions, with caving to fill the worked-out area.'

'Well, that does give 57s and 58s a free run of the shaft on nightshift,' said George. 'So they have no excuse for not doing a good performance on that shift.'

'That's what I am banking on, George,' replied Roy. 'I'm also hoping that Region will not ask too many questions if they keep seeing weekly outputs of twenty-one thousand tons. We'll be making a good profit on those tonnages.'

Friday 29 April 1966

Sandra had a call from her mother-in-law, Mrs Lacey, inviting her to a lunch in Doncaster with a few of her friends. When Terry came in from work, Sandra told him about the call and he encouraged her to accept the offer.

'I've already accepted, Terry. Because it's on a Wednesday, it doesn't clash with my childminding for Dawn. I just wondered who these ladies might be?'

'Oh, I have no idea. My mother has always had these friends, who have to fill their time up with something. I suppose they'll be well-provided for by their husbands, and they probably have help in the house and in their gardens.'

'I shall try to fit in,' said Sandra. 'I'll show them how happy we are, without saying too much about the Upthorpe mining community. Although, from what my dad says, Martins is now one of the most profitable pits in Yorkshire. There certainly seems to be plenty of money around, at the moment.'

'How will you get to Doncaster?' asked Terry.

'I shall take you to work in the car and then I'll do a bit of shopping in town before going to your mother's to get changed. I also want to go to the Building Society to put some more money into our savings account. We might not be in the same league as your mother's friends, but we are building up our savings very nicely, Terry.'

'If I get through the next stage of my exams I should also be due to a pay rise,' said Terry.

'You used the wrong expression, Terry. You should have said 'when' you get through your exams next month, not 'if'. I hope that you're using your lunch hours to do more swotting for the exams, with your mates.'

'We're working through old exam papers; there's not been a pack of cards on show for the last month!' Sandra came over and gave him a kiss.

'I am pleased to hear that, Terry.'

Wednesday 4 May 1966

The ladies' lunch was in a hotel on the outskirts of Doncaster. It was clear that this was a regular event, as the ladies were met by the head waiter, who had reserved an alcove where he served them with drinks. Sandra stayed on orange juice, but the others were mainly on gin-and-tonics. Their average ages would best be described as matronly, but their outfits were designed to contain the excess pounds while accentuating their figures. Sandra's mother-in-law made the introductions and was very keen to say how pleased she was that Sandra was pregnant, so that she would be presented with her first grandchild. Sandra's loose outfit disguised her condition, and she expressed how well she was and how pleased she was to meet them all. She sat next to Mrs Lacey, but in the discussions with the lady on her other side, she was able to tell her about her friends in Upthorpe, and particularly Dawn, whom she looked after for two days each week.

'So you will be an expert with babies and young children?'

'You could say that. I've certainly had some experience, these last two years, so a baby of my own doesn't cause me any fears.'

'I never had any children,' replied the woman. 'And I have always been terrified of them.'

'You poor woman,' thought Sandra, but she didn't say anything.

After lunch, Sandra went back to her mother-in-law's house and changed back into her casual clothes to go to pick up Terry from work. She was asked a lot of questions about their life, and about how Terry was coping. Sandra confidently responded to all the queries, and she was sure that Terry's mother got the impression that life was very good for 'the younger Laceys'.

Thursday 5 May 1966

At mid-morning, Roy took a call from George, who was on the Fuston face.

'It's happening, Boss. The coalface is alive. The roof's creaking and we can hear the pinging as the legs in the powered supports yield. The lads are a bit scared, so I'm going to stay with them. We've taken one shear off and there is a break in the roof over the panzer conveyor. I'm going to get these lads to stay on until the afternoonshift get here, because if we can get another shear off, that break will be over the powered supports, which should hold it. Once we get that break to the back of the powered supports I'm sure the roof will fall down. Can you stop the conveyors into the Low Moor seam? We don't want the conveyors to stop us here, as it's critical we get the next couple of shears off as quickly as possible. It won't take us long, because the coal is softer now.'

'Leave that to me, George. I'll arrange it.'

Roy rang the control room and asked them to get Jim Lord to ring him. They knew exactly where he was, so Roy's 'phone rang almost immediately.

'Yes, Boss, you want to speak to me?' said Jim.

Roy explained what George had told him. 'We must give total priority to the Fuston conveyors. Go to the bottom of the Cento conveyors. Stop the Low Moor conveyors first. Keep in touch with the pit bottom bunker and then, if necessary, stop the Benton seam conveyors. You'll see how much coal is coming from the Fuston seam conveyor, and whatever happens we mustn't stop it. At the present time they're getting the powered supports over without any major problems, so we want to shear our way out of this first weight on the coalface. You might find that the coal flow from the Fuston seam is quite big, which is what we want. So we won't lose any coal for the pit as a whole, it will just be coming from different sources for today.'

'Leave that to me, Boss. I'll be in position in five minutes. I'll ring you later.'

★

Jim rang back fifteen minutes later.

'Coal is pouring off the Fuston seam conveyor, Boss. I've stopped the Benton seam conveyors as well as the Low Moor ones. The shearer must be cutting faster now. I should be able to see the difference when the machine is lifting the bottom-coal, due to the size. There's a little room left in the pit bottom bunker, but this flow of coal will keep the shaft full.'

'Thanks, Jim. I'll be in touch if I get any more news from George.'

Roy listened to the steam exhaust from the winding engines and the rattle of the pit tubs being changed in the cages. He hoped that there would be no stoppages for the next few hours.

★

At twelve o'clock he got another call from George. 'I think we might make it, Boss. They've just set off on their third shear. The break is well over the powered supports now. The back legs of the supports have lowered quite a bit, but none of them are anywhere near solid yet. Luckily the belts have not stopped.'

'That's because you've got the run of the pit, George. Jim is managing the conveyors at the bottom of the Cento conveyors. He says that the flow from the Fuston seam has been enough to keep the shaft going, so everything else is stopped.'

'There's certainly been some coal come off this face today, Boss. You could say we've been running scared, but at least we've been producing some coal. I think I'll stay with the afternoonshift. These lads are settled now, but their mates will need to understand what's happening. Hopefully, later this afternoon we'll get the roof breaking down behind the powered supports. That should be an interesting experience.'

'I'll arrange to send you down some extra snap, George. Your experience will be vital to solving this first weight.'

'It is a new experience for me, Boss, but we wouldn't have solved anything by standing and watching. We had to get forward, and time wasn't on our side. These lads have done us proud this morning, Boss.'

'I'll see that they are compensated, George,' replied Roy, making a note in his workbook.

★

It was two o'clock when Roy got a further call from George Turnbull.

'We've completed the third shear, Boss, and I've had a talk with both teams together, before the dayshift left. The main effect of the roof weight is on about eighty yards in the middle of the coalface. Some of the roof may fall down after this next shear, but the rest will follow after the fifth shear. I'll stay with them, but we might need shaft priority again this afternoon. There's no sign of more breaks in the roof, forward, so if we get these two shears off and all the supports set, we should be alright for tomorrow. We can let somebody else have a go then. It's a bloody wonderful site now, Boss, when this shearer is in full flight. I've got the snap, Boss, and nobody seems to have tried to share it with me.'

'Thanks a lot, George. Jim will keep his eyes on the conveyors for you this afternoon. Enjoy your snap.'

What a treasure that fellow is, thought Roy. He's rescued Martins, again, by being in the right place when the problem presented itself and having the nerve to see the answer.

★

At five o'clock George sent a message to Roy that they were on their fifth shear for the day and he wanted to stay with the men to see the supports over and set after that shear. He would ring Roy at home, when he got out of the pit.

★

He rang at seven-thirty. 'We've made it, Boss. It's all supported, and the powered supports are set in the newly-cut ground. It was hairy when we pulled the supports over after the last shear. The rock was cracking and groaning and then it kept falling in behind the coalface with bloody great crashes. I think some of the lads might have scary dreams tonight. There's very little load on the powered supports, now, so I think conditions will be normal tomorrow morning.'

'You have done a great job today, George. Get off home and we'll talk this over tomorrow.'

When Roy rang the pit to get the scores for the shaft winding he knew that it had been a a very good day for Martins, even though some faces had performed well below their norm. He decided he must have a meeting with Cobba and his team, to review the production policy for the pit.

Tuesday 10 May 1966

Roy had the meeting with Cobba and his mates. He had the results for the previous week and they again showed a tonnage of just over twenty-one thousand tons. He expected that the financial results would be similar to those of the previous week, when a profit margin of well over thirty per cent of total turnover had been recorded, according to Jeff Briggs. That must put Martins as the most profitable pit in the Region, thought Roy. The financial figures were not for consumption by the union, but Roy knew that they would want to know about the Fuston coalface. There was debate around the pit, according to George, about the way that the rest of the pit had been restricted in order to allow the Fuston coalface to have first call on the shafts. This was a ticklish issue that would be hard to resolve with the union.

Cobba and Jimmy were joined by two other members of their union committee.

'I wanted a chance to talk to you to discuss the current situation at Martins,' Roy began. 'You could say that we are facing the problems of success. These are not easy problems to solve, but they are better than having to solve the problems of failure. For the second week in a row the pit achieved a saleable tonnage of over twenty-one thousand tons. This is near to the potential that the pit can produce in a five-day week. As you know, this was affected last week by a significant increase in the tonnage from the Fuston seam.'

'What was the Fuston tonnage, Boss?' asked Cobba.

'We estimated it as five thousand six hundred tons for the week; and on Thursday they produced sixteen hundred and fifty tons,' replied Roy.

'But on Thursday the other faces were stopped, to let them have full use of the shafts,' said Cobba. 'That can't be right.'

'I realise what you are getting at, Cobba, but I want to discuss Thursday in detail with you. It was a special situation. The general position that we're in is that we have too many production units at the present time. And I want us to discuss this first.'

'I knew this was coming,' said Jimmy. 'You want to shut the Low Moor seam and get rid of some men from the pit.'

'That is one solution, Jimmy,' said Roy. 'But it's not the one that I favour. When I came to the pit the overall manpower was around sixteen hundred. It's now fourteen hundred and twenty, and falling each week. I don't want to drop the manpower drastically, because we have another issue to consider.' Roy went on to discuss the impact of face changeovers in the Benton seam, and in the Fuston seam, which would cause very drastic reductions in the tonnage for the pit. There were also geological risks, which had affected other mechanised coalfaces in the Region. In this respect, Martins had been very fortunate, apart from the one face in the Low Moor seam.

'So, what I have been considering is an insurance policy for the future,' emphasised Roy. 'I want to keep the coalfaces in the Low Moor seam. In fact, I want to increase the production from them.'

'I am all in favour of that policy,' said Cobba, 'but how will you increase the production from the Low Moor?'

Roy went on to explain how he wanted to save the coal on 56s to cover the changeover from 57s face to 59s face. He showed the phased plans which indicated that, on current trends, 57s mechanised face and 56s hand-filled face would finish at the same time. The union saw the sense of this, but asked how it would be organised. 'What we have looked at,' said Roy, 'is to share the men between the three Low Moor faces, but they'd only fill half the face each day. This would give us four hundred and fifty tons per day, shared over the three shifts. Effectively this would make some men available for other work throughout the pit, especially for the intensive work on face transfers.' Roy also explained that he intended to operate the Fuston face on two shifts for the time being. There was some mumbling among the union men at this suggestion.

'Tell us about the Fuston face last Thursday, Boss.' asked Cobba.

'This was a new experience for all of us. As you all know, the Fuston roof is a thick bed of hard sandstone. This held up and didn't break down behind the powered supports for nearly three weeks. The floor is much weaker than the roof and the first sign of change was when the floor started to lift up behind the coalface. On Thursday morning it was clear that the coalface was going to have its first weight. What happened was that the chocks sank into the floor and, instead of the break line developing at the back of the line of chocks, it developed on the solid coalface. George Turnbull saw this happening and rightly decided that it was critical to get that break line in the roof to the back of the chocks, by moving the face forward as quickly as possible. The coal was much softer and the men did a brilliant job of taking five shears off and getting the chocks over before any of them got fast. The roof caved then and conditions on the coalface are now settled down.' He looked at Cobba.

'Before you mention it, I shall be paying the men well for their work on Thursday. There was a lot of skill and nerve went into their work that day.'

'Is that the end of the problem with this roof?' asked Cobba.

'We think so,' replied Roy. 'We will only know that it's broken fully when we get evidence of subsidence on the surface. It's estimated that the surface should lower by about fifteen inches. The Fuston coalface in under agricultural land, so the Surveyor is arranging to lay out some marker pegs. He'll subsequently be able to survey them to know when the full subsidence has taken place.'

'So we could have some more problems with the Fuston face?' said Cobba.

'Yes, we could. But we know what to do to get through a repeat of the problems of last Thursday.'

'In that case we certainly need to keep the Low Moor seam working as an insurance policy for the pit,' concluded Cobba, and his mates nodded in agreement. Roy was pleased to get that agreement, but he didn't think it would be as easy to convince Mr Jenkins of his plans for the Low Moor seam.

★

Reverend Folds went to the church when he knew that Peter Carter would be there doing some organ practice. He had a musical idea that he wanted to put to Peter. When James Folds went up to the organ, Peter stopped playing.

'I don't want to stop you, Peter, but I have an idea to put to you. I want us to try it at the Whitsuntide service here in Upthorpe, and then I'd like to take it, as a feature, when we both go to Birmingham three weeks after that.'

'This sounds interesting,' said Peter.

'I want us to close the services with the song that finishes the musical Carousel – you know the piece You'll Never Walk Alone. We have a young girl in the senior school here with a good singing voice. My idea is that she should sing it first, as a solo, and then the congregation should sing it for the finale.'

Peter played a few bars of the song on the organ. 'I'll have to get a copy of the song, to make sure we perform it in the right key.'

'I'd like you to do that, Peter and also arrange the accompaniment on the organ. You could try to put in some rumblings of thunder for the storm, and then there's the possibility of some suitable bird song. Let yourself go with the musical arrangement, and have some fun. It's a great climax and you'll be able to open up the organ here, and in Birmingham, to lift the congregation.'

'When do you want this?' asked Peter.

'I'm afraid as soon as possible, as I want time to discuss this with the people in Birmingham. We'll have to arrange to have a rehearsal with their soloist before the services. I thought of the idea to use the song a few days ago, when I heard it on the radio. It will be particularly apt for the Sunday afternoon service here, which is very special, as I'm baptising two young boys at that service.'

'I'll have it ready in a couple of days,' said Peter and his mind began thinking on what organ effects he could arrange to accompany the singing.

★

Reg Jenkins had talked to Roy about the production schedule for Martins. Roy had been deliberately vague, but said that his production plan was designed to fill the shaft with coal and it should give a weekly saleable tonnage of between twenty-one and twenty-two thousand for the week. Roy emphasised that this plan was based on security of output and making sure that the conditions on the Fuston seam were stable. Reg Jenkins had said that he would come and visit the Fuston coalface. In readiness for his visit, Roy had the surveyor make a chart showing the tons from each source in the pit.

The daily chart showed:

Benton seam faces	*2,370 tons*	*13 shears*
Development Coal (mainly Fuston)	*800 tons*	
Fuston seam face	*1,320 tons*	*4 shears*
Low Moor seam	*480 tons*	
Total Output (raw mine coal)	*4970 tons*	
Saleable Output	*4300 tons*	

Weekly Output, based on 1,000 tons per day to power station market 21,500 tons
Based on winding a total of 4,940 tubs per day, which is the critical objective for the mine.

Roy studied this chart and believed that it was the best way to demonstrate his plan.

'We'll see what Mr Jenkins thinks,' said Roy, but he was not full of confidence.

Thursday 12 May 1966

When Roy presented a copy of his output schedule to Mr Jenkins, as they were having a coffee before going underground, he glanced at it and threw it to one side. He was clearly not impressed with the logic. He suggested that they went underground. He couldn't understand why the Fuston seam was being restricted. He said he'd discuss it when they came out of the pit. He didn't seem to be in a very good mood.

★

They called first at the pit top tippler house and Roy showed him the screen taking out the raw coal. It was an impressive stream of coal, going straight to the power station bunker.

★

Underground, they went first to the loading point in the pit bottom. There was a full belt delivering into the tubs and the loader man was pulling his lever every few seconds.

'Where's it all coming from, Boss?' asked the loader man. 'We've had a few breaks loading into the bunker. I don't think he'll have much more room left. And the shaft is winding flat out.'

'It's a fine sight,' said Roy. 'You're doing a good job. You can only do your best, and when everything's full you'll have to run with the shaft.'

'We do usually get a chance to load some out from the bunker for the last hour.'

Reg Jenkins made no comment and they went through to the man-riding train to go to the Fuston face.

★

When they were walking along the conveyor to the Fuston coalface they remarked that there was very little coal on it, but when they got near the face the coal started to flow.

George Turnbull met them. 'How are things, George?' asked Roy.

'We've just started the second shear for this morning,' replied George. 'The roof conditions are good, but I did see a break over the powered supports, so we might get some roof collapse after this shear.' George had received a look from his boss to suggest that Reg Jenkins must be treated with caution.

Reg Jenkins inspected the roof conditions in the roadway.

'There's no sign of load on these roadway supports,' he said.

'This is true,' replied George. 'We did have one wooden support that broke last week, but that was just before we had to take it out anyway.'

'Can we get to see behind the supports, to see what's happening there?'

'It's not easy here, Mr Jenkins. It's better at the other end of the face,' replied George.

They went along the coalface, following the shearer. It was the expert driver and they could see how he managed to touch the sandstone roof, to check where it was, without cutting into the sandstone.

'This shearer driver is worth his weight in gold,' said Roy. 'The demonstrator from the firm told me he was a natural, and that we were lucky to have him in these special circumstances.' There was no response to this from Reg Jenkins.

They were with the shearer when it parked at the roadway at the end of its run. They saw the cowl turn over and the driver drop the disk to cut up the bottom-coal.

'I'll take it twenty yards and then we'll get this end over,' the driver said to the three men who were watching. He set the machine to haul on its return trip, and carefully watched to see that he was taking all the bottom-coal, but not cutting into the floor dirt.

'This fellow produces some excellent coal and avoids any unnecessary dirt,' said Roy. 'With the constraints on the shaft, I've explained to them that it's coal we want in the tubs, not dirt. They seem to have got the message.'

When the shearer stopped, George took Reg Jenkins to a place where it was possible to see behind the powered supports.

'You'll get the best view from this position, as they start to get the supports over,' said George. 'We'll leave one support back for the time being, so that you can see.'

Reg Jenkins and George shone their powerful spotlights into the area behind the coalface. They could see the rock that had fallen, but there was a clear cavity over the rock.

'It's not filled the void yet,' concluded George. 'But I think we'll get some more as they get the powered supports over this time.'

They followed the two men getting the supports over, after the third man had rammed the panzer over. When they were about one-third of the way along the coalface they could hear the roof grinding and the powered supports pinging as their legs reached yield load. Quite suddenly there was an almighty crash as hundreds of tons of rock fell behind the coalface. Reg Jenkins jumped to one side, but the men on the face just carried on with their work.

'It was a lot more violent, last Thursday,' said George. 'If that's all that happens every few shears, we can live with it.'

'This rock roof has some teeth,' said Roy, as they started to walk off to go out of the pit.

'I've never seen a mechanised face working under a sandstone roof of that thickness,' said Reg Jenkins.

'We're all learning, and gaining new experience, with this coalface,' said George.

★

After a sandwich lunch, Reg Jenkins looked at the daily schedule again.

'It just doesn't seem right to work that seam on two shifts for four shears per day.'

Roy went into the logic of his plan. The shaft capacity was full. More coal from the Fuston seam meant that he would have to stop some other mechanised face output. If he closed the Low Moor seam he would have to lose men from the pit, and he would have the union against him. The manpower was reducing anyway and there was the problem of manning when the pit had to transfer the face equipment to new faces. During both face-to-face transfers and with any breakdowns on the Benton seam faces it would be possible to get extra output from the Fuston seam. He emphasised that there were only eight men on the Fuston face team. He was sure that he could rely on those two teams of men giving him extra coal to keep the shaft full in an emergency. They had the privilege of being on days and afternoon shifts only, and they would be keen to retain that shift pattern. It was a plan for Martins that might not make sense to some people, but it included an insurance policy to keep the pit up to capacity.

'It doesn't seem right, to me,' persisted Reg Jenkins.

'Well, it does make financial sense,' put in Roy, to try to turn the argument his way. 'I'll show you the figures for the last two weeks.' He asked Gordon to get Jeff Briggs to come in, with his weekly finance figures.

Jeff arrived shortly afterwards, carrying his papers for the last two weeks.

Reg Jenkins looked at them.

'Are you sure about these figures?' he asked, looking at Jeff.

'I'm very confident, Sir,' replied Jeff. 'I always prepare the weekly figures this way for Martins. Usually when we get the monthly and quarterly figures later, they tend to give a slightly better result.'

'It's an unbelievable profit margin,' said Roy. 'And that is what my plan is seeking to protect on a week-by-week basis.'

'I'll have to think about it. I'll get someone from strata control to look at that coalface and get their views. After all, it was that department which specified the powered supports.'

'That would be helpful, Mr Jenkins,' said Roy.

He'd played all his cards to try to get the best deal for Martins. Would Reg Jenkins dare to propose changes? Roy thought he might do just that.

Friday 13 May 1966

Peter Carter had given James Folds his arrangement of the music to You'll Never Walk Alone, and he'd suggested that he should have a rehearsal with the girl, Maureen, who was to sing the solo at the Whitsuntide services. Maureen was a little younger than Peter, but he'd known her for several years through the church. She had a good soprano voice but she'd not received any voice training. James and Gwen had come to the church to see how the solo sounded. Peter had persuaded Maureen to rehearse at the front of the church, near the organ. They tried a run-through and then Peter suggested changes in the way she should stand and he told her that in the final phrases she should raise her arms and sing at full volume.

'I'll now put in the variations that I've arranged for the organ,' he said. 'You should hear thunder and rainfall, and a bird singing. But don't let any of that put you off; just go for it.'

This time, it sounded quite different. The finale was dramatic and Maureen hit the top note with real power. There was applause from James and Gwen.

'That sounded wonderful, Maureen,' said Gwen. 'You really got into the character of the role. It will be a great finish to both services.'

'What I'll do now,' said Peter 'is to play the short link that I've written to follow the solo, while everyone stands up.'

He played that and then suggested that they had another run-through of the solo and then James and Gwen should stand up and sing the chorus again, as though they were the congregation. Peter would then give the final chords on the organ. They did as he suggested and it worked perfectly for timing and, at the end, the chords on the organ were dramatic.

'Wow, that's going to be another of your magical music treats, Peter,' said James. 'If it goes well in the afternoon and people want an encore, they'll have to come to the evening service! Well done, Maureen and Peter.'

Monday 16 May 1966

The strata control engineer went underground and Roy arranged to meet him to discuss his findings. Jim Lord had accompanied the engineer on his visit and he came into the office with him.

'It was fairly normal, today, Boss,' said Jim. 'We saw them get their two shears off and we saw the powered supports pulled over twice. There was some load on the supports and after the second shear some rock came crashing down. I could hear a few of the chock legs pinging as they yielded.'

'What was your reaction to the conditions?' Roy asked the engineer.

'It is an exceptional case of strata control for a coalface,' he replied. 'We knew that the roof was a thick bed of sandstone, which would take some breaking, but we also knew that there was a band of hard strata in the floor. We expected that band to give a solid base for the chocks to sit on. However, it now looks as though the supports are pushing down into the floor and not providing enough resistance to make the rock break at the back of the supports. The only option is for the rock to form a break on the solid coal.'

'Does this mean that the supports are not up to their job?' asked Roy.

'It's difficult to answer that,' said the engineer. 'They are the highest-rated supports available, so we don't have access to any alternatives. Also, at the start of all mechanised coalfaces there are exceptional loads until the strata settles down. It could be that you will be alright from now on, but it will always be a violent occasion when the roof breaks. Your men seem to be acclimatised to the conditions, now, and they weren't disturbed by the thunder and crashing of the rock.'

'Our plan is to move the face forward in a controlled way and keep our eye on the conditions,' said Roy. 'For a week now, since the first heavy weight, there's been nothing that's affected the operation of the face.'

'It's a very good coalface, and the men are doing a fantastic job. You must be proud of them.'

'I am,' replied Roy.

'I will write a report and send it to Mr Jenkins and yourself,' said the engineer.

'I'll study it with interest,' replied Roy. 'And I will get in touch with you if we have any change in the conditions on the coalface.' The strata control engineer left the office.

'Well, according to that we have no other cards to play, Jim,' said Roy. 'So we'll have to watch that coalface like a hawk. Mind you, I'll settle for four shears a day if it'll behave itself.'

'We can't get anymore out of the shaft, Boss. The whole pit was stood several times this morning, with the pit bottom bunker full and I suppose it'll be the same this afternoon.'

'We're suffering with the problems of success, Jim; it's frustrating.'

Sunday 22 May 1966

Willie Carter was bustling around the church. It was Whit Sunday afternoon and he was checking that everything was ready for the capacity congregation that was expected. This was the big day for the Sunday School and preparations had been taking place for several weeks. The children had been coached in recitations and singing by the local schoolmistress. She was very experienced, and her very stature inspired obedience. As usual, the Sunday School had bought a special song sheet with suitable original hymns for the occasion. There were marching songs, cheerful songs about sunshine and smiles, simple songs that could be taken as solos for the young children, songs about Jesus, and a suitable song for the close of the service. The latter had been scrapped this year, in favour of James's proposal that Peter had been working on. Willie hoped that this would be a success, but he was inwardly confident, as Peter's musical ideas were usually successful.

The final preparation had started on Thursday night, when the men of the church had been down to the cellar to bring out the wood to make the staging that was erected at one side of the church, over the choir stalls. When assembled it gave six rows of seating, starting way up the wall and ending at floor level. Each bench on the staging took seven or eight children, depending on their size. There was competition to go on the top row, because they had the best view of the congregation, but the selection was made by the schoolmistress at the final rehearsal. At the opposite side of the church, the choir was squeezed into half their normal number of seats, with some additional chairs to take the full complement. Their role was to support the children's singing, particularly in the choruses.

The performance element of the service was only part of the special arrangements. The Whit Sunday service was the occasion for wearing new summer outfits. Girls had new dresses, with fancy shoes and hairstyles. Boys had new shirts, with ties, and often new trousers, too. It was the occasion for a boy to wear his first long trousers.

★

The children assembled in the schoolroom, with last-minute parental instructions ringing in their ears. 'Shout up when you have to say your poem', 'Don't dirty that new dress, it has to last you a full year' and so on. There was a tension in the air and the children had butterflies at the thought of being on display to the full church. Before they paraded in to church, the schoolmistress called them to order and lined them up in the right sequence. Then she gave them a commanding look and there was absolute silence.

'Remember these instructions: No fidgeting; no talking; look at me all the time and remember that you are singing for Jesus.'

In the church, parents had arrived early in order to get a seat with a good view of their offspring; mothers insisted on fathers attending, and there was a sprinkling of grandparents too. Willie knew that he would have to fill the extension as well as the church, and he'd the added complication of saving the front row for the christening party. Fortunately for him, Helen was aware of the problem, so they were there early. Janet and Bob, with Tony and Michael, along with Peggy with Dawn, and Sandra and Terry sat on the front row. Helen and Roy sat on the second row next to the aisle where they could get out at the appropriate time in the service.

The children paraded in, from the front door of the church, down the aisle, to a marching tune played by Peter on the organ. The choir followed them, and then the schoolmistress, who took her place by her music stand at the front. Finally, Reverend Folds walked in and climbed into the pulpit.

'We have a beautiful day, and we have the children looking very smart; we have a full church to support them and we have the spirit of the Living God here in our midst to welcome us all. Let us sing the first hymn, number three on your sheet.'

★

The service proceeded with its variety of items from the children. There were some forgotten lines that needed prompting and there were some poems that were merely whispered by frightened children, but there were also some moments that would be remembered for years. One boy, in a broad Yorkshire accent, recited a poem about a football match. It had humour in it, which caused laughter, and it finished with his team scoring the winning goal. The last line was 'It's a goal; it's a goal'. He shouted out these words as he jumped up and down and the congregation joined in cheering with him. Two sisters sang a duet in harmony. Peter had coached them and they sang with confidence and perfect harmony, as he accompanied them on the piano. The star of the show was a little girl of six-years-old who sang a solo. Again, Peter had coached her, and it was a sad song. She got the feeling into the words and there were tears around the church as she finished.

James Folds spoke to the children for a few minutes. He told them a story about two young children called Arthur and Olga, who ran their own company called 'The Surprise Package Company'. They secretly delivered surprise packages to old people who needed help in the community and, of course, in the end, they were found out and got their reward.

James turned to the congregation. 'I have nothing to add to those words, to you all as parents. Children are surprise packages all the time. Sometimes the surprise is that they are in trouble and need your help and guidance; sometimes the surprise is that they say something to you that shows they understand your problems; but all the time they need your love and they will repay it with their love for you. There is no better surprise package than the love of a child.'

He walked down to the front of the church and stood at the communion rail.

'Today is for children, and on this occasion, for the first time, we are to have a christening as part of the service. We're going to welcome two boys into the church and I think they'll be on the platform next year.' He asked the christening party to come to the front.

Janet and Bob stood with the boys, and Sandra and Terry with Helen and Roy, as godparents. Peggy stayed in her seat.

'We are not complete; we must have the mother, Peggy, with us, and little Dawn who was baptised here last year,' said James. Peggy came forward, with Dawn in her arms, and stood to one side. James Folds looked at the children on the stage. 'These boys are special because they have extra names. They are called Tony Moore-Hall and Michael Moore-Hall. So they will have trouble at school writing out their names. I don't think we have any other children on the stage who have double names, do we?'

The shortened baptism ceremony was conducted, and Tony and Michael stood at the front, as Janet had instructed them. Tony held Michael's hand. They both lifted up their heads as James made the sign of the cross, three times, on their foreheads. The water trickled down their faces. Tony took a handkerchief out of his pocket and wiped his face and then wiped Michael's face. Janet was so proud of Tony.

The parents and the godparents gave their responses and then James turned to the congregation.

'As many of you will know, these two lads lost their father, last year, through a fatal accident at the pit; they have been very brave and built a new life of love, with another family. But they need the love and friendship of this church, along with their new family and their mother. Will you in this church keep the flame alive so that these children can be swallowed up in the love of Jesus?' There were cries of 'we will' but some of the parents didn't understand that part of the responses.

'I usually carry the babies that I've christened around the church, to show them to the congregation, but on this occasion they're too heavy for me! But the two boys will be here at the end of the service, so please come along and shake their hands, and welcome them into the church.'

The christening party returned to their seats.

'We now come to our final hymn, which has been arranged by Peter, our organist. Maureen will sing it as a solo first, and then we will all join in. But I want you to think about the words of this song, because they were relevant to the Moore family last year. They had to walk through a storm in their lives; their hopes were tossed and blown and everything appeared lost for them. But they found that if they walked on, and on, with hope in their hearts, they would not be walking alone. The Lord be praised for what he has been able to do for them.'

Peter smiled at Maureen as she took up her place at the front. They'd modified the performance by having a break before the last phrase. Peter said that if it worked there should be an echo around the church. He played a few bars of introduction and Maureen began to sing.

When you walk through a storm
Hold your head up high
And don't be afraid of the dark.

At the end of the storm
Is a golden sky
And the sweet silver song of the lark.
Walk on through the wind
Walk on through the rain
Though your dreams be tossed and blown
Walk on, walk on with hope in your heart
And you'll never walk alone...

Maureen held the note on 'alone' and then she cut off at the same time as the organ. There was an echo effect around the church.

Then Maureen sang the last line at full voice with her arms raised and she went up to a high note at the finish.

You'll never walk alone.

The congregation was thrilled by the sound. The schoolmistress raised her hands to get the choir, the children and the congregation to their feet while Peter played the few bars of linking music. It was a dramatic and moving experience as the full church sang the song again and it ended with a great climax.

James Folds stood at the front and raised his arms to pronounce the benediction, but there was a catch in his voice, and tears in his eyes, as he said, 'May the blessing of God Almighty, and the fellowship of the Holy Spirit, be with these dear children, and with us all, now and for evermore. Amen.'

★

The children paraded off the platform and up the aisle out of the church. James then called Tony and Michael to the front and as they faced the congregation he put his hands on their shoulders. Quite a few of the congregation came and shook hands with them as Janet and Bob looked on with pride, particularly with Michael, who smiled and copied Tony. Some parents were keen to establish contact with their own children before they got up to mischief, so they rushed out of the church.

Helen Dobson went to James, at the front, and shook his hand.

'I didn't know what you were aiming for by having the christening on this day, but it was inspired and I will never forget the finale.'

'It moved me to tears,' replied James. 'I was struggling with the benediction, which is something that doesn't happen very often to me in a service.'

Peter was still playing an organ voluntary when Helen went and leaned over to him.

'That was truly wonderful, Peter. Your arrangement of the final song ought to be available for all churches to use, but I suppose it was particularly relevant to the christening service of Tony and Michael.' He reached the end of the piece.

'Thank you, Mrs Dobson,' he replied, as she squeezed his arm.

★

Back at the house, Roy was acting as host and he was in a relaxed mood. He decided to talk to Sandra and Terry, who were sitting on their own. Terry had been hesitant about being a godparent, but Sandra had insisted he joined her, after Janet's invitation. On this occasion she had left Janet and Peggy to organise the children with their sandwiches.

'You seem to be very fit, Sandra, and the baby's beginning to show now,' said Roy, looking at the bulge.

'I'm feeling very well, Mr Dobson,' she replied. 'We've started getting the things together now, ready for the baby. It'll be a bit of a shock for my dad and David, to have a baby around the house.'

'I hope your father doesn't get his sleep disturbed too much,' said Roy. 'It might make him more difficult in our meetings.'

'I think Terry will suffer the most,' said Sandra. 'I can't wait to train him in nappy-changing in the middle of the night!'

'I take a lot of waking up, in the night,' said Terry.

'I've noted that,' joked Sandra.

James and Gwen came and had some refreshments, but they couldn't stay long as James had to go back to lead the evening service, which in many ways was a repeat of the afternoon programme. Helen left with them, as she wanted to go to the evening service, so she left Roy to sort out the transport of everyone back to Martins Lane. Sandra looked after the Dobson children while Terry took Peggy and Dawn in his car, and Roy took Janet and Bob with the two boys, in his car.

'Thank you very much for bringing us back home,' said Janet. 'It's been a wonderful day for us. It was very kind of Helen to put on the food; she made it a real party day for us. Say thank you to Mr Dobson, for bringing you back in his car, Tony.'

'Thank you for the car ride,' said Tony. 'When are you getting a new car?'

'I'm thinking about it, Tony,' replied Roy, with a laugh. Everyone had a grin at this remark.

'You never can tell what they will say next,' said Janet. They waved to the car as it drove away.

★

When both cars got back to the Dobson's house they found that Sandra had tidied away the food and was doing the washing-up.

'You could have left that,' said Roy.

'Certainly not, Mr Dobson, Helen has done a wonderful job, getting it all ready, so she shouldn't have to do the cleaning up as well. Anyway, I have a good assistant to help me, haven't I, Terry?'

Terry took up a tea-towel as though he had some experience of that task in the kitchen. Roy's admiration for Mrs Sandra Lacey grew even stronger.

Chapter 22

The Enclosure team was in session but there was a sense of depression in the air.

'The ambulance took him to the hospital at about eight o'clock last night,' said Pat. 'It was only this morning when I heard that it was Cyril.'

'Nobody knew, in the Club last night,' said Charlie.

'I heard that he'd been warned by the doctor that he needed to lose a lot of weight, to help his heart,' said Cliff. 'Cyril didn't seem to take any notice of that advice.'

'I think he was upset by the stupid go-slow by their association,' put in Albert. 'Cyril had more sense than some of the silly buggers running that show now.'

'I suppose we'll go to the funeral, once we know when it is,' said Charlie. The others nodded.

'How are we going to find out what's happening on the surface at Martins now, without Cyril?' asked Charlie.

'We might have to get somebody else in the team,' said Cliff.

'That won't be easy. They'll have to be reliable, and not tell tales from our discussions,' said Charlie. 'You'll have to check them out, Cliff.'

'It's not a bloody secret society, Charlie!' said Albert.

'We have our standards, though, Albert,' replied Charlie.

'Well, Cyril would have seen that they are going flat out again this morning,' said Cliff, looking across at the shafts.

'I wonder if they managed a record tonnage last week?' said Pat. 'I heard that the manager wants to get twenty-two thousand tons for one week. They've not achieved that yet, but they are over twenty-one thousand tons every week.'

'There's plenty of coal going out every day,' said Charlie. 'One of the loco drivers was in the Club last week, and he said that they've never handled as much coal by rail. There's plenty going by road, as well.' He pointed to two full lorries going along Martins Lane.

'There are still men leaving the pit every week,' said Pat. 'Half a dozen men from the Low Moor seam left last week to go as a team to a Doncaster pit. I think they left because they didn't have regular jobs now.'

'Cobba should be worried about that,' said Albert. 'But I think he's done a deal with the manager to let the manpower go down. The silly bugger. He'll regret it.'

'The manpower is less than fourteen hundred, now,' said Pat. 'It was over sixteen hundred when this manager came.'

'But it's a different pit now,' said Cliff. 'They don't need as many men with these mechanised faces. And Martins must be making a lot of money, with the tonnages they're getting out each week.'

Cliff was proud of being associated with Martins Main. When he went umpiring around Yorkshire he usually managed to mention that he knew Martins Main very well. A lot of people commented that they'd heard that the pit was in the top league now.

Saturday 11 June 1966

Helen had decided that she would like to go to the church in Birmingham when James Folds was the visiting preacher and Peter Carter was playing the organ. She'd made a plan: they would go to Nottingham on the Saturday and visit Roy's mother, with the children, and they would stay there overnight. On the Sunday morning she and Roy would drive on to Birmingham for the morning service, leaving the children with Grandma Dobson. They'd travel back in the afternoon to Nottingham, pick up the children and then return to Yorkshire.

Roy believed it was a good idea. He arranged for George Turnbull, his undermanager, to cover the pit, so that they could leave on the Saturday morning and so spend some time with his mother.

Mrs Dobson senior was delighted to host them, although it was a tight squeeze for sleeping accommodation. The two Dobson boys had to sleep in the same bed, which they took as an excuse to lark about for an hour before going to sleep. Helen was on the point of getting cross, but Roy cautioned an overreaction and suggested that she let them have a bit of fun.

Sunday 12 June 1966

Roy and Helen left early, to leave plenty of time to find the church in Birmingham. Robert and John were just up out of bed as they left, and they looked bleary-eyed. Grandma Dobson said she would sort them out.

*

They found the church quite easily. It was in the tradition of a nineteenth-century stone-built, city-centre Methodist church, seating over a thousand in the congregation, with a balcony all the way round. The pulpit was in the centre, but elevated nearly to the level of the choir stalls that were on the balcony, in front of the massive organ. The organist was in full view of the congregation and had a series of mirrors to see what was going on in the pulpit and in the congregation. As they had an hour to spare, Helen and Roy looked around the building. At the front was a noticeboard announcing the special visit of Reverend Folds as preacher, and Mr Peter Carter, as organist for the day. They then found Gwen Folds and she suggested that they take seats on the front row in the centre of the balcony. She told them that Peter had been rehearsing the soprano soloist who was going to sing the final hymn You'll Never Walk Alone.

'Goodness me,' said Helen, when she saw the organ. 'Peter is going to feel very exposed, playing that massive organ.'

'Worry not,' said Gwen. 'We came and stayed overnight, so he had an hour on the organ last night. He made it sound magnificent. The minister for the church would like to keep him! We really are fortunate to have him at Upthorpe.'

'He might have another career, as an organist,' said Roy. 'He's a very good lad in his work at the pit, and he's so reliable. I see him making a success of his life, whatever career he follows.'

'We need to find him a very nice girlfriend,' suggested Gwen.

'He has no time for girlfriends, what with his engineering studies, his organ exams, his job at the pit and his organ playing,' said Helen.

★

Peter came and took his place at the organ half an hour before the service was scheduled to start. The congregation started to trickle in and Helen was pleased to see that there were a good number of young people who came up into the balcony. Gwen explained that they were from the university, as the University Methodist Society, or MethSoc as they were known, used the church as its base. Peter's presence caused some surprised looks from various people, because he looked so young. When he started to play, the congregation began to listen. He'd chosen a number of varied voluntaries, which was his usual style. After some conventional Bach church music, he played a Sousa march; then he played a bravura organ piece that had his hands and feet moving at break-neck speed and ending with a triumphant chord. There were even one or two tentative claps in the congregation, but tradition prevailed, and the congregation maintained its decorum. Before the choir paraded in, Peter had some fun playing an organ arrangement, in New Orleans jazz style, of classic songs from the 1920s. The students loved it. He also had an unusual piece to welcome the choir to their stalls and James into the pulpit: he played the triumphant theme from Judas Maccabaeus, by Handel. In the hymn format the words were 'Thine be the Glory, risen, conquering Son, endless is the victory Thou o'er death has won.' and it forms a chorus after each verse. The congregation wanted to join in and sing the words as Peter ended with a dramatic finale.

James surveyed the congregation. The church was not full, but he thought there were well over six hundred people present.

'Good morning to you all. I am delighted to be here to share the services with you today. But you will see that I have not come alone; I have brought with me a great friend, Peter Carter, to play the organ. You have just had a taste of his expertise and there will be more to come. Would you like to give him a welcome?' This time there was a burst of applause and Peter turned round on his organ stool to acknowledge it. When he turned around he looked even younger.

James then started the service with a prayer, before the first hymn. The rest of the service followed the normal 'hymn sandwich' format with hymns, readings, an anthem by the choir and then the sermon. James chose as his theme 'the call to service'. He spoke to all ages of the congregation: the need for young people to bring enthusiasm; the need for parents to bring patience and persistence; the need for older people to bring experience. He suggested that all these qualities were needed to satisfy the call to service. He concluded by saying that to all these qualities had to be added the love of each other, but that that can only be provided by the Spirit of the Living God working in the church. Helen knew his sermon was well-received as she looked at the reaction of the congregation around her.

When it came to the final hymn, James spoke to the congregation.

'Our final hymn will be a bit different, this morning. It was the Sunday School anniversary at our church in Yorkshire, a few weeks ago, and I baptised two boys at the end of the afternoon service. Just over eighteen months earlier these boys had been involved in one of those tragedies that usually destroy people. One boy was eighteen-months-old, the other was three-years-old. Their mother was in hospital expecting another baby and she was in very poor health. The boys were being looked after by a neighbour and friend of their mother. Before the baby was born, the boys' father was killed in an accident underground, at the mine. Can you imagine a worse scenario? It's very difficult. But if you funnel the love of God into these tragedies and you all work together, a tragedy can become a victory. The mother had a little girl, who is a real charmer. It was decided to let the boys stay with the friends who were looking after them. Their mother recovered her health and she was able to raise her daughter with confidence. Then, the idea was born that this might be a permanent solution. It called for prayer and fellowship together. The mother had to give up her children freely, and her friends had to willingly take on the responsibility of two young boys. I must add that this couple desperately wanted children of their own but had not been successful. So they lavished love on these boys, and they have now adopted them.'

'I heard the finale to Carousel on the radio, a while ago, and it struck me that it would make a good final hymn in church. I asked Peter to arrange the music. If you listen carefully, you should hear thunder from the organ, wind and rain, and birdsong. But I want you to think about the words. Those boys and their mother certainly walked through a storm when tragedy struck their family. Their hopes were lost and torn but they persevered and walked on and walked on with hope in their heart, and they found that they were not walking alone. The love of Jesus enfolded them and the help of friends built them up so that they entered a new episode of their life. Those boys are now baptised into the church. The soloist this morning is from your church, and after she has sung the song through, we will all join in.'

Peter played the introduction and a lady in the choir stood and sang the solo. She had a fine voice and understood the acoustics of the church. When they had the break, before the last line, there was a dramatic echo around the building. Then she sang the last line with a big crescendo. The congregation stood and sang with full voice and Peter had the organ at full power. After the final chord, and as the sound died away, a man near the front of the church raised his arms and looked up to the pulpit, and cried out in a loud voice.

'For the glory of the Lord, Sir, let us sing that again.'

James looked around at Peter, but he was already playing the introduction to the solo. No one sat down and, if anything, the second singing was more moving than the first.

James raised his arms to pronounce the benediction. His voice was loud and clear.

'Dear Lord, we have witnessed you in our midst this morning. Will you stay with us as we go our different ways, and may your Holy Spirit flood our lives this day and for evermore. Amen.'

When the service had ended, Helen and Roy walked round the balcony so that they could have a word with Peter who was playing a voluntary. He was obviously thrilled by the way the service had gone.

★

In the car as they were driving to Nottingham, Helen told Roy of her thoughts.

'We have to live life to the full now, because it cannot stay like it is.'

'What do you mean, Helen?' asked Roy.

'There will be changes. We won't be able to keep James Folds much longer, as the Minister at Upthorpe, and we've seen today that Peter Carter is already made for bigger things than our church. We'll miss them both very much and there'll be big gaps to fill in our lives.'

Sunday 26 June 1966

Roy Dobson was sitting in the lounge at home, supposedly reading the Sunday paper, but his mind had wandered and he was reflecting on Martins Main. There was one week to go before the end of the financial quarter for the pit. Martins had performed very well through the period and Roy was even anticipating the quarter's accountability meeting with enthusiasm. The results had been consistent and remarkable. There was nothing that anyone in the Region could question; all the figures represented achievements significantly better than budget. Martins' results must have had a very positive impact on the Region's results.

And then the telephone rang.

It was George Turnbull. 'I think we have a major problem with the Fuston face, Boss. The deputy doing his inspection has rung out to say that there's been a major weight on the coalface. A lot of the powered supports have been forced down to such an extent that that their legs are fully closed and the supports will be fast; they're so low that the shearer won't be able to get through the coalface. He's managed to crawl through, and he says that things seem to have settled down. It sounds very serious, Boss. I'm going to get changed and go down to inspect it.'

'Don't rush off, George, I'll come and join you,' replied Roy. 'While you're waiting, see if you can get hold of Jim Lord. Ask him to join us on the inspection.'

Roy regretted his previous thoughts about the accountability meeting; Mother Nature had a way, in mining, of demonstrating who was in charge of conditions, and she played her harshest cards when they were least expected.

★

On the coalface they found a remarkable situation. Yes, there had been a major application of pressure on the powered supports, but it was now a spent force. The rock had sheared at the back of the powered supports and it must have sheared to a great thickness, because nowhere on the coalface could they see any cavity. All that was visible was solid rock.

How could they go about recovering the coalface? The challenge was to take an eight-foot wide cut off the solid coal. They would then have to pull all the face equipment forward into the new ground, and reassemble it. There were several challenges involved in this. George gave his view.

'We can get a conventional coal-cutter through, Boss. We can under-cut to a six-foot depth and then fill the coal off by hand. We need to do that for the eighty yards of coalface that's too low for the shearer and where the powered supports are solid. The rest of the coalface, at each end, we can cut later with the shearer, and then straighten the coalface up. I'm confident that the conditions will be normal, going forward. They were last time we had a weight on the coalface.'

It was agreed to do this and George rang the Mechanical Engineer to ask him to get a cutting machine prepared to do the job.

The next challenge was how to get the powered supports free, so that they could be pulled over.

'We'll need to loosen them, if possible, by digging the floor out underneath them,' said Jim. 'The best way to do that would be using a compressed air pick. If we fire shots we'll damage the supports. We won't have to get all the dirt from under the supports − I'm confident we'll be able to pull them free if we cut out the majority of the floor dirt. Anything will be easier than trying to load-out the rock sitting on top of the supports.'

This approach was agreed and again the Mechanical Engineer was given a shopping list for a portable compressor with hose and a number of compressed air picks that could be coupled into a pressure line.

The final task was to assess the damage to the individual legs of the powered supports, but it was impossible to do this until the supports were pulled over. Roy decided to call in expert advice from the strata control engineers at Region and from the support manufacturers. He also made a note that he would have to decide on a temporary support system for the coalface, when the coal was filled-out but before the powered supports were pulled over.

The team decided that it would take two weeks at the very least to complete the recovery. Martins would see a dramatic drop in its output for the first time in several months.

★

When Roy, George and Jim reached the surface, their plans for recovery were scheduled with priorities listed for each item. Jim was left to finalise this while Roy spoke to the engineers to call out men to start assembling the equipment for transport underground. George considered calling men out to start on the mining work, but Roy suggested that, as the conditions were not going to change on the coalface, George should personally direct the work on Monday morning. Roy also decided that he would not report the matter to Reg Jenkins just yet, with it being Sunday. There was no risk to life, and he'd be able to explain the recovery plan in more detail on Monday morning when Jim had put it all down on paper. The question going through his mind, though, was why it had happened on that particular day.

Tuesday 19 July 1966

Roy had arranged to meet with the Regional Strata Control Engineer and the powered supports manufacturer to go over what had been discovered about the events on the Fuston face on that last Sunday in June. According to the regional expert, the incident had happened because the coalface had advanced to the square position on that weekend. The width of coal extracted on the coalface was two hundred and thirty yards, and the coalface had advanced about two hundred and thirty yards from its start line. This was often the time when the strata collapsed, particularly when very strong rock formations were involved. Having seen the evidence, the strata control engineer gave his view that the initial force had broken along the solid coal, but that once the powered supports had yielded so that their hydraulic legs were solid, the full force had sheared the rock off along the back edge of the powered supports. He arranged for a special underground camera to take pictures showing the solid rock filling the void at the back of the powered supports.

Roy said that he was not aware of the square position theory. Had he known the implications of the position of the coalface he would have aimed to keep it moving forward until it was past that position. He again raised the question of the strength of the legs in the powered supports, and the manufacturer reported that they were working on the design of a leg that would take an extra ten tons of load before it yielded. Surely the next coalface in the Fuston seam should have the higher duty legs, Roy thought, and he put this argument strongly to the strata control engineer. This would mean that each powered support would then take a total load of three hundred tons before it yielded, which represented a twenty-five per cent increase. The strata control engineer agreed that this would be worth considering.

It had been a time-consuming exercise to recover the coalface. In the first four days the coal had been extracted, and the panzer conveyor pulled over into its new position. Getting the powered supports over was a very tedious and difficult job, as they had expected. The compressed air picks were used to loosen the floor dirt under the supports. Access for this job was difficult and there was a premium on small, lithe men who could work in limited spaces. Only four or five supports were released each shift, but the success of the method was demonstrated by the findings that there was little damage to the powered supports. George was utterly frustrated, as his physique precluded him helping at all with the compressed air pick work under the supports. It was only now, nearly three weeks after the incident that all the face was reassembled and the shearer could be used to straighten off the coalface.

For three weeks the output for the pit had been reduced to seventeen thousand tons. This wasn't exactly a disaster, but the profit margin had been much reduced.

Sunday 24 July 1966

Helen came home from church eager to report some good news to Roy.

'You didn't tell me that Peter Carter had been successful in his engineering exams, Roy,' she said.

'I wasn't aware of that fact,' Roy replied. 'I've had a major incident with the Fuston seam, over these last three weeks, as you well know.'

'Well, he achieved the highest marks on the course, again,' she added.

'That is very good,' replied Roy, who was genuinely pleased for Peter.

'But that's not all. He's also passed the exams he was taking for the Royal College of Organists.'

'That's excellent. I'll congratulate him when I next see him at the pit.'

'But you might not see him for months,' said Helen. 'I have a better idea. I think we should send him a card, congratulating him. We can both sign it. I didn't get to know the news from Peter – it was Willie who whispered it to me, and he said Peter was keen not to make his results public. He can put some letters after his name now, but he wants to take two more organ exams in the next two years, to achieve a Fellowship.'

'He's a very nice lad,' said Roy. 'But I have one worry. I hope he doesn't get any injury to his hands, in the pit, that would affect his organ playing.'

'Oh dear,' said Helen, who was shocked at Roy's comment. 'I'd never thought of that.' She would pray for Peter's hands, in her prayers that night.

'There's one other piece of good news,' she continued. 'Sandra rang me up to say that Terry has passed his RICS exams for this year. She was very pleased because she has leaned on him to concentrate on his studies, as well as his sporting hobbies. He seems to be taking marriage seriously.'

'I think that young Mrs Lacey is a very formidable character,' said Roy, with a smile. 'I'm not sure I would want her as my secretary at the pit, breathing down my neck.'

'Roy Dobson, you are not telling the truth; you would love it.'

Helen went upstairs to say her prayers.

Monday 8 August 1966

It was the start of Bull week at the pit, and the coal shaft was winding at full speed. The Enclosure team had been depressed and subdued around the time they'd been to Cyril

Mann's funeral, but there was now a new member of the team, and life was perking up. Bert Wall had been the Surface Foreman at the pit for many years. He'd just retired, as he'd reached his sixty–fifth birthday. He was lean and fit; he played bowls at the Welfare sportsground as well as going for long hikes.

Cliff had made sure that Bert realised who was chairman of the Enclosure proceedings and he continued to ask questions to test the new member's experience.

'So, you saw some big changes at Martins, over these last few years, Bert?' asked Cliff.

'Yes, things changed when this last manager came. He had some trouble getting the surface men to change their shift times and wind the coal for longer periods, but they had no choice really. He was only asking them to do what they were supposed to do.'

'There must be a lot more happening on the surface, now?' suggested Cliff.

'There certainly is. We've never seen so much coal, on a daily basis, all the time I've been at Martins. It affects everybody, and it certainly affected my job. If anything stops or breaks down you have to get it going straightaway or you have to re–route the coal into railway wagons.'

'Why do they do that?' asked Charlie, who didn't understand why railway wagons came into the discussion.

'We had firm instructions from the manager that nothing was to stop the shaft winding coal. So if anything happened in the Coal Preparation plant, we switched the coal to a conveyor that loaded the raw coal into a special track with empty railway wagons. We once stopped the shaft because there was no wagons stood ready, so the manager laid down that there must be at least fifteen empty wagons stood on that track at all times, in case of a stoppage.'

'He certainly knows what he wants, does this manager,' said Cliff.

'He certainly understands the operations on the surface, though,' replied Bert. 'I never saw some of the previous managers, but this fellow often spends an hour walking round, and talking to the lads on the pit top. It all started with the scheme to put in the new cages and bigger pit tubs.'

'How was that?' asked Albert.

'Well, everybody said that it was impossible to do that changeover in the holiday week last year,' replied Bert. 'But the manager kept going around asking questions and getting things sorted out before the holiday week. I think we all got some confidence in him at that time.'

'Does he still do visits on the surface?' asked Charlie.

'Oh yes. A few weeks ago he spent a few hours riding up and down on the loco,' replied Burt. 'With a train a day going to the power stations, as well as the other trains of washed products, the lads were under pressure to fit everything in. They were having problems with marshalling the wagons for the mainline trains. He must have sorted it out, because British Rail has agreed to use an extra line alongside the mainline, just for the power station coal, which has made it much easier for the Martins loco.'

'I keep telling you that this fellow is a very good manager, Albert,' said Cliff, having a dig at Albert.

'He's not had it all his own way with the Fuston seam yet,' said Albert.

'They're planning to change all the legs in the powered supports to a higher rated leg before they go on the next coalface,' said Pat.

'Bloody hell, that'll cost a bomb,' said Albert.

'But Martins is making a lot of money now,' said Pat.

'That's what this manager is after, so that he can get promoted to a better-paid job,' said Albert. 'I've always thought that was his aim.'

'The manger never gave me the impression he was aiming to move on,' said Bert. 'He was always talking about the future of Martins.'

The Enclosure team realised that their new member knew quite a bit about the colliery manager.

★

Roy had revised the arrangements for the Bull week. He desperately wanted to achieve twenty-two thousand tons saleable in one week. So far, although the pit had exceeded twenty-one and a half thousand tons, it had not reached the twenty-two thousand tons figure. Operations had to be tweaked to get the extra performance. He'd arranged for the shaft inspections at the coal shaft to be done over a one-hour time period. This would give an extra one and a half hours of coal-winding on the night shift. He'd arranged for the Fuston dayshift team to start at three o'clock in the morning, take three shears off and then come out of the pit. The Coal Preparation plant would operate over longer hours on the nightshift, and extra coal would be prepared for the power station market and stored in the new siding by the mainline.

Discussing this plan with his staff, it was predicted that a weakness might arise with the surface organisation on the nightshift, so a deputy mechanical engineer was put in charge of surface operations on the nightshift. It was also decided to have the colliery loco in operation for the full twenty-four hours on the surface.

★

When Roy reached his office at eight o'clock he knew that his plan was working. The coal shaft had been winding coal since four o'clock and the Fuston face was on its second shear. The men completed three shears and got out of the pit at eleven o'clock. George reported that the face was in good condition and the shearer was in-cut, ready for the afternoonshift. Roy spent two hours on the surface. Everyone seemed set on achieving the best possible performance. When he went to visit the boilers, he found the men stripped to the waist and sweating profusely. Running chainlink boilers on a hot summer's day was not for the faint-hearted.

Friday 12 August 1966

Throughout the week there had been minor stoppages. Those on the surface didn't stop the shaft, but did present the challenge of feeding the wagons of raw coal back into the system, which was full most of the time. That problem would have to be solved by doing a special wash on Saturday morning.

There had been a scare on 58s face when the trepanner ceased hauling. Bob Hall was the fitter on the coalface and he flushed out some valves and added some new oil and the problem disappeared.

There were numerous occasions when the conveyors had been stood due to the pit bottom bunker being full, and some of the extra coal from the Fuston seam was lost by reduced tonnages from the Benton seam faces. However, the figures for the tubs wound each day suggested that the magical tonnage had been achieved.

Saturday 13 August 1966

The washer was run for six hours to clear the raw coal in the railway wagons. The figures were finalised by lunchtime and, including the saleable coal from the Saturday washing, gave a total of twenty-two thousand three hundred and fifty tons. Roy decided that this was an inflated figure and one that couldn't be expected on a regular weekly basis, so the figure was reduced twenty-two thousand one hundred and ten tons, and the rest was carried over to the following week.

★

So the potential objective set by Norman Pickersgill had been achieved. Roy felt no great exhilaration, just a sense of exhaustion. How should Mr Pickersgill be informed of the figures? Roy decided to let him see them through the normal channels. His job, he decided, was to thank his staff and the men who had performed beyond the normal call of duty to squeeze the pit until it squeaked. He knew that the men would be seeing compensation for their efforts – in their pay packets – and that this might increase their enjoyment of their holidays at the seaside during the holiday week.

When he got home, Roy gave Helen a big hug and kiss, without any explanation.

Then he fell asleep for the afternoon, sitting in a deckchair in the garden.

Saturday 20 August 1966

The number of people going away on holiday seemed higher than ever this year, according to the review by the Enclosure team. This was partly the consequence of no major tasks being undertaken at the pit during this year's holiday week. Roy had encouraged his staff to take their holidays and there was limited cover in all departments.

Monday 22 August 1966

It was a strange holiday week in Cobba's household. Terry was working, so that he could have some time off when the baby was born. Sandra was feeling the size of the baby, and the hot weather made her much more tired than she was normally. Cobba was not keen to leave her, but she insisted that he took David for three days to watch Yorkshire play cricket at Headingley.

After his football success, David had played a very successful season for the cricket first team at his school, despite being one of the youngest members of the team. On one Saturday afternoon, when Cobba, Sandra and Terry were spectators, he had scored an unbeaten seventy-four runs, and had then taken three wickets with his bowling. The school recorded a win against one of their arch-rivals and David was mentioned in the school magazine for his efforts. His performance was also acclaimed in the local paper.

'You have to go and watch Yorkshire, Dad,' said Sandra. 'Our David deserves a treat, after the way he's played this year. Don't worry about me; I shall be alright here on my own. The baby's not due for weeks yet. In any case, if anything starts, I can always get hold of Terry to come and get me. You know that I've got everything packed, ready to go into the maternity home.'

'We'll go for the three days, if you're sure, Sandra,' said Cobba. 'There's nothing of importance happening at the pit this year that needs me, and I'm certainly not going to the seaside when you're in this state.'

'We'd better enjoy this year,' said David. 'Because I suppose next year we'll be dominated by a little monster.'

'I heard what you said, David,' replied Sandra. 'But I know that you'll be an adoring uncle who spoils your niece or nephew, and teaches them all sorts of mischief. I've seen tough fellows like you before, who change completely when they see the new baby.'

'We'll see,' said David, who wondered if Sandra might know something that he wasn't aware of.

Thursday 25 August 1966

It was very exciting week for Peggy and Dawn. They had joined with Bob and Janet Hall and the two boys, in a bungalow they had hired on a holiday site in Bridlington. Their journey was by train. Initially they'd taken the local train from Upthorpe to Doncaster, and then a train to Bridlington. The bungalow was just off the beach, and the sunny weather was perfect for the children playing on the sands and paddling in the sea. Peggy and Janet did all the catering, while Bob kept his eye on the children. They ate very well and had treats, with ice-creams each afternoon. By evening-time the children were exhausted and all fell asleep as soon as their heads hit the pillows. The grown-ups were then able to have a leisurely evening, chatting and drinking the beer and cider that Bob bought from the local shop on the site. Peggy was encouraged by Janet to wear her new bikini, and together they were very attractive figures on the beach. Tony and Michael took delight in holding Dawn's hands and walking with her into the sea. Bob took both Tony and Michael into deeper water and Tony gained sufficient confidence, by the end of the week, to try swimming.

'What a difference a year has made,' said Peggy, as she licked her ice-cream cornet. 'I can't believe that I'm here with you.'

'I did say last year that you ought to be with us,' said Janet.

'Yes, and I didn't think it would be possible,' replied Peggy. 'Thank goodness for Martins Main.'

'We can all say that,' said Bob. 'We've earned some good money, this last year.'

Monday 5 September 1966

At the end of the holiday, Roy Dobson had a major issue that needed the full focus of his managerial skills. There were only eight weeks' life left on 57s coalface and then there would be the face-to-face transfer of the equipment to 59s coalface. Roy and his Surveyor agreed the stopline for 57s face, so that it would ensure conditions on the coalface were good. Roy had spent time with George and Jim, discussing the procedure to be followed to prepare the coalface for the salvage operations. The main aim was to get support behind the powered supports so that the roof could be held up. This would be achieved by placing weld mesh over the powered supports as the last six shears were taken off the coalface. The lengths of weld mesh would be connected together to form a complete lattice cover up to the roof. As the final shears were taken, this lattice cover would pass over the supports and then form a cage behind the powered supports that held the falling strata away from the supports. The whole process of the final eight shears needed to be done systematically and with great care to ensure the safety of the workmen involved. Roy went through this with George and Jim, emphasising that it would require their personal supervision, as safety was far more important than speed. The success of the exercise would be attained if the salvage operation of the powered supports was able to proceed without any adverse roof conditions. They agreed to have a training session with the men, a week on Saturday morning.

Saturday 17 September 1966

As well as fully briefing the men about the procedure to be followed in the face-to-face transfer, the training session also described the route that the salvaged powered supports would take to reach 59s coalface. At the end of that route a service station had been established, where the powered supports would be blasted with a compressed air jet to clean off the dirt. They would then be examined for any hydraulic leaks, which would be repaired. The supports would then be pressurised in a frame to check that they were taking the correct load, before they were installed on the coalface. 59s coalface was equipped with its panzer conveyors and all its other equipment, including a new trepanner, ready to start once the supports were installed.

As far as the operation of the pit was concerned, during this transfer period Roy had ensured that another machine driver was fully trained for the shearer on the Fuston face, so that it could operate on three shifts to keep the output up to the required level. 56s hand-filled coalface would be staffed-up on a daily basis. There would be no coal from the Low Moor seam, and Roy was satisfied that those coalfaces could now be closed. At his accountability meeting at Region at the end of July, Roy had described in detail these plans to keep the pit output up to nineteen thousand tons per week during the changeover period. He needed to deliver on his promises, and he hoped that the Fuston face would not be subject to any abnormal conditions during this time.

Tuesday 20 September 1966

Roy arranged a meeting with his management team, to go through the details of the face-to-face transfer arrangements. At the end, he closed the meeting with his review of the objectives for everybody.

'We have another challenge facing us all at Martins Main. I have explained to Mr Pickersgill what we have planned, and what the results of the pit will be during this changeover period, and he has accepted my plan. It is as important that we deliver this plan to our programme as it was that we delivered the commissioning of the Central Conveying Scheme on time. We can only stay top of the league of Yorkshire pits if we deliver top-class performances on a continuous basis. I rely on you to not let me down.'

Roy was confident that his team would not fail him.

Chapter 23

Wednesday 21 September 1966

Sandra Green gave birth to a baby girl in the maternity home. Although reasonably on time, Terry wasn't present at the birth, but he delivered a spray of flowers to his wife when he heard the good news. He was nervous, like the other newly promoted fathers, as they gathered in the waiting room before visiting time. When he got to Sandra's bed, he found her looking a little tired, but also very proud of her achievement in giving him a daughter.

'How was it?' he asked, as he gave her a kiss.

'It was not an experience I'm keen to have on a weekly basis,' she replied, 'but just look at her, Terry; isn't she beautiful?' She looked across at the baby, who was in a cot at the side of the bed and appeared to be sleeping peacefully. 'I expect I'll be feeding her myself very soon.'

'You are wonderful, Sandra. I'm very proud of you,' said Terry. 'Is there anything you need?'

'I think I have everything I want here. There's one thing I could do with, though.'

'What's that?' asked Terry.

'I want to show her to my dad,' replied Sandra. 'I'm sure he'll be very proud of his granddaughter.'

'I'll ask him to come with me tomorrow,' said Terry.

'Think on, Terry; just my dad tomorrow; you can bring your parents later in the week.'

'OK,' replied Terry. 'What about a name for her? We've talked a bit about names, but we never made any firm decisions.'

'That's why I want to see my dad,' replied Sandra. 'I want to talk to him about names. He was very close to his mother, but she died when I was a little girl, and I never really knew her. She was called Louise. I'd like to call our daughter Amy-Louise.'

'That sounds very good, Sandra,' replied Terry. 'I have no better ideas.'

So that settled the name.

'How are you getting on with your new housekeeper?' asked Sandra. Janet Hall had arranged for Bob's sister to go each morning to Cobba's, to tidy the house and do any shopping and to leave a meal for the men to cook in the evening.

'She seems to be OK,' replied Terry. 'I've only seen her once, as I've usually gone to work before she gets there. Your dad is the one who gives out the orders. I assume she'll be coming for a week or two when you get home? I shall see her then, as I'll be having a week off work to help you.'

'Oh, I don't think we'll need her for long,' said Sandra. 'There'll be enough, with two women in the house. And I think that this little lady will be the one giving orders for a while,' added Sandra, looking across at the baby.

Thursday 29 September 1966

Sandra had had a lot of visitors while she was in the maternity home. After Cobba, who was very thrilled to nurse his granddaughter, Terry had brought his mother and father. They'd admired the baby and Mr Lacey had given Sandra a five-pound note to put in a bank account for Amy-Louise. Terry's mother hadn't suggested that she nursed the baby. It was a different story with Sandra's other visitors, though: Helen Dobson, Janet Hall and Peggy Moore had all asked to nurse the baby and were thrilled at how she took to them.

Terry arrived when Sandra was feeding Amy-Louise. He was slightly embarrassed.

'You'll have to get used to this, Terry. It happens day and night, and when this little lady is hungry she has no patience waiting for me to provide.' Terry observed the baby suckling contentedly, with her eyes closed.

'Well, you seem to be well-up to the job,' replied Terry, looking at Sandra's full breast.

'You might have admired the look of my bust in the past, Terry,' replied Sandra. 'But they are working boobs now, and they have a very important job to do.' Terry had visions of kissing Sandra's breasts in their lovemaking, and he wondered when that would become a part of their life again.

Sunday 9 October 1966

At Upthorpe Methodist Church, the Harvest Festival again featured a very large piece of coal mined by Willie Carter and transported by special delivery from the pit. The incentive this year was purely commercial and not in any way related to the harvest message of the minister, Reverend Folds. The auction of the large lump of coal last year had yielded a substantial sum from a wealthy visitor who was determined to outbid Joe Norton, who had visions of a large coal fire in the winter months at his farm. Joe was pleased that, even if he had failed to win the coal, he had made the other bidder pay a high price that benefited the church funds. Those funds were in a healthy state, due to increases in the congregation and higher collections at the services. This meant that the loan which Joe had provided for the purchase of the organ was to be repaid to him after the annual church meeting. Joe had never doubted that he would be repaid, but he was wary of some church members proposing other spending, without giving his loan its due priority for repayment.

Once more, Roy joined Helen for the Harvest evening service, as she was reading one of the lessons. He was thankful for the harvest of coal that had been reaped at Martins through the year. The results for the third quarter of the year, to the end of September, were way above the previous year, and he knew that his pit was the most profitable in the Region. He was not completely relaxed, as 57s coalface had started to take the final shears to prepare for the face-to-face transfer. Various questions were running through Roy's mind, especially during the sermon: would the special arrangements work to control the roof for the salvage operations? Would the rest of the pit operate without major incidents through the transition period? Might it be the end of the golden run for Martins Main, with some unknown factor affecting operations?

When Helen wanted to discuss the sermon with her husband, in the car as they were travelling home, his guilt was evident as he groped for lucid comments.

'Roy Dobson!' said Helen. 'I do believe that your mind was on other things during the sermon. I should send you to bed in disgrace, only we have to entertain Sandra and Terry, with Amy-Louise, when we get back.'

Sandra had been out of the nursing home for just over a week, but she'd indicated that she was willing to take on her former role as babysitter for her friends. This had allowed Roy to go to the evening service instead of him looking after Robert and John.

When Roy and Helen arrived home, their boys were upstairs in bed and Terry was reading them a story. Sandra was in the sitting room feeding the baby, who had her eyes closed as she suckled contentedly. Roy backed out of the room as he thought he was embarrassing Sandra.

'Don't worry about me, Mr Dobson,' said Sandra. 'With three men in our house I'm used to men seeing me feeding the baby. I'm getting them trained to take her and get her to burp up any wind after she's finished.' She turned to Helen, who was watching the baby. 'Did Mr Dobson help with feeding-time for your boys, Mrs Dobson?'

'Sandra, you must be joking!' replied Helen. 'Tell her the truth, Roy.' She looked across at Roy who'd come back into the room.

'I was spending a lot of time at the pit, when our boys were little,' confessed Roy.

'At one point, he was at work so much that I think the children saw more of the milkman, than they did of their father!' said Helen. 'You'll stay and have a cup of tea, Sandra, won't you?'

'Yes, if it's no trouble, Mrs Dobson,' replied Sandra. 'Terry will no doubt be thirsty, after all the reading he's done; he's been upstairs with them for nearly an hour. I want him to get used to controlling children at bed-time, so that he can look after Amy-Louise when I'm out on an evening.'

Roy could see the way that Sandra Lacey was planning for the future.

Tuesday 11 October 1966

Roy Dobson was on 57s coalface. He'd been through the whole face and examined the mesh behind the powered supports. It was containing the caved roof, and stopping it flushing around the powered supports. At least that part of the exercise had worked, he thought to himself.

The first powered support had been withdrawn, and hauled through the coalface to the left-hand roadway. He was in position to see the extra wooden supports that had been set where the powered support had been withdrawn; these looked adequate to hold the roof. The second support had been disconnected from the hydraulic circuits and swung round ready for haulage through the coalface. The haulage rope was connected to the support and a man travelled with the support to signal to the haulage man if there were any problems. The system appeared to be working as designed. Roy checked his watch and estimated that it should be possible to withdraw one support every half-hour. That suggested that it should take four days to withdraw the chocks from 57s coalface. He decided to move to 59s coalface to witness the arrangements there.

When he got to 59s roadway, where the powered supports should arrive, he found the men waiting for the first support, but there was no sign of it. The face deputy told him that George Turnbull had gone off to see what was happening. After a few minutes, the haulage system started and George came down the roadway with the first powered support fastened to a tram. He was not very happy.

'The first bloody support, and we get a tram with a damaged wheel!' he announced to everybody. 'It got off the track three times before the lads realised what the problem was. We had to reload it on another tram. I'm sending the damaged tram out of the pit marked to go to the engineer's office. Let him try using that tram on a rush job!'

The men used a hoist to lift the powered support off its tram and onto the maintenance unit. They blasted it with compressed air to clean it, and then checked the hydraulics. All appeared in order, so it was passed by the deputy engineer as ready for installation. It was moved by the men along a specially-designed roller-track to the coalface and twisted to go through the face to its installation position.

Roy spoke to George about his inspection.

'As far as the salvage is concerned, George,' he said, 'I saw the whole cycle, and I think it should be possible to withdraw one support every half-hour. Of course, the travelling distance through the face gets less as we proceed, so it's not unreasonable to expect forty-five supports to be salvaged each day.'

'That sounds about right, Boss,' replied George.

'I don't see why the maintenance work and installation on the face here should be any different to that,' concluded Roy.

'I agree with you, Boss. I'm hoping that we can transport the supports in trains of five, once we get organised, so the transport shouldn't be a problem. We just have to hope that the roof conditions on 57s behave themselves.'

'I'm confident that they will, if we stick to the support system that we've specified,' replied Roy.

★

Roy got home very late, well after the boys were in bed. In mitigation, he explained to Helen the importance of the work being undertaken on the two coalfaces, and the fact that he was reassured that the plans he'd made were working.

Wednesday 12 October 1966

Roy reported to Reg Jenkins that sixteen supports had been withdrawn from 57s coalface and that twelve of them had been installed on 59s coalface; the face-to-face transfer was going according to plan. He communicated that the pit tonnage had been three thousand eight hundred for the previous day, which was in line with his expectations. However the good news was short-lived.

Just before eleven o'clock the hydraulic section failed on the trepanner on 58s coalface. More seriously, during the afternoon shift one of the gears in the ranging arm of the Fuston seam sheared. While the hydraulic section would delay operations for twenty-four hours on 58s face, the delay on the Fuston seam was more serious. It would take two days to get a replacement ranging arm from the manufacturers, so this signalled the end of coal production in the Fuston seam for the week. This was the one sequence of breakdowns that Roy had dreaded: two major breakdowns when he had no spare face capacity. The pit would be five thousand tons down for the week, and that would put the operations at a loss for the first week in months. Would it mark the start of bad news for Martins, he wondered. He determined to set an example that this wasn't the case, and decided to work through the weekend with the face-to-face transfer.

★

As soon as he arrived home, Roy told Helen that he would be underground at the pit on both Saturday and Sunday. She made no comment, as she was aware of the need for Roy to lead from the front during this difficult period at the pit. Instead, she gave him a hug.

'Do what you think is best,' she said. 'We'll be here waiting for you, when you get home. On Sunday evening I want to go to the evening service, so I'll arrange for Sandra and Terry to babysit, to cover in case you're very late back.'

'I would hope to be home earlier than that, but we never know. George summed up the situation the other day. He said some bugger has killed a robin, which will bring us bad luck, and we'll have to battle through until we discover who did it.'

'I think George is leading you into bad language!' said Helen.

'I know worse language than that,' said Roy.

'I don't want to hear any of it,' replied Helen.

Thursday 13 October 1966

Terry followed the new routine that had been arranged by Sandra for Thursday and Friday mornings. He got up an hour earlier than usual so that he could go to Martins Lane at eight o'clock to pick up Dawn and take her back to Cobba's house on Wilbur Crescent. There she was handed over to Sandra, with all her clothes and toys, to be a part of the household for the day. Terry then drove off to Doncaster as fast as he could, hoping that the traffic wouldn't delay him getting to his office on time. He wasn't happy about the arrangement, but Sandra had been firm and had insisted that she wanted to continue with her babyminding commitment to Peggy.

When Terry returned home in the evening, another journey had to be made, to return Dawn back to Martins Lane. On some occasions Sandra drove to Martins Lane and left Terry to have his dinner on his own. Whilst he didn't object to this, he had to keep a wary ear for any crying by Amy-Louise, who was always in bed when he got home. He was sure that Peggy was getting a very good deal. Dawn enjoyed her time with Sandra, so there was never any reluctance by her to join Terry in the car. Peggy was always very appreciative of Terry's help and she hoped that she'd be able to return the babyminding favour when Amy-Louise got a bit older.

★

Janet came to Sandra's house for lunch and a gossip. It was the first time Janet had been to Wilbur Crescent for many months. She brought only Michael, because Tony was now at school. Janet was finding her life very strange, now, with just one boy at home during school hours. Sandra asked about the change.

'How's Tony getting on at school?' she asked.

'He's settled down very well and seems to be quite happy,' replied Janet. 'It's me that has the problem.'

'In what way?' asked Sandra.

'I'm always looking around the house for him. I've become so used to having both the boys around all the time. I think Michael is missing him as well.'

'But they'll be together in the evening.'

'That's true, and Michael is keen to play with Tony, but after a full day at school, Tony's tired and he's happy to go to bed quite early.'

'I'm sure you'll settle down, Janet, and get used to the new routine.'

'How are you, and all your men, coping with Amy-Louise?'

'Amy-Louise is now settled here and she requires preferential treatment, especially at feeding-time. Mind you, I'm producing so much milk that I'm relieved, sometimes, when she needs feeding. Terry's getting his hand in with her, and last night I even got our David to nurse her, while I was serving the dinner. You could say that this is now a busy house.'

'If things are too hectic for you, I could always look after Dawn when Peggy's at work,' said Janet. 'It would be no problem for me, certainly during school weeks.'

'I'll bear it in mind, Janet, but I want to keep helping Peggy.'

Janet stayed for over three hours and she was able to talk freely to Sandra, as Michael and Dawn played well together. When Sandra was feeding Amy-Louise, both Michael and Dawn sat beside her and looked on with great interest, watching Amy-Louise suckling greedily. When the feeding was done, Sandra put Amy-Louise over her shoulder and allowed both the children to tap her on the back to get her wind up, although they were so gentle that Sandra had to help them in order to get the right result.

Janet was told that Sandra had no intention of having another baby until Terry had passed all his exams. She also learned that David was going to play more football for

Doncaster Rovers Youth team and that there had been other professional football teams watching him play. Cobba was very proud of David, but he was insisting that David passed his A-level exams and made a start on a career before he made any move into professional football.

Sandra heard from Janet how much time Bob was putting in at the pit, and some of the problems affecting Martins. She also learned that Peggy was doing very well with her job in the wages office and might be offered an extra day each week. Sandra suggested that Janet might be needed for one day each week, as a childminder, if that came off. Janet also divulged that she was beginning to think that Peggy had caught the eye of some man in the wages office, because she was now going to work dressed much more smartly, and wearing more make-up.

'Now, that would be a big news story,' said Sandra.

Friday 14 October 1966

'They missed a train for the power station market, yesterday,' said Bert.

The Enclosure team was discussing the lack of coal for the shafts.

'That's not surprising,' said Charlie. 'Both the mechanised faces were stood with major breakdowns. The Fuston face won't start again until Monday.'

'That's the trouble with these mechanised faces,' said Albert. 'The pit is buggered when they break down. When you had men filling the coal, if the men had shovels, you got the coal.'

'This week will be the worst week for output from the pit for months,' said Pat.

'They should be alright next week,' said Cliff. 'They're doing quite well with the face-to-face transfer, so 59s face should be in production at the end of next week.'

'I think it'll start earlier than that,' said Charlie. 'They were expecting they'd be working over the weekend with the transfer. In fact, some fellows in the Club thought that the job would be staffed-up on all three shifts on both Saturday and Sunday.'

'One of the engineers has pulled out of the football team on Saturday afternoon, as he'll be working,' said Pat.

'Well, they need something to change, next week,' said Bert Wall. 'They haven't pulled much coal this morning; the shaft's been stood as much as it's been winding, while we've been here.'

'George Turnbull will sort the job out,' said Cliff. 'He's played a major role in pulling the pit around. It's difficult to remember that the Welsh fellow tried to push him out.'

'He's a real bastard, is that Reg Jenkins,' said Albert. 'He keeps away from Martins now, but he's been causing trouble at some of his other pits, from what I hear. They should send him back to Wales.'

'They might not have him, Albert,' said Cliff.

Sunday 16 October 1966

Roy Dobson came out of the pit with George Turnbull. It was after six o'clock, the light was fading and the pit yard was deserted. The drone of the mine fan gave the scene a strange background, as though it was another world utterly unrelated to the activities in the houses of Upthorpe. Roy and George walked across the pit yard and the noise of their footsteps on the concrete was exaggerated. Neither of them spoke. They were tired; it had been a long day. The face-to-face transfer of the powered supports had proceeded steadily until near the end of the Saturday nightshift, when the weld mesh had fractured when one of the supports was being withdrawn on 57s face. There was a fall of roof that buried both the support being withdrawn and the next two supports. This resulted in a full shift of filling-out the fallen rock and slowly adding additional wooden supports and weld mesh to gain control of the roof.

George had been at the fall from the beginning of the Sunday dayshift, and Roy had joined him at mid-shift after examining the installation on 59s face. Roy was pleased with 59s face and was confident that it would quickly achieve good production when the remaining fifty supports were installed. On 57s face, he witnessed George using all his experience and skill at handling the bad roof and directing the men, step by step, to gain control of the situation. George also pushed the men to achieve continual top-class performances. As only one man could work in the enclosed position of the fall of rock at any one time, George kept changing the man in that role, so that he could work at full speed, shovelling the dirt onto the panzer conveyor. Each man worked until he was dripping with sweat and his arm muscles were clearly aching, before George gave him a breather. Eventually, this afternoon, after more than a full shift, the weld mesh was secured and the two difficult supports were withdrawn and normal salvage operations were resumed. It illustrated to Roy the narrow margin of safety that his system contained. He hoped that there would be no further problems.

★

As he drove home through Upthorpe he saw people going about their lives. He realised that some were going out to the Club; some were visiting friends and relatives; and some were enjoying an evening at home watching television and putting the children to bed. It was so different from the world underground: the cramped conditions; the noise of the machinery; the heat and the dust; the continual challenges of the geology, that it seemed unnatural for a man to be able to move in both those worlds. But that was the career that he, Roy Dobson, had chosen – a double life, in two completely different environments, both of which had the highs and lows of success and failure.

★

When he arrived home he was greeted by Sandra, as Helen was was not yet home from the evening service at church. She set about heating up the meal that Helen had prepared, and she laid out a place for him in the kitchen.

'You look very tired, Mr Dobson. Has it been a difficult day?' Sandra asked.

'It's been a challenge, Sandra. There was a fall of roof on the nightshift and it's taken most of today to sort it out and get back to normal operations.'

'Let me get you a beer, Mr Dobson. You certainly deserve a drink while the meal warms up. I'm sure I saw a beer in the fridge.'

'Now that is a good idea, Sandra.' Roy started to relax.

He'd drunk most of his beer, and was tucking into his hot meal, when Helen came home, accompanied by Reverend Folds and his wife, Gwen.

'James gave me a lift home from the service, so I've asked them to stay for a cup of tea. You're very late home; have there been difficulties?' Roy explained the problems on 57s coalface.

'At least Sandra seems to have been generous in quenching your thirst,' said Helen, looking at the glass of beer. 'Come and join us for a cup of tea in the lounge when you've finished your meal. I expect Sandra and Terry to stay as well.'

Helen bustled around in the kitchen, getting a tray of cups and plates ready. She went into the pantry and brought out a newly-made chocolate cake.

'That looks nice,' said Roy, as Helen put the chocolate cake near him on the kitchen table.

'You can have a piece when you come and join us, if you promise not to talk about Martins,' replied Helen.

★

When Roy went through the hall to the lounge, he caught sight of his face in the mirror: his eyes had the black outlines of dust on his eyelashes, indicating where he'd been all day.

James Folds immediately asked Roy about the pit and, despite Helen's request, he had to relate the story of a difficult week at Martins, and of the tricky problems on 57s face over the weekend.

'I hope the new week brings you better circumstances, and a new beginning,' said James.

'I hope so too,' said Helen. 'We've hardly seen him here, this last week, and when he was at home, his mind was elsewhere.'

'You must be very proud of him, though, Mrs Dobson,' put in Sandra. 'He has worked wonders at Martins, according to my dad. And the folk of Upthorpe have never been so well-off, as they are now.'

Roy was shocked and embarrassed by this remark, but before he could comment, James added his thoughts.

'I can agree with what you've said, Sandra. Upthorpe folk are very spare at giving praise to anyone's achievements, but numerous people in the community have told me, how much they respect the colliery manager at Martins. It's not just for what you do, Roy, but for the way you lead by example. And that includes being underground this weekend. I was told about that at this morning's service.'

Roy was speechless, and embarrassed, so he reached over and let Helen serve him a large piece of chocolate cake. She gave him a loving smile, as she slid it onto his plate.

The evening continued with chat about the church, the football success of David Green, Terry's job and his future exams with RICS, and Sandra's joy at being a mother. Amy-Louise was brought into the room as Terry and Sandra were getting ready to leave, and the baby gave the group a big smile, in her own way seeming to reflect the evening's atmosphere.

Wednesday 19 October 1966

The Enclosure was in session and they were watching the coal shaft, which seemed to be working at full speed.

'They're certainly pulling some coal, this morning,' said Bert Wall.

'The pit will be back to full capacity now,' said Charlie. 'According to reports in the Club last night, they took the first shear off 59s face yesterday morning, and it will be on three shifts from now on. The Fuston face is also back in business.'

'I've no doubt that the manager will be trying to get the pit up to full performance again, as quickly as possible,' said Cliff. 'When you have a successful pit, you want to keep it there.'

'The manager has certainly done his best over the last week,' said Charlie. 'He was down the pit all day Saturday and Sunday. George was also on the job both days. One of the lads said that it was a bit of bad luck when the weld mesh broke and allowed a fall of roof that buried two supports. It delayed them well over a full shift, otherwise the face would have been on full production from Monday afternoon.'

'How do you think Martins will be fixed, with all these pit closures that are happening up and down the country now?' asked Albert.

'Martins should be alright,' said Pat. 'The pits that are up for closure are those that have few reserves of coal and their costs of production are too high. Martins Main has been making very good profits. No one will want to shut that pit now.'

'There's plenty of scope for shutting pits in other coalfields, like Scotland, Durham and Wales,' said Cliff. 'Martins Main has plenty of reserves and all its coal is being sold into the markets. That's more than can be said for some other pits in Yorkshire. I think you've got to have a positive outlook for the pit, Albert.'

'There's too much politics in the mining industry,' said Albert. 'You've got to watch your back all the time. There are some militant young men, these days, getting jobs in the miners' union up and down the country. It only wants some strikes and all the political parties will have it in for the miners again.'

'The men at Martins would be fools to start striking again, like they used to do,' said Cliff. 'Surely they've learned some sense over these last three years under this manager.'

'There are still some silly buggers at Martins, who would rather stand on a picket line than do a shift's work underground,' said Albert. 'The problem now is that they have no one to lead them. Cobba has hung his boots up. He's no interest in fighting for the workers' cause any more. I still think he's done a deal with the manager. I'll bet he picks up a good pay packet every Friday, for what he does. And Jimmy Bell seems to have gone quiet these days.'

'He has been doing a lot more shifts underground this last year, doing workmen's inspections,' said Pat. 'I suppose that his money will have gone up for those shifts.'

The team looked across at Pat Mulligan, who again had revealed one of the secrets of the pit.

'Cobba's like a fellow who's won the pools,' said Charlie. 'He's got a real glint in his eyes these days. His lad is doing very well at sports and there are a few football clubs showing an interest in him. He's also a natural cricketer, and in the summer the local paper was forecasting a good future for him, even as a possible Yorkshire player. Then Cobba has got his granddaughter; the Stewardess in the Club says that she's a little charmer and that Cobba dotes on her. Cobba's family life has never been as good as it is now.'

'You're probably right there, Charlie. His wife was a really difficult woman to live with,' said Cliff. 'I know she had poor health, but she certainly made Cobba and the kids suffer with her.'

'That's even more reason for him losing his militancy at the pit,' put in Albert Dunn.

'Well, the pit is now producing plenty of coal,' said Bert. 'Look there, the loco is taking a run of full wagons with power station coal down to the mainline, and there are four lorries in convoy on Martins Lane taking coal direct to the power stations.'

'It certainly is a grand sight,' said Cliff.

★

Roy Dobson was having a special meeting with his Surveyor and his finance man, Jeff Briggs. They were looking forward. Two major questions about the future needed to be answered: when would 58s coalface reach the boundary and its equipment have to be transferred to 60s coalface? and when would the Fuston coalface reach its finishing line and have to be transferred to the second face? Whatever happened, Roy had to ensure that these two dates were well separated. The finish line for 58s coalface was ten months away, and this was a reliable date as the weekly performance of the face was consistent. This meant that the face could possibly finish in July next year. The best time for 58s to reach the boundary would be just before the pit holiday week, in August. Such a finishing date would allow work to be carried out during the holiday week and so reduce the time the pit was short of a coalface. There was attraction in that timetable.

With the Fuston face, it was more difficult to forecast its finishing date, as its priority had varied and there was always the risk of another serious weighting that could stop the face for a period. Using a figure of eighteen yards advance per week for the Fuston face, this gave a finishing date of the beginning of June. Roy looked at that date and shook his head.

'It's too close for comfort,' he concluded. 'There's no way that we can be in the position of having the two face-to-face transfers overlapping. And with the Fuston face there'll be the added problem of changing all the legs in each support. It'll need a mini-factory underground to do that, and it could take weeks.' Roy stood up from the table and walked around his office. 'There's only one thing we can do; we'll need to slow down 58s coalface and try to speed up the Fuston face. I need to work out how this can be organised.'

The rest of the meeting covered other aspects of the production faces and the finances of the pit. The Surveyor pointed out there was still a further one hundred yards for 56s coalface to advance to the boundary. Was that coal going to be worked now, or could it to be saved until the next face-to-face transfer? Roy said his preference was to save that coal until the Fuston face-to-face transfer.

The three men then had a discussion about manpower at the pit. This was still reducing on a week-by-week basis and was now at thirteen hundred and fifty total manpower. Roy asked Jeff to do an exercise to see how many men would reach retirement age during the next six months. Jeff explained to Roy that the tonnage needed for the pit to break even on a week-by-week basis was slowly reducing. He'd prepared a graph that illustrated this.

'That is a very useful way of demonstrating how we're increasing the efficiency of the pit,' said Roy. 'I might take a copy of that to my next accountability meeting, provided it still shows the same trend.'

'It should continue the same way, as long as we keep reducing the overall manpower and we avoid any very expensive purchases in one week,' said Jeff. 'I do apply a smoothing effect to the weekly costs, to avoid dramatic changes in the graph.'

Roy was pleased with his finance man and with the ideas he was putting forward.

After the meeting, Roy decided to think through the issues they'd discussed and then he would have a meeting with Cobba. In the meantime, he told George that he wanted to have six shears per day from the Fuston face, even if this meant less coal from the Benton mechanised faces.

'The Benton lads will not be happy if that reduces their earnings, Boss,' said George, with a worried look on his face.

'If that happens, George, we'll have to consider some changes. We need to fill the shaft with coal and get back up to over twenty-one thousand tons each week for the next two weeks. I have my accountability in two weeks' time and I want to explain that the pit's performance for the last two weeks was a one-off.'

'I'm sure we'll have a good run up to Christmas, now, Boss,' replied George. 'There was plenty of spirit on the Fuston face this morning, and they were keen to start on their third shear, but the belts didn't run well during the last hour of the shift.'

'I noted that, George, but the shaft was winding flat out. There was more coal than we could handle.'

Tuesday 25 October 1966

At the urgent request of Cobba, Roy was asked to attend a meeting of the Welfare Club committee. There were special items on the agenda, he was told.

'I've gathered that there are some wild ideas to spend a chunk of our financial surplus over the Christmas period, Boss,' Cobba had said. 'The Club is doing very well and the profits are higher than they have ever been. So I suppose that we can expect there to be ideas from the committee. It's what we spend the money on, that matters.'

'I'll be there, Cobba,' Roy had replied. 'If we get things sorted out I'd welcome a chat with you in the privacy of the Club rather than in the office here, when you would have to be accompanied by your mates.'

The Club committee agenda covered the routine accounts for the operations, with a comparison to the previous year. Roy was surprised at the figures, which showed a twenty percent increase in turnover and an even bigger increase in profits. There was no doubt that the increased earnings from Martins were resulting in higher spending at the Club. Under the agenda item 'Christmas Activities' there was an immediate move by members of the committee.

'Mr Chairman, can I suggest that we reduce the price of beer over the Christmas period? Looking at the profits, we can afford to do it.'

'Just a minute,' replied Cobba, looking directly at the committee-man making the proposal. 'How do our charges per pint compare with other local Clubs?'

'They're slightly lower,' replied the committee-man, hesitantly.

'Well then, you have the answer. Just because we operate an efficient Club, there's no need for us to give away our beer.' He paused for effect.

'What are we going to do then, Cobba?' asked another committee-man.

'Well, we do have a proposal from our excellent Stewardess,' replied Cobba. 'She wants to have two free parties this year for the children: one for kids under five, and another one for those from five to ten-years-old. There would be different entertainers suitable for the age groups. There would also be games and lots of prizes.' Cobba looked around to see the reaction of the committee.

'That sounds alright, as an initial proposal,' replied one of the committee, indicating that there was still a chance of cheap beer.

'The Stewardess has another proposal,' put in Cobba. The committee looked at him in expectation. 'She suggests that we hire buses and take trips of teenagers out to a show, or a pantomime, in Leeds or Sheffield.'

Roy decided to support this last idea. 'I think there are great possibilities in this last proposal. I think we should offer a range of trips, with a choice for the teenagers. We could include a play, or a classical music concert, as well as pantomimes, and let the teenagers make their own choice. It would be expensive for the Club, but it might give these young people an experience that they would not normally get.'

'Thank you for that, Mr Dobson' replied Cobba. 'You have identified a wider scope to that idea than I had first seen.'

'It will need a lot of organising, to offer a range of options,' said Roy. 'But I think it would be worth the effort and would do the Club a lot of good.'

'I think we should support this,' said another of the committee.

'You're taking on a lot of work,' said Cobba. 'It will need committee-men to be on duty at all these events and some of your wives would be required to help, particularly with the under five-year-olds.'

The rest of the meeting concerned other details for the Christmas period: applications for opening time extensions on Christmas Eve, New Year's Eve and New Year's day; which acts and bands should be engaged for entertainment (a higher grade than ever before at Upthorpe); special bingo prizes for the key dates; and finally, it was decided to have a fancy dress competition on New Year's Eve, with significant cash prizes. Roy raised the subject of the Aberfan disaster in Wales that had occurred on the previous Friday. A total of one hundred and forty-four people had been killed, including one hundred and sixteen children, when their school was swamped by a flood of mud when the pit lagoons burst in heavy rain. The committee decided to contribute £200 to the disaster fund. Cobba closed the meeting and, while the committee-men drifted off to the bar, Cobba and Roy went into the small Club office.

'That was an excellent meeting, Cobba,' said Roy. 'The Club is really doing good work for the community, now.'

'A bloody lot better than it would have been if we had just offered cheap beer,' replied Cobba. He looked at Roy for him to proceed.

'What I wanted to discuss, Cobba, is the outcome of a review we've undertaken,' began Roy. 'We've been looking at phasing output from the coalfaces for the next year. There's a risk of the face-to-face transfer from the first Fuston face to the second face getting mixed up with the face-to-face transfer from 58s to 60s face. That would be a disaster for the pit. What I want to do is to get more coal from the current Fuston face and slow down 58s face to two shifts per day. I also want to save the rest of the coal on 56s hand-filled coalface until the Fuston face finishes.'

'That will cause us some problems, Boss. Surely you'll have some spare men at the pit without regular jobs,' said Cobba.

'That is true, Cobba, but it will only be a short-term issue. We're losing men on a regular basis each week and there might be another option.'

'What's that, Boss?' asked Cobba, after a pause in the conversation.

'As you know, they are closing pits, mainly in other parts of the country, but there will be some closures in this region of Yorkshire before long. I understand that there are favourable redundancy terms being offered. Now, we've looked at the number of men who will reach sixty-five in the near future, and there's a steady stream over the next six months. If we look at the number of men who are over sixty-three-years-old, there's a surprising total of sixty-eight. I have an accountability meeting next week with Mr Pickersgill, and I have figures to show that if we could offer these men favourable terms it would increase quite significantly the results for the pit. I don't know if he will agree to this, but if you are in agreement, I would like to propose it to him.'

'That's a difficult one, Boss. My mates in the union are always raising the problem of the manpower reducing at the pit. As you know, one team of men who left and went to a Doncaster pit tried to come back to Martins, but they were refused jobs. That upset the union, and some of them are getting restless and mumbling about industrial action. Of course, I tell them that the wages at the pit have never been better, and the men would not tolerate a dispute now.'

'There is another issue on recruitment that I could offer to soften the pill,' said Roy. 'I think we should be taking on some juveniles, especially apprentices. We could start signing a few on each month, as the redundancies took place.'

'That would certainly be a good move. I'll think about it, Boss, and let you know before your meeting.'

'I've seen some figures that show that a man of sixty-three getting redundancy is very nearly as well-off as he would be if he worked the last two years.'

'That sounds a good deal. I'd like to see those figures.'

'I'll get you a copy and let you see the calculations,' replied Roy.

Roy joined Cobba for a drink at the bar and took the opportunity to talk to the committee-men and some of the Martins men that he recognised.

When he went home he was thankful that he'd had these opportunities at the Club, sounding out Cobba on major strategy moves at Martins.

Chapter 24

Thursday 3 November 1966

'They've left you to near the end of this round of accountability meetings,' said Diane, as Roy waited in her office before going in for his meeting. 'You must be in for an easy passage,' she added.

'Oh, I don't know about that,' replied Roy. 'We had some problems two weeks ago. But we're now back on stream again. How many more meetings are there?' Roy asked.

'They'll finish this morning,' said Diane. 'There's only one more after you. There have been some difficult ones on this round of meetings, with some managers coming out here in a state of shock after their meeting. I had to persuade one manager to stay and have a cup of tea to get him fit to drive his car back to the pit.'

Reg Jenkins had not briefed Roy about the accountability meetings for other managers, but Roy felt confident that he should not have unresolved major issues after his meeting. A colliery manager came out shortly afterwards and he seemed fairly relaxed. Roy was then called in and he took his place opposite Mr Pickersgill, who had his senior staff on each side of him.

The meeting followed the brief, which showed a good set of figures for the third quarter of the year, to the end of September. The figures were significantly better than for the same quarter in the previous year. There were some questions on the details, but Roy was able to answer them with additional information. The conditions in the Fuston seam were raised, and Roy explained that there were heavy strata loads on the powered supports from time to time, but that the face was moving forward and coping with the challenge. He also explained the plan to change all the legs in the powered supports to new, higher rated ones, before they were moved onto the second coalface.

When it came to the financial figures, Roy decided to play his card on cost control.

'We've set up a system of monitoring the break-even tonnage at the pit on a week-by-week basis and we've graphed the results.' He passed some copies of the graph to Mr Pickersgill. 'As you can see, Sir, the graph shows that the break-even tonnage is steadily reducing. This is what we would expect, as we are not doing any recruiting and we're letting men leave at every opportunity. We're also keeping a firm hold on materials costs.'

'That is a very persuasive graph,' said Norman Pickersgill. 'And it shows that increased efficiency is being turned into increased profits. What are your plans to continue to keep the graph going down?'

'We believe we can continue to keep the weekly break-even tonnage reducing. Actually, we have an opportunity, now, to make a step change in the total manpower at the pit.' Roy stated his intention to increase the output from the Fuston face, which he knew Mr Jenkins favoured. However, he explained, he would need to reduce it from the Benton faces, particularly 58s face. This would create a surplus of manpower at the pit, which was a concern for the union and might lead to some form of unrest. He added that exercises had been undertaken at the pit to try to find a solution to the problem.

'We have analysed all the men reaching retirement age in the next two years and it's a surprising figure of sixty-eight. What I would like to do is offer those sixty-eight men redundancy terms that would be attractive to them and let them leave as soon as possible. To sweeten the pill for the union I would then wish to recruit a few juveniles, particularly as craft apprentices, each month. I realise that this is an unusual approach, but it would give us the right manpower levels at the pit for the next few years. With a weekly output of over twenty-one thousand tons, and a manpower level of about twelve hundred and seventy, the profit margins would be very high.'

There were surprised looks at Roy from the senior staff alongside Mr Pickersgill; none of them had ever heard a colliery manager proposing to reduce the pit manpower, especially in an accountability meeting.

'Well there you are, Gentlemen,' said Mr Pickersgill, looking around his team. 'We have a colliery manager who comes before us with a plan to make more profit. All we have to do is help him to make it happen.'

Reg Jenkins quickly approved the option of increasing the output from the Fuston seam. Roy explained that he needed as big a gap as possible between the Fuston face finishing and Benton 58s face finishing. Mr Pickersgill looked across at the Personnel Manager.

'What about these redundancies? How are you going to organise them?' he asked.

'I'm not sure that we can, Mr Pickersgill. We have to identify the loss of jobs at a pit that is closing in order to apply the redundancy terms. Martins Main is not in that category.'

'But the men are surplus to requirements; if they are made redundant we will see an immediate increase in profits. Come on, use your imagination!'

'We could always make a transfer of the Martins men onto the books of a pit that is closing, once they have agreed to accept the terms,' suggested Reg Jenkins.

'There you are: that's one option. I don't mind how you do it, but give this fellow the details of the terms he can offer the men who would qualify for redundancy. I want action straightaway.'

'Yes, Mr Pickersgill,' replied the Personnel Manager, rapidly making notes. Roy noticed him briefly glance up at him; the look on his face was one of displeasure. This was another senior regional official, thought Roy, who had a debt to settle against him in the future, if he ever got the chance.

*

Later in the afternoon, when he was back at the pit, Roy got a call from Norman Pickersgill.

'I just wanted to be sure that you'll be attending the annual Christmas dinner dance, with your wife,' said Mr Pickersgill. 'I didn't want to ask you at the meeting today.'

'Yes, I'm sure we will be attending, Sir,' replied Roy.

'There is something that I would like your wife to do at the event. I'll have a word with her about it in the near future.'

'Shall I tell her that you'll be contacting her?' asked Roy.

'Yes, you can if you like. I've not worked out myself yet what there will be to do.'

'Right, Sir,' said Roy, as Pickersgill rang off.

Wednesday 16 November 1966

Helen Dobson was driving back to Upthorpe after spending three hours talking to Mrs Hazel Ackroyd at her house in the village of Flockton, on the hills above Huddersfield. Helen reflected on the challenge that she faced. She'd been asked to tell the story of Hazel Ackroyd's life, in just a few minutes, in front of a large audience of hard-faced colliery managers and their wives at the regional dinner dance next month. She would need some inspiration.

★

Hazel and Frank Ackroyd had both been born in the village of Flockton in 1902, of humble, working-class parents. They'd been in the same class in the village school and had both left school when they were thirteen, to start work. She'd worked in the local mill and he went to work at the mine.

'Were you always friendly with your husband?' Helen had asked.

'Not really,' replied Hazel. 'I remember looking across at him at his desk in the classroom and fancying him, but I was shy and didn't dare approach him. He came from a large family with nine children and he was next to the youngest; I came from a family with two children. My dad worked for the post office, so we were sort of a bit more secure than his family. His dad worked in the mine, with his five sons. Our families were very different. His dad was a strong man, who expected immediate obedience from his wife and children. All the children had jobs to do about the house, and if his dad asked for something, he got it immediately. The kids were all working, and when they got their wages on a Friday, they handed them over to their mother. That was her housekeeping because her husband used his wages for drinking and gambling. I couldn't believe it, but the children stood at the table for their meals – only his father and mother sat down. By contrast, my family were very close and we had fun together. It could have been because my parents were active in the church. The first time I took Frank home, he could not believe the difference. Mind you, that was after the war, when we had been seeing each other for a couple of years.'

After being told how Frank had progressed at the mine, through nightschool study and hard work, Helen moved on to the more intimate story of the couple's courtship and marriage.

'How did you eventually come to be married, after your strong pact of not cementing your relationship until after Frank's studies were complete?' said Helen.

'It was once again the mine owner, who intervened. When Frank got his Manager's ticket the owner immediately appointed him as a Deputy at the mine, and offered him one of the company houses in the village. So in one move, we had a house and better-than-average job security. We didn't know at the time how important that would be in the 1926 miners' strike.'

'I suppose you arranged the wedding without any delay, when there was a house on offer,' said Helen.

'Yes, we made all the arrangements in a couple of months and we were married in November 1924. 'It was a very cold day, with icy winds and snow showers, and my teeth were chattering as we had a few photographs on the church steps. Of course, it was a new way of life for both of us. Frank had to get used to handling the men underground, and of course some of them were his relatives. I had to get used to being a housewife, because when you got married in those days, you automatically lost your job in the mill. And here we are, still in the same village, after all this time. But we've moved up from the first house that we had,' she added with a smile.

'Did Frank not consider moving to other pits, particular the bigger ones, in Yorkshire?' asked Helen.

'Not really,' replied Hazel. 'He was appointed Undermanager for the mine, in 1936, and then the owner appointed him Manager in 1946, before the nationalisation of the industry. Frank knows all the men at the pit, and they are good workers, so he's had a very satisfying career. Flockton Moor's got a good name, even if it is small by some standards.'

They continued to discuss children and grandchildren, Hazel's life in the church, and finally the future after Frank retired.

'Now that's going to be a big challenge for him, and probably for me too. He's been a creature of habit and those habits have all revolved around the pit. There's going to be a big void to fill, but I'm sure we'll sort it out between us. It's been a wonderful journey together and, when I look back, I'm glad that I went and spoke to Frank, that day in the woods.'

Monday 21 November 1966

Roy was holding the official meeting with the union team to discuss the terms that were available for the men who qualified for the special redundancy offer. Cobba was familiar with the offers that would be made and he knew that they would be a big advantage for those men who were worn out by pit work. He also recognised that some men were effectively reducing their life expectancy by every additional month they worked. However he'd reserved his position, and made no firm commitment to Roy's proposal.

Roy made a presentation that he'd carefully prepared to prove his case. He showed the output patterns from the coalfaces and the timing of the face-to-face transfers of equipment. He then listed the staffing levels required throughout the pit for the production faces, the development work, the salvage work and the general maintenance of the mine. At each part of the presentation he stopped for any questions and comments. There were a few questions, and one or two comments, but there was no disagreement with his figures for the manpower required. Cobba made the point that no juveniles had been signed on at the pit for over a year, and he thought that it was disappointing that Martins was not offering any jobs for young lads in the Upthorpe district. This argument got support from Jimmy and the other union men. Roy was able to say that he agreed with them, and that he had plans to rectify the situation. The final figures showed that there was a surplus of manpower to run the pit. The union members couldn't argue with the figures, but there was some muttering about it being an unacceptable position.

Roy emphasised that there was a risk that Martins might be subject to a manpower audit because the number of men without a regular job was being discussed at the pit level and that this was bound to arouse interest at Region. This gave the opportunity for the union team to make comments about the useless team at Region. Roy then played his card.

'We've been trying to evaluate what we can do at the pit to resolve the problem to everybody's advantage. We've found that there are sixty-eight men who are within two years of retirement age. If these men were to leave, that would be a significant move to balance the manpower position. Don't be too harsh on the Region. The Personnel Department have had to be involved in order to provide a solution. With a lot of pressure from the top at Region, they've agreed to incorporate these men into the redundancy agreement at other pits that are to be closed. I have now received the terms for each man – what they will get as a lump sum and what their pension will be from the date they retire.'

'Are you prepared to show us the figures, so that we can decide if it's a good deal?' asked Cobba.

'I have nothing to hide and, having looked at the figures, I'm sure that the men will be very nearly as well-off as they would be if they worked. And when they get to the age of sixty-five they'll have the state pension as well. I'm prepared to discuss each individual case with you, provided that you treat the figures as confidential to this meeting.'

'We'll accept that condition, Boss,' replied Cobba. 'As far as I am concerned, I want the best deal I can get for our lads who have given a lifetime to this industry. I just want to be confident about the figures.' There were nods from the rest of the union team.

'Right, I will ask Jeff Briggs to go through the individual cases.'

Jeff displayed on the overhead projector screen the age of each man, what his average earnings had been, what his lump sum would be, and what his weekly pension would be. The figures were impressive, and each case was subject to comment by the union men who knew the people concerned.

'That bugger has never been able to hold down a regular job; he might as well go.'

'He's always done a good job and deserves to go, but will his wife let him retire? She wears the trousers at that house.'

'I never realised he was that age. I thought he was only in his fifties. He's wearing better than his brother.'

'That poor sod is knackered. He won't last until he's sixty-five. It will give him a few months of retirement, if he can go.'

At the end of the sixty-eight names, Roy put the question.

'Can I take it that you agree that this is a sensible way to proceed, for the men at Martins?'

'I think we can agree, Boss,' said Cobba. 'But I take it that this is voluntary. If a man wants to stay on, then he can do.'

'Yes, I accept that,' replied Roy. 'But there are two additional things you must consider. We want the men to accept these terms so that we can move forward. If the majority of the men agree to retire now, then I will be signing on a few juveniles each month as apprentices. I am sure you'll agree that that is a good move. The other factor I want you to honour is that this is a special deal for Martins. I don't want anybody bragging about it around the clubs, so that we end up with some sort of external investigation. Region is bending the rules a bit, to help Martins.'

'I understand what you're asking, Boss,' said Cobba. 'We will treat this whole exercise confidentially.'

'We'll arrange interviews starting the day after tomorrow,' said Roy. 'Jeff will see the men individually, and I'm quite happy if one of your team comes in with each man, so that they are comfortable with the discussions.'

'That's a very good suggestion,' said Cobba. 'I'll arrange for one of us to be there with every man.'

Tuesday 6 December 1966

There had been two weeks of intensive work at the pit. Each man who accepted the redundancy terms was cleared to leave within two weeks and on the Friday that he left, he received his lump sum as well as any wages due. It was a real Christmas present for all the men involved. Some of the men had never seen so much money at one time in their lives.

However the exercise also resulted in significant changes to the total manpower within the pit. For each man with a regular job who was granted redundancy, someone else had to be identified to fill that position. So there was a lot of shuffling around and changes in shift patterns. Roy was determined to finish all the changes before the Christmas break.

In all, sixty-three men accepted the terms, but there was pressure from ten men, who were slightly younger, to be released, and Roy was able to include them in the exercise.

In total, before the end of the year, seventy-three men would leave under redundancy and seven others put in their notice: a total manpower reduction of eighty men in just three weeks.

'This will have a major impact on the profitability of the pit,' said Jeff Briggs, during his weekly finance meeting with Roy Dobson.

'It will indeed, so long as we keep the output up,' replied Roy.

Monday 12 December 1966

The Enclosure was in session during the Christmas Bull week. There was discussion about the rate of production and also about the manpower position.

'They've laid two extra trains on, for the power station, this week,' reported Bert Wall. 'And they did an extra wash, on Saturday morning, to clear the raw coal in railway wagons. There seems to be no limit to the production from the pit at the moment.'

'The lads were talking in the Club, over the weekend, and they think they might be able to break the weekly record for output at the pit again this week. They're giving priority to the Fuston face,' said Charlie. 'The manager must be turning on all the taps.'

'I think the manager's leaving the production to George. Dobson's interest is sorting out the manpower and he's spending all his time on that,' said Pat.

'He's doing the right thing, in leaving the operations underground to George,' said Cliff. 'I think George has been the major influence in Martins' success and this manager is wise to leave it to him.'

'What's happening to the manpower then?' asked Albert.

They all looked across at Pat Mulligan, anticipating an answer to this question. He didn't hurry with his reply, and seemed to choose his words carefully.

'I understand that there is a proposal to let the older men at the pit retire early. They're all being interviewed personally, and their cases discussed.'

'Surely they are not being forced out?' said Albert.

'No, it's a voluntary decision by each man,' replied Pat. 'But I have heard that there is a lump sum on offer and an immediate pension. It sounds to be an attractive offer.'

'What on earth is Cobba thinking about?' said Albert. 'Letting the management have discussions with the men about such a thing.'

'I heard in the Club that either Cobba or Jimmy is going in with each man, to check what's on offer,' said Charlie.

'I understand that the manager has pulled off a very good deal for the men, from Region,' said Pat.

'This manager certainly produces some magic tricks out of the hat,' said Cliff.

'He's an advantage now, as Martins is the most profitable pit in Yorkshire, and in the top league of pits in the country,' said Pat. 'When he asks for some help he can expect to get it.' Pat had never been so much involved in the Enclosure discussions for a long time. He determined to keep his mouth shut for the rest of the morning.

'It's a bugger how he keeps doing it,' concluded Albert.

Saturday 17 December 1966

There was a new arrangement, this year, at the Dobson household, for babysitting on the night of the regional dinner dance. Peggy was on duty, accompanied by Dawn, and they were staying the night. Sandra had other commitments.

Peggy welcomed the opportunity to be useful, and Dawn was excited to be staying in the big house. Helen was resplendent in a new maroon, full-length evening dress, which had a low-cut back and a plunging neckline. Roy thought she looked very attractive, but he reserved comment until they were settled in the car.

'I think you will be a contender for belle of the ball tonight, in that dress, Helen,' he said, as he squeezed her hand. Helen didn't reply, as she was thinking through the two speaking jobs that she had to do during the evening. She was happy that the event would follow the normal format, and she was familiar with the arrangements, but she was challenged with saying the right words at the one new feature of the evening.

When they were circulating before the dinner was called, Roy was pleased that some managers had had a word with him when they passed. However he also noticed that other managers, at the opposite end of the bar, were casting looks in his direction, which might indicate that they were discussing him, and not in any favourable way. There could be some jealousy that he was on the top table again, with Mr Pickersgill.

Before the meal started, and when everyone was seated, Norman Pickersgill made his usual speech. However this year he was positive about the performance of his Region, and he complimented the manufacturers and mining companies for their support. He made reference to the overall reduction in the market for coal, nationally, and the effect this was having on pit closures throughout the country. He added that he feared it would also affect pits in his Region of Yorkshire. In conclusion, he indicated that this year there would be a special feature to the evening and that this would take place after the meal.

'In what's now becoming a tradition at this event, will you please be upstanding for Mrs Helen Dobson, who will say grace.'

Helen stood with her eyes closed and her hands clasped in front of her and waited for a silence to envelope the dining room.

'We would ask your blessing, Lord, on the coal mining industry of this country, and on all who work in the pits, and all who service them. We would especially pray that everyone in the industry will work together so that the pits become safer as workplaces and the mining communities become centres of prosperity and friendship. Also, for this meal, and the opportunity to mix with friends and colleagues, we give you our grateful thanks. Amen.'

When Helen sat down next to Norman Pickersgill, he squeezed her hand and whispered in her ear.

'That was a very wise move, Helen, to mention the whole of the mining industry and the need for everyone to work together for improved safety and health in the pits. Everyone needs to be reminded of these responsibilities. It will definitely follow that there'll be prosperity in the mining communities if the industry is safe and successful.'

★

After the meal was over, and coffee had been served, Mr Pickersgill had a word with the head waiter, who brought the microphone back to the table and gave a sign that cleared all the other staff from the dining room. Norman Pickersgill addressed the audience, who were wondering what the 'special event' might be.

'It seemed to me that this was the ideal occasion to recognise the long and distinguished service to the industry of one of our colliery managers who will be retiring in the near future. A lot of you have known Frank Ackroyd for many years, and I am pleased to have him and his wife sitting at my table tonight. Now Frank has a special claim to fame. He's been at Flockton Moor pit since he started as a boy, in 1916, and he's worked his way up from a pony driver, when he started, to be Manager of the mine. He was the pit Undermanager from 1936 until 1946, and from 1946 he has been Colliery Manager. This means that when he retires, in a few weeks' time, he will have been in senior management at Flockton Moor for nearly thirty-one years. As you can see, Frank is not a big fellow, but he must be made of special steel, because no one at that pit, even if they're well over six-feet tall, can put one over Frank. He has been proud of his pit and the men who work there. It is Frank who has been responsible for the high standards of workmanship that Flockton Moor has achieved over the years. His management style has safeguarded the results of the pit by always having production faces available if geological surprises arise. On cost control he has applied the West Yorkshire vigilance of avoiding any unnecessary spending. I remember, when I came into this Region, someone told me that I could rely on Frank Ackroyd to deliver his weekly tonnage and his weekly profit like clockwork. He has done exactly that, and I only wish that his pit had been four times its size. I have a presentation to make but that must wait a few minutes. Mrs Ackroyd is here, and I am sure that she has played a major part in the life of Frank. I have asked Helen Dobson to say a few words about Mrs Ackroyd.'

There was a surprised hush around the dining room as Helen stood in front of the microphone. She looked across the table to Hazel Ackroyd, smiled, and then looked around the room.

'I want to tell you a love story. Imagine a young girl, in the junior school, sitting at her desk and looking across the room to a young lad sitting at his desk, and fancying him. But she was too shy to approach him, so it never got any further. They both left school when they were thirteen-years-old; he went to work in the pit and she went to work in the mill. He still didn't know that she fancied him. Frank was in a family of nine children and he was next to the youngest. Two of his older brothers volunteered in the army in the First World War. They were very smart fellows, and Frank worshipped them as they paraded around the village in their army outfits.'

Helen paused as though she did not want to tell the next bit.

'Both the brothers were killed, in the same month, in 1917.' She said this in a low voice and she looked at Frank, who had put his hands up to his face.

'Frank was utterly devastated and he walked around the village and into the woods with his head down and in total despair. Hazel saw him, one day, walking in the woods and decided that he needed her, so she overcame her shyness and went to him. The only cure for tragedy in life is love. Imagine the scene, as they sat by a tree, with Hazel trying to console and comfort a heart-broken young man who had no faith in his future. She encouraged him and coaxed him to have hope, and she promised that she would stand by him. He trusted her and believed what she'd said, and that was the start. It was no whirlwind romance, however. When the mine owner suggested that Frank should go to nightschool and get some mining qualifications, Frank's father was dead against such a move, as he wanted nothing to do with mine owners or mine management. But Hazel encouraged Frank to take up the offer and she got her father to talk to Frank and help her to persuade him to go to nightschool. So Frank started his studies, and they made a pact: they agreed that they would remain friends but that their relationship would not become serious until Frank had finished his schooling. That was a four-and-a-half-year pact, and you can only honour such an undertaking if it's real love. When Frank was made a deputy, and with the job he got a pit house, they got married in 1924.'

Helen paused and looked around the room, where all the eyes were on her, keen to hear the rest of the story.

'The rest is the history of a family: three children all doing well in their careers now; both Frank's and Hazel's parents needing extra care and comfort in their old age; brothers and sisters seeking advice and help from time to time – the usual mixture. But Frank's and Hazel's responsibilities spread to the whole village of Flockton. Frank was involved with the Welfare and the Sports Clubs; Hazel had the church and her connections with the village school. So everyone came under the influence of two wonderful people who were happy to stay loyal to their community in West Yorkshire. I just can't quantify the friendship, the support, the advice and the kindness that these two have given over the years to Flockton, but what I can say, is that it is a love story between Hazel and Frank. They have poured out that love to each other, and then passed it on to everyone around them. Ladies and gentlemen, will you please welcome Mrs Hazel Ackroyd, and I can assure you that she still fancies Frank after over forty-two years of marriage.'

Helen went over to Hazel and they hugged each other. When they parted, Hazel wiped the tears from her eyes. Then they heard the applause and realised that everyone was standing on their feet, clapping. Pickersgill's secretary, Diane, handed a large bouquet to Helen, who presented it to Hazel, and the applause continued. Mr Pickersgill then called out Frank, and handed him an engraved oil lamp, to even more applause. A photographer appeared and took several shots of Frank and Hazel, and then a final one of the four of them: Mr Pickersgill at the side of Frank, and Helen at the side of Hazel. Everyone then resumed their seats and the staff appeared to clear up the tables and the band took up their position on the stage. Norman Pickersgill leaned over to speak to Helen.

'I wanted it to be something special for Frank and his wife, who must be a unique couple. But you made it extra special, Helen, and I do appreciate what you did.'

'I hope what I said was appropriate,' replied Helen, with relief that it was over.

'It was inspired,' he replied.

Roy took Helen onto the floor for the first dance, and held her tight.

'I said you would be the belle of the ball, but I didn't think you would also win the prize for the best speech ever to a retiring couple,' said Roy.

'You will have to try hard to get someone to make a similar speech for you when you retire, Mr Dobson,' replied Helen, with a grin.

As they walked off the dance floor several of the managers' wives thanked Helen for her speech.

★

Later in the evening, on her way back from visiting the cloakroom, Helen met Polly Jenkins and Denise Wallace, and they had a talk together at the side of the dancefloor.

'I've been hearing from Polly that Martins has been doing very well of late,' said Denise. 'I'd already thought that your husband was bound for promotion to senior positions in the industry, but after hearing you tonight, and seeing your relationship to Mr Pickersgill, I'm absolutely certain he'll have a great future.'

'Oh, I don't know about that,' replied Helen with a smile. 'Roy is always telling me that mining is a risky business.'

'Well, what you said tonight about that colliery manager's wife was absolutely excellent,' said Polly Jenkins. 'I have been to a lot of retirement functions, but I have never heard anything to compare with your speech.'

'I agree,' said Denise Wallace.

'Thank you very much,' said Helen, as she escaped back to Roy.

★

The dance band for the evening was a new one, and it was an improvement on previous years, both in the rhythm and the programme of music. There was also a female singer, with a fine voice and a sexy figure, and a style of performing that wooed the men. Roy was at the entrance to the gents' toilet, talking to Reg Jenkins, when he heard some comments, from inside, from a colliery manager. Initially he thought the speaker was referring to the singer.

'She's got everything: a lovely figure; a smart brain to be able to perform like that and a body that suggests that she's super-sexy in bed. He must be the luckiest bloody colliery manager in the country.'

Roy realised that they were talking about Helen. Whilst he agreed with their sentiments, he didn't say so when he passed them in the doorway.

★

Roy had an exciting evening, dancing with all the ladies at his table, but with extra dances with Helen, who was in demand from numerous men in the hall. He managed to have a quiet talk with Norman Pickersgill and informed him that Martins had exceeded twenty-two thousand tons for the Bull week, and so set up a new weekly output record. As the reduction of manpower was starting to take effect, he expected the profit margin also to be at a record level. Mr Pickersgill was pleased at the news, even though he'd been expecting it.

Wednesday 8 February 1967

There was a social evening at Upthorpe Methodist Church incorporating a a ceremony when the church handed over a cheque for one thousand pounds to Joe Horton, to repay him for the loan that he'd made for the purchase and installation of the organ. Reverend Folds thanked Joe for his generosity and commented on the impact that the organ had made on the services of the church. He then surprised those present, by making an announcement.

'I want to tell you myself, before you hear rumours from other places,' he began, and there was a hush in the schoolroom. 'Gwen and myself have had a wonderful time, here at Upthorpe, over the last five years, and we have made friendships that we will never forget. But we have decided that we must move on. So, in August we will be moving to a Methodist Circuit in Birmingham, where we will have four churches to look after. We'll miss the mining community here in Yorkshire, and I suppose we'll be involved more in the engineering works and the car plants of Birmingham. One of my churches is near Bourneville, and the Cadbury chocolate factories. I wonder if the Methodist minister gets free samples? But I know that Upthorpe Methodist Church will continue to prosper, because of the commitment and beliefs of the members here. And you can rely on Gwen and myself to serve you to the best of our abilities until the day we depart.'

★

It was at the same event that Helen Dobson heard from Willie Carter about a new assignment that his son Peter was to take on. His organ teacher, Dr Sloan, had been invited to spend a month in America, as the visiting organist at a large church in Washington DC. As Dr Sloan's deputy organist was going into hospital for surgery, he'd invited Peter to become organist, for that month, at the Parish Church in Leeds. He would only be required to play the organ, as another musician would take on the responsibilities for the church choir. Peter was excited by this opportunity, but he would have to solve the problem of reorganising his shift rota at the mine, to allow him to be in Leeds most nights of the week.

★

Helen was then approached by Gwen Folds with some news. Sandra had asked James to christen Amy-Louise, and of course he'd agreed. The date was to be finalised, but it would be after Easter.

'I have no doubt that Sandra will be carefully selecting her godparents,' said Gwen. 'She seems a very well organised young mother.'

'She is indeed,' replied Helen.

Monday 13 February 1967

Sandra called to see Helen and was invited to share a cup of coffee while Amy-Louise was sleeping. Helen had an idea that at some time during the visit there would be an invitation to be a godparent, and so it was. But Sandra was very keen that Roy should also be a godparent, as this was a request from Cobba, as well as from Terry and herself. Helen agreed to lean on her husband to get him to comply with the request.

Tuesday 14 February 1967

Cobba was in the manager's office, dealing with some pit issues with Roy. Cobba then went on to discuss the forthcoming meeting of the Welfare Committee.

'I hope you can come to the next meeting, Boss, as we've now got the annual accounts for last year, to be approved by the committee.'

Roy checked his diary and replied that he intended to be present next Tuesday. He asked if there was anything special about the accounts.

'They're very good, Boss, as you might expect, with the increased earnings for the men from Martins. The Christmas arrangements for the kids and the young people went down very well with the community and, as a result, we were packed out over the holiday period. I'm just a bit worried that some of the committee will come out with wild ideas again, to spend some of our surplus. I think we should invest it, so that we have increased reserves in the bank for the future.'

'I agree with that, Cobba, and I'll support you at the meeting,' replied Roy.

When they'd finished discussing the Welfare Club, Cobba asked if he could talk to Roy about another matter.

'I need a bit of advice, Boss, about a family matter,' said Cobba.

'I'm not the one to approach about family matters, Cobba; you should talk to my wife,' replied Roy, with a grin on his face.

'I think it's a man's issue, Boss,' replied Cobba. 'You see, our David has had a firm offer to be an apprentice with Sheffield United football club, and of course he wants to take it up.'

'I can understand that, Cobba. You must be proud of him for doing so well.'

'Yes, I am very proud of him, and I want him to do what is right for his future. I'm going over with our David to see the Assistant Manager who looks after the apprentices, to go through the terms of the apprenticeship. I wondered if it would be possible for you to go with us?'

'If you tell me when it is, I'll try to go with you,' replied Roy, somewhat surprised at the invitation. 'I suppose that the aim will be for him to continue his studies while developing his skills and fitness for football?'

'That's it exactly,' replied Cobba. 'I don't know if it will be possible to do that, and the trouble is that David will accept anything from the football club. If it means leaving school, that'll be a bonus for him. If you're with us I'm sure he'll listen to your advice.'

'I'll try to help, Cobba.'

Cobba decided to ask a final question.

'How did the accountability go, at Region, the other day, Boss?'

'It was fine, Cobba. As you'll appreciate, the tonnage for last year was the best ever for Martins, and our financial results are having a big impact on the region's figures. We discussed the market situation, and we may have to stock coal later in the year. The real challenge this year, at Martins, will be to move the Fuston equipment from the first face to the second face and upgrade all the powered supports in the process. If we can keep going at the present rates, we should be into that job at the end of May, or the beginning of June. We've a lot of planning to do to organise that.'

'I'm sure you will be able to fix it, Boss,' replied Cobba, who was happy that Roy had agreed with getting the right plan for David's future.

Chapter 25

Friday 7 April 1967

New developments at Martins were providing subject matter for the Enclosure during the week before the Easter holidays.

'They have a bulldozer at work in the fields behind the pit, preparing a coal stocking site,' said Bert. 'They've laid out quite a big area, so they must be expecting that there will be some thousands of tons to stock.'

'It's a sign of the times,' said Cliff. 'They're closing pits in Yorkshire, now, as well as in the rest of the country, because of the reduction in demand for coal. I saw in the paper a few weeks ago that the first gas from the North Sea was pumped ashore at Easington in Durham. Some folk are saying that there will be lots of gas and it will affect the demand for coal.'

'Will they stock washed coal, or raw coal?' asked Charlie Marshall.

'I don't know the answer to that,' replied Bert. 'It seems daft to stock washed coal, which will deteriorate on the stock pile so that it might want rewashing before it can be sold. There's no spare capacity in the washer.'

'They'll be stocking the power station coal,' said Pat. The team looked across at Pat, obviously wanting him to expand on this. 'The power station coal is of mixed sizes, and they hold big stocks of it at the power stations. If Martins get an extra order for the power stations, all they'll have to do is get some lorries into the field with a loading-machine and send it straight off to the power stations.'

'That makes sense,' said Albert.

'I've heard that the Martins Home Coal scheme is taking on deliveries of concessionary coal for the two pits that are closing in Yorkshire. So that will be some extra coal going to market,' said Cliff.

'I'll bet Cobba is rubbing his hands, with that extra business for the Home Coal delivery service,' said Albert.

'Cobba told some mate of his in the Club that he'll be taking on an additional lorry to do the job,' commented Charlie.

'That was always a mystery, finding out about the Home Coal service,' said Albert. 'I could never get a look at the accounts. Cobba just always said that it was paying its way. I suppose he gets a bob or two for managing the job.'

'It was always rumoured, from the men who worked for him, that he got more than a bob or two,' said Bert. 'Mind you, when they got their own bunker to load the lorries the job was much easier for his men. That might be why they've given him the extra business.'

'What on earth is on that lorry?' asked Charlie. A lorry was passing along Martins Lane carrying crates of white-painted hydraulic units.

'They look like hydraulic props,' said Cliff, 'but they have no tops on them.' He looked at the lorry for a minute and then he said. 'I know – they could be the new legs to change for the ones in the powered supports on the Fuston face.'

'They look bloody big,' said Albert.

'There will be a lot more loads, if they're for the Fuston face,' said Cliff. 'There must be well over a thousand hydraulic legs on the powered supports for that coalface.'

'The lads were saying in the Club that it will be a massive job, to withdraw all the supports, modify them and then install them on the new face,' said Charlie. 'They've heard George Turnbull discussing the problems with Jim Lord. They haven't decided how to organise the changeover yet. Apparently there's still a lot of rock load on the coalface every time the roof breaks behind the face. One lad said the risk is that the roof breaks down and flattens the supports, so that they can't be withdrawn.'

'I keep telling you that the Fuston seam has fooled most managers so far,' said Albert. 'No pit has made real money from that seam.'

'You can't say that, Albert,' said Pat. 'A lot of the profits made at Martins now must be coming from the Fuston seam.'

'Yes, but will it continue in the future?' said Albert.

'I understand that they're going to recruit some juveniles, after the Easter holidays,' said Cliff.

'There was a queue of lads, some of them with their fathers, at the pit yesterday, putting their names down for consideration,' said Pat.

'How many will they be taking on?' asked Charlie.

'I've heard they'll take on eight at Easter, and a further eight in the summer,' replied Pat.

'I think one or two fellows were talking about it to Cobba, in the Club last night, and asking him to put a good word in for their lads,' said Charlie.

'It's a bloody big change from a few years ago,' said Albert. 'They were begging anybody to come into the pits then. Now even sons of miners can't get a job. I suppose they'll want lads who are good at schooling. In my day they wanted lads who were strong in their arms and weak in their head. They made the best colliers.'

'Which category were you in, Albert?' asked Cliff, with a grin.

Monday 24 April 1967

Roy and Cobba were sitting in the pit conference room, in a circle of chairs laid out for the two of them and the eight new juveniles selected to start at Martins. The lads were nervous, and wondered why the Manager wanted to talk to them before they started their initial training course. One or two of them were sweating profusely at the thought of being asked questions by the manager. Roy noticed this, and decided to try to put them at their ease. He welcomed them to the pit and asked them, in turn, to tell him their names, which he checked off on the paper on his knee. Then he asked them if they had any relatives who worked at the pit. From the replies, he concluded that Cobba had been in discussions with the training officer, putting a good word in for the lads whose fathers and grandfathers had worked at the pit.

'I want to talk to you a little bit about Martins Main, and tell you what the job will offer you, and what I want you to do in return. Of course, you will probably realise that you are lucky to have been picked to have a job. I understand that we had nearly fifty young lads applying for these jobs. So the first thing is to remember that you have got an opportunity, so don't waste it. During the last three years we've invested a lot of money into Martins, to introduce mechanised coalfaces. So we now produce coal with horsepower and machines, not with manpower and sweat. But to do that we need men who are skilled at operating or maintaining those machines. Some of you will be going for training as craftsmen, so as well as working at the pit you'll have to go to nightschool and study to pass the required exams.'

'But you'll all be going to the training centres to learn mining skills. You might think this is a bit of a bore, but listen carefully, because you'll pick up lots of tips there, to help you have a safe working life. Let me tell you something that happened to me. I was underground, as a young man, and I'd rested my hand on a flat piece of steel, in a mine roadway. One of the workmen came over to me and held up his hand. He had a finger missing. He told me that he was resting his hand on a flat piece of steel when a small stone fell out of the roof and chopped off his finger. A chance in a million for the poor fellow, but you'll never see me underground resting my hand on anything that will make a chopping block. As you move around, you'll see lots more examples of good, safe practice when working underground: remember them all, and apply them. I want you all to develop into expert miners who can apply their skills throughout the mine.'

'Now, let me tell you what you will get back from working at Martins. Mining is a fascinating job and your working life will always be interesting and challenging. While we do have a factory process now, on the coalfaces, there is a great difference between a coal mine and a factory. Just think about this. In a factory, you bring the raw material into the factory and process it. With mining you move the factory forward, every day, into the raw material to produce the coal. Now the geological conditions around the coal seams vary from day to day. Sometimes the change is small and doesn't affect the operations, but sometimes Mother Nature, in the form of the geology, gives major surprises, which can interfere with the operations completely. These are the shocks that colliery managers dread.'

'The other subject I want to mention is safety. In my opinion, safety starts with everyone applying best practice. And 'everyone' means everyone. It's no use if most people are doing a good job if there are a few doing shoddy work. Best practice is what it says – the best way to do that job. At Martins, we try to plan jobs in great detail so that we spell out how the job should be done, for both efficiency and safety. You should be learning about best practice for different jobs all the time. If you're in a new situation and you're not sure, ask for guidance – there's sure to be someone around who can help you. The last thing we want to be dealing with is accidents to workmen, or worst of all fatalities, which result from workmen not knowing what is best practice.'

'Now, I would like to say a few words about the money you'll get for working at Martins. You'll get paid a good wage, whatever you're doing. When you get onto the production faces you will get an opportunity to earn high wages if you achieve high output. As a colliery manager, I'm not afraid to pay high wages if the output is high. One thing that's happened over the past few years at Martins, has been the increase in wages earned by men in return for improved output. This is obvious in the lives of folk in Upthorpe. They have more money to spend on their lives. They have better things in their homes, better holidays and more security. Just look around and you'll see this.'

'The other major change has been the reduction in disputes and arguments about pay rates. If you have any problems, you can always go to Cobba Green and your union men, who know how to resolve any anomalies without them becoming disputes. We've now arrived at the position that Martins is one of the most successful pits in Yorkshire. I am proud of the achievements, by everyone at Martins, to get to that position. We are like a successful football team: everybody works together and it's better to be scoring goals and winning, rather than losing.'

Roy paused and looked around at the lads, who'd been listening carefully. 'Would you like to say a few words, Cobba?'

'Yes, I would,' replied Cobba. 'I've been thinking, while you were talking, about the difference from when I started work in the pits. I turned up on the first morning, in the dark, with my snap-tin, and was put to work in the pit bottom. My training was a five-minute demonstration of how to handle the tubs, and I was left to it. If I made a mistake, I got a bollocking and learned never to make the same mistake again. You lads have had the advantage of meeting Mr Dobson on your first morning. It was months before I even saw my colliery manager, and years before he spoke to me. Think on what Mr Dobson has told you. Martins is now a successful pit, and it's your job to keep it that way.'

There was further discussion, and Roy asked if any of them played football. One or two nodded positively. Roy picked up on this and talked about the importance of fitness and told the lads about Cobba's son David, who was to be an apprentice with Sheffield United. He emphasised that David was to finish his schooling in Upthorpe and take his A-level exams. Cobba was proud of Roy's example.

The lads were offered the opportunity to ask questions, but only one lad asked about the reserves at Martins, and the life of the pit.

When the meeting was over, the lads went out to a pit van to take them to the training school, while Roy and Cobba went back to the manager's office.

'I think that meeting was a good idea, Boss,' said Cobba. 'There are some good lads there, and they now know what you want from them.'

'They should have a good career in the mining industry. But I'm worried about the reduction in the demand for coal. We'll have to start stocking coal this summer, unless demand picks up.'

'The Yorkshire Miners Union is talking about the problem of coal stocking. There've been some daft ideas floated around – that all the pits should ease back on output, to avoid any pit closures. I suppose they'll point to Martins, because it's well known now, that the pit is highly successful.'

'That is the last thing we want,' said Roy. 'We'll be stocking power station coal, but there might be a chance of an agreement for the power stations to increase their stocks. If they agree to that we want to be able to shift any stock quickly to them. I'm arranging to put some hard core down in the stocking area, to make roads, so that the lorries don't get bogged down, either when the coal's being stocked or picked up.'

'That should help, Boss. We'll be moving more Home Coal from next month, when we have an extra lorry on to deliver to the beneficiaries of the two pits that are closing. We might have some spare capacity with the lorries, during the summer, to take coal to the stocking ground. I'm sure I could agree a cheap price with you, for the extra work,' added Cobba, with a grin.

'That's good to know, Cobba. I suppose we'll have to arrange the stocking transport through Marketing, but if you let me know when you have some lorries available, I'll put a good word in for you.'

★

On the pit van going to the training centre, the new entrants relaxed and discussed the meeting with the manager.

'I can't understand why the manager wanted to talk to us,' said one lad. 'I thought he only made the big decisions at the pit. Talking to us must have been a waste of his time.'

'You weren't listening, mate,' replied another lad. 'He was telling us how he wanted us to behave, and how he wanted us to work at the pit. He was telling us what the deal was. My old man says that he's good at talking to the men as he goes round the pit, and that he listens to what they say. That's how he's got Martins to be a successful pit.'

'I agree,' said another lad. 'We're lucky to get a job at Martins, with a manager that sets an example to all his men. My mates, who've got jobs at some other pits, say that it's hell there, and the management treat them like dirt.'

The lad who had spoken first decided to keep his mouth shut and to listen more before he expressed his views in future.

Tuesday 25 April 1967

Roy had decided to brief all his senior staff on the results of the first quarter of the year and discuss the future action programme for the coalfaces and the timing of the face changes.

Yesterday he'd met with Jeff Briggs to focus on the finances. Jeff had had an estimate of the financial results for the quarter, up to the end of March, which showed that Martins had achieved a very good performance. The tonnage was up marginally on the previous year, but the profit was significantly higher, due to the reduced manpower at the pit and the re-use of salvaged equipment from the Morley and Low Moor seams.

Roy had spent time with the colliery Surveyor, to check the phasing of the coalfaces, and this information was put on a chart that was pinned on a blackboard in the conference room.

Roy had emphasised to his staff that the meeting must start promptly at two o'clock, because there was a lot to get through. He was relieved to see that his undermanager, George Turnbull, was there in good time and hadn't been deflected by some practical problem affecting his part of the pit.

Roy welcomed everybody and firstly explained the results for the quarter. The financial figures demonstrated the effect of the redundancies and the impact of the salvage programme. He complimented his staff on the way they'd operated the pit over the first three months of the financial year, ending his remarks with a simple statement.

'You all know that the results from Martins are having a significant impact on the region's results. Over the last three years, Martins has benefited by investment authorised by Region. In every investment case, we have delivered what we promised, or much better than we promised. Region now expects us to be the top pit for profits, and you are all respected for your part in this role. However that is the past and history; as I've said to you before, we have to plan the future so that we can continue to be successful.'

'I want to go through the action programme, to explain how we manoeuvre the operations on the coalfaces, to be able to achieve two face-to-face transfers in the third quarter of the year.'

Roy went to the blackboard and uncovered the chart. 'This shows that if we continue to achieve an advance of eighteen yards per week, the Fuston face will finish in the last week of May. We've scheduled the new face, Fuston Two, to start in the last week of July, so this gives us seven weeks to do the face changeover. Assuming that this is achieved, we've altered the priority in the Benton seam, to let 58s face be on three shifts, so that it reaches the finish line by the holiday week in August. This would allow us to use that holiday week to do as much as possible of the face-to-face transfer. This plan would reduce to a minimum the impact of these two face changes on the pit performance. That's the gist of our plan, and the objectives we must achieve. Are there any comments on this?'

'If we're to use the pit holiday week to do salvage and installation work in the Benton seam, we need to be getting men organised for the work as soon as possible,' suggested Jim Lord.

'You have spotted why I wanted this meeting now,' replied Roy. 'It's not only men that we need to identify, it's management cover as well. You all know what we did two years ago, when we were challenged by the Central Conveying Scheme. We have to repeat that exercise. So the senior management team need to plan their holidays outside of the pit holiday week in August.'

'The changeover of the Fuston face is going to be much more complicated than the

Benton seam faces, Boss,' said George. 'I've been discussing it with Jim. Changing over thirteen hundred legs in the supports is a very big job in a factory, when they have all the power tools and lifting gear on the job. How we create room underground for this is a major problem.'

'There is another issue, Mr Dobson,' said the Mechanical Engineer. 'Getting the old hydraulic legs out of the supports will be very difficult. We've examined the designs and they're held in place by a collar at the top, which is fastened to the canopy, and a collar at the bottom, which is fastened to the base. There are pins in these collars that stop the hydraulic legs rotating. It's going to be a devil of a job to get these pins loose after they've had a year underground.'

'I did have a look at this, with the face fitter, a few days ago,' said Jim. 'And we were stumped for ideas. I suggest that we try to get a few pins loose, to see if there's a way to do it underground.'

'Agreed,' said Roy. He looked at the Mechanical Engineer. 'I suggest that you go with Jim on this exercise, and take the best practical fitter at the pit with you, to pick his brains.'

There was further discussion of the phasing of the development work for the Fuston Two face and for the Benton 60s coalface, to meet the action programme, but all this work was either up to schedule or in front of the programme.

'From the discussion this afternoon, it seems that it's the work involved in changing the hydraulic legs in the powered supports for the Fuston Two coalface which is the main problem that needs to be solved,' concluded Roy. 'When the exercise on the coalface has been done, we'll meet again to review the position. I think we should discuss this problem with the manufacturer of the powered supports and seek their input.' The Mechanical Engineer agreed to contact the support manufacturer.

Friday 28 April 1967

The Mechanical Engineer, Jim Lord, a pit foreman fitter and a service engineer from the support manufacturer, went underground to examine the problem with getting the old hydraulic legs out of the supports. After two hours of applying penetrating lubricants, and trying to get at the pins with hammers and special tools, no progress had been made. They even lowered-off the hydraulic legs, to see if that made any difference, but the pins were stuck fast.

'The way we do this job, back in the factory, is to have a special power tool that's clamped to the hydraulic leg, to push the pins out,' said the service engineer. 'That's the only way to get these pins out. This changeover is definitely a workshop job, not one to be tackled underground.'

All the Martins staff on the job agreed with him and it was suggested that he should be around when the management team reconvened with Roy.

Jim took George to one side for a private word. 'We have to give the boss an alternative, George,' said Jim. 'If we have to send the supports out of the pit to get the hydraulic legs changed, that's not a long job. It means we can draw off the supports as fast as we can and dispatch them to the surface, then when they're modified they'll be sent back underground. We have to arrange the transport routes for the chocks going out, and the up-rated chocks coming back into the pit, so that they're completely separate and the flow in one direction doesn't affect the other. It doesn't need to extend the total job time, provided we organise the transport teams. There's no doubt that changing the hydraulic legs in the workshop will be much faster than it would be underground.'

'I agree, Jim,' replied George. 'We'll plan the haulage routes, and get them drawn out on a plan, so that we can explain them to the boss.'

'This is a transport challenge,' said Jim. 'As well as transporting the powered supports to the surface and back, the plan must show the installation of a double-row of wooded chocks, when the powered supports are withdrawn. It'll need thousands of pieces of wooden chock pieces, six-inch by six-inch square and three-foot long. We can arrange for these to be underground, and stocked near the finish line of Fuston One coalface, before it finishes. In other words, instead of there being a stock of this wood on the surface, it would be underground.'

'There's a length of roadway that we could get tidied up and levelled, so that these wooden chock pieces can be stacked near the face finish line.'

'You might not be able to get the full number underground, but certainly the vast majority,' said Jim.

'You leave that to me, young man,' said George. 'Just work out the total number that we'll need and I'll arrange a pattern of stocking that gets them on the job.'

Tuesday 2 May 1967

The senior staff reconvened their planning meeting at two o'clock. The service engineer from the support manufacturer was at the pit, and Roy had agreed that he should attend. He gave him the chance to open the discussion of options.

'What do you suggest as the best method to tackle this change to the powered supports?' asked Roy.

'It has to be done in a workshop, where powered tools can be applied, Sir. Getting the old legs out will not be easy, but there are methods that we use in the factory that could be used in the pit workshop. I've discussed this with your engineer and we've identified an area in the workshop that can be set up as a production line to undertake the work. There'll be power tools available at each point to assist the technicians working there. It should be an assembly line process, like building up a new set of supports.'

'What rate of throughput do you envisage?' asked Roy.

'If the line is staffed at its different points, I would be looking at completing two units per hour,' replied the service engineer. 'To be honest sir, the chocks should only be on the surface for a few hours before going back underground.'

'So the upgrading will be able to keep pace with the salvage operation?'

'That's how we see it, Boss,' put in Jim. 'And we've sorted out transport routes to keep the salvaged supports and the upgraded ones separate.'

George put the plan on the table, showing the routes marked in separate colours.

'That seems a good arrangement,' said Roy, when he'd examined the plan.

Jim also explained how a dedicated number of trams would be used in the circuit, for the whole job.

'There's another transport issue that we have solved,' said Jim, looking across at George.

'We intend to have all the wooden chock pieces stacked underground, near the face finish line, while the face is in operation,' said George.

'That's a good move,' said Roy. 'They form the insurance policy, making sure that there's no collapse of the roof that will prevent efficient salvage operations on the old face line.'

There was further discussion on details, and a plan was agreed: the Mechanical Engineer would be responsible for the production line in the workshop, to operate on three shifts, changing the support legs; Jim Lord would be in charge of the salvage operation on the Fuston One face, and dispatching the supports on the haulage system to the surface; George Turnbull would have responsibility for the operation of the haulage systems and for the installation of the powered supports on Fuston Two face; and there would be a service engineer from the company to assist in resolving any problems, who would concentrate on ensuring that the new installation was to the correct standard.

★

Roy Dobson went home that night feeling that the plan was now a sound practical operation. It would not be easy to do it in the set timescale, but he felt that his team had faced the problems and teased out the right approach.

Thursday 4 May 1967

Helen spoke to Sandra about the christening arrangements. It was to take place at the morning service a week on Sunday, and Helen wanted to provide a lunch for the main participants, afterwards. This would follow the format used for Tony and Michael's christening, but Helen wanted to know who would be attending from Terry's family.

'Will Terry's parents be coming, Sandra?' she asked.

'I expect that they will, but we have not confirmed that yet,' replied Sandra. 'There's a possibility that Terry's Grandma may decide to come too.'

'That would be no problem, but might Mr and Mrs Lacey invite some of their other friends as well? There's a limit to how many people we can accommodate here.'

'I think it's very unlikely, Mrs Dobson, that there'll be more than the three of them. Their friends are more for going out to Sunday lunches, rather than going to a church service.'

'I do want to invite Peggy and Dawn, and also Janet and Bob, with Tony and Michael.

We've all worked together over the past three years, so we have all an interest in Amy-Louise,' said Helen.

'That would be very nice, but are you sure you can cope with all the catering?' asked Sandra. 'I can give you a hand with some baking?'

'We'll plan this together, Sandra, so that it's a special day for you and for Amy-Louise. Will your brother be coming?'

'I'm sure that he will be under pressure from my dad to be there, but he's getting involved with his cricket commitments at school, and occasionally they have a Sunday fixture. I've invited my friend, Pauline, to be a godparent, and I am sure she'll help looking after the little children.'

'I think that adds up to twenty-one in total. We'll arrange to feed the young children in the playroom upstairs, but our two boys are getting more grown-up now, so they can help with entertaining the adults downstairs.'

★

Helen explained the arrangements to Roy, and emphasised that he would need to be a host, looking after the guests, particularly the Laceys. Roy thought that his wife would also need to be free to mingle with the guests, so he made two suggestions. Firstly, he proposed that they should use the gardener, Dennis Gates, to drive his car to take people to the church and, at the end of the service, bring them back to the house. Secondly, he suggested that they should have the gardener's wife, Joan, helping with serving the food and drinks. Helen had already met her and noted her practical housekeeping skills. Helen was impressed by Roy's ideas on this occasion.

Sunday 14 May 1967

As the christening date had approached, Sandra had announced that there had been a change of plan, and that her brother would also be a godparent. When Helen had asked the reason for this, Sandra explained that David had been very hesitant about the event, so Cobba had laid the law down and insisted that David should show some responsibility to his wonderful niece, by being a godparent. David had seen that there was no way out of this so, for peace and quiet, he'd agreed. It would mean that Helen and Roy would be joined by Pauline and David, to stand as godparents for Amy-Louise.

The planning paid off and the event caused much interest among the congregation at the church. Peter Carter wasn't the organist, as he was on his four-week secondment to the Parish Church in Leeds. Peter's substitute was in a different league though, and gave a poor lead to the singing as she struggled to hit the right notes and used only one manual of the instrument.

At the end of the christening, James Folds carried Amy-Louise around the church and she beamed at the congregation with her charming smiles. Sandra was so pleased with her that she gave Amy-Louise a kiss when she was returned to her arms.

★

After the service, Mr Lacey offered to give two people a lift, in his large car, back to the Dobson house, and Roy suggested that Peggy and Dawn should travel with him. This may have been behind some questions to Gwen Folds, who was sitting with the Laceys at lunch, about Peggy and Dawn. Gwen Folds had taken the opportunity to relate, particularly to Mrs Lacey, the full story of Peggy and her children and the tragedy of Gerry's death. She explained the part Helen had played, along with Sandra, in supporting Peggy through her time in hospital, and then the final solution with adoption of the two boys by Janet and Bob. She finished her tale with these words.

'You see here today the team that came together and worked to solve a tragedy for the benefit of everyone. There were lots of prayers for guidance and advice, and the Good Lord led us on, step by step, to a wonderful solution.'

Mrs Lacey was quite touched by the story, and her mother summed it up in the car as they were on their way back to Doncaster.

'It's a long time since I've met such a crowd of very good people.'

Mr Lacey had also been impressed by the people at the reception. He'd lifted his assessment of the Dobsons, and he was surprised, yet again, by the way his daughter-in-law was accepted on a par with these people. He'd managed to avoid direct discussions with Cobba Green, but he noticed that Cobba was also at ease with everyone there. He concluded that his granddaughter was in good company. It was on the journey back to Doncaster that he had the idea of inviting Terry, with Sandra and Amy-Louise, to join him and his wife on the holiday that he was planning, to Cornwall, in September.

Monday 15 May 1967

The Enclosure had a morning session. They noted that the pit was having a good run, with output on a regular basis.

'The trouble is that they're not selling all the coal, now,' said Bert.

'There seems to be plenty of coal going out by road, and they're always lowering wagons down to the mainline,' said Charlie.

'Yes, but you can't see from here how they are stocking coal in the area behind the pit,' said Bert. 'There's a footpath that goes out that way and, if you take it, you go alongside the stocking area, so you can see what's going on. I've been along there a time or two.'

'We ought to go along there then, and have a look,' said Charlie.

'I think that's a good idea,' said Cliff. 'Why don't we go this afternoon, while the weather's good?'

The suggestion was accepted.

★

The team met at the end of Martins Lane and followed Bert Wall, who led them along the route of footpaths to the stocking ground. They leaned on the fence and surveyed the large area that had been prepared with hard-standing tracks for the lorries and a series of levelled areas that were twenty yards wide and two hundred yards long.

'Bloody hell, they're planning to put a lot of coal down,' said Albert, as they looked at the stockpile being built on the first levelled area. 'How much do you think that bay will hold, Cliff?'

'I can't estimate that, Albert,' replied Cliff. 'They're building the pile about twenty-feet thick and it's at least fifteen yards wide at the top. Along that length there'll be a few thousand tons.'

'I've heard that the Surveyor has to survey the stockpile at the end of each month and calculate how much there is,' said Pat.

'Why's that?' asked Charlie.

'Stocked coal is a nightmare to get right,' said Bert. 'There have been some right cock-ups in the past, at some pits. The manager includes the coal stocked each week in his saleable tonnage for that week. If he's a bit generous with the estimate, it shows he's doing better than he really is. So it's always a temptation for a manger to overestimate the coal put to stock. There have been cases when all the coal is cleared from a site and they find that there's still some tonnage shown in the books as being on stock. In one or two cases, the manager has moved on and someone else has had to sort out the deficit.'

'How do they do that?' asked Charlie.

'They have to reduce the pit output declared by a figure each week, and reduce the book stock figure. It's alright if it's a small figure, but if it's many thousands of tons, somebody has to carry the can, and usually gets sacked.'

'This manager will not get his stock coal wrong,' said Cliff. 'He's too wise to make that sort of mistake.'

'He's told his surveyor to reduce the figure down by five per cent each month, so that there'll be no shortfall,' said Pat.

A lorry came from the pit yard and went up the ramped road onto the stockpile. At the end, it tipped its load.

'That looks like one of Cobba's,' said Albert Dunn.

'Yes, it's one of the Home Coal lorries,' said Bert. 'Cobba is delivering the Home Coal during the mornings and then in the afternoons all his lorries are taking power station coal from the bunker onto the stocking site.'

'I wonder how he's pulled that off?' said Albert. 'Somebody's looking after Cobba these days.'

'He'll have got a price per ton, but he'll be able to offer flexibility by having his lorries available on site,' said Pat.

'They're weighing-off each loaded lorry at the land sale, to be sure that they know how much coal is going to stock,' said Bert. 'They're only stocking the surplus power station coal. On Saturday morning all three lorries did a shift stocking coal, but that's not surprising, given the pit had a very good week for tonnage, and they had to do a Saturday morning shift washing coal in the Coal Preparation plant.'

'Cobba was in the Club last night, and he was full of beans,' said Charlie. 'It had been the christening of his granddaughter at the Methodist church, yesterday morning. He thinks the world of that kid.'

'They had a reception for the christening party at the manager's house, after the service,' said Pat.

'I'm sure that Cobba's in the manager's pocket,' said Albert. 'There are too many things happening where they are both involved.'

'But Cobba has also got contacts in other places,' said Cliff. 'I know that he sees the big boss at Region, Mr Pickersgill, at the Yorkshire Welfare meetings. It must be Pickersgill that's agreed to put the money into Martins. If Cobba has played a part in that he's done a good job. Three years ago, none of us dreamed that the pit could be anywhere near as good as it is now. And think about what that's done for the folks of Upthorpe.'

'There is certainly some money being spent in the place now,' said Charlie. 'Every day there seems to be deliveries to the houses – furniture, televisions and all manner of stuff. The women in the Club are flashing new clothes around all the time.'

'If they're getting so much extra money, they ought to be saving some for a rainy day,' said Cliff.

'A few of them might be saving some of their money,' said Charlie, 'but Upthorpe folk have never been good at saving for a rainy day.'

'I'll bet Cobba had got some stacked away,' said Albert. 'He's always been tight with his money, and he's got his finger in a lot of pies.' Nobody in the Enclosure disagreed.

'I wonder why they're not using big dump trucks to take the coal onto the stocking site?' asked Cliff. 'It's alright for Cobba's lorries now, in the summer, but it'll be a different story in the winter, when it's wet or icy.'

'There's an answer to that,' replied Bert. 'They designed the power station bunker to take normal lorries or railway wagons. The dump trucks are too wide and too tall to go under the bunker to load, so they'll have to use lorries. The Home Coal lorries only take about five tons. They could hire bigger ones, but I suppose Cobba's men are on site, so he can fit in with the demand.'

'His men are staying on overtime during the evenings, on some nights,' said Bert.

★

The Enclosure team stayed at the stocking site for over an hour, watching the lorries tipping the coal and a bulldozer levelling off the stockpile.

'It's a bloody bad sign, seeing all that coal being stocked,' said Albert. 'I wonder if it will ever get picked up and burnt.'

'Stocking has happened before,' said Pat. 'It will get picked up if we have a bad winter, and it might be needed when they've closed some of the pits that are running out of reserves.'

'I heard that they're now proposing to close some pits that are losing a lot of money, even if they have plenty of reserves to go at,' said Cliff.

'That'll cause some problems with the unions,' said Albert. 'I can't see the Yorkshire NUM standing for that. They'll be thinking about an overtime ban, or a strike, before long.'

'Don't be so sure about that, Albert,' said Charlie. 'They were talking in the Club about a pit, near Wakefield, that was put forward for closure a few weeks ago. The Yorkshire NUM went to the pit to tell the men to reject closure and say that they'd be backed by the local union. The men told them to bugger off, because they wanted the pit closed so that they could have the redundancy money.'

'You have to remember that a fellow who has never had any money spare in his pocket is going to be tempted by the offer of a lump sum and a chance to get out of the pit,' said Cliff.

'Yes, and the management know this, and they know how much to play that card,' said Albert.

Thursday 18 May 1967

Roy was having a meeting with his management team, to go through the detailed plans for the final shears on the Fuston face and the support system to be used. There were only two weeks to go before the date for the predicted finishing position. Detailed support plans, provided by the Surveyor, were on display. After the plans had been scrutinised, Roy asked for any comments.

'I'm puzzled that you're proposing to use weld mesh over the supports for the last six shears, Boss,' said Jim Lord. 'It's so difficult to get the mesh into place on the coalface and it slows down the operations. With the rock roof, I wonder if we need it on the Fuston face?'

'I hear what you say, Jim, and the Fuston face is indeed very different from the Benton seam faces,' replied Roy. 'But you'll see that I'm proposing that we try and get a thick wooden prop set up to the weld mesh, behind the powered supports, before we start to salvage them. Hopefully this will hold the roof up, so that we have enough room to get the wooden chocks in as soon as each support is withdrawn.'

'I understand that, Boss,' replied Jim. 'But you are trying to hold up more roof than we did on the Benton face. Might that tempt the roof to put its foot down?'

'I've discussed this with the Regional strata control team. They've calculated how much resistance this extra wooden prop and the wooden chocks will give, in place of the powered supports. They concluded that we cannot do any more than shown on this plan. The trouble is, Jim, we do not get a second chance. If we haven't got enough support in to hold the roof after the powered supports are withdrawn, the coalface might close up on us. If it does that before we've completed the salvage, we're knackered. I'm trying to design a system that reduces that risk to the minimum.'

'I've got the majority of the chock pieces stacked ready, underground, Boss,' said George.

'And when I look at them I think there's enough timber there to hold the sky up. You'll be in charge of the salvage, Jim. Just work to this plan and keep your fingers crossed.'

'I shall be doing that, George,' replied Jim. 'But time is also an important factor; the longer it takes us to salvage the powered supports, the greater the risk of the coalface sitting down on us.'

'I accept that, Jim,' replied Roy. 'We need to make sure that we reduce the time factor to the minimum, by planning to operate continuously. What I want us to do now is to go through the manpower plan, to see that we have enough strength through the twenty-four hours, so that no part of the process stops.'

★

The team spent the next hour checking the number of men to be deployed to each position to cover the total operation. They then went through the supervision, by all departments, of the different operations throughout the twenty-four hours. There were some changes to the original proposals to ensure that there would be equable senior staff supervision on all shifts.

'Is there anything we've missed?' asked Roy. There was general agreement that everything had been covered. Roy then turned to the Surveyor.

'Right, I want all this putting on paper, including the men's names, and we'll have that on display in various places at the pit. I want everyone to know what we're trying to do. I also want another plan, which shows what is achieved on each shift. You'll have to think about this,' he said to the Surveyor. 'We need to see where each powered support is at the end of each shift. I want these plans to be on show around the pit and they'll need to be updated each shift.'

'That's a good idea, Boss,' said George. 'We want the rest of the pit to look after themselves for a week or two, while we're concentrating on this job.'

'I am sure they will not let us down,' said Roy.

★

Roy Dobson went home that night with his mind full of the detailed plans that had been agreed. Just before bedtime, in answer to quizzical looks from his wife, he described to Helen what had happened at the meeting, including lots of details that had been agreed and how it was to be monitored. She asked a few questions and was impressed that Roy was confiding to her his serious thoughts on the plan, and its risks. It was a new approach by him; he was usually reluctant to talk at length about the pit.

'I feel a bit like an army commander, who has made elaborate plans for a major battle,' said Roy after a while. 'The officers in the field have been briefed on what they have to do, and all the soldiers have been identified. The equipment is in place and the plans will be explained so that everyone is in the picture. The whole pit will see how the battle progresses, with the bulletins each shift. I don't think I can do anything else.'

'Oh yes, there is one thing you've forgotten,' said Helen. 'If you are Napoleon, and I think you could be, you have one last thing to do before the battle.'

'What's that?' asked Roy, with a puzzled look on his face.

'You must visit Josephine and use all your manly skills to show her your love. You must leave her physically satisfied, with memories of passion that will last her throughout the time of the battle.'

She stood up and turned towards the stairs. 'I will see you in bed later, where you can complete your battle plan.' Helen Dobson went off to say her prayers. Roy wondered if he was up to his final challenge for the day.

Friday 19 May 1967

'Dad, can I have a word with you?' Sandra wanted to talk to her dad before he went out to a Council meeting.

'Sure. What is it, Sandra?' replied Cobba.

'Terry's dad rang him last night and suggested that we join them when they go on holiday to Penzance in September. He said they would pay for us and they thought it would be good for Amy-Louise to go to the seaside. They've obviously thought about it, because they said that they would babysit so that Terry and me could go out on a night, after dinner. They also said that the hotel is one that they've stayed in before and they're used to having young children.'

'So what's the problem?' asked Cobba.

'I'm not sure I can stand a week with Terry's mum, and I don't want to leave you on your own with David,' replied Sandra.

'Don't worry about me and David. If it's in September, David will be up to his eyes in football and we can sort things out here. What does Terry think?'

'Oh, he's all in favour of it, especially as his Dad is footing the bill.'

'Well, there you are then,' said Cobba. 'You go and enjoy yourself, and help to spend a bit of your father-in-law's money. Amy-Louise might be walking by then and she won't be put off by being in a hotel. She'll use that smile of hers to charm the other visitors and the hotel staff.'

'Ok then,' replied Sandra. 'I wasn't worried about Amy-Louise, she'll take it in her stride. It's how I can cope for a week with Mrs Lacey that was bothering me. I'll have to get Terry to concentrate on his mother, while I concentrate on his dad and Amy-Louise. Thanks, Dad. I'll start to make plans, then.'

'You do that, Sandra,' said Cobba, as he went off to his council meeting.

Chapter 26

Friday 9 June 1967

The Enclosure was in session.

'They're starting to take the last shears off the Fuston face today,' said Charlie. 'The lads were saying that they're just over a week later than they planned, but they still hope to have the face changeover done so that they can start the Fuston Two face by the end of July.'

'They'll be working the Benton faces flat out now, to get the tonnage as high as possible. All the tonnage has to come from the Benton seam,' said Cliff.

'They've started up Benton 56s face again, to get the last coal from there,' said Charlie. 'They say that most men at the pit are not keen to go back to hand-filling, now they've got used to driving machines and turning handles on supports, rather than swinging shovels.'

'That's bound to happen,' said Albert. 'All this mechanisation will breed a crop of weak-armed miners. In my day miners were real men. They were physically fit and proud of it.'

'Yes, but the lads at Martins have picked up other skills now,' said Cliff. 'They tell me that some of them can make these machines talk and make coal-getting look easy and they've all had to learn how to help with the engineering systems at the pit. I say good luck to them. Miners have always been adaptable to new mining practices, from the earliest days of the coal industry.'

'That's true,' said Albert. 'But look what good it's done them. The mine owners and the government have always forgotten about these skills, because they have no idea what goes on down the pit. They've never paid miners what they're worth because they never knew how men had to work underground. When politicians and VIPs have a visit underground the management always lays it on so that they only see the good bits. And they only stay underground for a couple of hours. It's different if you have to work eight hours underground.'

'You have a point there, Albert,' replied Cliff. 'But I think things might be changing. You can't put this manager in the same class as some of the old managers.'

'They say that he's planned this face changeover right down to the last detail,' said Charlie. 'Everybody at the pit is talking about it.'

'I understand that there are plans already up in the baths, in the lamp room on the surface, and also underground, in the pit bottom, showing the names of every man and what he'll be doing on this changeover,' said Charlie.

'Not only that, but the Surveyor has to provide an update at the end of each shift showing where every powered support is. These charts will be posted up so that everyone at the pit can see what progress is being made,' said Pat.

'The manager has certainly given this job top priority,' said Cliff.

'I'm not surprised,' said Albert. 'This bloody Fuston seam has caused all sorts of problems in the past, at other pits. If that rock roof decides to put its foot down, nothing can stop it.'

★

Roy was underground on the Fuston coalface, watching the operation of laying lengths of weld mesh over the powered supports and connecting each length of weld mesh to the next one. Jim Lord was supervising the work. His method was to run several lengths of weld mesh down the panzer conveyor to where they were needed. He then stopped the conveyor and had the men in pairs fixing the weld mesh and pulling the supports over.

'It might seem slower to stop the conveyor to do this job, Boss,' Jim said to Roy, when he joined him on the coalface, 'but we have found that it's actually quicker, and a lot safer. We should be able to complete one shear in the shift and leave it ready for the next shift to start on the next shear.'

'D'you think that it'll take six shifts to do these last six shears, Jim?' asked Roy.

'I do, Boss. I shall be happy if we can get this face set up for salvage in six shifts.'

'Well, I'm keen that you should be here when the last shear is taken, to supervise installing the wooden props behind the powered supports. It'll be a tricky job, but I feel it's the one aspect that might help to reduce the risk of major strata control problems. Will you do that, Jim?' concluded Roy.

'Yes, you can leave that to me, Boss,' replied Jim. 'It might be on the nightshift tomorrow, or it could be the following dayshift. Whichever it is, you can rely on me being here.'

★

Roy was sure that Jim was beginning to be an important member of the management team. He could certainly be trusted to be present when his supervision was required. Roy went through the coalface and saw that the conditions were good for a salvage operation. He'd seen the thousands of hardwood pieces that George had stacked near the coalface, ready to set when the powered supports were withdrawn. He then went onto the Fuston Two face-heading. It was in good condition and all the equipment, except the powered supports, was installed for the face to start production. He went out of the pit satisfied that everything was in place for the face changeover. This would be the most important job at the pit for this year.

★

Roy rang Reg Jenkins and gave him the up-to-date position. Reg made no comment, but wished him good luck. Martins Main would now be highlighted in the regional results, as it would be producing significantly lower tonnages than it had done throughout the year. The pressure would be on, but Roy was confident that his management team, and the men at the pit, would not let him down.

Monday 12 June 1967

Jim Lord was on the coalface. He could see that the weld mesh was over to the back of the supports and down to the floor. The shearer had taken the last shear off and the panzer conveyor had been rammed over to the solid coal. The task now was to move the powered supports over by about one foot and install a wooden prop behind each support, between the floor and the weld mesh, at roof level. Jim had organised the wooden props to be run down the coalface and placed in front of each powered support. Now he had the job of organising the setting of the wooden supports. One man summed up the problem to him.

'How the bloody hell are we expected to get behind the chocks to set the wooden props, Boss. We'll have to be a contortionist to do that.'

'I'll show you,' said Jim. He'd been reviewing the options on the best way to do this task. 'We need to get these wooden props behind the powered supports. They don't need to go directly behind the centre of the powered supports, so we'll do it this way.' He wriggled his body between the first two supports and fed the wooden prop over the connecting hydraulic hoses. He then raked the loose dirt from the floor and set up the wooden prop with a wooden pad on top of it and tapped it with a hammer until it was firm, but not tight. 'There, you can see how to get the wooden props into place. As soon as we've withdrawn the powered support, you'll have room to get in and hammer up the wooden prop until it's tight to the roof. Have you got that?'

'Yes, Boss,' replied the workman. 'I hadn't thought of doing it that way. We can sort these wooden props out now.' The other men who'd been watching nodded in agreement.'

'Right, I want two of you to go down the coalface, setting these wooden props,' said Jim. 'It's a bit tight getting between the chocks, so you two go on that job.' Jim pointed to the two thinnest workmen in the team. 'The other three, stay with me and we'll make a start with salvaging the first powered support. This'll be the difficult one, as there's not really enough room to swing it round for transport through the coalface.'

They set up a ram to pull the powered support forward, but it was still wedged between the supports on either side.

'We'll have to jack it up and pull the front over the panzer conveyor,' said Jim. 'It's only this first support that'll be a problem.'

It took a further half an hour to get the support forward over the panzer conveyor and then swing it round into the track for it to be hauled through the coalface. They connected the haulage rope to the support and spoke to the man who was driving the haulage engine at the end of the coalface.

'You travel through the face with the support, and stop the haulage engine if the support looks like getting fast on any obstruction,' said Jim to one of the men. 'When you've got the support into the roadway, leave it to the men there to load it up ready for transport out of the pit. You crawl back through the coalface, dragging out the haulage rope. We'll make a start on getting the next support out. We'll get that out before we start setting the wooden chocks, so that we have room to swing it.'

The second support was lowered-off, pulled forward and swung around, ready for hauling through the coalface before the man returned with the haulage rope. One of the workmen hammered up the wooden props, that had been set to the roof, until they were vertical and absolutely solid tight.

'Now for the big job,' said Jim. 'We need to set the wooden chocks in the space where the first powered support was set.'

Jim had the floor cleaned up so that the hardwood chock pieces were set level. There was just room to get two wooden chocks set from the panzer conveyor to the position where the wooden prop had been set. Each wooden chock had thirty-four pieces, each six-inch by six-inch square and three foot long. They were run down the panzer conveyor and passed to one man who put them in position. Thin wooden wedges were then driven in to make sure that the chock wood was set tight to the roof.

'Bloody hell, Boss, it's like a timber yard,' said one of the men. 'Is it necessary to set all these chocks?'

'It is if you want the roof to hold until we've withdrawn the last powered support. All these wooden chocks are our insurance policy, to avoid us being chased-off the coalface with a major weight.'

'I understand that, Boss,' the workman replied, 'but look how long it's taken us. We must have been well over half an hour setting these first two wooden chocks.'

'Don't worry about that,' said Jim. 'You'll get faster as we go forward.'

★

The second powered support had started its journey through the coalface when they started to withdraw the third. When it was turned into position they started setting the next two wooden chocks. Jim kept his eye on his watch and worked out that they were already withdrawing the powered supports at the rate of one per hour. If that converted into twenty supports per day, that would mean that all the supports would be withdrawn in eleven days. He was sure that Roy Dobson would settle for that timescale. He was also sure that if there were other parts of the system that hit snags, Roy would sort them out.

★

At the end of the shift, four powered supports had been withdrawn and were in the roadway at the end of the coalface; three supports had started their journey to the surface; wooden chocks had been set in place of the first three powered supports and the fifth support was being turned ready for hauling through the coalface. Jim decided to stay on and supervise the next shift to guide them on the method of salvage and the way of setting the wooden chocks. One slight snag was that the use of the wooden chock pieces was faster than had been anticipated, so Jim had to arrange additional men transporting the chock pieces from the underground stockpile to the coalface.

★

Jim spoke to Roy and gave him a full report on the progress for the shift.

'You've made a good start, Jim. Do you think the other shifts will be able to achieve a similar result?'

'I'm staying on for an hour or two, to make sure that the afternoonshift understands what to do,' replied Jim. 'And I'll come back to see the nightshift and brief them. If I've any doubts I'll go back underground tonight, to have an hour or two with them.'

'That shouldn't be necessary, Jim, but I'll leave it to you. I'll see how the production line copes with the supports when they get to the surface.'

'I've set my sights on twenty salvaged supports each day, from now on, Boss,' added Jim as a final comment.

'If you can achieve that, then we'll have cracked it,' said Roy, who was impressed by Jim's analysis of the possibilities. He decided to keep that forecast to himself, though, and not pass it on the Reg Jenkins.

★

Roy rang Helen and informed her that he would be late home, as he wanted to see the powered supports going through the production line in the fitting shop. The first powered support came to the surface at half past four. Roy went down to the fitting shop and was surprised to see little activity. He could only conclude that they'd not anticipated the arrival until much later in the day, or even before the next morning. He burst into the Mechanical Engineer's office and found the engineer there, with his deputy engineers, discussing some other technical issue.

'I don't want to worry you chaps, but you have powered supports from the Fuston seam waiting for your attention in the fitting shop. I've just come from there and there doesn't seem to be anyone there to deal with them. So you'd better get your glad rags on and start the production line.'

'No one let us know that they were on their way,' said the Mechanical Engineer, defensively.

'They're still underground, making sure that the flow of salvaged supports keeps going. You're going to look mighty embarrassed if there's a queue of supports on the surface, waiting for you to sort them out. After all the planning that we've done, you've taken your eye off the ball just when it was needed to get things moving to a good start.'

Roy was seething, but he didn't want to lose his temper openly.

'We'll get men onto the job straightaway, Mr Dobson,' said the Engineer. 'Men have been trained on all aspects of the production line work, so we'll get them moving.'

'I'll come back down in an hour, to see what progress is being made,' said Roy.

★

When Roy returned to the fitting shop, the first powered support was in position for dismantling and there were men and engineers working on it like bees around a honeypot.

The pins were being withdrawn and the legs released. There was no doubt that they had the right tools available, and within an hour the first support was moved forward into position to have the new hydraulic legs installed. The men then split into two teams: one team to dismantle the second powered support, while the other team started to install the upgraded hydraulic legs and re-assemble the canopy. When Roy left the fitting shop, the first powered support was nearly ready to go to its final position to have the hydraulic hoses coupled-up and the support tested under load. He left instructions that the upgraded powered support was to be sent underground as soon as possible, so that it arrived at the Fuston Two coalface ready for the installation team on the following dayshift. He was fairly confident that the engineering team had been caught with their trousers down, but that they were organised to carry out the upgrading work on the powered supports at a rate that would keep pace with the salvage operations.

★

Roy reviewed the output figures, now that there was no coal from the Fuston seam. Even with good performances by the two mechanised coalfaces in the Benton seam, the daily output would be just over three thousand tons. Clearly Martins would be conspicuous at Region, with such a reduction from its recent tonnages. He hoped that Jim's projections for the salvage operations would be proved correct.

★

When he arrived home, Roy had his warmed-up dinner. Having relaxed for half an hour, he was on the point of ringing the pit, to get the afternoonshift reports for the production faces and the salvage operation on the Fuston face, when Helen spoke to him.

'Before you get immersed in the pit again, I want to remind you that we have an important engagement here, on Saturday night. You may have forgotten about it, so I'm reminding you now so that in your detailed planning you can ensure that you have four hours with someone else covering the pit.'

'Yes, I had forgotten,' admitted Roy. He paused. 'What's happening on Saturday night?' he asked tentatively.

'I suspected that you'd forgotten. We're having James and Gwen Folds to dinner,' replied Helen. 'There'll only be the four of us and I'll organise all the food. All you have to do is open the wine and be the perfect host.'

'Oh, yes, I remember now,' said Roy, with a note of relief in his voice.

'We're having them early as there will be a few goodbye events at the church, before they leave in August. They have been a wonderful couple, and so helpful and sincere in their work at the church and in the community. I'm going to miss them very much.'

'Who's coming to take their place?' asked Roy.

'I'm told that it's a young man who has just completed his training as a Methodist Minister. He's not married, so he'll be a complete contrast to James.'

'I'll organise for Jim Lord to look after the pit on Saturday night. There'll be work going on through the weekend on the Fuston face changeover, but it should be straightforward because we've got off to a good start.'

'That's fine,' said Helen with a smile. 'I've always thought that you weren't indispensable.'

Friday 16 June 1967

The Enclosure was in session.

'It's a completely changed situation, now,' said Bert. 'They're recovering coal from the stocking ground to meet the power station orders. They've installed a short conveyor so that they can feed the coal straight into the power station coal bunker, without it going through the Coal Preparation plant. They've also reduced the hours of washing on the nightshift.'

'Is the output down so much, then?' asked Charlie.

'I understand that they're only producing about three thousand tons per day,' said Bert. 'They were producing well over four thousand tons per day when the Fuston face was working.'

'They've had five days now, on the salvage operations,' said Cliff. 'I wonder how that's making progress?'

'The lads in the Club said it was going OK, last night,' said Charlie. 'But they're all amazed at how much timber they're setting, where the powered supports have been.'

'That's the manager playing it safe,' said Cliff.

'I have the position as it was this morning, at the end of the nightshift,' said Pat. He took a piece of paper out of his pocket and the Enclosure was impressed by this stop press news. 'They'd withdrawn fifty-four supports from the old face and installed thirty-nine on the new face, and there were four supports available for immediate installation first thing this morning.'

'That means that they're about a quarter of the way through the job,' said Cliff. 'That's pretty good progress.'

'They're staffed-up to keep working through the weekend,' said Charlie.

'Is it Cobba's lorries that are picking up the coal from the stocking ground?' asked Albert. 'Cobba will be laughing all the way to the bank if he gets paid for putting the stock down one week and then paid again for picking it up the week after.'

'No, Cobba isn't involved in the pick-up,' said Bert. 'They've brought another team in, and they have bigger lorries, which can move twelve tons each load. The lads were saying that they think there might be a change in policy, as they're having extra trains on each week now, for the power station coal.'

'It might be the holidays at some other pits,' said Cliff. 'It shows that Martins coal is a popular product.'

A large car turned into Martins Lane, moving at speed towards the pit gates.

'There goes the Welsh dragon,' said Albert. 'I wonder what he wants?'

'Probably come for some lunch,' said Charlie, with a laugh.

★

The presumption that Roy Jenkins had come for lunch was partially right. He'd rung Roy and asked to come over and have a chat with him, over a sandwich lunch. Roy had agreed, although this would stop him going underground to see the state of the Fuston face salvage operations. When they were having their sandwiches, Reg Jenkins explained what he wanted to discuss.

'Pickersgill has asked me to put a proposition to you, that has come out of some meetings he had in London recently. Apparently, the National Board feel that success stories are not being publicised enough in the industry. They want the courses for managers at the Staff College to concentrate on actual successes within the industry, instead of spending all their time on management theories and the latest consultant's reports on management styles. He said that he could provide a good example of a success story, but he didn't disclose which pit it was.'

'I've only been to one short course at the Staff College, when I was an undermanager,' said Roy. 'I got the impression that the tutors there were all semi-academics.'

'That's the bloody trouble,' said Reg. 'The Minister for Power in the government is always complaining about the lack of productivity in the industry. He pushes the National Board to call in consultants from America, or universities, and that's it. Nobody gets to know where we're successful, and they're not encouraged to follow those examples.'

'What does Mr Pickersgill want me to do?' asked Roy.

'He wants you to prepare a presentation about your time at Martins. It needs to have lots of visual aids, and last about forty-five minutes. You need to show what the pit was doing when you came, and spell out the issues that had to be addressed. You can then work your way forward, describing the actions that have been taken and how they were organised. He particularly wants you to show how each action impacted on the finances of the pit.'

'What about the industrial relations side?' asked Roy, who was wondering how he could cover his relations with Cobba, and the effect that that relationship had had on the performance at the pit.

'You can say that the union was a problem when you came, but that you've worked with them and they can now see the benefit of a successful pit giving higher earnings for the labour force. Pickersgill is keen that you describe how Martins dealt with the winding enginemen's dispute.'

'This is a challenge,' said Roy. 'What sort of timescale is Mr Pickersgill setting? All my attention is focussed on the pit at the moment. I want to get this Fuston changeover done so that the pit can get back to full capacity. Then we'll have the face-to-face changeover in the Benton seam, which we hope to start in the holiday week.'

'I don't think he'll want to wait for that length of time,' replied Reg. 'What you need to do is spend a bit of time each day getting the headings down. You can then get the Surveyor preparing slides and let Jeff Briggs start working on the financial figures.'

'Has he got a date for the presentation at the Staff College?' asked Roy, who was getting more worried about the proposition as Reg Jenkins provided more information.

'His idea is to let you give the presentation to him first, so that he can advise on any changes that he thinks are necessary. When he's satisfied, he'll offer it to the Staff College.'

'Good grief,' said Roy. 'It gets worse and worse. What a prospect, giving a presentation to Mr Pickersgill and then, if he's satisfied, having to give it at the Staff College!'

'You'll be alright at the Staff College, because I think Pickersgill will make sure he's there with you. He has strong views about how that place should be run, and this will be his way of putting one over on the college Principal. He has a very high opinion of himself, apparently, and Pickersgill would like to bring him down a peg or two.'

'Mr Pickersgill is very clever at using other people to push forward his ideas,' said Roy. 'I seem to get into the firing line quite a bit.'

'Don't complain, it's better to be firing bullets for him, than having him firing bullets at you. There are a few colliery managers in this region who would willingly change pits to be in your position!'

Roy agreed with that statement, so he decided to take a positive approach to the proposal.

'I'll do as you suggest, Mr Jenkins, and make a start straightaway, laying out the topics to be raised. If you agree, I would welcome your comments on my ideas, as soon as we have them listed.'

'I'll certainly help, if I can,' replied Reg Jenkins. 'But you need to remember that Pickersgill is a shrewd fellow and he's likely to have a clear idea in his mind of where he wants the emphasis placing in your presentation. So you'll have to be ready to accept some changes.'

'I expect him to want changes,' said Roy. His mind was working on how he would approach the subject matter.

'If Pickersgill is happy about the presentation, I wouldn't put it past him to arrange for one or two of the Board members to be present at the Staff College presentation.'

'Oh, don't say that!' exclaimed Roy. 'You'll make me even more nervous than I am already.'

★

When Reg Jenkins left the pit, Roy immediately called the Surveyor and Jeff Briggs into his office. He explained what had to be done, and that the matter had to be treated as confidential. It would be the three of them who would meet for an hour each day to agree what would be in the presentation, and who would do what. Jeff Briggs would handle all the secretarial side as well as the financial figures, and Roy would arrange a typist to work exclusively for him, who had no other responsibilities at the pit. In the next half-hour they listed twelve topics, in chronological order, that should form the main part of the presentation. They agreed to meet tomorrow, for an hour, to study the financial figures to be used to describe the state of the pit when Roy took over as manager. He was warming to the task, and even a belt breakage on 58s coalface, that cost an hour's delay, did not depress him. He was satisfied that the progress on the Fuston seam salvage was encouraging, as the dayshift had salvaged seven more powered supports in the shift.

★

That night Roy discussed with Helen what Mr Pickersgill was proposing, and how he could well do without the extra work at the present time.

'I'm aware, Roy, that Mr Pickersgill comes up with ideas for other people to carry out and that they initially might seem strange, but they turn out to be inspirational. I was very sceptical of his idea for the presentation to Frank and Hazel Ackroyd, but in the end it was a brilliant success.'

'That was because of a certain Mrs Helen Dobson, who did it just right,' said Roy.

'But who asked Helen Dobson to take on the job?' replied Helen. 'And that is why he's asked you to do this presentation: he knows that you will do it right, because you know what has happened at Martins, and why the decisions for change have been made. You are a privileged man, Roy Dobson. You have a mentor and senior manager who is always pushing you to achieve higher performances from yourself and your pit.'

Helen paused and then added another sentence. 'And he knows that you have a wife who will ensure that you will deliver the goods.' She went over to him and gave him a big kiss and hug.

Saturday 17 June 1967

As planned, Roy met with Jeff Briggs and the Surveyor, and they had an hour sorting out the financial figures that were pertinent when Roy started at the pit. They decided to have a slide that showed how many disputes there had been during the three months before Roy took over as Manager, how much output had been lost, and the impact the disputes had made on the finances.

'There'll be no difficulty in painting a fairly desperate financial picture of the pit before you arrived,' said Jeff. 'I've been looking back at the figures, and I'm amazed that you accepted the job!'

'I have to admit that I never expected to be offered it,' replied Roy. 'And I certainly had no idea how bad the financial results were.'

'Have you decided what your main themes will be?' asked the Surveyor.

'I think there should be four main themes. Firstly there'll be the restructuring of the pit, to concentrate the workings; secondly we need to make the case for the Central Conveying Scheme and its impact on the pit's performance; then there's the mechanisation programme, which would not have been effective without the other changes; and finally I'll draft a section on industrial relations, explaining how better performance and better wages helped to reduce the disputes and achieve better cooperation with the unions.'

'There is talk at the pit that Cobba is far more positive than he used to be, Boss,' said Jeff Briggs. 'And he certainly keeps Jimmy Bell from causing problems like he used to do.'

'That's right, Jeff,' replied Roy, wanting to avoid any further discussion on this subject. 'But Cobba knows the deal, as far as Martins is concerned. I have no doubt that he's picked up the same story from Mr Pickersgill as he's been told by me. The deal is that if you deliver the goods, then you'll get more investment. It's as simple as that. Cobba is not against success in principle. He shows that with the way he gets the Club to operate, and he has the same approach to the Home Coal scheme. I'll cover this in the section on industrial relations.'

They then agreed what overhead projector slides should be prepared, and they decided to meet at eight o'clock on Monday morning to prepare the next section.

★

When James Fold's car drew up in the drive, Helen went out to meet their guests. It was a fine, warm, summer evening and they walked around the garden admiring the vegetables and fruit before entering the house.

'It's a fine garden,' said James. 'There's a lot of expertise on show; you must have a good gardener.'

'He is a fine gardener, and you'll be able to sample his fruit and vegetables in the meal, tonight,' replied Helen. 'I do feel so guilty about tonight, though,' she added.

'Why's that?' asked Gwen Folds.

'Well, here we are, and it's the first time we've invited you to have dinner with us, and you'll be leaving in a few weeks,' said Helen.

'But we've been here when you've entertained the christening parties. They were excellent occasions.'

'Yes, but tonight there will be just the four of us, and we'll be able to talk freely about things.' Her guests didn't ask for elucidation on what they were to talk about.

★

The menu was a simple, three-course meal, but it was all made from the garden produce. The starter was a vegetable soup, with a tomato base, using tomatoes from the greenhouse; the main course was chicken in a white sauce with carrots, potatoes, peas and broad beans; and the sweet was a choice of strawberries or raspberries, with fresh cream.

'That was a wonderful meal, Helen,' said Gwen afterwards. 'You can compliment your gardener on his produce. I've never tasted food so fresh. You must find the gardener a great asset.'

'He is there to ensure that the colliery manager can give his total attention to the pit,' said Helen. 'I don't think Roy has ever been noted for his horticultural skills – not according to his mother, anyway. He doesn't know the difference between a flower plant and a weed. When we were in our first house, and Roy had to look after the garden, he laid it down to grass and concrete. I have to say, though, that we are very fortunate to have all the vegetables and fruit from this garden.'

'I suppose there's a similarity between your life and ours,' said James. 'You have to move around to be near your pit.'

'Most managers have a house provided by the British Coal Executive near their pit,' replied Roy. 'Just a few have started to buy their own houses, so that they are on the property ladder, but we haven't opted for that, at this stage.'

'You must find it a challenge to have to up-sticks and move on every five years?' said Helen.

'I suppose it's in the tradition of the early Methodist preachers,' said James. 'John Wesley travelled around and preached to open-air gatherings, before the Methodist churches were built. And, of course, the ministers are only one element of the preaching in the Methodist church, as there are hundreds of local preachers who take the majority of services. Some of these local preachers are real challenges to us ministers, as they are men of great faith and from their working life they bring reality to their message.'

'But the preaching is only one aspect of your work,' said Helen. 'I believe that your major input to the church and this community has been the way you have both related to people and helped them in their lives. I am not in any way belittling your preaching, James, but you will be remembered here by more people than the congregation at the church.'

'Moving on is a shock to the system, and tinged with a lot of sadness,' said Gwen, with a depressed note to her voice. 'We have to tear ourselves away from all the friends we've made, and move into a new situation, where we're often regarded, at first, as strangers and visitors. We have to work hard to develop new relationships and find out who needs us and who will support us.'

'We will miss you very, very much,' said Helen. 'You have been a source of guidance and strength to us all. When I told Peggy Moore that you were leaving, she openly wept. She said she would never have got through that period in hospital, when Gerry was killed, without your help. How do you prepare for your move?'

'When we leave, we review what has happened in that ministry, and we take the experience away as inspiration for the next posting. Our inspiration is all the memories of the great moments, when the spirit of the Living God has been on display,' said James. 'And we have certainly got many memories of those moments at Upthorpe.'

'We, also, will remember your time here, for some amazing evidence of the Spirit at work,' said Helen. 'I will never forget the christening of Tony and Michael at the Sunday school anniversary, and the singing of You'll Never Walk Alone at the end. I get goosepimples every time I think of that. And I have the picture of Tony holding his brother's hand, and then wiping his face with his handkerchief, as the christening water ran down.' She paused and choked before she could continue to speak. 'Do excuse me, it moves me to tears every time I think of that scene.' Helen stood up and left the table with tears streaming down her face.

'I'll go and comfort her,' said Gwen. She left the room and went in search of Helen.

★

'Your wife is a woman of deep faith,' said James. 'We'll miss her very much, as we move on.'

'I am very fortunate to have her as a support at all times,' said Roy.

'There is one thing that I have failed to do, while I've been at Upthorpe,' said James, who wished to change the subject.

'What is that?' asked Roy, who was interested to learn of the failure.

'I have never been underground in a coal mine. And I feel that I'm at a disadvantage with a number of Methodist ministers, some of whom have entered the ministry from the coal industry.'

'Oh well, we can put that right,' said Roy. 'When do you actually leave Upthorpe?'

'We'll be flitting to Birmingham in the second week of August,' replied James.

'Things are a bit hectic, at the moment, at the pit, as we're changing the equipment from one coalface to another in the Fuston seam. That should be finished by the end of July, so if you can spare a day in the first week of August, I'll arrange a visit underground, and I'll try to accompany you myself.'

Roy was pleased to have the chance to give James the opportunity to increase his experience. James took out his diary and selected the Tuesday of that week and wrote it in his diary.

★

When the two ladies returned to the table, with Helen looking calm and her face carrying a new application of lipstick and eye-shadow, Roy decided to mark a change in the conversation.

'We're getting a new recruit at Martins,' he said. 'James has agreed to do a shift at the pit before he leaves Upthorpe. He's going to have an underground visit on the Tuesday of the first week in August.'

'That's something he's always wanted to do,' said Gwen. 'He does seem to have conveniently timed it to avoid a day of packing before our move, though!'

'I plead guilty for that planning,' said Roy. 'I asked him to make it after we've finished the face changeover in the Fuston seam. It will also be an easier trip for him, because if we go to the Fuston coalface he won't have to crawl through a Benton seam face which is only three-feet thick.'

'I'm quite excited about the visit,' said James. 'It should give me some new material for my sermons.'

'Can't you re-use your sermons, when you move to a new church?' asked Roy.

'It's not easy,' replied James. 'Often they seem out of date, when I check them, and rather than updating them, it's sometimes easier to prepare a new one.'

'Some of his colleagues have a different approach,' said Gwen. 'They specialise in using old material and consider it a success if they get several repeats out of one sermon.'

★

Helen and Roy went with James and Gwen, through the hallway and out of the front door, to see them off. All four paused and put off the moment of departure. They stood in the garden and silently watched the evening sunshine filtering through the trees and playing on the flowers and vegetables. It was a peaceful evening scene and a calm finale to a day. But to those there it also seemed to signify the end of an active, deep friendship, that no one wanted to face. No one tried to put their feelings into words. There were hugs all round, and then Gwen and James drove off, with waves of farewell from Helen and Roy. Helen was clearly very sad.

'I'll go and say my prayers, Roy,' she said, when they were back in the house. 'We have so much to be thankful for, from our friendship with Gwen and James. I want to pray for them in their new life in Birmingham. Then I want to pray that their work will be continued by the new minister at Upthorpe.'

Roy realised that his wife was facing the future in the Upthorpe church with some apprehension.

Monday 19 June 1967

Roy met with Jeff Briggs and the Surveyor. Jeff had drafted the text for the review of the state of Martins when Roy had arrived at the pit. The Surveyor had prepared overhead projector slides showing the financial position of the pit, and also the disputes that had affected the pit before Roy arrived. They agreed some revisions of the text, to better reflect the impact of the slides. They then went on to cover the production faces and the way the pit was spread out in three seams, with a large number of men on the haulage systems servicing the coalfaces.

'We have to finish this section with a positive conclusion that there had to be a concentration of the workings and a review of the haulage systems,' said Roy. 'This can lead on to the next section, on the Central Conveying Scheme. We can describe the scheme, and the timing of it, to allow commissioning over the pit holiday week.'

They discussed what needed to be included in the text, and what illustrations of the Central Conveying Scheme would be needed.

'Tomorrow, we'll include the section on the first mechanised coalface, and the good fortune of having a coalface nearly developed when the equipment became available,' said Roy. 'Now, I must get underground to see the progress on the salvage of the Fuston coalface.'

*

Earlier, Jim had explained to Roy, over the telephone from the face, that there was some strata pressure now affecting the operations. Roy wanted to go underground to see how this extra pressure was affecting the salvage of the powered supports, as this was the critical path for the face changeover. It was clear that there had been a reduction in the number of powered supports salvaged on each shift over the weekend. Was the reduction a reflection of the smaller teams working on each shift? Or was it due to a reduction in senior management supervision? Or was it that the men were getting stale, due to working seven days a week without a break? He needed to know the answer to these questions.

★

When he arrived at the coalface, at the end where the first supports had been withdrawn, he could see the impact of the strata forces. The wooden chocks that had been set in place of the powered supports had been crushed until they were reduced to little more than half the height they were when they were set. This meant that the travel way through the coalface was a crawl, whereas it had been walking height when the coalface was working. The men who were feeding the wooden pieces of chock wood onto the panzer conveyor saw Roy looking at the effects.

'Mother Nature is putting her foot down, Boss,' said one of the workmen. 'There was a lot of bloody creaking and cracking, yesterday, at this end of the face, but it's quieter this morning.'

'Yes, I can see the effect that the weighting has had on the wooden chocks,' said Roy, pointing to the squeezed chocks at the start of the coalface.

'It's a crawl, now, on the panzer conveyor, to get through the coalface,' said one of the men. 'While you're crawling through we won't run the conveyor, but you'll need to signal us when you get to the salvage team. They should be nearly ready for another run of wooden chock pieces, any time now.'

'Right, I'll give you a signal of seven when I'm off the panzer conveyor,' replied Roy, as he bent down to crawl through the track to the salvage team. It was a travel way between the solid coal and the wooden chocks, of about two-feet six-inches square, and he could see where the sandstone roof had fractured along the edge of the solid coal. This had been his worst fear. What would be the conditions where the powered supports were being withdrawn? Roy wiggled his way forward as fast as he could, so that the panzer conveyor could be released. The height was too low for him to crawl freely, and as he moved down the coalface he could hear the roof creaking and the wooden chock pieces splintering. For any inexperienced mining person this journey would have created fear and claustrophobia, he thought to himself. When he got to the salvage position, Jim was in charge and greeted Roy with a summary of the position.

'This is going to be a race against both time and the conditions, Boss,' he said. 'As you've seen, the strata pressure is following us along the coalface. The powered supports are yielding, which we can hear from the pinging of the yield valves. So far, none of them has lowered so that they are solid, but we've still got ninety supports to go, before we reach the end.'

'How much progress have you made this morning?' asked Roy.

'This is our third support that's ready to be hauled to the face-end,' replied Jim. A man signalled the haulage rope to pull the support and he set off to follow the support along its journey.

'You can clear the face panzer,' said Roy. 'I said I would give a signal of seven when I got to you.'

'Right, Boss,' said Jim. 'We need the panzer running, to get the chock wood pieces down to set, now. We're doing everything we can, Boss, to set the wooden chocks as tight as possible, to try to hold the roof.'

'The men said that the roof has stopped lowering now, at the face-end where you started the salvage process,' said Roy.

'I'm aware of that, Boss, and it's the best bit of news we've had today. It does give us some hope that things might not get any worse than they are now.'

★

Roy stayed for over an hour and saw the wooden chocks set and then another powered support withdrawn. He followed it through to the end of the face and saw it being loaded on a tram for transport out of the mine. He then went round to the new coalface, where George was supervising the installation of the refurbished powered supports.

'Morning, Boss,' said George. 'How's the salvage job going? We're waiting for refurbished supports to keep us going.'

'I've just left Jim, and it looks as though they might salvage five supports this morning, and that will be about the best we can expect per shift, from now on,' said Roy, who wanted to give a fair report. 'Hopefully, the weight on the coalface will not get any worse, and none of the powered supports will get solid before they're withdrawn. The wooden chocks that we're setting are taking a massive load.'

'Yes, Jim was saying that the support system is doing its job so far,' said George. 'As you can see, the conditions here are very good and we should have no difficulty finishing off the installation very quickly, once the salvage is complete.'

Roy talked to the men, who were confident that the coalface would be very successful, once it was in production. That can't come soon enough, thought Roy.

He went out of the pit and realised that the next seven days were critical with this face-to-face transfer.

Chapter 27

Monday 31 July 1967

Fuston Two coalface started to cut coal today.

Roy had decided not to go underground onto the Fuston coalface on its first production shift. George Turnbull was there and he reported to Roy that they'd completed one shear and the shearer was in-cut ready for the next shift.

★

Roy spent the morning with Jeff Briggs and the Surveyor, going through his presentation. Over the last ten days they'd completed a first draft of the presentation, and Roy had tried to put together a suitable conclusion. He was having great difficulty sorting this out, as he seemed to be repeating parts of the paper.

'What I think it needs, Boss, is a very short paragraph with some slick comments to summarise options that could be tried by other pits. This seems to be the objective of Mr Pickersgill in having the presentation made at the Staff College.'

'Right, that's a good idea, Jeff,' replied Roy. 'We'll now have to put our heads together to find the right words.' It took nearly two hours, and many attempts, before they ended up with an acceptable draft.

'Martins Main had been struggling for years, showing little progress and continued frustration for everyone involved with the pit. It needed a series of shocks, with the introduction of changes. Firstly, the change to concentrate the operations; secondly, it needed a capital project to give the pit additional capacity, and then it needed the introduction of mechanisation to produce the coal with horsepower not musclepower. But finally, and this was probably the most important change, it needed the conversion of everyone at the pit to a new way of thinking. They had to become confident in the belief that Martins Main could be successful, and then they had to recognise that success is sweeter than failure. None of these changes by themselves could be classed as major, but together, along with the new way of thinking at the pit, they have produced dramatic financial returns that could be achieved at other pits.'

'I wonder what Mr Pickersgill will think about that for a conclusion?' said Roy. They agreed to get a draft of the text and the overhead projector slides ready the next day.

★

Roy reported to Reg Jenkins that Fuston Two had started production and that he'd completed the first full draft of his presentation on Martins Main.

'What should my next move be, on the presentation?' he asked.

'Get in touch with Diane straightaway,' replied Reg. 'Pickersgill is going away on holiday in about a week, and I'm sure he'll want to see it before he goes.'

★

An hour later Roy rang Diane. He was dreading giving the presentation to Mr Pickersgill, but he felt that he had to get it over with.

'Diane,' he said. 'Mr Pickersgill gave me a task to prepare a presentation on Martins Main. We've completed the first draft, with suitable illustrations, but I am sure that Mr Pickersgill will want to suggest some revisions. Can you advise me on the next move?'

'He has already mentioned it to me,' replied Diane. 'I'll have a word with him and get back to you.'

'Thank you, Diane,' replied Roy, 'I'll wait to hear from you.' Roy put the 'phone down and realised that his hand was shaking. He was now committed to a new and terrifying experience. In only a short while he found out exactly when that would be.

'He has altered his diary and he wants you to come over to his office at three o'clock on Friday afternoon, to give the presentation. I'll arrange an overhead projector, and I assume you'll bring someone with you to work it.'

'Right, I'll be there,' said Roy. He rang Jeff Briggs and the Surveyor, and arranged that they would have a dry-run in his office tomorrow morning.

★

Roy took his draft copy home and went through it during the evening. He explained to Helen what was planned, and how he was dreading the reaction of Mr Pickersgill.

'I think you should read it out to me,' said Helen. 'I may be more critical than Mr Pickersgill.'

So Roy read through the text and Helen listened. She didn't have the benefit of the overlays, but she got a clear picture of the arguments.

'It sounds very good, to me,' she said. 'The text flows well and you haven't got any tongue-twisters to trip you up. But I would like to bet that Mr Pickersgill will want you to compare the financial results before you started at the pit with the ones you've achieved during the last few months.'

'We deliberately didn't do that,' replied Roy. 'We've illustrated how each of the major changes has contributed to the improved financial results, but decided not to show how much the reduction in the total manpower has affected the finances, as this was a very big figure. I'm under no illusions, Helen, that Mr Pickersgill will have some suggestions to make. I'm certainly not going to argue with him.'

Friday 4 August 1967

Roy was sitting in Diane's office, with Jeff Briggs, well before the three o'clock appointment. He had his copy of the text on his knee and he kept looking at different parts of it to refresh himself with the words. He was also thinking of the state of the pit, in case he was asked about the face-to-face changeover. The Fuston Two coalface was settling down, and for the last two days the pit output had reached four thousand tons. They would be starting the final shears on 58s coalface in the Benton seam in one week, which was just before the pit holiday week. This should allow some progress to be made in that face-to-face transfer during the holiday. Everything at the pit was fitting into a tight schedule.

★

Mr Pickersgill was ready on time, and he had Reg Jenkins with him, to hear the presentation. Roy took a deep breath and commenced speaking and Jeff put the overhead projector slides on the screen at the point they were marked in his text. There were no pauses in the presentation, except when Roy had a drink of water from the glass that Diane had placed on the table. He noticed that from time to time Mr Pickersgill scribbled on a notepad on his knee. Roy read the final paragraph, and felt a sense of relief as he waited for reactions.

'I am very pleased with what you've prepared,' begin Norman Pickersgill. 'And I think that the illustrations provide some startling facts and figures in a visual way. But I do want to sharpen the focus of the arguments, in one or two places.'

'I will be glad to do that, Mr Pickersgill,' said Roy, who was genuinely keen to make any improvements required.

'There are four places that I want you to modify what you say, and I'll be glad if you would comment on these, Reg,' said Mr Pickersgill, turning to Reg Jenkins, who nodded his willingness to help.

'Firstly, I want you to make the case that the winders' dispute gave you an opportunity to take on the winding enginemen and to prove that they were not capable of holding the pit to ransom. You should also say that you got support from Region to take a very positive approach. Secondly, I want you to quantify what impact the general reduction of manpower at the pit has made on the financial results. Work out what the reduction in profit would have been had you kept the manpower at a fixed level instead of taking positive action to reduce it. Thirdly, I want you to develop the argument that the attitudes of the union officials was changed by giving them defined jobs to do and responsibilities for communications to the manpower. You might get asked whether the union men were rewarded for this additional responsibility, and you can say that the union officials were paid the appropriate rate for the work they did. You can add that they benefited from the men having higher wages and being less likely to raise issues that led to disputes. Do you agree with my comments, Reg?'

'Yes, I do, Mr Pickersgill,' replied Reg Jenkins. 'I think it covers the changes at Martins very well. There are other things that could be added, but I think the presentation is long enough.'

'Finally,' said Mr Pickersgill, 'I like your concluding paragraph, but I think it needs an additional sentence. You should add, 'There must be other pits in the British Coal industry that could be subject to similar changes to Martins Main, and could be expected to improve their results in the same way."

'We'll work on the changes you've suggested, Sir,' said Roy. 'We did identify the benefits from the reduction in the overall manpower at the pit, but we were shocked by the size of the impact this had on the finances.'

'That is exactly why I want you to identify this particular financial result. There are many pits that don't face up to their realistic manpower requirements: they hang on to men for comfort in emergencies, without realising how much it's costing them. That was one of your good moves at Martins – to reduce the manpower in anticipation of the benefits of the investments made in the pit.'

'We'll complete the revisions to the text and the illustrations in the next few days,' said Roy. 'Do you want me to send a copy to your office?'

'Yes, please,' replied Norman Pickersgill. 'And I want the illustrations converted from the overhead transparencies into slides, which will be more professional for the presentation at the Staff College. Now that I can see what's available, I will probably arrange a date for the official presentation there, before I go on holiday.'

'I would like to be there on that occasion, if it was possible,' put in Reg Jenkins.

'That will certainly be the case, Reg. We will both be there, as we've both had a little to do with the changes at Martins.'

As the men packed up their papers and overlays, Mr Pickersgill commented that he had noticed that Martins was now showing daily tonnages back up to the right level.

★

As they drove back to the pit, Roy and Jeff discussed the meeting at Region. The story of Martins over the last three-and-a-half years was a good story, and Roy thought they'd represented it fairly. He also emphasised that everyone at Martins and in Upthorpe had benefited from the success of the pit.

★

When Roy got home that evening he described to Helen Mr Pickersgill's reaction, and his intention to get a date in the calendar for the Staff College presentation. Every time he thought of that commitment his heart missed a beat. It would be a major event in his career, to be on display, there, explaining the success of his pit. He was bound to get asked some searching questions, and he would have to ensure that his answers satisfied Mr Pickersgill and Mr Jenkins, as well as the questioners.

Helen gave him a smile, which showed how much she was proud of her husband and his talents. As it was Saturday tomorrow, and the weather forecast was good, she suggested that they go off for an afternoon to the Yorkshire Dales, with the boys. She reminded Roy that he'd been underground at the pit during the last four weekends, and so he needed a break.

Roy didn't disagree, and he made arrangements for Jim Lord to cover the pit.

Monday 7 August 1967

The Enclosure was in session. It was a bright, summer day, with a gentle breeze that brought the sounds of the operations over to the team as they gazed towards the mine. Against the hum of the mine fan they could hear the pulsing of the steam from the winding engines and the thump of the pit tubs as they were pushed into the cages.

'It's the holiday Bull week, this week,' said Charlie. 'I suppose they'll be trying to produce a record output, to get their money up for the holidays.'

'They've extra trains on this week, for the power station coal,' said Bert.

'They've got the Fuston Two coalface going now, so they should be filling the shafts with coal,' said Cliff.

'They'll be taking the final shears off the Benton 58s face later this week, and getting it ready for salvage and transfer to 60s face,' said Charlie. 'They've arranged some men to work over the holiday week to start the face-to-face transfer.'

'That means they'll need more coal from the Fuston face,' said Cliff.

'There was no problem getting extra coal from the Fuston face when they did the last Benton seam face-to-face transfer,' said Charlie. 'The lads were talking about the powered supports having up-rated hydraulic legs on the Fuston Two face, and they think there should be no trouble with the roof conditions now. They were saying it should be a coal factory.'

'The manager's taking the parson from the Methodist church down the pit tomorrow,' said Pat.

'Why's that?' asked Albert. 'Is the manager trying to organise some divine help for the pit?' he added, with a laugh.

'No, it's not that,' replied Pat. 'He's leaving Upthorpe, and going to some churches in Birmingham, in a few weeks' time, and he's never been down a coal mine. So he wants to get a pit visit in while he has the chance.'

'I understand that he's done some very good work, while he's been in Upthorpe,' said Cliff. 'He seems a very genuine fellow, from what I've heard.'

'He might change a bit, when he's been underground,' said Albert. 'In the old days, when the owners or VIPs came underground, they used to send a man in front, telling the men to watch their language and not swear when the visitors were there. One or two fellows then used to swear with a posh accent and it caused a few laughs.'

'They're going flat out,' said Bert, looking at his watch. 'They're winding through snap today. That's a sign that there's a lot of coal being produced.'

Tuesday 8 August 1967

Gwen Folds dropped off her husband at the pit at nine o'clock, which had allowed Roy plenty of time to discuss with his staff the state of the pit.

James had been told to bring some old clothes that he could wear underground, but

Roy had arranged for him to be provided with safety boots, a boiler suit and safety helmet. The visit was to the Fuston Two coalface and, over a coffee, Roy gave him a brief description of the pit before they went underground. He showed him the plan of the Fuston seam, and the route they would travel after they'd seen the operations in the pit bottom at the coal-winding shaft. Roy had also arranged for George Turnbull to meet them at the coalface and to have Willie Carter there, to go through the face with James. He wondered how Willie would perform as a tour guide.

James was amazed at the activity in the pit bottom and the speed with which the full tubs were loaded into the cage. At the loading point he saw the full flow of coal being loaded into the pit tubs, and how coal was diverted into the pit bottom bunker when the flow rate was beating the shaft winding rate. He kept making comments to Roy.

'It's truly amazing. I never could imagine that there was this world underground, with all this activity going on. I can appreciate how the different skills of the men blend together to make it all work.'

'You've only seen a few of the skills, here,' replied Roy. 'You'll see some exceptional skills on the coalface.'

★

When they reached the coalface, George was there and he shook hands with James and then introduced him to Willie Carter.

'You might not recognise this fellow, in his pit clothes, but this is one of your key men at the church.' Willie came forward, with a smile on his face, and James recognised him.

'So this is your world, Willie,' he said. 'I am very impressed with what I've seen.'

'Is Peter around this morning?' asked Roy.

'Yes, Mr Dobson,' replied Willie. 'He's working on a section switch in the other roadway. We should see him when we get through the coalface.'

'Right, you lead the way and answer all James's questions, Willie,' said Roy. 'Where's the shearer, George?'

'It will be over half-way through the face,' replied George. 'We're on the second shear and if we go through we should see it coming back and lifting up the bottom-coal and the men getting the supports over. As you can see, Boss, the roof has not broken behind the coalface yet, so there's no pressure on the coal and so the cutting speed with the top-coal is fairly slow.'

They walked through the coalface and Willie explained all about the panzer conveyor and the powered supports. They stopped when they were behind the shearer and about twenty yards from the end of the face. They watched the shearer park at the end, swing the cowl over and then start the trip back, lifting up the bottom-coal. There was a full load on the panzer conveyor and the machine was moving quite fast.

'Wow, look at that, Willie,' said James. 'What a sight, to see all that coal being produced by one man and a machine.'

'He's a very skilled driver,' said Willie. 'He has to be careful not to cut into the roof, as the sandstone produces sparks and damages the cutter picks.' They then watched as the men rammed the panzer over and started to get the powered supports over, following the shearer through the face.

'That was quite staggering,' said James. 'It's an amazing system of mining you have here. How much coal is the machine producing?'

'Each shear produces three hundred tons of coal. To get that, the shearer has to pass through the coalface twice, cutting the top-coal one way, and then lifting up the bottom-coal on the way back,' said Roy. 'And this morning they'll certainly complete two shears, which will give six hundred tons of coal. That compares with about fourteen or fifteen tons that one man could fill in a shift on a coalface.'

'It's certainly a lot easier than hand-filling, Boss,' said Willie, with a grin.

★

As they went further along the roadway, they came to Peter Carter, who was working on a spare electrical section switch carrying out some tests. James spoke to Peter, who then explained what he was doing and how the electrical system to the coalface was organised. Willie then left them and went back to the coalface and George accompanied Roy and James to the man-rider and travelled out of the pit with them.

★

In the office, over a sandwich lunch, they talked about the visit and Roy explained that the mining system on the Fuston coalface was really state-of-the-art, and how fortunate Martins had been to get that new type of power loader.

'You've made a great success of the operations, and everybody says that you've a very profitable pit, now,' said James.

Roy outlined to him the main arguments in the presentation that he'd prepared on Martins, which explained the changes that had contributed to the success. James particularly probed him about the change in the attitudes of the men at the pit. After some general comments, Roy quoted the statement in the conclusions. 'It needed the conversion of everyone at the pit to a new way of thinking. They had to be confident in the belief that Martins Main could be successful and then they had to recognise that success is sweeter than failure.'

James wrote the quote down in his notebook, and thought about it for a moment or two.

'That is some statement,' he said. 'It's almost biblical, and it's certainly evangelical, with the concept of conversion. And that's what you think has been the major change at Martins since you came here?'

'Yes,' replied Roy. 'All the technology in the world, however good it is, will only succeed if the people using it believe in success. Changing their minds, so that they believe in success, is a complex process, made up of all sorts of little changes, examples and influences that make people think differently.'

★

Before he left, James thanked Roy for a visit that he would always remember, and stated that it was a privilege to have seen the new Martins Main in action. He had one last comment.

'I will never forget seeing Peter Carter at work underground, doing his skilled job as an electrician. He's an outstanding young man, who manages to lead a double life. He works in the hurly-burly of the mine, and then he produces the most wonderful music on the organ,' said James. 'Willie says that you were the inspiration for Peter working in the mine. You must be very thrilled by the result.'

'I remember when Peter came see me, with Willie, and I can see him now, standing by my desk and asking my advice,' replied Roy. 'He impressed me straightaway at that meeting. I gave him a suggestion and he's gone away and put in the work and gained experience and he's going from strength to strength. He works very hard and he'll not let anyone down. I am aware, though, that the time may come when he chooses music, rather than the mining industry, for his main career.'

Wednesday 9 August 1967

Helen had decided not to ask her husband about the visit the previous evening, as Roy had had several telephone calls from the pit. However, today she was given a full report from Gwen Folds.

'James has never stopped talking about his pit visit,' said Gwen. 'He was fascinated by what he saw, and all the skills he witnessed underground. Roy cleverly let Willie Carter show him through the coalface and he also saw Peter Carter at work underground. He couldn't believe the technology he saw for producing the coal, and the efficient way it's transported out of the mine. Roy also filled him in on the way the manpower at Martins has been motivated to become successful. James said that it was better than a seminar on the best practice in business management! You must be very proud of your husband, Helen, and of what he does.'

'Indeed, I am,' replied Helen. 'I am proud of him because it's not an easy job having responsibility for all those men and for all the operations at the mine.'

Friday 18 August 1967

It was half past six, and Peggy Moore was very late getting back from the wages office. Being the day before the start of the pit holiday week, it was the busiest day of the year there, with men collecting the money they'd spend on their holidays. Peggy knew that Sandra would have left Dawn at Janet's house, as this was the arrangement when Peggy was delayed. She went straight into Janet's house and flopped into the nearest chair.

'You looked shattered, Peggy,' said Janet. 'Has it been one of those days?'

'It really has been a killer,' replied Peggy. 'I've never seen so much money in all my life. There have been some massive pay packets today, with the Bull week earnings and then the holiday pay. But it all went wrong this morning, when one of the girls gave out the wrong pay packet to one of the nightshift men. We only found out when there was no pay packet for the right man when he came for the pay packet that had been handed out in error. He happened to be one of the big earners, so he was very put out. It caused all sorts of investigations and checks, and we got way behind, and there were some grumbles about the delays.'

'How did it get sorted out?' asked Janet.

'The nightshift man brought the pay packet back, but that was after he'd been in bed for a few hours. Apparently he was so tired when he got home that he'd gone to bed and left the packet in the kitchen, without checking it. It was only when his wife came home from shopping in Doncaster, and saw that it had the wrong name on it, that the error was found. The girl who made the mistake was given a real telling-off and she was in tears. It made us all nervous and we all double-checked each pay-out, after that.'

'Well, don't rush off,' said Janet. 'Stay and have a bite of tea with us. Bob will be back with the boys, shortly, and they'll be glad to see you. Dawn would like to stay, wouldn't you, Dawn?'

'Yes, Aunty Janet, I'd like to stay for tea,' replied Dawn, very precisely.

'There you are then, that settles it,' said Janet, and she started to set the table with six places – which was quite a squeeze.

'I wish we were going away on holiday next week, like most of Upthorpe,' said Peggy. 'I'm ready for a holiday, after this last week.'

'I know you must be,' replied Janet. 'Bob has agreed to work the holiday week as there's another of these rush jobs on at Martins, moving a set of face equipment. But we've only got three weeks to wait until our holiday, and everything is booked, so Bob won't be able to put the holiday back.'

When the kettle was boiling, on the hob over the fire, the boys burst in with Bob.

'Look who's here, boys,' said Janet. 'And your Mummy and Dawn are going to stay to tea with us.'

Peggy smiled at the two boys, and brightened up as they came to her and gave her a hug.

'Have you been in the money again, today?' asked Tony.

'Yes,' she replied. 'There was lots and lots of it today – many, many hundreds of pounds.'

'Did you bring any for us?' asked Michael, with a grin on his face.

'I gave yours to Uncle Bob,' replied Peggy.

They had the sandwiches and talked about what the boys were going to do before they went away. Peggy asked Tony about school, and after he'd described what they had been doing, Janet passed Peggy the school report that Tony had brought home. Peggy was very pleased to see that it was a good report, and praised Tony's hard work and success in the various subjects.

'You've done very well at school, Tony,' said Peggy, 'That is a good report and I am very proud of you.' She thought she would give Tony a reward, when they were at the seaside, to encourage him to go on trying at school. She could tell that Janet and Bob were also very pleased with Tony's first year at school. Michael seemed very keen to start at school, too, and Janet was hoping that he'd be able to start after Christmas. Peggy realised it would be a real test for Janet, when both the boys were at school. She made a mental note that she'd have to visit Janet more often, then.

When Peggy got home she put Dawn straight to bed, and then followed her half an hour later. She was exhausted, but she was pleased to have the extra money from her two days each week in the wages office. She was working three days during the holiday week, but that should be much less stressful. The seaside holiday, again with Bob and Janet, would be a well-deserved treat for Dawn and herself, but this year she would have more money to spend, as a result of her job. She'd make sure that she was generous with spending on all the children.

Monday 28 August 1967

On the first day back after the pit holiday week, the Enclosure was reviewing events that had happened over the holiday. Cliff Smith had been watching cricket at Headingley and he briefed the team with his views of the Yorkshire players. Pat Mulligan had been over to Ireland to see some of his relatives, and he described the rainy weather there and expressed his relief to get back to Yorkshire. Bert Wall had been walking in the Yorkshire Dales, and he claimed to have walked over one hundred miles in the week. There was some doubt about the mileage but when he described the places he'd visited and the routes he'd taken, the team realised that he had indeed covered that mileage. Albert Dunn had been to stay with his sister for two days, in Bradford, but he was glad to get back home.

'My sister's a miserable bugger. She never has a good word to say for anybody.'

'It runs in the family, then,' said Cliff.

Charlie burst out laughing. He'd stayed at home and spent many hours in the Club. He was able to fill the team in on the progress at the pit, with the face-to-face transfer of 58s supports to 60s coalface.

'They only really worked two full shifts each day, on the job, but by the end of the week they'd drawn off more than half the supports. So the manager decided to carry on with the job on the Saturday and Sunday. They were saying in the Club, last night, that they could have the face starting production later this week.'

'They've done very well, then,' said Cliff. 'That'll be another feather in the manager's cap.'

'Most of the management team were working through the holiday week,' said Charlie. 'They were all required to stagger their holidays until later in September.'

'This manager certainly makes his staff pull their weight when there's a big job on,' said

Albert.

'There's something else going on as well,' said Pat. 'The Surveyor and the finance man were working through the holiday week. I don't know what it is, but they must have been preparing some document or report. They've had one woman working on this for the last few weeks, doing all the typing.'

'Could it be another capital project?' asked Cliff.

'I don't think that's likely, because there would be the engineers involved if it was a capital project,' replied Pat. 'And they've all been working on 58s transfer or other maintenance jobs.'

'It's strange that you've not been able to find out what's going off,' said Cliff.

'Yes, it is strange,' agree Pat. 'But someone will spill the beans before too long. I'll keep my eyes and ears open.'

'Well, they're certainly pushing some coal out this morning,' said Bert. 'They're winding through snap on the first shift back after the holidays!'

'George arranged for Fuston Two team to come on very early, so that there was plenty of coal at the shaft at the start of the dayshift,' said Charlie. 'He's expecting the Fuston face to have its first weight, this week, and the rock to start breaking. He says he wants to get that over with and see what a difference these up-rated powered supports make.'

'The management are still wary of this Fuston seam, then,' said Albert.

'They're just being careful,' said Cliff. 'But I have heard that the equipment on that face is the very best in the country, so it should be well up to the job. I think George just wants to get that face hitting the headlines. After all, it gives three hundred tons for every shear, and they only have eight men on the coalface team. Just think, they can get a hundred tons for every man-shift worked on the coalface. No wonder the pit's showing a big profit.'

Friday 1 September 1967

The new 60s coalface, in the Benton seam, had started cutting coal on the afternoon shift yesterday, which gave the pit its full production capacity since the beginning of June.

Roy Dobson had decided to have a meeting with his management team, to review the experience of the last three months and to discuss plans for the future. He laid on a sandwich lunch and asked all his senior management team to be present. It was the last chance to get everyone together before they started to take their delayed holidays. After they'd all finished their sandwiches, they gathered in the conference room and Roy faced them, with the screen behind him, where he intended to show them a few overhead projector slides.

'Firstly, I want to thank you for your efforts over the last three months when we've all been challenged by the two face-to-face changeovers,' he said. 'We have completed them satisfactorily, within the time scale that we planned, which has limited the impact that they've had on the pit's performance. Shortly I'll show you what has happened to the results over the last three months, but to get those figures into perspective I want to go back to my early days at Martins. Jeff has prepared these overlays. Firstly, they show the number of days lost by disputes in the three months before I arrived. They were nearly as bad in the first three months after I started, but these figures come into perspective when we show what the disputes did to the finances of the pit. It's sobering to see how much money the pit was losing at that time. As we move forward in time, I'll give snapshots of the financial results as they improved when each technical change was made. With the pit in its settled state now, you can see that the profit margins are among the very best in the country.'

Roy went through the overheads and made comments.

'There is one change we made that needed the support of all of you, and I think it's important to quantify this in financial terms. I know that some of you were a bit sceptical about that change. Running down the manpower, in anticipation of the manpower reduction from job savings schemes, had a major impact. Had we not done this, and kept on the manpower, this is the reduction of profit which would have resulted.'

Roy paused as he showed these few overheads. There were comments from members of the staff when they realised the significance of these financial figures.

'There's another way to express this,' Roy continued. 'We're now plotting a graph on a week-by-week basis to show the break-even output figure for the pit. Obviously, as the manpower reduces and the total wages costs reduce, that break-even figure slowly falls and, consequently, the profit margins increase.'

Roy took questions from his management team. There were some technical issues and he answered them and encouraged others to join in before he carried on.

'The real point of this meeting is to discuss with you where we go from here. We need to exploit what we now have at this pit. We've been entrusted with the latest coalface equipment, on the Fuston Two face. We should get better support from the up-rated powered supports, but we have to take action to help them. When we get near the square position, which will be when we've advanced two hundred yards, we must work the coalface continuously, seven days a week, to reduce the risk of major strata pressure and bad roof conditions. I'll discuss this with the union, to get their agreement. We should get the first break of the rock within the next few days, and it will be interesting to see how the up-rated powered supports cope with that. What's your view, George, of the likely effect?'

'My impression is that these supports are going to do a better job than those on Fuston One coalface, Boss,' replied George.

'The aim now is to produce, on a regular basis, over twenty-one thousand tons per week,' said Roy. 'We have one advantage to help with this objective in that we've now got a bigger weekly order for the power station coal. They want us to prepare two trains per day, as well as some coal by lorry, so stocking should be minimal.'

★

There was some further discussion about routine pit issues but, when this was finished, Roy had the last word.

'I know that most of you have not had your summer holiday, yet. You all deserve a break, so I wish you the best of holidays and also some late-summer sunshine.'

★

'That was a very good meeting, Boss,' said Jeff Briggs, as they spoke in Roy's office, later in the afternoon. 'You were able to use some of the information that we'd prepared earlier, and they won't suspect that it was put together for a different presentation.'

'But these are the fellows who made the changes happen,' said Roy. 'They need to know the financial results of all their efforts.' Jeff had not thought of that approach.

Monday 4 September 1967

Roy got a telephone call from Mr Pickersgill's office, telling him the date for the presentation at the Staff College. It would be during the second week in October.

Chapter 28

Friday 15 September 1967

Roy was sitting at home with Helen. He was relaxed, and relieved that Martins was back up to full output. 60s coalface, in the Benton seam, was working well, and the team of men were competing with 59s face to see who could produce the most coal and earn the highest wages. Both the Benton coalfaces had minor frustrations that they were not able to operate flat out as the Fuston Two coalface was producing well and the total tonnage was in excess of the shaft capacity. Roy was relieved that the rock roof was breaking behind the powered supports on the Fuston Two coalface, and that it seemed that the up-rating of the support hydraulic legs was working. The Coal Preparation plant was now back to operating on the nightshift and all the coal was being treated as there were now extra trains for the power station market. The weekly saleable outputs would be around twenty-two thousand tons per week, as the power station coal had a higher ash content but a lower selling price.

'You seem very relaxed tonight, Mr Manager,' said Helen. 'Shall we have more of your attention now, for a period?'

'Yes, I'm hopeful that Martins will now have a good run. Of course, I'll have to face the additional challenge of the presentation at the Staff College next month and I'm not looking forward to that evening.'

'You'll have the benefit of a week's holiday before then,' said Helen. 'You seem to be the last of the management team to be taking a holiday this year.'

'That's right. They have done me proud, so I wanted them to have first choice for the weeks in September. George is away from tomorrow, for a week.'

'Everybody seems to be away next week,' said Helen. 'Sandra and Terry are going to Cornwall with the Laceys. Sandra has been making elaborate plans for her and Terry to sample the nightlife while Mrs Lacey supervises Amy-Louise on an evening. She thinks it will be quite a challenge for her mother-in-law. Bob and Janet and the two boys are repeating the same holiday as last year, with Peggy and Dawn, in Bridlington. They're going by train. I've agreed to give them a lift to the station. Janet says that they seem to have far more luggage than last year and it's a long way to walk from Martins Lane with the three children. It won't take me long to do the two trips.'

'If you like, I can do that job in the morning,' said Roy.

'No, I want you to have a quiet day and relax a bit. Anyway, I want to see them off. Dawn is very excited about the holiday and she was talking to me about what she will be doing on the sands and in the sea. She's quite a bright little girl now, and very proud of her older brothers.'

Saturday 16 September 1967

When Helen dropped off Peggy and Dawn at the station, with their luggage, she observed the strong bond between the three children. When the boys saw Dawn arrive, they ran along the platform to greet her. Tony took her little case and held one of her hands, while Michael held the other, and the three of them walked along the platform to Bob and Janet. There were smiles of excitement all round.

'What a wonderful sight, Peggy,' said Helen.

'It's unbelievable,' said Peggy. 'It really is one happy family.' Bob came and took Peggy's case and Peggy turned to thank Helen for the lift to the station.

'You have a wonderful holiday, Peggy,' said Helen, as she gave her a hug.

Back in the car, she wiped her eyes before she drove back home. The scene with the three children and the three parents was truly moving, and she whispered a prayer of thanks to her Living God.

Saturday 23 September 1967

When the holidaymakers returned, there was much to talk about and Helen was a good listener. Sandra told how her holiday had been very good in many respects, but had one flaw. Mr Lacey had persuaded the hotel to give them adjoining rooms, so that they could easily babysit for Amy-Louise. The hotel had done this by using one of their suites with a connecting door between the two rooms.

'It worked for their babysitting, but it was a disaster for any passion between Terry and me,' said Sandra. 'You could hear what was happening in the other room, so there had to be no noisy lovemaking. Then there was always the risk of the door opening and Mrs Lacey coming in to see Amy-Louise, so it was difficult to relax. We cheated, one afternoon, by pretending to go shopping in the town, but we went back to our room for a real romp!'

'But it was a success overall?' suggested Helen.

'Oh, definitely,' said Sandra. 'And it was very cheap for us, as Mr Lacey paid all the bills. Amy-Louise gave plenty of smiles in appreciation. I think he would be shocked if he knew how fast our bank account is growing, as our expenditure is so low!'

'You save some money, Sandra,' said Helen. 'You never know when you might need some.'

★

The other holiday group came back showing evidence of their sunny holiday.

'I've never, in all my life, been exposed to so much sun,' said Peggy. 'I seemed to spend all the time in my bikini. So much so, that half-way through the week I went shopping and bought another one. And it was the same with the children. It was all sand and sea, and they got browner and browner as the week went on. They ate everything that was put in front of them, and then they slept like logs. It was paradise, Helen.'

'When are you having a holiday, Helen?' asked Janet. 'Bob said that all the management at Martins were taking late holidays this year.'

'Yes, we're last in the queue,' said Helen. 'Roy will be off for the first week in October. I'm making plans behind the scenes, but Roy doesn't know about them yet.'

'Oh, we'll keep it a secret,' said Janet.

★

The plans that Helen was making were for a week's holiday in Paris. She had to arrange for Grandma Dobson to come and stay with the Robert and John, who would be at school that week. She'd enlisted the help of the gardener, Dennis, with various tasks related to looking after the house and the children. She had agreed with him that he would bring in his wife, Joan, if Grandma Dobson needed any help. She also briefed Janet about her plan, and asked her to keep an eye on the boys, in case Grandma Dobson found them too boisterous. The plan was that her and Roy would drive to Dover, cross the Channel by ferry, and then drive on to Paris. They would have a one-night break in a hotel near Dover. Helen made all the necessary reservations. She sought advice from a travel agent and settled on a small, distinctive hotel that had lots of history and character. Her real problem was when to tell Roy about the plans: it had to be soon, as she didn't want him to get tied-up with any commitments at the pit, but she had to have everything in place so that he couldn't start changing things. She checked with Gordon, at the pit, to make sure that Roy had booked that week off as holiday, and he confirmed it. Grandma Dobson agreed to stay in charge that week, and Helen arranged to fetch her on the Friday before the start of the holiday.

Sunday 24 September 1967

The holiday grand plan was revealed to Roy when Helen returned from the evening service at church.

'I have a couple of things I want to talk about tonight, Roy,' she said, as she sat down beside him on the settee. 'Firstly, I'm very disappointed with the new minister at church. He's preached three times now, since he arrived, and I've tried to be sympathetic to him, as he's a young man, but it just doesn't seem right.'

'Oh why, what's the problem?'

'The problem is that he's not James Folds; and the real trouble is that he will never be a James Folds. He doesn't preach, he just comments on the scriptures, like in a Bible study class. He doesn't refer his preaching to the real world and its problems. I can feel a sense of disappointment in the congregation. There's no spiritual atmosphere. And I can't think that anyone would go to him, like we went to James and Gwen, for involvement in solving people's problems. I am trying to be sympathetic to him, but I get the impression that he thinks he's a chosen one, and that he therefore must be right.'

'Isn't it a bit too early to make an evaluation of him as a person?' said Roy.

'Maybe it is,' replied Helen. 'I'll try to be patient and see if he'll modify his style in the weeks to come.'

'What's the other thing you want to discuss?' asked Roy.

'This is much more positive. I have decided that we need a holiday. Everyone else seems to have had a holiday, so I've arranged one for us and I've got everything organised. We are going to Paris for a week, next Saturday.'

Roy's face told her that he was completely surprised and before he could comment, Helen continued.

'You can relax. All the arrangements have been made and you have just to accompany me and be a good consort and protector from the wily Parisians.'

Helen explained all the detailed arrangements she'd made, and how all her plans fitted together.

'You seem to have thought of everything,' said Roy. 'There seems to be nothing left for me to do.'

'Yes, there is,' replied Helen. 'You have to sort out Martins Main, so that they can manage without you for a week. I checked with your secretary, Gordon, and he confirmed that you had booked next week as holiday and I assured him that you would be taking it as holiday.'

'You are a very clever wife,' said Roy and he gave Helen a kiss and a cuddle before she went upstairs to say her prayers.

Tuesday 26 September 1967

Roy had taken the final draft of the presentation on Martins Main, along with a set of slides, to Mr Pickersgill's office when he was away on holiday, but Roy had not heard anything back. He decided to have a word with Diane, to explain that he himself would be away on holiday the week before the presentation and that he needed to be sure that Mr Pickersgill was happy with the final version.

'I'll speak to him, Mr Dobson. The presentation was left for him, with lots of other papers, to go through when he came back from his holiday. I'll be in touch.'

'Thank you, Diane,' replied Roy, and he waited for a call.

In fact, it was not Diane, but Norman Pickersgill himself, who called back. After the preliminaries, and some initial questions about the immediate prospects for Martins, Mr Pickersgill gave Roy the answers to his questions.

'I've gone through the final draft of the presentation and it's fine. I also feel that the slides are much better than the overheads. On the day of the presentation I want you to travel down to the Staff College in the morning, to arrive for lunch. You can ring up the college and arrange this with the course organiser. It'll allow you to have a run-through during the afternoon, with your fellow Briggs, so that you're both confident about the set-up. It's a multi-discipline course of thirty-six members, with colliery managers, regional staff and senior engineers from headquarters. You'll get a chance to see them at lunchtime, but I suggest that you avoid any close contacts prior to the presentation. I suspect that there could be some negative reaction to having an evening presentation by a colliery manager on this course. I shall come down, with Reg Jenkins, during the afternoon, so I'll see you at the dinner. I'll make sure you're introduced to the college Principal, then, and to the senior staff from headquarters. There might also be two members of the National Board there.'

'Thank you, Mr Pickersgill,' replied Roy. 'I will make the necessary arrangements.'

'I've had one final thought. You might get asked about the latest results from the pit. It would be a good idea to have a slide showing the figures for the last few weeks in September and the first week in October. Hopefully they'll be impressive?'

'I am confident they will be, Mr Pickersgill,' replied Roy.

He put the 'phone down and took a deep breath. So he was going into the lion's den for Norman Pickersgill, and the audience could be antagonistic. This was going to be a real challenge. He decided to have a session with Jeff Briggs to try to anticipate any difficult questions he might be asked, so that they could work out their responses. Helen might have planned a holiday in Paris for him to get away from all his responsibilities, but one essential item for his packing would be the presentation document. He would have to hide it in the luggage without her knowing.

Tuesday 3 October 1967

'So, the Boss has left them to it, this week,' said Charlie, when the Enclosure members had gathered and settled. 'They were saying in the Club that he's gone off with his wife and it's his mother who's looking after the kids. No one seemed to know where he's gone.'

'He's gone to Paris,' said Pat. 'They're driving there, but having a night near Dover on the way.'

'Taking his wife to Paris!' said Charlie. 'He must be trying to impress her. It'll cost a bob or two, to stay there for a week.'

'My understanding is that it's his wife who's arranged this holiday,' said Pat. 'So she is taking him.'

'He must have set the pit a big target for this week,' said Bert. 'They're winding flat out and it seems routine, now, to run through snap. And they're selling all the coal and not stocking any.'

'It must be the extra orders for the power station coal,' said Cliff.

'They sent ten trains to that market last week,' said Bert. 'And we also saw quite a few loads go out by lorry. There goes the loco with another run of full wagons down to the mainline.' They all looked across at the activity in the sidings.

'The pit must be doing very well,' said Cliff. 'I expect that George Turnbull will be trying to have a good week while the boss is away.'

'What sort of weekly tonnage are they doing now?' asked Albert.

'I should think they will be doing about twenty-two thousand tons saleable, now that they've got all the coalfaces working,' said Pat.

'Mr Dobson, as the colliery manager, must have his name up in lights now,' said Cliff.

'I don't know about that, but there is something special happening during next week, when he comes back from his holidays,' said Pat.

'What's that, Pat?' asked Charlie.

'I'm not sure what it is,' replied Pat. 'But I know that a rep from a manufacturer, who wanted to meet him next week, was told that Mr Dobson would be away at the Staff College, in London, for two days. It could be that he's been asked to give some paper, or report, about Martins Main.'

'Wow. Now that would be something very special,' said Cliff. 'That's the place where they take the very best management in the industry and prepare them for the biggest jobs.'

'Did you go to the Staff College, Cliff?' asked Charlie.

'No, we weren't in that league,' replied Cliff, with a laugh. 'We had to go to a place in the North East. It was good, though, and made us think about our responsibilities, and how we could do a better job.'

'We might get to know what's happening next week, when the manager gets back from his holidays,' said Cliff.

Sunday 8 October 1967

Roy was driving his car up the A1 in the early afternoon. The traffic was light and there was a relaxed atmosphere in the car. Helen was sitting quietly, reflecting on their holiday. She reached over and squeezed Roy's knee, from time to time, and gave him a smile. Roy's thoughts scanned the memories of a wonderful week when they had both been so in tune with each other that everything had worked out wonderfully well.

The hotel manager had befriended them and directed them to the best restaurants in that part of Paris; he'd met them at the breakfast table each morning and discussed their planned visits for the day, and then suggested they visit little additional gems, near the main attractions. When he'd realised that Helen wished to concentrate on the cathedrals and churches of Paris, he guided them to small, intimate churches, in localities that were not on the tourist trail, as well as the larger Sacré Coeur and Notre Dame. Roy had images of Helen knelt in prayer by his side at each place of worship they visited, often with her eyes tightly closed, but with a smile on her face. Was she saying thank you for this time together? He hoped so. He also wanted to thank whoever was watching over them and providing them with memories that would stay with them forever.

Roy's thoughts turned to the physical and emotional experiences of the week. On the first night at the hotel in Paris, he'd noticed that Helen was wearing a new, silk nightdress.

'This week, Roy, we are going to love one another, physically, more intensely than has ever happened before,' Helen had said provocatively. She hadn't expected to get an immediate response, but Roy showed immediately that he was on the same wavelength, as he took her in his arms and slowly laid her on the bed. He'd gently removed her nightdress as he stroked and kissed her, so that she completely relaxed. Instead of entering her straightaway, he'd continued to stimulate her breasts by kissing and touching, and then, with his hand and fingers, he opened her up and massaged her until her body arched and she exploded in his arms. She collapsed, gasping for breath. When Helen had recovered, in the lovemaking that followed she climaxed again when he came inside her. Whether it was for real or simulated he didn't know, because it had never happened twice before, in all their married life.

On the last two nights, Helen had had another surprise for him. Her night attire was baby-doll pyjamas, in pale-pink, see-through nylon, that left nothing to the imagination.

'I think I'm a bit old for this outfit,' she'd said, 'but I understand that men are turned on by this nightwear. At least Sandra Lacey said that Terry raised his game when she wore a set on her holiday.'

'You look ravishing,' Roy had replied. 'I'm sure I will raise my game tonight, but I hope that you won't feel you have to report back to Sandra!'

'This is just for the two of us,' said Helen, clasping him to her and giving him a passionate kiss.

Roy gripped the steering wheel tightly and concentrated on his driving as he recalled the image of their lovemaking that night, with Helen mounted astride him, wearing just the baby-doll top.

★

In addition to the fond memories going round in their heads, the other reason why their drive home was so relaxed was that Helen had made two 'phone calls home, during the week, to ensure that Grandma Dobson was coping with her responsibilities. On both occasions she'd got Dennis, the gardener, who had given her a full report of events – who had visited them; how both the boys had behaved themselves, and how Grandma had rested every afternoon when the boys were at school. He also said that his wife was cooking a meal each evening, so that Grandma Dobson could treat the week as a holiday. Helen thanked him for bringing Joan onto the scene. Dennis had assured her that everything was under control. He'd even suggested that they could stay away for another week, if they wished.

'They are managing without us, Roy,' Helen had said, after the second telephone call. 'I'm satisfied, now, that your mother is not being stressed. They're happy for us to stay away another week!'

'There's no chance of that,' replied Roy. 'I have my challenge at the Staff College next week.'

'That should be no problem,' said Helen. 'I know you've been doing some revision each evening. I didn't object to you sneaking a copy of the presentation into your case. I found it before we left home, when I was doing my final checks on the packing.'

'I've no secrets from you, Mrs Dobson,' answered Roy, with a smile. He was feeling more confident now about the presentation, and he was sure that he had answers to many of the questions that might be raised.

★

When they arrived home there was a joyful reunion with John and Robert, and Grandma Dobson, who was full of praise for the way they'd behaved and looked after her.

Helen decided to go to the evening service at church, after tea, and she left Roy in charge. He took the opportunity to ring George, to announce his return, but he had a clear view of leaving pit business until morning.

'I am just ringing to let you know that we're back home, George. It's been a wonderful holiday. I don't want to talk about the pit this evening, unless there's something very serious. I suggest that you don't go down the pit first thing in the morning, but that you fill me in on what's taken place. I expect to get to the pit at about eight o'clock and we can have a talk in my office.'

'There's nothing that can't wait until the morning, Boss,' replied George. 'I think you'll be quite pleased with how the pit's done while you were away.'

'That's good, George. I'll see you in the morning.'

Roy put the 'phone down and went to spend the evening with his boys and his mother. It was a first, for him, to put off being briefed about the pit. Maybe the holiday had done him good and altered his priorities a little.

★

When Helen returned from church, Roy asked how she'd found the service.

'How did the new Minister perform tonight?' he asked.

'He wasn't preaching at Upthorpe tonight, he was planned at another church. It was a wonderful service, led by a local preacher from another church in the circuit. He's a very devout Christian, and an experienced preacher. He speaks slowly and only has a few notes on a piece of paper, but it all makes sense. I could listen to him all night. I'm glad I went to the service, but I'm ready for an early night.'

They all went to bed early. Roy held Helen in his arms. It was not an occasion for passion; he just wanted to thank her.

'You did a brilliant job organising that holiday, Helen,' he said.

'It's been a wonderful week, I have to agree,' Helen replied. 'Life can't ever get better than this, Roy,' she added with a sigh.

Monday 9 October 1967

George Turnbull was in his pit clothes, waiting outside the manager's office when Roy arrived before eight o'clock the following morning.

'Right, George,' said Roy, as he sat at his desk. 'Fill me in on the news.'

'We did pretty well, Boss,' replied George. 'The output was just over twenty-two thousand tons. I think there was a bit more, but Jeff Briggs thought that you'd want to hold that back.'

'Yes, George, Jeff was right. I don't like to go much over the twenty-two thousand figure. Well, you've done well then. Were there any problems?'

'We had to nurse one of the cutting ends on 60s trepanner. It was losing oil and sounded a bit noisy all day on Friday, but it lasted out and we've changed it over the weekend.'

'Did anything else of note happen during the week?'

'We had a pit visit from Mr Jenkins,' replied George.

'Now that is a surprise. Where did he go, underground?'

'He eventually went to the Fuston Two face, but he spent some time in the pit bottom and then he walked along the conveyors down to the Fuston face. I let Jim look after him. I thought it would do the lad good, to be on display to Mr Jenkins. I met them when they got to the coalface. Mr Jenkins seemed reasonable happy, as the face did well that shift, and completed two-and-half shears.'

'Did you have lunch with him?'

'Yes, I came out of the pit with him. We were a bit late and we travelled out with the main shift of men. There was a bit of shoving and shouting when we went to the front at the pit bottom to get on the cage first. I gave a few of the men a good cursing for behaving like hooligans.'

'What did he say to that?'

'I think he was a bit impressed, because they did quieten down quickly.'

'Did he make any comments over lunch?'

'He said we needed a good output for the week. He explained that you were going to give a presentation at the Staff College on Wednesday, and that you might be asked some questions about the latest results at the pit.'

'Yes, it's going to be a challenge for me,' replied Roy. 'I was going to brief you all about this. I'll be going on Wednesday morning, with Jeff, and we'll be staying overnight, but we should get back by Thursday lunchtime.'

'Mr Jenkins said that he's going down, with Mr Pickersgill. I hope that it goes well for you, Boss. Me and Jim will keep things going here.'

'I'm sure you will, George. Just carry on where you left off last week.'

George hesitated, as though he expected Roy to explain more about the presentation, so Roy decided to satisfy his curiosity.

'You grab a chair, George, and I'll fill you in on what's at stake.'

He spent some time explaining how Mr Pickersgill had set up the presentation and the line he wanted Roy to take. He expressed his views on the risks that he would have, as a colliery manager, giving such a paper at the Staff College, where evening speakers tended to be very senior men from business and industry. He also hinted at the difficult questions that he expected to be asked, and his hope that he could give answers that satisfied Mr Pickersgill. His great dread was that Norman Pickersgill got involved in the discussions if he wasn't satisfied with Roy's performance.

'Bloody hell, Boss, I don't envy you taking on that job. You really are going into the lion's den. I'll be thinking about you, but I'll be a lot more comfortable looking after the pit, that night.'

'It's certainly a trip into the unknown,' replied Roy. 'Along with Jeff, I've put a lot of work into the text, and we've got plenty of slides to illustrate the arguments. Mr Pickersgill has approved what we've prepared and he'll be there to back me up. It's a good story to tell, George, and everybody at the pit can be proud of what we have all achieved at Martins Main.'

'I still sometimes think that it's a dream, Boss, how the pit is performing, now, when I think back to all the years when we were working hard and getting nowhere.'

'You get off, George, and carry on the good work. I'll be finalising all that we need for Wednesday, so I don't expect to get underground today.'

★

Roy spent the day sorting out lots of paperwork that had come in while he'd been away. He also spent some time with Jeff Briggs and the Surveyor, agreeing a further two slides that would illustrate the very latest weekly results for the pit. Reg Jenkins rang and they had a chat about his visit underground. Reg also explained the arrangements that had been made for himself and Mr Pickersgill to travel during Wednesday afternoon to the Staff College. Norman Pickersgill was staying on for a meeting the following day, in London, so Reg begged a lift back to Yorkshire with Roy and Jeff.

Wednesday 11 October 1967

Roy turned the car off the main road into the Staff College site. It was set in fifty-five acres, six miles northwest of central London. A millionaire engineer, who'd made his money providing equipment for the railways, and other industries, during the rapid expansion of the economy, had built the original property in the early-Victorian period. The house was built in brick, with stone-carved decorations above the windows and doors. In its life as a Staff College an annexe had been built, in the same style, to provide additional rooms for course members and visitors. The grounds included extensive flower borders and lawns, but there were recreation facilities in the form of tennis courts and a croquet lawn. At one side of the house, a grassed area dipped away steeply to a lake, which was surrounded by a natural wooded area comprising mature trees. There was adequate space for students to get exercise and to find some privacy for discussions in the fresh air.

The house had been adapted internally to have a lecture theatre and several syndicate rooms. There was also a bar, alongside the dining room, that had been equipped with expensive tables and chairs, so that it was more similar to an expensive hotel than to a school dining room. As well as a large lounge with comfortable seating, and an adjacent television room, there was a table-tennis room and a large snooker room.

There were small offices for the staff, who were mainly members of various management disciplines in the industry who'd been seconded from their jobs for two or three years. The house manageress was known throughout the coal industry as Formidable Fiona, as she ruled over the housekeeping and kitchen with a rod of iron. She was a big woman, in every respect, and had a powerful voice and a look that would spike any course member who took a familiar approach to herself or any of her staff. She always amazed the course members, however, by the way she adopted a gentle, subservient approach to distinguished guests. The domestic staff was made up mainly of young women from overseas, on short-term contracts, who were trying to improve their English. Fiona guarded them and herded them to their rooms each evening, so that there could be no exposure to course members who might have an upsurge of needs for female company. Some course members were sure, though, that the diet was laced with bromide, because their normal sexual appetite seemed subdued.

The college Principal had a large office on the first floor. It was lined with books and had an antique desk with an impressive swivel chair and a bank of telephones on the desk. The rest of the room was furnished with leather settees and chairs, where the Principal could have meetings with his staff and the continuous flow of distinguished visitors. His education had been classics, at Oxford, and in the Second World War he'd been successful in the Secret Service. A spell in the civil service, after the war, brought him to note at the right time to join the flow of additional management into the nationalised coal industry. His spell in the marketing department at Headquarters prepared him for the role as Principal of the Staff College. He believed that he could make a difference to the industry if the College could educate its senior staff in the latest techniques of management. He had never been down a coal mine.

★

Roy parked at the front entrance and unloaded his luggage. At the reception desk he introduced himself and the receptionist called for the Course Director while she presented Roy and Jeff with keys for their rooms in the annexe. The Course Director welcomed them and explained that there was a plenary session taking place in the lecture room until lunchtime. After lunch, the course members would be working in syndicates, on their projects, and it would then be possible for Roy to set up his slides and have a run-through of his presentation. It was suggested that they move the car to the car park and go to their rooms until lunchtime, when he'd meet them and introduce them to other members of the staff.

When they were settled in the annexe, Jeff shared his first impressions.

'This place has some atmosphere, Boss,' he said. 'I've only to put the slides on, but I'm terrified. I don't know how you feel?'

'It is a bit daunting, Jeff,' replied Roy, 'but we'll get through. You're supposed to be here to help me keep calm and not get stressed, so don't you get all nervous!'

'You are right, Boss. I'm letting you down. I'll pull myself together,' said Jeff, and he immediately took several deep breaths, straightened his back and assumed an attitude of confidence.

'That's much better,' said Roy. 'We'll have half an hour of relaxation now, before we go down for lunch.'

★

Forty minutes later, Roy and Jeff were met by the Course Director, who took them into the bar and bought them drinks. Jeff had half a pint of beer, but Roy decided to stick to orange juice. Other members of staff came and joined them and Roy realised, when they were introduced, that they were of different disciplines and came from various parts of the country. There were a few course members in the bar, but most had gone into the dining room. The Course Director explained that lunch was a buffet and that some syndicates ate together and had a brief lunch so that they could get to their syndicate room and continue work on their projects. He explained that each syndicate had been given some aspect of the British Coal Executive's business to study and were required to present their views on how that business could be changed so that it achieved much higher efficiency over the next five years. They would have to make a presentation on their findings to the Deputy Chairman of the Executive, on the final day of the course. It was proving to be a very challenging exercise, and some syndicates were struggling to reach any noteworthy conclusions. Roy thought that this was another reason why his evening lecture might not be popular.

After lunch, while they were still chatting generally, a younger member of staff suddenly introduced Roy's presentation into the discussion.

'This is a very special occasion, Mr Dobson,' he said. 'I'm very much looking forward to your presentation tonight. We often talk about pits, in discussions between course members, but I can never remember a full presentation about a specific pit. Will you be giving us the full picture, with all the results?'

Roy gave him a smile and decided to take his comments seriously.

'Yes, we'll be giving you the bad, as well as the good,' he replied. 'And all the way, we'll be trying to quantify in financial terms the impact changes have made,'

'That will be really interesting,' said the young man.

Another member of staff chipped in. 'I've been trying to get some financial figures about your pit, from the Regional finance office, but they've not been forthcoming, as though there's something to hide.'

'I can't comment about Region,' said Roy, diplomatically. 'If we can't use the finance figures we'll not be able to use half our slides.' The group laughed at this.

'It could be that the Regional General Manager didn't want the finance figures to be available here, before the presentation,' said the Course Director. 'I understand that he will be here tonight.'

'Is that true?' asked another of the staff, with a sound of shock in his voice. 'Norman Pickersgill is coming tonight? Bloody hell, it will be some occasion.'

'It will certainly be some occasion for me, with Mr Pickersgill in the audience,' said Roy, trying to pass it off as casually as possible.

'I'll have to smarten myself up for tonight, then,' said the young man who'd opened the discussion.

★

Roy was sitting at the front of the lecture theatre while the Course Director introduced him. He was feeling relaxed, having survived a pre-dinner session with the College Principal and Mr Pickersgill, in the Principal's office. At the dinner he'd been on the same table as the College Principal, along with Norman Pickersgill and two members of the National Board. He'd eaten sparingly of the meal, and drunk mainly water, along with one glass of white wine. At no time had he faced awkward questions, and Mr Pickersgill had been lavish in his comments about his colliery manager. Roy felt he needed to put on a confident display with the presentation, to repay the confidence shown in him by his boss. The Course Director had carefully checked with Roy his educational achievements and management experience so far and Roy had insisted that he mention that he was from Nottingham and had been brought into Yorkshire to take over Martins Main.

The course Director ended his introductory remarks with a synopsis of the presentation.

'This is the history of the last four years at Martins Main Colliery.'

Roy moved over to the lectern and gave the audience a smile as the lights were lowered and the screen was filled with a photograph of the shafts and surface buildings of Martins Main. The plumes of steam clearly showed that the steam engines of both shafts were in operation. The position of the pit when Roy took over was the starting point and Roy detected an interest in the figures presented and a realisation of the dire financial results. The next theme was to emphasise the need for concentrating the workings and he explained the concept of the Central Conveying Scheme, and its objectives of manpower efficiency and lifting the shaft capacity by a third. Getting mining contractors to make a contribution to that scheme was stressed, as was the success of getting the union to change its policy, by involving them in inspections of the work.

Roy stated that the first mechanised face presented itself as an opportunity because the pit was well in front with the development of new face capacity. The build-up of the face equipment on the surface, and the interest it generated at the pit, was shown by slides of the men watching the training sessions. The commissioning of the Central Conveying Scheme over the pit holiday week was covered in detail, and the audience reacted with surprise when Roy explained that all the senior management at the pit were on duty that week. He stated that the manpower savings from this scheme had been achieved by stopping recruitment at the pit well before the scheme was commissioned. The slides showed what the financial impacts of this had been.

The second mechanised coalface demonstrated the need for additional bunkers in the pit bottom, and this was illustrated with several slides of the bunkers and how they were used. It was described as a 'pit improvised solution that worked'. Again, its impact was reflected in the financial results.

'No pit works in isolation,' read out Roy. 'And just when we had the pit working well, we were faced by an overtime ban and a go-slow by the Yorkshire Winding Enginemen. We could have accepted this as outside of our responsibility, but we did not want it to affect the men and their earnings. There was a chink of light which turned into a golden opportunity.' The text then identified the one winding engineman who was not in that union, which gave one normal shift operation at the coal shaft. There was laughter when Roy explained how one of the union winder men put in a sick note that guaranteed his absence for the duration of the dispute. This was equivalent to a major football pools win. The training of other staff on the engines had identified one member of staff who was as effective as the full-time winders, and this had meant that the coal shaft could give near-normal results. The support of the Region in the actions taken at Martins had helped to defeat the dispute, added Roy.

The challenge of the Fuston seam was explained in detail, as was its need for the latest technology in powered supports and the use of a ranging drum shearer. Its real impact was achieved by operating the seam with retreat coalfaces which used very small teams of men. This allowed a further step change reduction in the total manpower at the pit. There was a section on the face-to-face transfer in the Fuston seam and the up-rating of the powered support hydraulic legs, in the production line which was set up in the surface fitting shop.

Marketing changes, with the introduction of a power station fuel, was the change that made it possible for the Coal Preparation plant to handle the higher weekly outputs without any major up-rating of the plant, Roy continued.

While there had been examples of the financial affects of the different initiatives, the final sequence of slides reflected the quarterly results throughout the total period covered. When the latest quarterly figures were shown for the last year of operation there were gasps of surprise at the profit margins shown. The weekly break-even tonnage trend was then shown and it was referred to as a barometer for the pit to measure the conversion of its performance into profits.

Roy turned over the page and saw that he was nearly at the end. He took a deep breath and stated the final heading, 'Conclusions'.

'Martins Main had been struggling for years, showing little progress and continued frustration for everyone involved with the pit. It needed a series of shocks with the introduction of changes. Firstly, the change to concentrate the operations; secondly it needed a capital project to give the pit additional capacity and then it needed the introduction of mechanisation to produce the coal with horsepower not muscle-power. But finally, and this was probably the most important change, it needed the conversion of everyone at the pit to a new way of thinking. They had to become confident in their belief that Martins Main could be successful and then they had to recognise that success is sweeter than failure. None of these changes could be classed as major by themselves, but together, along with the new way of thinking at the pit, they have produced dramatic financial returns. Similar results could surely be achieved at other pits.'

Roy sat down, to generous applause. The Course Director said that there would now be an opportunity for questions. The first one came from a Yorkshire colliery manager.

'Mr Dobson, the results of Martins Main have been noticed throughout the Yorkshire coalfield. The one factor that has amazed a lot of us is the change in the union position. Cobba Green was well known as a left-wing union man who was always looking for trouble. That seems to have changed. How have you sorted Cobba?'

'Cobba has been a part of the total manpower at the pit, and he has changed his position, like the rest of the pit. He is not against efficiency and success. As Chairman of the Upthorpe Welfare Club he demands hard work and efficiency. He's also in charge of the Home Coal delivery service and he had a problem when several of his men were retiring. He asked me if it was possible to provide the Home Coal into a small bunker where the lorries could load directly instead of the men having to shovel the coal out of railway wagons. It was possible to do this and the pay-off for the pit was that the Home Coal was altered so that it contained about one-third smaller coal. This gave us more large coal for the premium market, and Cobba could manage with one less lorry. Everybody benefited and Cobba saw that he would get fair treatment from me if he supported the policies we were following. He knows the score, and he's committed to it; we have to produce the results specified for any capital invested in the pit, before we get any more money.'

Another question was asked, this time regarding accident rates at the pit and absenteeism.

'I would expect improved figures in both these aspects, with the introduction of mechanised faces. I think we can show both these improvements with additional slides, if Jeff can find them.' Jeff adjusted the slide carousel until he got to the appropriate slides.

'Mr Dobson, you have shown some very impressive improvements in the financial results for the pit. Do you think you can maintain them?' asked a Welshman.

'Yes, I think we can maintain them,' replied Roy. 'I can show you the results for the last three weeks, and last week was one of our best weeks ever – and I was away on holiday!'

Jeff put the slides on and they showed a very high percentage profit margin. There were murmurs of amazement around the room at a profit margin of over forty per cent of turnover.

A vote of thanks was given by one of the course members.

'It seemed strange to several of us on this course, that a colliery manager should be coming to speak to us this evening. We usually get very senior executives from other industries or companies displaying their expertise and telling us how we should operate. Tonight, we have been given a detailed report on how a pit was changed from a desperate failure to be one of the most successful in the country. The impressive part of the presentation has been how each change has been measured, and its impact shown on the finances of the pit. Mr Dobson, you have given us much to think about. Thank you very much for your presentation and we all wish you well at Martins Main.'

He walked over and shook Roy's hand. Roy gave him a big smile and simultaneously he felt a weight taken from his shoulders. He had succeeded in front of a critical audience.

The rest of the evening was spent in the bar, and Roy was the centre of attention. He fielded questions from the Board Members, from the College staff and from members of the course. Norman Pickersgill stayed in the background, but before he left he took Roy to one side to have a word with him.

'You did a very good job tonight, Dobson. They were hooked by the way you illustrated the results in financial terms, for all the changes made. I also liked your answer on Cobba Green. His support has certainly been a bargain at the price. You've left the Principal with some issues on the course content to think about, and both the Board Members were very impressed. Enjoy the rest of the evening and I'll have a talk with you when I get back to Yorkshire.'

'Thank you very much, Mr Pickersgill,' replied Roy.

He went back to the bar and had a quick word with Reg Jenkins, who was sitting with several Welshmen, in deep discussions on mining matters. Roy didn't stay long, as he wanted an early start after breakfast, to make his journey back to Yorkshire.

Thursday 12 October 1967

Roy and Jeff's departure from the Staff College was later than planned, as Reg Jenkins hadn't appeared for breakfast until nine o'clock. Roy rang Martins and got a report from George, who, surprisingly, was still on the surface.

'We had a right cock-up yesterday, Boss,' said George, when he came on the 'phone. 'Early on the afternoon shift, the gearbox collapsed on the main screen which takes the coal from the wash box. It stopped the washer and we had to improvise.'

'Were you able to repair the breakdown?' asked Roy.

'Luckily, we had a spare gearbox available at the pit, but it was a difficult job to change the damaged one. It took until the middle of the nightshift, to get the washer working again. It didn't affect the pit, because we ran the raw coal through into railway wagons to stock it until we can wash the coal. There are bloody full wagons of coal shunted all over the sidings, Boss.'

'Never mind about that, George; we'll have to put an extra shift on, to wash the coal on Saturday morning.'

'Some of the washermen say that we're squeezing too much coal through the plant and not doing enough maintenance work, but I told them to stop belly-aching and get on with the job. How did your session go last night, Boss?'

'I think it went OK,' replied Roy. 'Mr Pickersgill seemed satisfied, and we had answers to all the questions that were asked. You keep the pit rolling, George. I suppose we'll be in the spotlight a bit more, now that we've publicised our results, so we can expect a few more visitors coming to have a look at Martins. I'll get back as soon as I can, but we're waiting for Mr Jenkins, who seems to have had a lie in this morning.'

'I'm going down the pit now,' said George. 'I've told the Mechanical Engineer to keep his eye on the Coal Prep plant today, to avoid any further stoppages.'

★

It was a quiet drive up the A1 to Yorkshire. Reg Jenkins sat in the front seat, dozing most of the time, with no wish to discuss either the previous evening's presentation or the circumstances at Martins Main that morning.

★

As soon as Roy got back to the pit in the afternoon he toured the pit top to assess the number of wagons of raw coal that needed to go through the washer in addition to the coal being produced from the pit. He realised that it would need a full shift of washing on Saturday morning and that there would still be some coal left in railway wagons to treat during the following week. Martins Main was going to have another week with twenty-two thousand saleable tonnage.

Chapter 29

'I want us to take an initiative with the new minister, Roy,' said Helen Dobson, after she returned from the Sunday evening service. 'There are mumblings in the congregation about him and his style of preaching. I think we should invite him over for a meal and have one or two of the key church members present. We could class it as a welcome dinner from us, and that should disguise any discussions that take place.'

'I'm quite happy to do that. It will be interesting to meet this fellow who's causing my wife such apprehension about how he does his job. Who will you invite from the church?'

'That is a good question,' said Helen, as she carefully considered the options. 'We don't want to invite too many, but we must have a representative selection of the membership. We must have John Warwick, who's chairman of the trustees; Joe Norton will speak his mind, which could be useful; and the same goes for Willie Carter. But we need some young people, so Peter Carter could be the right person to invite, and Maureen is a very sensible young woman, and she's playing an increasingly important role in the singing in church.'

'You need an even number, so I would suggest you invite all those you've just mentioned, and assuming you need me there, that'll make a total of eight people,' said Roy.

'There is no way that you are skiving off from this event, Roy Dobson,' said Helen. 'I need your support, but we'll also need your skills in human relations, to influence this young fellow and make him recognise how he needs to change so that he can deliver a full ministerial role to the Church.'

'I think you're attributing skills to me that I don't recognise, or understand. If I don't recognise that I have these skills, how can I be expected to produce them on demand? I'm happy to be present, and listen to the discussions, and I'll contribute if I see an opportunity, but I cannot promise that I'll be able to produce some life-changing formula. Can you tell me a bit more about this young fellow?'

'Benjamin Sorrell is in his late twenties. There's no doubt that he's bright, because he did well at school studying classics and then he went on to university, to study Theology and Philosophy. I don't know what first degree he got, but he stayed on at university to do some research so that he obtained a PhD. He was already qualified as a local preacher and he was put forward for the ministry immediately, before he got any job. He did two years at the Methodist Training College in Manchester, and he's now a probationary minister. So it's actually Reverend Doctor Benjamin Sorrell, as he's keen to present himself. He'll probably get tired of church members at Upthorpe wanting his advice on their obscure ailments!'

★

Helen Dobson set to work inviting the members of the church to her dinner party. All the people she approached expressed a willingness to attend, and favoured this attempt to find out more about the new minister. It wasn't easy to agree a date, however. Benjamin Sorrell said that he couldn't attend a Saturday evening dinner, as he required Saturday evenings to prepare himself for his Sunday preaching. He emphasised that, as far as he was concerned, Sunday was the most important day of the week. In the end, a date was arranged for the last Friday in October.

Monday 16 October 1967

The Enclosure was reviewing the performance for the week during which Roy had given his presentation at the Staff College.

'They had to wash a full shift on Saturday morning, to get rid of most of the coal that they stocked when the washer broke down,' reported Bert.

'The lads in the Club were saying that it was another good week for output,' said Charlie. 'Have you got any idea of the figure, Pat?'

'I understand that the pit achieved just over twenty-two thousand tons, which is the third week on the trot that they've done this,' replied Pat.

'They also sent out a train to the power stations, on Saturday morning,' said Bert. 'Martins definitely has some good customers for its coal, these days. Some other pits are having to stock coal and there are rumours that more pits will have to close.'

'Yes, I've heard that if there is no demand for coal from any particular pit, they can expect to be considered for closure,' said Cliff.

'The market is not the only thing in favour of Martins,' said Pat. He paused for effect and all the members looked at him.

'What news have you got now, Pat?' asked Albert, who sensed that Pat must have something very important to disclose.

'The manager gave a paper last week, at the Staff College, about the last four years at Martins and it was regarded as an excellent presentation. There were very senior people from the Coal Executive there, and they were most impressed. It was considered worthy of wider distribution within the industry. Mr Pickersgill was there and it was him who suggested the paper.'

'Does this mean that the manager will be moving on, then?' asked Albert. 'I always thought that he would get promotion, if the pit did well.'

'I've not heard anything about that,' replied Pat, 'but he must be regarded as a top-league manager now.'

'He's done a very good job at Martins,' said Cliff. 'We don't want to lose him now. I think that Roy Dobson and George Turnbull must be one of the best management teams in Yorkshire.'

'The lads were saying that the young fellow, Jim Lord, is making a good mining engineer,' said Charlie.

The Enclosure members were agreed in their assessment of the management team at Martins. There was a sense of pride that they represented a supporters' club for the pit. During the rest of the morning they watched the relentless bustle and thrust of the winding engines and the clang of the pit tubs as they were changed in the cages. The continuous flow of coal from underground also produced a sense of urgency on the colliery surface to wash the coal and present it in railway wagons or lorries for despatch to the customers. Martins Main was on song.

Friday 27 October 1967

Helen Dobson checked the extended table that was laid out with the best family cutlery and crockery for the eight people who were coming to dinner. She'd arranged for Joan Gates, the gardener's wife, to be on hand, to carry out the final stages of cooking the meal and also to serve it. She wanted it to be a leisurely meal, and it was timed for a seven o'clock start, to allow half an hour of chat before the meal.

Helen had planned the menu to provide a meal typical of the mining community. She had no idea whether Reverend Doctor Benjamin Sorrell had any dietary problems, but she'd decided that they'd have water to drink at the table, as he had already spoken, in one of his sermons, against strong drink.

The first course would be tomato soup made with fresh tomatoes from the greenhouse. The joint was roast pork, which Roy was to carve in advance of the visitors arriving. It would be served with fresh vegetables, also from the garden. The sweet would be a plum crumble, served with custard.

The transport had been carefully organised. John Warwick was nominated to pick up Benjamin Sorrell, while Joe Horton agreed to bring the Carters and Maureen. On the journey, John Warwick explained the important role held by the colliery manager in the community, and he also explained the impact that Helen Dobson had brought to the Methodist Church since she became a member.

★

Helen welcomed John Warwick and Benjamin Sorrell, who arrived first, and settled them in the sitting room, where she introduced her husband to the minister. There had been no chance for anything other than small talk when the rest of the party arrived. Joe was dressed casually, but Willie Carter was in his best suit, and obviously somewhat nervous to be dining at the manager's house. Peter Carter was very relaxed, and so was Maureen. It was Maureen who put the first searching question to Benjamin Sorrell, in the pre-dinner discussion.

'We've made great progress at the church with music over the past two years,' she said, 'with Peter's initiatives and his organ playing. What are your interests in music, Dr Sorrell, and what particular styles do you prefer?' She asked these questions with the innocence and enthusiasm of youth.

'I am not musical, at all,' replied Benjamin. 'So I have no preference in styles. In fact, I sometimes think that hymn singing plays too big a part in our services, and distracts from the message.'

'Nay, lad, you can't deny the importance of music in the Methodist church. Just think of the power of the words in Charles Wesley's hymns,' said Joe Horton. 'We have certainly had some wonderful occasions at Upthorpe, with music.'

'And not only with traditional music,' said Helen. She went on to explain the use of the song You'll Never Walk Alone, at the Sunday School anniversary service, and the relevance it had to the christening of Tony and Michael, which was made a key part of the service. She looked across at Maureen. 'I am sure, Benjamin, that if you had heard Maureen singing it, as a solo, you would have been moved to tears, like many of us in the congregation.' Maureen blushed at these words of praise. Benjamin Sorrell decided not to make any further comments on music.

John Warwick then discussed the importance of Martins Main in the life of the Upthorpe community. He encouraged Roy to outline the current facts about the pit, its weekly output, the number of men employed and the wealth it put into the community each week. Roy also explained how the pit was training young people for technical jobs in the coal industry, and how these skills would be transferable to other industries. He asked Peter Carter to give an outline of his job, and of his training and education. Peter did this enthusiastically, and it was obvious to everyone that he was proud of his progress to date. Peter also described the team spirit that applied underground, between the men on the coalfaces. Roy picked up on this and stated that everyone at the pit had a part to play in handling the coal and preparing it for dispatch to the markets. He expressed the view that all the men at the pit had increased their efforts recently and that this had led to an improved team spirit at the mine. Benjamin Sorrell made no comment about the mine.

'Have you spent any time in industry, or agriculture, during your training?' asked Joe Horton.

'Not really,' replied Dr Sorrell. 'Throughout my university time, and when I was training for the ministry, I concentrated on my studies. I read more widely than other students, so that I became an expert at my subject. That was my priority.'

Helen realised that the conversation was getting really serious, so she called a halt and announced that dinner was ready. In the dining room, the table was set with three places down each side and one at each end. Roy took one end, and Helen the other. Down one side, starting with Helen, she placed Benjamin Sorrell, John Warwick and Maureen; down the other side were Joe Horton, Willie Carter and Peter Carter.

Helen asked her guests to stand while she said grace.

'Dear Lord, we are privileged to be members of your church, and thankful that we can meet together with a common purpose. We want to serve you, and the community, and by our example bring others into your fold. Thank you for this food and bless our time together, tonight. Amen.' Willie Carter gave another loud 'Amen'.

The meal progressed smoothly, and the conversation was mainly about the meal and mundane local issues. Roy revelled in having the two young people to talk to, and was glad that any discussion of church affairs would be left to Helen's end of the table. He learned from Maureen of her plans for going to university, to study English, while Peter explained how he would be taking further exams for the organ, as well as another year's exams towards his Higher National Certificate for Electrical Engineering. Maureen described her life as a sixth former at the Grammar School in Doncaster, and Peter gave her some humorous stories about life underground at the pit. They both spoke of their love of music and their hopes of performing more musical events at Upthorpe Methodist Church. Roy predicted that there would be little support for these ideas from Benjamin Sorrell, given the conversation earlier.

From the other end of the table Roy overheard snatches of Joe Horton talking about his farm and explaining to Helen the commitment that was needed, every day of the year, for his herd of milking cows.

'There's one advantage of being a Methodist minister; you don't have to start at five o'clock each morning,' commented Joe.

'Farming is definitely a way of life that calls for continuous commitment,' said Helen, showing sympathy to Joe's case.

'Don't be too sympathetic to Joe, Mrs Dobson,' said John Warwick, with a mischievous smile. 'He might appear to be a hard-working farmer, but he's an astute businessman. It's on land that was part of Joe's farm that the new housing development is taking place in Upthorpe. There are rumours that Joe got a very good price for that deal!'

'Now then, John, you should not spread rumours,' replied Joe. 'I might have got a good price for that land deal, but I've spent it buying more land for the farm, so we're now working harder than ever. We're keeping the livestock at the old farm, but we plan to use most of the new land for arable crops. To do that we need new tractors and ploughs, and we might even have to buy a bigger combine harvester. So you see, John, I'm worse off than I was before I sold the land. I might want to borrow a bit from you, to tide me over until the next harvest.' He looked across at Helen. 'That is unless the colliery manager can give me a sub.' This banter caused some laughter at that end of the table.

There was praise for Helen's meal, and she suggested that they go back into the lounge where she would serve tea or coffee. Maureen offered to help serving the drinks, but Helen assured her that Joan, who had provided a professional service to the diners, would do the rest of the clearing up and washing-up. When they were all settled, John Warwick decided to open the discussion.

'You've had a look at us for a few weeks, Benjamin; what plans are you thinking about for the future of our church?' asked John Warwick. Dr Sorrell saw this as his opportunity to express his views.

'My vision is for a church steeped in the Bible,' he replied. 'With my academic qualifications and my training, I think I'm the right person to make this happen.' He looked around the room, but there were no great signs of enthusiasm.

'How do you propose to do that?' asked Helen.

'I propose holding Bible classes one or two nights per week, going through sections of the Bible in detail. I want the members to see that this is the way to grow their faith. I hope that they'll end up with the same enthusiasm that I have for following the truths of the Bible.'

'I can see that there's a role for Biblical knowledge to be prominent in the church,' said Helen, 'but we've developed links into the community through social activities, to attract people into the church. And these activities have certainly brought some new people into the church. Where does community work fit into your plans?'

'It doesn't feature at all, really,' replied Benjamin Sorrell. 'I do not attach any value at all to coffee mornings and social events; they might bring people into the church building, but only a deep knowledge of the Bible can make people real believers.'

'Are you sure that you're right in rejecting community work?' asked John.

'Yes, I'm quite sure that I am right,' replied the minister. 'When you are called to God's work – and I am sure that I have been called – you know quite clearly what it is you have to do.'

'I've had a long lifetime of being a member of the Methodist church,' said Joe. 'And I've seen a good number of Methodist ministers and local preachers. Those that have made the most impact, and brought in new members, have been those who have had liberal views and preached a welcome for anyone to come into the church.'

'That's been my experience, as well,' said Willie.

'Don't you think it's a bit premature, to have such rigid views of your role, when you're just at the start of your ministry?' suggested John. 'We want to grow our church, and we want to have a welcome for anyone who needs the love of the Lord Jesus. And we'd like to help you in playing your part in this mission.'

'A minister must have a vision for his church,' replied Benjamin. 'So often, churches are locked into traditions that have been around for years, and the members reject any changes, and don't want to grow their faith.'

'But we have accepted changes at Upthorpe: we've started to build up youth activities, and we now have some young people active in the church,' said Maureen. 'Surely you want that to continue?'

'Yes, I'm keen to involve young people in my Bible study groups,' he replied. 'I know that if I can get young people converted to a Bible-focussed life, they will become real Christians.'

'But the first challenge is to get young people into the church!' said Helen. 'We have to have some activities that attract them to the church, rather than the alternatives; the Bible studies follow later. Surely you accept that approach?' Helen was feeling that they were not making any progress in the discussions.

'You could be suggesting that the end justifies the means,' said Benjamin, 'and that's a dangerous philosophy, which I'm always wary of following.'

'What do you mean by 'real' Christians?' asked Peter. It was clear from Willie's nodding head that he too wanted an answer to that question.

'I mean a person who has had a call from God, and who has answered that call,' replied Benjamin. 'There are many members of the church who are regular worshippers, and also workers in the church, but they have never had the call.'

'They might not have had a dramatic moment of conversion, but they are prepared to grow in faith,' said John. 'And it's our responsibility in the church to nurture these people, so that they become the reliable core of God's mission.'

'I agree with that,' said Willie.

John Warwick continued his theme. 'I've known several tragic cases of people who had the call, and were full of the spirit, but it didn't last, and they faded from the church. Having one moment of calling, you seem to be suggesting, Minister, is the only way to enter the faith.'

'Yes, that is my belief,' said Benjamin Sorrell.

'I am afraid that I am not in agreement with you on that rigid definition,' said John. 'I believe that there are many routes to a deep and lasting faith.'

It seemed that a clear picture had been obtained of the minister's views, so the discussion reverted to trivial matters. It was Benjamin Sorrell who brought the evening's gathering to a premature end. He thanked Helen for a magnificent meal and the church members for the discussions but, if John wouldn't mind, he felt he should be getting back to the manse. John left with Benjamin. Shortly afterwards Joe said he would take the others home, but whilst getting ready to go, he assessed the outcome of the evening.

'We have got a young fellow here who has a very narrow view of the church, and he's only at the start of his ministry. But it's our church, and we must take it in the direction that we want. We have to continue to grow the church, despite the minister, so you young folk can carry on with your plans,' he concluded, looking at Maureen and Peter.

★

When all the guests had gone, Helen was sad that the aim of the dinner had not been achieved, and she expressed that thought to Roy, but he had another view.

'You now know where you stand,' he said. 'He showed no signs of any compromise. You can now plan how you will organise the activities in the church. If he doesn't want to be involved, then you'll have to manage things yourselves. If all his initiatives fail, then he has the chance to join you in what you're trying to achieve. If he doesn't want to do join you, then he'll have to move on to another posting.'

Helen was heartened by Roy's conclusions from the meeting, and she communicated these thoughts to John Warwick.

Thursday 2 November 1967

Following on from the dinner party hosted by the Dobsons, an unofficial meeting had been arranged, at the home of John Warwick. Significant members of the church council decided who would do what was necessary, among the lay members, to keep the church moving forward with its current policies. They declared that there would be support for the minister in his initiatives, but that those initiatives would be additional to the current activities in the church. It was clear that, if it came to a vote at the Church Council, Benjamin Sorrell would have little chance of stopping any of the current church activities or of allowing his initiatives to have priority.

Tuesday 28 November 1967

Everything was looking good at Martins Main and there had been a clear run of outputs of over twenty-two thousand tons per week.

★

The Enclosure was in session when an ambulance, with its blue lights flashing, turned along Martins Lane. It went to the pit entrance but, instead of going forward into the pit yard, a workman directed it in the direction of the sidings.

'It must be an accident on the surface, for the ambulance to take that route,' said Bert. 'It must be serious, because usually anyone injured is taken up to the ambulance room, and the ambulance goes there.'

'Could it be one of your mates, Bert?' asked Charlie.

'It will be somebody that I know, because I know everybody on the surface,' replied Bert, who was anxiously looking across to the pit sidings.

It was fifteen minutes later when the ambulance reappeared onto Martins Lane, travelling at speed with its blue lights flashing and its siren sounding. It turned off to go on the Doncaster road.

'They seem to be in a hurry to get the injured fellow to hospital,' said Cliff. 'It must be an emergency.'

★

Roy was underground when he got a call from his secretary, Gordon, asking him to come out of the pit, to the surface, as quickly as possible. One of the shunters, who had been marshalling railway wagons under the screens, had slipped and fallen as he was applying the brake, and his leg had gone under a wagon wheel. His leg was badly damaged and he'd lost a lot of blood. It would need expert surgery if the leg was to be saved.

From the telephone underground, Roy gave Gordon clear instructions. The accident site had to be preserved, for examination by the Mines Inspector, who was to be informed to come to the pit as soon as possible. The Surveyor was to measure up the accident site, make a plan of it and take witness statements. He should also take photographs of the site. The Mechanical Engineer should route the run of mine coal into railway wagons as the Coal Preparation plant would soon not be able to treat any more coal until the site was cleared by the Mines Inspector. Cobba should be informed so that the union could also inspect the site.

Roy came directly out of the pit and the accident, along with its consequences on the pit and the next of kin, kept him fully occupied for the next two days. Ben North, the experienced workman, was in a critical state after operations to try to save his leg.

Wednesday 29 November 1967

Another major incident was to have a severe impact on Martins Main.

It started with a telephone call from underground. 'Boss, we appear to have a sizeable fault which has come into the left-hand end of 60s coalface,' reported George Turnbull. 'I've just had a look at it. The strata conditions are pretty good, but there's no sign of the coal seam beyond the fault.'

'I'll come down to see it for myself,' replied Roy. 'And I'll get the surveyors down to plot it. Is it going to affect the coalface?'

'It certainly is, Boss. It looks to me as though it will cut the face off at an angle of thirty to forty degrees. We need the surveyors to check this. If we're to shorten the coalface, we'll need to make our minds up quickly, so that we can turn the roadway and have a plan to salvage the powered supports.'

'We'll sort the plan out when I've had a look at it,' replied Roy.

He discussed the situation with the Surveyor. There were no projections of faults in this area of the pit, so a team of surveyors went underground with instruments to get an angle on the line of the fault. Roy went underground and saw the conditions, with George. They agreed to stop 60s coalface temporarily, to carry out drilling with long holes to find out where the seam was beyond the fault. Roy rang out of the pit to get the experts on long-hole drilling from the Region, with some of their equipment. In the meantime, Roy asked Jim Lord to concentrate on Fuston Two coalface, to get additional coal from there to balance the pit tonnage. This would be an opportunity for the Fuston seam to have access to the shaft capacity without any constraints. Roy's mind was working on how they could achieve at least twenty-one thousand tons this week.

Friday 1 December 1967

Roy had continued to receive daily reports from the hospital about the Ben North's progress and he was pleased to learn that he had now been taken off the critical list.

★

It had taken two days of drilling, measuring and plotting on the plans to evaluate the impact of the geological fault on the operations. When Roy saw the plans from the

Surveyor, he realised that the impact on the Benton seam workings was very significant. The fault had a vertical displacement of twenty-one feet, so there was no way the coalface could work through it. It would be possible, though, to turn the left-hand roadway of 60s coalface at the angle of the fault and shorten the coalface. As the coalface advanced, it would be necessary to salvage the powered supports, along with the other face equipment. Roy estimated that it would be possible to advance the coalface until the length of the coalface was reduced by a hundred yards, but the angle of the fault also showed that it would cut off 59s coalface within the next two to three months. The plan also indicated that the development of 61s coalface would be aborted in its original position. The only option was to push the trunk roadways forward, to see if the Benton seam was fault-free in the position of 62s coalface.

Roy reported the implications of the fault to Reg Jenkins. He called a meeting of his management team to explain what actions had to be taken as a result of this fault. He held the meeting in the conference room, where he had a large plan displaying the projection of the fault and its impact on the Benton seam operations. He started by discussing the reportable accident to the workman on the surface.

'It's been a poor week for Martins. As you know, we had the very bad accident to the surface worker in the sidings. I understand that he's now off the danger list, and I shall be going to see him tonight, with my wife. It's still too early to know if his leg can be saved, but we must hope for the best. This was a chance-in-a-million incident. He was applying the brakes to one of the wagons, with his brake stick, when he slipped on some oil on one of the sleepers. As he fell, he rolled over and his other leg went across the rail and was caught by the wagon wheel. His leg was badly damaged, but the actions of his mates and the pit first aid man, managed to reduce the bleeding. He was removed to hospital in quick time. I don't think anything more could have done for the unfortunate fellow.'

'Then we had the fault that appeared at the left-hand end of 60s coalface. This is a major problem for Martins Main, in the Benton Seam, and we have to limit the damage as much as we can. That's the purpose of this meeting. We will agree what we're going to do, and we'll list all the actions, so that everyone at the pit is clear what's to happen. Let me deal with 60s coalface first.

We will produce coal on two shifts each day. Then, on the third shift, we'll have a team of men who will shorten the panzer conveyor and withdraw the appropriate number of powered supports. It will be complicated to work that end of the coalface and keep it tidy and safe, so I am only expecting four shears per day. We need to perfect this method of operation, as it will be needed on 59s coalface, when the fault affects that face in the New Year. Any there any questions?'

'No, Boss, no questions,' said George. 'But we'll need extra craftsmen on that third shift, to help with the salvage work.' The Mechanical Engineer agreed to organise his fitters.

'The next thing we need to consider is the main roadway developments in the Benton seam,' continued Roy. 'As you can see, there's no chance of having a 61s coalface, due to this fault. We therefore need to give top priority to driving those roadways forward, to see if there is a 62s coalface. There is another reason for these roadways to push forward as fast as possible: the hole drilled through the fault indicated that the seam section was much less than the section on 60s coalface. What's the position with the main roadway developments, George?'

'I've already spoken to the men, Boss, and I've shuffled some very good development officials into those roadways. They will be given top priority.'

'The real challenge is how we are going to keep the pit tonnage at a respectable level, with these problems in the Benton seam' said Roy. 'I believe the answer rests with the Fuston Two coalface. That face will now have the run of the shaft capacity and it should be able to keep the pit up to twenty thousand tons per week. You'll recall that we had a serious problem with roof conditions when the first Fuston coalface had advanced to the square position. The Fuston Two coalface will have advanced to its square position in the next two weeks, and we cannot afford for the coalface to stop in the same position for any period of time and so allow a major strata weight to affect the roof conditions. We'll therefore arrange to operate the coalface on all shifts over the next two weekends. I'll be arranging that with the unions later today. My thoughts are that we have been given another challenge by some surprise geology, and we'll have to rise to meet it.'

There were other matters of detail discussed, but Roy thought that he had set a plan before his staff that would retain the pit in its successful role.

After the meeting, he saw Cobba and his union colleagues, to brief them on the implication of the geological fault in the Benton seam. It wasn't a controversial meeting. Cobba openly expressed the view that the manager was taking the right actions, in the circumstances, to safeguard the pit's performance. That also applied to working the Fuston Two coalface on every shift during the next two weekends.

★

Once home, Roy discussed with Helen his plan to visit the injured surface worker in hospital and he was grateful when his wife offered to go with him. Cobba had said that he knew the family, so Roy arranged to pick up Cobba so that he could accompany them.

At the hospital there was a crush of visitors at the entrance to the ward, waiting for the start of visiting time. The patient had now been removed from the intensive care unit into a general ward. Cobba spotted the man's wife, and brought her over and introduced her to Roy and Helen. She was obviously very nervous at meeting the colliery manager, but Helen took her to one side to chat with her and learn the latest position with her husband. Cobba went to have a word with the Ward Sister and explained that the colliery manager and his wife were visiting the patient and he persuaded her to allow two extra chairs at the side of the bed, for Roy and Helen. This caused some curious looks from the other visitors, when the four of them walked down the ward, accompanied by the nursing sister.

It was clear which bed they needed, as there was a large cage over the injured leg and the man was laid down. Cobba went straight up and spoke to the man.

'Now then, Ben, how are you getting on? You have some extra visitors tonight,' he said. Ben turned his head and looked at Cobba, who was standing next to the bed and in front of his wife.

'I'm better than I was, Cobba, but I'd be a lot happier on the pit top at Martins, instead of in here.'

'That will come, Ben,' replied Cobba. 'You'll have to be a bit patient.'

'He has no patience at all,' said his wife, who came forward and bent down to give him a kiss. 'If you look the other way you'll see that the colliery manager and his wife have come to see you.' The man's position in the bed was fixed, to avoid any movement of his injured leg, so he had to swing his head over to see Roy and Helen. It was a surprise to see them and he didn't know what to say.

'Don't worry about us,' said Roy. 'And certainly don't move if it affects your leg. We've come because there are a lot of people at the pit who keep asking about you, and they want to know that you're improving.'

'I think I'm improving, Boss,' he replied. 'It was a bad break of the leg, but they say that it's healing now. But I've not seen it yet. They always move this bloody cage so that I can't have a look.'

'Why do you want to look?' said his wife. 'Leave it to the doctors; they know what they're doing.'

'It's my bloody leg!' said Ben. 'I'll have to get to know it again, sometime before long.'

'I agree with you, Ben,' said Helen. 'It is your leg, but your job will be to persuade it to do what you want it to do, in the future, when it's healed. You'll get to be the boss over it, then, and you'll have to coax it and exercise it until it's back to normal. I shouldn't worry about seeing it now. It will be all yours to sort out in the future. Just concentrate on getting your strength up, and think of all the people who are willing you to get better.'

'Aye, I suppose that's good advice,' Ben replied. There was a look of conspiracy between Helen and Ben's wife, who gave Helen a smile.

After some more general talk, with Cobba and Roy adding some snippets about the pit, Cobba, Helen and Roy left Ben with his wife. At the end of the ward the nursing sister in charge was on her own in her office. They went into the office to have a word with her about Ben's prospects.

'It was a very serious accident to that leg, with a wound that will take some time to heal,' she said. 'It will be a while before we know that the wound will fully heal. Then there's the further question of damage to the muscles, and how much use he might have in the leg, in the long-term. He's made good progress, compared with his condition when he first came into the hospital, but there's still a long way to go. He'll need a lot of support to keep his spirits up, in the next few weeks.'

'Thank you for that appraisal,' said Roy.

'We'll come again to help to keep his spirits up,' said Helen. 'I think his wife will need some support, as well, if it takes as long as you're suggesting.' Cobba looked across at Helen, as he was not certain that her offer was a genuine one. Going back in the car, though, his cynicism was dispelled when Helen asked Roy to provide her with the man's address, so that she could visit his wife during the next few weeks.

Monday 4 December 1967

'Everybody in the Club last night was discussing the Benton seam fault that's come onto 60s coalface,' said Charlie. 'They say that it could be serious.'

'It's worse than that,' said Cliff. 'I got a copy of a sketch plan that's been prepared, and this same fault will affect all the plans for the Benton seam.' He produced the sketch plan and the members of the Enclosure gathered round.

'There is no way that they can get another coalface developed by the time 60s ceases production,' concluded Cliff.

'That means that they'll be a coalface short then, in the Benton seam,' said Albert.

'It does,' said Cliff. 'But if the worst comes to the worst, they could be two coalfaces short, if 59s finishes before they've developed a new coalface in the Benton seam.'

'This manager's policy, of working less coalfaces, has come home to roost,' said Albert.

'The pit still expects to produce over twenty thousand tons saleable a week, in the short-term,' said Pat.

'How will they manage that?' asked Charlie.

'They'll get more coal from the Fuston Two face,' said Pat.

Some concern was expressed, within the Enclosure, that the prospects at Martins were not looking anyway near as good as they were a few weeks ago.

★

Helen came home very distressed from a Church Council meeting. She wanted to discuss it with Roy.

'You won't believe this, Roy, but Dr Benjamin Sorrell tonight proposed that the traditional services for Christmas should be discontinued – no nativity play, no carol service and no Christmas concert by the Junior School choir. He says that they take the focus from the real message of Christmas. We were all speechless to start with, but then John Warwick challenged the proposal. He reminded the meeting that the Junior School had given a Christmas concert in church for as long as anyone can remember. He said he thought that it was important for the concert to be held as usual, as it brought the children into the influence of the church, and it was supported by many of their parents who didn't normally attend. Benjamin Sorrell said that this was part of the froth of Christmas, and that it had no real spiritual significance. However, there was a long discussion and then Joe Horton put a proposal to the meeting that the pattern of services for Christmas should stay the same as in past years. This was carried by a large majority. Benjamin Sorrell then expressed his disappointment that the church was not supporting, and I quote, 'his powerful ministerial message and leadership'.'

'It sounds to have been a stormy meeting,' replied Roy. 'Did you take part in the discussion?'

'Yes, I'm afraid I did,' said Helen. 'I was so cross that I reminded him that the church has a duty to nurture all its members and also to nurture and serve the community. I asked him how it's possible to show real Christian love if one doesn't show it to the community.

I drew reference to the Good Samaritan. Some of the Church Council members voiced their agreement to what I said.'

'Did he answer you?'

'No, he didn't, he just gave that fixed smile that he shows when someone disagrees with him – the smile that's intended to say that he's right and they're wrong.'

'Calm down, Helen,' said Roy. 'I think he'll have met his match, with your Church Council. How did you find Ben North when you visited him today?'

'I was going to tell you. I picked up his wife and took her to the hospital. She's a nice woman, when you get to know her. Her husband's worked at Martins since he left school, but he didn't fancy working underground, so he stayed on the surface. They've two teenaged children and she has a part-time job to increase the family income. They live in the small village of Clinton, three miles from the pit, and he travels to work each day on his push-bike. It's really a small cottage that they rent, and she keeps it neat and tidy. She insisted that I had a cup of tea with her, when we got back from the hospital.'

'And how was Ben?' asked Roy.

'He seemed to have improved, from when we saw him on Friday, and he was very appreciative of the bunch of grapes I took. But he's still laid down, with the cage over his leg. His wife says that it'll be another week before the dressings are taken off his leg wounds. How was your meeting at Region today?'

'We had a long planning meeting, trying to sort out where to develop another coalface in the Benton seam. The fault that's run in has really ruined the pit plans. It's doubtful whether there'll be any reliable coal for quite a long time. In the end, we decided to develop a coalface opposite 58s. It will only last for three or four months, as it's a small piece of coal, so it's just an emergency plan.'

'Are you worried about the pit, now?' asked Helen. 'Everything seemed to be going well for you.'

'There is always a risk, in coal mining, that the geology will change suddenly and disrupt the best of plans,' replied Roy. 'That's what's happened to us at Martins. We'll have to get ourselves reorganised, but it will take us at least a year to sort out the Benton seam.'

'Has Mr Pickersgill said anything about the new situation?'

'I understand from Reg Jenkins that he's had a meeting with the Regional Planning department, to check why the fault wasn't projected. They produced all the plans from surrounding pits and there was nothing to suggest there would be geological problems in this area of the mine. One thing that will be put on hold is any more presentations of the paper I gave on this pit at the Staff College. While this year will be the best ever for Martins, in terms of output and financial profit, the prospects for next year are very uncertain at this stage.'

'Could this invalidate the information and conclusions of the paper?'

'It might; but in the meantime we'll be able to produce good levels of output and remain highly profitable. The real risks will show themselves in about four months.'

'Don't you worry, Roy,' said Helen, as she came over to give him a hug. 'I'm sure you'll sort it out. What will be the reaction at the Regional annual dinner dance? Do you think we'll be on Mr Pickersgill's table again?'

'We are not normally on Norman Pickersgill's table for any reason to do with Martins Main, Helen; it's all because of a certain Mrs Helen Dobson. She's a personal friend of Mr Pickersgill, and he thinks very highly of her as a woman of distinction.'

'Don't you tease me, Roy Dobson,' replied Helen, smiling at her husband. 'I'm going upstairs to say my prayers now. I have to ask for forgiveness, tonight, for what I said at the Church Council meeting, and I want to pray for Ben. And I might spare a few requests for Martins Main and its manager.'

Wednesday 6 December 1967

Mr Pickersgill was in his office with the Regional Personnel Manager. It was another of many meetings discussing staffing issues. With the closure of pits and slimming down, the Region had been offering redundancy terms to many staff at different grades within the organisation. Today's was somewhat different, as it affected a senior appointment.

'These are the terms that will apply, Sir,' said the Personnel Manager, placing a copy of the figures in front of Mr Pickersgill. 'He has a good number of years in the Staff Superannuation Scheme, and the redundancy will give him a significant lump sum as well. He lives in his own house, which I think may by fully paid for, as he has no loan from the Coal Executive. So he will have a good pension to live on.' Norman Pickersgill studied the schedule of figures.

'We will see how the discussion goes, but we could sweeten these figures with three months' pay in lieu of notice, if he leaves in the next few weeks,' said Mr Pickersgill. He rang his Secretary and asked her to send Mr Ralph Lacey into the office.

'Take a seat, Mr Lacey,' said Mr Pickersgill. 'We want to take the opportunity that is available at the present time to put a proposition to you.' Mr Lacey moved nervously in his seat, uncertain what the proposition was going to be. He had a notebook in his hand to write down any instructions he might receive about mining matters.

'As you are aware, the industry is contracting quite quickly and, as well as pits closing, regions are being merged in other parts of the country. The British Coal Executive has agreed to provide funds to offer very favourable terms to senior staff, to make the contraction work smoothly. As you are approaching sixty years of age, when we have looked at your terms we think that we can offer you a deal that is too good to refuse. What's your reaction to the opportunity to retire early?'

'To be honest, I've not thought about it, Mr Pickersgill. I always assumed that I would be required to work until I was sixty-five.'

'As I see the future of the coal industry, no one will be working until they are that age,' said Mr Pickersgill. 'Although I have to say that I cannot see the current favourable terms being available for much longer. Do you agree with that statement?' He turned to the Personnel Manager.

'The financial terms are exceptionally good at the present time, Mr Pickersgill,' agreed the Personnel Manager.

'What I suggest is that you go away and have half an hour discussing the build up of the figures with the Personnel Manager. Then you will no doubt want to discuss them with your wife. When you have made your mind up, if you let me know, I can set the wheels in motion, and then you can have a very significant financial Christmas present.'

'I will do that, Mr Pickersgill,' replied Mr Lacey, and he stood up to leave.

'By the way,' said Mr Pickersgill, stopping Mr Lacey in his tracks. 'How is that granddaughter of yours, now?'

'Oh, Amy-Louise is doing very well, Sir,' he replied with pride. 'She's growing up to be full of beans and a real charmer.'

'Well, there you are,' said Pickersgill, with a wave of his hand. 'I am offering you a deal that will let you spend more time enjoying your granddaughter. What more could you ask for?'

Norman Pickersgill was confident that Mr Lacey would opt for the early retirement terms. It would allow him to make the appointment of a younger mining engineer, with a very high reputation, who was surplus to requirements in the North East of England.

Friday 8 December 1967

Helen Dobson called on Sandra Lacey to make arrangements for the babysitting on the night of the annual dinner dance. Sandra was keen to chat.

'We have major news in the family,' Sandra said. 'Terry's dad has been offered early retirement, with a generous lump sum payout and access to his pension in three months' time. He's jumped at the offer. He's relieved to get out of his job with the Coal Executive, as he has not been happy in the Region, since Mr Pickersgill came. He sounds to be a bit of a tyrant.'

'I don't know about that, Sandra,' replied Helen. 'I've always had a good relationship with Norman Pickersgill, but then I don't have to work with him every day.'

It was agreed that Sandra and Amy-Louise would stay the night on the occasion of the annual dinner dance.

When Amy-Louise went to lie down for a morning nap, Sandra provided coffee and gave Helen an update on the state of her extended family. Cobba had got the chairmanship of the housing committee on the Borough Council, Sandra reported, and she said that he was keeping quiet about it as he didn't want everybody in Upthorpe approaching him about their position on the housing waiting list. Her brother, David, was enjoying success with his football career and was regularly playing with the reserve team for Sheffield United, where he had an apprenticeship. Terry was to be upgraded in his office, in the New Year, but he was working very hard to prepare for his RICS exams.

'So, things are going pretty well, here,' concluded Sandra. 'How are things with you, Helen?'

'I'm alright, Sandra,' Helen replied. 'But there are problems at Martins, due to some geological problems which are giving Roy some challenges.'

'I've heard about them from my Dad,' replied Sandra. 'But Dad is confident that Mr Dobson will sort them out.' Helen hoped that the confidence, shown by so many people, in Roy, was well-founded.

Tuesday 12 December 1967

It was the Tuesday of Bull week, and the Enclosure was discussing the latest information about the pit.

'They're winding plenty of coal,' said Bert. 'All these problems in the Benton seam don't seem to be affecting the output from the pit. How can that be?'

'The reason is that the Fuston Two face is doing very well,' said Cliff. 'And they're still getting some coal from 60s coalface, although it's getting shorter. The troubles will start when they have to stop that face.'

'The talk in the Club is that it will stop at the Christmas holidays,' said Charlie. 'They'll then salvage the rest of the equipment from the face. It will be wanted for 58Bs face.'

'When will that be ready?' asked Albert.

'They'll start opening out the coalface after the Christmas holidays, so the earliest that it'll be installed and ready, will be the end of February,' replied Cliff. 'I've seen a programme with all this drawn out. The trouble is that it'll only last a few months.'

'What happens then?' asked Albert.

'Nobody seems to know,' said Charlie. 'They've not found any decent coal in the forward headings in the Benton seam. It's all faults and thin coal.'

'Bloody hell,' said Albert. 'It sounds to be a real mess.'

'You have to remember that Martins will achieve its best results ever, this year,' said Pat. 'You can't take that away from the manager.'

'That's OK; but what about next year?' put in Albert.

'We'll just have to wait and see,' replied Cliff.

Thursday 14 December 1967

Roy Dobson had arranged to hire the conference room at the Club to have the annual meeting with his staff. He considered it was more important than ever to have the meeting, this year, due to the changed circumstances at the pit. He'd spent several days preparing his talk and Jeff Briggs had worked on the financial figures and the Surveyor had prepared the slides. Roy wanted it to be as professional as his presentation at the Staff College. He wanted to get the perspective right.

The conference room was full and the audience expectant.

'I want to tell you of the very good results that will be achieved by Martins Main for the year that finishes next week,' he began. 'It will be the best year ever, for Martins, and its financial results will show profit levels higher than any other pit in Yorkshire. So, it's well done to all of you who have contributed to that excellent performance. I would have hoped to be able to go on to project performances for next year at the same level, however that is not possible.'

Roy showed information on possible output patterns for the forthcoming year, and emphasised the importance of achieving higher performances from the Fuston seam. He concluded his presentation with a carefully crafted statement to his staff.

'Next year we are to be tested as much as we have ever been while I've been your manager. We have to re-establish ourselves in the Benton seam, but at this stage we are not sure where that will be. So we have to be able to react quickly to the opportunities when they arise – we've done that in the past. We have to build up equipment and mechanised systems very quickly and efficient – we've done that in the past. We have to produce top-class performances from our coalfaces, when they are available – and we've done that in the past, too. So next year will be nothing new for all of us, but we will need to work as a team. But next year there will be one difference: we will need to keep the team spirit high through the periods when the results are poor – that will be a new challenge for us.'

After the presentation there were lots of questions. These mainly centred on reserves in other seams, rather than the Benton seam. Roy had to say that there were no plans to access other seams at the present time. He came away from the meeting aware that there were serious concerns among members of his staff that the current plans did not give long-term confidence in the pit.

Saturday 16 December 1967

It was the evening of the annual dinner dance and Sandra came to the Dobson's house, as planned, with Amy-Louise. Amy-Louise immediately went off, with Robert holding her hand to help her up the stairs, as they headed for the playroom. Sandra stayed with Roy as he waited for Helen to come down from her bedroom where she was applying the final touches to her make-up. As she descended the stairs she looked magnificent in a full-length dark-blue satin evening dress with long sleeves with lace around the cuffs. It was shaped to emphasise her figure and had a belt around the waist. Helen wore it with a matching stole and shoes.

'Mrs Dobson, I always look forward to seeing you when you go to this function, because your outfits are so beautiful,' said Sandra. 'But tonight you look absolutely stunning. How do you do it, getting the colours just right and your dresses such a perfect fit?'

'Believe me, it's more by good luck than by skill, Sandra,' replied Helen. 'I need to look good, as we're usually on the top table and I can't wear the same dress twice.'

'I hope that Mr Dobson gives you a special allowance for your wardrobe,' said Sandra. 'He's a fortunate fellow, to have you as his partner all night.'

'He has to share me with other dancing partners,' replied Helen. 'But he's no use at shopping for clothes; he just says yes to anything. So I wander around the shops on my own until I see something that attracts me. Fortunately, over the past few years, I've always managed to spot an outfit that's suited me.'

Outside, Dennis Gates, the gardener, was holding the car door open for them.

'Good evening, Mrs Dobson,' he said, as he made sure that her dress wasn't trapped in the door. He enjoyed these occasions, when he was able to mix with the other chauffeurs who were driving VIPs to the Christmas event. He was enjoying his life as the Dobson's gardener; it was much better than delivering Home Coal.

'You do look wonderful tonight,' Roy whispered in Helen's ear, as the car started down the drive.

'I am dressed to impress your boss, so that he doesn't lose confidence in you,' replied Helen with a smile.

'You should have saved it for a few months' time,' said Roy. 'This will be the best year ever at Martins, so Mr Pickersgill should not be de-rating me yet. It might be a different story in three months, though.'

★

In the hotel banqueting suite, Roy went to get Helen a fruit juice from the bar, and then he checked the seating plan, just to confirm that they were sitting at the top table. He wasn't sure if he was imagining the reaction of some of his colleagues, but he thought he detected a few smirks on the faces of some of the colliery managers. They'd obviously heard of the faults affecting the Benton seam faces at Martins. Had he been in the toilet when several managers were there together he would have been shocked at their other comments.

'He needed to be brought down a peg or two,' said one manager. 'Giving a presentation at the Staff College as though he had the answer to every pit's problems; suggesting that his solutions could be applied at other pits! He stuck his neck out; well now he's got real problems to sort out. This will test him. We might find out just how good this bugger is.'

'I'm not bothered about him,' said another manager. 'But I still fancy his wife. Have you seen her tonight? She looks smashing. Just imagine going home on a night to wrestle with that woman in bed. It would be even worth suffering an accountability meeting with Pickersgill, to have that body to look forward to.'

'It's not on offer without strings,' put in one of his mates. 'She's very religious. You'd have to go to church and get down on your knees.'

'I don't mind getting down on my knees if she'd get down on hers, for a bit of variety, you understand!' There was raucous laughter from the managers as they left the gents.

★

Mr Pickersgill gave his welcome to the assembly and said that he would speak after the dinner. He asked Helen to say the grace. There was a shuffling of chairs as everyone stood.

Helen detected, in the silence that followed, a keen attention to what she would say this year. With her eyes firmly shut and her hands clasped before her, she spoke into the microphone.

'Good Lord, we thank you that, in this industry that is continually faced with hazards and challenges, you have been there throughout the past year to guide and protect all who work in the mines. You have also prompted and influenced all with responsibilities in management, to make the right decisions and to ensure it is a safe and successful industry. We would pray for your continued guidance in the year ahead, which we know will have shocks and surprises for us all. We now thank you for this food and for the opportunity that this function offers us to meet with friends and colleagues. Amen.'

When they sat down, Norman Pickersgill turned to Helen and clasped her hand.

'I wait for your grace each year, Helen, in expectation for what you will say. It is always different, but strangely relevant. Thank you very much.'

★

When Mr Pickersgill spoke, after the dinner, he was slightly subdued. He acclaimed the success of the Region, which was at the forefront of performance in the country, and he thanked everyone for their efforts to achieve that success. He was, though, disappointed at the rate of contraction in the industry and he feared that there might have to be more pit closures in Yorkshire and in his Region. He concluded by stating his confidence that his staff would be able to meet and resolve all the problems they were faced with in the coming year.

In the dancing that followed Roy danced mainly with Helen, but did have dances with the other ladies from the top table. This year, Mr Pickersgill had Richard and Denise Wallace on his table, representing the mining contractors. So Roy had Denise as his partner in a slow foxtrot, and he experienced once more the closeness of her body as she adopted her intimate style of dancing. He observed her in other dances and realised that she adopted different styles with different partners.

The other exceptional event on the dancefloor occurred later in the evening. The colliery manager who earlier had been fantasising about Helen was sitting at the table next to Mr Pickersgill's table. His colleagues, fuelled by alcohol, suggested that he should take the opportunity to invite Helen for a dance. He rejected this at first, but when Helen was sitting on her own while Roy was in conversation with Mr Pickersgill, they increased the pressure and, on the spur of the moment, the colliery manager went across to Helen.

'Could I invite you to have this dance with me, Mrs Dobson?' he said, with a slight bow. Helen stood up and gave him a smile and joined him on the dancefloor. He adopted a serious approach and consciously aimed to disguise the effect of the alcohol he'd drunk. He explained that he was a colliery manager and how much he admired what Roy had achieved at Martins. He said that he appreciated the pressures that affected colliery managers and their wives. Helen responded to his conversation but also noticed that he was a good dancer and could improvise clever moves, so she had to concentrate to follow his lead. It was a quickstep and he held her very close as they sped around the floor, finishing the dance with several rapid reverse turns. Helen was glad to cling onto him, to avoid falling, and he held her tight. He led her back to her table and again gave her a slight bow as he thanked her for the dance. Helen thanked him and decided to have a break, to get her breath back, by visiting the ladies cloakroom.

When the colliery manager got back to his table his colleagues asked for a report. The men were on their own as their wives had also gone off for a break.

'That was bloody marvellous,' said the colliery manager, as he took a long drink from his pint of beer. 'I have had my Christmas present for this year.'

'You seemed to be holding her a bit close,' said one of his mates.

'She's a good dancer, and you have to hold a partner close if you're putting fancy bits in the dance. She followed me very well.'

'Was she as good as you expected?' asked another colleague.

'Even better,' he relied. 'She has a beautiful body and I've felt most of it, during that dance. The way she followed my lead in the dance makes me imagine what it would be like if she followed my lead in other ways.'

'Watch out,' one of his mates said. 'Your wife's coming back.'

Sunday 17 December 1967

The Christmas period was to be busy for both Helen and Roy. They both agreed to support each other over the coming festive season. Roy agreed to attend the special events at the church, and Helen agreed to present prizes to the children at two special children's parties at the Welfare Club.

'We need to attend the Junior School Choir concert and the Church carol service,' said Helen. 'These Christmas events are well attended and I'm not sure if Dr Benjamin Sorrell will even put in an appearance at either of them. They are both organised so that we can manage without him, though. I've ended up being in charge of the carol service, and introducing the hymns and doing two of the readings. I'll not be able to sit with you in the congregation, but I've arranged that Willie will sit with you.'

'Why don't we invite my mother and sister up for next weekend?' suggested Roy. 'If they come up on the Saturday morning they can go and see you presenting the prizes at the children's party on the Saturday afternoon and then go to the carol service on the Sunday night.'

'That's a good suggestion,' replied Helen. 'Will the boys be invited to the Welfare Christmas party?'

'They're definitely invited, and Cobba said that he hoped they would be at the party, now that you're presenting the prizes.'

'Well, that's alright, as the whole family will be there. I hope that the boys don't scoop too many prizes!'

'Cobba said that Sandra was planning to go, and enter Amy-Louise into the Bonny

Baby competition.'

'If she enters, with her charming smiles, it will be a tough contest for the others,' replied Helen. 'I'm pleased that I'm only presenting the prizes, and not one of the judges.'

Friday 22 December 1967

The Stewardess of the Welfare Club had planned more elaborate parties than those she'd organised the previous year. She anticipated that there would be a bigger attendance of children, so the food was more varied, and there was more of it. The games and competitions were also more extensive. She had all the committee members helping her control the events, so that they finished with adequate time to tidy up and adapt the Club for the evening session. On Friday afternoon there was a party planned for the children under five-years-old. On Saturday afternoon it would be the turn of the five to twelve-year-olds, but also, in another room there was to be the Bonny Baby contest. She'd arranged this to engage those parents bringing older children to the Club.

Helen was at the Club throughout the afternoon, helping with the organisation and then presenting the prizes. She gave a very favourable report to Roy, when he came home from the pit.

'You have a genius, with the Club Stewardess. Everything was very well organised and she had time to encourage the shy children to join in and enjoy themselves. She also contrived to share out the prizes, so that no one got more than their share. The mothers, who stayed on, clearly have a great respect for her. I was most impressed.'

'It was one of my more inspired ideas to keep her on, when we had to kick her husband out,' replied Roy. 'Did you enjoy yourself?'

'Yes, I did,' replied Helen. 'And I came away feeling that the Club is playing a positive role in the community, in parallel with the church. Janet Hall was there and she brought Dawn, as well as Michael. Michael was keen to tell me that he'll be starting school after Christmas. He's a smart little lad now. I marvel every time I see those boys, and think about the wonderful way that Janet and Bob are bringing them up. What really gets me moved, though, is the relationship between Dawn and her brothers. Today, Michael kept his eye on Dawn all afternoon and, when it was time for the food, he took her hand and led her to the table so that she could sit next to him.'

'You played an important role in finding the right family solution for those children,' said Roy.

Saturday 23 December 1967

The Saturday afternoon party for the older children was equally successful. Roy's mother and his sister observed the event with lots of smiles and laughs, particularly at the antics of the older boys who were trying to cheat, despite Roy's efforts as referee. Again, the prizes were awarded equitably, but when Helen was asked to present them at the end, she applied a variation to the procedure. She took a letter out of her pocket and used it to explain to the audience why she was presenting the prizes.

'Father Christmas should really have been here this afternoon presenting these prizes, but he's sent me this letter asking me to stand in for him. He wants me to explain why he cannot be here. He has so many presents to get ready for the children in Upthorpe this year, that he's working overtime to get them all made and packed up, ready for him to deliver on Christmas Eve.'

Helen looked round and saw one or two cynical looks on the faces of some of the older boys, while the younger children were amazed that Helen had received a letter from Father Christmas. 'Anyone who does not believe this letter from Father Christmas will be excluded from receiving a prize.' This caused the older boys to change their cynical looks and when Helen asked if they would all join in three cheers for Father Christmas, everyone cheered at the top of their voices.

Amy-Louise got second prize for the Bonny Baby competition. Cobba was relieved at this result, as he didn't want anyone to think that his granddaughter had been given preferential treatment by the judges. He was sure, though, that Amy-Louise should have won.

Sunday 24 December 1967

The evening carol service brought a full congregation to the church, but no Rev Dr Benjamin Sorrell. The choir was augmented with additional singers, including some from the Junior School choir. The hymns and special items were conducted by the schoolteacher who'd conducted the Sunday School anniversary. Four young girls sang Away in a Manger. One very young girl sang a modern song that had been a part of the Sunday School nativity play. Her clear, sweet, bell-like voice had so impressed the audience at the nativity play that she'd been persuaded to repeat the solo at the end the play. Once again her solo, which was quietly accompanied by Peter Carter on the piano, captivated the congregation and there was absolute silence during her performance, followed by murmurs of wonder when she finished. The choir sang Hark, Hark What News the Angels Bring, to a local Yorkshire tune that used all the vocal parts in runs and harmonies and ended in a climax that Peter exploited with the organ at full blast. The carols were performed with solid Methodist enthusiasm and the readings told the full Christmas story, although some of the readers were hesitant and far from word-perfect.

When it came to the final item, Helen explained that this was a break in the normal tradition of the church carol service.

'It's not really a Christmas piece,' she said, 'but it's a wonderful finale and captures the real aim of a Christian going along life's journey. We finished this year's Sunday School anniversary with this song, arranged by our own Peter Carter. It will be sung first by Maureen, and then we'll all join in the second time through. Please keep standing at the end for the final prayer. You'll Never Walk Alone.

It was a glorious finish to the evening, and when Peter took his hands off the organ keyboard there was an echo around the church. Helen waited for there to be complete silence and then, with her hands clasped in front of her and her eyes tightly closed, she prayed.

'Dear Lord, tonight we have celebrated the coming of Christmas. We thank you that you sent your son to earth, at Christmas, to live among us and show us your ways and your truths. But most of all, we thank you that you gave us the assurance that we will never walk alone if we put our hands into your hands, and allow you to lead us and guide us wherever life may take us. Now may the spirit of the Living God, which has been here with us tonight in this service, go with us and stay with us for evermore. Amen.'

As she got down from the pulpit, Helen thanked the choir, the children, the conductor and the organist for their contributions to the carol service. However before leaving the church, she herself was thanked by many in the congregation for the part she'd played in leading the service. The comment she would always remember was from Willie Carter, who approached her, hesitantly, as she walked towards the door. He took her hand and held it.

'Mrs Dobson,' he said, struggling for the right words. 'We have never had a carol service like that before. Thank you so much. We saw the Lord in this church tonight.'

She squeezed his hand. 'Thank you, and God bless you, Willie.' She left the church, with a lump in her throat, and went to join Roy and the rest of the family who were waiting in the car.

Back at the house, Roy's sister had a few words with her brother, when they were in the kitchen together.

'It's been a wonderful break for me and Mother, this weekend,' she said. 'But it's also been a revelation to me. I have seen what an amazing woman Helen is, and how she complements you in your work. Also how deep her faith is. You made a very good choice when you picked her for a wife, Roy.' She squeezed his arm and he just nodded in agreement and dare not look her in the eye, as he was deeply moved by his sister's words.

Chapter 30

Friday 5 January 1968

It had been an excellent Christmas for the Dobson family. The Club had been packed throughout the Christmas period, and Cobba had rung Roy to remark on the record financial takings. Maintenance work at the pit had gone well, and Roy had only visited the pit on one morning, to check on the reports. Helen was very happy with the events at the church over the Christmas and New Year holidays, and the Church Council members expressed their relief that they had insisted on carrying out the traditional programme. It was noted that the minister, Benjamin Sorrell, was having only limited support for his Bible study classes.

★

Roy went back to work ready to face a challenging time. There were significant changes to be made in the organisation of the pit. 60s coalface had ceased production and teams of men were deployed to salvage the rest of the equipment and prepare it for installation on 58B coalface. Two development teams were deployed to open out the 58B coalface. They started at each end of the coalface and it was a race to see which team got to the mid-point first.

'I've talked with the lads, Boss,' reported George Turnbull. 'They've guaranteed to have the face opened out in three weeks. I'll make sure that they have all the supplies they need.'

'If you can do that, George, it will be a big help,' replied Roy. 'In those three weeks we'll need to have all the equipment from 60s face salvaged, ready to do a quick installation on 58Bs.'

'Don't worry about that, Boss. I'll sort that out. When do you think we'll hit the fault on 59s face?'

'According to the Surveyor, it should happen in the next two to three weeks,' replied Roy.

★

In a detailed discussion with the Surveyor and Jeff Briggs, Roy drew up the potential production figures for the coming weeks. The estimate showed a daily total of three thousand nine hundred tons. So, allowing for some breakdowns, they calculated that it should be possible to average a weekly saleable output of seventeen and a half thousand tons. That tonnage would give a profit each week for the pit. These were the figures Roy would want to present at his accountability meeting scheduled for the third week in January.

'The output will reduce the time before 59s coalface has to shorten off, when it hits the fault,' said Jeff.

'That is true,' replied Roy. 'But, if George keeps to his timetable, we might be able to have 58Bs face in production by the middle of February. That will keep us right for at least three months.'

They then considered the plan for the next coalface in the Benton seam.

Assuming that the next coalface would be 63s, it was clear that there would be over a thousand yards of roadway to complete and then two hundred and fifty yards to head out the coalface. Roy gave instructions to the Surveyor.

'Talk it through with George and Jim, to agree the quickest way to access that coalface. When that's done I need an action programme that I can discuss with the management team and the unions. I'll also want to explain it when I have my accountability meeting at Region in three weeks' time.'

'It's a challenging time for Martins, Boss,' said Jeff, as he gathered up his papers.

'This is why we need detailed plans, so that we can establish the right priorities,' replied Roy. He wanted to encourage a positive approach to the situation at the pit and avoid anyone showing fear and despair.

Tuesday 23 January 1968

Helen Dobson was holding a coffee morning for her friends Janet, Peggy and Sandra. Sandra had brought Amy-Louise, and Peggy had brought Dawn, but both Janet's boys were now at school. Amy-Louise had climbed the stairs with Dawn and they were playing with the toys in the playroom, so the ladies were on their own.

'How are you enjoying life now, Janet, when both the boys are at school?' asked Sandra.

'I've only had two weeks,' she replied, 'so I've been busy doing all the jobs that got left until I had more time to fit them in! But I am seriously thinking about the future, now.'

'What does that mean?' asked Helen.

'I'm wondering whether I should go back to work. The shop in Doncaster has kept in touch with me, and is offering to have me back part-time. They've been doing quite well lately, and they've bought the shop next door so that they can do an extension. They say they'd welcome my experience.'

'You don't need to go back for the money, do you?' asked Helen. 'I thought Bob was earning plenty at Martins.'

'Yes, Bob's doing very well, but we've been thinking about changes in the future.'

'What changes are those?' asked Sandra.

'Well, it's nothing definite, yet, but we've been wondering if we should consider buying one of the new houses in Upthorpe. It would be much better for the boys to live there. It is only talk at this stage, though.'

'Oh, Janet, don't leave me on my own in Martins Lane,' cried Peggy, with a look of horror on her face. 'I'd miss you and the boys so much. There's no way that I can consider moving into my own house in Upthorpe.'

Helen moved over to where Peggy was sitting, and put her arm around her.

'Peggy, don't worry, you'll not lose Janet and the boys, whatever happens. We've all stuck together for the past few years, and that will continue, I'm sure.'

'It certainly will,' replied Janet. 'I've not mentioned it before, because I knew it would be a shock to you, Peggy. There's a lot to happen before we make a decision to buy our own house. It might take years.'

'You never know, Peggy, you might move first,' said Sandra. 'My dad was telling us that the time will come when the Council will want to clear out the houses on Martins Lane, and move people into new council houses. It's all a case of getting money from the government.'

'There you are, Peggy,' said Helen, in a much more cheerful voice. 'There are all sorts of changes going to happen in the future, that will affect all of us. Let me get some more coffee.'

'What days would you consider working?' asked Sandra.

'We've mentioned Monday and Tuesday, to start with, but I could do Saturdays as well, if Bob was available to look after the boys,' replied Janet.

'I would be glad to help on the days you're working, by taking the boys to school and having them after school,' said Peggy. 'But I want to keep my part-time job at the pit on Thursdays and Fridays. That's made such a big difference to my life.'

'You won't need to do it all, Peggy; I'll be able to help,' said Sandra. 'Amy-Louise loves Tony and Michael and often talks about them. I wouldn't be surprised if she doesn't suggest that she needs a brother, before long!'

'Have you got any plans in that line?' asked Helen, as she returned into the room with a full coffee pot.

'Not yet,' replied Sandra. 'I'm adopting a very chaste life, for Terry, until he finishes his RICS exams. Since his promotion, he needs all his strength for his work and his studies.'

'Sandra Lacey you are a cruel wife, denying your young husband his desires,' said Helen, with a grin.

'The door is not completely closed,' said Sandra with a laugh, as she stood up to fill her cup with more coffee. She looked directly into Helen's eyes as she added. 'I have my ways to ensure that if he does not get quantity then he certainly gets quality. You needn't worry, Helen, Terry Lacey thinks he's a very fortunate young man. I understand that things are not too good at Martins. How is the manager bearing up?'

'He's working very intensively,' replied Helen. 'He describes the situation as 'challenging'.'

'I don't know how he copes with all the pressure,' said Peggy. 'I keep hearing snippets in the wages office. There are all sorts of views about the underground problems. It must be a terrible responsibility to be a colliery manager.'

'Yes, it is a big responsibility,' replied Helen. 'But Roy has got a good deal of experience, now, and that certainly seems to help him when difficulties arise. It will be a difficult evening with him tonight, as it's his accountability meeting at Region tomorrow. He'll spend all evening, and part of the night, going through figures about the pit, to be ready to answer any questions he'll be asked.'

There was a noise as Dawn and Amy-Louise came running down the stairs, and the conversation changed to discussions with the children.

Wednesday 24 January 1968

Roy entered the waiting room in Mr Pickersgill's office. He was surprised, and a little flustered, to see the other senior regional staff waiting to be called into the meeting. Diane Parks was not in her office, so he presumed that she must be in with Mr Pickersgill.

'First in to bat, for this series,' said Mr Jones, the Regional Production Manager, giving Roy a grin which indicated that he was aware of the changed circumstances at Martins Main.

'Yes,' replied Roy. 'It's a new experience for me, to be first in the accountability programme.'

Reg Jenkins sidled over to Roy and whispered in his ear.

'Don't read anything into being first on, and don't let Jones rattle you. You have an amazing set of results for last year, but you need to explain how you're going to get out of the present problems.'

Diane Parks came rushing out of Mr Pickersgill's office, carrying her shorthand book and a sheaf of papers.

'You can go in now,' she said to the regional team. 'You'll have to wait a bit longer, Mr Dobson. Mr Pickersgill wants a brief pre-meeting with the rest of the panel.' Mr Jones's face dropped at this information, as it did not bode well for the mood of Norman Pickersgill.

'You seem to be under pressure, Diane,' said Roy, giving her a smile.

'We have been buried with lots of paper since Christmas. I think everyone in London is asking for as many reports and answers to questionnaires as they can possibly think up. All that happens here is that Mr Pickersgill gets more and more irritable.'

'I'm not looking forward to today's meeting,' said Roy.

'But I thought you had a very good set of annual results?' said Diane.

'Yes we did, but some unexpected geology has hit us, and it will take us some time to get everything sorted out.'

'I'm sure you will sort it,' replied Diane, who was showing a more positive attitude than Roy felt.

★

The buzzer sounded, and he was shown into the office to sit opposite Mr Pickersgill.

Roy spread out his papers on the desk in front of his chair, and then looked straight into the eyes of Regional General Manager.

'Good morning, Mr Dobson,' said Norman Pickersgill. 'This is a story in two parts: an excellent year last year, which we will deal with first, but then a future that is uncertain and difficult to evaluate.'

There were comments of praise from all the members of the regional team, and Roy was able to answer quite easily their questions on financial matters. He tabled his graph showing break-even weekly tonnage for the pit and this clearly demonstrated that all the increases in efficiency had been converted into increased profits. Mr Pickersgill summed up that part of the meeting by congratulating Roy on the pit's performance for the year.

'Now for the future. What is your present output?'

'We are producing over seventeen thousand tons per week, and that is making the pit profitable on a week-by-week basis. We expect to hit the fault on 59s coalface at the end of next week, and we'll then be shortening the coalface as it advances. We still expect to produce around seventeen thousand tons per week and keep the pit profitable. 58Bs coalface will be developed by the end of the month, and we expect to have it in production before the end of February. That will take over from 59s coalface, but it only has a short life, of about sixteen weeks. The real problem is the development of the next Benton Seam coalface, which we think will be 63s coalface. I can show you a detailed plan of this work.'

All the regional team left their seats to gather around the table as Roy displayed the detailed plan showing the disturbed geological problems and the faults which confirmed that there would be no 61s or 62s coalfaces. He then laid out the plan of the trunk roadways in the Benton seam, phased out to be driven by the three development teams, to prepare 63s coalface.

'This shows that there'll be a gap, of about four months, when we will have only a Fuston seam coalface in production. And it could be that during this period that we'll have to do a face-to-face transfer of the Fuston seam equipment.' Roy paused and the implications sank in.

'So, that will be a period when the Martins results will significantly pull down the Regional results?' said Mr Pickersgill. 'Has anyone any comments?' he looked around the regional team.

'These plans clearly show the effect of the fault and the disturbed ground on the Benton seam output,' commented Mr Jones, who thought he should make a contribution. 'They also show the time factor in resolving the problem. I agree with you, Sir, that a gap without any coalface in production at Martins will have a serious impact on the Regional results.'

'Is there anything that can be done to reduce, or eliminate, this gap in the Benton seam production?' asked Mr Pickersgill.

'If we could install a roadway drivage machine in one of these Benton seam developments, we could increase the drivage rate significantly, and so reduce that gap,' said Roy. 'It would also help us to get 64s coalface ready earlier.'

'There you are, Mr Jones. We need you to find a modern drivage machine, as a matter of urgency, to help to reduce this output gap.'

'I'll get onto that straightaway, Sir,' said Mr Jones.

They all resumed their seats, for the summing up by the Regional General Manager.

'Have you any comments, Mr Jenkins?' asked Norman Pickersgill.

'I am very hopeful, Sir, that this will be a short-term problem. The Fuston seam has still more potential to give and there are very large reserves of coal in that seam. Martins needs one Benton face and one Fuston face to be comfortably profitable. If we get two Benton seam faces, along with one Fuston seam face, then there is no reason why Martins should not be able to repeat last year's performance, on a regular basis.'

'I agree with you, Mr Jenkins,' said Mr Pickersgill. He looked at Roy. 'Mr Dobson, you are facing a real challenge now. You'll need to motivate your team to do everything they can to close this output gap in the Benton seam. You know what the pit can achieve, and I look to you to get Martins back to those high levels of output and profitability later in this calendar year.'

'We will be doing all we can, Sir, to achieve just that,' said Roy. He gathered up his papers and left the meeting.

★

In the car, driving back to Martins, Roy reflected on the accountability meeting. It hadn't been as difficult as he'd feared it might be. Mr Pickersgill and his team had recognised the excellent performance from Martins for the last financial year. And on the future prospects for the pit, Roy was satisfied that he'd provided the information in a way that exposed the problems, along with his plans to deal with them. It seemed that these plans had been accepted, without too many questions and offers of alternative solutions. He'd also got a roadway drivage machine that would double the rate of progress in one of the Benton seam trunk roadways. It had not been an unproductive morning.

Saturday 27 January 1968

Roy was holding a meeting with all his staff, to go through the detailed arrangements for the next few weeks.

'I am sure that you'll understand that the next few weeks will be very important for us, with significant changes taking place. What's the position on 58Bs developments now, George? Let's start with that,' said Roy.

'There's just five yards between the two development teams, and they're deployed on the face this morning,' replied George. 'They'll complete the opening out this morning, and they'll then get the two coal-cutters into position in the centre of the coalface. We're going to use the coal-cutters to haul the line pans for the panzer conveyer into position. This method has been done at other pits, and we have an expert from the regional mechanisation department to supervise the job.'

'When will this be done?' asked Roy.

'We plan to do it tomorrow morning,' replied George. 'All the line pans and panzer chains are available on trams at each end of the face. The job should be completed in one shift. Jim and myself will be on the job, and it'll be a bit of a race between us to see who gets his half of the pan line done first. It might be tricky, coupling the two halves of the line pans together, but that's why we need the regional fellow.'

'What about the rest of the installation?' asked Roy.

Jim Lord stood up and rolled out a detailed action programme for the installation.

'We've prepared this, Boss, which has been agreed by all departments,' replied Jim. 'There's a lot of work to do, but we think it can be done in the next four weeks. You can see that there are men deployed on three shifts to do the installation work, and that they have the backup of craftsmen who are familiar with the equipment. I think all the equipment is available underground, or at the pit, except the trepanner, which is being supplied from the workshops.'

'We've been promised it in two weeks time,' said the Mechanical Engineer. 'That timescale will be OK, as that will be the last thing to be installed.'

'Let's now cover 59s coalface, as that will start shortening next week,' said Roy. 'Is that all organised?'

'Yes, Boss, we shall carry out the same system that we used on 60s coalface – cutting coal on two shifts and then shortening on the third shift,' said George. 'All the men are deployed and I've swapped the deputies round, so that two who got experience on 60s face shortening will be on 59s for the next few weeks.'

They discussed where to stock the salvaged equipment from 59s as the face was shortened, as this would be needed for 63s coalface, at some time in the future.

'We need now to consider the installation of the road header machine for the Benton trunk roadway. When will that be delivered to the pit?' asked Roy.

'It's promised for delivery on Monday,' said the Mechanical Engineer.

'Right,' said Roy. 'Let's agree what will happen. I know it's a new machine, as far as the pit is concerned, but there's no time for looking at it and admiring it. It goes straight into the fitting shop to be stripped down and sent off underground. Some of the pieces will be large, and difficult to transport, so the sooner they set off the better. Arrangements can be made underground to store the units and send them into the drivage in the right order for assembly. Is that clear?'

'Yes, Mr Dobson,' said the Mechanical Engineer. 'I'll arrange for it to be stripped down on three shifts, by the fitters who'll have the job of reassembling it underground. I've arranged for an engineer from the company to be on hand to give us advice.'

'Good,' said Roy, noting a better approach from his Mechanical Engineer. 'I think you're all aware of the importance of getting 63s face into production as soon as possible. Getting this new road header allocated to us reflects the support that we have from Region to help us get out of our problems. We must get the improved performance from that machine, George.'

'I am sure that those lads will give us what we need, Boss,' replied George. 'I've talked to them and they've accepted that they should be able to set two supports each shift, with the machine doing all the cutting and loading of the materials. On that basis we should advance more than thirty yards each week, which is twice the current rate. I understand that the manufacturer will be sending a demonstrator, to show how the machine should be operated.'

'That's what we need, George,' replied Roy, who was pleased to learn that such results would substantially reduce the gap in the Benton seam tonnage. 'Right, we all know where we're going for the next few weeks, and we need to get on with the job,' concluded Roy.

He didn't want to extend the meeting longer than necessary. He was aware that he hadn't raised the matter of the Fuston Two coalface, but that was performing satisfactorily.

Monday 29 January 1968

'More changes at the pit this morning,' said Charlie, to his Enclosure colleagues. 'It was all the talk in the Club last night. 58Bs face is now being installed on three shifts. That was the main talking point last night.'

'Why was that?' asked Albert.

'Well, they only finished opening out the coalface on Saturday morning,' replied Charlie. 'Apparently, they left the coal-cutters in the middle of the coalface and used them to pull the line pans onto the face. It's a new method and both George Turnbull and Jim Lord were on the job. They installed the face panzer conveyer in the shift. It was a bit tricky, coupling the two halves together, but they were all out of the pit by four o'clock.'

'That is some achievement,' said Cliff. 'On 57s coalface, which was the first mechanised coalface at Martins, it took days to install the panzer conveyor. This manager is certainly on the ball for trying up-to-date methods.'

'The lads in the Club said it was George who was behind this idea,' said Charlie. 'He'd picked it up that another pit had used that method, and he got a Regional mechanisation engineer involved to advise him. They said he was on top form yesterday, driving everybody on to get his half of the face done before young Jim Lord finished his half.'

'There's no doubt that George has taken to this mechanised system of mining better than a lot of men much younger than him,' said Cliff Smith. 'He's always been keen to get involved himself, whatever's going on.'

'Who won the race?' asked Albert.

'I think it was a draw,' said Charlie. 'Nobody would say who'd won. I think that both pan lines got to the middle at about the same time. They said that George was over the moon that the method had worked.'

'The pit still seems to be getting quite a bit of coal out,' said Bert. 'And they're still sending two trains a day to the power stations. Have you any idea what the weekly output is, Pat?'

'My understanding is that they're getting just over seventeen thousand tons per week. I also think that they're still making a profit on those tonnages.'

'They must have been making a bloody fortune, then, when the weekly tonnage was over twenty thousand tons,' said Albert.

'They were doing just that,' replied Pat.

A low-loader lorry turned onto Martins Lane, driving slowly. It had a track-mounted machine on it, which had a centrally-mounted arm which pointed forward, on the end of which was a cutting drum. The front of the machine had a wide blade at floor level, in the centre of which was a chain conveyor. Two rotating spinners at the side of the blade were designed to push any cut material onto the central conveyor.

'What on earth is that bloody thing?' said Albert. 'I've never seen anything like that. It looks like a real monster.'

'The only thing that I can suggest is that it's some form of machine to go into one of the development roadways,' replied Cliff, 'but I can't think where it'll go. I think I've seen a photograph of these machines in the technical press; I think they're referred to as road headers.'

'Nobody mentioned anything about a new machine in the Club, last night,' said Charlie.

'I'll have a word with my mates on the pit top,' said Bert. 'They'll know what it has come for and where it's going. I'll let you know tomorrow.'

'Thanks, Bert,' said Cliff. 'It's not often that something like that is delivered to the pit without us knowing about it.' He was pleased that Bert had been a good addition to the Enclosure team.

★

Janet Hall was on the bus, travelling to Doncaster to start her second week back at work at the dress shop. She'd got over the hurdle of the first day back, and it hadn't been as difficult as she'd expected. Some of the staff had been in the shop when Janet had worked there before, and they welcomed her back. There was excitement at the work going on to extend the shop to the property next door. Janet had worked Monday and Tuesday on her first week, but had agreed to also work the Saturday at the end of the second week. Bob was on afternoon shift, so he wouldn't be working the Saturday morning. Peggy would meet the boys from school on Monday and Tuesday and she would give them some tea and look after them until Janet got home.

The plans to care for the boys were working well, and Tony and Michael seemed quite happy with the new arrangements. They'd asked Janet numerous questions about the shop, and what she did there. Janet had been surprised when Sandra had visited the shop, on her second day back. Janet served her and Sandra made several purchases of skirts and blouses, and some designer underwear. Janet's customer impressed the shop manager.

'I know it's only the end of January,' Sandra had said, 'but I think we'll be having a holiday with the other Laceys at Easter, so I need to get my wardrobe organised. I've spent quite a bit on Amy-Louise, who is getting very clothes-conscious for a little girl. Today she's staying with Terry's mother, so I'm going to spoil myself.'

'You're quite right to do that,' said Janet, as she took the money from Sandra, who peeled the pound notes from a roll that she took out of her handbag.

Janet didn't feel at all guilty about going back to work, and she was enjoying her various responsibilities and the staff gossip in the shop. Her colleauges had asked lots of questions about her boys, and she'd put some photographs in her handbag to show them.

She was really proud of Tony and Michael. She thought for a minute how life had changed for her, compared with the previous time she was working in the shop. As regards the possible house move, there had been discussions with Bob and they'd decided not to pursue it any further, at least for the rest of this year. They would certainly not talk about it, and if anyone asked any questions they'd be told that it was not being considered now.

Despite the cold January weather, Janet was feeling quite happy about life for the Hall family.

Friday 9 February 1968

Roy was underground, in the Benton seam roadway, where the road header had been installed. He wanted to see it in operation, to assess what impact it might have on the performance in the roadway. It had taken a week to strip the machine down on the surface, transport it to the roadway underground and then build it up. This meant that the men had been operating it for four days under supervision by the demonstrator from the company. George had left the 58Bs installation to join Roy on his visit. As they walked along the roadway they could see a flow of dirt and coal passing them on the conveyor. There was a good load on the conveyor.

'That's an impressive rate of loading, George,' said Roy.

'The lads are getting used to it, Boss. I've not spent much time in the roadway, but the deputies tell me that it is a fine machine. The challenge for the men is to cut the roadway profile with the machine so that the arched steel girders fit snugly. If they cut the profile too large then they lose time packing wood behind the arches to fill the gap. I'm sure they'll get the hang of it, and I'm told that one or two of the men will make excellent operators.'

They walked further along the roadway and came to the fault. The gradient dipped as the roadway descended through into the seam. As they walked along Roy inspected the coal seam in the side of the roadway and noticed the other small displacements caused by the disturbed geological conditions. He saw the thinning of the seam section and the extensive slips and cracks in the coal seam and the shale roof above the seam.

'This is certainly very different from the Benton seam that we've been used to, George,' said Roy.

'We would certainly have had some bad roof conditions on the mechanised faces, if we'd been working in this area of the seam,' replied George. 'The view of the men and the officials in this roadway is that there are signs that the conditions are getting back to normal, but the seam is generally less than three feet thick.'

When they reached the operations they were able to watch the men setting one of the roadway supports which was made of four-inch by four-inch H-section steel. It was composed of three sections – one up to the roof in the centre of the roadway, to which was connected legs down either side of the excavation; the cutting arm of the machine had a bracket on it which held the roof section of the girder in place up to the roof, while struts were connected to the previous support. Before the support was set, weld mesh was put next to the strata all round the excavation. The result was a steel reinforced tube, which would hold the strata in place and prevent pieces of shale dropping onto anyone or anything passing along the roadway. The men used the power of the machine to do the lifting and manoeuvring of the support system into place.

'This looks to be a versatile machine,' commented Roy, as he watched the operation.

'It's bloody good one, Boss,' replied one of the workmen. 'It takes quite a bit of the sweat out of the support setting, now that we're getting used to what the machine can do for us.'

'When will you decide to put the roadway in for 63s face, Boss?' asked another of the workmen.

Roy explained the options, which required good roof conditions.

'It would be much quicker using this machine to cut out the rock and set the special girders.'

'That's a good suggestion,' replied Roy, who turned to George. 'You could order the special junction supports, George, and get them down here ready, so that these lads could immediately make the junction and drive the first twenty yards of 63s roadway, once we decide the position of the coalface.'

'I'll do that, Boss. I agree that we should take advantage of this machine to do as much work as possible for us to speed up this job.'

★

Roy spent another half an hour talking to the men and establishing with them that it might be possible for them, on occasions, to set three arches during a shift. He also spent time answering their questions about the pit. He came away satisfied that the visit had been a good communications exercise. He was sure that a lot of the views he'd expressed, and the information he had quoted, would be talking points in the Club that night.

Sunday 11 February 1968

Dr Benjamin Sorrell had conducted the Sunday evening service at Upthorpe Methodist Church. The attendance had been less than the normal attendance for a Reverend Folds service. Dr Sorrell gave his normal form of sermon, with commentary on the Old Testament book of Daniel. Before he started his sermon he'd informed the congregation, with some pride, that he'd been invited to return to his old university, for a week, in the near future, to lecture on the book of Daniel.

There was to be a special meeting, at the home of farmer, Joe Horton, after the service. Farewells were quickly made at the end of the service, and key members of the Church Council headed to the farm. John Warwick had suggested the meeting, and he was pleased when Joe offered to host the event, which was to be confidential. It was the same six church members who'd attended the dinner hosted by Helen Dobson for discussions with Benjamin Sorrell. There had been no noticeable change in the way the new minister had carried out his duties since that occasion.

John Warwick opened the meeting with a short prayer, and then he expressed his views of the situation.

'In my opinion, we have a very difficult situation developing at the church. And it's not one that is likely to go away with time. Church members are making comments to me, and no doubt to some of you as well, that the spirit of the church is fading away. We've seen the attendance at services declining, and there seems to be a sense of despair in evidence within the church. I accept that it was going to be difficult for anybody following Reverend Folds, because of the strength of his faith and his ability to relate to everyone he met. But Dr Sorrell is a complete contrast, and he's shown no signs of modifying his rigid views to better meet the needs of the church. I would welcome your input to the discussion.'

'He seems to me to be only interested in studying the Bible,' said Joe. 'He never puts in an appearance at events at the church, and I don't think he does much visiting of sick members, or those in hospital. To be honest, I don't know what he does with his time.'

'Thanks for those comments, Joe,' said John.

'I was once told that being a Methodist minister could either be the hardest job in the world, or the easiest,' said Helen. 'And the difference depends on how the minister views his responsibilities to the church members. We all know that James Folds set himself the highest possible standards, and that he was determined to serve everyone in the community as well as church members. With Dr Sorrell, he aims to convert the church members to his way of worship and study, and if they don't join him, he rejects them altogether.'

'Mrs Dobson is right in her comments,' said Willie. 'He's pushing people away from the church, not trying to gather more in.'

'I agree with all that's been said,' offered Maureen. 'But what can we do about it? I thought that we were stuck with him for the next few years.'

'Well, that's the point of this meeting,' said John Warwick. 'If we are sure at this meeting that we cannot accept Dr Sorrell as our minister, then there are things we can do.'

'What are they?' asked Maureen.

'Firstly, we need to expose the problem to the Circuit Superintendent Minister. I think he may be aware of our problems, as he's had representations from other churches about Dr Sorrell. If we can convince the Superintendent Minister of our case, he will then refer the matter to senior ministers in the Methodist church. After all, Dr Sorrell is in his probationary year, so his performance has to be assessed.'

'But what can they do to resolve our problem?' persisted Maureen. 'And when could any changes take place?'

'I'll answer your second question first,' replied John. 'Any change would be made for next September, at the start of the Methodist year for all new ministerial postings. That's why we need to act now. There are several actions that the Methodist Church could take. They could move him to a different church, one that would accept his style of preaching or they could find an academic posting for him, somewhere that's more suited to his interests. It's unlikely that they would decide that being a Methodist minister is the wrong vocation for him, but they might. However we must make a strong case, now, that the current position is unacceptable.'

The meeting quickly came to a conclusion that what they needed was a different minister, and then they sorted out the steps that they would take to achieve that result. It was agreed that John, Joe and Helen would jointly take the actions. They would have a meeting with Benjamin Sorrell to explain the conclusions that had been reached about his ministry in Upthorpe. John would then organise a special meeting to get the Church Council's agreement to the actions that had been proposed. Meetings would then take place with the Circuit Superintendent Minister and, if necessary, with other senior ministers in the Methodist church.

'Methodist ministers have followed an itinerant life over the centuries, moving from church to church,' summarised John Warwick at the end of the meeting. 'There are often cases where ministers do not fit in with the needs of congregations. Usually those congregations accept what they have been given and wait, in hope, until the next changeover of ministers. But this is our church, and we can see, in God's name, that we need to take action. We have to pray for His guidance in all that we do to resolve this situation.' There were murmurs of agreement from the other members of the meeting.

When Helen got home, she explained to Roy all that had gone on at the meeting, and the role that she would be playing as this issue progressed. He suggested that the church had been subject to a seismic event similar to the geological disturbances affecting Martins Main in the Benton seam. To get over the disturbance, he said, just like at the pit, decisions had to be made, and actions taken, to recover the situation and ensure the future success of the church.

'I'm going up to say my prayers now, Roy. As you've seen a connection between the pit and the church, do you want me to offer prayers for Martins as well as for the church?'

'Helen, I always need your prayers,' replied Roy.

She gave Roy a searching look and then she realised that he really meant it.

Monday 19 February 1968

There was a positive atmosphere in the Enclosure.

'A new coalface goes into production today,' said Charlie. 'They were saying in the Club last night that they've got 58Bs face in operation three days earlier than the plan. George is chuffed at the outcome.'

'Does that mean that they've an additional coalface then?' asked Albert

'The message is that they're going to work 59s face for another two weeks, shortening it down to eighty yards long,' replied Cliff. 'That means it will be shorter than 60s coalface when that was stopped. They're effectively salvaging the coalface equipment and getting some output at the same time. I think that's a sensible decision. This manager makes good decisions.'

'They're certainly producing more coal this morning,' said Bert. 'They're winding through snap again. They've not had to do that for a while. There goes another run of wagons for the power station market.' He pointed across to the loco moving wagons down to the mainline. 'They're still managing to send two trains a day to the power stations.'

'I thought the pit was in big trouble, when they hit the faults in the Benton seam,' said Albert. 'Are they over their troubles?'

'Oh no, not yet, Albert,' replied Cliff. '58B will only last about four months and then there'll be no face in the Benton seam. All the output will then have to come from the Fuston seam. I realise the Fuston is not your favourite seam, Albert.'

'I know what you're getting at,' replied Albert, somewhat crossly. 'I did say that they would have trouble in that seam. I have to admit that they've done better than I expected. Let's hope that the good run continues.'

'The Fuston seam has been doing well because they've managed to get seventeen thousand tons saleable during the last few weeks,' said Pat. 'And the pit has been making a profit each week.'

'There goes the Welsh bastard,' said Albert Dunn, as Reg Jenkins' car drove at speed along Martins Lane. 'I wonder what mischief that bugger's up to, today?'

★

Reg Jenkins' objective was to discuss with Roy Dobson the exact same subject that was under discussion in the Enclosure.

★

Roy had assembled all the detailed plans of the Benton seam trunk roadways, and he had the Surveyor standing by to answer any questions. The better progress with the road header had provided more information about the geology, but it had not all been good news. After the preliminary discussions about the output and the position on 58Bs face, while they drank a cup of coffee, Roy laid out the plans on his desk.

'The first plan shows the progress with the Benton seam trunk roadways,' began Roy, pointing at the plan. 'This is the position of the two roadways this morning. You can see the impact that the road header machine has had, with one roadway well in advance of the other. This roadway is proving the geology. About ten days ago we were confident that we'd got into better conditions and we could lay out 63s face where it had originally been projected. But then two days ago we hit another fault, and some disturbed strata, so we decided to advance further before making the decision.'

'How big is the new fault?' asked Reg Jenkins.

'I can show it better on this plan, which is a section along the roadway,' replied Roy, laying out the second plan on his desk. 'You can see that it was two-feet six-inches, nearly the seam section.'

'That isn't a face-stopping displacement,' said Reg Jenkins. 'There are a lot of mechanised faces in Yorkshire that have to operate carrying that size of fault on the coalface. Bloody hell, in Wales, most faces have faults on them, and a lot of the faults have much bigger displacements than two–feet six-inches.'

'We didn't want to set the face off with a fault on it if, by moving the face position by twenty yards, it could be totally clear of any faulting,' explained Roy.

'You're looking for perfection, young man,' exclaimed Reg Jenkins. 'You cannot afford to delay the availability of 63s face by even one day. Pickersgill is leaning on me to tell him what effect the road header has had on the availability of more faces in the Benton seam. If Martins ends up without a coalface at all, for any period of time, the Regional results will be knackered. We cannot have perfection; half a loaf is better than no loaf at all.'

'I hear what you say, Mr Jenkins,' replied Roy, somewhat shocked that Norman Pickersgill was asking questions about his management decisions.

'Right then, what are you going to do about 63s?' asked Reg, looking straight into Roy's eyes.

There was a long pause as Roy realised that he was being asked to make an instant decision. The decision would be made without the full, detailed geological information to back it up. He was being asked to approve a plan that carried a risk of failure. He hadn't done that in all his time at Martins. This was a new situation. Actually, he realised, he wasn't being asked to make a decision; he was being instructed what he should do. He needed to be clear on the mandate that Reg Jenkins was carrying, and whose authority was behind his instructions.

'I am aware of the importance of getting new capacity in the Benton seam, but I have been aiming, if possible, for the new coalfaces to be able to produce at the rate of the past ones,' began Roy, in reply to Reg Jenkins' question. 'What you seem to be saying is that we cannot afford to wait for a guaranteed top-class coalface, but that we have to get the best we can. Am I right in assuming that?'

'Of course you are, man,' replied Reg Jenkins, testily. 'You are desperate; you can't have perfection. You have to get the best you can.'

'In that case, Mr Jenkins, we'll have to open out 63s coalface in its planned position, even though it will be carrying a fault on it for the first part of its life. I will instruct the Surveyor to prepare a plan that can be signed up. In the meantime, I'll assume that the plan will be signed, so I'll withdraw the road header back, and make the junction for 63s roadway.'

'Right then, we have a decision,' said Reg Jenkins. 'We're making progress.'

★

Reg Jenkins left the office shortly afterwards. Roy was fuming at the way he'd been forced into making an instant decision. He decided to call a short meeting of his staff, for the following afternoon, to agree what should happen with the Benton seam developments. He called the Surveyor into his office and instructed him to prepare a plan for 63s coalface. When Roy indicated the position of the coalface he received some questioning looks from the Surveyor. Roy didn't make explicit the link between his instruction and his meeting with Reg Jenkins, but he knew that a number of people would see it.

★

When Roy arrived home that night, Helen realised that he was very upset about something. She waited until after they'd eaten their evening meal and the boys were in bed, before she asked what was the matter.

'Mr Manager Dobson,' Helen began. 'I detect that something at Martins has happened today that has caused you to be in a very tense mood. It's not the normal Mr Manager Dobson that I'm used to and I think I need to be told.'

Roy initially declined to tell Helen anything about the matter, but she persisted.

'Roy, if I can tell that you're tense and very angry,' she said in a very serious tone, 'everyone at the pit will see that you're very different from your normal self. I don't like what I'm seeing, Roy, and I'm concerned that, in your present state, you will be at risk of making poor decisions and upsetting people. Please tell me what has happened?'

Roy explained the full story of his meeting with Reg Jenkins, and the instruction that he'd been given. He explained that he had never been in that position before, as manager of Martins Main. He expressed his worry that Mr Pickersgill might have sent Reg Jenkins with a mandate to get a decision. That was something that had never happened before. Previously, he told Helen, it had been his plans that Norman Pickersgill preferred, rather than Reg Jenkins' ideas. It would also present a new situation with the management team at Martins. In the past he had been able to motivate his staff because they knew that it was his plans that they were being asked to support. They knew what he was planning for 63s face, because he had told them. Now he would have to sell them a revised and risky plan that had been thrust upon him.

Helen asked more questions about the pit to get clarity on the problems Roy was facing. Roy was able to explain that progress was being made towards a solution for the future of the pit. He explained at length how his plan, to ensure 63s was in secure geology, was better than the risky plan which was being signed.

'Roy, I want you to try to lose your anger and return to your normal style of management,' suggested Helen. 'You don't want to lose the loyalty and full support that you've had with the management and the men at Martins. After all, if the decision you've been forced to make proves to be the wrong one, you want the men to understand that it was not your decision.'

'I know what you're saying, Helen, and I suppose you're right.' Helen moved across to where Roy was sitting and hugged him.

'You'll have another decision to make in the next few days, and I'm confident that you'll get that one right. I paid my monthly visit to Ben North and his wife today, to see how he's recovering from his accident.'

'How is he?' asked Roy. 'I've been wondering. I had a word with Cobba, recently, but he didn't know.'

'He's making good progress. He showed me the wound on his leg. It's healed, but it's left a major scar. I can understand how near he came to losing the leg. He's exercising to try to get his leg muscles working and he hobbles about with a stick. But he wants to get back to work, Roy. After I asked him a good few questions about his plans he confided in me. He knows that he might never be able to return to his old job, but he said that he intends to see Cobba, to ask him to use his influence to get him a light job somewhere on the surface. You'll be able to find him something, won't you, Roy?'

'When Cobba brings his case to me I'm sure we'll fix him up with something,' said Roy. 'If there's a risk that he might never be able to go back to his old job, we need to try to set him up in something useful and interesting for the long-term.'

'Forget about Reg Jenkins, and his needs, Roy. Concentrate on Ben, and make a good decision for him and his family. He really deserves it because he's being very brave, every day, as he tries to get fit enough to get back to work.'

'Leave it to me, Helen.'

'Do you want a progress report on the church problems?'

'Yes,' replied Roy. 'The church and the pit are running in parallel with their problems, so a bit of cross-fertilisation might be desirable.'

'Well, we met Dr Sorrell, today, and told him our views of his ministry. The meeting only lasted half an hour and he made no concessions whatsoever to our requests for him to change his style of ministry. Joe Horton got quite forceful in the end, and asked him how he spent his time. The answer was that his time is spent studying the word of God. His aim is to become a recognised Biblical scholar. When Joe reminded him that his main responsibility is to serve the members of the church, he just smiled. John Warwick has arranged a Church Council meeting for next week. We're seeing the Circuit Superintendent Minister tomorrow. John has heard that the Super has already been approached by other churches with complaints about Dr Sorrell. So, the plan of action goes on.'

'You have a lot to pray about tonight, Helen,' concluded Roy, as Helen headed for the bedroom.

Chapter 31

Tuesday 5 March 1968

Roy attended the Welfare meeting at the Club. The financial results for the Club continued to be excellent and the attendances were very good. There were special events organised for the forthcoming Easter weekend. Pressure from one or two members of the committee led to an agreement to have additional prizes for the bingo evenings during Easter week. Cobba was not too pleased that this had been raised in the committee without pre-discussions with him, however he knew that the Welfare could afford to be generous, and there was the chance that publicity about the prizes would increase the attendance and cover the extra costs. At the end of the meeting, Roy agreed to go into the office for a chat with Cobba.

It was the usual session that they had after Welfare meetings. Cobba asked lots of detailed questions about the pit, and Roy willingly gave him full answers that included some confidential information not usually released at pit level. As a consequence, Cobba knew more than anybody else on the union side and he also knew what Roy's plans were. There had been a lot of changes again over the short-term. 59s coalface had ceased production and was staffed-up to salvage the rest of the equipment; 58Bs coalface was producing well, but Roy explained that he didn't want to push it too hard, because it would only last a further three months. Roy explained fully the meeting with Reg Jenkins, and the decision to develop 63s face in its original position. The road header had made the junction and was driving 63s main roadway to the coalface position. The coalface could then be opened out while the road header continued to drive the Benton trunk roadways. When 63s started, the coalface would have to carry a fault, which would affect operations. Cobba asked what the gap would between the end of 58Bs face finishing and 63s coalface starting. Roy explained that his latest best estimate was about eight weeks. Cobba had a final point to discuss with Roy.

'I'd like you to spare a few minutes, Boss, to see Ben North with me, later this week. He's keen to start work as soon as possible but he'll not be able to go back to his shunting. He's made a remarkable recovery, but it'll be a long time, if ever, before he gets his leg muscles anywhere near normal.'

'I'll be glad to see him,' replied Roy. 'Bring him up to the office on Thursday afternoon. I'll have a discussion with my surface staff to see if there's a suitable job that he can do.'

★

Roy's exploratory talks with his surface foreman had revealed two pieces of information. Firstly, that Ben North had been a reliable and conscientious workman; secondly, that the surface foreman was sure that Ben would want a real, productive job and not some invented role that would allow him just to attend the pit and get paid. After some thought it was agreed that there were two options, both of which would require Ben to undertake some training. He could train as a lamp room attendant, which would require him training in the operation and maintenance of electric cap lamps and flame safety lamps, or Ben could be trained as the Coal Preparation plant's control room operator. The control room started up all the equipment in sequence and there were displays to show how the process was working and the loads being carried in various parts of the plant. Roy decided to wait until he had seen Ben, and assessed his degree of recovery, before he pursued any job options further.

Thursday 7 March 1968

Cobba brought Ben North into Roy's office. Ben was walking with the aid of a walking stick, and he had a pronounced limp. Roy stood up and went round his desk to welcome him.

'Come in, and take a chair,' he said. 'I'm delighted to see you back at the pit. You've made a remarkable recovery.'

'There is still a long way to go, Mr Dobson,' replied Ben, 'but I'm doing as much exercise as possible, to build up my leg muscles.'

'My wife told me that she's seen your scar, and it's a big one,' said Roy.

'It's not pretty sight, Boss,' said Cobba, 'but Ben says that he's improving every week, in what he can do and how much he can walk.'

'I think if I can get back to work, Mr Dobson, it will be an incentive for me to keep improving,' said Ben.

'I'm sure you're right,' said Roy. 'And we are keen to get you back. Obviously you're not able do your old job, at this stage.'

'No, I couldn't run up and down like I used to,' replied Ben. 'And I don't have the strength to control the wagon brakes like I used to.'

'We have been wondering if we should train you to do a different job, but one that is important for the pit,' said Roy.

'I don't mind trying something different, if you think I can do it. But I'm not a brainbox, Mr Dobson,' replied Ben.

Roy explained to Cobba and Ben the two roles that were up for consideration. They discussed the possibilities and Ben said that he would prefer the Coal Preparation plant job, as he liked to be involved with the coal. Cobba encouraged Ben to go for that job, pointing out that the control room operator would get a higher grade of pay than a wagon shunter. It was agreed that he should start his training in the Coal Preparation plant the following Monday. Ben was over the moon, and couldn't wait to get home and tell his wife the good news that he'd be starting work again, and possibility with an increase in pay as well.

'That Mrs Dobson is a very kind and wonderful woman,' said Mrs North. 'I'll bet she had a word with her husband, after she last saw you.'

Monday 18 March 1968

Ben North started back at the pit, in the Coal Preparation plant control room. It was an important day for him. Little did he know that the following day was a much more important day for Martins Main.

Tuesday 19 March 1968

Roy arrived in his office at eight o'clock. He glanced at the sheet on his desk, which showed the results for the previous day. The tonnage was down, so something was wrong. There was a note opposite the figures for Fuston Two coalface – 'weight on the coalface on the night shift'.

'Gordon, get me George Turnbull on the 'phone, please.'

'He's left a message, Mr Dobson, that he's gone to Fuston Two face with the dayshift men. Jim Lord is also on the face. There seems to be some problem getting an answer from the 'phone at the face, but I'll keep trying.'

Roy sorted out other reports on his desk, but he was getting restless when there was no message from the face.

It was nine o'clock when the call came through.

'I have Jim on the 'phone, Mr Dobson. I'll put him through.'

'It's Jim, Boss. I've escaped with three men and we've come off to the end of the main roadway for Fuston Two face. We have a major incident here, Boss.' He was gasping for breath. 'Just let me get my breath back and then I'll try and describe what's happened.'

'OK, Jim,' said Roy. 'Take your time. I will get the details down as you talk.'

'I was with the two men getting over the roadway supports. We knew there was pressure on the supports, because we could hear them pinging when they yielded. We could even hear the pinging as the panzer conveyor was stood, because the shearer was fast under the supports in the middle of the coalface. It was on the return run, cutting up the bottom-coal and coming back to the main gate. Quite suddenly the pinging got more intense, affecting the roadway supports and the face supports. We could see the supports actually lowering. Then there was a great grinding and thundering of the rock roof, the support legs went solid and I actually saw a leg shear. I shouted to the three men to run for it, as the whole place was collapsing, like we were in an earthquake. It wasn't easy to get along the roadway, as the wooden legs under the girders were shearing like matchsticks and letting the girders down onto the conveyor. We had to climb over some of the girders. The coal was also bursting off the sides of the roadway, so that instead of being twelve-foot wide it must have ended up seventeen-or eighteen-foot wide, and the rock was lowering down across the full width. The roadway was affected for nearly a hundred yards back from the coalface. One of the men with me is injured. He was hit in the face by coal bursting off the side of the roadway. I've patched him up and tried to stop the bleeding, but I think he'll need some stitches. The other two are not injured, but we're all very shocked.'

'Where's George?' asked Roy.

'He was in the middle of the face, with the shearer,' said Jim. 'I can't imagine how they will get off the coalface,' he added.

'What about the other men?' asked Roy.

'I'm going to send for the men in the development heading to come to help the injured man to get out of the pit. I'll go now into the return roadway of Fuston Two and see if there are any men there who've managed to get away from the coalface. Then I'll ring you back, Boss.'

'Do that, Jim,' replied Roy. 'I'd like to have a bit more information before I report the position to Region.'

★

In the return roadway, Jim saw the lights of three men and went to meet them. There was an electrician and a workman and they were assisting a man who'd broken his leg when he was trapped by a roadway girder that had fallen on him.

'He was behind us and we heard him cry out,' said the electrician. 'So we went back and managed to get his leg out from under the girder. We were lucky not to get hit by other girders that were being forced to the floor when the wooden legs broke.'

'What length of the roadway's affected by fallen supports?' asked Jim.

'At least two hundred yards,' said the electrician. 'There's no way any other bugger will get off that coalface. I looked along just before we decided to leg it and the roof supports were down onto the panzer and their steel legs were actually shearing. There was no travelling track at all along the coalface.'

They helped the injured man through into the main roadway to join the other three men. The men from the development heading came up then, and Jim organised them into a team to carry the stretcher, with the man with the broken leg, to the man–riding train. The other injured man, with the gashed face, was given a new dressing by the development official who was carrying a first aid box. Jim went back to the telephone to ring Roy, who answered straightaway. Jim gave him the facts.

'I've been into the return roadway and two men and an electrician have managed to escape. One of the men suffered a broken leg when he was crushed by a falling girder. They say that two hundred yards of the return roadway is affected and it's virtually impossible to travel through it. The electrician looked down the coalface just before he left, and the supports were down on the panzer and the chock legs were splitting and shearing. Effectively, the powered supports are destroyed, Boss. He could see no travelling track at all.'

'How many other men are still on the coalface?' asked Roy.

'There will definitely be George, and four workmen,' replied Jim. 'I suppose there could be another craftsman, but I'm not certain.'

'Is the ventilation flowing normally?' asked Roy.

'Well, there is a flow of air around the coalface,' replied Jim. 'It's nowhere near the normal quantity, but it's sufficient to dilute any methane. I tested for methane in the return roadway and there was only a small showing. I think you should get some first aid men down here, Boss. And the ambulance room will need to be ready to receive the two injured men who are travelling out now.'

'I need to speak to Region, now, to let them know of the incident,' said Roy.

'It's very serious, Boss,' said Jim. 'From what I saw, and the information I got from the electrician in the return roadway, I think it's very doubtful if we'll be able to rescue the men on the coalface.'

'Don't say that, Jim, at this stage,' replied Roy, who was shocked at the thought of five fatalities. 'Surely there's something we can do to get onto the coalface.'

'Wait until you see it, Boss,' said Jim. 'I want to go back along the main roadway to see what the position is now, and if the weighting of the strata has calmed down. But I need somebody with me. In fact, Boss, I think you should consider calling out the Mines Rescue team. They might have the skills we need in a situation like this.'

'Do not go into the district on your own, Jim,' said Roy, giving Jim a clear instruction. 'When I've finished telephoning, I'll come straight down.'

'You might find that you are tied to the surface, Boss. There will be all hell let loose when news of this gets out. You'll have Regional staff, police, ambulances, Mines Inspectors, newspaper and television reporters. You'll have your hands full. I'll try to get some men and officials to come down here from the Benton seam, so that we can do an inspection. I'll not leave this 'phone to go into the district until I've spoken to you and agreed who's going where. I'll set up a board, so that we can keep a list of anyone entering either roadway.'

'Right, Jim,' replied Roy. 'Let me have any further information that becomes available.'

Roy's mind was in a whirl. He didn't know what to do next, nor did he feel that he had enough information to assess the magnitude of the situation. However, his mind did register that it was a major mining disaster.

★

'Gordon, get hold of Cobba and send him in as soon as he gets here, even if I'm on the telephone to Region. Then get me Mr Jenkins on the 'phone.'

'Cobba is on his way up, Boss,' said Gordon. 'I'll get Mr Jenkins now.'

The telephone rang. It was Reg Jenkins.

'Mr Jenkins, we have a major incident at Martins,' began Roy. 'There has been a massive weight on Fuston Two coalface. The information is sketchy, but it sounds as if the powered supports are destroyed and the chock legs are actually breaking. Both roadways have been affected and the wooden legs have broken and the steel girders are down on the floor.

This covers nearly a hundred yards in the main roadway, but even more in the return roadway. Coal has peeled off from either side of the roadways and the rock roof has lowered. So far, three men and Jim Lord have escaped along the main roadway, and two men and an electrician have escaped along the return roadway.' Cobba came into the office and Roy pointed him to a chair but continued with his account to Reg Jenkins on the 'phone. 'George Turnbull and four men are on the face line, and doubts are being expressed about the possibility of getting to them, whether they're injured or not.'

'This sounds really serious,' said Reg Jenkins. 'Are there any injuries, so far?'

'Yes, one man has a badly cut face and another has a broken leg. Both of them are on their way out of the pit.'

'I will let Pickersgill know and get some experts from Region out to you,' said Reg Jenkins. 'What's the plan now?'

'I'm going to talk to Cobba, who is here now. Then I'll ring the Mines Inspectorate,' said Roy. 'I wonder whether I should call out the Mines Rescue team? And I think I ought to set up an Incident Room to monitor what's going on. I do want to go underground, myself, to assess the situation.'

'Ring the Inspectorate and set up the Incident Room. I'll get over as soon as I can, and we'll decide then what to do about the Mines Rescue team. Don't go underground until I get to you.'

'Thank you, Mr Jenkins,' said Roy, who was pleased that he was getting support from his boss, rather than criticism.

★

Roy briefed Cobba on all the information he had so far.

'What is going through my mind, Cobba, is that we have a disaster on our hands. I can't help thinking about George and those men trapped on the coalface. I feel so helpless in not being able to know the facts well enough to plan to rescue them.'

'I'll sort out who was on the coalface this morning,' said Cobba. 'I'll see the injured lads and those who've come out with them, who were on the face. That should tell me who's still not accounted for.'

'When you've sorted that out, Cobba, pass it on to the Incident Room,' replied Roy. 'I'm going to get Jeff Briggs to set up the Incident Room in his office.'

Roy spoke to Jeff and made the arrangements. A sign was posted on the finance officer's door to indicate that it was now the Incident Room. Roy rang the Mines Inspectorate and said that there had been a reportable accident during an incident at the pit. At this stage he didn't want to give the Inspectorate the impression that it was a very serious incident. While he was waiting for Reg Jenkins to arrive he rang home. After a few preliminaries, Roy came to the purpose of his call.

'Helen, we have a major incident at the pit, and it may develop into a disaster. Five men are cut off in one part of the pit and we may not be able to get to them for some time. One of them is George, and I want you to go to see his wife with the news and look after her until she gets support from the family. All the facts are not certain yet, and we have more inspections to carry out. I'll ring you when the position becomes clear.'

'Roy, I'll do anything you ask. I'll be thinking about you. Please be careful, darling.'

★

The Enclosure team was all assembled and its members were in good humour in the warm March sunshine. It was Bert Wall who detected that something was not normal at the pit.

'There must be something wrong this morning,' he said. 'They're only winding coal in fits and starts, and they're obviously stopping for snap at the coal shaft.'

The team concentrated their attention on the mine and what they could see.

'There was no talk of problems in the Club last night,' said Charlie. 'Some of the lads on 58Bs face were downing lots of beer and they seemed to have plenty of cash in their pockets. One of them even bought me a pint.'

It was at that point that an ambulance turned into Martins Lane and went into the pit yard and turned up to the ambulance room.

'There must have been an accident,' said Cliff. They watched for the ambulance to return to the road, but it remained parked at the ambulance room.

'Whoever is injured must not be out of the pit yet,' said Charlie. 'The ambulance is waiting for him.'

The coal shaft started winding again after snap, but only wound for ten minutes before it stopped again.

'It can't be just an accident,' said Bert. 'There must be something wrong with one of the coalfaces.'

Reg Jenkins' car turned into Martins Lane and drove into the pit yard.

'Bloody hell,' said Albert. 'It must be serious if it's brought the Welsh wizard to the pit.'

A stream of unfamiliar cars began arriving at the pit, mainly carrying Regional staff. The Enclosure members didn't know who they were, but they did know that it was unusual for that number of cars to arrive at the pit on a Tuesday morning.

'It must be something big,' said Cliff. 'I wonder what's happened?'

Half an hour later a Mines Rescue van turned along Martins Lane.

'That's the Mines Rescue team,' said Cliff. 'I've never seen them at Martins Main, in all the time I was at the pit. This is very worrying. It must be a serious incident that the pit can't sort out on its own. I wonder how we can find out what the problem is?'

'We should get to know when the dayshift men come out at the end of their shift,' said Charlie. 'They're sure to know what's going on. One of my neighbours is on dayshift, so I'll ask him. I'll let you know this afternoon.'

'That'll be good, Charlie,' said Cliff. 'Give us an update this afternoon.' The others nodded in agreement, accepting that whatever they'd had planned for the afternoon would have to be postponed, as the Enclosure would have to be in session.

★

Roy was changed, ready to go underground, as soon as Reg Jenkins arrived. He'd had another call from Jim Lord.

'I've got some men and a couple of deputies down from the Benton seam, so that we can do an inspection of both roadways, Boss.'

'I'm changed and will be coming down to you in a few minutes, when Mr Jenkins arrives. We'll take one roadway each. You can make a start on the return roadway and I'll take the main roadway. I've set up an Incident Room on the surface, so you must ring and report the names of the people going with you into the return roadway. I take it there've been no other men who have managed to escape from the face?'

'No, Boss,' replied Jim. 'I think we know the real problem now. How do we get to these fellows on the coalface?'

'We do know that the number involved is five – George and four men,' said Roy. 'We've accounted for everyone else and so we now know the names of those involved. I'll see you in the next half an hour.' Roy had arranged to have the man-rider available so that he could get there as quickly as possible.

When Reg Jenkins entered the office he reported to Roy that he'd called out the Mines Rescue team from Region, and that he'd seen their van in the pit yard. Roy explained the position underground, and the plan for the inspections. He agreed to ring out with the results of the inspections, to brief Mr Jenkins, as soon as they were completed. Mr Jenkins would hold the Mines Rescue team on call at the surface until Roy had reported on the situation and whether they would be needed. Reg would also explain the situation to the Mines Inspector, when he arrived, and persuade him not to do an underground visit at this stage. The last thing Roy did was to give Reg Jenkins a list of the five men who were trapped on the coalface.

★

Roy arrived at the Fuston Two main roadway, where two men and a deputy were waiting for him. Jim Lord had started his inspection of the return roadway forty minutes earlier. The first three hundred and fifty yards of travel, for Roy and his team, was easy and the roadway supports were normal. Then there were signs of some load on the supports and some of the wooden props were splitting. This gradually got worse and, at the five hundred yard-mark, the wooden legs were broken and the steel roof girders had fallen to the floor and were straddled across the conveyor. Progress was difficult, and Roy decided to leave the deputy and one man at that point and he went forward with the other workman. It was a scramble, and in some places they had to climb over the girders and wooden props and in other places crawl under them. There was really no support to the roof, but it wasn't broken down. When they'd travelled a further fifty yards, the situation changed completely. Coal had burst off from both sides of the roadway; the wooden props and steel girders were all down on the conveyor, and partially buried with coal. As they shone their lights forward they could see that massive blocks of sandstone had fallen out of the roof and were blocking off most of the roadway.

'You wait here,' he said to the workman. 'Everything is quiet now and it seems that the weighting of the strata has finished. So I'll just go on a bit to look along the side of that sandstone rock that's blocking the road, and check what the position is forward.'

'Be careful, Boss,' said the workman. 'I've never seen anything like this. Nothing could have resisted this pressure. There must be a risk that some more rock may fall. I don't think you should stay any longer than is necessary.'

'I agree with you,' replied Roy. 'I'll only be a minute or two.'

Roy moved forward to the rock fall. He shone his light along the side of the rock but as far as he could see there were falls of rock nearly continuously along the roadway. They must have come down with such force that they'd flattened all the equipment in the roadway. Roy was thinking of the implications of what he could see, when a piece of rock fell down with a clatter about five yards in front of him.

'Are you alright, Boss?' the workman shouted.

'Yes,' Roy shouted. 'I'm coming back now. There's no way we can get any further forward.'

Roy wrote down the distances that were affected along the roadway and he checked these figures with the deputy. They worked out that Roy had been within sixty yards of the coalface, but when he described the conditions on that final length of the roadway, they agreed that it would be impossible to use that route to get to the workmen.

When they got back to the end of the main roadway, Jim and his party were waiting for them. Jim gave his picture of the return roadway, which was worse than that for the main roadway.

'It's just as I imagine it would be if a bomb had dropped, Boss,' said Jim. 'We couldn't get any nearer than two hundred yards from the coalface, and from there forward there are big slabs of sandstone blocking the roadway. There's no way we can get to the coalface along that roadway,' said Jim. One of the men who had been with Jim added his views.

'It was bloody scary. I've never seen anything like it. We'll all be having nightmares tonight.'

Roy explained what he had seen, and the fact that the main roadway was also blocked for access to the face.

'Where do you think George and the men will be on the coalface?' Roy asked Jim.

'From the message that George sent off about the shearer being fast, I would think they're around the middle of the coalface,' replied Jim.

'The only idea that I can come up with is that we drive a new roadway from the main roadway across to the middle of the coalface,' said Roy. 'It only needs to be about seven or eight feet wide and we could drive it just in the coalseam. It'll be a bit tricky when we break through to the coalface, but we should be near the men.'

'I know what you're suggesting, Boss, but it'll take us days to do that,' said Jim.

'I understand, Jim,' replied Roy. 'But it will take us weeks to reach them by any other method. I'll ring Mr Jenkins now and then I'll go out of the pit and discuss the options.'

★

Roy rang Reg Jenkins and described what they'd gathered from the inspections. He told him that they wouldn't need the Mines Rescue team and that they could be released from the pit. He indicated that he had a plan to get access to the coalface, and that he would be setting men on to get started with the preparations straightaway. Roy then instructed Jim to get a team of men into the main roadway, resetting the girders and wooden props so that the roof was supported to within seventy yards of the coalface. Another team should get the coal-cutter that was in the nearby heading and take it along the Fuston Two main roadway. He said that it would need to be modified so that the new access road would be in the coal seam. Roy also described the work that needed to be done on the conveyors to get the conveyor in Fuston Two main roadway running at a shortened length. Then a small conveyor would be needed to convey the coal along the access road. As all the electrical equipment at the coalface was destroyed it would need a new power supply connecting for the cutting machine, conveyor, auxiliary fan and drilling machines. Roy would arrange this as soon as he got out of the pit.

'These jobs are top priority, Jim,' said Roy. 'And they must be covered over the full twenty-four hours. There are men's lives at stake. I want you to concentrate on organising the job down here while I sort out with Mr Jenkins all the other arrangements.'

★

Roy arrived on the pit top as the afternoonshift men were preparing to go underground. He got some strange looks from some of the men, but he didn't have time to stop and talk to them. He got the Surveyor in to his office and instructed him to prepare a plan for an access roadway starting at seventy yards back from the coalface position and connecting to the middle of the face. He saw the Electrical Engineer and instructed him to organise the new power supply. He briefed the Mechanical Engineer on the needs for conveyor equipment. In all cases he emphasised that everyone was to be asked to work flat out to try to save five men's lives. Roy stated that he intended to come back to the pit on the nightshift and that by then he wanted the access road in operation. He then sent for Cobba and explained the position of the Fuston Two roadways, and his plan to drive an access road to the middle of the coalface.

'I want you to sort out the men for this job, Cobba. I want four men in each team and I want four shifts each day, starting with a team at six o'clock tonight. I want the job never to stop. They are driving a road to try to save five men's lives. I can't think of any better motivation. They know they'll get paid well.'

'What's going to happen to the pit, now?' asked Cobba.

'That's something that we'll have to sort out,' said Reg Jenkins. 'But we must try to get these five fellows out first, Cobba. The poor sods are trapped and probably not able to move. They must be waiting for a miracle to happen.'

'What's the position regarding publicity about this incident?' asked Roy, when Cobba had left.

'There will be some pressure for information when it leaks out,' replied Reg Jenkins. 'And it will get out before long. It might well get into the national news by tomorrow. Pickersgill does not want us to release the names of the five men involved, until we've had a chance to talk to their next of kin.'

'I've arranged for my wife to visit George Turnbull's wife, when I give her the green light,' said Roy. 'She would help with the others if necessary. We'll talk to Cobba about that.'

★

The Electrical Engineer gave Peter Carter the job of sorting out the power supply for the access drivage.

'If they're taking the coal-cutter from the Fuston heading we might as well take the electrical switch gear,' said Peter. 'They're very near, and it won't take us long to get them onto the job if you will let me have some strength. We can then break into the cable that's along the main roadway and power up the switchgear.'

'You can have as much strength as you like, Peter, but get power onto the job before you leave,' said the Electrical Engineer. 'Mr Dobson says that he's going to be on the job, tonight, to supervise the start of the access road.'

'Leave it to me, Boss,' said Peter, and he led the team of six electricians and cablemen to move the equipment and connect the power.

★

The Enclosure was back in session, but it was nearly three o'clock when Charlie Marshall came hurrying up with his news.

'I'm sorry I'm late,' he gasped. 'But the neighbour was on overtime, so he's only just got home. Wait while you hear this. He says that there's been a massive weight on the Fuston Two coalface and the word is that all the equipment's been flattened. Not only that, but part of the roadways to the coalface have also been destroyed.'

'That bloody Fuston seam,' said Albert. 'It's done it again. When it puts its foot down it's a killer. I've always been worried that this might happen.'

'I have to admit that you've always expressed doubts about that seam,' said Cliff.

'That's not all,' said Charlie. 'There's worse to come. My neighbour says that although some men got off the face before it totally collapsed, there are five men cut off on the face. He didn't know the names of the other men, but George Turnbull's one of them.'

'My God,' exclaimed Cliff, in a state of shock. 'Not George, cut off on the face. What are they going to do to get them out? This is a major disaster.'

'My neighbour didn't know what's happening, but the manager has been down to do an inspection,' concluded Charlie.

★

At three thirty Cobba came back into Roy's office.

'I've brought the list of men who will do that access road for you,' said Cobba. 'The first team will be at the pit for six o'clock tonight, and the others will follow on. They know what's at stake, and they've promised to go flat out.'

'I am sure they will, Cobba,' said Roy. 'I'll see some of them, because I'm coming back tonight to take over from Jim Lord. He did well to get three men to run off the main roadway at the right time – they just made it. Jim has been on to me this afternoon and there are lots of men deployed to get the equipment ready to start the access tonight.'

'How long will it take?' asked Cobba.

'If your lads do their stuff, we should be there in four days,' replied Roy.

'Not much chance for those that are trapped, then?' said Cobba.

'You never know,' said Roy. 'We have to hope. There is another matter, Cobba. We need to tell the next of kin for the four workmen who are affected. My wife will be seeing Mrs Turnbull. We have to do it in the next hour or so, as their families will be wondering where they are already. Who do you want to do it?'

'I have the names, Boss, and I've been thinking about it. One fellow is single and still lives with his mother – that might be the difficult one. The others, I will see to. I'll probably take our Sandra along to the two of them who are young wives with young children. It would be helpful if Mrs Dobson could cover the fellow who lives with his mother. He's not a young chap, and his mother is in her sixties. I know Mrs Dobson does a wonderful job in these circumstances.'

'I'll arrange that, Cobba. You have to give these next of kin some hope, Cobba,' added Roy. 'You can tell them all that we're doing to try to rescue their men.' Roy had picked up that Cobba was clearly not hopeful of a successful rescue.

Roy rang his wife and made arrangements for her to visit the mother of the single man, as well as Mrs Turnbull. Helen said that she wished James and Gwen were still around, to give support in these circumstances.

★

There was pressure from newspapers and television reporters, asking for information about the incident. They were ringing the pit and asking questions. Reg Jenkins rang Region and arranged for a British Coal Executive press officer to come to the pit to help with the media issues. Roy jotted down some notes for a possible statement. One reporter got as far as the manager's outer office before being asked to leave the site. Reg rang the local police and asked for a presence on site to contain the media.

★

The Enclosure team was watching Martins Lane for signs of activity. Their interest in the shafts and normal operations at the mine had disappeared; their only concern was the incident. When the Mines Rescue van left Martins Lane, Cliff had a view of the significance of this.

'That is a good sign,' he said. 'That means that the pit can sort out the incident with its own resources.'

'It might mean that there's no bloody hope for the men that are trapped,' said Albert. Cliff was very quiet when he thought about that possibility.

They saw a police car turn along Martins Lane.

'Does that mean that there are fatalities already?' asked Charlie.

'The car's stopped at the pit entrance and they've got out,' said Bert. 'They might be there to stop anybody who's not associated with the pit from getting into the pit yard.'

A few minutes later a television van was pulled up by the police and refused entrance to the pit premises.

'There you are,' said Bert. 'I suppose there'll be a lot of press interest when the story gets out.'

They saw the reporter get out of the TV van and a cameraman set up his camera to shoot film with the Martins Main notice board as a background. A young man came out of the pit yard, followed by several reporters with notebooks. The TV reporter joined them. The young man read out a statement to them and they all took notes.

'We'll have to watch television, tonight, to get to know more,' said Charlie.

'You'll be lucky,' said Albert. 'The management will keep us all in the dark as long as possible. They always do in major accidents like this.'

'This manager is usually good at communications,' said Cliff.

'It won't be him that's handling this,' said Albert. 'It'll be some smooth-talker from Region, or London, that's deciding what to say. When you've been involved in a major incident, like I have, you realise who calls the tune in a case like this.'

★

The TV man was an experienced journalist and his report given to camera was used by the local and national evening news programmes. It was in his usual, precise and factual style.

'I am standing at the entrance to Martins Main pit in the Yorkshire mining community of Upthorpe. At around eight o'clock this morning, on a coalface in the Fuston seam, there was a major geological disturbance that affected the coalface and the roadways leading to it. Four men escaped along one roadway before it closed up; three men escaped along the other roadway before that too was closed. Of those men, two were injured, but not seriously. Five men remain trapped on the coalface. The management have deployed men to make an alternative access to the coalface as quickly as possible. The community of Upthorpe is in shock tonight, and its hopes and prayers are that the rescue bid will be successful.'

★

Helen Dobson had arranged for the Dennis, the gardener, to collect his wife, Joan, so that she could accompany her on the two visits. The gardener had the job of staying behind to look after Robert and John when they came home from school. Helen had been in her bedroom for twenty minutes, praying for guidance as she carried out her task to deliver the potential bad news to the two women. She was determined also to bring them support and hope. When Joan Gates arrived, Helen briefed her on the position at the pit, and the role that they had to play.

'I've never done anything like this before,' she told Helen.

'It's not what you do on these occasions, it's who you are that matters,' said Helen. 'I know that you'll be a great help to me. We have to listen, and then we have to give support. You'll be surprised how simple things can give vital help to people in these circumstances. I know you are able to offer practical help, which we will sort out. I think we'll start with Mrs Jones, the lady whose son is still living at home with her. She lives on Martins Lane. I think I know where her house will be.'

Helen parked the car outside the house and went up and knocked at the door. It was opened by a small, dapper lady with short, tightly-curled, grey hair.

'Can I come in, Mrs Jones?'

Mrs Jones held the door open wider, and Helen Dobson and Joan Gates went forward into a neat kitchen-cum-living room. Mrs Jones sat in a chair by the open fire while Helen and Joan sat on chairs by the kitchen table.

'I am Helen Dobson; my husband is manager of Martins Main, and he's asked me to come and have a word with you. This is my friend, Joan Gates.'

'Is something wrong at the pit? I wondered why he was so late getting home. His dinner is spoilt,' Mrs Jones said, in a matter-of-fact way.

'You are right, Mrs Jones,' replied Helen. 'There is indeed a problem at the pit and that's why we have come to see you.'

'They can be dangerous places, can pits. But my Jack has not done so badly, he's never had an accident. His dad was not so lucky though. He was killed in a pit accident thirty years ago. What's the problem, then?' Helen was completely shocked by Mrs Jones's calm approach. She decided to state the facts in a simple way, because that seemed to be what Mrs Jones wanted.

'There's been a major geological movement on the coalface where your son was working. It's also affected the roadways leading to the coalface. Some men escaped, but there are five men trapped on the coalface, and your son is one of them. My husband is arranging to drive a new roadway to the coalface, to rescue the trapped men.'

'I suppose we have to hope that they get there sharp,' said Mrs Jones.

'I think you can rely on them trying their best,' replied Helen. 'We're sure to get to know the progress they're making. My husband will see to that.' Mrs Jones nodded and seemed to accept what Helen had said.

'Is there anything that you need, Mrs Jones; any arrangements we can make to help you?' asked Helen. 'Have you any relatives that we could get in touch with, who could support you?'

'I'm alright, love,' Mrs Jones replied. 'I keep myself to myself, but I have some neighbours on Martins Lane that I talk to. I'll not fret. Whatever has to be, will be. Don't worry about me.'

'You are a very wise woman, Mrs Jones,' replied Helen. 'We admire how brave your approach is to the situation. We'll keep in touch with you. I have friends on Martins Lane

— Peggy Moore and Janet Hall. Do you know them?'

'Peggy Moore lost her fellow in the pit, didn't she?' I nod to her when I see her on the road,' replied Mrs Jones.

'I will let them know how you're affected by this incident. If you need any help at all, just have a word with them, and they'll get in touch with me,' said Helen. 'We'll leave you now, but at least you know what's happening.'

Helen and Joan went out to the car. There were some children around the car, and some women were out in the street looking to see at whose house Helen had been. She realised that the people of Martins Lane now had an idea of the identity of one family affected by the incident.

'That was a surprise,' said Helen, when they were in the car. 'Mrs Jones is a really cool customer. I never expected her to be like that. I'm going to call on my friend, Peggy Moore, who lives a bit further along, and tell her where we've been.'

Helen stopped the car again and they again noticed several neighbours watching them. It was busy at Peggy's, as Tony and Michael had just landed home from school and were playing with Dawn in the kitchen. Peggy confirmed that Mrs Jones was well known as an independent woman who looked after herself. Peggy promised to drop in on her in the next day or two, while the emergency lasted.

★

The visit to Mrs Turnbull was very different. Helen had met her before, but when Mrs Turnbull saw Helen, rather than being reassured, she knew that something serious must have happened. She became very distressed and upset. While Helen comforted her, Joan made a cup of tea in the kitchen and brought it in. Helen and Joan stayed for over an hour.

Helen rang the Turnbull's daughter, in Kent, and explained the position to her. She said that she would come up to Yorkshire first thing in the morning to stay with her mother. Helen also rang their son, in Derby, who said he would come up that evening and stay with his mother for a few hours, but that he had to be in Derby for important meetings the next day. Helen arranged for Joan to come over in the morning and stay with Mrs Turnbull until her daughter arrived.

★

When they arrived back at the Dobson's house, Helen looked back on the afternoon's work.

'Many thanks for going with me, Joan,' she said. 'You've been most helpful. It wasn't what I expected at all. I thought we would have to give a lot of support to Mrs Jones, but not to Mrs Turnbull, but as you saw, it was the other way around. You never know how people will react in these situations.'

'I'll telephone you tomorrow afternoon, and let you know how Mrs Turnbull is after her daughter has arrived.'

'Yes, please do, Joan,' replied Helen. 'That will be most helpful.'

★

Roy arrived home at six o'clock. He ate some of the meal that Helen had prepared for him, but he wasn't hungry. He watched the evening news and saw the report from the pit gates of Martins Main. The implications of what had happened were beginning to register. His whole world was collapsing. Helen tried to calm him, but she failed. He was quite honest with her.

'Helen, it is my pit. I have worked hard to make it what it is, and I dare not think of what might happen. I can't rest until I have done everything possible to get those five men out. I'll have to be underground as much as possible. Please keep saying your prayers.'

'You know I'll be thinking of you all the time, Roy,' Helen replied. 'Martins Main and all its men will be constantly in my prayers.'

★

Roy left for the pit at eight o'clock to go underground with the nightshift men. Just after he'd left, Helen had two telephone calls. The first one was from John Warwick, the headmaster. He asked Helen how Roy was coping, and enquired about the latest situation with the five men who were trapped.

'I'm ringing you because I know that the community will need a lot of help from the church,' he said. 'I rang Benjamin Sorrell to explain the challenge that's facing us.' He paused before continuing. 'I cannot believe this, Helen, but he says that he's leaving in the morning, to go back to his university for the next week. He said that it's an important commitment that he has to keep.'

'Thanks for letting me know,' said Helen. 'I was going to speak to him, but now I needn't bother. We're on our own, John, but the Good Lord will be with us.'

'Let me know, Helen, if there's anything I can do to help.'

The second telephone call brought the offer of unexpected help.

'Helen, it's James Folds, here. We've seen the news flash about the men trapped at Martins Main. Have you time to talk?'

She spent ten minutes explaining the situation, and the work that she'd been doing. She also discussed what a tragedy it was for Roy, and how his whole world was collapsing. James explained that he was speaking from Cornwall, where they were just starting a holiday. Was there anything they could do to help? Helen explained how there would be no Methodist minister in Upthorpe for the next week, at a time when so much was likely to happen.

'I would give anything to have you and Gwen here,' Helen said, and then she added as a throwaway line. 'You could stay here with us.'

'We'll leave for Upthorpe first thing in the morning,' said James. 'I now know why there was a force telling me to ring you after I saw the news bulletin. God bless you, Helen.' Helen fell to her knees by the telephone. She was weeping and praying at the same time.

★

At the pit, Roy rang the deputy at the access road, where a new telephone had been installed. A lot had happened over the afternoon shift. The conveyor along Fuston Two roadway had been shortened, and was running; the coal-cutter was on the job; and all the electrical equipment was powered up. Roy was pleased to hear that the coal-cutter had made the first cut. In the background he could hear shouting, and men shovelling coal.

As he went across the pit yard, he noticed that there was an eerie quiet among the men waiting to go underground. They looked across at him, but there were no comments or questions. They didn't know what to say, and they were not surprised to see him going underground. After Roy had passed, one of the men spoke to his mates. 'The poor bugger, he's in the shit up to his neck, and he has no George Turnbull, now, to help him sort it out.'

★

When Roy reached the end of the Fuston Two main roadway he saw a face that he recognised. Peter Carter, with several electricians, was pushing a tram, with an auxiliary fan on it, into the roadway. They were all sweating profusely, and they were black with coal dust, and looked exhausted.

'How are things going, Peter?' Roy asked.

'This is the last piece of equipment, as far as we're concerned, Mr Dobson,' replied Peter. 'We sorted the power out and they've started the access road. They'll need this fan, later tonight, so we want to get it into position and powered up before we leave.'

'Well done, lads,' said Roy and he walked behind them as they pushed the tram along the roadway.

★

The entrance to the access road was a hive of activity. The men were stripped down to just their shorts, and they were covered in sweat and dust. When he saw Roy, the deputy came over.

'We've managed to get two cuts off, Boss, and they're pushing the machine back to cut a third. We're getting the little conveyor in as well, now. It will mean that the job is then set up completely. There'll be the auxiliary fan to couple-up later tonight. Roy stood back and watched the men at work. There were grunts, and a few swear words, but he'd never in his experience seen such intensity of work. A faint flicker of hope stirred in him. One man was clearly in charge and giving instructions.

'Don't start cutting until we've got this conveyor running,' the chargeman shouted, to the man on the machine. 'Drill the boreholes next. We'll only be a few minutes, packing up this tail end and coupling the belt. We've got to get another cut filled-off before our mates get here.'

Within twenty minutes the little conveyor was running, the coal was undercut and the shotholes stemmed. The men came out of the heading to a safe position, while the deputy fired the shots. In the meantime the men grabbed a drink of water.

'That looks a lot better,' the chargeman said, as he observed the fired coal. 'One down either side, and me and Joe will go on top of the pile.'

Roy stood and watched and was amazed at the speed their shovels were moving and how quickly the coal disappeared onto the conveyor. He calculated that there was eight tons of coal, but that it was all filled-out and the heading cleaned up in half an hour. The men then set two wooden supports.

'We'll not extend the conveyor, but do another round first,' said the chargeman. He set up the stake for the rope to haul the machine forward.

'Your mates are here,' said the deputy.

'We'll keep going until they're ready to take over,' said the chargeman. When the coal-cutter was staked into position, the machine-man started to undercut the coal. He kept his hands on the controls until a man from the new team knelt beside him and took over the controls. Roy went out into the roadway where the men were putting on their clothes ready to travel out of the pit.

'You've done very well to set up the job and then get three cuts off. The other three shifts will have something to live up to,' he said to the team.

'Do you think we'll get there in time, Boss?' the chargeman asked.

'I just don't know,' replied Roy. 'But I have more hope now, having seen what you lads have done on your shift.'

'We'll be here tonight,' said the chargeman.

'I might see you,' said Roy.

'We'll get the auxiliary fan running now, Boss,' said the deputy. 'I have some men getting more wooden supports, and some more conveyor structure and belting onto the job.'

'You're going to need plenty of supplies, to keep these lads going,' said Roy.

Wednesday 20 March 1968

The new team were different to the previous team. In charge was an older man, who had his two sons and another relative in the team. There was no shouting or instructions, but each man knew what he had to do and an odd look by the older man established any change in priorities. After they'd filled-off the first cut they extended the access road conveyor and then coupled the flexible hose onto the auxiliary fan and started it. This gave a cooling flow of air into the new roadway. The team carried on, taking the second and third cuts off. Work never stopped, and one man at a time, in answer to a nod from the older man, had a few minutes off to eat a sandwich and have a drink of water. Roy looked at his watch. At the rate that they were going they would certainly complete four cuts, and they might even have started on the fifth cycle by the time they were relieved. He stayed with them to the end of their shift and saw the changeover to the third team. That team took over the drivage with the eighth cycle fired, for them to fill-out.

★

Roy got to the pit top just before eight o'clock. He was exhausted but he knew that there was a lot for him to do on the surface. He was sitting in his pit clothes, in his office, having a cup of tea, when Reg Jenkins came in.

'What's the position?' asked Reg.

Roy described the progress in the access road and Reg was clearly impressed.

'I have never seen men so motivated,' said Roy. 'I've witnessed a mining miracle taking place underground. If we can keep up this rate of progress, we should get through by Friday afternoon.'

'It will certainly be an achievement, if you can do that,' said Reg. 'We shall have much more interest from the media today. It's been a major story on television and the radio, this morning. We'll have to sort out the press briefing for later this morning. I'll go out and brief Pickersgill on the progress you've made so far.'

Reg left the office and went to ring Norman Pickersgill.

'Pickersgill thinks that you should be at the press briefing to explain the latest position and answer questions,' said Reg, when he returned.

'What I've been thinking is that we should show the press a plan of the access road that we're driving,' said Roy. 'Do you think that Mr Pickersgill would approve of me showing the plan? It would give the press some facts to work on.'

Reg left to have another talk to Mr Pickersgill.

'He approves of the idea, but he wants to see the plan first,' he said, when he returned.

Roy sent for the Surveyor and asked him to prepare a large-scale plan. He told him the length of roadway already completed, which he could show on the plan. He emphasised the urgency of the plan as they'd need to rush a copy over to the Regional office.

Roy then rang Helen to report that he was alright. He wasn't sure when he would get home for a few hours' sleep. She said that she was thrilled that James and Gwen Folds would be coming to stay with them.

'We'll be able to support to the community really well, with their help,' said Helen, who was feeling more hopeful.

★

The Surveyor brought the plan into Roy's office at ten o'clock. It was approved by Roy, and by Reg Jenkins, and was sent over to Regional office to be cleared for the press conference at eleven o'clock.

★

The Enclosure was in session, though Charlie Marshall was late arriving.

'Here comes Charlie,' said Cliff Smith. 'He looks as though he's something to tell us, from the way he's rushing. Morning, Charlie, what do you know?' asked Cliff.

'One of my neighbours is working on the Fuston face rescue road, and he was on the midnightshift last night. So he's only just got home, so I now know what's happening,' said Charlie, visibly sticking his chest out. 'They're driving a rescue road in the seam, from the main road to the centre of the coalface. That's where they think the shearer was when the weighting happened, and where they hope to find the men. It will be a hundred and five yards long, to get to the face line. It's about seven foot wide, and they're only taking the seam. From six o'clock last night to six o'clock this morning, they'd taken seven cuts off. That's an advance of fourteen yards. My mate says that the manager was down the pit with them last night, and he's hoping that they'll be able to get eighteen cuts off per day. If they can do that they'll be about half-way to the coalface by tomorrow morning.'

'That is an amazing rate of progress,' said Cliff. 'They must be very good men.'

'Apparently Cobba picked the men,' said Charlie. 'There are four men in each team and four shifts for the day. He's asked each man to give everything he can, to try to get through to the trapped men. My neighbour said he's never worked as hard in all his life in the pit. He thinks they'll get through sometime on Friday, if they can keep going.'

'Goodness knows what they'll find,' said Albert. 'I dread to thing how those poor buggers have suffered on that coalface.'

Albert's comments caused a sombre mood to fall on the Enclosure. Their attention was then attracted to the number of cars starting to pass along Martins Lane. There was also the television van that had been there yesterday. Now they could see that the cars were being allowed into the pit yard, and all parked together.

'There must be a press conference, or something,' said Bert Wall. 'From the look of it, they're being directed up to the conference room.'

'I wonder who'll have the job of giving the report, and answering the questions?' said Albert. 'Some of those reporters are bastards, and they're clever at asking trick questions.'

'It might be the manager,' said Cliff.

'The poor bugger,' commented Albert. 'It was him that wanted to work the Fuston seam in the first place.'

'The pit has done well in the Fuston seam until this happened. You have to bear that in mind, Albert,' said Pat Mulligan.

'Fat chance of it doing anything much in the future,' concluded Albert.

★

At the eleven o'clock press conference, Roy sat at a table with the British Coal Executive public relations man by his side. They'd agreed that the PR man would manage the meeting and issue the statement, but that Roy would speak to the plan that was on display. Roy was surprised by how many reporters were present, and noticed that there was a TV camera at the back of the room.

The prepared statement was short, and said that an access roadway was being driven to reach the coalface at the point where it was anticipated the men would be found. Roy then took over and explained the plan pinned up on board at the front. He told them how the two roadways had been cut off by falls of rock, and that this had determined where the access road could be started in the main roadway. He outlined the work that had been done to assemble the equipment to do the drivage, and explained that there were four teams of men working throughout the twenty-four hours driving the access roadway. Finally, he pointed out the shaded area on the plan, that represented the fourteen yards that had been completed to the end of the nightshift, of the total length of one hundred and five yards.

There was an opportunity for questions, and they came thick and fast:

Were the management sure that the men would be safe on the coalface? The conditions on the coalface were not known.

When would the access road reach the coalface? At the present rate of progress, some time on Friday afternoon.

Could the access road be driven any faster? Roy elaborated on his previous answer. 'I spent last night underground with the teams. I have never, in all my time in the mines, seen men work so intensively, and skilfully, to get this roadway through. I checked before I came down to this meeting and another six yards has been completed.'

Had the management anticipated an incident such as this? The supports on this coalface are the highest-rated supports in the UK coal industry, and strata control engineers considered that they would be adequate to control the sandstone rock.

Martins Main has been a very successful pit over the last year. How much contribution has come from the Fuston seam? Roy had to think quickly. More than a third of the pit output came from the Fuston seam over the past year.

So this incident was a surprise to you? Yes.

There were other questions, of a more general nature, about the coal industry and the PR man handled these. Once it was his turn to field the questions he quickly brought the press conference to a close, and promised that there would a further update tomorrow, on progress. After the reporters had closed their notebooks and started to leave the conference room, the TV reporter came forward and asked if he could record his report, with the plan as a background. The PR man suggested to Roy that this would be acceptable.

The outcome was another incisive report.

'Today, the people of Upthorpe have been given some slight hope for their five trapped miners. The management has presented a progress report on the new access roadway that is being driven to the coalface. This plan shows the new roadway, which will be one hundred and five yards long, and the progress so far. The Manager assures us that four teams of men are labouring every minute of the day to push this roadway forward. He is full of praise for their efforts. He said that he has never, in all his experience in coal mines, seen men working so intensively and skilfully to get a job done. But it will be quite a wait, and no one knows what they will find when the roadway is through. The good people of Upthorpe remain very tense and shocked. Their pit has been very successful over the past year and the last thing they expected was to be involved in a mining disaster. Spare a thought for them tonight, and also for those miners toiling underground to rescue their colleagues.'

★

Roy spoke to Jim Lord in the early afternoon, before he went home for a few hours' sleep. Progress with the drivage was very good, but Jim raised another issue.

'I've been thinking about what we may find when we get through, Boss,' he said. 'It's likely that there'll be a twisted mess of metal, with the trapped men behind it. We'll need some power metal saws, with lots of blades, so that we can tackle the problem in various places. I've arranged to have compressed air available, but I would doubt if the Mechanical Engineer will have a stock of cutting tools.'

'That is a very good point, Jim,' replied Roy. 'I'll tell him to get the necessary tools and to line up some skilled fitters to be available on the job to help clear equipment out of the way.'

★

When he'd made the arrangements, Roy was cross with himself that he hadn't spotted that need. He realised, then, that he was nearing exhaustion and must get some sleep. He left Reg Jenkins to look after the pit while he went home. He intended to be back at the pit with the nightshift.

When he walked through the front door, he was greeted by Helen, who asked him to welcome James and Gwen, who had just arrived. After just a few words he was hustled upstairs by Helen, who'd detected his exhaustion and suggested he get some rest. She was going to visit Mrs Turnbull, with James and Gwen, and she would ensure that Roy wasn't disturbed by John and Robert when they came home from school.

'Please get me up at eight o'clock, Helen, no matter how difficult it is to wake me. I must be back at the pit for the nightshift.'

'Have you got to go back again tonight, Roy?' asked Helen.

'Yes, it's essential.'

★

There was a different mood in the pit yard, compared to the previous night, when Roy went to go down the shaft. The men nodded to him and one or two spoke to him. He gathered that he had their support for what he was trying to do. Everyone knew the yards driven in the new access road and the rapid progress was giving the men some hope for a good outcome. Roy stayed underground until the end of the nightshift, but he then came out of the pit to talk to Jim Lord. The Mines Inspector had persuaded Reg Jenkins that he must go underground to see the conditions on the Fuston face, as the Chief Inspector of mines wished to report on any political questions about the rescue.

Roy had agreed to take the inspector underground at eleven o'clock. This meant that the British Coal Executive PR man would be handling the press conference today. Roy considered that there should be no problems, as the total advance for the day was forty yards, making a total length drive of fifty-four yards. Roy's instructions to Jim were to keep the men going flat out in the drivage. Roy would deal with any issues raised by the Inspector, and would get him away from the coalface as quickly as possible. Jim reported that he'd arranged for some hydraulic rams to be available to move the coalface equipment. Knowing Jim's skills at improvisation he asked him to be available on the Friday afternoon, when the access roadway should be through to the coalface.

Chapter 32

Thursday 21 March 1968

It was as good a day as it could have been, overall, for Roy. The visit by the Mines Inspector passed without any adverse comments; the press conference noted the good rate of progress, so the press reports were positive; it was agreed that there should be a further press conference tomorrow afternoon, when there might be more information about the trapped men.

Roy slept at home that night, leaving the pit in the hands of the workmen and officials, who knew what they had to do.

Friday 22 March 1968

At breakfast, Helen was trying to persuade Roy to eat a good meal, but he had no appetite.

'You need to eat to keep your strength up, Roy; this will be a big day for you,' she said.

'My heart keeps missing a beat every time I think of it, Helen. It will either be a day of great joy, if we get the men out, or it will be a day of utter despair, if we're too late. I just can't think about the consequences if I lose George. His whole life has been at Martins Main and all the men trust him. It will be a tragedy beyond belief if he has given his life for the pit.'

'Roy, I will be thinking of you all day, and praying for you,' she said, as he left the house.

★

James and Gwen deliberately came down to breakfast after Roy had left. They questioned Helen about the position at the pit and she explained what Roy had said. When the children had left for school, James said that they must have a time of prayer. Dennis Gates walked past the living room window on his way into the house to speak to Helen. When he glanced in and saw the three of them kneeling in a circle, with their hands clasped in prayer, he quietly went back to his work in the garden.

James Folds spoke the final prayer.

'Dear Lord, we stand at the gate of Gethsemane this morning, with the people of Upthorpe. We do not know whether we will see the crucifixion or the resurrection by the end of the day. It could be a day of rejoicing or a day of tears. Whatever is the outcome, we know that you will be with us, and that your strength and guidance can cover all our needs. We pray especially for Roy, today, who carries such responsibility and challenges at the mine. We pray for all the workmen who are striving so hard to reach the trapped men. For all the people of Upthorpe who are affected by this disaster, we pray that they are not left to suffer alone. We pray that they may be led by word, or contact, or action, to find a channel to your overpowering love that can lift them up into your arms. We pray that their fear and despair is overcome by hope and faith as they face the future. We dare to ask these prayers, Lord, because we know that you answer all our prayers in your own way, and that you never, ever let us down. Amen.'

★

Roy and Jim went underground with the afternoonshift. There was a feeling of anticipation among the men going underground, as they knew that the access roadway should break through to the coalface during the shift. The report from the face was that the coal was softer as they neared the face line, and that the sandstone roof was not broken down. Roy had agreed to ring Reg Jenkins, in the manager's office, when they had any news of the men. Reg would pass the information on to the press officer, who would decide what to tell the correspondents at the press conference.

Roy inspected the access roadway and saw that the wooden supports were being set nearer together, to avoid any roof breaking down as they broke through.

'This next cut might be the last one, Boss,' said the chargeman. As he swung the cutter jib round, he noticed that the resistance of the coal was much reduced. 'We must be just about there, Boss,' he said.

When they fired the shots there was a hole through to the coalface.

'We'll fill this out, and we can get the rest with our picks without any more shotfiring,' said the chargeman.

The air was flowing through, so Roy and Jim went out of the drivage and switched off the auxiliary fan while the men filled-out the coal.

'You have a minute here, Boss,' said Jim. 'I'll have a look as soon as I can get in, and I'll come and tell you what the prospects are.' Roy accepted this offer.

Ten minutes later Jim came back, while the men were still filling-out some more coal.

'It does not look good, Boss. It's a wall of twisted metal. It's not possible to see in to check the bodies, but I can't imagine anyone surviving there. They must have been crushed when the supports collapsed. I'll take the fitters in, and we'll make a start on cutting the metal to get a better look. It's going to be a mammoth job, recovering the bodies. You stay here, Boss, and have a few minutes' rest. I'll fetch you in when there's something to see.'

Roy did as he was asked. He felt physically sick and in utter despair. He didn't want to fail the men at this crucial time, but he knew that Jim was better able than he was to carry out the next tasks. He sat in the side of the roadway, with his helmet at his side and his head in his hands. The men carried on with what they were doing and bustled around him, but they left him to himself. They were sympathetic to his status – a lonely man facing defeat.

★

Jim came back about thirty minutes later and touched Roy on the shoulder to bring him back from his thoughts.

'We've cut the first plate so that we can get our head through to see the men,' he said. 'George is the first one we can see, but I think there are four bodies there. The other one must be further down the face line. I'm organising the fitters and the men to strip out the equipment, so that we can get through to the bodies.'

'I'll come and have a look first,' said Roy. He pushed his head through the gap and looked both ways. He could see the body of George Turnbull, crushed by the collapsed supports, his oil lamp by his side. 'I'm not leaving, Jim, until I can take George with me.'

'That's OK, Boss, but I think you should ring Reg Jenkins in the office, now, and give him the sad news,' said Jim. 'It's going to be very difficult to get the bodies out, so the next of kin should not expect their men to be available on the surface until tomorrow.'

Roy gathered his thoughts and then rang Reg.

'The position is the worst that we had feared, Mr Jenkins. The bodies have been crushed by the collapsed supports. We can see four, but we think that the fifth body will be further down the coalface. The plan is to strip out the face equipment and work has started on that. It will be difficult to release the bodies and get them out from the powered supports. The first body will be George, and I'm going to stay here until I can bring him out of the pit.'

'This is very bad news,' said Reg. 'Now I suppose we will have to tell Region, and all the media.'

'Will you do me a favour, Mr Jenkins?'

'Sure, Roy, what is it?'

'Will you please ring Helen and tell her straightaway,' said Roy. 'I am sure she will want to go to the relatives and tell them before they hear it on the radio and television. You can also tell her that I'll be staying here until I can bring George out of the pit. I think you should also tell Cobba.'

★

Helen got the message within minutes and she set out with James and Gwen to visit the relatives. It took them several hours, and they realised that there would be follow-up work to do over the coming days, offering support to those women faced with the misery of a death in the family. Helen was very moved by the young children at two of the families, who stared at her with puzzled looks on their faces, as their mothers shed tears of panic.

Mrs Jones reacted in her normal way. 'You have not surprised me with your news,' she said. 'I thought it was a lost cause when you came the first time. So I never had much hope of seeing him alive again. I'll start sorting out the funeral arrangements now. I'm not having that new minister who's come to the Methodist church. He's a right queer stick.' James and Gwen had to smile at this comment.

'I can help you to have another minister for the funeral,' replied Helen, who wasn't surprised by Mrs Jones' comment about Benjamin Sorrell.

★

The press conference took place at four o'clock. It was delayed until clearance had been received from the headquarters of the British Coal Executive to release the information. The reporters were restless as they wanted to send in their copy to their newspapers. The television reporters were at crisis point to get the film to the studios for the evening news. The headquarters PR man read a short report stating that the access roadway had reached the coalface and that an initial inspection had unfortunately revealed that the men had not survived. Work had commenced to recover the bodies, but this would be a difficult process due to the conditions on the coalface.

The television reporter stood in front of the plan on the wall and recorded his report to camera.

'I have stood in front of this plan for two days and admired the progress taking place to get an access roadway to the coalface to free the trapped men. We now know that all the efforts have been in vain, as an inspection has revealed that the men have not survived. We also know that it will be a long and dangerous process to recover the bodies. So the worst fears of the people of Upthorpe are now a reality. Children have lost fathers; wives have lost husbands and mothers have lost sons. More than that, Upthorpe, which before this incident was a prosperous and successful mining community, has been stopped in its tracks and is not sure of its future. The British Coal Executive will have to answer questions about why this disaster took place. Where did the plans and the designs go wrong. But before all that there will be the funerals and the heartbroken tears and pain of all the relatives and friends of the five men who have given their lives in the quest for coal. Think of these folks of Upthorpe in the next few weeks.'

★

It took four hours of cutting, sawing and pulling to get the equipment out. It was apparent that George had been forced into the ground and trapped by the disintegrating powered supports. It took a further two and a half hours of digging and scraping before George's body was released and pulled out into the access roadway. He was placed on a stretcher and cleaned up by the ambulance man, and then covered by a white sheet. Roy placed his helmet beside him on the stretcher, along with his oil lamp, before the party started the long journey out of the pit. Roy realised that it would be after midnight when the party got to the pit top. This was probably how George would have wanted it, for him to be quietly coming out of the pit for the last time. But when the party came out of the cage at the pit top Roy saw about thirty men forming a channel for the stretcher to pass through, headed by Cobba and his union colleagues. They all stood there, bare-headed, and while their presence was a shock and surprise, he realised that it was the best possible tribute to a wonderful man.

Saturday 23 March 1968

Work had continued through the night to release the next two men. Roy had made it clear that he would be going down the pit in the morning to bring the men out.

It was after ten o'clock when the two stretchers were ready to begin the journey out of the pit. This time, when they came out of the cage on the surface, there was a much bigger crowd. The surface men who were on maintenance work had been allowed to leave their jobs to pay their respects to the men. There were many other men who had given up their Saturday morning to come from home to line up. Some of them had brought their wives along. There were also press photographers taking pictures of the two stretchers and of people in tears in the crowd. The procession from the shaftside started in absolute silence. Then someone started clapping and the whole crowd took up the applause. As one newspaper reported the next day. 'This unusual display was a statement of defiance. It said, 'these are our men and we are proud of them and the sacrifice they have made.'

★

Cliff Smith and Charlie Marshall had been in the crowd and they'd also joined in the applause. They went from the pit yard back to the Enclosure.

★

Getting the last two men out presented exceptional difficulties. The shearer driver was behind the shearer, so he had to be approached from the side. The fifth man was located forty yards down the face from the others, and it was difficult to get in to strip the panzer conveyor out of the way. Roy realised that it would take the whole day to get these men released, so he arranged that he would go underground and bring them out on Sunday morning.

★

The Enclosure members were all in sombre mood.

'We've been meeting here for years,' said Cliff. 'But this is the worst day there's ever been at Martins Main. I don't know what's going to happen to the pit in the future.'

'They can't carry on with the pit if it runs out of coalfaces,' said Albert.

'You are surely not suggesting that they'll close the pit, are you, Albert?' said Charlie. 'There's plenty of coal left at Martins.'

'It's no use having plenty of reserves if the pit isn't producing any coal,' said Albert.

'I've heard that they've hit another fault in the Benton main roadways,' said Pat Mulligan. 'So they'll be months preparing a new coalface there.'

'I hadn't heard that,' said Cliff. 'It's all tragic news, these days.'

'I got that information from the Surveyor,' replied Pat. 'It got buried in all the efforts to rescue the trapped men this last week. I don't suppose anything will happen about the future until after the funerals.'

'I expect the funerals will take place next week,' said Cliff. 'There'll be a huge crowd there for George Turnbull's funeral. They'll never get everybody in the church.'

★

Helen Dobson was working on the funeral arrangements. She'd discussed the situation with John Warwick, and expressed her view that James Folds should take the funeral services that were scheduled for the Methodist church. He knew more about the pit and the community than Benjamin Sorrell, who would be away for most of the next week anyway. This plan was agreed by the Circuit Superintendent Minister and had the full approval of members of the Methodist church. James accepted this commitment, and got to work meeting the families involved. Three of the funerals would be at the Methodist church, one at the Anglican church in the next village to Upthorpe, and one at the Catholic church in Doncaster.

Helen agreed with James that Roy should give the eulogy for George Turnbull.

'I know that it'll be a great strain on Roy, to take on that responsibility, but I'm sure that I can persuade him that it's the right thing to do,' said Helen.

'We can all work together to share the preparation of what is said at the service,' said James.

Sunday 24 March 1968

Roy went underground with Jim Lord at nine o'clock in the morning. The report from the nightshift indicated that one body was recovered, and the other one should be available by the time they reached the Fuston coalface. In fact, there was a delay in recovering the second body, so they didn't start the journey out of the pit until ten thirty.

With the publicity given to the reception at the surface the previous day, Roy expected a crowd on the surface, but he was shocked to see at least two hundred people lined across the pit yard to form a passageway for the stretcher-bearers. The difference, on this occasion, was that there were at least fifty schoolchildren, who had been placed on the front row. This had been organised by John Warwick, the Junior School headmaster. Roy was moved by the young faces, which displayed a mixture of fear and respect as they realised that there were dead bodies under the white covers on the stretchers. They joined in the applause with the rest of the crowd, but this also puzzled them.

The scene was captured by press reporters and photographers, but it was also filmed by a television camera. The TV report, screened on the news that evening, covered the whole of the journey across the pit yard and there were images of people with tears streaming down their faces while they lifted their hands in applause. Roy, who walked in front of the stretchers, and Jim, who bought up the rear, were both overcome by tears at the reception by the people of Upthorpe.

Friday 29 March 1968

For Roy, the week had been dominated by the funerals. He went to them all, accompanied by Helen. There had been two on Wednesday, two on Thursday and today it was the funeral for George Turnbull.

Mrs Turnbull and her two children realised that this was a funeral that would affect the whole community, and they'd agreed to it being planned with that in mind.

The route of the funeral cortege was extended, so that it didn't go directly from George's house to the Methodist church, but first went from his house to the pit yard – a route that George had travelled thousands of times. The pit yard had been cleared so that the funeral cars could do a sweeping turn that took them alongside George's office, before they went back along Martins Lane. Both sides of Martins Lane were lined with people and the funeral director walked in front of the hearse for that part of the journey. Police stopped all other traffic and there was a respectful silence from the watchers made up of men, women and children, the youngest ones held in the arms of their mothers.

At the church, there were crowds of people outside who couldn't get a seat, but they heard the service through loudspeakers that had been set up especially for the occasion. Willie Carter acted as steward, and squeezed as many as possible into the seats in the main part of the church and the extension. Peter Carter was playing the organ and he'd chosen the music after discussions with James Folds. The coffin was carried into the church by six miners who had worked for George over many years. George was a big man, but they lifted the coffin with ease, evidencing their strength and skill.

Reverend Folds welcomed everyone to the funeral service, including those who were standing outside the church. He encouraged those outside to take part fully in the service, by using the service sheets that had been distributed and by joining in the hymns. He finished his introductory remarks with the following words.

'We have many things to do in this service today. We have to pass George on from this life on earth to the life beyond; we have to mourn with the family and offer them support and strength in this time when they are required to face life without George and the presence of you all here today is contributing to that support; but most of all, we have to celebrate the life of a man who had humble beginnings, but rose up to take a lead in the very demanding job of managing the underground operations in a coal mine. In carrying out that role he influenced the lives of thousands of people in the community of Upthorpe, and gained their respect for his practical skill and hard work. When the service is over and the coffin is leaving the church it will be accompanied by the organ playing See the Conquering Hero Come. Surely that is how we want to remember George Turnbull.'

The service followed the usual format of hymns and prayers, and then it came to the turn of Roy to speak about George. Just before he stood up to go to the front, Helen squeezed his hand. She knew what a challenge this was for Roy, and she hoped that he could contain his emotions while he spoke. Roy went to the front without any introduction and a hush fell over the congregation. He stood at the lectern and looked up at the congregation before he started to speak.

'It is an impossible task, to speak adequately about George Turnbull in a few minutes. I have known him for four years, but I was always learning more and more about his skills and his expertise, right up to the end. He was born in Martins Lane and followed his father into the pit when he left school. But he had ambitions and was not satisfied in just being a workman, so he went to nightschool to study mining. He stopped studying when he got his Under-manager's Certificate and he became a deputy. That was the start of his career in management and eventually he became Undermanager of the mine. So George has worked at Martins Main for forty-three years. No wonder he was so knowledgeable about the pit. There are some who say that George should have carried on studying and got his Mine Manager's Certificate, because he would have made a good manager. I have to agree with them.'

'However George's qualifications were just a small part of his expertise. He loved mining, and he revelled in all its complexity. He wanted to know how everything worked and he wasn't satisfied until he knew how to do the different jobs that were necessary to make the mining operations produce the coal. So he didn't tell men what to do, he showed them. He lived through many changes in mining systems. I saw him accept, and master, the new mechanised mining operations installed at Martins in my time.'

'He was a very hard worker. He could never leave a job half-finished; he always stayed on to complete it. This must have been very inconvenient for his wife, who never knew when he would come home. And she was not sure how long he would stay at home because, if he had any doubts, he would go back to the pit at night to ensure that the nightshift men knew what they had to do next.'

'George was completely reliable, and he had his own high standards of integrity. He told the truth as he saw it. This was the case whether he was dealing with his workmen or with his bosses. As a member of the management team at Martins, he was a tower of strength. One of his regular answers to me, when we were making plans, was 'Leave that to me, Boss, I'll sort it', and I knew he would do just that.'

'He had no illusions of status; to everyone at the pit, he was George. That was the name that he had when he started at the pit, and that was what he was called by everyone when he finished.'

'It's tragic that George should have died the way he did, but it was true to his character. He was in the middle of a very difficult mining situation that he was trying to sort out. That was bravery of the highest order.'

Roy paused and took a deep breath.

'Away from the pit, George was a family man – a husband, a father and a grandfather, and his devotion to all his family was as complete as it was to his job. We mourn, today, with all of you in the family, and share in your pain with the loss of George.'

'Everyone here today, and many more in this community, has had the privilege to know and work with George Turnbull.'

Roy paused and cleared his throat. He was having difficulty saying the last two sentences. 'None of us will ever forget him. He was truly a super man.'

Monday 1 April 1968

Roy was sitting in his office. The nightmare of the last two weeks was over, but the pit that was left was a mere shadow of what it had been. The atmosphere was one of despair. One seam completely lost; the other seam staggering along with just one coalface that would last a little over two months. Its replacement was now months away, due to another fault in the Benton seam trunk roadways. How to manage such a situation was the conundrum going round and round in Roy's mind.

And there was no George Turnbull; there was a vacuum. Roy knew that there were lots of people at the pit forgetting that George was no longer there. They set off to do what they'd been doing for years.

'I'll ask George's advice.' 'George will arrange that for me.' 'We need to ask George what he thinks.'

Jim Lord was standing in for George's responsibilities and, despite his keen approach and the respect that people at the pit had for him, he was a poor replacement for George, and he knew it.

★

When Helen and Roy had been saying goodbye to James and Gwen Folds, yesterday afternoon, and thanking them for all that they'd done during the disaster, James had asked Roy what would happen next at Martins Main.

'I really have no idea, James,' Roy had replied. 'Not only is the physical state of the pit extremely bad, but there must be negative effects on the morale of the men. I don't know how much the loss of George will affect the men, but my guess is that it will be significant. George was a hard taskmaster to satisfy, as far as the men were concerned, but without him they'll find just how much they respected him and relied on his judgement.'

'What about yourself, Roy?' James had asked. 'What does the future hold for you?'

'James, I have no idea. To me the future looks like a dense fog. I have no idea what is in front of me, nor do I know which way to go.'

James had shaken his hand. 'We will be thinking of you, Roy, and continuing to pray for you,' he'd said. The two couples had clung to each other as they parted. James and Gwen sensed the fear and despair surrounding Roy and Helen.

★

Roy looked at the figures on the papers on the desk in front of him. The results for Martins during the last two weeks gave a measure of the problems. On the week of the incident the output had been just over six thousand tons; during the last week the output had been just below five thousand tons. Roy knew that with those tonnages the pit would be showing a significant financial loss, though he was in no hurry to actually get the financial figures. His concern was that he could see no actions that he could take to rectify the situation.

★

Later in the morning he got a message to attend a meeting about the position of Martins Main, in Mr Pickersgill's office, at nine o'clock tomorrow morning. It might be that decisions about Martins were to be taken away from the pit.

★

Roy spent the rest of the day with the Surveyor, getting an up-to-date set of plans about the pit, and then, with Jeff Briggs, getting the latest financial figures. Unlike an accountability meeting, Roy was not sure what questions he would be required to answer tomorrow.

Tuesday 2 April 1968

In the outer office, waiting to go into the meeting with Mr Pickersgill, Roy's feelings were different to any that he'd experienced before. He felt that he was in a dream.

'It's been a very difficult two weeks for you, Mr Dobson,' said Diane, who was trying to be sympathetic.

'Yes, Diane, it has,' Roy replied. 'I can only describe it as a nightmare. And I'm not sure I'm out of it yet.'

★

When he was called in, Roy was surprised that there was only Reg Jenkins and the Personnel Manager alongside Norman Pickersgill.

'Mr Dobson, we all know that you have had to handle a very difficult situation over the past two weeks,' began Mr Pickersgill. 'As well as having the media spotlight on the mine, you've also had to deal with very sensitive personnel issues, with the relatives of the five men killed. I am told that Mrs Dobson played a very fine role in this respect.'

'She was very helpful, Sir,' replied Roy.

Mr Pickersgill was still looking at Roy, so he decided to add to his reply. 'While we've been in Upthorpe she has been involved with several difficult issues affecting people. I think she is accepted as a sincere woman who will bring help and support to people in distress.'

'I am aware of what she has done, and I will be speaking to her to express my appreciation,' continued Mr Pickersgill. He paused before continuing. 'We are now left with the problems of Martins Main to tackle. I am sure that you are clear that the pit is in a very serious position.' He looked at Roy.

'I am, Mr Pickersgill,' replied Roy. 'I do not see any solution that will bring the pit back to viability in the short-term. Assuming that the Fuston seam is not workable with current technology, then the pit doesn't have the prospects of achieving the highly profitable performance that we achieved last year.'

'Good. You have drawn the right conclusions on the present situation. And I can inform you that there have been detailed discussions here at Region, which came to the same conclusions. I have also had meetings in London, with Board members of the Coal Executive, to agree a policy with them. They are concerned at the excess capacity within the industry and they cannot agree to any protracted plan to invest in a pit, over a long timescale, to make it viable.' He looked at Roy. 'You might be shocked at this, but we have decided that Martins Main should be closed.'

Roy was visibly shocked. It had crossed his mind that this might happen, but his instinct was that Mr Pickersgill would want Martins to continue, after the success he had seen at the pit.

'It is the only decision to make, Sir,' said Reg Jenkins, in support of his boss.

'So now we have to decide how to proceed,' said Mr Pickersgill. 'We will want you to manage this policy of closure, Mr Dobson.' He looked at Roy.

'Right, Sir,' replied Roy. 'It will be a new experience for me.'

'We do not want you to announce the closure immediately. We think to make an immediate announcement would be tactless, so soon after the disaster. What you can say is that a review of the plans for the pit will be taking place in the next two weeks at Region. You can also say that a full investigation into the failure of the support system in the Fuston seam will be taking place at the Headquarters Research Establishment. The supports were the most highly-rated powered supports in the country at this time, so that should indicate that the prospects of further workings in the Fuston seam are very doubtful. You can thus stop any further development in that seam. If it is at all possible, we would like you to salvage the ranging drum shearer from the Fuston coalface.'

'It will be a difficult exercise, Sir, but we'll attempt to get the shearer out.'

'We would like you to send the powered supports from 59s coalface out of the pit so that they can be deployed to another pit, after repairs in the workshops. This will send the message to the pit that the future of the Benton seam is doubtful.'

'We can do that immediately, as the majority of the coalface equipment is salvaged already,' replied Roy.

'These decisions will give you a significant surplus of manpower. There are vacancies at other pits in the Region, and they will be offered to Martins men. The Personnel Manager will have one of his staff at Martins, full-time, to handle this. You'll have to negotiate this immediately with the union. If any men want to take redundancy, that will be arranged.'

'When will the announcement of the closure be made, Sir?' asked Roy.

'We think in about two to three weeks,' replied Mr Pickersgill. 'The date of closure will be the end of production on 58Bs coalface. There will be some men retained to salvage the pit. Whether or not we decide to keep the shafts open for the time being will depend on the outcome of a review at Region. My initial view is that we'll close the pit completely and seal the shafts. The site will then be available for future development, when finance is available. Our job used to be focussed on developing mines and getting coal out of them; more and more it looks as though we'll be involved in closing mines and preparing the sites for future use.'

The meeting continued for a short while, going into more details of the plan. It was agreed that Jim Lord should be given a temporary appointment as Undermanager. It was also agreed to transfer some junior engineering staff and craftsmen to pits that had vacancies. Roy had one burning question, which concerned his own future, but he didn't dare raise it.

★

Roy went to Reg Jenkins' office and continued discussing practical issues. Reg wanted the road heading machine from the Benton trunk road developments for one of his pits. He hadn't managed to get agreement at Region for this transfer, but he told Roy to let him know if anyone else was claiming the machine. Roy had the impression that he was now running a second hand car depot, with people looking for bargains. It was a long way from being a colliery manager.

★

Back at the pit, Roy had immediately arranged to meet Cobba and Jimmy, as union reps, later in the afternoon.

It was a strange atmosphere, with unwillingness on the part of the union to ask the critical question - is the pit going to be closed? Roy explained the meetings that were to take place at Region to evaluate the options for the pit. He also described the investigation that would be undertaken at the Headquarters Research Establishment, on the failure of the powered supports on the Fuston Two face.

'I thought they were the best supports available in the country?' said Cobba.

'They were,' replied Roy. 'That was why we were confident that we could work the seam.'

'There can't be much chance of more workings in that seam then?' concluded Cobba.

Roy was able to confirm that there was no purpose in further development work in the Fuston seam and the roadway development there should be stopped.

'What are you going to do with all the men, then?' asked Cobba.

Roy explained the arrangements to transfer men to other vacancies in the Region.

'This sounds like closure without announcing it,' said Jimmy. 'If it was closure there would be redundancies.'

'If men want to take redundancy, I can arrange that,' replied Roy.

'I know it's very difficult for you, Boss, to give us an answer, now, as far as Martins is concerned,' said Cobba. 'And I know that there are problems with over-capacity in other parts of the coal industry, so there's no recruitment taking place. Will you promise to tell us as soon as you know what's going to happen here?'

'I will do that, Cobba, and I would expect to be able to give you an answer in about two weeks,' replied Roy.

'We want the best possible outcome for our men at Martins,' said Cobba. 'Three months ago I thought we had the best pit in Yorkshire. We have been dealt some cruel blows, by Mother Nature, and we'll have to face the consequences.'

'It is because I want to do the best for the men at the pit that I have agreed to make some transfers to vacancies in the Region straightaway,' replied Roy.

★

They discussed other details about the pit, including the appointment of Jim Lord. Then the discussion reverted to the disaster and the funerals.

'It's been a traumatic two weeks for Martins, and it would have been better to be in the national media for some better news than a disaster,' said Cobba. 'It must have been traumatic for you and your wife, Boss. I think the folk of Upthorpe appreciate what you both did.'

'Thank you, Cobba,' said Roy. 'It was a nightmare, and it's not over yet. Managing this situation at the pit is very new for me.'

'I understand that, Boss,' said Cobba. 'I think a lot of folk are realising that Martins Main will never be the same again, without George.'

'I can agree with you there, Cobba,' said Roy.

Roy believed that the meeting had gone well. He decided to see how things developed, but there was a possible opportunity to bring forward the date of the pit closure announcement. He would need to clear that with Mr Pickersgill.

Wednesday 3 April 1968

The Enclosure was in morning session and the mood was depressed.

'The news in the Club last night is that Cobba has called a special union general meeting tomorrow night, to discuss the position,' said Charlie Marshall.

'The union had a meeting with the manager yesterday afternoon,' said Cliff. 'What came out of that?'

'Nobody seems to know,' said Charlie. 'Cobba came into the Club for about half an hour last night, and the lads were asking him questions, but he said he didn't know what's going to happen.'

'I've heard that a man from Personnel Department is going to have an office at the pit. So they might be moving some men out to other pits,' said Pat.

'Surely Cobba should have known about that,' said Albert. 'I'll tell you this; we are going to see all sorts of things happening now at Martins, and we'll be bloody lucky to get to know anything.'

'One of my mates on the surface says that some powered supports will be coming out of the pit and sent off to the workshops for repair,' said Bert Wall.

'Will they be coming back to Martins?' asked Cliff.

'There's no bloody point, Cliff,' said Albert. 'There's no coalface to put them on. The pit is buggered.'

'Yes, and three months ago it was one of the best pits in the country,' added Cliff.

Friday 5 April 1968

Helen Dobson received a telephone call from Norman Pickersgill.

'Mrs Dobson, I want to thank you for all the work you did in the community during the disaster,' he said. 'In an emergency like the one at Martins, which lasts over several days, there is growing despair and fear that needs sound counselling to keep people going. You certainly filled that vacuum, from what I have heard from various sources.'

'Thank you, Mr Pickersgill,' replied Helen. 'In fact, I had wonderful support from other people and I could not have done it on my own.'

'How is your husband settling down, after the ordeal?'

'It was a great test for him, particularly the funerals. I think it will take him some time to fully recover. I'm doing all I can to support him. We shall get through, though, Mr Pickersgill.'

'I am sure you will, Mrs Dobson,' replied Norman Pickersgill, before he rang off.

★

Cobba asked to see Roy after the union general meeting.

'How did the meeting go, Cobba?' asked Roy.

'It went in a direction that none of us expected, Boss, and that's why I wanted to see you. We covered the points that you made, and I think that we'll get some men wanting to go to other pits. Also some will be interested in redundancy. They were all puzzled as to why we don't have a decision on the future of the pit. I think the sooner it's finalised, the better.'

'I hear what you say, Cobba, and I will pass on your views.'

'The thing that surprised us was a very bitter attack on you, as manager. They blame you for the decisions that have led to the present position. Closing the Morley and Low Moor seams was condemned. It virtually throttled the pit, was one comment. Going into the Fuston seam was a terrible mistake, they said. No pit has done anything in that seam. It was stupid to expect those powered supports to withstand the forces of such a thick bed of sandstone. It went on and on, and it got very nasty at the end.' Cobba paused.

'In what way, Cobba?' asked Roy.

'Well they're blaming you for the deaths on the Fuston coalface. One fellow stood up and said 'that manager, through the decisions he has made, has the blood of five men on his hands.' I tried to call the meeting to order, and closed it as soon as possible.'

'That is a very strange reaction,' said Roy. 'I can understand the men's disappointment with the present position of the pit, but I didn't expect such bitterness directed at me. How many men have these views?'

'I don't think it's a lot of the men,' replied Cobba. 'But once they got started nobody else could get a word in, so it's difficult to know how widespread the view is. There's the danger of some of them going to the press. I think you should be wary of this.'

'This is a shock for me,' said Roy. 'I have tried to lead the men and communicate with them at all times. I've searched my conscience about the decisions that I've made at

Martins but, as you know, the policy for the pit has not been mine alone. Senior staff at Region have been involved in the decision making process. There's also been input into the technical side of the equipment on the Fuston seam coalfaces. This will be assessed by the Research Establishment investigation. I don't think that I can say anymore. I'm really puzzled at what you've told me, Cobba. Is there anything else that you want to raise about the future?'

'There is one thing, Boss, that directly affects me. If the pit closes, I hope that the arrangements for the Home Coal delivery service can be left with our system. As you know, we currently cover two other pits, besides Martins. I wouldn't like to see all that handed over to another pit.'

'I'll bear that in mind, Cobba,' said Roy.

★

When he got home, Roy reported to Helen what Cobba had told him about the union meeting.

'It felt a bit like a man being kicked when he was on the floor anyway,' said Roy. 'I suppose that there must be anger and bitterness among some of the men at the present position. They seem to have forgotten the good times that they've had at Martins. It's a strange way to let it out at a union general meeting, though.'

'I think it's a release of feelings that have been stored up over the last few weeks,' said Helen. 'They feel that somebody has to be blamed for what's happened. Try not to let it affect you, Roy. I don't think the majority of the men at Martins will take that view against you.'

'I'll be going underground next week, so I'll see if I get any reactions from the men as I go around the pit. I intend to speak to Mr Pickersgill, to see if we can bring the announcement forward to the end of next week. Cobba thinks that it would be good to do that.'

Tuesday 9 April 1968

Roy had managed to arrange a short meeting with Mr Pickersgill.

He explained the position, and the view of Cobba, that the announcement should be made sooner rather than later. He also explained the concern that Cobba had about the Home Coal delivery scheme. He informed Mr Pickersgill of the view of some of the men that Roy's decisions had led to the failure of the pit. His visit to 58Bs coalface on the yesterday had met with some coolness from some of the men, but he thought they were in a minority. He warned of possible bad publicity.

Decisions were made quickly.

Norman Pickersgill established the policy that the Home Coal delivery service for all the retired miners in the Region would be handled by the Martins scheme. Cobba was delighted that the scheme would get its coal from one of the long-life pits in the Region that had a bunker system for Home Coal.

Roy would announce the closure to the union on Friday morning and the information would be released to the press later that afternoon.

Regarding the aim to blame the colliery manager for the failure of the pit, Mr Pickersgill was sceptical of it having any momentum, but he asked to be informed of any incidents.

Friday 12 April 1968

The meeting at ten o'clock was interesting to Roy because of the different approach by Jimmy Bell and Cobba. Jimmy was challenging the decision and talking of action against the closure, without having any specific suggestions. Cobba was quite clear that the aim of the union was to get the best deal possible for the Martins men. He warned Jimmy that there were opportunities available, at the present time, to get Martins men settled at other pits and that these opportunities might not be available in the future. In the end, Jimmy fell into line with Cobba, and they agreed to hold a meeting on Saturday night to pass a motion accepting the pit closure. Roy assured them that, if they did that, he would do all in his power to arrange transfers or redundancy, according to the men's wishes.

Roy wan't sure if Cobba could deliver such an agreement if there was resistance from some of the men.

Saturday 13 April 1968

At nine thirty in the evening Roy got a 'phone call from Cobba, from the Club, to say that the motion had been accepted by the union.

'How did you manage that, Cobba?' he asked.

'Well, we didn't get a great attendance tonight. I think some of the men probably didn't get to know about the meeting, with it being Easter Saturday. There wasn't much opposition. I'll see you on Tuesday morning, Boss. We'll have to get busy sorting the men out. I've heard that there may be another closure in the Region. We don't want them taking any of the vacancies. How long are you going to run 58Bs, Boss?'

'I'm suggesting it closes after four weeks and is then salvaged,' replied Roy.

'That should finish before the other pit closes,' said Cobba.

Tuesday 16 April 1968

There had been some press coverage of the closure in the weekend press. There were stark headlines – Disaster Pit to Close – but little comment behind the headline.

Today, however, there was a more detailed report in the local paper.

'Martins Main pit, the scene of a recent mining disaster where five men were killed, has been announced for closure. The union has accepted the closure. Cobba Green, union chairman, says that his concern is to get

the best jobs possible for Martins men at other pits. The union is working with the management to achieve this. He also said that the Home Coal delivery scheme at Martins is to be retained and all retired miners can rely on the service continuing. Another union official, who cannot be named, reported that there is a view at the pit that bad decisions by the colliery management over the last few years have led to the closure of the pit. There was no comment from the colliery management at Martins Main about this claim.'

Roy hoped that report might be the end of the criticism of him as colliery manager.

Tuesday 23 April 1968

Roy had entered a new phase of his management. He was organising the salvage of equipment at the pit, to satisfy the needs of various pits in the Region. The road header had been brought to the surface and transferred to one of Reg Jenkins' pits; the ranging arm shearer had been successfully salvaged from the Fuston Two coalface, after a week's work, and transferred to the workshops; all the powered supports from 59's coalface had been brought to the surface and sent to the workshops. There then followed a continual stream of conveyor belting and electric cables, which were in high demand at other pits, being removed from the pit. For the beneficiary pits this was of course a cost-saving exercise, as the cost of salvage was being posted to a closure account on Martins Main.

In parallel, there had been meetings with groups of men each day and arrangements made for them to be interviewed at other pits, or processed for redundancy. Cobba was active in this work, and he tried to keep the men together as teams, which made the transfer more acceptable to them. For some men a move to another pit was a traumatic experience, after they'd worked at Martins for over twenty years, especially for those who lived in the houses on Martins Lane and who walked the few hundred yards to work. The prospect of taking a bus ride, for several miles, to another pit, was daunting.

During the last two weeks of production on 58Bs there was a sense of panic, as though they were on a sinking ship, and men were pressurising Cobba to get them into the transfer process. Rumours started circulating that the vacancies in other pits were nearly all filled, and men might have to move to another coalfield to get a job. Roy did all he could to calm the fears and to reassure the men that there would be jobs for everybody who wanted one. He detected looks from some of the men which indicated that they didn't believe him.

Wednesday 1 May 1968

Helen and Roy were sitting in their lounge in the evening when there was a mighty crash as a window was broken.

'Don't go near the window, Helen,' shouted Roy. 'Go upstairs. Somebody must have thrown a brick from the lane at the side of the house. There might be more.' Roy picked up the telephone and rang the local police. He went upstairs and from the bedroom window he could see a group of men in the lane. They aimed several more stones and broke a number of panes in the greenhouse, before moving off. Roy couldn't recognise who the men were, but he assumed they were some of the disgruntled men from Martins, who blamed him for the pit's closure.

Thursday 2 May 1968

Helen rang Roy in the afternoon and asked him to come home as soon as he could.

'Is it another attack on the house?' he asked.

'No, it's worse, Roy,' replied Helen. 'There's been an incident at the school.'

Roy dropped everything and went home. His eldest son, Robert, had obviously been in a fight and was bruised about the face and body and very shocked. Helen was comforting him and trying to calm him down.

'Don't say anything, Roy,' said Helen. 'I'll tell you in a minute what happened.'

'I don't want to go back there, Mum,' Robert said, through tears that had started to flow again.

'You won't have to go back,' said Helen. 'You sit here and rest while I have a talk to your dad.'

Helen and Roy went through into the kitchen. 'Apparently, two or three of the older boys picked on Robert in the playground, and said that you were responsible for Martins Main closing. As you would expect, your son argued that it was not true and he defended you. It got into a fight and the teachers found Robert curled up on the floor in the playground, with cuts and bruises. John Warwick is making enquiries to try to find out who the culprits are, but there's little that can be done, even if he does find the culprits. First an attack on the house, and then an attack on the children. What will happen next? I'm feeling scared, Roy.'

★

Roy made a telephone call and arranged to see Mr Pickersgill tomorrow afternoon.

Friday 3 May 1968

Helen accompanied Roy to Norman Pickersgill's office.

'I did intend to see you in the near future,' said Mr Pickersgill. 'But tell me why you asked for the meeting first, and particularly why Mrs Dobson has come along?'

'We are having problems, Sir, which are affecting the family,' began Roy. 'And we don't know what will happen next, or whether the problems will get more serious.'

Roy explained how the house had been attacked and damaged. Helen then described what had happened at the school. She apologised for having to raise it with Mr Pickersgill, but she explained how the children didn't want to go to school again.

'It won't matter for the next few weeks, and it's not as though the teachers aren't trying to protect the boys. I know the headmaster very well, but he accepts that there are some children at the school who will act as bullies, and they have no discipline from their parents,' said Helen.

'I had not heard about these incidents,' said Mr Pickersgill. 'I thought the run-down was proceeding very well. I was told that the issue of the responsibility for the situation at Martins had fizzled out in the press, which is what I expected. Is there any change that's sparked this behaviour?'

'This week there have been rumours around the pit that the availability of jobs for Martins men is drying up. So Cobba has been pressed by men to get them into the redeployment scheme. I have to add, Sir, that Cobba has done a great job with the closure. I was surprised that he got the union meeting to agree to the closure in the first place. I suspect that some men, presumably the opposition, did not get to know about the meeting. That's typical of Cobba. But throughout, and in the press, he's stated that his policy is to do the best for Martins men. It's not the men's fault that the pit has suffered from major geological problems.'

'I hoped for his support, after we gave him the Home Coal contract for all retired miners in the Region,' replied Mr Pickersgill.

'Let me get down to the serious problems you've raised. We cannot accept such behaviour, and I will have a word with my senior contacts in the police force and then I think you'll see more police around your house. But the real solution is what's next for Roy Dobson. I've been working on this, and there's a plan that I will now finalise as a matter of urgency. At the Mining Research Establishment, which is near Burton-on-Trent, there's an initiative to set up a Mining Systems Branch. This will focus on spreading the best practice of mining systems around the coal mines. They're looking for an experienced young mining engineer to lead this. I have put your name forward, because I think you're ideal for the appointment. Also, I'm sure that you'll benefit from a break from colliery management. The new job will get you familiar with the latest technology and you'll see pits throughout the country, so your experience will be broadened to prepare you to come back into senior roles in line management in a few years' time. You will also be in the right place for the investigation about the equipment on the Fuston coalface. Your input will be critical to that investigation. What do you think about that?'

'It's a change in role, but I am sure it will be a challenge that I can take up,' replied Roy.

'I will clear the position with you in the next few days. Your salary will be on a headquarters grade, but it will be higher than your current colliery grade, so it is really a promotion, which I think you deserve after the results you have achieved over the past two years. In the meantime, you might like to visit the area to prospect for a house in some place near the Research Establishment. That will also solve the schooling problem.'

'Thank you very much, Mr Pickersgill,' said Helen. 'We came here with a problem and we're going away with a future for Roy and the family.' She shook hands with Norman Pickersgill. He held on to Helen's hand as he said his goodbyes to her.

'Mrs Dobson, it has been a great privilege for me to meet you, and to have your support at Regional events. I do hope that we will be able to renew our friendship, later in your husband's career.'

Tuesday 7 May 1968

The offer of the post came through from Headquarters. Its terms were very favourable for Roy, so he accepted immediately. The start date was only three weeks away.

Roy made plans to visit the site, to meet the Director General of Research, while Helen toured the area looking at houses. As they wanted to move quickly in order that the children could start at a new school, they decided to rent a house in a village near the Research Establishment. Roy would take a week off on holiday before he started his new job.

Thursday 9 May 1968

The Enclosure was in session on the last day of coaling at Martins.

'What a sad day for the pit, and us,' said Cliff.

'We shan't be watching the coal shaft and hearing the tubs clattering into the cage, and counting the tonnage ever again,' said Bert.

'They say that some men are blaming the manager for getting the pit into the state it is,' said Charlie.

'I think he was a good manager,' said Cliff. 'He just had bad luck with the geology, and it all came at the same time. There's always bad luck in mining.'

'I wonder what's going to happen to him?' asked Charlie. 'They've moved a lot of men away from the pit, but he's still there.'

'I understand that he's doing a wonderful job at salvaging the pit and transferring materials to other pits,' said Pat. 'I understand that the profit has jumped at one pit, that got in first for electric cables and conveyor belting.'

'Every lorry that goes along Martins Lane with salvaged stuff on it is like seeing the guts of the pit pulled out,' said Albert. 'I don't think I'll be able to keep coming here, and watching it all going on. They ought to shut the shafts and be done with it. And then close the pit gates. It's all over now, bar the shouting.'

'But we've met here for years,' said Cliff. 'We can't stop now.'

'What's the point,' said Albert. 'We shall just be standing here watching everything fall to pieces. It's not just the pit that'll die, the whole bloody community will collapse. Just think about it – no work, no jobs. Well over a thousand men worked at Martins and lots of other local firms were doing work for the pit. Where will they find companies that provide anywhere near that number of jobs? There'll be men wandering about all over the place with nothing to do. Kids's leave school, bored to death and get up to mischief. We've been watching something that was alive and fighting to get bigger and better. From now on, Cliff, we'd just be watching a corpse withering away. I can't face that – you can count me out,' Albert said, and walked off homewards.

That was the beginning of the end of the Enclosure.

Friday 10 May 1968

When the news of Roy's appointment was made public, there was a whirlwind round of farewells, particularly for Helen. She invited Janet, Peggy and Sandra over for tea. Janet said she was glad that she was back at work as Bob had transferred to another pit, but he wasn't sure what overtime he would get. Peggy was not sure what would happen in the future to the wages office, but her boss had said he would want her to move if he was in charge in a new location. Sandra reported that Cobba was happy that he would be busy with the Home Coal scheme, the Welfare Club and his Council work. He'd considered it a tragedy that the geological problems had hit Martins, because he thought Roy was one of the best people he'd ever seen in colliery management.

Sunday 12 May 1968

After the last service that Helen was to attend at church, she was surrounded with well-wishers: John Warwick, Joe Norton, Willie and Peter Carter, and Maureen. Helen hugged them all and thanked them for their support during the past few weeks. She learned that Peter was accepting a transfer to another pit as an electrician but that if he passed his final Royal College of Organist's exams, he would then consider applying for a church organist post if one became available. Last to speak to her was Willie Carter, who had accepted redundancy.

'Mrs Dobson, we will miss you very much,' he stammered. 'You came into this church like an angel, and we all felt the spirit of God at work again. God bless you.' He broke down. 'I'm sorry, I can't hold the tears back.'

Peter came and held his father in his arms. Helen then went and took hold of Willie in her arms and hugged him.

'May the good Lord bless you, Willie, and help you to keep the flame of faith alight, here in Upthorpe.'

She left the church with immense sadness, but also with the hope that she could find another religious refuge near her new home.

★

Roy and Helen went to see Mrs Turnbull for an hour. She was more settled than at the time of the funeral and she had decided to sell up in Yorkshire and go to live with her daughter in Kent, and then find a house there.

Tuesday 14 May 1968

Roy went to his last committee meeting at the Club and was thanked for his work on the committee. In the office with Cobba afterwards, they had their last conversation. 'I'm sorry that it has ended like this, Cobba,' said Roy. 'We worked well together, and I thought we had a winning formula, but Mother Nature can be very cruel.'

'With all the geological problems coming together there was no option but to shut the pit, Boss,' replied Cobba. 'We have been successful so far at getting the lads into pits which should give them a good future. I'm alright, with the Club, the Council work and the Home Coal scheme. I have no bitterness and in any case my kids are set up. And I have a wonderful granddaughter in Amy-Louise,' he added with a grin.

'You'll be alright, Boss. Pickersgill is looking after you and he'll go a lot higher in the British Coal Executive.' They shook hands and Roy left without going into the bar. He thought it was the wisest move.

Thursday 16 May 1968

The furniture removal van left the house mid-morning to go to the new house. Roy and Helen and the boys walked around and checked that nothing had been left behind. They had a final look at the garden and passed the key on to Dennis Gates who was staying on to look after the house and garden until the Region decided what to do with the property.

'Right, that's it,' said Roy. 'Come on, into the car and let's go.' Helen was in the front, and the two boys in the back.

'Are you driving to the pit before we leave Upthorpe?' asked John, the youngest, in the back. 'When you leave the house in the car you usually go to the pit first.'

'No, John, we're going to a new life. Martins Main is history now, for the Dobson family,' replied Roy, who knew what the boy was referring to.

He turned the car southwards, towards Doncaster, and the route through Derby to Burton-on-Trent.

'Why's Mum crying?' asked John.

His bother dug him in the ribs and told him in a whisper to 'Shut up'.

Helen wiped her eyes, and when she calmed down, replied, 'I am sad, John, because of all the friends and people we're leaving behind. Just think, we won't see Tony, Michael, Dawn and Amy-Louise growing up. And I had so much more that I wanted to do in the church. The last few years here have been as near paradise as we will ever experience. But it's all collapsed in the last three months. So now we will have to start and build it all up again.'

'We'll help you, Mum,' said Robert. Helen burst into tears again.

About Trevor Massey

Early days

Charles Trevor Massey was born and bred in Barnsley, West Yorkshire. His family are Methodist through and through, and mining is in his veins.

A working class upbringing, where money was in short supply, provided a solid grounding in life. Trevor's mother managed the household income by dividing the weekly wages into a row of egg cups on a shelf in the kitchen cupboard. Mr Massey senior was a property repairer for colliery company houses in two pit villages, though he supplemented his meagre wage by doing a variety of other jobs. A room in the family home was let out to the local doctor to use for his surgeries. Yorkshire thrift was the basis of family life, with luxuries only purchased once there was sufficient money saved up. Trevor recalls that his mother cooked plain food in the same open fire coal oven for over 65 years, always using vegetables and fruit from the garden. Family meals might not have been adventurous, but they were healthy.

Trevor was an only child, born in May 1934. He attended Barugh Green Junior Mixed & Infant School until passing the eleven plus exam. Winning a George Beaumont Scholarship allowed him to move to Queen Elizabeth Grammar School in Wakefield. Inspired teaching and good friendships were the hallmarks of his time there, and he mixed with many fellow students who went on to great things, such as Ronald Eyre, the renowned television producer, and David Storey, the famous and prolific author who wrote 'This Sporting Life' about his experiences as a Rugby League player.

Passing on the mining baton

Trevor tells the following story to illustrate the mining influence of his forbears and how his interest in mining was sparked.

Grandad had three greenhouses on his smallholding. There was 'the Big Greenhouse' which was about 40 feet long and 15 feet wide. It was made of wood, with glass along one side, the roof and both ends. The other side was a wall to a storage shed and the coke shed. The greenhouse had beds around both sides and along one end and then there was a wide one along the middle. There was a well under one end of the greenhouse that collected water from the house and the greenhouse which was used for watering the plants. The main crop was tomatoes and when it was fully set it held around 80 plants. There were large diameter heating pipes around the greenhouse that were fed by a boiler to provide heat in the springtime when the plants were first set.

The other two greenhouses were 'the Little Greenhouse' and 'the Other Greenhouse'. The Little Greenhouse was quite small, no more than 10 feet by 6 feet, but it had a boiler and circulated hot water so that it was used to raise plants from seed. The Other Greenhouse was attached to the Little Greenhouse but it was much bigger, 15 feet by 12 feet, and it was possible to open a valve and let some hot water circulate around it. Its main role was to grow lettuce and cucumbers as well as tomatoes.

Once the fire was lit in the Little Greenhouse in the early months of the year, and the seeds were set, it was kept in day and night. It was a cosy place and it was not uncommon for Grandad to spend his last hours of the daylight there tending his plants or just sitting and talking to anyone who had come to see him. As you sat you could hear the hiss of the boiler and hot water circulating through the pipes and you could almost feel the plants growing.

I recall one night sitting with him as a young lad of about ten years old, when he reminisced about his time as a coal miner. He described the coal seams and how they had to drive roadways forward to open up the reserves. He explained how they had to use their picks to undercut the seam and then use the cleat lines of the coal to break it down and fill it into the pit tubs. He talked about setting the wooden supports and coping with difficult roof conditions. The talk went on for a long time about many different incidents he recalled. In fact, a lot of the facts and information was way over my head and I could not understand it at all. But he presented his story with enthusiasm and pride. There were no regrets. He was assured about the skill and expertise of himself and his mates. It went on so long that it was dark by the time he decided that we should pack up for the night. He regulated the boiler so that it would stay in overnight and filled it with coke. We then went into the house.

Grandma was not pleased. 'Where have you been while this time? It's dark outside.'

'We've been in the Greenhouse,' replied Grandad.

'What have you been doing?'

'I've been talking to the lad.'

'What on earth have you been talking about for so long to let it get dark?'

'I've been telling him about my experiences in the pits.'

'You don't want to be filling his head with all that rubbish. He'll never have to get involved with pits and mining.'

Grandma might have been cross because Grandad had stayed out longer than usual, but she was wrong about the value of that evening. Grandad's father, as well as his grandfather, had been miners and that night I was given an injection of the family history and heritage in the mining industry. It became a part of me. When I chose mining as my career some years later it stayed with me and I became a part of that heritage.

The motivation in any career can have many sources. For some people their motivation is to be better than their peers; for others it is to earn money and security for themselves and their families; for yet others it is to achieve a position of status or fame; some are attracted to becoming a celebrity. For me, the challenge was to achieve approval from my forefathers for what I was doing throughout my career in the coal mining industry. I was always sad that my grandfather died before I could take him underground and show him the modern coal mining methods and the equipment involved. I think he would have been impressed by the horsepower that mined the coal instead of the sweat and toil of the miners with picks and shovels. But I was forever thankful for that night in his Little Greenhouse, when he passed on to me the baton of his experience, skill and enthusiasm for being a miner.

Doing it the hard way

Trevor left Grammar School Sixth Form with A-levels in English Literature and History. During the Christmas break in his final year at school, a group of three friends arranged some visits in a plan for self-help careers advice. The first visit was to a woollen mill in Huddersfield. Trevor's obligation was to arrange a visit to a coal mine. His uncle worked on the coalface at Woolley Colliery and fixed up a Saturday morning visit. The sixth form students saw a coalface in production and the transport arrangements to move the coal to the pit bottom and wind it up the shafts. Trevor was fascinated by what he saw and determined on a mining career, despite the fact that his parents' aim was that his education would mean he didn't enter the mining industry.

A senior mining engineer, friend of a friend, advised young Trevor that he should go to university to get a degree in mining engineering. This was more easily said than done without science A-levels.

Trevor started work on the surface at North Gawber colliery in Mapplewell. He travelled to the pit on a push bike and returned home in his pit clothes as there were no spare lockers in the pit head baths. The National Coal Board organised an induction period which incorporated classroom work such as first aid and pit operations as well as practical 'on the job' training and visits to working coalfaces to see various operations in practice. The 'passing out' from the course involved the presentation of the most impressive certificate Trevor has ever seen. Alongside the pit work Trevor enrolled at Barnsley Technical College to study for A-levels in Chemistry, Physics and Mathematics through day release and evening classes.

Aiming to win a Coal Board scholarship to help with finances at university, Trevor was summoned to what he describes as the most terrifying interview of his life. About twenty people - the great and good of the NCB staff department, and professors from all the university mining schools - were arranged on one side of a long table. A single chair in the middle of the room faced the Chairman of the panel. An innocent question 'What are you reading at present' led to a prolonged discussion between Trevor and one of the panel. He'd replied that he was reading 'Rommel's Papers' by Liddel Hart, a detailed analysis of the war in the African desert. It just so happened that Professor Whetton from Leeds University had been a Colonel under Montgomery throughout the desert campaign! The interview was a succcess.

The four-year course at Leeds University resulted in Trevor being awarded a first class honours degree. On the day the results came out he went home to tell the good news to his parents. His mother was visiting a friend in Wakefield, so Trevor decided to call there to see her. He parked his Lambretta scooter and went in carrying his helmet. His mother was in full flow of a conversation, which she was reluctant to close. At one pause for breath, Mrs Massey looked across to her son and said, 'Did you get a first?' On receiving a positive reply she simply resumed her conversation without further comment.

As a graduate, Trevor followed the NCB's Directed Practical Trainee course, taking him through all aspects of pit operations, from mechanical engineering, the wages office, through to colliery management. In parallel he studied for his Mine Manager's Certificate and took the exams of the Institute of Mining Engineers, which would lead to chartered status after the required management experience.

A start in management

Trevor's first management post was at North Gawber Colliery, where the colliery manager was C W Turner. Charlie was a progressive and successful colliery manager, and Trevor reflects that his influence was great. Trevor recalls a saying of Charlie's – 'don't play the ace in any negotiations if you could win with the nine.'

A driving inspiration

At Easter 1956 Trevor was commissioned to be the chauffeur at a wedding in Cawthorne. His mother had worked with the bridegroom's mother and the families had maintained their friendship after their marriages and through the Second World War.

Trevor got the bride to the church on time, despite the challenge of finding the middle gear of the Vauxhall Velox's steering column gear change. The chief bridesmaid was the seventeen year old sister of the groom. Trevor made up his mind that day to woo her. He offered her driving lessons and devised other activities to establish contacts, but there was strong competition. Enid Herbert was a prize worth working for, however, and after three years of courtship, she and Trevor married in 1959. Enid has provided constant support and inspriration for Trevor, as well as keeping the home fires burning and nurturing their two sons and one daughter.

An illustrious career

Trevor Massey amassed a wealth of experience, expertise and tremendous respect within the mining industry. His management career progressed through Undermanager at two collieries, Deputy Manager at two collieries, Manager and General Manager at specific Yorkshire mines, through to Group Manager, Chief Mining Engineer and Deputy Director Mining at Yorkshire Areas and then Deputy Director of Selby Coalfield. His career culminated as Head of Mining and then Head of Technical Department at British Coal Headquarters.